I0772337

Revelation Trilogy

Pacifica - Judgement - Sovereign

T. E. Burrell

ISBN: 979-8-9914559-3-0

DEDICATION

The Revelation Trilogy is dedicated to the two women who made it possible.

My mother Mickey, FORCED me to read for an hour every day during my summer break between first and second grade. It started an obsession that I am forever grateful for.

My wife Becky supplied an amazing level of patience and understanding along the journey. Those who know me well can attest this is no small feat. Without her advice and support this story would still be rolling around in my head all by itself.

CONTENTS

Book One: Pacifica

ACKNOWLEDGEMENTS

My thanks to Jordan for his insightful feedback, questions, ideas, and encouragement during the writing of this trilogy. His developmental editing was incredibly helpful.

Thanks also to Jess and Emmaleigh for their help with the cover art. Their advice, energy, and creativity is greatly appreciated by someone who is significantly artwork challenged.

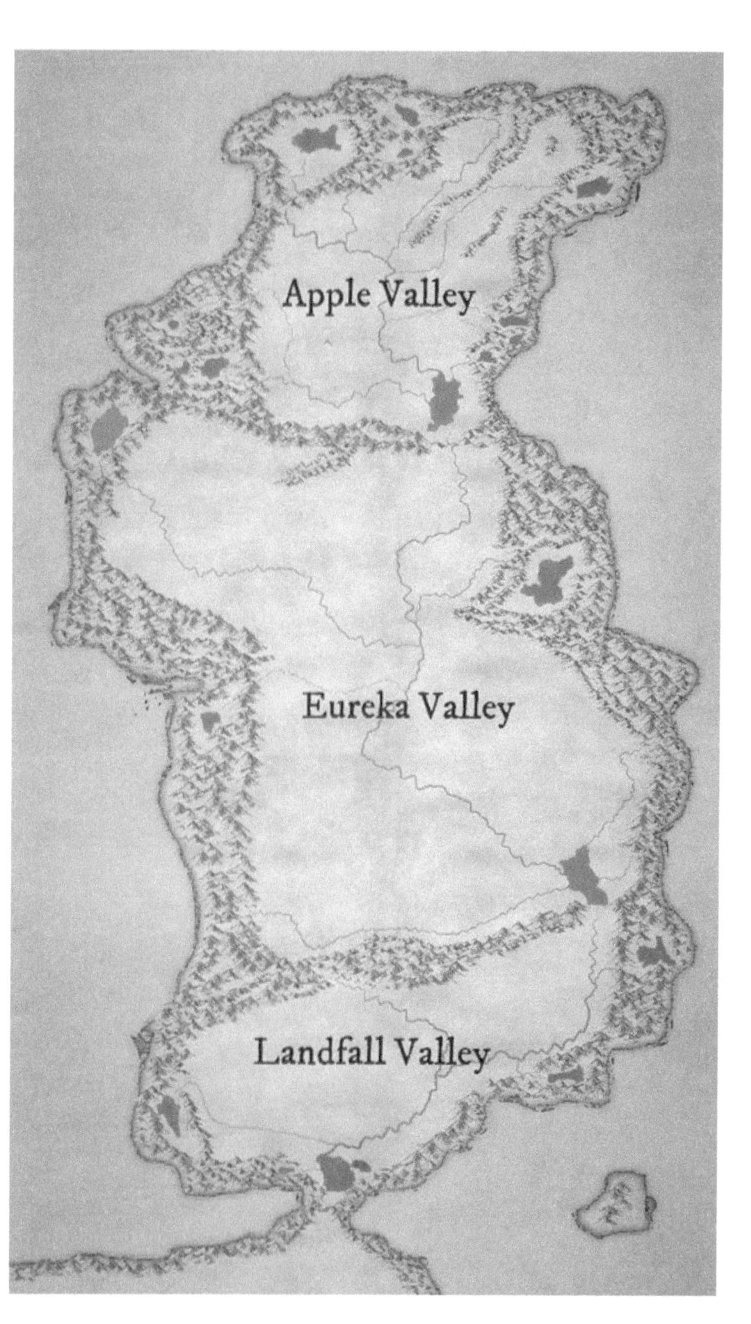

Apple Valley
Eureka Valley
Landfall Valley

Pacifica

CHAPTER 1

SURVEY

"These people have no idea what is about to hit them," the anthropologist said quietly to himself. The ocean planet below was a beautiful blue. The single large landmass directly below him had a few swirls of white above it, but was mostly clear. He was observing two primitive civilizations from an altitude of twenty-five hundred kilometers.

His survey ship and its network of satellites had a wide and diverse array of sophisticated surveillance equipment. The instruments could visually zoom in with incredible resolution and even listen in on conversations given the right atmospheric conditions. Grant Parson could peer into the intimate private lives of the people below while remaining completely anonymous and invisible.

These primitive cultures were living in an inhospitable world. They had evolved to thrive in spite of the challenges. But each had lost their technology since emigrating from Earth nearly two millennia ago. The mutants were slowly but surely assembling an enormous horde. They would soon overwhelm the true humans. It would be a massacre.

This was unfortunate in Grant's mind. So many interesting things to study and time was running out. But he was excited about the carnage that was soon to come. Because he was an anthropologist, he felt he had the inside track on how this would play out. He had already placed a large bet. The true humans' main line of defense would fail in the next battle. He would be rich! Grant was looking forward to multiple days of live streamed watch parties, followed by his payout. It would be memorable.

Stuck in a survey ship out in the middle of nowhere was not the exciting life Grant had envisioned as an anthropologist. He sometimes regretted his choice of profession. But having a front-row seat to this spectacle was worth all the long and lonely hours.

Pacifica

CHAPTER 2

APPLE FALLS

Del could hear Apple Falls before he could see them. Rounding a bend in the road, he stopped to admire the stark beauty of the main waterfall. It was still a long way off, but the sound of the falling water already drowned out everything else. It never ceased to make him homesick. He had moved away to attend university many years ago. He would likely never move back.

Del was Dean of Landfall University and enjoyed his work and his life. But he still got homesick. As he got nearer to the falls, the power of the enormous volume of water seemed to press in from all sides. This was the first of three falls that rose a combined eighteen hundred feet above the Eureka Valley. He thought the view from the top of the falls was the prettiest place in all of Pacifica.

Del was tall, broad, olive-skinned, and of late, a bit portly. An ordinary man with the exception of his eyes. It wasn't the color or size that caught your attention; it was their intensity.

It was a bright, brisk morning, and Del had been up early. He was enjoying the hike alongside the turbulent Apple River leading to the falls. Having spent the previous night in a small village inn he had started his day well rested. His mood alternated between joy at the beauty of the hike and berating himself for not exercising more often. He could feel his back, knees, and leg muscles as he labored up the road. Even more troubling was his heavy breathing. He was ashamed. Middle age and the sedentary nature of a university professor had taken its toll.

There was a strong bias among his people to stay in excellent physical condition. Pacifica had been in a long-standing and brutal war between the peninsula and the continent for well over a thousand years. Everyone was expected to be prepared to serve as a soldier at a moment's notice. His position as university dean meant his direct participation in the fighting was extremely unlikely. But everyone was expected to be able to contribute to the common defense.

Traversing the Falls was the only way to enter the Apple Lakes region. This region was located at the tip of a peninsula. It consisted of a main valley that was both long and wide. A deep lake fed the falls at one end. The main valley was surrounded by mountains on the other three sides that plunged steeply from cliffs into the ocean. Arranged like a fan were a half dozen smaller valleys with their own lakes and waterfalls draining into the central valley. These smaller valleys were sparsely populated and purposely not developed. Apple Lakes was a natural fortress. It was the last line of defense for Pacifica. There had to be room to expand if the worst occurred.

Del was on his way to evaluate two students at the Apple Lake's school for admission to the university. It was unusual for more than one applicant from this rural region to be accepted. Many years there were none. Del suspected the local teacher might be guilty of overstating her student's capabilities.

Given they were Dr. Dorothy Esper's twins, she could be excused for perhaps being a bit overwhelmed by their mother. He had high regard for the teacher, who had been a recent university graduate. A teacher being overly enthusiastic about her students was not unusual nor a bad thing. If Del found even one of them qualified for university entry, the trip would be well worth it. If not, it would be a good learning experience for the young teacher.

Del thought teachers ought to aggressively advocate for their students. He would be warm and supportive with his mentoring, regardless of how the applications for admittance worked out. He knew he had a reputation for being intimidating. So, he needed to take special care to not dampen a young teacher's enthusiasm.

His plan was to avoid climbing the long narrow switchback trail that snaked its way up alongside the Apple Falls's lowest and largest waterfall. It rose eleven hundred feet above the Eureka Valley floor and was a very challenging hike. This plan took on more significance once he realized how badly out of shape he had become. The trail alongside the falls took advantage of a natural cleft in the sheer granite wall.

The cleft made a trail possible up this lowest section of the waterfall. From there, a proper road was available that snaked its way up the steep incline past the two upper falls that were much less daunting. It must have taken many years and enormous effort to chisel out the narrow path to the top of the lower falls. He planned to avoid the arduous climb by riding the Tram.

The Tram was a recent marvel of Pacifica engineering. Del participated in the design portion of the project by providing historical examples of trams and assisting the responsible engineer in calculating stresses and safety margins. It was water powered and comprised of a complex system of cables, pulleys, clutch, and brakes. Technologies that were commonplace to his ancestors.

The surviving accounts described the Colony Wars as so devastating that civilization was lost for a time. His people had gone from traversing the galaxies to engaging every ounce of energy they had in the struggle to grow enough food. The fact their civilization had survived at all was a miracle. Del was proud of this step forward.

The Tram investment was justified by its ability to transport fruit, lumber, and metals from the Apple Lakes region to the two larger and more densely populated valleys below. Apples, plums, peaches, and sweet cherries were grown in abundance in the Apple Lakes Valley. Their export to the lower two regions was a vital part of Pacifica's food supply.

In return, Apple Lakes received manufactured goods and a variety of grains, including rice, wheat, barley, and corn. A secondary motivation for the Tram was that the Apple Lakes region was the last redoubt for their people. This uplifted portion of the end of the peninsula formed a perfect defensive castle for the region. Care had been taken to ensure it could be self-sufficient if needed. It could end up being critical for their very survival.

As Del strolled over to the Tram, a booming voice called out from behind him. "DELLLLL." He slumped down a bit as a deep sinking feeling appeared in his stomach. He knew his plan to take the Tram was gone. "You're not thinking of risking your life on that ill-conceived death trap, are you?"

Del turned and looked back toward the voice. Walking toward him was Griff. An extremely robust man with a closely shaven head, dark eyes, and copper colored skin that advertised a lifetime spent outdoors. Even when speaking in a conversational tone, Griff's voice carried everywhere.

"I know the Tram is difficult to understand. I know it's scary. Try and show a little courage," Del said, motioning toward the Tram operator and group of men loading it who had stopped to watch them. "And no,

I am not riding the Tram. I am going to have it take my backpack to the top." If he had to hike to the top, he was damned if he was going to carry a heavy backpack up the trail, too.

"Call me coward, but I am smart enough to know certain death when I see it," Griff bellowed with a harsh laugh. "I'm not going to risk my change of underwear to that rickety contraption either," Griff boomed and chuckled some more.

Griff could be accused of many things, but a coward wasn't one of them. He was Master Sergeant of the Guard. The Guard was Pacifica's elite group of professional full-time warriors and there was only one master sergeant. While every citizen of Pacifica were part time warriors, the Guard was its base for strategy, training, leadership, and special assignments. Griff's rank was not ceremonial. In battle, he was often in the front line. Typically, in the most vulnerable position. Between wars, he was responsible for guiding recruitment and training.

Griff was short for a member of the Guard, which Del knew he was a bit sensitive about. But he was massively built with a reputation for being quick as a panther. Once Griff got inside your Guard, the fight was over. And he always got inside your Guard. Only Vic had been held in higher regard. Vic was legendary, nearly a deity in Guard lore. He was the previous master sergeant and had been Griff's mentor. Vic was the one fighter Griff could never best. Vic simply disappeared one day twenty years ago, adding to the reverence.

Anyone observing this would wonder if these two were old friends or bitter enemies. Del knew Griff was pretending to be suspicious of the Tram. He was also publicly giving him a pass on having to cart his heavy backpack up the switchback trail. While neither would ever admit it to the other, there was long-standing respect and trust between the two. They were friends. They had met twenty years ago when Griff was a Newbie attending a Guard required history of warfare course at the university. Del was a graduate student teaching the course.

When Del announced the required reading, Griff asked with his affected 'slow learner' facial expression and voice, "Does that big book have anything useful in it?" As if that were a serious question.

"Only if you know how to read," replied Del, staring him down. They held the stare for several seconds until Del said while still looking at him, "Any more stupid questions?"

Griff just grinned back at him. There weren't many that were brave enough to stare Griff down. The clash of egos continued to this day but had mellowed as friendship and respect slowly overtook their competitive natures.

Del knew Griff was intelligent, even if he did consistently play the fool around university staff for fun. In his training role, Griff had worked with Del to develop specialized university classes for the Guard. They both saw benefit to their partnership. Some of the university professors privately scorned the Guard, believing they should just stick to fighting and leave education and decision making to those better suited for it.

"Why the trip to Apple Lake?" Del asked. He knew it was either to evaluate the defensive capabilities of the region or for recruitment.

"Heard there's a boy showing promise for the Guard. His father was accepted into recruit training but didn't make the cut. Rumor is he's been training the boy his entire life to accomplish what he couldn't." Griff paused, then asked, "How about you, recruitment visit?"

"Yeah, it's that time of year," Del replied.

"Given the history of Apple Lakes scholars, I would think you would be looking elsewhere," Griff said with the corners of his mouth slightly upturned. He knew Del had been born and raised in the Apple Lakes.

Del ignored the good-natured dig and said, "There are two candidates the local teacher has referred. I'll spend the week looking over their work, discuss their potential with the teacher, and decide if either merit an invitation."

"Well, looks like I'm going to have to put up with you for a few days," Griff commented and then turned and started up the trail.

Del smiled, admitting that a few days with Griff would be professionally useful and privately enjoyable. He sighed deeply, synched up his belt, and grimly followed.

CHAPTER 3

ARCHERY PRACTICE

Tee was running ten feet behind Diana on a well-used trail that wound its way through the trees. They were headed to the last station for today's training. There was a long-standing agreement that Diana would take the lead when a fast pace was required. Tee was the faster runner, and this ensured the quickest pace while still keeping them together as a team. It also supplied Tee with the guilty pleasure of admiring Diana's butt. Which, in his opinion, had much to be admired. They broke out into the clearing and discovered their last stage. The target was sixty yards away on a hill above them.

Diana grabbed one of the two bows at the station, notched an arrow, pulled back, and placed it just inside the red circle. Tee had simultaneously pulled back as well, centering on the bullseye. Then he almost imperceptibly adjusted his aim and launched an arrow. It landed just outside the red circle. They had both launched second arrows before the first ones had landed. These were both inside the bullseye.

"You win, Diana," Tee said with a groan.

"You're getting worse, or you just let me win," she responded with a smile that included a question in her voice and on her face.

Tee threw up his hands and said, "No, you won fair and square." An electric smile replaced the questioning one with her obvious pleasure at besting him. It was worth the lie. Diana was tall, robustly athletic, and had a smile that exploded onto her face when she was amused. Tee glanced up and caught his mother frowning at him. She knew he had intentionally lost and then lied about it. It was also possible she saw where his attention had been when they came into the clearing. He would get an earful later tonight.

Diana was one of his oldest friends and his mother's protégé. But she was not the archer he was. His mother was the only one who could beat him. She was Lead Archer for the Apple Lakes Volunteers and perennial winner of the yearly archery competition in the Pacifica Games. Arti was a legend in Apple Lakes.

Being a small rural community, there was great civic pride in her winning the archery competition year after year. The Pacifica Games were based on a wide range of abilities and skills related to warfare. Arti was a name known throughout Pacifica for her dominance with that weapon of war.

Almost all the winners in the fighting skills events were members of the Guard. But it was not unusual for the foot races, weightlifting, and archery events to be won by regular citizens. Women dominated the archery competitions. That domination came partly from a belief that archery was for women and old men. Boys and young men concentrated on hand-to-hand combat. Their weapons were sword, knife, and spear. Skills that were needed for battle on and below the Wall.

Arti had decided today's last challenge was to take them through a running course with random bows at each of ten stations. These bows had a variety of draw weights. The objective was to run up to each station, gauge the bow with the first arrow, then be precise enough to place the second arrow in a small red circle anywhere from ten to seventy-five yards away. For this exercise, Arti required the second arrow to be loosed within three seconds of the first. It took much practice to do this accurately. The wind tended to pick up and swirl in the late afternoon, making it all the more challenging. Tee thought his mother was a bit obsessed with unlikely scenarios.

For today's challenge, her argument was that chaos was a common condition on the Wall and if your bow was damaged, you needed to quickly grab another and be accurate. Tee had to admit that with practice not only could he get his second arrow in the circle, but his first arrow more often than not hit dead center. His mother was always coming up with unique challenges.

Arti looked sternly at Tee and said, "Diana and I are going to walk the course a second time. You can go down to the lake if you want, but be home by suppertime."

"See you down at the beach later, Tee," Diana said with an amused smile still in place.

Tee smiled back and just raised his hand in acknowledgement as they walked back down the trail. His mother dismissing him like that was a rebuke. She had warned him before about letting her other archers beat him. She said it wasn't kindness. "The girls are very competitive," his mother had said again just yesterday. "When you let any of them tie or beat you, it just makes them complacent. There are good reasons why I never let up on you or any of them." Tee had to admit she was probably right. His obsessive practice with the bow was partly driven by wanting to beat his mother. As daunting and elusive as that was.

As Tee entered puberty, he had become more and more in turmoil around Diana. He loved her as his childhood friend. That had matured into something much more. Lately he had been tongue tied or, worse yet, saying stupid things when she was around. She didn't seem to notice his attraction to her, which was a relief. But it was embarrassing all the same. She was his cousin Ansen's girlfriend. His perfect cousin had the perfect girlfriend. He was jealous. He could admit that. But they were both so caring and kind to 'the freak' that he could not be resentful or angry about it.

You need to stop being delusional, Tee, he thought. They will get married, have beautiful children, and we will all be friends forever. It was a pleasant thought, but the turmoil remained. As his mother and Diana disappeared down the course path, he casually picked up the other bow, notched an arrow, and neatly dropped it dead center in the target.

Tee ran at a fast pace for the three miles to the lake. He arrived breathing easily, but with a sheen of sweat. He took off his clothes until all he had on was a pair of swimming trunks Grammy had made. He dove into the shockingly cold water but acclimated quickly as he swam and fell into a rhythm. Tee's mother knew he needed a swim. Which is why she mentioned the lake. She might be angry with him, but didn't let that interfere with what she knew he needed.

Swimming burned off energy and anxiety like nothing else for Tee. Swimming was an odd thing to be able to do. It often made him a target for bullies. But it was worth it. Quinn and Hestie's mother explained why he could swim so well when others struggled. She was a well-known medical researcher before she converted into one of Apple Valley's family doctors. She had done some research on his unusual ability. Tee was short and slender.

His bone structure, although solid and well formed, was unusually light. He also had a less dense musculature than others. If he relaxed and simply laid on his back, he could actually float in the water. Nobody else could do that. Everyone had to learn to swim. It was so they wouldn't drown if they accidentally fell into the lake. Being able to make it fifty feet was the requirement. Most could barely do that. A normal person dropped to the bottom of the lake if they stopped swimming vigorously.

Dr. Espers had stressed that there wasn't anything wrong with him. He was just different. He overheard her telling his mother that he was a "Throwback."

Years later, in history class, he finally figured out what she meant. He was like the original colonists. Smaller and lighter before they naturally evolved to live on Pacifica. They were initially worried about him breaking bones, but so far that wasn't a problem. His bones were lighter than normal, but strong enough for his frame.

Tee swam to a private beach on the far side of the lake. He thought of the small sandy beach nestled in the cliffs as his. The only way to get there was by boat or to swim. It was a good place to think when he was troubled. Being outside under the sun or stars had always calmed Tee. It was his place to solve problems or control anxiety.

As the sun started to dip, he decided he needed to swim back. When he reached the other side, he saw Hestie standing on the beach. She and her brother were his next-door neighbors and close friends. At first glance, Hestie was a pretty girl, but not someone who stood out in the crowd. However, there was a warmth that emanated from her. She had a way about her that made people instantly like and trust her. The more you got to know Hestie, the more attractive she became.

As Tee stood and started to walk out of the lake, he raised his hand to wave. Then he noticed Hestie had a worried expression on her face. He realized with a start that Angus and his two brothers were also on the beach. He could tell that they had been harassing Hestie.

"Looky here, a turd washed up on shore," Angus declared to the laughter of his brothers. "You know, people don't float. But turds do. We should bury it. That's the sanitary thing to do, right?"

With that, Angus tackled him and held him while his two brothers dug a hole in the sand. Hestie was pleading with them to stop, but they paid her no mind. They buried him with his arms shoved underneath his legs in a seated position with just his head above the beach. Tee tried to pull his arms out, but the sand was too heavy. He was trapped.

"Show him what we found in the rocks," Angus told the youngest brother. The next thing Tee knew, a Viper snake with its fangs unfolded was being waved in front of his face. Vipers could kill you if you got too much of their venom.

"Leave him alone, Angus!" Tee relaxed, recognizing Ansen's voice.

"Don't ruin all the fun," Angus replied, turning. With that, Diana, Ansen, and Ansen's younger sister Tia walked out of the woods and onto the beach. Ansen was an impressive looking young man. Tall, broad, and muscular, his usual easy-going manner had been replaced with anger. "I said leave him alone."

"It's no big deal. We were just having a little fun with the dwarf." Angus put his face close to Tee and whispered, "You get to float away today, turd, but your cousin won't always be around."

As Ansen walked off, Tia hurried over and said with concern in her voice, "Are you okay, Tee?"

"Now that you're here to save me, I am," he said, smiling. Tia was Ansen's youngest sister and a joy to everyone. He was horrified that Diana had witnessed this. He hoped he covered it well. Having Ansen save him while Diana watched was especially embarrassing. But having Tia there made it impossible not to smile. "Did you help Aunt Arti up at the archery range?" he asked Tia as Ansen, Diana, and Hestie used their hands to dig him out.

"Yes, I'm retrieving arrows and learning to fix them," Tia said with excitement in her voice. Tia worshipped Diana. She had been her shadow since she was a toddler. Whatever Diana did, Tia wanted to do. Being too young to be accepted for training as a potential Wall Archer, she had talked her Aunt Arti into helping out on the archery range after school and chores.

"Did you get a chance to shoot today?" Tee asked.

"Yes," gushed Tia. "I used Diana's short bow and got two arrows in the red."

"Practice pays off, Tia," said Tee with a smile.

"It's not my bow, Tia, I told you it's yours," said Diana.

Tia beamed.

As they walked back toward town, Ansen pulled him off to the side and said, "Tee, you need to watch Angus. I don't trust him. I've seen him intentionally hurt people while sparring. He covers it well, but I can tell it's not an accident. He definitely has it out for you for some reason, and I wouldn't put anything past him." Tee nodded in agreement. This wasn't news to him. But it was significant that Ansen was so concerned.

CHAPTER 4

SCHOOL PROJECT

Emily Clarkson walked to the front of the room. She was young and enthusiastic. As she leaned forward to start her lecture, it was apparent she enjoyed what she was doing.

"Good morning," she said, smiling. "We will complete our study of Pacifica emigration history by examining the moral questions that resulted in our planet being divided between true humans and GEMs. As you know, our people ventured far from Earth and into another galaxy to escape the brutal Mutant Wars. While GEMs, Genetically Engineered Modifieds, are different from us, we consider them to be human. We were determined to avoid taking part in the genocide of those considered non-human. "Our people hold the belief that we need to keep humankind free from genetic engineering. We do not believe we have the knowledge to predict all the impacts that might result from editing our genome or epigenome. If history has shown us anything, it's that playing God has unintended consequences. While we are firmly against genetically altering humans, we do not believe we have the right to exterminate other humans just because they have been altered.

"This moral stance has come at a high cost. The GEM race was designed to be aggressive, thrive in hot and cold environments, and have a high reproduction rate. These attributes seem reasonable as advantages to surviving across the many challenging environments of Pacifica. Implementing this genetic engineering had serious unintended consequences. We do not believe the designers intended their progeny to lose most, if not all, of their empathy. We believe this loss of empathy is what enabled the development of a culture that glorifies subjugation and brutality.

"In short, GEMs are a race of psychopaths. There seems to be something innate in their makeup that causes them to enjoy the pain and suffering of others. They appear to have no remorse. The very worst of human traits. As our enemy, their selfishness and desire for individual dominance is a weakness, since it interferes with their ability for large-scale coordination.

"Our ancestor's view was that genetic engineering was not necessary for survival on this planet as long as we restricted colonization to the coastal, mountainous areas. Our peninsula is perfectly placed for us to thrive. It is much milder than the majority of the continent. Even given that restriction, we knew our people would have to evolve to be stronger and more resilient.

"This is a difficult planet for humans to thrive on compared to our home planet of Earth. We know we are larger and stronger than the original colonists based on the few surviving medical records from that period. While we avoided genetic engineering, there was a mandated breeding program in place for roughly fifty generations. This was a dark period in our history where some men and women were not allowed to have children. Others were forced to conceive with multiple people who were selected based on their physical attributes.

"You can imagine raising children with your wife that had come from a variety of donors. Or a wife not allowed to have children but having to accept that her husband was being used as a donor to impregnate a variety of women. Somehow, traditional marriage survived. But it survived by placing an extremely high emotional cost on those who had to live through it.

"The desire to be allowed to have children with your spouse explains in large part why there is still a strong cultural bias toward visible robustness. People were driven to marry those who were viewed as desirable breeding stock. Logically, this shouldn't matter anymore. We have evolved and we thrive. Evolution no longer needs to be directed or encouraged by social norms.

"Your assignment, due a week from today, is to select one of two topics. For either topic, write an essay describing the moral dilemma and why colonists made the decision they did. Summarize agreement or disagreement with those decisions with clearly worded arguments.

"Choice number one. Knowing what we know now, should we have gone against our moral stance of not eliminating the GEM race when we had the chance? Are there situations when genocide is a good and moral choice? Does it matter whether genocide is carried out on true humans or genetically enhanced humans?

"Choice number two. Should we have resisted mandatory breeding programs? Should we have had faith that evolution would naturally occur? Would we have a heathier society today if different decisions had been made? What should we do, if anything, to adjust the cultural bias toward size and strength resulting from this?

"When I have reviewed and graded all the papers, I will select a few contrasting opinions, and we'll have a debate."

"This afternoon we have a special guest," Tee's teacher continued. "In the back of the room is Professor Delvin Dacy, who is Dean of Landfall University." Heads turned around. "His specialty is technology and engineering with an emphasis on antiquities. He was involved with the design of our Tram and will give a lecture on that topic after school for those who are interested. He also chairs the admittance board for university applicants. He will be observing for the next two days and will interview those of you interested in the university. He is also well informed on technician training schools in Landfall City and is available to answer any questions you might have."

Tee wasn't surprised. Everyone knew the professor had come to see his next-door neighbors Quinn and Hestie. They would definitely be offered admittance to the university. Both were scary smart. Everyone said they were the best students coming out of Apple Valley in a generation.

For most, a decision for vocational schooling or an apprenticeship was worked out with parents. For families who owned a business, a child's apprenticeship was simply moving full time into the family business. For a rare few, a position at the mysterious university was offered.

Quinn was one of his best friends. He supposed they were friends because they were both a little odd. Quinn's oddity was his incredible intelligence coupled with an incurable good nature. Quinn was always happy and positive, no matter what was going on. He assumed the best in everyone, even when there was ample evidence to the contrary. He seemed to have an inability to recognize evil intentions. Unlike Quinn, Hestie was reflective, shy, and quiet. A deep thinker. She had an uncanny ability to read people. Diana and Hestie were best friends, so the four of them hung out a lot together at school.

Tee was daydreaming. It was always a negative mark on his school evaluations. Every year it was the same thing "Tee needs to stay engaged in class," "Tee is intelligent but lacks focus," etc., etc., etc. He was mentally planning his next hunting trip when Diana suddenly shot him a glance, looking horrified.

Turning to look at Hestie, she seemed concerned as well. Tee shook himself and re-played what had been going on in class. They had moved from history to math. Angus had been asked a simple math question related to fruit farming weights and measures. He was unable to answer. No surprise there. Pear farming was his family's business.

But Angus was not very bright. He was large, athletic, extremely bad tempered, and quick to imagine insults. In short, he was a bully. If there was a shared goal at school, it was to avoid Angus getting angry. Everyone except Quinn understood the right thing to do in this situation. Hope the teacher didn't call on you, and if she did, struggle to answer. Or even better, give a wrong answer.

However, Quinn, as usual, head in the clouds, didn't understand the danger. He probably answered quickly because the professor was observing. Quinn's only goal in life was to go to Landfall University and study engineering. Angus had turned bright red when Quinn correctly answered the question. Diana's and Hestie's horrified looks said it all.

When recess was called, the teacher asked Quinn and Hestie to stay behind. Tee relaxed. If Quinn missed the first recess, maybe a confrontation in the schoolyard could be avoided. Knowing Angus, Tee knew something would happen, eventually. Oh well, hopefully that could wait for another day.

CHAPTER 5

RECESS

Griff was well hidden in the brush wearing his camouflage cape and waiting for recess. The school was on the edge of the woods, so it was a simple matter to get close. The boys and girls separated into various groups, some talking and a few boys sparing. Everyone was avoiding being near or even looking at the large, brooding boy with an angry expression on his face. He guessed this was Angus. The region VC who had recommended the boy had said, "He has a few personality quirks and a quick temper."

Physical contests between the boys were encouraged. The constant war with the GEMs meant they needed to be prepared. It was normal for boys to agree to spar at recess as long as no hard punches were thrown.

Sometimes surreptitious surveillance was a waste of time, and it looked like this was one of those times. Then a heavy-set sort of nerdy looking boy walked out. He had a big grin and greeted one of the groups. The angry boy, he had guessed, was Angus walked over and, with no warning, punched him. The nerdy kid was still smiling when Angus's fist hit him square in the jaw, knocking him to the ground. Angus then started kicking with obvious intent to cause damage as the downed boy rolled into a fetal ball.

Griff was getting ready to rise when a short and slender boy stepped up and said, "He's yielded Angus."

"Stay out of this turd," replied Angus, and kicked hard again.

The smaller boy jumped forward and pushed Angus away, then backed up and said, "Leave him alone, Angus. If you want to fight someone, fight me."

Well, thought Griff, this is interesting. Bravery is one thing, but this kid has a death wish. Just then, the small boy darted in, landed an ineffectual punch, and darted out again. Well, at least he's quick, thought

Griff. Angus lost his temper, abandoned his training, and threw a wild punch, which the smaller boy ducked. The small boy then stepped in and tried to take Angus out with an uppercut. He missed. After that, it got ugly really fast, since the smaller boy was now inside Angus's reach.

Griff got himself ready to rise once more as Del and the teacher walked out. They quickly broke up the beating, well it wasn't really a fight anymore. As Griff settled back down, the smaller boy looked directly at him with anger and accusation written all over his face. Even more interesting, thought Griff.

CHAPTER 6

VOLUNTEER COMMANDER

Major Richards greeted Griff with a firm handshake and said, "Griff, it's been too long. Don't see a lot of the Guard up here. Gets a bit lonely in the wilderness."

"When does your rotation end, Major?" Griff responded.

"One more year, then someone else gets to look after these yokels. I will admit they are a sturdy bunch, and their reputation for honesty and decency is understated. They've made me feel at home. So much so, I've given some thought of retiring here."

Major Richards was the Apple Valley Volunteer Commander, or VC. He was still a vigorous-looking man, but the years showed. Richards looked noticeably more tired than the last time Griff had seen him. It might be time to find Richards something less demanding than region VC when this year was up. These assignments were typically given to older respected Guard officers as the first stage of retirement.

Every man, woman, and child in the region was in a volunteer unit. These units had their own officers, non-com's, logistics, and support staff. The VC was in charge. His duties included a full understanding of the capabilities of the region and being on the lookout for potential Guard recruits. If the unit was called to the Wall, the VC reported into Commander General of the Guard, or CGG.

"I heard you might have a recruit for us," Griff offered.

"Yeah, his name is Angus, and he's a brute," Richards replied. "You may or may not remember his father, Asher Willard. He was a recruit twenty years ago but didn't make the final cut. Evidently Asher didn't take his failure well. He's been obsessively training that boy and his younger brothers ever since they could walk. Wants them to accomplish what he himself could not.

"Angus's fighting skills are excellent. His flaws are that he's a bit dimwitted, loses his temper easily, and tends to underestimate his

21

opponents. This has been encouraged by the fact the competition up here isn't what it is in the lower valleys. When he does lose, it's usually because he gets impatient and is out maneuvered." Richards hesitated, then said, "The other thing is a tendency to over dominate. Once we get him out from under his father's influence, I think these traits can be ironed out."

"As you know, I've been here for a couple of days," Griff said. "First day, I covertly observed the schoolyard during recess. I saw all the flaws you mentioned during a fight he initiated with another boy in the yard."

"Let me guess," said Richards. "Was it Tee Stone?"

"Yes, how did you know that?" asked Griff, surprised.

"Tee won a bout against Angus a couple of weeks ago and it embarrassed and infuriated him," Richards replied.

"Let me guess, he outmaneuvered him," Griff said with a smile and they both laughed.

"I think it did Angus some good to realize every enemy is dangerous. However, it is troubling that he doesn't accept his fault in this. He tells the others Tee cheated. As you know, there is no such thing as cheating in a fight," Richards said, smiling.

"But given the faults, your recommendation is that we invite him to recruit training?" Griff asked.

"Yes, his potential is too good to pass on. We need to fix the flaws."

"Tell me more about Tee," Griff said.

Richards was surprised. He hesitated as he thought it over and then responded, "To be honest, I wish he weren't so small. He's a tough nut, I can tell you that! He rarely wins hand-to-hand matches, but he never gives up. It isn't lack of practice, skill, or effort. Everyone eventually realizes they just need to overpower him. That is when he doesn't trick them into doing something stupid. Which he does more often than you would think. I've often thought the perfect warrior would be a combination of his cousin Ansen's athleticism and Tee's smarts and toughness. Ansen has the physical skills but doesn't have the drive, motivation, and ruthlessness necessary to make it in the Guard.

"He's a natural leader. Tee was picked the past two years to lead Apple Valley's capture-the-flag team. Another reason why Angus might resent him. During those two years, Apple Valley has won every match. The consensus of the other regions is that 'Tee is a tricky bastard.'

"In the tournament this year, he won in the early rounds by employing multiple probes designed to evaluate his opponent's decision processes and biases. These resulted in some sophisticated envelopment maneuvers both offensive and defensive in nature. They get worn down by losing lots of little battles until he's stripped a strategic portion of their defense. Then he goes in for the kill. He somehow convinces his opponents they know what he is up to. They don't.

"In the final he bunched his team in the center, stripped his own defenses, and gambled it all on a mass charge right up the middle. His opponent was Landfall City. He knew the quality of that team was far above his. Leaving your flag naked is not a recommended strategy, but it worked.

"The reason it worked is he had gotten everyone to expect a defensive posture with multiple light probes. His standard war of attrition. He started by probing the middle in every previous engagement. So they didn't take the initial attack seriously until it was too late.

"Outside of his leadership capabilities, he's an excellent runner and has unusual skill in swimming and archery. He can actually swim all the way across Apple Lake, bizarre, huh? While nobody can touch Arti, he comes closer than anyone else to beating his mother."

Griff paled. "Tee is Arti's son?" he asked.

"Yeah, can't you see the similarities?" Richards replied.

In a flash, Griff realized that Tee's slender frame was similar to his mother's with facial features suggesting a family connection. Griff was stunned, but hoped it didn't show. He was embarrassed to admit, even to himself, that he was obsessed with Arti.

It had started years ago. He was below the Wall with a squad. They were outflanked, overwhelmed, and in danger of being decimated. Arti had shown up and quickly cut down enough of them for the squad to retreat back to the Wall. How she had placed arrows between Guard members on the move was incredible. More impressive was her choice of targets. She understood the flow of the battle and strategically cut down just the right GEMs to open up a path for retreat while protecting their flanks. The combination was awe-inspiring.

Once they reached the Wall, he realized his Newbie hadn't retreated to plan. He had veered down the Wall and was now separated from his squad. Wading back into the fray with his squad along the Wall, cursing loudly as he went, he was surprised to see he still had archery support. An archer should not have an angle along the Wall for this.

Looking up, he couldn't believe what he saw. Still starkly vivid in his memory was Arti standing exposed on the top of the Wall instead of safe behind a crenation. She stood tall against a clear blue sky like an angry goddess. Tall but unusually slender, her red hair was tied back but flowing with the wind as she dealt death one arrow at a time. She saved his life. She saved the whole squad. He was thunderstruck.

Thanking her for what she had done later, he discovered that while she was intense, she was also surprisingly warm. Still angry, he had marched the Newbie up to her to apologize for his idiocy. She couldn't have been more gracious. She actually thanked the Newbie for "protecting all of us."

And with that, Griff was lost. Asking around he found out she was married. He then firmly tamped down his attraction, but retained his admiration for her courage. Now the fantasy came rushing back.

"Griff, are you okay?" Richards asked with concern.

"Yeah, sorry, what did you say?" Griff replied.

"I said, Tee is on my list for volunteer officers' training. He isn't meant for work below the Wall. But he certainly has potential to provide leadership and decision making on and behind the Wall. When he graduates this spring, I'll let him know and start his training."

They spent the next hour discussing the overall defensive capabilities and logistical status for the upper lakes area. At the end of the discussion, Griff asked, "Are the volunteers on the cliff top lookout posts staying diligent?"

Richards reddened and replied with embarrassment, "To be honest, I haven't hiked up for an inspection in a while."

The upper valleys were remote mountainous areas with their outer boundaries jutting out of the ocean. The cliffs were sheer and high, with large waves crashing into them. However, the GEMs were smart, aggressive, and persistent even in the face of overwhelming challenges. Twelve Guard posts had been strategically set up high in the cliffs to look for boats and directly observe the few beaches that might allow a team to land and scale the cliffs. It was windy, cold, and utterly boring. But it had to be done. So, two men per Guard station were always in place.

Surprise inspections were needed to keep the volunteers diligent.

"Probably a good idea to go scare the hell out of them," Griff suggested. He could tell Richards was not looking forward to the strenuous hike. It will be good to rotate him out next year, Griff thought.

As he walked back to the inn, he scolded himself for his juvenal obsession. The Guard was a small elite group that stuck together. So much so that Guard member families were a close-knit community, spending considerable time together at Guard events. It was an extended family. If he proposed Tee for recruit training, and he somehow made it, there would be events where he would interact with Arti. "I can't let this craziness interfere with making the right decision on Tee. God help me get ahold of myself," he prayed.

CHAPTER 7

FRIDAY NIGHT BONFIRE

Starting in spring and throughout the summer and early fall, Tee and his friends built a bonfire on the beach every Friday evening. Those were magical evenings. Laughing, eating, joking, telling stories, playing games, and just being young. Others would come and go, but the core group of five would always show up.

Tonight, Tee was sitting off to the side and watching. School would be over next month, and the world would change. This didn't seem to be bothering anyone else. Hestie was shaking with laughter, listening to Ansen tell one of his ridiculous stories. They had heard all his stories many times. That didn't seem to make them any less funny.

Ansen could make anyone laugh, even the ever-serious Hestie. Diana was on the other side of the fire, smiling and faking interest in whatever Quinn was trying to explain to her. It was likely incomprehensible. Quinn was always animated, happy, and enthusiastic about whatever his latest interest was. He made you want to be interested, even when you had no idea what he was talking about.

The five of them had been together forever, it seemed. Uncle Hugh, Ansen's father, had stepped into a parental role when Tee's father had died. He treated Tee like a son and included him in all family events, great and small. A year older, Ansen was more like a brother than a cousin. While Ansen had a biting wit, he also had a big heart and took on the role of protective big brother. Quinn and Hestie lived next door.

Their mothers were good friends and, as children, they wandered back and forth constantly between the two houses. He could always count on Quinn for a smile and Hestie for deep, serious conversations. She always pointed out the best in everyone. Both had been good and loyal friends to the slender and short oddity they lived next to. Not that the twins were any less odd. Tee could remember thinking he was stupid until he realized everyone was stupid compared to the twins.

Finally, Diana. Tee fondly remembered the first time he met Diana.

He had been told two days before that his father had died at the Wall. He was in his second year in school, so he must have been six. All the kids knew what had happened and were avoiding him. Apple Lake was a small community.

During recess, Tee was sitting by himself under a large oak tree when a small voice said, "I'm sorry about your dad. My dad says he's a hero." Tee looked up to see a pale face framed by long soft hazel colored hair. Her blue eyes were shining with unformed tears and her lower lip was quivering. Tee's mother had not yet come back from the Wall. Tee was terrified she might be dead, too. Diana's compassion broke the emotional dyke he had been defending.

Tears started to silently stream down as he turned his head away. Diana sat down, reached out, and put her hand on his. She didn't say anything, just sat with him as he quickly got his tears under control. Tee was very embarrassed. Warriors don't cry. If any of the kids found out, he would be humiliated. Diana never said a word about it. Not to him. Or anyone else. Ever.

Hestie and Diana were fast friends. A few weeks later, Diana found out from Hestie that Tee's mother was Arti. "Is Arti really your mother?" Diana had asked, her eyes wide. Tee shook his head yes and Diana continued. "My mom was classmates with her and says she's really nice." Tee beamed. Most people only seemed to care that his mother was a famous archer. They didn't realize what a great mom she was. "Can I meet her?" Diana asked quietly.

"Sure," said Tee. With Diana's mother's approval, Tee brought her home and proudly introduced his friend Diana.

Arti smiled and asked, "How is your mother? I haven't seen her in a while."

Diana replied. "She's fine. She says to send me home if I pester you too much."

"Pester me? Whatever about?" Arti replied with warmth.

"Well, I like archery. She's worried I will bother you asking too many questions," Diana responded with a worried expression on her face.

Arti laughed loudly and said, "Archery questions never bother me." Arti looked at them both with a smile, thought a minute, then said, "Tee goes most evenings with me and shoots at special targets while the

Archers practice. He has an extra bow that would be right for you; would you like to join us tonight?"

Diana's blue eyes grew impossibly larger, and she said breathlessly, "Yes, I would love that." Diana had been a part of his and his mother's lives ever since.

Ansen suddenly called out, "Hey, Tee, what are you doing over there in the dark? I thought I told you to only do that in private." They all laughed. Tee blushed and was glad it was dark. Ansen could say things nobody else could get away with. If Tee or Quinn had said the same exact thing, it would have come across as creepy.

"Sorry Ansen, just thinking. I understand your confusion, since you don't know how to do that." A good comeback that got a few smiles. You had to fight back carefully with Ansen. The last thing you wanted was an insult competition because you would lose.

"Come over and warm up by the fire, Tee," Hestie said. If anyone understood the need to just sit and think, it was Hestie. Tee walked over and plopped down next to her and Ansen. Guessing what troubled Tee, she asked, "What are you going to do after school lets out?" It was a little spooky how Hestie seemed to know what people were thinking and feeling.

Tee shrugged and said, "I'm not sure."

"We need help in the blacksmith shop. Dad keeps giving you hints, Tee," Ansen chimed in.

"I know, but Pete is perfect for that and almost ready. I don't want to be in his way," Tee said with a sigh.

"Knock it off, Tee," Ansen said angrily, "You are part of the family; didn't we all make that clear years ago? You have just as much right to join the family business as my brother does."

"I didn't mean it that way," Tee replied. "I'm just not as interested in blacksmithing as Pete is." He hesitated a moment and then said, "I talked to the professor today after the Tram presentation. There is a mechanics training program down in Landfall City. Ever since they put in the Tram, I've been interested in machinery. The sawmills and food processing plants running off the Apple River above and below the falls are fascinating. Maybe we can find a way to expand the blacksmithing business into machinery. I just need to figure out how to afford the school."

Tee then looked at Hestie and asked, "How did your interview with the professor go, Hestie?"

"Good. He's nice, in a gruff sort of way. He told Quinn and I that he will be putting both our names forward for admittance. He's pushing Quinn toward the engineering department but wants to know more about what I'm interested in."

"From what little I understood about what Quinn was saying earlier, I don't think he has to push him very hard," Diana said, smiling as she looked warmly over at Quinn.

Quinn had just opened his mouth when Ansen jumped in with a plea, "Diana, please don't get him going again."

Quinn smiled and said, "Okay, okay, no more trying to educate Luddites tonight."

"I would ask what a Luddite is, but I really don't want to know," Ansen said.

"So, what are you interested in, Hestie?" Tee asked.

"I'm not sure. I know I want to help people. Becoming a doctor sounds interesting, but I'm not sure what kind. Pediatrics and psychiatry both seem interesting."

Ansen smiled devilishly and said, "So little kids or crazy people."

"Well, knowing more about both might help me understand you a little better, Ansen," Hestie said with a rare jibe, causing everyone to laugh.

Tee sat back, completely at ease. Life couldn't get any better. He wished it could stay this way forever.

CHAPTER 8

DINNER AT THE INN

Del sat in the dining area of the bar at the Apple Lakes Inn waiting for Griff to arrive. His back was stiff. His legs ached from the hike up the falls. He had been walking gingerly since he had arrived. I really need to get more exercise, he thought.

Growing up in Apple Valley, he had gone up and down the falls trail more times than he could count. It seemed so easy when he was a young man. It was especially galling how cheerful Griff had been when they reached the top. Pointing out how perfect the weather was for hiking and with a sweep of his arm pointing out the tremendous view from the top. Griff wasn't normally this cheerful and Del knew it was his way of poking fun at Del's state of fitness.

He knew it was ridiculous to compare himself to a professional soldier. Especially one who thrived on exercise. But it was galling all the same. If he was fair, Griff had suggested stopping and resting several times. He knew it wasn't because Griff needed it. Anyone else from the Guard would have been trying to walk him into his grave.

Although Griff had a gruesome reputation within the Guard, he hid a dark secret. The man was, in reality, a bit of a softy. That is, if he respected you. He was especially polite with women.

Neither of them were married. In his case, he simply didn't have time for a wife. Academics was what he lived for. He had an occasional woman friend from time to time. But more often than not, it was someone he was collaborating with. It was lonely sometimes, but he had accepted many years ago that he would be a lifelong bachelor.

Del didn't know why Griff had never married. That wasn't a topic anyone was brave enough to bring up with him. Griff actually seemed to be a bit afraid of women. Which was somewhat endearing in such a gruff and violent man. Del certainly wouldn't tell anyone he suspected Griff had a soft side; he wasn't stupid. But it did cause him to smile.

Griff walked into the inn, sat down heavily, and without any pleasantries said with a grimace, "Do you have real beer up here? Or is the fruity crap all there is?"

"Good evening to you, too. As for the beer, you'll just have to tough it out, Griff," Del said with a smile. Before the Tram, it wasn't reasonable to cart much up the falls, even alcohol. At this point, there was pride in being different." Del moved a bit closer and whispered, "Not that you care, but the locals heard what you said and are smirking." Griff just rolled his eyes and shrugged.

Del ordered peach whiskey. When it arrived, Griff tasted it tentatively, made a sour face, and exhaled with a loud sigh, shaking his head in disgust.

"The good news is fresh venison is available tonight if we order quickly. Some local hunter just brought it in," Del said.

"It won't make up for the crappy drinks, but that is good news," Griff said with a sour grin. He then turned serious and said, "What do you know about Tee Stone?"

Del's face scrunched up in surprise and he said, "Strange you ask about him. In a normal year, I would be putting him forward. He's no genius, but his leadership potential is unusual. Strong enough academically, but with skills in mediation and negotiation beyond his age. He has a knack for organizing and collaborating. His teacher says everyone likes him."

"I know of at least one person who doesn't," Griff said, smiling, and they both chuckled, remembering the fight, or more accurately, the beating.

Del continued, "There are a pair of twins that are special, truly special. I will get them both admitted. I'm from this region so it will look preferential proposing two candidates. I can make that work by calling in a few favors. Once the other professors get Quinn and Hestie into class, any questions about preference will disappear. However, I can't make three work, no matter how well deserved."

"So, he's less irritating that your typical university know-it-all." Griff scoffed.

Del hesitated as his eyebrows came together. Then he smiled slowly and said, "I guess that's the truth of it. You have to admit the Guard has more than its share of overly large egos."

Griff smiled back at him and said, "You realize we are likely the worst of them." They both laughed.

"So why ask about Tee? He definitely doesn't look like Guard material," Del observed.

Griff chuckled. Shaking his head, he sighed and looked out the window with a troubled expression. Then he said, "He's unusual." Griff paused and sipped his whiskey, then said, "When I'm evaluating someone for the Guard, I sneak close to the exercise yard on the first day to observe how they interact with the other boys. Aggressiveness, ruthlessness, and a desire to win at all costs are Guard virtues. But so is teamwork. Bullies make poor additions to the Guard. They can be useful below the Wall but more often than not create more problems than benefits."

Griff took a deep breath and continued. "You saw the end of the fight at recess," Griff said. "First, it wasn't Tee's fight. He was protecting another kid who got sucker punched and was being viciously beaten. Having the smallest boy out there trying to break it up was weird. That it clearly didn't surprise any of his classmates made it even weirder. Second, instead of delaying for the teacher to come out, he pushed him hard, causing him to lose his temper and swing wildly. It was obvious he expected this, as he avoided the punch. Then he stepped inside for the kill. It was very aggressive. As you saw, the result wasn't pretty. His counterpunch had to be perfect, and it wasn't. That's when you walked out."

"I was horrified to see how badly beaten Quinn was," Del said.

Griff sighed and said, "So, that's one of your geniuses. Good thing he's smart because he's useless in a fight. If Tee hadn't stepped in, I would have. Given that he did, I decided to see what would happen." Griff smiled. "I expected him to get his ass kicked. And he did. What really shocked me was the realization he knew I was watching the whole time. When the teacher broke up the fight, he looked directly at me. He held his stare just long enough for it to be an accusation. I'm guessing he thought I should have stepped in. When I didn't, he made a snap decision to defend. Maybe to force me out of hiding. I was really well hidden and camouflaged. He should not have noticed me. That level of awareness in someone who hasn't been trained is unheard of."

Griff took another sip of his whiskey and continued. "To make it even more interesting, I had a recruitment meeting with the Apple Valley commander. He immediately started campaigning for Angus. No surprise there. Was quite effusive about it. Described him as skilled, tough, and highly motivated. He did observe that Angus was 'overenthusiastic in dominating others,' Guard speak for bully. He thought teamwork might be a problem, but thought he was worth a try.

"Then I asked about Tee. He was surprised at first. Then he said he wished Tee were bigger. He had the toughness, motivation, and instincts to join the Guard but clearly didn't pass the eye test. What really interested me was his success in the regional capture-the-flag games. As you know, that game mirrors aspects of military strategy, and he seems to be some kind of savant."

"Okay, so Tee has traits you like. You can't seriously be thinking of him as a recruit," Del said with surprise.

Griff sighed again and said, "Warfare isn't one dimensional. The most successful scouts are not always the best fighters. The best scouts seem to be those with endurance, awareness, patience, but most of all, judgement. Being a good officer is all about judgement and an ability to get others to follow you. As you know, our selection criteria are focused on hand-to-hand fighting skills and the ability to survive below the Wall. This is critical, but not sufficient, in my opinion."

Del held up his hand and said, "Hold on, I've met Dee. He would chew someone like Tee up and spit him out the first day. And the CGG would be applauding while he did it."

"Probably, yes," Griff replied with another troubled sigh.

"Tell me more about your geniuses. What makes them so special?" Griff asked.

"They're twins. A boy and a girl. Their father was an engineering student of mine years ago. Someone I collaborated with on the Tram design. He's a smart guy, easygoing, a bit odd, but does good work. Not a standout. Their mother Dorothy is another story. She is a once in a generation intellect. She was recruited and groomed to join the university staff as a researcher. Her mentor thought she would end up as chair of the university's medical research department someday.

"They're both from Apple Lake. Childhood sweethearts. They wanted to move back. She is one of the local doctors but consults with the university on a regular basis. She gets asked to help researchers filter out complexities to help in identifying cause and effect in their research data. She has an amazing and unique ability to see information in massive and confusing data sets."

Del paused to take a sip of whiskey. "Hestie is gifted, but perhaps not as unique as her mother. What is different is she has an abundance of empathy; reading people and situations extremely well. As you know, it's not unusual for really smart people to have limited social intelligence. Her mother, for instance, has a reputation for making blunt observations she doesn't realize are quite insulting. Hestie has the potential to be an excellent medical research doctor working directly with patients. Will be interesting to see what she eventually decides to do with all that.

"Quinn is brilliant and passionate about technology and engineering. The projects he showed me in his rickety workshop are far ahead of anything I've seen in a student entering the university. He has been engaged in an extensive self-study of topics that interest him since he was able to read. He will likely jump ahead at least a couple of years right away. I'm already convinced he will make enormous contributions. The challenge is that Hestie seems to have gotten all the social skills their parents had to give. It's entertaining to watch the two of them interact with others.

"They're extremely close and both well-liked by those who know them. Hestie for obvious reasons, but Quinn because he is always in a good mood bubbling over with happiness and enthusiasm about whatever has caught his fancy. Hestie artfully sooths over the bruised feelings Quinn creates for those who don't know him, while their friends just accept that Quinn is Quinn."

"Not sure I've seen you this enthusiastic about university candidates before," Griff observed.

"We'll we've had several whiskeys which might explain part of my enthusiasm."

"You've had several whiskeys; I could only stomach the one," Griff said with a sour look and a shudder. "I'm going to stay a few extra days. I want to do a little more background on Angus and talk with him. It turns out they have a capture-the-flag scrimmage this weekend. I want to observe and maybe talk to Tee a bit too. I may deliver recruit invites if I'm convinced they deserve them. I expect you're heading back tomorrow."

"Yeah, I'll be away before breakfast, so I'll see you at the next planning session," Del said.

Griff stood up from the table and as he walked away, he turned and said with a sarcastic grin, "Enjoy the Tram ride down."

Del just waved Griff away, smiling. I will definitely enjoy the ride down, he thought. I probably revealed more enthusiasm than I should have. I am wildly excited. But unfortunately, I can't reveal why my friend.

"Barmaid, one more whiskey please," Griff requested. After it arrived, he continued to sit, privately delighted, sipping his drink slowly, and making plans.

CHAPTER 9

INVITATION

Griff could hear the yelling before he rounded the corner and could see the farmhouse. He was surrounded by a pear orchard, so decided it must be the Willard farm. The house and the orchard didn't look well maintained. Most farmers were diligent with their crops and farming equipment. Some less so with their houses, but most kept things clean and orderly. This farm was neither.

Standing in front of the barn was a tall, broad, overweight, red-faced, scruffy looking man about Griff's age flailing a young boy's bare bottom with a belt. He was screaming, "You worthless piece of shit! You're not worth the food I give you."

The boy had his pants down around his ankles, blood dripping down one leg, and tears streaming down. His mother just stood there watching. Terror evident on her face. Angus and two other boys were standing in the background. Angus was showing a very thin smile, as if he might be enjoying this.

They all suddenly spied Griff approaching. The man stopped beating the boy and in a challenging voice said, "Who are you and what do you want?" Before Griff could answer, he added, "Whoever you are, I don't like strangers on my property, so state your business and then get the hell out of here."

Griff continued to walk up without responding until he came face to face with him. "My name is Griffith Ricks. I'm Master Sergeant for the Guard. I'm here to talk to Angus on Guard business."

The man looked surprised, and now perhaps a bit embarrassed. How he could be surprised that Griff was in the Guard given he was in uniform was hard to understand. He held the blood splattered belt in one hand while gripping the boy with the other. Now that Griff was closer, it was obvious he was drunk. His breath and clothes reeked of alcohol. His features firmed up and he shoved the boy to the ground and said sternly, "Get back to work." Then, looking back at Griff, he said, "You talk to me about the Guard, not Angus."

Griff's face froze, he stared him down, and then calmly said, "You must be Asher Willard."

"Yeah, he's my boy, and he does what I tell him to do. You here to invite him to recruit training?" Asher said, glaring back.

"Angus has reached his maturity and doesn't need your permission for anything anymore," Griff said. "I'm happy to explain Guard recruit training with parents once an invite has been given so they can advise. I'll come back after I've talked to Angus to answer any questions." Griff then turned to Angus and said, "Come take a walk with me."

Asher Willard's brows crashed together. He opened his mouth as if he would object but then turned and while walking away yelled, "Woman, get me a whisky."

Griff walked back down the path away from the farm and said, "Angus, I would like to invite you to Guard recruit training. The next session starts in two weeks."

"Thank you, sir. I was expecting an invite. I think I'll like being in the Guard," Angus said without a shred of humility.

"You'll have to get through training to get into the Guard, and it's going to be difficult. We don't take everyone we invite," Griff said.

"The only thing I'm worried about is whether some current Guard's kid gets pushed ahead of me. I deserve to be in the Guard, just like my dad deserved it. Everyone knows getting in isn't all about merit," Angus said in a challenging voice.

Griff stopped, turned to Angus with a frown, and said, "I always encourage recruit invites to say or ask anything in the initial conversation. If that was a question, let me assure you merit is the only criteria for entry into the Guard. If that is an accusation, be very careful who you voice it to in the future. Guard members, including myself, don't take kindly to false accusations." This was delivered as an obvious threat.

Angus leaned forward with a look on his face as if to argue, thought better of it, and said, "I accept the invitation. I just want to make sure recruit training is fair."

Griff was watching Angus carefully. This kid was a volcano ready to erupt. After seeing the heartbreaking scene in the yard, he could understand why Angus might have some issues. He hoped the thin smile he saw on Angus's face was a nervous one and not enjoyment. It had taken every shred of control Griff had not to thrash the father. He would report the boy's abuse to the local sheriff when he got back to town. He would strongly recommend the sheriff make sure the woman was okay. He was especially worried about her.

"One other thing, Angus," Griff said, reverting to his calm voice. "There are two invites this year for recruit training."

"So, you invited Ansen?" Angus said with a tinge of a sneer.

"No, I'm going to invite his cousin Tee," Griff said in a bland voice.

"What! You're kidding me," Angus said, laughing. "No way that little turd is qualified for the Guard."

Griff's face clouded as he started to get angry again, told himself to calm down, and said in a stern voice, "I decide who's qualified for an invite, not you. I know there have been some issues between you and Tee. That stops now. Guard members are brothers from the moment they are invited. You will put away any ill feelings toward him now or turn down the invite. He's going to be told the same thing."

Griff watched Angus as he looked to the ground, obviously trying to control his anger. Angus took a big breath, let it out slowly, and looked back up. Griff stared him in the eyes for a few moments and said, "Are you accepting the invite to recruit training?"

Angus looked down again and said in a flat voice, "Yes, sir."

With that, Griff turned around, and they walked back to the farmhouse. Asher Willard was sitting on the porch drinking from one glass while another was sitting on the table beside him. He said, "We got started on the wrong foot. Sit down and have a drink."

"No thank you. I don't drink in the middle of the day," Griff said, not willing to pretend this was going to be a cordial conversation. "Your wife should join us so she can ask questions, too."

"She's too stupid to have anything worth listening to. Making dinner, cleaning the house, and warming my bed are the only uses I have for her," he said, chuckling as if Griff would get the joke.

He didn't. "Any questions?" Griff asked curtly.

"No, I know everything about the Guard. I want to hear you promise Angus won't get cheated out of a spot in the Guard like I was," Asher said in a challenging voice.

"Our selection process is based on merit. Those who don't get in are simply those who don't measure up. Any other questions?" Griff said in a tense voice.

"No," Asher said, fuming.

As Griff walked around the bend in the road, the loud and angry voice of Asher Willard could be heard again. Evidently, Angus had told his father that Tee had been invited. He couldn't make out all the words, but scrawny and turd came through clearly. Then he heard Asher say in a clear voice that Arti must have spread her legs to get Tee an invite.

Griff stopped, gritted his teeth, and took a deep breath. He stood there stiffly for almost a minute until his anger was under control and then walked on. He knew what he would do if he went back. He decided the best thing was to pretend he didn't hear it and move on. Was Richards right? Griff wondered. Could they really fix Angus by taking him away from his father? Could they instill Guard values? He didn't have a good feeling about it.

After giving a report to the Sheriff, Griff asked where he could find Tee. "He's likely up at the archery range. Practices all the time," the sheriff reported and then said, "Thanks for the information on Asher. We are constantly going out there to resolve problems with neighbors and making up excuses to check in on Sara and the kids. Sara won't say anything bad about her husband and makes up stories to cover her and the kid's injuries. 'I walked into a door, he fell down the stairs,' etc. She's terrified of him. I know somebody is eventually going to get seriously hurt. But I can't do anything until they do."

Griff was nervous about the next stop. He hadn't spoken with Arti since her heroics at the Wall those many years ago. But first he had to go find Tee and make the invitation. Deciding to invite Tee had been a hard decision. The easy part was the leadership, intelligence, creativity, and boldness he exhibited in Apple Valley's capture-the-flag games. It was a child's game, but it showed attributes he thought were sorely needed in the Guard.

By itself, it wouldn't have been enough. Griff had to be confident an invitee could get through recruit training. Tee's immediate defense of his friend on the playground was what ultimately swayed him. The boy had courage. He was willing to fight a losing battle. He just didn't have the size the Guard was looking for.

Griff walked into the clearing and saw Tee with a very pretty, tall, and athletic looking girl. They were shooting arrows at a distant target with impressive accuracy. Griff stopped and watched for a while, finally deciding Richards wasn't exaggerating Tee's expertise with a bow. The girl was getting all her arrows inside the red circle, but spaced somewhat randomly. Tee's were all grouped dead center. He guessed having Arti as a mother probably had something to do with that.

He walked up and interrupted them saying, "Excuse me, Tee, do you have a few minutes?"

Tee and the girl turned around, both surprised to see him there. "Yes, sir. Diana, I'll be back in a few minutes." He gave her a quick smile, turned around, and walked off with Griff to a bench just out of earshot.

"Are you here to ask questions about Ansen?" Tee said.

"No son. I actually here to offer you an invite to Guard recruit training."

Tee's mouth opened, shut, opened again and with a shocked look on his face he sputtered, "You have to be kidding me."

"To be honest, if you accept, everyone is going to think it's a joke of some kind," Griff said in a quiet voice.

"But I'm way too small to be in the Guard," Tee said.

"Everybody has deficiencies. As far as I can tell, this is your only significant one," Griff said seriously.

Tee stopped and looked down at the ground. He started to say something, stopped, and thought some more. Finally, he said, "Thank you for the offer, sir. I don't know what to say. I never imagined anything like this. Can I talk to my mom and think about it before I give you an answer?"

"Of course. I'll need to have your decision by this time next week since I'll make someone else an offer if you refuse," Griff said kindly. He thought it was a good sign that Tee wanted to think it over.

"Ansen would be a much better choice for this," Tee said.

Griff's face softened, then he said in a soothing voice, "These discussions we have before you accept or reject my offer are completely private. Anything you say will be kept in confidence, never to be shared with anyone. Can you promise the same before I comment on Ansen or tell you about the challenges you'll face if you accept?"

"Yes, sir, I will keep what is said between us," Tee said in a serious tone.

"Your cousin has a lot of good qualities. He's an exceptional athlete, but just an excellent fighter. He's not exceptional because he doesn't have the drive and passion to persevere, no matter what. This isn't a bad quality in a person. It's completely normal. But normal is a bad quality for a Guard recruit. If he was going to be invited, it would have happened last year when he graduated," Griff said.

"I understand," was all Tee had to say.

"I've invited you because the Guard needs to expand its capabilities. All our lives are at stake. Fighting it out below the Wall is a vital part of our defense, but it isn't adequate. You've shown great skill in discovering weaknesses in your opponents and creatively taking advantage of them. While capture-the-flag is a child's game, you've shown exceptional leadership, planning, and execution in those contests these past two years. I think those skills translate to the future of the Guard.

"Unfortunately, you are small in stature and that is going to cause you a lot of suffering if you accept my offer. Fortunately, you are large in heart, incredibly large, it seems. You'll need all of it because it won't be easy, and it won't be fair. If I thought you might quit once you start, I would never make an invite to you," Griff explained. Then he waited patiently for Tee's reply.

Tee thought some more, looked up and with fire in his eyes said, "I have been bullied my entire life. I know recruit training would be far worse than anything I've overcome. But, If I can make a difference to keep my family and everyone else safe, then I don't see how I could do anything other than say yes and see it out until the end."

Any doubts Griff had vanished. He was right about Tee. Recruit training was going to be extra ugly. But this is what a leader in the Guard should look like.

"A little background, in case you don't know this already. Recruit training consists of forty-five days of shake out, or as we call it IH, In Hell. A large number of those invited quit voluntarily during this. It is brutal, degrading, and only the very strong survive. Next, we have ninety days of combat training with an emphasis on learning to fight as a team known as AH, After Hell. Some drop out in this phase. Usually because they realize they won't make the cut.

"We limit graduation to the top fifty recruits based on a point system you can learn about later. After that, we spend another ninety days on basic training that assesses each recruit for various training regiments that will last for another year to eighteen months. Everyone is extensively trained for fighting below the Wall. But some are given extra training, such as scouting or development for promotion into the officer ranks.

"However, remember, everyone is a fighter first. Talk it over with your mom and let me know your decision, Tee," Griff said, smiling. He then handed him a piece of paper and said, "Here is where you can reach me. Get your decision to me by this time next week. Now, how do I find your mother so I can answer her questions?"

"She's down at my aunt's below the falls, and it's not clear when she'll return. My aunt has been really sick, and Mom is taking care of her and my cousins," Tee said.

A huge weight came off of Griff, and disappointment quickly replaced it. He was embarrassed that Arti had such an impact on him. It was ridiculous at his age. He didn't even really know her, for heaven's sake. He shook off his jumbled thoughts and said to Tee, "Give her the address and I'll try and answer any questions she has. Given she's spent so much time at the Wall, and much of that supporting the Guard, she probably has a good idea what you're getting into."

Griff's face took on a softer appearance, and he said, "Some advice if you're open to it. You'll learn in the Guard that you never reveal strengths or weaknesses to an enemy. You are going to have to think of the instructors and the other recruits as enemies until graduation. Your bunkmate being the only exception. With that in mind, keep your swimming ability a secret. Letting it be known will just offer another avenue for abuse."

Tee certainly understood that one, he thought. His most recent nickname was a perfect example.

"Last item. The other invite from Apple Valley was given to Angus Willard. I know there is history and you two don't get along. The minute you accept the invitation, Angus is to be viewed as a brother. That means you have to let all the history go. Do you understand?"

"I understand and I will do that," Tee said.

Griff was pleased. He was a little surprised that he had been harboring more doubts than he realized. Those doubts had been erased. Now he concentrated on how he was going to win the initial fight with Nate and Dee. Nate was the CGG, Commander General of the Guard, and Dee was the head drill instructor. He knew both of them really well, having served together in various capacities. He knew they would hate Tee on sight. Griff relished a good fight. Especially one with no rules.

CHAPTER 10

OBLIGATION

Tee told Diana about the invite as soon as Griff left the archery range. He guessed he should have kept it a secret so he could be sure to be the one to tell his mom. 'That bird has flown,' as Grammy liked to say. Diana had given him a strange look when he first told her. She seemed sad instead of the mixture of excitement and worry he had expected. Then she continued the oddness by saying how much she *and* Ansen would miss him if he accepted. How proud *they* would both be.

Diana had never spoken of her and Ansen like that before. She always spoke in terms of herself and let Ansen speak for himself. It was strange and perhaps a subtle message that she perceived his interest and was letting him know it would lead nowhere. That certainly made it easier to consider leaving Apple Valley for good. Guard members spent the bulk of their time near the Wall or at the numerous ocean cliff side forts. It stung, but it was also the type of thoughtful, caring gesture Diana would make.

His mother heard about the invite almost immediately, of course. She asked him to come down the falls and stay with her at his aunts for a few days. His aunt lived with her husband and his other cousins just outside Apple Falls. Tee didn't know these cousins as well. They lived below the falls, and they were much younger. His aunt was the youngest of Grammy's children and much younger than his mom and uncle.

Arti gave her son a big hug and pulled him into the chaos of a home with four children ranging in age from six months to four years. Tee had been an only child but was used to the hum of activity from the time he spent at Uncle Hugh's with his Aunt Anny, Ansen, Pete, and Tia. It was a familiar and welcome feeling.

"So how long was it going to be before you told me?" Arti asked with hands on hips and a stern expression.

"It's only been one day, Mom," Tee replied. "I should have kept it private until I got down here."

Arti's eyes softened and then she said, "I'm very proud of you, Tee."

"Thanks, Mom, but I don't know if I'm really cut out for the Guard," Tee replied.

"The Guard doesn't offer invitations to recruit training unless they're certain you are," Arti said firmly.

"Their master sergeant who invited me claims I have capabilities the Guard lacks. He told me it would be especially hard for me as the instructors and other recruits would resent someone of my stature getting invited," Tee said with a questioning face.

Arti's face softened again, and she said, "I am slender and have lived with the jibes and offhand remarks my whole life. One of the reasons I have worked so hard on my archery was a desire to feel better about myself. Your father was short. You got the worst of that combination. Your father was also very smart, loving, and charismatic. I'd like to think you got the best from both of us instead of the worst."

Arti hesitated, then continued. "Regardless of your blessings and challenges, you've been asked to sacrifice. To make a difference for your family and all of Pacifica. Your Friday night bonfires only happen because of the sacrifices made by your father and countless others." Arti stopped and waited for Tee to respond.

"Grammy says protecting others isn't a choice, it's an obligation," Tee said.

"My mother is a wise woman. She lost two sons and a son-in-law at the Wall but has never wavered," Arti said softly.

"To be honest, I don't have questions about whether I should do this or not. Guess I've spent too much time with you and Grammy for that," he said with a sad grin. "I just want to make sure you're okay with it."

"I won't lie and tell you I'm not worried. But I would be disappointed if you chose not to accept this invitation. All our lives depend on being able to defend our little piece of heaven. The Guard has recognized that you are a special young man. Embrace it, Tee."

CHAPTER 11

CELEBRATION

The plan was to get together Friday night at the beach for a sendoff for Hestie, Quinn, and Tee. Then Grammy declared she was showing up. If Grammy was showing up, then everyone from all four families would be there. Grammy had been a big part of all their lives. Babysitting, entertaining them with stories, telling fortunes with her deck of cards, and occasionally applying consequences for their youthful indiscretions. She had this head thumping thing she did. She would flick her middle finger hard alongside your head. It stung, but didn't actually cause any damage. They had all gotten head thumped at some point, even Hestie.

Ansen joked that he had a permanent indentation on the side of his head from the number of times she got him. You had to be on the lookout for her if you had done something wrong. She also provided an ear for anything and everything. You could tell Grammy your deepest secrets and know they would remain private. Of course, you were required to receive her 'good advice' in return. It was advice you might not want to hear. But you knew the advice was good even when you chose to ignore it. Although not related, Hestie was eerily similar to Grammy in that regard.

Years ago, Tee had told Hestie, "Grammy is who you'll be in sixty years." He'd meant it as a joke.

Hestie hesitated, looked at him seriously, then her face slowly transformed into a shy smile. "That might be the best compliment I've ever had. Thank you Tee."

He had been taken aback by her reply. Older now, he was starting to really see and appreciate Grammy. It really was a nice compliment. Tee sat down next to his grandmother on the rough bench he and Ansen built for her years ago. "Why did you come down to the beach tonight, Grammy?"

Grammy looked at him with a sparkle in her eyes and said, "There are important events in life, Tee. You ought not to miss them. I've known all of you since you were babies. You are as important to me as you are to each other. Sorry I'm invading your bonfire, but I wanted to enjoy it with all of you. Don't worry, I'll go early and leave you young people to your fun. Just humor an old woman for a couple of hours."

Tee raised his hands palms up, shook his head side to side and said, "Grammy, don't be silly. You're welcome to stay as long as you want. I'm glad you decided to 'Invade.' It's fun having everyone here. Much better than our typical Friday. Maybe we should have been doing this all along."

"Nonsense. Young people should get away from old people and have a little fun," she said with a warm smile. She lowered her voice. "Are you nervous about recruit training Tee? Before you answer, you should know I won't accept lies from you tonight," Grammy said with a fake stern look on her face.

Tee loved that his grandmother could be blunt and empathetic all at once. It was quite a skill. "Yes, very, but don't tell anyone," he whispered with a smile.

Grammy smiled back nodding and said, "Your secret is safe with me. What worries you?"

"The Guard recruiter told me I would have an especially hard time. He said there will be instructors at the school offended I was offered a slot in recruit training and will try and get me to quit."

"We were all surprised when you were chosen. Not because you don't deserve it, but the Guard does seem to have its standard look," Grammy said thoughtfully. "You can do this Tee. You've been pig-headed, stubborn, and prone to single-mindedness since the day you were born. You don't give up even when you should. So, I pity those who try to get you to quit."

"Well, thanks for the compliment, I think," Tee said, smiling warmly. "Quitting isn't what I worry about. I'm worried that however hard I try, I still won't make it."

"If you give it everything you've got, and don't make it, we'll all be proud. Especially your mother," Grammy said confidently. "I'm not worried about that, and you shouldn't be either." She searched his face until she was satisfied he had really heard her and then said, "One last question. Are you going to tell Diana how you feel?" Grammy asked with softness in her eyes and voice.

"No, she doesn't need that, and neither does Ansen. If I tell her, it will be uncomfortable forever between the three of us. She loves Ansen, and he loves her. That's the end of it." Tee wasn't sure how Grammy had extracted his feelings for Diana from him. She had a way of getting people to tell her things they hardly admitted to themselves. At the time, it had felt good to tell her, but she needed to stop harassing him about that.

"Okay, Tee, I will stop. For now, anyway," Grammy said with a wicked smile. "I do need to tell you this. We ALL believe in you. Remember that when it gets tough. Now, go, have fun with your friends. This time next week you'll be on an exciting adventure. Be sure to enjoy it, especially the tough times."

Grammy watched Tee walk back toward the fire and his friends with love and sadness swelling in her breast. She would miss him, Hestie, and Quinn terribly. They would never know how much she would miss not having them nearby. The three of them needed to move on with their lives and I need to support that, she thought. Just think of how Tony and Dorothy must feel. Both their children are moving away at the same time. At least she would still have Ansen and Diana nearby. She loved her grandsons fiercely, and Diana was a wonderful girl. She would be thrilled to have her in the family. Shaking her head, she marveled over how blind and stupid young people were. Diana and Hestie love each other and all three boys. Tee and Ansen are more like brothers than cousins. But none of them seem to have a clue about what's really going on. I'm glad I'm an old woman and don't have to live through the stupidity, pain, and suffering of being young.

As the fire died down, Grammy decided the young people had had enough of old people for the evening. She gave Anny 'the look' and Tee's aunt said, "Pete, Tia, let's go, it's time."

"I want to stay. It's Friday night. No school tomorrow," Tia said, pouting dramatically.

Tee's aunt hesitated. Everyone knew that Ansen and Diana would stay at the fire after everyone else had gone. This had been their pattern all spring. It would interfere with their blossoming romance if Ansen had to walk Tia home.

"Tia's no bother Aunt Anny. If you let her stay, I'll walk her home," Tee said. He had a special place in his heart for Tia. It was impossible to be unhappy around her. Tia was responsible for everyone calling him Tee. She had had trouble pronouncing his name as a toddler and when she started reading, she noticed their names started with the same letter. "Everyone says his name wrong. It should start like mine does," she said. Then she started just calling him Tee. It stuck.

His aunt looked at Tee warmly and with a smile said, "Okay, we'll have a little peace in the house this evening. Make sure it's not too late."

Tia ran over, jumped into his lap, and gave him a huge hug, "Thank you, Tee!"

"No problem, squirt," he said, smiling with a warm glow inside. Tia was always so endearingly dramatic with her affections.

"I want to stay too, Mom," Pete said with a slight whine for effect.

"If Tee walks you home with Tia, then fine. In the meantime, you listen to Ansen. When he says it's time to go home, you go. Do not overstay your welcome. If you give Ansen any trouble, you'll have your father to answer to," his mother said with a stern look on her face and his father nodding in the background.

"Okay, Mom," Pete promised, while showing a little frustration in his voice. Pete was a mirror image of Ansen halfway through his final growth spurt. He would grow to be as large or larger and was already quite the athlete for his age.

Instead of having Ansen's easygoing nature, he was intense and focused. He thought he was old enough to walk Tia home. Just like he thought he should already be working in the family blacksmithing business. Tee was his latest hero in getting an invitation to Guard recruit training. This was something he hoped to do someday, and so he peppered Tee with questions.

"How long is your training? When will you know you've made it? Do recruits really die during training? Will they send you to the Wall? Can you send letters telling us how it's going? Can I send you a letter? Why did you get an invitation and Ansen didn't?" This last question was an obvious dig at his older brother, and Pete had glanced sideways at his brother when he said it.

"Whoa Pete, one question at a time," Tee said, laughing. "I'll send letters to your Aunt Arti, and she'll read them to everyone. You can send me letters too. But I won't receive or be able to write letters for forty-five days. They call that In Hell, the first part of the Shake Out. I know training is intense, but I'm pretty sure they aren't trying to kill us. I don't know much about the Wall other than your Aunt Arti's stories. The Guard is secretive about their training, so can't answer questions because I don't know."

"Pete, give it a break. You've been after him all night. As far as why he was selected, it's pretty simple. Tee is the toughest dude you'll ever meet, and he's really smart about warfare stuff. I am neither of those things." Then, with just the right hesitation, he added, "I am, however, much better looking," Ansen said while glancing over at Tee with a smile. Everyone groaned.

Ansen's self-awareness and self-confidence were amazing to Tee. Ansen knew what he was, and he knew what he wasn't. His little brother's insult was quickly shrugged off with a joke. What had become an uncomfortable situation became comfortable again. Not that Ansen wouldn't get even with Pete, that would come later. Pete was destined to suffer from a barrage of not so good-natured ribbing when Ansen decided it was time for payback. Pete really ought to know better.

"What made you write the 'little people' essay, Tee?" Diana asked, with mirth dancing in her eyes. I've never seen Ms. Clarkson so frustrated. The best part was when she chose you to debate your 'opinions' against Hestie, who made exactly the opposite arguments."

"That was fun," said Hestie, smiling. "I do think you pushed it a bit too far in the debate by suggesting genocide against little people to free up resources might have been the morally correct decision. You were supposed to pick one topic after all."

Tee, smiling with an evil grin, said, "I don't know. She looked right at me as she was describing the effects of negative cultural biases against those of small stature. It was the sympathetic part of the look that did it. I actually got a really good grade. She said irony combined with sarcasm and humor are an effective means for getting people to think. To question their belief systems. She told me that after her initial shock, she decided Hestie and I had coordinated our papers and the debate as a political protest. As you know, she is all about the downtrodden. She said I ought to consider a career in social work or politics. I laughed all the way home."

"That was probably the most fun I had in class all year. Everybody talked about it for days," Diana said, her eyes bright.

The chatter continued until Tee was sitting with Pete, Quinn, and

Hestie, watching the fire as it burned its way down to the embers. He looked over to where Ansen, Diana, and Tia were sitting and could tell it was time to call it a night. Tia was entertaining Diana, as only Tia could do. But the look on Ansen's face said he had had enough of his sister's theatrics for the evening. "Well guys, I think it's time for me to go," Tee said.

"No!" said Tia. "It's still early and I won't see you before you leave."

"I promise to come by the house before I leave, Tia," Tee said.

"Pete, Tia, it's time to go. Tee agreed to walk you home, and it's time," Ansen said with a firm look going back and forth between them.

"Hestie and I will go with you guys," Quinn said, getting up and perhaps showing one of his rare instances of social awareness.

So, the five of them headed down the path toward Apple Lake, with Pete barraging Tee once more with questions as Tia glued herself to Hestie, chattering like a bird. Quinn brought up the rear, deep in thought. Tee had snuck a quick look as they left the clearing. He saw Ansen and Diana leaning their heads together and fought down his rising jealousy. I really need to get a grip, he thought. He was lucky to have Ansen as his cousin. And lucky to have a lifelong friend in Diana. He would get past this. They would all be friends forever. He just needed to keep reminding himself.

As he was sorting through his emotions, he heard the menacing voice of Angus say, "I told you your cousin wouldn't always be around, turd." Tee stopped as Angus and his two younger brothers stepped out onto the trail.

"We're supposed to put the past behind us, Angus. We're brothers now, remember?" Tee said with steel in his voice.

Angus stepped forward and said, "I kick the shit out of my brothers all the time. Why should you be any different?"

"I don't want to fight, Angus," Tee said firmly.

"You don't have a choice, turd," Angus said as he rushed forward, diving toward Tee's knees. He was intending to get him on the ground to negate Tee's quickness. Tee knew once he was on the ground, he was lost. He had seen Angus employ this tactic before, and in an instant, he stepped forward and planted his knee directly into Angus's nose with a loud crunch.

Angus held both hands to his nose, swearing as the blood rushed out and said, "You're dead, turd."

Tee backed up to give himself more room. He had noticed out of the corner of his eye that Tia had kept her head. When Ansen and his brothers showed themselves, she immediately ran back toward the beach to get Ansen. If he could delay long enough for Ansen to show up, this would turn into a fair fight. He knew Angus would likely back away at that point.

Tee didn't notice that Angus's youngest brother had gotten behind him. So, when he shuffled backward, he unknowingly backed right into him. He got pushed forward, right into Angus's arms.

Tee was forced to the ground, and Angus started beating him viciously. Chaos erupted. Hestie was screaming for everyone to stop. Both Quinn and Pete had jumped in to help but were pulled off Angus and into separate fights by the brothers. Quinn was quickly knocked to the ground by Angus's youngest brother, who pummeled him as he lay curled up on the ground. Pete was faring better, fighting off the older of the two brothers when Ansen slammed into Angus, knocking him off Tee. The two of them stood up and squared off.

"This isn't your fight, Ansen," said Angus, sounding like he had a cold from the blood in his nose.

"It is now, asshole," Ansen replied as he surged forward with a series of punches, driving Angus backward. After a hard punch to the stomach, Angus dropped his guard, and Ansen nailed his broken nose with a hard left jab. That dropped Angus to the ground where he stayed, holding his nose and swearing. All the fight had gone out of him.

Hestie touched Tee's shoulder lightly and asked, "Are you okay, Tee? You got hit pretty hard in the head." Then Diana came over to examine him as well and they both started treating him like a toddler who had just skinned his knee. Tee didn't know which was worse. Getting beaten up by Angus or getting sympathy and ministering from Hestie and Diana.

He had never felt so humiliated. Why did anyone think he could become a member of the Guard?

CHAPTER 12

ANGUS

Griff arrived in Apple Valley early in the morning. He was very grumpy. He had been riding a horse or hiking most of the day before and all night. He had gotten an urgent message from Richards the morning before that Tee had been ambushed by Angus and his brothers and was injured. By sheer luck, he had been up toward the north end of Eureka Valley, which made a quick trip possible. No sleep, but possible. The week before the start of each recruit class was very busy for Griff. He was not happy to start it off this way.

Griff's main concern was whether Tee was so injured he couldn't start training. Missing a cycle would mean his invitation to Tee might be discovered and that would make it harder to force him through. Unless Richards was misrepresenting what happened, his next task was to tell Angus his invitation was being revoked. He was sure that was going to be an interesting conversation, especially with Angus's father.

Griff knocked on Tee's door and a badly bruised Tee answered the door. "Good morning sir, would you like to come in?" Tee asked with deference.

"Are you okay, son?" Griff asked with obvious concern.

"Yeah, just a few bruises. I'll be fine," Tee answered back while limping slightly into the front room of the home. Sitting in the front room was an old woman with bright, warm eyes. Tee motioned toward her and said, "This is my grandmother."

"Pleased to meet you, ma'am," Griff said.

"Mr. Ricks is Master Sergeant for the Guard, Grammy," Tee said to complete the introductions.

"So, you're the one who invited Tee to attend recruit training," Grammy said, locking eyes with Griff.

"Yes, ma'am," was all Griff said.

"Good, you're polite. You must also be smart if you understand Tee's worth," Grammy said and gave him a devilish smile.

"I'm not sure about the smart part, ma'am. But I am impressed enough to want him in the Guard," Griff said respectfully. He hesitated while Grammy continued to examine him and then said, "Tee, can we talk somewhere privately?"

Grammy stood up and walked toward the door. She hesitated with her hand on the doorknob and said, "I'll head out. Time to get home and feed the animals. Tee you stop by later, okay?"

"I will Grammy. Love you," Tee said.

"Love you too, my boy," Grammy said as she closed the door behind her.

"I need to hear your version of what happened, Tee," Griff said.

"It's pretty simple. Angus attacked me while I was walking home from our regular Friday night bonfire. I had my two younger cousins with me, as well as my next-door neighbors, Hestie and Quinn. He stepped out of the dark and told me he wanted to fight. I reminded him of what you said. I told him I didn't want to fight. Then he attacked me," Tee explained.

"I've heard he has a badly broken nose," Griff said questioningly.

"I kneed him in the nose when he dove at my legs. Tia ran to get Ansen, who showed up pretty soon after the fight started. He pulled Angus off me and hit him in the nose again. It did look pretty bad," Tee said.

Griff stared at him for a while and then said, "I believe you."

"Just like that?" Tee asked.

"Just like that," Griff confirmed. "Will you have any trouble making it to training?"

"I can make it to training, but am wondering if I'm really who the Guard needs," Tee said. "My cousin Ansen had to save me. I'm doubting whether I can make a difference."

"You can make a difference," Griff said firmly.

Tee hesitated, took a deep breath, and said, "Well then, the choice is easy. Grammy was just here repeating what my mom said. If you can make a difference, then it isn't a choice, it's an obligation." And then Tee visibly relaxed and with one corner of his mouth raised, said, "Recruit training can't be worse than having to face Grammy if I fail to make good on an obligation." Tee then turned serious and said, "I will treat Angus as my brother in the Guard. I'm sorry things spun out of control."

Griff relaxed inside. This just confirmed once again that he had made the right decision.

"Okay, we'll expect you next week. Do not be late," Griff said with steely eyes. "Is your mother back yet?"

"No, my aunt is still sick but getting better. It's going to be another day or two. She said she really doesn't have any questions. Just wants to make sure I recognize and honor my obligations," Tee said.

As Griff left Tee's home, he was angry. Really angry. He knew he should have calmed down before he went out to the Willard farm. But he was on a mission. As Griff rounded the bend and saw the farmhouse, he could see that Asher Willard was on the porch drinking again. And early in the morning too. He took a deep breath to calm himself and walked up without announcing himself.

"What are you doing back here?" Willard said. "Guard training doesn't start until next week and Angus has work to do until then."

"Where is Angus? I need to talk with him," Griff said.

"You can tell me whatever it is he needs to know," Asher Willard said. Just then, Angus came out of the barn, stopped, and then casually approached the two of them.

"Angus, I'm here to tell you not to bother coming to Guard training next week," Griff said sternly. "Your invitation has been revoked. I told you to treat Tee as a brother and yet you decided to ambush him. And you couldn't even do that by yourself. You had to have help."

"That's not what happened," Angus shouted back. "Ansen, Pete, and Tee ambushed us while we were walking home."

"So, you're a liar as well as a coward," Griff said firmly.

"Don't you call my boy a liar. Real men scare you, don't they? You don't want them in your precious Guard. I've had enough of you wimpy Guard bastards. It's time you get your ass kicked by a real man," Asher said as he stepped forward.

Mrs. Willard took one step toward him meekly, put her hand lightly on his chest and said to her husband, "Let's just calm down and talk this over."

Asher's face exploded with anger. He backhanded his wife, sending her head over heels off the porch, and charged Griff.

He thought later that the backhand was what did it. Usually, he would have simply restrained someone in this situation until they calmed down. Especially someone drunk, out of shape, and no threat to actually hurt him. Instead, Asher was being tended to by the local doctor for a broken sternum. He had hit him with enough force that it looked like Asher would likely have a permanent deformity from it.

Angus had stepped in to help his dad and gotten his nose broken again for his troubles. Griff actually felt a bit bad about that. It was sort of mean. What bothered Griff more were the sobs coming from Sara Willard. He couldn't imagine what her life must be like living in this household.

The incident cost Griff the rest of the day. A day he could ill afford. The sheriff had to get testimony from him and all the witnesses at the farm. If Griff had not been Master Sergeant of the Guard. And if the Sheriff hadn't already been looking for reasons to lock Asher up, he might have been held longer. Hope for the family arrived in the form of Dr. Dorothy Espers.

Griff was impressed with the local doctor's no-nonsense approach. She insisted that all members of the family undergo a medical evaluation. When she finished the examinations, she presented the Sheriff with her written opinion that the wife and youngest son were being subjected to life-threatening physical abuse. She recommended they get the judge to issue a restraining order and move Sara Willard and her youngest son to a safe location. They ended up spending some time that afternoon talking about medical procedures at the Wall and what could be done to improve them.

Griff realized he had met her before, but in the heat of battle, he really hadn't paid her much attention. He took a mental note to set up some time with her and the Guard medic corps to discuss some of the improvements she suggested.

As the sun was setting, Griff reached the bottom of the lower falls. Another hour and he would be at the Apple Falls Inn. Two whole days and one night wasted.

IN HELL

It was a cold, brisk, clear day and Dee was in an extremely good mood. He was nearly forty years old with dark hair, icy blue eyes, and a bulldog face. With massive arms and legs, his strength was legendary. His fighting skills were second only to Master Sergeant Ricks. He was bundled up against the cold with his heavy parka. Steam was coming out with every breath.

He always looked forward to training up the future of the Guard. Dee was short for "Drill Instructor." A nickname given to him years ago. He embraced this assignment so much that he encouraged its use. By now, everyone had forgotten what his real name was.

In Dee's mind, there was no contribution higher than taking boys with raw ability and turning them into Guard Newbies. He was pleased and honored that he was the one who owned this critical function. Dee gladly dedicated his life to making the Guard better.

IH was always interesting. You learned who was mentally tough, and who wasn't. It was always surprising who stood out and who quit early. The Hell part was a bit misleading because the physical fitness and depravity portion of training was done at a training facility in a high valley. It was cold at any time of the year. The elevation mixed with the cold was a challenge all by itself. They would move to their main training facility down below the Landfall Dam once this portion was complete. This allowed for better skills training and taught them to deal with the heat as well.

He expected this was going to be a special group. Not all recruit classes were equal. Some were weaker, and some were stronger. This class had a lot of Guard members' sons. It wasn't nepotism. In fact, the bar was a bit higher for them as nobody wanted to be embarrassed. Growing up, they understood what life in the Guard was all about. They also had a parent who was an elite warrior helping them perfect their fighting skills. He was especially enthusiastic that Barin Phillips's son Jay was in this class. He had watched him win the youth hand to hand combat championship the previous spring.

In his opinion, Jay was a unique talent. Likely better than his father, and that was saying something. Not that he would let any of them think they were better than pond scum. You had to knock them down before you could build them up. He smiled, thinking about the shock some of the city boys would feel being cold all day long. They were used to warm buildings and thick coats in this type of weather.

As he walked toward them, standing at attention, he saw a short, skinny kid with lots of bruises. He had to look twice because he couldn't believe his eyes.

Dee marched up to him and said, "What the hell are you doing?"

The boy hesitated, then said, "I was told to report here, sir."

"By who?" Dee asked, glaring at him.

"Master Sergeant Ricks, sir," Tee answered.

"For what?" Dee shouted.

Tee hesitated again, looking confused. Then he finally said, "For Guard training, sir."

"What's your name son?"

"Theron Stone sir. But most people call me Tee."

"I don't care what people call you. Wait here," ordered Dee.

With that, he turned away from the muster and walked away without an explanation. The quartermaster who had mustered them saw one head turn to look, and he marched over and screamed in the offender's face, "You are at attention! You will not move until Drill Instructor Dee tells you otherwise, understood?"

"Yes, sir," the recruit barked out in a nervous voice.

"I don't have time for this nonsense. What is Griff trying to pull?" Dee said as he walked purposely away from the muster, "It's got to be a practical joke. The kid is short, skinny, and looks like a good stiff breeze would take him away."

He first went and found Sergeant Derick, his physical fitness instructor. "Why do we have some kid who clearly can't pass your entrance test in my muster this morning?"

"He passed all the tests, Dee. I know it's weird, but he's actually in exceptional physical condition. Minus the bruises, of course. Came in first by a large margin on the ten-mile run. Wasn't even breathing heavy at the end. One third of the recruits were bent over, gasping for breath as soon as they crossed the finish line. The big city boys are used to a lower elevation, but that's no excuse. We'll need to run them hard for a few weeks."

"Where did the kid get the bruises?"

"One of the boys from his hometown beat him up last week. Heard the other kid didn't get hurt at all," Derick said with a sneer.

"Oh, for God's sake. So, he couldn't even fight off some random hick?"

Dee walked toward the officers building, fuming. When he got there, he knocked hard three times on the CGG's door.

"Who is it?" the CGG asked.

"Dee sir."

"Enter." While he was walking through the door, the CGG said with irritation in his voice, "What do you want, Dee?"

"A midget showed up to report for training, sir. Says his name is Theron Stone," Dee said.

"So, reject him as unfit," the CGG said.

"He's passed the physical fitness entrance exam and Griff is the one who gave him the invite," Dee replied.

The CGG breathed out hard, dipped his head in frustration, snapped it back up, and barked out, "Corporal! Go find Master Sergeant Ricks and tell him to report here immediately."

"Yes, sir," came the reply.

After enough time had passed for them both to recognize that Griff didn't report immediately, he opened the door without knocking and casually walked in with a smile, "Good to see you Dee, it's been a while."

"You can't seriously be proposing some undersized kid for the Guard," said the CGG, looking at him sternly.

"He's not a typical recruit, sir. He has skills and potential in areas the other recruits do not have. The Guard needs to broaden its capabilities,"

Griff said firmly.

"Dee has rejected him for not passing the entrance test," the CGG said.

Griff looked over at Dee in surprise and asked, "What test did he fail?"

"The eye test," Dee said.

Griff hesitated and then said with a frown, "You can't reject him because you don't like the way he looks. If that were a test, you wouldn't be in the Guard either."

"Very funny, Griff. What are you trying to do? Make a mockery of us all?" Dee continued angrily. "He got the crap kicked out of him just last week. From what I heard; the other kid came out of it without a scratch. Recruits ought to at least be able to defend themselves from the local yokels. They are supposed to be the best of the best."

"That local yokel was originally invited to recruit training. He ambushed Tee with his brothers due to some imagined past insult. He knew they were both headed for Guard training. I told both of them to bury any animosity and treat each other like brothers. I withdrew his invitation because we don't need that type of kid in the Guard," Griff said with conviction.

Then, in a frustrated tone, Griff said, "I'm trying to get both of you to realize that hand to hand combat is not the only tool we should be utilizing against the GEMs. I understand every recruit needs to be effective below the Wall. Size and strength are not the only weapons that can be deployed."

Griff hesitated a few moments and then said, "By the way, Dee, you should at least get your story straight. The other kid has a badly broken nose and won't look quite the same going forward."

As Griff swung his head back toward the CGG, Dee shrugged, stepped back, and leaned against the door with his massive arms crossed. He smiled as the CGG and Griff argued back and forth. CGG said that the integrity of the Guard was at stake. Griff went on and on about the benefits of offensive and defensive diversity in battle. He knew Griff would win. He was the CGG's first sergeant years ago and CGG idolized Griff almost as much as everyone else did. Even if he did yell at him a lot.

Dee reflected on the time when the CGG as a Newbie had wandered away from Griff's squad during a retreat at the Wall. Griff immediately ordered them all back out there to save him. When they finally returned to the safety of the Wall, the volume, variety, and duration of Griff's obscenities had been a thing of beauty. Griff even made the CGG go apologize to a Wall Archer who had helped them.

The truth was that Griff would be the CGG today if he had wanted it. And if that had happened, Dee would probably be master sergeant. It was frustrating, but he knew he wasn't in Griff's league. Nobody was. On the other hand, he honestly thought he made a bigger contribution as a drill instructor than any other job the Guard might assign him to.

So, in the end, it was what the Guard needed. And that was all that mattered. Having admiration for Griff didn't mean he wouldn't enjoy watching Griff fail with one of his crazy experiments. Especially one Dee felt threatened the integrity of the Guard.

As Griff continued to bludgeon the CGG, Dee could see the end was near. He appreciated the CGG standing up to Griff. Most of the officers did everything but salute when Griff 'suggested' a course of action. While it was good to see a fighting man making the life and death decisions on the battlefield, this was wrong. That skinny kid had no business being considered for the Guard.

"Okay, Griff, enough," the CGG said, ending the debate. "Dee, start him with the others, but let me know when he quits," the CGG said, looking back to Griff with a challenging smile.

"Yes, sir," snapped Dee. Then he pivoted around and walked out.

After the door was closed, Griff said with a cold stare, "Nate. You know he's going to do everything he can to run the kid out of training."

"Good, the sooner the better. If a miracle happens and he gets through training, I'll buy you a drink at the graduation ceremony," Nate said with an even bigger smile. "If not, you'll owe me a drink and Dee a drink and an apology."

As Dee walked back to the muster, he wondered how to best orchestrate a quick exit. The recruits had been standing in the cold at attention in their light exercise garb this whole time. He could see some of them shivering. He knew they were jealous of his thick parka. Does them good, he thought. The city kids had no idea of how severe the elements could be. How the cold could suck the strength and willpower out of a man. They would learn quickly, or they would be gone. "At ease," he ordered and picked up the clipboard he had been looking at when he first noticed Tee.

A sudden thought hit him. *Why don't I assign Jay Phillips as Tee's bunkmate?* As the son of a solid Guard member and winner of the youth combat competition, he was entering the Shake Out with very high expectations. Jay was taller than most, with a physique even Dee was jealous of. Handsome with red hair, blue eyes, and light skin blushed red by the sun. Hyper competitive with a reputation for ruthlessness in the fighting ring. Dee thought Jay would be extremely pissed off getting an albatross as a bunkmate. He'll help me push him out, thought Dee, smiling inside.

Of course, he couldn't smile on the outside. That would lead recruits to the conclusion he was human and not the devil himself fresh from hell to torture them. He would make the next forty-five days hell on earth for these recruits. Then the work would begin.

"Pay attention. I'm not going to repeat myself," Dee barked out. "Most of you are not good enough for my Guard. The sooner you leave, the better. Better for you, better for the Guard. I've seen poor recruiting classes before. This has to be the worst. One out of five failed to meet the physical fitness entrance exam yesterday. They are gone. The entrance exam was a warmup. It was easy. Going forward, it's going to be hard. Anyone ready to quit?"

Dee stared at them and then locked his icy glare onto Tee, letting him know he wasn't wanted. "So, I guess this recruiting class is not only physically weak, it's filled with morons," Dee said, continuing his cold stare at Tee.

"We only allow fifty recruits into the Guard with each recruiting cycle. That means that more than half of you will not graduate. I don't believe there are fifty in this class worthy of the Guard. If all of you quit, and we have nobody in this cycle, I will have done the Guard a service. If we have more than fifty left at the end of training. The top fifty recruits based on points awarded will be admitted."

"The Guard relies on teamwork. We all win, or we all fail. You will be assigned a bunkmate who will stay the same until one of you quits. When that happens, a new bunkmate will be assigned from those that are left. You will eat, shower, and shit at the same time as your bunkmate. They will be your partner in all things. Points are awarded individually or as bunkmates, depending on the exercise. You cannot make the top fifty if you haven't accumulated a large number of bunkmate points. If you have bad teamwork, if you have a bad bunkmate, you won't make it."

"Quartermaster will announce the bunkmates list. When your name has been called, go with your bunkmate to the barracks and pick out your bunk bed. This will be your home until you quit. Next, go to the quartermaster. He will provide you with uniforms, bedding, and supplies for personal hygiene. Quartermaster will then muster you all back out here so we can get to work."

Dee then stepped back and let the quartermaster call out the list. He had instructed him to leave Jay and Tee until the end. That way, he could watch the tension slowly grow into horror as Jay realized Tee might be his bunkmate. It also meant they would get the worst bunk bed available. Dee had to fight to keep the smile off his face as the second to last bunkmates were named. The look on Jay's face was priceless. Frustration, fear, and anger all mixed together. This was going to be fun.

The first few days, Tee felt like he was actually in hell. Then it got worse. They were up before dawn and still at it until well after dusk. Sometimes they were rousted out of bed after an hour or two of sleep for an all-night march. One time, they were awakened in the middle of the night to wade quietly up a stream for hours through freezing water, learning to 'hide their movements.' They had twelve recruits quit during that exercise, to the delight of the instructors.

Tee thought his normal, heavy exercise routine would help. It didn't matter. The instructors knew your weaknesses and were brutal in exploiting them. Jay, his bunkmate, was a machine. He was strong as a bull and quick as a cat. A natural athlete with excellent endurance. He was the ideal bunkmate, from Tee's perspective. Jay had a different perspective. He was not happy having Tee as his bunkmate.

On their first day of training, Jay had pulled Tee off to the side in the barracks and said in a harsh whisper, "I don't want you as a bunkmate. Quit now and stop wasting everyone's time."

Tee locked eyes with him. Looking upward at a steep angle, he calmly said, "I will get through this whether you want me as a bunkmate or not. We're bunkmates until you quit," parroting what Dee had said. Tee then turned around and walked off.

Jay was taken aback. He wasn't sure what he expected Tee to do, but turning the tables on him, staring him down, wasn't it. Tee didn't seem to be intimidated by him at all. That put him in rare company and earned some private grudging respect.

It was a truce of sorts. Other bunkmates shared stories, joked, practiced together in the rare downtimes, and most seemed to be on the path to becoming good friends. Jay was a good bunkmate when it was required. But nothing more. It was obvious to the other recruits that Jay was not happy with Tee. It was also obvious after a few days of competitive training that Jay was likely the top recruit among them. This led to Tee getting increasingly harassed. Recruits with weak bunkmates had gotten the idea that when their bunkmate quit, they might get Jay if Tee quit at the same time.

Tee was taking a shower when he heard a voice say, "Time to quit you little shit."

Tee hunched over a little and breathed out with a sigh. *Why do I keep getting compared to excrement?* he wondered. At least it rhymes, which shows some creativity. The speaker was Kale. His bunkmate had quit the day before. He was the clear runner up to Jay in the recruiting class. Jay and Kale would make an unbeatable team. Tee just continued his shower and didn't respond.

"I said it's time to quit," Kale said as he stepped closer.

Tee turned to him, looked him squarely in the eyes and calmly said, "I'm not going to quit."

"You're going to regret not taking my advice," Kale said with menace as he moved within reach of Tee.

"You touch him, and you'll have me to deal with," Jay said as he entered the shower room. Everyone paused, showering to watch this play out.

"Why do you care Jay? He's just holding you back," Kale replied, trying to reason with Jay.

"He's my bunkmate. If you attack him, you attack me," Jay said firmly.

"Okay, Jay. But you're going to regret not doing what you can to get rid of him," Kale said with disgust and then walked away.

Tee was privately relieved. The harassment had been escalating and there were too many times when Jay wasn't around. Making a statement like that in a shower room full of recruits meant the story would go everywhere. Nobody took Jay lightly. They wouldn't risk his wrath.

"Thanks, Jay," said Tee in a low voice.

"Don't thank me. I'm just doing my job. Make sure you do yours," Jay said sternly and walked away.

The next day, the first two weeks' point awards were posted. Jay was on top, and Tee was not far behind him. Jay had consistently won various competitions during the week. Tee had come in first every day on the morning run. He also outscored everybody by a huge margin in archery. This impressed some while disgusting others who believed that archery was for women and old men.

The Guard tied bunkmates together in everything. If your bunkmate won points, you were automatically awarded half of what they had earned. The same was true for point deductions. If your bed wasn't made correctly, or your uniform wasn't perfect, or you came up short on a thousand other trivial details, you both lost points. Sometimes points were deducted because Dee didn't like the way you looked.

"How in God's name did Tee Stone accumulate so many points?" Dee bellowed. He was incensed. That skinny little kid hadn't quit yet and was near the top in point totals.

Sergeant Derick shook his head and said, "If you remember, we put a high bonus on endurance and speed for the morning run because of the poor endurance this recruit class came in with. Tee has won the morning run by a wide margin every day. When we did the mountain run, it was even worse. If it were just the runs, he would be in the middle of the pack. But Jay is winning the majority of the sparring sessions, so Tee gets points from that too."

"Okay, it's just the first two weeks after all," Dee said, "Let's take the bonus away and downgrade points for the morning run. I don't want the endurance runs to award so many points going forward. Keep them practicing their archery. Griff was right to insist Guard members be competent with all weapons of war. But we don't have to give significant points for it. We aren't Wall Archers after all. Two more weeks and we'll be ramping down the heavy exercise. After that weapons training will start along with team competitions. Jay will not appreciate going from winning to losing."

"The kid is scrawny, but he's tough, Dee. He was blue and confused when he got out of the stream march exercise. I was worried we'd lose him. I'm not sure he'll quit. I also heard Jay let it be known that an attack on Tee was an attack on himself. Nobody is going to poke that bear," Sergeant Derick said.

Dee sighed and said, "I heard that too. Have to admit it makes me even more impressed with Jay. Tee is a major problem for him, but he's being a good bunkmate. Best traditions of the Guard and all that. On the bright side, with team competitions, it's going to get even more challenging having the wrong bunkmate."

CHAPTER 14

FRESHMAN ORIENTATION

Matthews, Chair of the mathematics department strolled into Del's office, plopped down in a chair, and said, "I'm not sure there is anything we can teach Quinn."

"What do you mean?" Del asked, confused.

"The first day after class, he came to my office and said with that big cheesy grin of his that he had a few corrections to submit for our textbooks. I thought great. When Quinn doesn't understand something, he is going to waste my time claiming the book is wrong. I have to admit, I cursed your name when that thought crossed my mind," Matthews said.

Del's eyebrows came together, and he asked, "So what happened next?"

"I was busy, so I told him to come back the next week and we would discuss it. After looking over his proposed corrections, I pulled Newton in. We spent the next few days checking and rechecking his work. While a few were simple typos, most were legitimate errors no one had spotted before. One was an obscure mistake in an incredibly dense derivation in differential geometry that hurts my head just thinking about it."

"Was he right?"

"Yes. We substantiated all of his claimed errors. Newton and I decided Quinn ought to be teaching our higher math courses instead of the two of us. The only problem with pulling him into the math department is his claim that 'math is easy and boring.' He only likes it because it's a tool he can use to do 'interesting things.' He told Newton and I this with such joy and delight that it was even more insulting than it sounds. And I thought bland and monotone Dorothy was irritating."

"So how did he get the knowledge? They don't teach that in high school."

"I asked him that. Turns out Dorothy has been checking out textbooks from the university library on her regular trips down here.

She's been home schooling Quinn and Hestie since they were in grade school. My guess is that home schooling Quinn consists of handing him books."

"So, what do you and Newton propose we do?" Del asked.

"Newton and I will sign off on Quinn satisfying requirements for an advanced degree in math when he completes his non-math requirements. We did our due diligence in a day long exam. By the end of the day, all the blackboards in the room were filled and Newton and I were feeling stupid. Quinn passed, but I think we failed," Matthews said with a wry smile. "He actually turned the test around and started asking us questions we couldn't answer. Then he gleefully supplied the answers. I think he thought we were all just having fun."

"Okay, I wondered how much of the lower-level course work he would test out of. Let's do this. His passion is engineering. I will pull the department together and come up with a plan. I suspect he will test out of most classes like he did in math. If so, I have a number of challenging special projects he can be assigned to. He will still need to take his required courses in the other subjects. Rounding him out can only be good. I think I'll pull in Phillis from the social work department and see if there is anything we can do to improve his social awareness. He is a happy and bubbly version of his mother, and you already mentioned how irritating that is at times."

"Yeah, nobody likes their stupidity pointed out to them. Especially when it's pointed out with such enthusiasm," Matthews said with a smile. "By the way, Newton and I decided over drinks that we will always have our PhDs to separate us from Quinn. He would never waste his time doing anything as easy and boring as that," Matthews said.

Del smiled and said, "If nothing else, Dorothy and her son will help keep all our egos in check."

"Amen to that," Matthews said with a smile.

Phillis, the dean of the social work department, was in Del's graduation class years ago. She was a dark, complected woman who exuded calmness wherever she went. Phillis had a way of listening that encouraged you to tell her your innermost thoughts. She seemed to understand everything you said. She seemed to be interested. Del had walked away from conversations with her in the past, wondering how in the world she had gotten some private part of him exposed. So, he was always a bit cautious approaching her.

"Good morning, Del. It's good to see you," she said in a way that indicated to him that she really was glad to see him.

"Good morning Phillis, hope all is well with you," Del responded cautiously. "I came by to talk to you about Quinn Espers, Dorothy's son."

"Oh. What did you want to discuss?" she said with a concerned smile.

"I wanted to get your advice on what we can do to help with his social integration here at the university," Del said a bit cryptically.

Phillis laughed softly with eyes bright. Her laugh had a bell-like tone. It really was quite endearing. "That's an interesting way to put it, Del." Then her features warmed and with compassion she said, "I've met both Quinn and Hestie. Of course, I know Dorothy quite well. Probably the best thing we can do is set up some interaction coaching for Quinn."

"What's that?" Del asked.

"It starts with a psychological evaluation to understand how Quinn sees the world and reacts to it. We then work with him to understand how others see him and techniques he can use to avoid making them uncomfortable. Most likely, he doesn't understand why his blunt, truthful statements bother others. If so, he will likely appreciate blunt statements in return and act on them. I get along with Dorothy really well. She is a very compassionate and caring person. It's just hard for most people to see it," Phillis said.

"Dorothy, compassionate?" Del said with surprise.

"Yes. She loves her husband and kids fiercely. The work she does assisting university researchers is because she cares about the students and wants to help them. Most of their research doesn't really interest her all that much. Ask around Apple Valley and they'll tell you she's a saint. Your kid's sick at 3:00 AM? Just go knock on the Espers's door and Dorothy will walk back with you for a house call. She just referred a woman and child to me for trauma counseling to help them deal with years of physical and emotional abuse. She found an older woman willing to take them into her home until they get settled. Most doctors would just suggest their patient seek counseling. They wouldn't worry about things like accommodations. Dorothy made sure they were taken care of and safe," Phillis observed.

"I would never have guessed that," Del said with surprise.

"Well, perhaps you should pay closer attention to social cues," Phillis said with a gleam in her eye.

"So, you're comparing my lack of seeing the real Dorothy with Dorothy's lack of social awareness," Del said with a small frown.

"Yes, that's exactly it. It's good to see you making progress," Phillis said with an even bigger smile. Del appreciated her wit, but quickly clamped down on that appreciation. Then Phillis gracefully said, "With Dorothy, you have to get past the flat affect and language she uses. Look at her actions and work your way back to what her motivations must be. This is true for everyone. But it's especially critical in understanding people with Dorothy's personality. To help Dorothy understand you, avoid tact and tell her the unvarnished truth. She won't be insulted; she will be appreciative. I know it seems counter intuitive, but most people want to be communicated with in the manner they themselves communicate."

"Should I do the same with Quinn?" Del asked.

"Let me spend some time with him and get back to you," Phillis said. "I'm guessing yes. But he has a sister who is super empathetic and some of that awareness may have rubbed off on him. It might change the plan a little bit. By the way, I've been trying to talk Hestie into social work. She has enormous potential. Unfortunately for me, she wants to focus more on the medical end of things. That got me thinking again about the connection between the two.

"Many times, when someone calls on a doctor, it's an emotional or life choice issue that needs attention. Doctors need to recognize this and respond accordingly. I would like to propose upgrading our medical degrees with social work classes designed to help them recognize when a problem may have its origins in something not strictly medical."

"Okay, Phillis, that does make sense. I'm not sure the medical board is open to more requirements right now. But putting it in front of them can't hurt. Let me know when you have a proposal on how to help Quinn."

"I will, Del, take care of yourself," she said with warmth.

He knew it wasn't just words. She meant it. Which warmed him. That woman was dangerous. He needed to avoid her as much as possible.

CHAPTER 15

AFTER HELL

The day started early with the good news that IH was officially over. They were told to quickly pack up because they were moving from their high valley training grounds to their main training camp. This was located below the Landfall Dam and just behind the Wall. The peninsula consisted of three regions spilling downhill, starting at the highest elevation in Apple Valley.

The two lower valleys had dams defining their southernmost boundary, with large lakes and broad fields. The valleys all had spectacular steep mountains on each side, with a few smaller valleys in the mountains on each side spilling into them. The two lower valleys were agricultural, with towns and a few cities dotting the landscape.

After a few hours of double time march, Tee worried that After Hell might be worse than In Hell. Tee's thoughts drifted to Grammy, and then to her advice to "Enjoy it." He looked up from the trail and realized how beautiful it was. The narrow trail followed a swiftly moving stream swelled with glacial melt and surrounded by green forest-covered hills. Eventually, the trail rounded a corner, and a stunning view of Landfall Valley far below appeared. This was an adventure. He had the choice to embrace and enjoy it, even if it was physically challenging.

Under his breath he said, "Thanks, Grammy."

The trail continued snaking its way alongside the steepening slopes of the stream, then widened out with another view of the Landfall Valley below. Just barely visible was a city sitting on the northeast end of a large lake. This was Tee's first glimpse of Landfall City. Hestie and Quinn were living there now and attending university. Of course, he wouldn't get to visit the city until Shake Out was over. He was really looking forward to seeing his two friends as soon as he could.

A sudden pang of homesickness hit him as he wondered how everyone was doing. This eventually had his mind wandering back to Diana with the familiar anxiety that caused. He slapped himself mentally and again elicited Grammy's advice. Life was wonderful, and this was a grand adventure.

They reduced down to march cadence once they entered the valley. The road was well maintained, flat, and easy to march on. Tee decided they had double marched them through the mountains because it was difficult. He had to admit they were better at it when it ended than when it began.

Late in the afternoon, they passed through Landfall City, skirting the lake until they reached the dam. From there, it was a switchback road down alongside the dam, ending in a canyon at the bottom. At the top of the road, Tee got his first glimpse of the Wall. It dominated the end of the canyon and was impressive. The canyon in between was entirely dedicated to military purposes and was a buffer between the GEMs and the dam. It included a small city to supply labor and support for the warehouses stuffed with weapons, food, and materials of all kinds needed for the defense of the Wall. Separate from the city, and near the Wall, was the main camp and headquarters for the Guard.

The area between the base of the dam and the Wall was sandy, hot, and very dry. The Landfall Dam had spillways that could direct water over cliffs directly into the ocean or down the natural waterway that had existed before the dam was built. Dumping the overflow into the ocean prevented the GEMs from having a local source of fresh water to support their attacks.

They finally reached their new camp in the late afternoon. The good news was that they had a much better bunk bed. Jay had walked in and claimed one off in a corner, away from the bathroom. Their old one had almost been in the bathroom. They had spent all of IH dealing with the dampness, smells, and noise. While the barracks didn't have privacy anywhere, their old spot was basically on the highway of recruits going back and forth to the bathroom at all hours of the day and night.

The room in the new barracks was identical to the one in the mountains, so the owners of that particular spot objected. Jay told them this was a new camp and so all the bunks were open until claimed. This ended up sparking an argument and mad scramble for bunk beds, getting louder and louder until Dee walked briskly into the barracks and said, "What in God's name is going on?"

"Salad stole our bunk bed," came the answer. Many of the bunkmate teams had nicknames given out by the instructors. It was a compliment of sorts because it meant you had been recognized. Not having a name meant you were beneath contempt. Salad was a derogatory name for Jay and Tee. One of the standard items for lunch was an apple and grape salad. The joke went that Jay was the apple because he was always sunburned, and Tee was the grape because he was always sporting purple bruises. It also referenced the comical size difference between them.

"If it's yours, take it back," said Dee, looking as if he expected them to do that right there and then. Silence was his only answer.

Dee stared at the complaining bunkmates for a while then said with a sneering smile, "Well, looks like it's not yours then." The two turned around and joined the scramble for a new bunk bed.

The demanding physical activities did ramp down, but stayed at a high level. More and more time was spent developing hand-to-hand skills and introducing weapons training. There were additional instructors now that the goal was to improve the recruits' skills in a wide range of capabilities. Midnight marches were few and far between, but common enough that you couldn't depend on getting a full night's sleep.

Tee was in the best shape of his life. He was also putting on quite a bit of muscle, which surprised him, given his slender frame. This motivated him to work even harder in his spare time, as strength was his biggest deficiency. His hand-to-hand combat instructors told him they were going to concentrate on defensive skills. In other words, you have no business attacking anyone. Tee thought this was a mistake, but he took what instruction he could get and practiced hard.

While individual combat was always a focus, teamwork was increasingly emphasized. Two on two sparring with short sword and shield had been going on for over two weeks with Tee and Jay having some success. Without discussing it with Jay, Tee had decided the best course of action was for him to delay his opponent long enough for Jay to win his bout and then double up on the remaining adversary. He could engage enough to protect Jay's back without risking a quick loss for himself. This culminated in an end of phase competition with a high number of points to be awarded to the winning team. Second place would get nothing. Dee had barked out the point rules for this event, "Fighting is about winning; we don't award points to losers."

They had gotten to the finals with a combination of luck, extraordinary skill, and effort. Primarily on Jay's part. Tee had done a good job of staying alive long enough for Jay to free up and double team

Tee's opponent. They narrowly won the last few rounds.

Now, however, they were going to go up against Kale and his bunkmate Zeb. This pair had been racing up the point totals while Tee and Jay had been slowly going in the opposite direction. While Jay had the edge on Kale, he wouldn't be able to put him down easily or quickly. Zeb, on the other hand, was nearly at Kales level and would easily dispatch Tee.

While Kale and Zeb had quickly dispatched their respective opponents. Jay and Tee's bouts had been messy affairs, with Jay basically having to win two fights. Jay was exhausted. Kale and Zeb were openly bragging that they were going to steal Jay and Tee's strategy by defeating Tee fast and then doubling up on Jay. There was no doubt in anyone's mind how this was going to turn out.

"Do you want to concede? You have zero chance, Jay; it will just be embarrassing. Everybody is watching, you know." Kale smiled, taunting him as they lined up to start.

Dee had shrunk the circle for the final round, declaring, "I want to see a good fight. That means I don't want to watch Tee run around all over the place." Dee had clearly understood the strategy Tee employed and decided to eliminate it. Tee, having gotten used to Dee's insults, just ignored the comment.

Zeb smiled meanly at Tee and said, "You're dead in ten seconds," which Tee realized was probably true if he didn't think of something quick.

The whistle blew and Tee dropped his sword and, holding his shield in front of him with both hands, darted sideways past Zeb. He charged right into the side of a surprised Kale, knocking him to the ground. Kale had reacted quickly, scoring a kill on Tee as they went down. But, in doing so, it opened him up to Jay, who darted in and scored a killing blow of his own. That left Jay and Zeb to fight it out one on one. It was a good fight, but Jay eventually won.

The crowd of recruits erupted. Some were delighted with the trickery, but some were offended. A voice in the crowd shouted, "That wasn't fair!"

Dee bellowed out, silencing them. "There is no fair in a fight. The only rules we have in recruit training are for the quitters. We have safety rules in place, so they have a chance to be useful citizens after they leave. Sacrificing yourself for the good of the team is in the best traditions of the Guard. And in case you're confused, whining is not."

That Dee had actually given him a compliment had momentarily swelled Tee's chest with pride. Dee then ruined it by observing, "That cheap trick will only work once, Jay." With that parting comment, Dee turned and walked off.

Jay walked over to Tee, let out a big sigh, and said, "That was smart. You surprised me as much as you surprised them. I almost didn't react fast enough."

Tee hesitated, checking Jay's face twice, looking for sarcasm, smiled, then said with a grin, "So, I'm not completely wasting your time."

Jay was startled by Tee's response. He had changed his mind about Tee. With the world against him, the little guy had steadfastly moved forward, regardless of the odds. He had to admit that Tee was hard not to like. And by now, pretty much everyone respected him. Perhaps he was due a little ribbing.

"No, not completely," he said with a smile, then turned serious and said, "Let's start planning these bouts, agreed?"

"Sounds good to me. The other bunkmates have weaknesses we can take advantage of. We aren't the only team with a major deficiency," Tee said, getting Jay to smile again with the obvious self-deprecating reference to himself.

As they walked back to the barracks both basking in the win, Tee suddenly turned serious and asked, "Could we trade knowledge as well?"

"What do you mean?" asked Jay, confused.

"You teach me how to fight and I'll point out weaknesses," Tee said with a grin.

"Weaknesses?" asked Jay.

"How do you think I win the occasional match? It isn't because I'm a better fighter. I study everyone to figure out their strengths, weaknesses, and tendencies. It's the only advantage I have."

He had to admit it was surprising Tee won any matches. Thinking back, he realized that although Tee lost most of his sparring sessions; he had enough wins for it to be something other than luck. Jay was also reflective enough to realize he was winging it most of the time. While he was good at reacting to situations, having a plan with contingencies to go along with that would probably be an improvement. "Okay, I'm in," said

Jay.

The Salad team was going to give him a heart attack. Dee had announced a bonus for the team winning the first bunkmates' competition with weapons. He had done that to put more distance between the Fish and Salad teams. Kale and Zeb were called the Fish because Zeb had failed his initial swimming test. While not required for entrance, it was a required skill to graduate from IH. The instructors had roused both Zeb and his original bunkmate extra early to practice swimming in the freezing cold lake every morning for a week until Zeb passed. Thus, Dee started calling them the Fish. Kale had inherited the name when he joined Zeb.

Salad winning the first bunkmates' competition had backfired, putting them back in the lead. Before this fiasco, Tee had been below the cutoff with little chance of catching up. Now he was in the mix again and it would take continued manipulation on Dee's part to fix it.

Over the next few weeks, Dee carefully picked opponents and situations so Jay would earn enough points to stay solidly in the top fifty while limiting what Tee earned. It had gotten to the point where even the other teams noticed.

When Jay first realized this, he was dead set on confronting Dee. "That SOB is doing everything he can to knock you down. I'm going to go tell him what I think about that," Jay said with fury in his voice.

"It won't change anything, Jay. He's in charge and doing what he thinks best. Getting a rise out of either one of us will just encourage him. Let's prove him wrong instead."

Training had progressed from small to large squad training in realistic scenarios. The goal was to quickly form up, select a sergeant in charge, access the situation, and deploy. Central to their training was how to attack or defend a wall. Pacifica's strategy was based on defending cliff side fortifications and the Wall. The Wall was Pacifica's weakness, so a major focus of training.

Getting near the end of the Shake Out, Dee was carefully selecting Tee and Jay's opponents to get the result he wanted. He and his instructor core had completely failed to get Tee to quit. Worse, Jay and Tee had formed a close friendship which provided Tee with a supporter who could make a difference. Dee remembered his own Shake Out and understood. It was you and your bunkmate against the world. That tended to form close and lasting relationships. Jay would make the point total with just individual contests, so didn't need the bunkmate points. Tee, on the other hand, needed them. In fact, he was below the top fifty cut list again with little hope of making it.

At the end of another long day of weapons training, Tee was sitting in a tub full of hot water. He thought he could feel every muscle in his body. As the hot water did its job, a pleasurable dull ache took over. Strange how wonderful it was to go from the physical pain of IH to the feeling of bliss that came from working out to his limit, but not beyond. Sergeant Derick alternated them between ice baths and hot baths, driven by a carefully designed workout schedule. Since the Salad team did everything together, they were on the same schedule, although concentrating on improving different physical attributes.

"This is heaven," Jay said with a big sigh. "I love this as much as I hate ice baths."

"Grammy tells me to find enjoyment in everything," teased Tee.

"Your grammy sounds as crazy as you," Jay said, hesitated, and then added, "You realize you're crazy, right?"

Tee looked over with a wry smile and said, "It's been suggested a few times, yeah." Tee let out a big sigh and asked, "What does your dad do in the Guard, Jay?"

"He was a large squad staff sergeant, fourteen members. They focused on destroying siege towers, battering rams, and anything else that gets built on our side of the moat. He's now in phase one of retirement acting as a recruit combat instructor," Jay said.

"Why isn't he here?" Tee asked.

"When an instructor has a kid in recruit training, they take a break and wait until the next class. The Guard doesn't want any hint of preference."

"I guess that explains your skills," Tee said. "Who gave you the invite to join?"

"Griff. I've known him since I was a little kid. I wouldn't say he's a friend of my dad's. According to him, Griff doesn't have any friends. Well, none that are alive. The story is that when his mentor disappeared, Griff sort of went mental. Already intense, he became obsessed with improving all facets of the Guard. His mentor was master sergeant when he disappeared, and Griff was the obvious choice to replace him."

"Do you have any idea why he gave me an invite," Tee said hopefully. He really couldn't figure it out.

"He must hate you for some reason," Jay said, smiling, then he turned serious and said, "I was angry and confused when you showed up. I just knew Griff must have been the one to invite you. He has a reputation for shaking things up, which isn't appreciated by everyone in the Guard. It took a while, but I think I understand why. Your instincts and ability to plan an attack or defense based on an enemy's strengths and weaknesses are what he wants. It's unique. I heard him tell Dad one time that the Guard should be more than a bunch of brutes bashing about. Coming from the head brute that seemed strange and funny. I can remember my dad and I laughing about it. I think I get it now."

"So, you're saying Griff isn't a complete idiot and neither am I," Tee said with a smile.

"You need to stop making fun of yourself. It gets irritating. Accept an honest compliment when it's offered," Jay said with a frown.

Tee hesitated, took a deep breath, sighed, and said, "You're right. It does feel good to be appreciated. It's just hard for me to take a compliment. Thank you, Jay."

After a few minutes of silence, Jay asked, "So, what are we going to do with the large squad exercise tomorrow?" Once they had started planning their bouts, Jay quickly realized Tee was an incredible strategist. His plans didn't always work, but they were always well thought out. They had a chance of success even in no-win situations. Tee and Jay eventually converged on a division of responsibility to take advantage of each other's strengths. Tee would put together a general plan with contingencies and Jay would execute it. That meant Jay would assume the role of sergeant when a squad was formed, making all the real-time decisions once engaged.

"My guess is that Dee will have us go first and give us teams with generally weak offensive skills. Then he will assign us to take the Wall. We'll likely go up against Fish and teams with strong offensive skills," Tee speculated.

"Why offensive if they are assigned to protect the Wall?" Jay asked.

"Dee doesn't just want us to fail to capture the Wall. He wants us to get decimated below the Wall. Embarrassment is what he's after," Tee said.

"Sounds like he might get what he wants."

"It's okay, Kale will take charge of their squad."

"I don't understand why that's good news," Jay said in confusion. Tee gave him a knowing smile until Jay's face slowly transformed into a smile and said, "I know that look. What's your plan?"

It was another bright, cool day that promised to heat up quickly. At first muster, they saw they had an audience today. Everyone recognized Griff, and most recognized the CGG. All the instructors were there in person as well. With one week to go, this looked like a final exam of sorts.

For the past few weeks, their training had taken place at the training Wall. This was an 800-foot-long replica of the real Wall. The only difference was that it had more posterns, or small doors, than the actual wall. The small doors provide an element of surprise, as a squad can pop out quickly and have multiple locations for a retreat. Since the recruits knew where all the posterns were, more of them simulated the ability to stage a surprise attack from the Wall.

Dee explained how the large squad exercise would work. "For the next two days, you will be formed into squads of ten bunkmates each. Each day, two squads will be named and assigned to either attack or defend the training Wall. You will have ten minutes to form up, choose your leadership, and come up with a plan. The exercise will end in two hours unless it ends sooner because the attackers have captured the Wall, or the defenders have decimated the attacking squad. We will then muster for a critique from your instructors. Any questions?"

They had all learned that awful first day that asking Dee questions meant you either "hadn't been listening" or "you wanted to waste everyone's time." So, after a few seconds of dead silence, Dee gave the instructions. "Today the Defend squad will be Fish, Stumble, Tree, Baffled, Reckless, Flee, Dense, Annoy, Feeble, and Oh No. The attack squad will be Salad, Neander, Witless, Late, Nervous, Sloth, Reek, Scum, and Squirrel. You have your instructions. You are excused." He then turned and looked right at Jay and Tee with glee leaking onto his face.

As they turned to go, Jay carefully guarded his features and said in a whisper, "You are one scary dude, Tee." They both smiled.

Jay quickly pulled the nine other bunkmate teams together and declared, "I'm in charge. Any questions?" There was a grunt or two, but no real opposition. Jay had that effect on people. They would have voted him leader anyway, so the direct approach simply saved them time. "Now listen up. Tee will explain the plan."

Tee turned to face everyone and said, "The plan depends on Kale being chosen to lead the squad. As you know, he is a solid leader and a tremendous fighter. He's also super aggressive and will look for a quick kill. We are going to take advantage of his lack of patience. We will grab scaling ladders and attack to the left of the Portcullis. But it needs to be a lackluster attack, with Jay and a reserve holding back. Act confused, argue with each other, look frustrated and defeated. Get a few scaling ladders up but let them throw them back down.

"At some point, Kale will get tired of waiting and order an all-out attack through the Portcullis. When they do, Jay is going to call a retreat. Let them collapse your right flank and retreat toward the left flank in a sweeping movement. Stay close in a good defense. The left flank will attempt—but fail—to envelop the attack by controlling the base of the Wall in an obvious attempt to take the portcullis. Moose, Rilla, and I will duck down behind the line of boulders and get split off from the right flank as it collapses.

"Once their attention is distracted by the sudden envelopment attack, we will sneak away from the skirmish and down the Wall, away from the action."

Moose and Rilla were collectively called Neander, which was short for Neanderthal. This was an old earth pre-human known for its robustness. Dee assigned the name to insinuate they weren't quite human. It was not a compliment. He even gave Moose and Rilla their nicknames. They were the only two in their recruit class he had done this to. Rilla was short for Gorilla. What did ring true is that they were both extremely strong and had an oddly prehistoric sort of look to them.

"We will retreat to the sixth postern. It will look like we're trying a rear assault with too few warriors. Once we are in position, Jay will call for a mass charge, followed quickly by a retreat back to a packed line. This time, while they are distracted, Neander will hook hands and throw me to the top of the Wall. I'll open the postern, and we'll attack the back of the Portcullis and lock the attacking defenders out below the Wall. If we accomplish this, the exercise will have ended, and we win."

"Sounds like a suicide mission," said Moose.

"Tee specializes in suicide missions," Jay said, smiling at Tee, then turning serious, "It's that or a protracted fight below the Wall that we lose. We all know we're outmatched."

"We're betting they commit to an all-out attack and leave minimal Guards for the Portcullis. Best-case scenario is they ignore us while we circle behind them and don't see me get thrown up onto the Wall," Tee explained.

Dee was standing on the observation platform with Griff and the CGG when the whistle blew. They all watched the slowly developing unorganized attack with Dee huffing and puffing, clearly disgusted. "You would think after all the training they've had, they could mount a decent attack. This is embarrassing," Dee said angrily.

"I'm sure that's what the Defend team is thinking," said Griff blandly.

Just then, the Portcullis burst open and the Defend team surged out, driving the Attack team backward. They watched as the Attack team's left flank tried to envelop the attack and force it toward their right flank in an obvious attempt to threaten the Portcullis. It was unsuccessful. The result was a tight defensive line angled with the attackers' backs toward the Portcullis and the Wall beyond it.

"Well, look at that. Tee left his bunkmate and is running away with Neander. Some sort of rear attack?" Dee said with a sneer. "Just more incompetence."

"The left flank envelopment failure has set the line so that none of the Defend team are paying attention to their rear," said Griff. Again in a bland voice.

They continued to watch the slow systematic destruction of the Attack team. Then Griff observed with a chuckle. "Don't look now, but Neander just threw Tee up on the Wall. Looks like they overdid it a bit."

Tee hit the inside railing wall hard. He slowly crawled to his feet, slowly shaking his head. His vision cleared, the pain subsided, and he suddenly remembered what he needed to do. Careful to keep hidden from the Guards, he made his way down inside the Wall. He opened up the sixth Postern and now there were three of the Attack team inside the Wall.

Dee watched dumbfounded as the three of them surprised the two guards watching the final stages of the assault from just inside an open

Portcullis. After dispatching the guards, they shut and locked the Portcullis, climbed to the top of the Wall, and declared victory. The recruits watching all this went wild.

Dee had the recruits form up below the observation deck for a critique. In his usual brusque fashion, he looked directly at Kale and asked in a sneering voice, "What did you learn?"

Kale looked up at Dee with a forlorn look, hesitated a moment, and then, in a clear voice, said, "It's better to be on Tee's team." The crowd standing around broke into loud and prolonged, uproarious laughter. Dee scowled but then failed to keep a tight smile off his face.

At week's end, they marched up to Armstrong Reservoir, just above the capital. It was an artificial lake created by the original colonizers to provide clean water for the city. It was in a relatively small but wide valley that was also maintained as a nature park with numerous trails spiderwebbing across forest land on both sides of the lake. They had spent a week at the reserve earlier in their training as part of their scouting basics. Everyone was familiar with the layout.

At one end of the lake was a long dam and at the other, a single trail connected the two sides. When they arrived, they set up camp and goofed around like the young men they were. Training was almost over. Tomorrow, they would participate in their last exercise. After that, they would either go home or be Guard members for life.

As soon as Tee saw the forest, he wanted to go on a hike. Nothing relaxed him as much as the quiet solitude of the forest. Jay decided he would go with him, even though he didn't understand why anyone would want to simply walk around in the woods. He was a city boy.

"Well, it's almost over," Jay said.

"Yeah, can't believe we'll be done after tomorrow," Tee replied.

"Are you sure you can pull off your end?" Jay asked.

"Not a problem. Just get to the choke point as soon as possible. Anyone you can defeat on our list will help the point total."

"However this goes tomorrow, Tee, you're stopping by to meet my family on Sunday before you head home," Jay said.

"Don't worry. We're both going to make the cut and continue training. Just make sure you do your part."

"I'm never going to hear the end of that, am I?" Jay said with a grin.

"No, you're not." And they both smiled.

Dee was up early, as usual. He found pleasure in being up before everyone else, enjoying the quiet of the morning. He thought this was the best recruitment class he had ever produced. It was something to be proud of. It was also the strangest. Dee wasn't the reflective type. He spent his time in the here and now, working to achieve his objectives. Every problem had an answer. Mistakes were merely a mechanism for learning.

When he heard people talk about the gray areas, he interpreted that as an excuse for not being able to make decisions. He knew most in the Guard thought him to be insensitive and uncaring. Nothing could be further from the truth. He cared deeply for his recruits. Whenever he heard one had gone down at the Wall, he wondered what he could do better with the next batch of recruits.

His real problem with Tee was that he would never be able to forgive himself if one of his boys died, because Tee didn't measure up. Once they graduated, they all became his boys. He never called them that out loud, but that was how he felt about them.

Contrary to all evidence, Dee had developed a high level of respect for Tee. Although he respected everyone who made it through recruit training, he had special regard for him. He was tough! Dee wasn't sure he could have overcome the challenges that had been thrown at Tee.

Well, after today it will be over.

Jay will make it no matter what happens, and Tee would have to race around the lake in record time, encountering no one. He had set up the staged release in opposite order of their endurance run point totals. Tee would leave last, which meant he had a gauntlet to get through, as everyone would challenge him to spar if they saw him. He might finish, but it would be really slow and not enough to get over the hump.

This last competition was constructed to test the recruits' scouting abilities. The day started on the south side of the lake at the dam. It would end sometime two to three days later at the north end of the dam. A large bonus of points was reserved for the first ten recruits to make it around the lake to the end point. These points were ratioed by the difference in arrival times, so relative speed was highly rewarded. Some of the trails had instructors positioned as pickets. If you failed to spot them, your day was over. If another recruit spotted you, they could challenge, and the loser's day would be over. You only got points if you or your bunkmate finished.

The recruits were assembled and ready to go. It was a cool, windless morning as the valley became visible in the dawn. No clouds in the sky and not a ripple on the lake. A perfect day, Dee thought. Dee and Griff were watching Sergeant Derick release the recruits one at a time. As they were called up, Dee would give a short description of the recruits' strengths and weaknesses with his recommendation for the next phase of training. When Jay's turn came, Dee turned to Griff and said, "That may be our next master sergeant."

Griff turned, nodded, and said, "He certainly has all the physical attributes. I liked what I saw during the Wall exercise. He carried out the ruse perfectly. We'll put him on a non-com training program, then wait and see what happens in real action."

Dee winched at the ruse reference and then eventually said, "I understand why you invited Tee. His ability to outmaneuver his opponents is impressive, unique even. He's gained the respect of everyone. However, he's not going to make it."

"Explain to me why you're so opposed to having him in the Guard," Griff said without malice.

"If he's in the Guard, and below the Wall, somebody is going to die because he can't do his part," Dee responded.

Griff nodded thoughtfully and said, "I understand your concern, but I disagree with your conclusion." He hesitated, then added, "I do admire your passion and hard work to ensure every Guard recruit is able to step up to the challenges."

It was a rare acknowledgement from Griff, and Dee appreciated it. Griff could be very hard on people, which Dee also appreciated. It took a little of the sting out of a feeling that he had been unfair to Tee, and Jay for that matter. But in his mind, the integrity of the Guard needed to be protected at all costs.

When at last Tee's name was called Dee went through his analysis. "Tough, smart, but with significant physical limitations. He shows an aptitude for scouting in the wild. Best in his class. Scout Instructor

Walker was very impressed. Perhaps his hunting experience. His inability to win individual sparring matches will disqualify him from the Guard after today based on points. His real value is as a strategist. I will strongly recommend him for volunteer corp. officer training. Your recommendations for making a few of these roles full-time jobs make sense to me. Perhaps he is the natural place to start."

Dee noticed that Griff was looking over his shoulder at something behind him and smiling. That wasn't good. Dee turned around and watched Tee finish taking off his clothes. He folded them, then placed them with his boots into the waterproof backpack the recruits had been issued. He had taken out his food and water to make room and discarded them. He put the backpack on and tied the front straps together tightly. Then Tee, completely naked with a backpack snuggly strapped to his back, turned toward them and smiled.

"Is he giving up? Is this some kind of protest?" Dee asked, confused.

"Maybe he's too warm. Perhaps he's not hungry," Griff said, his sarcasm heightening Dee's concern.

Then they both watched him turn around and casually walk down to the lake, wade in, and start swimming swiftly for the other side.

Dee was speechless. He had never seen anyone swim like that. He remembered back to when the recruits passed their tests. He clearly remembered Tee splashing around wildly with everyone else and finishing in the middle of the pack. Now he was swimming swiftly and smoothly with what looked like little effort.

Griff interrupted Dee's astonishment by saying, "Looks like Tee might set a new record."

"That's not possible. And if it is, it's got to be against the rules. This is clearly a race around the lake, not across it," Dee spluttered.

"Crossing the dam is forbidden, but there isn't a rule prohibiting swimming across. We had a recruit try to paddle a log across, remember? We had to go find a boat and save him. The idiot almost drowned. But we only added a rule that the recruits couldn't use logs or rafts to cross the lake. There is no restriction on swimming across." Griff's smile widened.

"You knew he could do this," Dee said, glaring at Griff.

"I always do a thorough investigation before I invite anyone to recruit training," Griff admitted.

"This is wrong," Dee said, glaring.

"You're right, it is wrong. It's also wrong for you to manipulate point awards to unfairly drive someone out. So, we're even," Griff said calmly.

Dee knew he had been outmaneuvered. Tee would get an outrageous number of points for this. It explained why Griff hadn't been complaining about Dee playing games with the point system. One or more of the instructors must have told Griff long ago. Dee took a deep breath and relaxed. He often told the recruits that it's better to be smarter than stronger than your opponent. It wasn't lost on him that he didn't say that as often to this class. Tee was going to become one of his boys, and as such, he would worry about him like all the others. Perhaps even more so.

CHAPTER 16

INDUCTION CEREMONY

Your father would be so proud of you, thought Arti. He took jibes for being short but never let it affect him. You have his charisma, which seems to serve you well. In many ways, you really did get the best of us. Arti knew the Guard functions were lavish affairs. This, however, was even grander than she imagined. Being a member of the Guard was difficult for families. The constant worry about safety combined with frequent absences was a burden few appreciated. The annual induction ceremony was just one event sponsored by the Guard to pull these families together. Being around others who understood the challenges and stresses was helpful. The Induction Ceremony was not just about celebrating each new Guard member. It was about adding to the extended Guard family.

Arti was met at the door by a handsome and polite young man who introduced himself as Jay. He was decked out in a dress uniform and smiling broadly.

"I was Tee's bunkmate in training. It's tradition for bunkmates to escort their bunkmate's family to their assigned table."

"It's very nice to meet you, Jay. Thank you for the escort," Arti said with a warm smile.

"I've been looking forward to this. Been wanting to meet the person who is better with a bow than Tee," he said, smiling back at her.

"Tee's been bragging about me," Arti said with a smirk.

"Someone commented that he was the best archer they had ever seen. To which Tee said, 'you haven't seen my mother,'" Jay said. "He talks about you quite a bit."

Arti smiled and said, "You've often shown up in his letters home. Seems the two of you have become good friends."

Jay winched a little and said sheepishly, "Not at first. But once I got to know him, he won me over."

"He tends to do that. I might be biased, but I think you've made a very good friend," Arti said.

Just then they were stopped by a large intense man who asked in a booming voice, "Jay, is this your mother?"

Jay and Arti were both startled. They turned and looked hard at each other, then broke into laughter. Recovering, Jay said, "No, Sergeant Dee, this is Tee's mother. You're right, we do look related." Dee wouldn't be the only one making that mistake this evening. Both being tall with red hair and pale skin, they stood out. It was an obvious assumption to make.

"My apologies. You must be Arti. Sorry I didn't recognize you. My name is Dee, and I lead recruit training." Dee hesitated a moment and then said, "Your son is unusual to say the least. You must be proud he made it through training."

Arti's smile turned into a frown as she said, "I'm not surprised he made it. I'm proud he's willing to endure the insults and barriers put in his way so that he can dedicate his life to protecting us all."

Dee put up both hands with palms out and, looking embarrassed, said, "I meant no disrespect, Arti. I've gained a lot of respect for Tee. Please enjoy the celebration. You have much to be proud of." And with that, he turned around and walked off.

After Dee had gotten out of hearing, Arti said in a low voice, "I heard all about Dee and his attempts to get Tee to quit."

"It ended up motivating both of us. Dee was obviously trying to get Tee to quit. And you know Tee, that wasn't going to happen. It ended up making Tee the most popular person in training by the end of it. He was the recruit who showed up Dee. To be honest, I wasn't happy when Tee was assigned to be my bunkmate. I knew having a good bunkmate was crucial. I wanted my bunkmate to be physically intimidating. I wanted him to have a mean disposition. Tee just looked so harmless. To everyone's surprise, Tee was the recruit everyone needed to watch out for. I was lucky to get him as a bunkmate."

Arti beamed.

Arriving at the table, Jay turned to a robust couple both with blue eyes and red hair and said, "Mother, Father, this is Tee's mother, Arti."

Jay's mother gave her a warm smile and said, "It's a pleasure to meet you. My name is Pam, and my husband's name is Barin. You just missed Tee. What a nice young man you've got. He stayed with us for the past two weeks. I've been telling Jay to pay attention to Tee. He's been the perfect houseguest."

"You never miss an opportunity for a lecture, Mom," Jay said with an amused look at his mother.

Pam turned to Arti and said, "Here, sit by me. I can tell from Tee that you're someone I'd like to get to know."

Arti wasn't quick to warm up to most people. But Jay's mother was so open, genuine, and warm it was hard not to instantly like her. The table she was seated at had Jay's parents on one side and two other Guard families on the other. One of them included a Wall Archer Arti was familiar with. The organizers had taken care to seat people with similar interests together. Instead of the lonely and emotionally draining experience she had expected, this was turning out to be a pleasant evening.

The ceremony started out with the CGG, narrating a memorial of family members of the recruits who had died protecting Pacifica. It was startling how many of the recruits had members of their immediate families who had lost their lives at the Wall. When he got to Tee's father, he mentioned the lives he had saved helping halt a sudden breach of the Wall. Arti couldn't help it; she hadn't known they would do this. The tears she tried to hold back started to fall. Jay's mother reached over and gently patted her back and whispered, "Thank you for your family's sacrifice, Arti."

What would have felt overly familiar coming from anyone else was strangely comforting. That phrase was a common one. But she could tell Pam meant every word. She had a feeling they would become good friends. Tears came for both mothers when Jay and Tee were called to receive their insignias. Even Jay's father's eyes seemed to shine a bit. The CGG announced that Jay and Tee had the highest bunkmate's score. This meant they would have a thin red stripe running diagonally through their single band insignia. Everyone kept their original Newbie insignia on their uniform, even the CGG. That thin red stripe would be part of their uniforms forever. The Guard was all about achievement as part of a team.

After the presentation, Jay and Tee joined them at their table. Arti gave him a huge hug and held on until Tee said, "Enough, Mom. You can give me more hugs later," to which the table exploded in laughter.

"You look good, son," Arti said quietly, wiping away tears of happiness.

Tee smiled and said, "I feel really good. I'm glad I decided to go ahead with this. It was the hardest thing I've ever done." He gave a grim smile and then said, "I would not have made it if Jay hadn't been assigned my bunkmate."

"He said you've become friends," Arti replied.

Tee smiled. "We have. He's a lot of fun. Reminds me of an intense version of Ansen. How are Ansen and Diana doing?" Tee asked with a wistful look.

"Ansen has been taking on more of the family business responsibilities. He's really matured. And just in time. My brother works too hard and I'm really glad to see Ansen step up and take some of the load off. Diana is Diana. Nothing much has changed other than her constantly asking about you," Arti said.

Nodding, Tee just said, "Good."

Dinner followed, with the recruit instructors serving both the recruits and their families. They were a dangerous-looking group of men, but extremely polite and attentive. After dinner, the crowd started moving around the room, greeting old friends and acquaintances.

Arti smiled as she watched Tee joking around with Jay and some of the other Newbies. A short but sturdy man suddenly appeared and introduced himself with an uncharacteristically soft voice. "Hi, I'm Griff. I don't know if you remember me, Arti."

She looked him in the eyes, studied him for a while and then said with a small grin, "Of course I do. I remember everyone who almost gets me killed," she said, turning the grin into a warm smile.

Griff chuckled and smiled warmly back. "Perhaps I should go get Nate and have him apologize again." They both laughed softly. "You must be very proud of Tee. He had an especially tough time, and I apologize for putting him in such a difficult situation."

Arti's face took on the intense look he remembered from the Wall and said, "Risk is part of life, it's what enables our survival. I'm very proud that he's willing to step up and do what he can to protect us all."

Arti's face softened, and she continued. "I am appreciative that you looked past his stature and saw his worth. That took an open mind and guts. Your support helped him get to where he is."

Griff nodded and smiled at the compliment, but thought. Oh, Arti. You have that wrong. Those who would love to see me humbled worked very hard to make my experiment fail. Which reminds me, he thought, I have to go find Nate for that drink.

They stood off to the side for a long time, talking and laughing about everything and nothing at all. Tee finally came up and said, "Jay's parents have invited us to their home for a nightcap. Do you want to go?"

"Yes, let's do that. I really like his mother and would like to get to know Jay and his father better."

Arti turned to Griff and said, "It was good to talk to you, Griff. Next time you're in Apple Valley, come to an Archers practice. I am interested in your thoughts on what we can do to better support the Guard."

Griff smiled and said softly, "I would enjoy that, Arti."

As Griff walked away, Tee glanced back at his mother and said, "I didn't know you knew Master Sergeant Ricks."

"I don't, really. We were involved in a firefight at the Wall years and years ago. I was able to support his squad with a difficult retreat and he remembers."

"Oh," said Tee, thinking there was much more to the story. His mother always downplayed what she had done on the Wall. When Tee first saw his mother with Griff, they looked like they were flirting with each other. He almost choked on his beer.

As a teenager, he thought it would be good for her to find someone. Not that he needed a father. But he would eventually be gone and didn't want her to be alone. But Griff? He was a crusty old bastard, and scary as hell. He is the one who got me into the Guard, though. But Mom? He had once bluntly asked her about finding someone.

She had stopped what she was doing, captured him with that intense gaze of hers and said, "Once you're on your own, if I stumble on someone who can hold a candle to your father, it's possible."

And that was all she ever said on the topic.

96

CHAPTER 17

GUARD EDUCATION

"How was the graduation celebration last week?" Del asked.

"Pretty much like all the others. Caught up with old friends and spent time with the Newbie Guard members and their families," Griff replied.

"I was surprised to see Tee made it," said Del.

"It was a close thing. Dee did everything he could to get Tee to drop out. When that didn't work, he altered the award system to limit his ability to earn points. You have to be in the top fifty by points to be in the Guard," Griff explained.

"Yet somehow he made it," Del replied.

Griff smiled and said, "The somehow is the fun part. Tee ended up out of the top fifty the last week of training. Recruit training has a final test with a large number of points available. We set them loose one at a time on the south side of the Armstrong Reservoir dam. They race around the lake to the north side. Few rules, but one is that you cannot cross over the dam. There is a large variety of trails you can take. Some are direct and fast; others allow you to stay hidden if you're careful. You can challenge anyone you see on the trails to personal combat.

"Guard members act as referees to keep it clean. The loser's race is over and the winner gains points. The strategy for those slow of foot is to win as many personal combat matches as possible and finish. The strategy for the quick is to avoid combat and get to the finish line as soon as possible. There is a large pool of bonus points for the top ten finishers. They divide up the bonus points by the ratio of the difference between the top ten finish times."

"Armstrong Reservoir is huge," Del observed.

"And lots of trails on both sides," Griff said. "We place pickets along some of the trails so you can't just run the whole way. If you miss a picket, you're out. It's usually the evening of the second day before the first recruit finishes. This year, Tee finished in just over an hour."

"Impossible. It's easily twenty miles around the lake," Del said.

"Yeah, but it's only two miles across. Dee wasn't aware that Tee can swim like a fish."

"And you didn't tell him," Del said.

"Guilty." Griff beamed, and they both chuckled.

"Well, I'm glad he made it. I'm guessing he'll be on an officer's track," said Del.

"Ticks all the boxes. He earned respect from the other recruits and the instructors. Toward the end of training, everyone was rooting for him. Even Dee came around," Griff explained.

"Before we get started discussing this year's education plan, I have a question. While I credit the Guard with more common sense than to offer it, why aren't you an officer?" Del asked with a serious look on his face.

"I joined the Guard to fight. Not point the way to battle." Griff scoffed.

Del laughed. "They do a bit more than that. And the lower-level officers do fight."

"Officers start out standing near the battle and pointing. Then they promote you away from the battle to sit down and point some more. It's just not the same."

Del smiled and asked, "So, if you don't want to be an officer, why are you the one defining class requirements for the officers?"

"Because I'm stupid," Griff replied.

"Come now, there's a reason," Del pressed.

"The CGG told me I got this job because I'm opinionated and irritating," Griff said.

"I'm sure that part is true," Del said with an amused expression. "But stupid, you're not. What's the real reason?"

Griff sighed, and with a thoughtful expression said, "Command doesn't see the need for expanding knowledge of warfare outside our current defensive strategy at the Wall and on the cliff forts surrounding the peninsula. We are extremely vulnerable if the GEMs break past the

Wall. Once they do, they can threaten the Landfall Dam. We have to be prepared for a retreat to the Eureka Dam. Then, if it all goes to hell, a phased plan to evacuate all the way to the Apple Lakes region. Successfully managing a retreat is difficult.

"Decisions must be made quickly, and they must be the right decisions. Less important, but still critical in my opinion, is that we aren't prepared to go on the offensive. Sure, we make limited forays below the Wall, but it's not the same thing as a concentrated, well-managed offensive campaign with contingencies. While that might seem crazy now, if there is an opportunity to deal them a serious blow, we should be prepared to take advantage of it."

Del was secretly delighted with this answer and was careful not to show his enthusiasm. An opportunity to train officers for broader military roles and expose them to the technology of the past was urgently needed. I can't tell Griff why we need this, but he's just given me the excuse for a course of study that could sneak some of that in.

"Okay, that actually makes sense. Would you like me to propose something?" Del offered with a bland voice.

"That's why I'm here," Griff replied.

"You realize this is a pretty big change from what we've been doing," Del said.

"Yeah, but it can't look like we're making a big departure from the past. We have to slip this past the CGG."

"Off the top of my head, it sounds like a program that reviews military history, strategy, and weapon systems. We can test their ability to respond to new military objectives with war games."

Griff stared back at him a bit confused and said, "I'm not trying to turn them into history students."

Del leaned forward and said, "If you want them to think outside the current strategy, you need to broaden and deepen their education. If retreat planning is important, we can focus on understanding retreats in the past that were well executed. We can compare them with those that were disasters. Many times, they were both. Dunkirk on old Earth is an example of disaster being turned into success. To understand the decisions that were made, you have to understand the era's technical capabilities. We can specifically design one of the war games as a sudden retreat from the Wall to Eureka Valley and then continuing on to Apple

Lakes under various conditions."

"That sounds good to me, but we don't have lots of study time with all their other responsibilities," Griff countered.

"We can phase in the education and have it increment based on rank level. That way, we spread it out over time. Go more in depth for the higher ranks, or those with high potential for promotion. You'll have to convince them that newly promoted officers need a special set of classes in addition to the ongoing education we already do. You guys like to haze Newbies and newly promoted officers. Make it sound like they are paying their dues or some such BS."

Griff thought for a bit. With concern on his face, he said, "When can I see the details?"

"Tomorrow afternoon if you buy me dinner tonight," Del said.

"Done, but you're buying the drinks. A real beer this time!" Griff said sternly.

CHAPTER 18

BLUE HERON TAVERN

Tee and Jay's lives fell into a routine. They each worked hard at training five days a week and hung out with Guard Newbies from their recruit class most nights below the dam. On weekends, Jay and Tee would hike up to Landfall City and spend Friday and Saturday nights there. The Phillips embraced Tee like he was one of the family. He had his own bedroom. When he was ready to do his university classes, they insisted he stay with them. Tee, Quinn, and Hestie replaced Friday night bonfires with dinner and drinks at one of the taverns in the center of town. Jay was usually at home with his parents and brothers or hanging out with his old school friends. Tee thought he might have a girlfriend, but didn't talk about her.

One Friday evening Jay said, "Tee, can I come and meet Quinn and Hestie?" I've met their parents and the rest of your friends in Apple Valley but not them yet."

"Absolutely," Tee said with enthusiasm. "They've asked lots of questions about you, and I know they want to meet you." He hesitated, smiled, and said, "How are you going to explain that shiner?"

Jay narrowed his eyes and gave Tee a look that said back off, "I walked into a door, Tee."

Tee was unconvinced, but decided they each had their secrets, so perhaps he should just let it go. It was drizzling as they quickly walked to the Blue Heron Tavern, trying not to get too wet. Tee turned to Jay and said, "One word of warning. Quinn doesn't have any tact whatsoever. He is brilliant. But whatever part of the brain manages social interactions is busy doing something else. If he says something odd, or even wildly insulting, just ignore it. He is completely genuine, harmless, and doesn't have a mean bone in his body."

"He's like his mom, then," Jay said.

"Exactly. Except a happier version," Tee explained, smiling.

"No problem. His mom told me with a straight face at the bonfire that personal hygiene was important for good health," Jay said smiling, "We really should have bathed after we got back from hunting, Tee."

Tee chuckled and said, "Yeah, ran out of time. But I'll remember to plan better next time."

They walked into the tavern and spied Quinn and Hestie in a back booth. Tee made introductions, and they ordered drinks.

"Can I try a sip of whatever that is you're drinking? I've never seen anything with that color before," Jay said.

"Sure," Tee said.

Jay tentatively tried a sip, screwed up his face, and said, "Yuk. A drink shouldn't taste like that. Is this an Apple Valley thing? You people do the most disgusting stuff."

Tee grinned, turned toward Quinn and Hestie and said, "He's referring to our hunting trip. I took the big tough city boy with me to Apple Valley. He almost puked while I was dressing the deer we shot."

"You shot, and then talked me into carrying most of it back."

"You had to earn your meal somehow. Just wasting my time otherwise," Tee said, earning a knowing look from Jay.

"You are never going to let that go, are you?" Jay said with an affected grimace.

"Not likely," said Tee with a grin.

"I did like the bonfire at the beach and roasting venison over the fire," Jay said.

"Did you meet everyone?" Quinn asked.

"I met Ansen, Diana, their parents, their brothers and sisters, and Grammy. Oh, and your parents were there too," Jay said, "It was quite the party."

"Did Grammy get you off to the side and extract your secrets?" Hestie asked with a warm smile.

"I like Grammy," Jay said enthusiastically, "And we did have a long talk." Jay hesitated and then confessed sheepishly, "Which included some advice." Everyone broke into raucous laughter.

"I can't believe what I ended up telling her," Jay said, shaking his head to even more laughter.

"You have to watch Grammy," Tee said. "Her advice tends to get repeated more and more firmly until she's satisfied you've followed it."

"It means she likes you, Jay," said Hestie. "It means you're officially part of the group," she added warmly.

Tee turned to Hestie and said, "How are your medical classes going?"

"Well, we've been dissecting, so I'm not sure it's a good topic just before dinner," Hestie said softly, then glanced over at Jay and gave him a shy grin.

Tee chuckled and said, "Wouldn't want anybody to get queasy."

Jay narrowed his eyes at Tee and said, "Okay, little man. Enough!" Then he looked at Hestie and said with interest, "What are you studying?"

"It's mostly basic biology and human anatomy. My mom's a doctor and I've been helping her with patients for a while. I know most of it already. I'm not sure if I want to be a doctor like my mom or something else. I'm also studying genetics, which I love and want to explore more deeply. I know I want to help people, so I'm trying to figure out what that means," Hestie said.

As Jay and Hestie continued their conversation, Tee turned to Quinn and said, "How is the mad scientist training going?"

"It's wonderful having access to the whole library and Professor Dacy's lab. It's like going to heaven. I was worried I would get stuck in lower-level classes for a few years, but they let me test out," Quinn said with enthusiasm.

Quinn being worried about anything was a significant event. Must have been a full-blown crisis. Tee thought wryly. "So, what did you test out of, Quinn?"

"They gave me all the credits for undergraduate degrees in mathematics, physics, chemistry, and mechanical engineering. I still have to take the required courses in history, English, biology, debate, and a special class in social awareness before I get those degrees," Quinn said casually.

Tee was stunned. He knew Quinn was smart, but it was hard to believe he had tested out of all the non-biology science and technology classes the university had to offer. He smiled about the "special class in social awareness." He bet the professors had scrambled trying to figure out how to deal with Quinn. What they would discover was that Quinn was exactly what he appeared to be. Crazy about science. Kind to everyone. No hidden agendas. And no tact whatsoever. Quinn told the truth without the limitation of worrying how it would affect others. He was a wildly enthusiastic and visibly happy version of his mother.

"So, if you tested out of all those classes, what do they have you studying?" Tee asked.

Quinn's face suddenly became guarded. He collected himself and tentatively said, "They have me doing special projects that involve reviewing incomplete archives from long ago. I'm being asked to reverse engineer what is missing in the archives."

Tee's face clouded. He knew Quinn really well. His explanation sounded like something he had memorized. Quinn was hiding something. Tee was sure he hadn't seen Quinn try to do this since they were little kids. He was bad at it then, and he is bad at it now. Well, the Guard has its secrets too and Tee didn't want to stress Quinn out by asking more questions about his 'special projects'.

"You mentioned Professor Dacy's lab. What does he have in it?"

"Everything!" Quinn burst out in excitement. He went on and on about the measurement equipment, lab supplies, reference materials, and notebooks from previous special projects. Tee sat, nodding his head, understanding some of it, but just letting Quinn rattle on and on. Much of it was interesting, and it gave him pleasure to watch his old friend be so excited about what he was doing with his life. They both had blessings. Tee was thankful for his, and for Quinn's.

As Quinn droned on and on, Tee stole a glance over to Jay and Hestie. They were both leaning in toward one another slightly and talking intently, eyes locked. Well, that's interesting, thought Tee. A good match. While Jay was a monster in the Guard, he had a soft side he wasn't afraid to show once he trusted you. Hestie was a lot like Jay's mother in temperament and where Tee thought Jay's soft side came from.

Quinn suddenly said something that piqued his interest. "They have electrical equipment in the lab?" Tee asked to confirm what he thought he heard.

Quinn froze, looked down at the table, looked up, and said, "Some really basic experimental stuff."

"Oh interesting, I bet that's fun," said Tee, knowing Quinn had just lied to him. He was stunned by that realization and his interest peaked.

"Yes, it is," said Quinn as his face turned a light shade of red.

Just then, Jay saved the day by saying, "Tee. Hestie wants to know what training we're both doing. I explained what they have me doing, but you should explain yours."

"I haven't started it yet, but I'm scheduled to take a bunch of history courses focused on military strategy. It's organized by maneuver. For instance, one of the first classes is dedicated to retreat planning and execution. It reviews significant failures and successes in the past when an army has had to retreat. I was told I'm going to have to understand military technology for each era examined. The idea being that to understand why certain choices were made, you have to have the full context of the situation. When I get to that point, I'm hoping Quinn can help me," Tee said, stealing a glance at Quinn as he sat stone faced. Gotcha, thought Tee. He's studying something along the lines of what they have me signed up for.

"What will be fun are the war games we get to play once the class has finished. It's coordinated with Jay's training. We will be part of a team. We are given starting conditions and have to quickly plan and execute a retreat. It's interactive with Guard officers, non-coms, and university staff, giving us situational updates as we work through the exercise. Should be fun," Tee said.

"Sounds like being on the losing team in capture-the-flag," Hestie said.

Tee hesitated, thinking about Hestie's observation, and said, "That's a good analogy. It's like we're moving the flag to somewhere we can protect it," Tee said thoughtfully.

The conversation continued briskly for quite some time and then started to slow as it got late. Tee, reading the room, finally said, "Well, Jay and I better go. We have physical training that starts early and goes all day."

As they said their goodbyes, Hestie turned to Jay and said, "I hope you can join us again, Jay. I enjoyed talking to you."

Jay smiled warmly and said, "Goodnight, Hestie, I'm sure I'll come with Tee again one of these nights."

They walked back toward Jay's home in silence for a while. Jay broke the silence with, "I wouldn't mind coming along next week if it's okay with you."

"You're always welcome, Jay. Both Hestie and Quinn like you, and it was fun tonight," Tee said.

"They both seem pretty smart," Jay offered.

"That's the understatement of the year," Tee said, amused.

"Does Hestie have a boyfriend?" Jay asked tentatively.

"Is that your way of asking me if I'm interested in her?" Tee said in an amused tone.

"Yeah, that, and whether there is anyone else," Jay said.

"The answer to both is no, unless there is someone I don't know about. And I doubt that because she would tell me. I love Hestie. But not like that. She and Quinn grew up next door, and she's like a sister to me. One I care deeply about, so don't you dare hurt her," Tee said with his voice getting slightly strained.

"You know me better than that," Jay said, obviously more than a little offended.

Tee stopped, looked at Jay, sighed and said, "I'm sorry I said that. I do know who you are. Hestie means a lot to me. You won't find a nicer person, or one who cares as much about others as she does," Tee said, which seemed to satisfy Jay.

They continued to walk in silence until Jay said, "You need to work on getting that chip off your shoulder. You have no reason to be suspicious, defiant, or worry like you do."

Only a true friend would take the risk of saying something like that, Tee thought. Jay was right, and he needed to stop. "You're right, Jay, I'll work on it."

And with that admission, they both relaxed and retreated to their own thoughts.

Tee's thoughts turned back to the evening. He knew when Hestie had gone from interesting to exciting for Jay. Quinn said something socially unacceptable and then left to go to the men's room. Jay had looked questioningly in Hestie's direction as she watched Quinn walk away. With fondness in her voice, she said, "The world would be a better place if everyone could just say what they think without anyone taking offense or judging them." Jay's gaze went from questioning to thoughtfulness until Hestie turned toward him, and he quickly looked away. They really would make a great couple.

Pacifica

or judging them." Jay's gaze went from questioning to thoughtfulness until Hestie turned toward him, and he quickly looked away. They really would make a great couple.

GLORIA

Hestie thought one of the best things her mother had done for her children was to show them how to learn. It wasn't enough to sit in a classroom and follow a carefully laid out plan of study. It was about being curious and following that curiosity wherever it took you. With their mother's help, Hestie and her brother had been involved in self-study at the university level since primary school. Quinn had tested out of his lower-level classes so he could take on challenging work.

Hestie had taken a different path. She kept hidden what she already knew. This allowed her to breeze through her lower-level biology and anatomy classes, giving her plenty of time to delve deeply into topics that interested and challenged her. The one that most absorbed her was studying the intricate blueprint and construction plan of life. DNA was the blueprint. The construction plan was a complex set of organic and chemical signals that determined when and how that blueprint was executed.

Evolution was driven by the dance of random changes to both the blueprint and the construction plan. Sometimes these changes were beneficial and carried forward. Sometimes they were detrimental and resulted in a dead end. She was fascinated by the incredible intelligence behind all of it. She was determined to learn as much as she could. The fact they had never found complex life outside of that originating on Earth was mind-boggling. In addition to making terraforming easier, it fed the bright fires of theological debate. Atheists used this fact to claim that the low probability of complex life forming naturally was verified by how rare it was. Believers in an intelligent creator used that same knowledge to claim it proved God uniquely created everything, just as the ancient texts claimed.

Hestie thought it was silly to use science to prove or disprove God's existence. Both camps' beliefs were faith based. Only an agnostic was devoid of faith. Hestie had a strong faith in God, goodness, and the obligation to fight evil. Grammy had instilled that early on and the more she knew, the more that strength grew.

It was unfortunate that studying genetics was considered suspicious. The horrible wars and pogroms that resulted from humankind experimenting with artificial evolution made it a touchy topic even two millennia later. The one thing that could automatically get you thrown out of the university, and perhaps into jail, was to attempt to artificially alter any of the drivers of life.

Hybridization was acceptable since it simply favored beneficial characteristics already present. Nothing was invented or created. Change by direct manipulation was the most heinous crime imaginable. The reality of GEMs was all the evidence one needed to understand the danger.

Given the fear and anger surrounding the topic, Hestie had decided at a young age to keep her talents hidden. She had an ability to read and understand this complex dance. What genes described. Why some turned on and some turned off. How cell specialization was generated. It scared her to realize she had the ability to design genetic changes to achieve a desired outcome. It scared her further when she realized she had a deeper understanding of these mechanisms than her mother did. Her mother was thought to be the smartest person on the planet.

It was embarrassing to think she knew more than her mother, at least in that one area. Perhaps she was arrogant. Maybe she didn't really understand as much as she thought she did. Hestie, by nature, was most comfortable in the background. It was an easy decision to hide her gift.

"Hestie, you need to come up for air," Gloria said with an affected frown, which transformed into a smile once she had her attention.

"Sorry Gloria. I just get so absorbed in this stuff sometimes." Gloria was Hestie's new friend. Gloria was extremely attractive. It was odd walking around with her since men of all ages would be staring at her while trying to look like they weren't. They would engage Hestie in conversation with the obvious end goal of meeting Gloria. That part of the friendship was uncomfortable. They had met in the university dining hall one night when Gloria bumped into her.

After both taking turns taking the blame and apologizing profusely, they laughed and eventually sat down and had dinner together. Since then, they had started studying together in the library most evenings. Gloria was in her biology class, so Hestie would help her from time to time. While Gloria wasn't Diana, she was beginning to be someone she could call a friend.

"I don't understand how you can get anything out of looking at pages and pages of A's, C's, G's, and T's. I know that has to have something to do with DNA. Isn't it undecipherable to just look at the letters?" Gloria said.

Hestie had to be more careful with her private studies in public like this. Gloria was anything but stupid. And now she was suspicious. She hadn't even noticed Gloria sitting down across from her. "You're right, it's a waste of time trying to make sense out of it," Hestie said as her eyes adjusted from her work to her friend.

"You need to get out more, girl. A friend of mine saw you studying with me the other day and he is very interested in meeting you, very interested. He's a nice guy and is having a small party Friday night. Do you want to go with me?"

"I've already got plans for Friday, Gloria. My brother and I are meeting up with Tee. I've told you about him before. He was our next-door neighbor growing up in Apple Valley. I've known him all my life. He's in the Guard and taking military history classes at the university this semester." To say nothing of the fact that Jay would be there, Hestie thought.

Jay had been on her mind a lot lately. Meeting up on Friday nights had become a regular thing and the more she got to know him, the more she liked him. He was kind, gentle, witty, and intelligent. The knowledge he was capable of protecting her against just about anything was also a little exciting. The fact she thought he was the most attractive man she had ever seen didn't hurt, either.

Better yet, he didn't seem to know how handsome he was. Best of all was that he was solidly, emotionally secure. He didn't need her help to understand himself. Didn't need a shoulder to lean on. They could just lean together. They had met up a couple of times on Saturdays. He had been the perfect gentleman every time. No pressure for anything physical, which she especially appreciated, given how physically imposing he was. She was starting to think she was going to have to be the one to initiate things if it went any further. She felt valued, appreciated, happy, and safe around Jay. She was in danger of falling in love and wasn't fighting it.

"Either you don't like men or you're hiding a boyfriend, Hestie. You've avoided every attempt I've made to introduce you. The only other thing I can think of is that you don't like my company," Gloria said with a rare frown, inviting disagreement with her last comment.

Hestie stared at her for a few moments, wondering where to go with this. There was something different about Gloria, and she couldn't figure out what it was. Of course, she was the last one who should be critical of anyone being 'unusual.' Her entire family was strange. Perhaps she was reluctant to talk about Jay because she was a little afraid of how serious it was becoming. Deciding to open up, she said, "Tee has a friend from the Guard that I've been spending time with. I'm not someone who sees more than one guy at a time. It just doesn't seem right for you to introduce me to anyone right now."

"Ohhh!" Gloria said, clapping her hands together, obviously delighted with the news. "Tell me everything."

Hestie smiled thinking about Jay and proceeded to list his attributes, getting enthusiastic as she warmed up to the idea of sharing this with Gloria. When she said he was raised in the Landfall City, Gloria stopped her and said, "What's his name?"

"Jay Phillips," Hestie responded, smiling.

Gloria just stared back at Hestie with shock showing clearly on her face. As the shocked look turned into concern, she said, "I hate to be the one to tell you this, but Jay Phillips is not a good guy. I went to school with him. He's beautiful, and he's charming. I'll give him that. But he's the worst kind of bully. He randomly targets popular boys and stalks them until they are alone and then beats them up. I heard he got caught by the friends of one of his intended targets a few weeks ago and was beaten badly. I spied him in town with a black eye just after that. It delighted almost everyone he went to school with. Worse, he takes advantage of girls and laughs about it later. The only thing he wants is their virginity."

Hestie was stunned speechless. She just stared back at Gloria, not knowing what to say. She finally looked down, gathered her books, and got up to leave.

"Don't run away, Hestie. I'm here for you. I'm sorry, but it's kinder to warn you about what type of man you're seeing. I just couldn't stay silent."

Tears were spilling from her eyes as she turned away and almost ran from the library. How could she have been such a fool? Girl from Apple Valley taken advantage of by the big city boy. She felt completely humiliated as she ducked her head and walked out into the rainy streets of the capital.

A few days later, it was Friday evening. Hestie was walking along crowded streets to meet Tee, Quinn, and Jay at the Blue Heron Tavern. It was a popular medium-sized place to have dinner and drinks located in the center of the city. It was frequented by a wide mix of people and had a rustic feel to it that reminded Hestie of The Apple Lakes Inn. The familiar atmosphere was likely why Tee originally suggested it.

She had spent two days berating herself for being fooled and almost told Quinn she was skipping Friday night. Then she realized the story didn't add up. First of all, she had high confidence in Tee's ability to read people. He would not be friends with a bully or someone who treated women badly. Of that, she was sure. He would certainly not be okay with someone he didn't trust dating her.

She smiled, thinking about the one kiss they had shared a few years ago. It was a quick one. They had immediately pulled away from each other and broke out laughing. Ansen had been pushing the idea that they should be a couple and that influenced them both. It was their secret. Having anyone else know would just cause embarrassment and confusion. Tee was her other brother. She was his sister. They loved each other. He was as close to her as any family member could be. He was the brother she didn't need to explain to others. The one she could open up to and would understand.

Could Tee have been fooled about Jay's true nature? That was certainly possible. Tee tended to believe in the best in people. But it seemed unlikely that Jay could have fooled them both. While she wasn't perfect, everyone said her ability to read people was extraordinary. All of her senses, all of her intuition, said that Jay was simply what he appeared to be. But she needed to confront him. Grammy always said it's better to fess up first to yourself and then everyone else in matters of the heart.

She smiled at the thought of Grammy wearing her stern face while lecturing all of them. Grammy's advice was always helpful if you bothered to follow it. When Hestie entered the tavern, Tee, Quinn, and Jay were already there.

She walked up to the table, skipped her normal greetings, looked directly at Jay, and said, "Jay, there is something I'd like to talk to you about. Can we go to another table?"

Well, that certainly caused an emotional upheaval for both Jay and Tee. Her empathy was so strong that their reaction caused a jolt of emotional pain for her. It was not in her nature to be blunt. She could feel the waves of anxiety flowing out from both of them. Quinn, of course, was oblivious. She didn't need to worry about him for now. Tee's face quickly went from anxious to throwing a questioning look at Jay. Perhaps there is something to what Gloria told her after all, she thought, with a sinking feeling in her gut.

"Sure," said Jay in a soft voice and got up from the table. He followed her over to a private table in the corner and sat down.

"What's this all about?" he asked, worry written all over him. Jay was an observant man, something she liked about him.

"You told me a few weeks ago that I could ask you anything. Can I?" Hestie said with a flat and slightly stern expression.

"Yes, you can ask me anything," Jay said, leaning back from the table a bit, concern clearly growing.

"The day we met, your face was bruised. Tee was teasing you about how that happened. He clearly did not believe your story. How did your face get bruised?"

Jay's face showed surprise and confusion. He hesitated, then said, "Not sure why it matters to you, but I'll tell you if you promise to keep it a secret from Tee."

Hestie's eyebrows narrowed with suspicion. She hesitated a few moments and then said, "I won't promise that. If there is something going on that Tee ought to know, I'm going to tell him. He's family to me."

Jay pondered that for a minute, clearly concerned with the direction of the conversation. Then he took a deep breath and said, "You clearly don't trust me for some reason. But that doesn't mean I don't trust you. I'll tell you what happened, and you can decide whether to tell him or not." Hestie nodded for him to continue and her features softened just a bit.

"Tee had a horrible time in recruit training. It's still hard for me to believe anyone could take that kind of abuse and just keep going. After you get to know Tee, you learn to expect uncompromising bullheadedness out of him. Since you've known him your whole life, I'm sure you're not surprised."

Hestie nodded at that, and the corners of her mouth bent up a fraction. "Tee is a force of nature at times."

Encouraged, Jay continued. "If you know that you also know how much be berates himself if he has to rely on anyone for protection. Nothing worse for Tee than not being able to personally take care of his own problems."

Hestie thought about this and then said, "You're right. It's stupid, but he hates having to rely on anyone. So, what happened?"

"You know that Tee and I are Newbies." Hestie nodded to show she understood. "We aren't considered full Guard members until we complete our training. That means we get some good-natured ribbing when we run into the various Guard units. The night before we met, I was at a bar near the Wall with a guy named Kale having a few beers. Kale was in the same recruit class as Tee and I. He was horrible to Tee throughout most of our training. Then he completely turned around and became one of Tee's biggest supporters. We're all good friends now.

"Anyway, five members of Scout Team 2 came into the bar, noticed us, and started with the common insults thrown at Newbies. We laughed along with them at the first few jibes and then ignored them. They were a little drunk, and ignoring them made them angry. That's when the largest of them asked if we knew the midget who had just graduated. We continued to ignore them, so he walked over to Kale, poked him in the chest, and said, 'I'm talking to you, Newbie.'

Kale took a step back, looked him up and down and said, 'His name is Tee, and he's a better man than you are.' The next thing I knew, Kale and I were in a brawl with all five of them. The Guard police showed up, and we spent the night locked up."

"Were you hurt?" Hestie asked, clearly concerned.

"Not really. But I do know that Scout Team 2 has readjusted their opinion of the latest Newbie class," he said with a self-satisfied smile. "The best part was when Master Sergeant Ricks showed up the next morning. He told Scout Team 2 in front of their staff sergeant that they were lucky Tee wasn't with us. He's tougher than either one of these guys, pointing his thumb over at us.

"Kale and I nodded in agreement at that. He told all of us he doesn't want to hear this being discussed. He told us we were an embarrassment to the Guard. Then he slowly looked around the room, looked all of us in the eye, and said he would personally make life a living hell for anyone who talks about the incident or doesn't treat other Guard members like brothers going forward."

"So, you're under orders not to talk about it and you're also worried Tee will feel bad about himself if he knows," Hestie said.

"That's about it," Jay responded.

Hestie considered this for a few moments and said softly, "I won't say anything, Jay. I don't want to get you in trouble. I agree there is no reason for Tee to know."

Jay looked at her suspiciously and then asked, "What is this really all about?"

"One more question," Hestie said with an intense look back in place. "Are you trying to trick me into giving you my virginity?"

"What?" exploded out of him loudly enough that it caused people at the tables nearby to turn and look at them. Even Quinn turned around with a rare look of concern on his face. Jay looked at her sternly for a while and whispered, "No. I'll only ask that of my wife on our wedding night."

Although she saw he was clearly offended, Hestie relaxed. There was no doubt in her mind he was telling the truth. She was surprised how important this was to her. There would be so much more than just humiliation if the accusations had been true. Gloria was lying about all of it. But why?

"I'm truly sorry, Jay. I really am. I was told some things about you that were just horrible. It was so bad I wasn't able to just trust my instincts and ignore it." A moment passed and then she said, "Do you know Gloria Binder?"

Jay's eyebrows crashed together. He turned a bright shade of red and was obviously working hard to keep his anger in check. "Yes," he bit off. "We were dating at school and then for a brief time after I came back from recruit training. We broke up before you and I met."

"Why did you break up?" Hestie asked.

Jay considered this for a few moments and then said, "Let's just say our ethics and morals weren't in alignment."

Hestie appreciated that Jay didn't say anything more than that. Clearly, something disturbing happened. She wasn't going to ask him about it. Now she had a different problem. She had broken trust with Jay. She should have just trusted him. Told him about the accusations and let him explain.

"Jay, I am truly sorry. I should have come straight to you with what had been said. I know deep down that you're trustworthy. I won't make that mistake again."

Jay just glared back at her for an uncomfortable minute. Then he said in a stern voice, "I have a serious question for you."

Hestie's insides roiled. If her mistake meant he wasn't interested in her anymore, it would be terrible. She was frightened by how important he had become to her. Taking a shallow breath, she nodded for him to continue.

Jay's frown grew even deeper, and he said, "How do I know this isn't some elaborate plan to take *my* virginity?"

Hestie just stared at him dumbly for a few moments, her brain not able to make sense of what she had just heard. Then she burst into laughter, rocking slightly back and forth, trying to gain control. Jay was smiling broadly and chuckling at the spectacle, clearly pleased with himself. She got up, went around to the other side, jumped in his lap, and gave him a huge hug.

"Thank you, Jay," she said softly into his ear. "I really am sorry." Then, turning around, she saw Tee and Quinn staring at them. "We should probably go over and save the evening. Tee has been stealing anxious glances at us the whole time."

Later that evening, after dropping the twins off at their dorm rooms, Tee and Jay were walking back to Jay's house and Tee asked, "Everything okay with you and Hestie?"

"Yeah, just boyfriend girlfriend stuff," Jay said.

Tee smiled and said with a touch of sarcasm, "So it's official, the two of you like each other."

"Yes we do, smartass," Jay replied.

Tee put his hand on Jay's shoulder and with an honest and earnest expression said, "Jay, I couldn't be happier for you, or for Hestie."

Jay was touched. He remembered their first conversation about Hestie and Tee's initial concern with him being interested in her. Tee was rarely serious about these sorts of things, which made it all the more genuine. An affected frown was on Jay's face and turning the tables on

Tee, he said, "You Apple Valley people have trust issues." Seeing the confused, questioning look he expected, he turned away and hid a smile. Let him sort that one out, he thought. They continued their walk to Jay's house in silence.

CHAPTER 20

DIANA'S HUNT

Diana was getting more and more frustrated with Ansen. Ansen decided he would go hunting with her because he thought it was dangerous for her to be in the woods alone. This was reasonable on the surface. It was rare, but there were panthers and bears who had been known to attack people. Not that she couldn't take care of herself. But it did sound nice to hunt with someone again.

Ansen was LOUD. He walked loudly. He breathed loudly. He would not stop talking. She enjoyed Ansen's banter most of the time. He had an unusual way of looking at life, which was entertaining and very funny. But damn it, this was a hunt, not a party at the beach. She finally decided it was her own fault. Ansen was always loud, so why should this be any different? So, she came up with a plan.

"Let's walk up to the beach lookout and see the guys," Diana said.

"So, you going to give up on hunting with me?" Ansen asked suspiciously.

Diana rolled her eyes upward and said, "Yes! Let's go see the guys and you can hang out with them. That way, you can stop pretending to enjoy the woods while I go hunting in peace for a couple of hours."

Ansen looked a little hurt and said, "Am I that bad?"

Diana smiled and said, "The worst! You are unbelievably loud. You're scaring all the game away."

"Fair enough," Ansen said.

Then, to Diana's amazement, he stopped talking. Diana really missed hunting with Tee. He had been gone for almost six months now and only came back once in all that time. He had his friend Jay from the Guard with him and the two of them had gone hunting. Diana wasn't invited. Tee and Diana had been roaming the woods together since they were old enough to be allowed to wander off. The woods relaxed her. She really liked supplying fresh meat for family and friends.

Being honest with herself, she had to admit she just plain missed Tee. It wasn't just the hunting trips. It was hard to be completely honest with herself, but Tee leaving left a hole. She could feel it in the pit of her stomach. Hunting just made the pain more pronounced. She adored Ansen. He was kind, witty, funny, and trustworthy. But she loved Tee. There, she admitted it. She knew deep down it was true. She had been in denial. He was not as funny or entertaining as Ansen, but you could have deep, soulful conversations with him. He understood her like no one else.

When he was around, she was simply at peace. He was short and slender, shorter than she was. But he always seemed to be the largest person around when there was a crisis or threat of some kind. She might have been surprised when he was chosen for the Guard. Everyone was, including him. But she wasn't shocked. How did I get myself into this situation, she thought. Everyone, including Ansen, thinks we'll marry this year.

Why did I run away from Tee for so long? Why were those feelings so scary? Well, some serious thinking to do and the woods have always been the best place for that.

"How do you think Quinn, Hestie, and Tee are doing?" Diana asked. She figured they might as well talk until they got to the lookout.

Ansen replied, "I haven't heard anything lately. It sucks that all three of them are gone. I miss them even more than I thought I would. But I'm really glad they are all in the capital and see each other regularly." Ansen sighed and then continued. "To be honest, I wanted Tee to get kicked out of recruit training. But he made it to graduation, so he's Guard for life." Diana just nodded in agreement. "I gave him an earful the last time he was up here about Hestie," Ansen said. "She has a heart of gold, loves him to death, and just keeps getting prettier. I do not understand why he doesn't pursue her. She isn't going to be available forever."

Diana spoke up with resignation, "I always dreamed the four of us being close forever. I imagined being on the beach Friday nights with Hestie and I trading kids back and forth while you and Tee trade insults." She smiled a wry and somewhat guilty smile."

Ansen said, "I think he's confused...LOOK OUT!"

They had rounded a curve in the trail and standing in a small clearing were three GEMs looking right at them. The GEMs didn't hesitate. They immediately broke into a run, pulling out wicked looking short swords. Diana didn't hesitate, either. She immediately drew back her already notched arrow and placed it in the throat of the lead GEM. This didn't slow the other two down at all.

A few feet away now, Diana had just enough time to draw a second arrow from the quiver, pull back and let fly. She watched in amazement as the arrow buried itself deeply in the second GEM's left eye socket. He dropped like a stone. She said a quick prayer and silently thanked Arti for all the endless crazy battle scenario drills she used to make them do. She had instinctively avoided their torsos because she didn't have time to decide if they had on armor or not.

Without that training, she would be dead or at the mercy of the GEMs. And the GEMs had no mercy. She quickly turned and saw that Ansen was wounded and barely holding the last GEM off. He was using a tree as a shield of sorts, but it was clear he wouldn't be able to hold him off for long with just his knife. Diana took another arrow and pulled back. She slowly circled the fight, looking for an opening.

There was a lot of quick movement by both of them that was hard to predict. If she missed, she would hit Ansen. Again, she heard Arti in her head telling her to concentrate, focus on getting a good shot, don't wait for the perfect shot. She let go, and the arrow grazed Ansen's forearm before burying itself in the GEM's side just below the vest and into the rib cage. This distracted the GEM enough that Ansen was able to step in close and drive his knife deep into the creature's chest.

Diana notched another arrow and looked around wildly. Two of the GEMs were quite dead. The one with the arrow in his neck was noisily bleeding out, so no threat there. The three GEMs had yelled loudly when they saw Diana and Ansen, so she believed others must be nearby. Ansen seemed to be in shock, but his wound wasn't serious enough to worry about it now.

"We have to run back to Apple Lake Ansen," Diana said.

"Shouldn't we rouse the guys at the lookout instead?" Ansen countered.

"They're dead Ansen. The only way those GEMs are here is by scaling the beach cliff. They must have surprised the lookout." Diana realized Ansen was not thinking clearly. So, she grabbed his shirt, gave him a pull back down the trail and broke into a run, hoping he would follow.

After they had been running for several minutes, her panicked mind settled down. She wondered if they should both run back to Apple Lake. There was another lookout just a bit further south, about twenty minutes or so off this main trail. The cliff below this lookout had no beach. Large waves pounded directly into the sheer granite wall, so very unlikely it had been directly assaulted.

Since they had surprised the scouts fairly close to the beach lookout, she hoped the GEMs weren't there yet. The lookout was there for one reason: a signal fire could be seen from Apple Lake and the next signal fire station in Eureka Valley below the falls. The quickest way to get a response team was to get that signal fire lit. The only problem was that it was a dead-end trail. If GEMs were following, they would come up that trail and trap them at the lookout.

"Ansen, you keep going down the trail to Apple Lake and report to Major Richards. I'm going to light the southern cliff top signal fire. We have to make sure this invasion is known all the way to the capital as soon as possible."

"No, Diana!" Ansen yelled with a wild-eyed expression, "I am not leaving you!" He grabbed her arm tightly, pulling her away from the branched trail to the cliff top lookout and down the trail to Apple Lake.

Diana calmed herself, stopped, and with her free hand slapped him hard, saying, "Get ahold of yourself! This isn't about you and me. It's about everyone in Pacifica. We have to split up to give a better chance of getting the news out." Ansen's expression changed from wild-eyed to shocked. He took a deep breath and said, "You're right, I'm sorry. Just please make sure you live. I will never forgive you if you don't." Even at the worst of times, Ansen was trying to joke. It fell flat.

Diana stopped running as she approached the lookout. She left the trail and carefully crept through the woods toward the clearing at the top of the cliff. She saw the huge stack of wood comprising the signal. She stopped, listened, and looked for GEMs. The two lookouts who were supposed to be there seemed to be missing. It was completely silent, with no one in sight. The small fire that was supposed to always be going was cold. Luckily, her mother insisted she take flint and steel with her when she went hunting. "You never know when you might get stuck out there for the night and a fire can come in handy," her mother had said.

Diana took a deep breath and shaved off some chips. With time, she got a small ember going. Then some smaller pieces of wood and was finally able to get the end of a dead tree branch glowing. She got up quickly, sticking the burning branch into the signal firewood stack, and WHOOSH the whole thing exploded. She fell back on her butt, smelling burned hair. She had forgotten the signal firewood was soaked in a flammable liquid just for this purpose. Quinn would know exactly what. Right down to the chemical bonding diagram.

She smiled and realized she was a bit loopy thinking about Quinn's weird store of knowledge at a time like this. She needed to focus. Checking herself over, she wasn't injured. She thought her hair was singed and worried her eyebrows might be gone.

"Now is not the time to worry about how pretty you are, Diana," she said out loud with a nervous laugh.

Gazing out to sea, she saw three large vessels on the very edge of the horizon that seemed to be heading north of the cliff lookout and toward the beach. Given the strong headwinds and choppy seas, it was going to take a while. She was terrified of what it would mean if hundreds or thousands of GEMs were able to scale the cliff and get entrenched in the upper east valley. She shuttered as she thought back to the demonic vicious smiles of the GEMs.

Her immediate problem, however, was she had just advertised to the GEMs where they could find her. She shouldn't go back down the trail and waiting by the signal fire seemed incredibly stupid. Walking around, she carefully studied the perimeter of the clearing. She found a faint game trail heading down one of the steep slopes opposite the trailhead. She thanked Tee. He was always exploring game trails, trying to figure out what their purpose was. This one meant there was a hidden way off the cliff.

If she was lucky, it would lead to water, which might then lead downstream toward Apple Lake. It might not be easy, but it was a better plan than waiting for the GEMs. Hopefully, the game trail didn't circle back to the cliff trail. Crossing her fingers, she carefully eased her way down the steep trail. She was careful not to fall or disturb anything that might be used to track her.

With luck, the GEMs wouldn't be as good at wood craft as she was.

The game trail led to a small stream and then alongside it downhill. It was narrow but eventually widened out enough that Diana could jog if she kept the pace slow and was careful. It suddenly veered south and past a small waterfall. She recognized the waterfall and headed off toward where the main trail should be. The main trail appeared suddenly and with that, she was running as fast as she could toward Apple Lake.

INVASION

Griff was observing Scout Team 2 performing climbing and repelling exercises. The team was working their way up the steep cliffs near the eastern sea. It wasn't far from Apple Falls. This area was perfect for this type of training because the granite walls were sheer, with just enough imperfections in them to allow for pitons to be driven in for support, but not enough to make a path to the top easy. You had to select your path carefully. It was grueling exercise.

The entire team knew they were there because of the bar brawl. Over the past month, just when they thought their punishment was over, Griff would show up and take them on another exhausting venture. He called it training. They knew it was punishment.

Griff was pleased with Sergeant Glenn's handling of all this. He had punished the offending members appropriately and never complained about Griff's extra assignments. Griff was delighted by the brawl, although he would never admit it. In his opinion, Jay and Kale were the future of non-com leadership.

The two of them thrashing five seasoned veterans from one of the better scout teams sent a strong message. Even better was that the brawl started because of insults thrown at Tee. News of this would make Tee's entry into the officer ranks easier. He ordered them all to be silent. But he knew that just meant they would whisper about it instead of talking openly.

Just then, he noticed smoke on the horizon above the cliff edge. It was in the general direction of where a signal fire might be, so he ordered Scout Team 2 to repel back down immediately. When down, they took off at a run for Apple Falls. The team of fourteen scouts plus himself rode the Tram up the lower falls. This thing is useful, thought Griff, silently thanking Del. Once on the road, they ran to Apple Valley, which was in total chaos when they arrived.

Major Richards and Arti were trying to organize, but the crowd was out of control. Griff's booming voice called out, "QUIET!" One of the burly villagers turned in his direction and kept shouting, so Griff walked up and coldcocked him. Casually placing his boot on the unconscious man's chest, he asked with malice in his voice, "Anyone else have an opinion?" That shut everyone up.

"Major Richards, what is the situation?" Griff demanded.

"A couple of hunters surprised GEM scouts up by the upper southeast beach lookout. One of them ran to the southernmost cliff lookout and, not finding anyone, lit the signal fire. She saw three large troop transport ships heading for the southeast beach. We were just discussing whether to attack their position or set up a defense."

"We don't have time for a debate. If they get control of the upper east valley we're screwed," Griff said with disgust. Griff then barked out orders to Richards, "Select fifty warriors and ten archers based on their endurance. I will take this advance team to the beach lookout and engage. Send another fifty warriors and ten archers at a quick march behind the advance team as a reserve. Assign a leader for the reserve team. All others are going to set up a defensive line blocking the upper east valley entry into the main valley just above the falls. Richards, you are in charge of the defense. Arti, stay here and support Richards. Assign leaders to be in charge of the archers for the advance and reserve attack teams."

Everyone started moving at once. Although Richards was officially in charge, nobody questioned Griff's orders, including Richards. In minutes, Griff and the advance team were jogging up the trail to the upper east valley. He had wanted to have Arti with the Reserve team. But he had lost all confidence in Richards. He thought she would keep things under control now that they had a plan. He shook his head. Richards had to go.

Puffing heavily as he ran up the trail, Griff had to admit he was impressed. The majority of the Advance Team was keeping up with Scout Team 2. The leader of the Advance Team Archers was a young woman named Diana. He remembered her from when he had delivered the recruiting invite to Tee.

At first, he thought she was too young for this assignment. But it turned out she was one of the hunters who surprised the GEM scouts. That she and her hunting partner had killed three of them was impressive. It had been her idea to split up with her partner, warning Apple Valley while she went to light the signal fire. Since she had no idea if that outpost had also been overrun, it was incredibly brave.

So far, they had been lucky. Devine intervention level of luck. He realized a full-scale invasion of the upper peninsula was detected because Diana's boyfriend was a lousy hunter, and she had superb judgement and courage. He prayed for their 'luck' to continue.

Diana had been a good choice for leader of the Advance Team Archers, thought Griff. As an avid hunter, she knew the area extremely well. She correctly guessed where the GEMs might place pickets. Which allowed them to be quickly taken out without setting off alarms. Better yet, she knew a back way into the beach lookout they could use to their advantage. Griff sent Staff Sergeant Glenn with six other scouts, five of the archers including Diana, and ten volunteers, all known to be good hunters. They would know how to sneak up on the beach cliff top without making noise.

"Stay hidden until you see them pursue our retreat," Griff told the team tasked with sneaking around the back. Your objective is to cut the rope ladders that will likely be in place. While we want to kick them all off the cliff as quickly as possible, it's more important to slow their progress up the cliff."

Turning to the main group, he said, "Main attack group will engage and then fall back into a defensive position. The main attack team archers will stay at the defensive position and cover the retreat. Your job is to slow the GEMs down as much as you can so the men can take their positions. Our goal is to draw the bulk of them away from the cliff. It's critical for us to buy time for our reinforcements to arrive."

Sergeant Glenn motioned Diana to his side as they carefully made their way up the back entrance trail. He whispered in her ear, "Follow us to the trail opening after the attack begins. Group your women on both sides of the trail as it opens up on the clearing on the summit. We will already be engaged when you get visuals on the GEMs, but provide whatever support you can. Your main role is to help cover our retreat."

Diana considered this for a moment and said, "I know the area. With a little time, I can have our archers dispersed along the entire back side of the clearing. We can hide far enough back in the foliage to blend in, but still have clear lines of sight. If we open the attack with a flight of arrows, they will be confused and looking for cover. If we are properly positioned, they won't be able to tell where the arrows are coming from. That should soften them up a bit for your attack."

Sergeant Glenn's thinking was much like most members of the Guard. Wall Archers had their place. Their place was up on the Wall, doing what they could in a support role. It wasn't generating battle plans. It wasn't leadership. But her plan sounded like an improvement. If the archers were discovered while dispersing, they could immediately launch the sudden assault he was envisioning, with little downside. Diana's plan had a chance of creating confusion and, with luck, panic.

Hesitating for a few moments to think it through, he said quietly, "I like it. Let me get into position before you disperse your archers. If you are detected, we'll attack immediately. Do you have some way of coordinating the first flight of arrows?"

"Yes. I can use a signaling arrow. It creates a high-pitched whistle. I'll launch that at your signal, and the other archers will launch immediately. I've told them to look to you for direction once we're engaged. If you want us to concentrate on any specific target or area, just wave and point. If not, they will pick off random targets as quickly as they can in support of you cutting the rope ladders," Diana whispered.

As soon as Sergeant Glenn gave her the hand signal Diana let her signaling arrow fly. She hit what she guessed was the senior GEM square in the back, driving him to his knees. Arrows sprouted immediately on GEMs located near the ropes anchored on the cliff edge. Her team was operating in what Arti called zones. Each woman took out everything in her zone until it was empty. They then moved to the right or left adjacent zones based on volume of targets. Sergeant Glenn had decided to use the whistling arrow to launch the ground attack as well. By the time Glenn and his attack team got to the cliff edge, most of the GEMs left behind were down or wounded.

There was a brief, brutal skirmish to take out those GEMs left who could still fight. The ropes were quickly cut, which elicited loud screams from below the cliff edge. Glenn immediately called for a retreat, and they hurried back toward the narrow trail they had used to sneak up the back side of the cliff. The archers quickly abandoned their posts and took their own paths back to the trail, weaving their way through the trees and stones. Sergeant Glenn had initially argued that they should stay and make the GEMs fight two separate battle lines. Griff had countermanded that saying Glenn's objective was to cut the ropes with as few losses as possible and then rejoin the main group. "Once the ropes are cut, they won't be able to replace them before our reserves arrive."

Griff was pleased. Unlike most plans, this one had been executed more or less as designed. The initial attack had drawn thirty or so GEMs away from the cliff edge and the rope ladders had been successfully cut. The change he made on the fly was to abandon his defensive position and throw everything into an all-out attack.

Once the rope ladders had been cut, screams from the falling GEMs had alerted them that they had been flanked. This had drawn the bulk of the GEMs back toward the cliff. Now that he had an idea how many GEMs were there, he confidently took the initiative. He was delighted to see Glenn had called off his own retreat once he realized Griff was attacking. Caught between the two battle lines, the GEMs had been quickly and efficiently dispatched. He noticed that many of the GEMs near the cliff edge had arrows in them.

When he first looked down over the cliff, he saw hundreds of GEMs on the beach. The sight made him shiver. From the bodies at the base of the cliff, quite a few had been on the rope ladders when they were cut. The trebuchet intended to harass ships attempting to land on the beach had been destroyed by the GEMs. But they hadn't bothered with the piles of stones stored for that purpose.

Glenn had the volunteers throwing these down into the crowd of GEMs milling around in confusion below. He also had a group gathering the dead GEMs up and chucking them over the cliff as well. A brutal message and an efficient way to clean up the mess. The ocean would do the work of disposing of GEM bodies for them. Knowing they had lost their chance, the GEMs organized themselves, turned around, and were going back to their ships for a retreat to sea.

"Sergeant Glenn, casualties report," Griff said firmly.

"One volunteer from my team killed and eight from the main attack team. Another ten wounded. Guard scouts are okay with Bill having a minor wound he's already taken care of. None of the volunteer wounds are life threatening, although two may need a doctor's attention before we try and move them back to Apple Valley," Glenn reported.

"The archers?" Griff asked.

"None killed or wounded. Diana spread the advance team out along the back of the clearing and far enough back in the woods that the GEMs couldn't tell where the arrows were coming from. She was perched on an outcropping so she could see the entire clearing. The rest were hiding behind bushes, rocks, and tree trunks. They made taking out the GEMs left behind after the initial assault easy. We just had to finish a few off and cut the ropes. Those women are deadly!" Glenn said with a smile, admiration shining in his eyes.

As the sergeant was finishing his report, Diana wandered over and showed them two dozen special arrows the women had brought. "Should we try and set those ships on fire?" she asked. The arrows had blown glass vial arrow heads filled with a flammable liquid. Oil-soaked rags were wound tightly around the shaft just below the arrow heads.

"Let them fly," Griff said with a determined grin. "But pick one of the ships and focus on starting fires that are spread out. You'll need to create enough separate fires to overwhelm their ability to fight the flames."

Two of the ships got away, but the third caught fire and was eventually taken by the sea with all hands. The other two ships didn't even attempt to save anyone. Griff wondered again if a full-time archers auxiliary ought to be part of the Guard. It was silliness not to include them in scout teams. Their value in situations like this was enormous. Most of the Guard belittled the women's abilities and contributions. Well, Glenn was certainly a convert. Griff took a deep breath and told himself it was another quest to be put on the back burner for now.

Griff didn't let them cut down the four lookout guards until the reserve team showed up. He wanted everyone to see what happens when you aren't diligent. More than a few people had to step into the forest to empty their stomachs. Evidently, the southern cliff lookout had been abandoned for a card game. From the mess in the guard shack, the four had been drinking and playing cards when they were surprised. The attack was likely a small boat floating in at night, then pulled up high on the beach out of sight.

A few of the GEMs must have climbed the challenging cliff at night and surprised the lookouts. Four horribly mutilated bodies were tied to trees just outside the shack. The GEMs had taken their time. It was obvious the four lookouts died horribly. They all heard the stories of what GEMs did to prisoners. But seeing it firsthand was gruesome. Griff ordered the four to be cremated in the signal fire pit.

They didn't deserve a resting place in the Hall of Heroes, and he didn't want their families to see how they had died. It seemed appropriate that their final resting place would put them on lookout duty for eternity.

I deserve to be in that fire pit as well, thought Griff. One derelict lookout team was bad. But two at the same time was hard to accept.

Richards was clearly not keeping up with his duties. But this was incompetence that went beyond one person. When he was here the last time, he should have spent a week hiking to all the lookout spots and performing surprise inspections. He suspected things might be a little lax, and he had a responsibility to chase that suspicion down.

Griff shook off his guilt. It wasn't the time for self-recrimination. He could beat himself up later. A major probe like this was highly unusual, and he wondered if it was part of some larger objective. It was time to anticipate the worst and mobilize at the Wall.

"Sergeant, I need to get to Landfall City as soon as possible. Get both lookouts cleaned up and provisioned. Scour this area and make sure we don't have any GEMs hiding in the woods. Diana can recommend volunteers who know this area your team can work with. You are in charge until orders from the Guard arrive. You understand?"

"Yes, Master Sergeant," Glenn said, then hesitating he offered, "I'll tell Major Richards I'm operating on your orders until I hear from the Guard."

Griff nodded and said, "I'll likely see you at the Wall. Good luck." Griff turned away and headed down the trail toward Apple Valley. The fact that Glenn understood his intent immediately was proof Richards's ineffectiveness was obvious to everyone. He really should have done something sooner.

COUNCIL VOTE

Del was surprised when Griff walked into his office. The master sergeant was a meticulous man. He was always clean shaven with a perfectly pressed uniform. He looked like he had slept in this one. Maybe rolled around in the dirt a bit, too. He looked worn out and sleep deprived. The smell of horse sweat now permeated his office. Del would usually start off with banter. The state of the uniform, the three-day-old beard, or the smell would be good places to start. However, something was seriously wrong here.

"What's wrong, Griff?" Del said with concern in his eyes.

"We need to mobilize, but I can't get CGG's support to go to the president to propose it," Griff said abruptly.

"Back up. Why do we need to mobilize?" Del asked.

"Three days ago, we fought off an attack in Apple Valley at the southernmost upper east side beach lookout. There were five to six hundred GEMs on the beach when we finally threw their advance team off the cliff. I believe this is part of something bigger," Griff said.

Del was shocked. Three days to get from Apple Valley to the capital meant he had been on horseback without sleep since he left. Griff wasn't prone to overreaction, so Del cautioned himself to listen carefully.

"What makes you think this is something major?" Del prompted.

"There were three ships involved in the landfall. Two of them sported a common flag, but the third was different. That means at least two war lords are cooperating. As you know, this is unheard of. Next, their target is strange. Strategically gaining control of one of the upper east valleys is limiting. While highly defendable, the valley is also a bottleneck if you're trying to get out. In other words, it's an excellent fort but almost as good of a jail."

"Why would they want to do that?" Del asked.

"It potentially pulls warriors away from the Wall. They are smart and have been watching us for as long as we've been watching them. They know if they capture even a small inconsequential piece of land, we'll throw everything against them until we kick them out. As you know, it would take six days, best case, to call troops back from Apple Lake. It's a clever diversion. My guess is that they will accelerate a major assault against the Wall once they hear of their failure to take the upper east valley. I believe we have less than a week to start mobilizing."

"We have watchers up on Mount Anderson with an antique telescope looking for GEM movement," Del said. "So far, we haven't seen any signs. In fact, it's been unusually quiet."

"That's just another sign of trouble, Del. Why should it be quiet? They know they have attacked us up north. They are obviously trying to lull us into a false sense of security at the Wall," Griff said.

As Griff started to add to his explanation, Del held up his hand to pause the conversation. He needed to think. How much could he tell Griff? He suspected Griff was right based on developments he had become aware of just that morning. But he couldn't reveal his knowledge of events beyond the limits of the telescope up on Mount Anderson. Griff's analysis was solid. Del was impressed once again with Griff's intelligence. Unfortunately, his arguments were weak in terms of what was politically acceptable. Mobilizations were very expensive and extraordinarily disruptive. The early spring planting season would start in a few weeks and none of the agricultural districts would be happy with a disruption. The council would want hard evidence of an impending attack before committing to a full-scale mobilization.

Del eventually looked up with determination. "I'll go see the president. It's better if I go alone because she is new and a bit suspicious of the military," Del said, the lie coming easily. "Give me a full rundown of the attack and walk me through your logic one more time."

After carefully describing the events surrounding the upper east valley, Griff added, "Since I'm in charge of training, it's within my authority to call a special Guard training event at the Wall. The CGG will be pissed off. Probably turn purple yelling at me. But he won't countermand it because he specifically gave me that authority. At least the Guard can be mobilized."

Del walked briskly from his office in the university to the small unassuming building that housed Pacifica's Administration, Judiciary, and Council functions. The military was a separate function reporting into administration. The president led government administration. Each of these functions was strictly limited by Pacifica's constitution. The original colonizers were minimalists when it came to government.

The constitution conferred specific authorities to each function and clearly stated that any powers not specifically conferred did not exist. They adhered in spirit to Plato's belief that governments are best led by philosophers. The idea being that government was a civic duty that should be completely separate from personal power and monetary considerations. Therefore, all civil servants took a vow of dependance on government support for their lifetime. They discarded all personal wealth, current or future.

The original colonists from Ships 1 and 3 had studied the long history of governmental failure and agreed that money was indeed the root of all evil. Therefore, public servants had political power but could not benefit financially from it. Since the constitution had a balanced budget requirement, this meant the size of government was forced to be small, frugal, and efficient.

Del walked into the president's office and asked the receptionist for the soonest appointment available. Turned out she had an opening in thirty minutes, so Del just sat down and waited.

Jennifer Malrey walked out of her office and greeted Del warmly. She was young and newly elected to her role. Although small in stature, she tended to fill the room with her presence without being intimidating. It was a calm and comforting presence.

The President of Pacifica was a ten-year term with no term limits. It typically only ended with death, retirement, or a vote of no confidence by the Pacifica Council. The previous president had retired after thirty years and was now serving Jennifer in a support role. This was common in Pacifica. Becoming a civil servant was a lifetime decision.

"It's good to see you, Professor. Come on in," President Malrey said, motioning him into her office. After they sat down at a table, she said, "What can I help you with?"

"It's not good news. I strongly believe we need to call for full mobilization," Del said with gravity.

"I haven't heard of any sightings," she said, confused.

"There was an attack we fought off in the Apple Valley region. They attacked one of the few beach sites and succeeded in reaching the top of the cliffs. Fortunately, they were defeated and retreated back to the sea. There is more to the story, but I strongly recommend calling the council together for a decision," Del said.

The president thought about this for a few moments and said, "We're lucky. All of the council members are currently in the capital. In another week, they would all have been home on spring recess. I'll call an emergency meeting. Can you come to the council chambers this evening after their regular sessions end?"

"Yes. I'll also go down to Guard headquarters and bring the CGG back with me. His opinion and advice might be needed," Del said.

"Thanks for bringing this to my attention. I sincerely hope we don't need to mobilize. But if there is evidence of a threat, we need to act," she said.

"One last item, Ms. President," Del said in a hushed voice, "The committee has just gotten evidence this morning strongly supporting the need to mobilize. As you know, I won't be presenting that evidence to the council members."

She rocked back slightly, locked eyes with him, and then said a voice that didn't go any further than Del's ears, "Understood."

There was a regular Tram that went between Landfall City and Guard headquarters down by the Wall. It was water powered and similar to the one traversing Apple Falls. The difference is that this one was larger, simpler, and faster, given the elevation change wasn't as extreme. This cut travel time down to a couple of hours, enough time to fetch the CGG and bring him back for the council meeting. Del would have to tread carefully. The CGG was a reasonable man, but one under the shadow of Griff, which irritated him. He would have to explain this as his concern rather than Griff's while using the information from the raid to support the need for mobilization. Everyone told him he was good at politics. It was not something he enjoyed.

Perhaps that is why he liked Griff as much as he did. No BS, just say what you think and work it out from there. Of course, Griff had his own agenda, just like everyone else. The difference was that Griff didn't hide his. All of his agendas were out in the open for everyone to see.

Del noticed that the council members were tired. They were at the end of a long day and nearing a much-needed recess. He couldn't decide if this was a good thing or not. It might make them more disagreeable, or it might make them open to good arguments. He would just have to wait and see how it played out.

There were a total of six council members, two from each region. When they formed the first government, a debate had sprung up on how to make sure their government didn't end up controlled by a patriarchy. While the original colonists thought of themselves as non-biased and open-minded, history was riddled with male dominated governments. It was pointed out that a healthy family consists of equal partners, each having their own responsibilities. So, the proposal was to have each region elect one man and one woman as representatives. Men would vote for the male representative and women would vote for the female. All other democratically elected positions, like president, were open to all. Just the main council was forced by the constitution to be split equally by sex. To the surprise of many, this worked amazingly well.

President Malrey walked in, sat down at the head of the council table, and brought it to order. "Thank you for staying late after a long day. The agenda tonight is an emergency proposal for full mobilization at the Wall. We have two guests. Professor Dacy brought this request and will review why he believes full mobilization is required. Our Commander General of the Guard is here to answer any questions on mobilization timing and alternatives."

Councilman Barlow, one of the representatives from Eureka, raised his hand and said, "Ms. President, might I request that we expand this discussion to include plans to negotiate for peace with the GEMs?"

"I am happy to table that discussion for another time, Councilman Barlow. Our work tonight is time critical. We need to quickly come to a decision on mobilization," President Malrey replied.

"I propose a vote to overrule your decision to limit the agenda to mobilization. The proposal is to include plans to negotiate with the GEMs," Councilman Barlow said in a challenging tone.

The president's role within the council was to organize, facilitate, and vote to break ties. She owned presenting and keeping the council on track with a clear and concise agenda. The council could overrule and propose an alternative agenda if four of the six councilpersons agreed. The president would then facilitate the new agenda to completion. Any of the six councilpersons could propose an alternative agenda.

"Okay, let's vote on whether to include discussions and possible votes on a GEM negotiation strategy, or offer," President Malrey said. They then went around the table with each councilperson voting on the altered agenda.

"Apple Councilwoman Ricks?"

"Nay. We were informed of an invasion of one of the Apple Lakes upper valleys by the Master Sergeant of the Guard. It's clear we need to be worried about our survival, not ridiculous proposals for peace," Ricks responded with anger in her voice.

"Apple Councilman Rickets?"

"Nay. Agree with Councilwoman Ricks. Let's get on with the proposed agenda."

"Eureka Councilwoman Rivers?"

"Nay. But I agree with Councilman Barlow that we need to consider concessions for peace. I would like to see a future agenda on this topic."

"Eureka Councilman Barlow?"

"Yea. We must stop acting like children and find a way to end these brutal wars."

"Landfall Councilwoman Pierce?"

"Nay. Our survival comes before any fantasies of peace with the GEMs."

"Landfall Councilman Barrett?"

"Nay. Peace negotiations are worth time on another day. I see little evidence they would be successful, but that doesn't mean we shouldn't try."

"The Nays carry the vote. Professor Dacy, you have the floor."

Del described the assault on the upper east valley in detail. He made sure to vividly describe the mutilation of the four lookouts. Then he mentioned the evidence of war lords cooperating in the assault. This caused a few gasps. One of Pacifica's perceived advantages was the historic inability of the GEMs to cooperate across the various tribes. That advantage was now in question.

Councilman Barlow raised his hand and, turning to the CGG, asked,

"Was your master sergeant in charge of the assault on the GEMs?"

"Yes. We were extremely fortunate that he was training a scout team close by. If not, we would likely have an entire valley full of GEMs to worry about now," the CGG said.

"Did he try to negotiate with the GEMs before slaughtering them?" Barlow asked with anger clearly evident.

"We don't negotiate with GEMs. We kill them," the CGG fired back.

"Well, perhaps that's the problem."

As Barlow opened his mouth to say more, President Malrey raised her hand, interrupting him. Then she firmly said, "Councilman Barlow. Please control yourself and stay on the agenda. We voted to table discussions of peace negotiations for another time."

He mumbled something, clearly very angry, but complied with her request. Del then presented a completely fabricated analysis showing a high probability of an immediate and large-scale assault on the Wall.

Del ended with a summary. "Observations from Mount Anderson show haze consistent with a large encampment just over the horizon. While there might be a natural meteorological reason for this, it would be unusual at this time of year. Our long-term analysis suggests that with their reproduction rates and expected mortality, the GEMs are likely running out of room. Instead of just coveting the peninsula, it is highly likely they need the space and agricultural output to support their growing population. My belief is that extreme conditions inland are forcing the war lords to cooperate. This will greatly enhance their ability to break through at the Wall."

"Are there any questions for Professor Dacy or the CGG?" President Malrey asked.

Councilwoman Rivers raised her hand and, when recognized, asked, "Can we discuss alternatives for a limited mobilization? It's close to the start of planting season. A full mobilization will mean our food stores could be diminished for up to eighteen months."

Jennifer nodded. "That is a reasonable request. However, let's vote on the proposal for a full mobilization and then table other alternatives, as necessary."

It was a split vote. As Del feared, the agricultural concerns of Landfall and Eureka overwhelmed their fear of a major assault on the Wall. He knew this was predicated on confidence that the Guard could hold off the GEMs long enough for a full mobilization if needed. Del had not worked with Jennifer for very long. He didn't know what she would do. The right move politically would be to abstain and table more palatable alternatives.

An expectation of the president is that they do everything possible so that a final decision was a majority vote by the council. Something that was jointly hashed out. Del was sure some level of mobilization would pass. This is what the council expected. While not everyone would be happy, they would all be satisfied.

President Malrey took a deep breath. She looked down at the table in front of her for a few moments, obviously collecting her thoughts. "We are deadlocked, but I am convinced the threat is real. I vote Yea."

Del could see that a few of the council members felt betrayed. This went against the long-standing practice of ending with a majority vote. There was a general belief that deadlocked proposals merely meant further negotiation and compromise was needed. It was rare for a president to be the final deciding vote on a major topic. She had to be careful because the council could force an election off cycle with a vote of no confidence. This only took a majority vote and was a real threat.

As they walked out of the council chambers, Del turned to the CGG and said quietly, "Well, we have a gutsy president."

"Thank God! I think we're going to need one," said the CGG. "You obviously think Griff is right about the upper east valley attack being part of a larger strategy."

"Yes, I do. We have tracked major assaults on the Wall over the years. Its past due for one and the size of the army attacking us has grown larger with every cycle," Del said.

"My biggest worry now is that they won't show up. That would create an atmosphere of suspicion of anything the Guard or university proposes in the future," the CGG said.

"I'm not hoping they show up. But I don't want our recommendations to be ignored in the future either. It's a lose-lose scenario," Del said. "We'll just have to focus on mobilizing. I truly hope we're lucky enough to end up with loud and divisive arguments instead of the alternative."

CHAPTER 23

MOBILIZATION

Apple Valley was in an uproar. There had been many partial mobilizations over the years. But this was the first major one in twelve years. Arti was spending as much time calming people down as she was planning the trip to the Wall. Thank goodness for Diana, she thought. That girl was a godsend. Arti had known Diana would eventually replace her as Apple Valley CA, Captain of Archers. But in the midst of the chaos, Arti realized how good that decision was.

Diana had organized the packing of their extensive store of bows, arrows, and support equipment. In addition to their existing supplies, they had to bring along all the tools and raw materials to make the wide variety of arrows that might be needed. This involved gathering all the women together and assigning them tasks. She showed real leadership. It allowed Arti to work with Major Richards and get everyone else organized for the long trip to the Wall. Major Richards was still in charge but had delegated much of his responsibilities to Arti, which was a good thing for the Apple Valley Volunteers.

"Diana, is everything ready to go?" Arti asked.

"Yes. We're first up for the Tram tomorrow morning. I'll have all the packing cases down there by nightfall," Diana replied, wiping sweat from her brow. "Most of the unit has already started down the trail and when the supplies show up in the morning, we won't waste any time getting started."

"Did Tia's parents agree with her joining us?" Diana asked in a hopeful voice. Full mobilization meant they would bring the arrow monkeys with them. These were girls who had shown interest and aptitude in becoming Wall Archers. They repaired equipment, made arrows, and supplied everything needed to the archers on the Wall.

"Tia has been harassing them non-stop since the call for mobilization came out," Arti said with a smile. "I was her age when I first went to the Wall as an arrow monkey. My brother clearly remembers it and feels it's time for her to get the experience."

Arti hesitated and then said, "Pete is the only one unhappy. He's going to work behind the Wall supplying food and water in the mess hall. He'll also train with the boys' reserve unit on his downtime. They never see any time on the Wall, but it's good training. You know Pete, he was going on and on about being good enough to fight on the Wall. I think he's jealous of Tia being able to work on the Wall at such a young age," Arti said.

"He'll get over it. Pete wants to do his part. He imagines his part should be bigger than it is. He'll be an excellent warrior someday, but he's still a boy," Diana said, smiling. Then, in a serious tone, "Ansen is a bit unsettled. Angry. Facing those GEMs made it all very real for both of us. My nightmares were pretty bad for a while. It was the same one every night. I'm being chased through the woods by GEMs and suddenly realize they have me trapped. I'm not going to get away. Then I wake up in a panic. One night in my dream, I turned and fought. I haven't had that nightmare since."

She hesitated a few moments and then said, "I wonder if Ansen is dealing with something like that. He changes the subject every time I bring that day up."

"Men can be hard to figure out. They appear to be strong and tough, a rock to stand beside in hard times. But at the same time, they can hide their fear. It can slowly tear them apart," Arti said softly. "Anger comes from fear. Keep trying to get him to talk about it. I'll talk to Grammy and encourage her to sit down with him before he heads off."

"Grammy really helped me with all of it. She has a way of putting things into perspective," Diana said, then changing topics she asked, "Will we run into trouble in Eureka Valley?"

"Had a long talk with Councilwoman Ricks about the troubles down there. She said Councilman Barlow has been stirring up the farmers. He's telling them they are going to suffer two years of hardship as a result of Apple Valley overreacting. Barlow claims we convinced the university to conspire with the Guard to overstate the risk," Arti said with frustration. "He says Del's an Apple Valley bigot and is using the university's prestige to force the mobilization. He's saying President Malrey is young and naïve. She's been fooled by the university. He questions her ability to lead.

"That's unfair," Diana said. "I don't think the university, or the

Guard, would create a problem that doesn't exist."

"I agree. The protests have been peaceful so far. She thinks portions of Eureka will defy the council and only do a partial mobilization. Hold enough of their volunteers back to ensure a good harvest next fall. Ricks plans to ask the council to censure Barlow if that happens. In the meantime, our plan is to travel in small groups. That's why we're traveling separately from the men's volunteer corp. We'll camp away from the cities on our way down. Once we get to Landfall Valley, it will be calmer."

"There was a rumor that Ricks was going to pick her bow back up," Diana said, grinning.

"She actually asked me if she could rejoin for the battle," Arti said, smiling back. "I laughed and asked her if she had been practicing. She admitted it had been a while since she picked up her bow. I gave her my stern instructor look and offered to let her try the Wall Archers qualification test. She held up her hands in mock horror and told me she had barely passed the test fifty years ago. She laughed and offered that maybe it was best if she just made sure the council gives us what we need."

"She's older than Grammy but I can see her on the Wall with a bow," Diana said smiling, "That is one tough woman."

"That she is. We couldn't have a better councilwoman," Arti said with admiration.

Arti was pleased with the speed and ease of travel through Eureka Valley until they got to Leucadia. To avoid the town, they would have had to add a day to their travel time and were under orders to get to the Wall as soon as possible. Until the GEMs actually showed up, they would hurry but not exhaust themselves. The plan was to camp an hour north of the city and traverse it in the early hours before the sun came up.

The hope of avoiding conflict ended early the next morning when a large contingent of Eureka Valley farmers blocked the road just outside the town's entrance. "I guess getting up early in the morning isn't the best way to avoid farmers," Arti said with a wry expression on her face.

"What are we going to do?" Diana asked.

Arti turned to her and said, "What would you recommend?"

It's mentoring time again, thought Diana wryly. She stopped and gave it some thought. After reflecting on the alternatives, she said, "I would stop, set up camp, and force them to make the next move. If they don't approach us, we'll just wait until the next company of Apple Valley volunteers shows up and decide whether to force the issue or not," Diana said thoughtfully.

"You're on the right trail, Diana. The only thing I would change is to go ask them for permission to use the road and see what happens. We'll ask respectfully, listen, but not argue." Arti paused a moment and then added, "But first, let's make it clear we're setting up camp so that any hotheads over there don't have an excuse to escalate the situation. They are unlikely to attack women, but you never know what angry people will do. Meet me here in an hour and we'll go talk to them."

Arti and Diana walked slowly up to a large cart set sideways on the road. There were about thirty men sitting around a fire off to one side, watching them as they approached. One of the older ones got to his feet and, with an entourage of younger men, approached them well in front of the cart.

"Do you need some help getting your broken cart off the road?" Arti said with a smile.

"This isn't the time for jokes, Arti. Yes, I recognize you, Arti Stone. Turn around and go back to Apple Valley. We have no beef with the Wall Archers. You Apple Valley people are overreacting to a few GEMs climbing a cliff. Full mobilization now will cause many of us in the Eureka Valley to go hungry next winter. Fruit trees will continue to produce crops regardless of whether you take a spring vacation to the Wall."

"Since you know my name, can I have yours?" Arti asked in a calm voice.

"My name is Will Evans and I'm mayor of Leucadia."

"We're not arguing for you to join us," Arti pointed out.

"No, but a message needs to be sent to the president and her council. We aren't going to stand for an unnecessary full mobilization that unfairly punishes us and our families," Will said angrily. "Councilman Barlow has explained how you used the university dean and the Guard to scare the government into mobilizing."

"Okay, I understand your position, Will. We're going to camp here and wait for the council to resolve your issues. We don't want conflict.

We aren't responsible for the mobilization. But we are obligated to support the council's decision," Arti said.

Will visibly relaxed, realizing Arti wasn't going to press the issue. "I have a lot of respect for you and your Wall Archers, Arti. This isn't personal," Will said in a placating voice. "If you need supplies from town, we'll let a few people through for that."

"I appreciate your flexibility and thoughtfulness, Will. Apple Valley wouldn't survive without its trade with Eureka Valley. We greatly appreciate all that you do," Arti said, smiling back at him.

Will brightened and actually smiled at the compliment, waving goodbye as they turned and walked away. As Diana and Arti headed back to camp, Diana turned to Arti. "Well, you charmed him. He went from belligerent to flirting," she said, with the corners of her mouth turning up.

"Men are men, Diana. Let them blow off steam, acknowledge their point of view, and then compliment them. It works every time. Another of Grammy's lessons," Arti said with a smirk. They both chuckled as they entered the camp.

The next morning Arti wandered down to the road blockade, intending to try to work out some sort of compromise when she saw a commotion in town. She squinted her eyes, trying to see what was going on, and then smiled. It was Griff with Scout Team 2 on horseback, moving quickly toward the blocked road from the other side. She recognized the scout team from the upper east valley invasion. Griff looked especially grumpy.

Griff skidded to a stop just behind the cart, recognized and nodded to Arti, turned and demanded in a commanding voice, "Whose cart is this?"

The crowd of farmers looked around at each other for a few uncomfortable moments. Will Evans grunted and turned toward Griff. "Doesn't matter whose cart it is. It's not moving."

Griff got off his horse and walked slowly, but with a belligerent swagger up to Will. Arti was impressed with how threatening Griff could be without saying a word. It was especially appealing knowing his secret. Griff was actually a softy. He stopped and stared at the man for a moment and then said, "Who are you?"

"My name is Will Evans and I'm the mayor of Leucadia," he said in an angry voice.

"Who is the assistant mayor?" Griff said.

"Why do you want to know?" Will answered with his chin thrust forward but a bit of reluctance in his stance.

"Because after I execute you for interfering with a mandated mobilization, I need to know who to talk to next," Griff said, stepping closer, daring the man to do something.

Both of Will's hands shot up palms forward as he took a step back and spluttered out, "You can't just kill me. We have a right to protest."

"You do have the right to protest. You don't have the right to obstruct a council ordered mobilization. The law is clear. If a citizen interferes with Pacifica's ability to wage war, including mobilization efforts, summary execution is an option at the discretion of the highest-ranking Guard member present," Griff said as he pulled out his sword. "As Master Sergeant of the Guard, I have the authority to act."

Will put up both hands, backing away quickly. "Okay, we'll move the cart and leave."

"You and your followers will not leave," Griff said, sweeping his gaze around to lock eyes with all of them. You are ordered to the Wall to protect Pacifica." Griff then looked over his shoulder and barked out, "Sergeant Glenn! Round up these volunteers. Take each of them home to get their weapons and provisions. Make sure none of them sneak off. If any of them try to avoid their obligations, bring them to me for judgement." Turning back to the mayor, Griff said, "I'm confiscating the cart for your equipment and provisions. You need to supply a couple of horses to pull it."

Will was defeated and speechless. When Griff took a step toward him, he quickly turned and motioned to a couple of the young men to pull the cart off the road. Arti glanced over at Sergeant Glenn and his team. She saw amusement dancing on their faces. I bet they have all been on the other side of Griff's displeasure, thought Arti.

After the logistics had been worked out, Arti walked back to camp with Griff. "You aren't the most subtle of men," Arti said with a serious expression on her face.

"There are times when the direct approach works best," he replied uncertainly. Griff was obviously unclear whether Arti was displeased with his actions or not.

Arti couldn't hold it, and her face broke into a smile and said, "I imagine the direct approach works really well for you in most circumstances." Then, hesitating a moment, she said softly, "Thank you Griff. We were stuck. You did exactly what was needed. We have to get to the Wall, not get embroiled in a political discussion." Griff blushed and Arti moved closer as they walked toward the Wall Archer camp together. Arti turned toward Griff and asked in a soft voice. "How is Tee?"

"Healthy and working hard," Griff replied, then remembering the bar brawl, smiled and said, "Don't tell him I told you this, but he's developing into a good leader. The veterans are noticing how much the Newbies in his class respect him and that bodes well for his acceptance."

Arti smiled with pride. Her husband had died before they had more children, and that pained her. But she was blessed with her only son. Satisfied Tee was doing well, her mind transitioned back to Griff walking beside her. He was all work and no play. Being honest with herself, this was an observation that accurately described her as well. Now that Tee was an adult on his own, perhaps it was time to live a little.

She was very attracted to Griff. She knew he was kindhearted when she first met him. Not sure how she knew this, given his fearsome reputation, but she knew. He was intelligent, thoughtful, and his insights on a wide range of topics were interesting. It didn't hurt that he was a ruggedly handsome man who took great care of his appearance. She had always liked the rugged look, and cleanliness was a big deal to her. When he was close, she ran the risk of turning back into the giddy teenager she had once been. She knew Griff had never been married and wondered about that. Lifelong bachelors were more common in the Guard. It was a hard life that made it difficult to have a family.

For a man with such a brutal exterior, he seemed to be exceedingly shy around women. She was pretty sure he liked women, and she in particular. The occasional flush of his face, hard to see with his dark skin, betrayed him. Well, perhaps after this upcoming battle with the GEMs is over, she would have to make a move. The worst thing that could happen was embarrassment, after all.

The rest of their travel down to the Wall was uneventful. Griff and Scout Team 2 decided to travel with them. They rode out early each morning and returned as camp was being set up in the evening. Traffic on the road was increasing substantially. It was pretty obvious that whatever Griff and Scout Team 2 were doing was accelerating Eureka

Valley mobilization.

Diana and Sergeant Glenn had taken to sitting by one of the campfires most nights and talking. "Where do you go every day?" Diana asked Glenn.

"We go out into the countryside and 'encourage' the volunteers to speed up mobilization," Glenn said with a smile.

"I'm guessing Master Sergeant Ricks is doing most of the encouraging," Diana said, smiling back.

"Yeah, we're just there for a show of force. He's such a force of nature that he hasn't had to do anything except show up and explain the law. To be honest, him just showing up is threatening. Griff doesn't really need us. But since we're on his shit list, we have to follow him around," Glenn said with a sigh.

Diana smiled and asked, "What did you do to earn his attention?"

Glenn sighed again and said, "A few of the boys got into a bar brawl with some other Guard members. To be honest, we deserve the extra work we've gotten. The only reason we were so close to Apple Valley when the GEMs invaded was because Griff had us climbing up and down the cliffs just east of Apple Falls. One of the many special training assignments designed to make his displeasure clear."

"Well, I guess I'm glad for the bar brawl then. I don't know what would have happened if your team hadn't shown up when they did," Diana said.

Glenn sat back on his elbows and asked, "How well do you know Tee Stone?"

Diana felt the question deep in the pit of her stomach. She suddenly felt guilty enjoying Glenn's company. Not because of Ansen, but because of Tee. A wide range of emotions cascaded through her mind until she realized she needed to answer his question. "Yes, I know him. We have known each other since elementary school."

"What can you tell me about him?" Glenn asked.

Diana looked down as she gathered her thoughts. She wasn't sure what to say. Clearly not that he was the most wonderful man she knew. That she was wildly in love with him. What would a member of the Guard want to know? She finally settled on, "He's very unusual. Everyone who knows him was as surprised as everyone else when he was selected for the Guard. But we weren't shocked. The surprise was that the Guard saw past his stature. He's a natural leader and highly intelligent. Apple Valley won the Pacifica capture-the-flag last year purely on Tee's abilities. He has a way of getting people to want to follow him."

Glenn clearly had questions he wasn't going to ask. Diana could tell he had seen the impact of his question. It was to his credit that he wasn't rude enough to put her on the spot. He only said, "I keep hearing impressive things about him. I'm looking forward to meeting him."

After a few moments Diana abruptly stood, said her goodbyes for the evening, and wandered back to her tent, clearly troubled. As she walked away, Glenn watched her with lots of unanswered questions held back.

CHAPTER 24

PEACE NEGOTIATIONS

Jennifer Malrey had avoided tabling the peace negotiations agenda for as long as possible. Mobilization was nearly complete. Eureka had been slow to comply, but had finally sent a reasonable contingent. She heard Master Sergeant Ricks had been sent to get them moving. She didn't want to know what his arguments were because she suspected it involved more than encouraging words.

The council's role in mobilization had faded to dealing with minor issues. Therefore, she could avoid it no further. Attempts had been made over the years to make peace with the GEMs and all had been disasters. A peace commission would be sent out and never heard from again. The last time a negotiations team had been sent out, some of them had been brought back on a moonless night and tortured within hearing of the Wall.

A Guard rescue team was immediately sent out. After a protracted melee in the dark, they returned with only the dismembered body parts from the male members of the peace commission. The GEMs had left it to their imaginations what had become of the two females. It was crazy to consider this. Jennifer had spent some time with Del a few days before trying to understand Councilman Barlow.

She had greeted him in her office saying, "Thanks for meeting with me, Professor. I'll be blunt and save both of us time. I try not to talk about council members behind their backs. But I'm having trouble understanding Councilman Barlow. I know he used to be a professor of history at the university, so I was hoping you could help me. My goal is to better understand him so I can make the council's agendas go more smoothly."

Del smiled grimly and said, "He can be a handful. In summary, he is brilliant, hardworking, and has a prodigious memory. His passion as a young scholar was the history of Pacifica, especially the decisions and events that led to our troubles with the GEMs. He knows the original colonists were committed pacifists, and he desires we return to those philosophies."

Jennifer wrinkled her brow and said, "An in-depth understanding of history would seem to me to be an attribute of someone with views completely the opposite of Barlow's."

Del nodded in agreement and said, "In my experience it's the brilliant who sometimes latch onto ideas and beliefs that defy logic. They know they are smarter than everyone else and so when they get off track, you can't bring them back. The basis of his defiance is his conviction that the official history of Pacifica has been systematically altered. He has created a compelling story based on a fairly substantial number of minor contradictions in the record. The history department is unified in believing this is simply the natural result of chaos from the Colony War and the collapse of civilization. Post-Colony War historians living in abject poverty took oral descriptions of events and wrote them down as history. As you might suspect, individual oral traditions, especially those several generations removed, are not considered dependable by serious historians. He claims the number and type of contradictions shows a clear intent to deceive."

"If he doesn't believe the official history, what does he believe?"

"Barlow believes that Ships 1 and 3 cheated the GEMs out of Pacifica. He believes this planet should have been left to the GEMs who were specifically altered to thrive here. We were supposed to emigrate to one of the more habitable planets in the sector. The basic story he's constructed has our ancestors breaking their word to Ship 2 and colonizing the peninsula with plans to conduct genocide on the GEMs. The surprise attack didn't work as planned and we got stuck here. He believes the GEMs have good reasons not to trust us and the current situation is the fault of our ancestors."

"Okay, this is starting to make some sense. Well, not literally. But it does explain some of his extreme statements and proposals. To be fair, he is very helpful on most topics that come before the council. As you said, he is intelligent and hard-working. He takes his role as councilman seriously and serves Eureka Valley citizens as best he can. He asks excellent questions, making us think critically about all aspects of our agenda items. I just wish the weird stuff would go away."

"There is little hope of that. I've spent many hours arguing with him when he was at the university. He would have become chair of the history department if he were a little more mainstream. He thinks I'm the one who blocked him, so I won't be much help trying to talk sense into him," Del said.

"Thanks for coming. The background helps. Let's keep this conversation between us. It will just make things worse if Barlow thinks I'm conspiring against him."

"Any time, Ms. President," Del said as he got up and strolled out of her office.

President Malrey brought the council to order and announced, "This morning's agenda is to discuss options for pursuing peace negotiations with the GEMs. Councilman Barlow has proposed assembling a negotiations team under his leadership and approach the GEMs in person. He desires the team to have the authority to negotiate with the GEMs under provisions agreed to by this council. Councilman Barlow, do you have anything to correct, clarify or add to the proposed agenda item?"

"Your description of the proposed agenda item is accurate, Ms. President. I would like to emphasize that my proposal has the council in complete control of decisions regarding any treaty or agreement we can obtain. I know some of you fear I might exceed my authority in discussions with the GEMs. I want to assure all of you I am in complete agreement with the importance of majority support for every aspect of negotiations."

"Are there any questions about the proposed agenda?" Jennifer asked. As she looked around the table, it was clear from the body language how this would go. Eureka would align around some sort of plan to offer peace to the GEMs while the other two regions would be reluctant to offer any concessions.

Councilwoman Ricks raised her hand. "Can we start with a discussion of what should be negotiated before we decide how to negotiate? Every peace team that has approached the GEMs in person has disappeared. Well, sometimes body parts come back. Consideration of safety for the negotiating team will need careful planning."

Jennifer was nodding as she said, "That seems reasonable. Let's vote on whether to start with the specifics of the negotiation. This only refines the order of discussion and voting, not the proposed agenda by

Councilman Barlow. All in favor of the revised agenda, raise your hands."

Looking around the table, Jennifer smiled and said, "The agenda is approved with the first order of discussion and vote focused on an agreement of negotiation details. After we agree on what we want to concede, and what we want in return, we'll turn to how we will approach the GEMs." Jennifer once again looked around the table for head nods of approval and continued. "Councilman Barlow, you have given this more thought than anyone. Do you have a specific proposal or framework?"

Barlow smiled, looked around the table, and said, "Thank you, Ms. President, I do. I believe our goal ought to be a world where we live side by side without regard to genetic origins. GEMs ought to be our neighbors, not our enemies." Looking around the table, Barlow recognized the look of shock and horror on the faces of his fellow councilpersons. He held up his hands, palms forward, and said, "Not immediately, but over time. I think it's important to have a goal in mind."

Several voices broke in loudly, shouting over one another. "Come to order!" Jennifer said firmly, with steel in her voice. She was usually so soft-spoken that this unusual show of sternness shocked everyone into silence. Jennifer glanced around the table until it was clear everyone was in control of their emotions. She turned to Barlow and said, "Councilman Barlow, could we stick with the agenda as it stands and delay a discussion of long-term goals for another time? I'm concerned the council will get off track and we won't make progress today."

Barlow grunted his agreement and said, "Okay, okay, we can dive into the specifics, but we need to get on the same page on where we want to eventually end up. Ignoring that for now, here is a list of concessions I believe we should make.

"One: turn the fresh water back on. A good-sized region of the continent used to get all its fresh water from what flows through Landfall Valley. With water turned back on, it opens up an area of land three times the size of the peninsula for agriculture. Dumping all that fresh water into the ocean is what our ancestors would have called a war crime.

"Two: encourage trade with the GEMs. We should set up a trading post in what are now Guard barracks and supply warehouses.

"Three: concede territory. There are several undeveloped valleys in the Apple Valley region. From the Guards report on the latest incursion, my understanding is that it's possible to bottle up the GEMs in these high valleys if problems arise. We owe them restitution for the wrongs of the past. Conceding territory should go a long way to convincing them we are finally acknowledging our responsibility for the horrible treatment they have endured."

There was stunned silence in the room. Councilwoman Ricks raised her hand and said, "May I be recognized?"

"You have the floor, Councilwoman," Jennifer responded.

Ricks took a deep breath, clearly trying to gain control of her anger. She looked around the room and said, "I propose we take each of these points separately and vote on them. I also propose we start with a vote on item one, turning on the water. We can likely come to some sort of agreement on this and having success early will help the rest of the discussions."

Councilwoman Ricks once again impressed Jennifer. Ricks was clearly the unofficial leader of the council. She had a way of dividing up agendas and proposing votes that moved the council down the road she wanted it to take. It was like watching a chess master systematically orchestrating the game and controlling an opponent.

"Before we vote on your proposal Councilwoman Ricks, let hear from the rest of the council on whether they have additional concessions for consideration," Jennifer said, looked around the table and when no one raised their hand she continued. "Okay then let's vote on whether to discuss and vote on each proposal separately."

The entire morning went by with one heated discussion after another, with an occasional personal insult thrown in. Jennifer had been forced to stop the discussions several times to remind everyone of the council's engagement rules. She was exhausted. She felt like she had been walking a tightrope all morning.

Jennifer worried that the growing divisions between the regions risked pushing the council into dysfunction. Eureka Valley was often in conflict with both Apple Valley and Landfall Valley. The physical land size and population were equal to the combination of the other two valleys. They provided sixty percent of the food for Pacifica. They believed they ought to have more say in council decisions. Taking yet another deep breath, she said, "Let's review decisions from this morning's official notes and close off this agenda item. Here are the decisions from Councilman Barlow's agenda proposal.

"One: an offer to turn on fresh water will be made under the condition that all hostilities cease.

"Two: any hostilities after the water is turned on will result in it being turned back off.

"Three: if we still have peace five years after the water is turned on, we will offer to set up a trading post outside the Wall and on the other side of the dry moat.

"Four: GEMs will not be allowed past the boundary of the dry moat.

"Five: no land concessions will be made.

"Six: the offer of turning on fresh water in return for a long-term commitment of peace will be made in written form. Councilman Barlow will sign this treaty offer for the council. The Guard will construct a kiosk on the GEM side of the dry moat with the offer posted."

Barlow was visibly angry. He took a deep breath, let it out, and then said, "I am extremely disappointed in our inability as a council to consider a legitimate offer of peace. We are the ones responsible for the horrendous death and destruction on both sides. I am disappointed that we are not taking responsibility for our past actions. I understand the council has spoken and this agenda item is closed. However, before we break for lunch, I have an emergency agenda item for this afternoon's session."

"Go ahead, Councilman Barlow. What is your proposed agenda item?" Jennifer asked.

"I propose a vote of no confidence in President Malrey," Barlow said, smiling smugly and looking directly at Jennifer. Turning toward the other councilpersons, he said, "She is not equipped to execute the duties of the Office of the president. Her incompetence in allowing full mobilization when no threat is apparent is proof of this. Her inability to shepherd the council to a responsible peace offer is further proof. The damage caused by her incompetence is serious enough to negate her ability to continue in her post."

Councilwoman Ricks shook her head from side to side. Clearly frustrated, she said, "President Malrey, would you mind stepping out while we discuss this? The constitution calls for us to convene in your absence for this process. We will first vote in a temporary head of the council, then discuss the proposal at length, and finally vote. We can call witnesses if necessary so this could take days, perhaps weeks, to execute.

As you know, it will take a two-thirds majority to instigate a general election to select a new president. If the two-thirds vote is successful, the temporary head of the council will take over your responsibilities until an election can be held."

"Who made you leader of this?" Barlow asked hotly.

"Nobody. I'm going over the process so we can excuse the president from the meeting," Ricks said with her eyes boring into Barlow's. "We'll communicate progress as we work through this, Ms. President."

"Thank you, Councilwoman Ricks. I will comply with whatever the council needs from me throughout the process," Jennifer said as she stood, turned, and walked briskly from the room, clearly shaken.

Jennifer was sitting in her office late that afternoon thinking about the possibility of being the first president voted out in her first month in office. The newspapers and history books would have a field day if that happened. They would make much of the fact that she was the youngest president to be elected in the history of Pacifica. She knew she had made the right decisions, given the information she had. There was a lingering doubt whether Del had provided false information to her. She had watched him spin a completely made-up analysis to the council. If she didn't know it was false, she would have believed him completely."

Her door suddenly burst open and one of her aides came in, out of breath. "They're here!" he said.

"Who's here?" she asked, confused.

"GEMs! Thousands of them! They're setting up camp on the horizon," the aide said in a panic.

And just when I thought I had problems, Jennifer grimly mused.

As the aide back ran out, Councilwoman Ricks calmly walked in, her demeanor a welcome change. "It's done; you've been exonerated. The vote was five-to-one," she said, a little out of breath. "Once the GEMs showed up, the posturing and silly debating ceased. The accusation ended up being poor judgement in voting for full mobilization. We shot down the leadership in the peace process complaint as ridiculous since we did the voting with no tie breakers needed.

"The council's opinion now is that you may have saved us all. I don't know what Barlow was thinking, voting for no confidence. Doing that after a massive number of GEMs show up on our front door was not a good move politically. That rash act destroyed his credibility with the other council members. Even Councilwoman Rivers, who has consistently supported him, is disgusted."

"Thank you, Councilwoman. I assume they voted you temporary head?" Jennifer asked.

"Yes, the majority wanted this over quickly. I have a reputation for little to no patience," Ricks said with a smile.

Jennifer stood up, took a deep breath, and prepared herself to become a wartime president. "Well, let's go take a look at them," she said as she motioned Ricks to follow her up to the roof of the government building. From there, they would have a view beyond the Wall and discuss what needed to be done next.

THE WALL
DAY 1

Tee and Jay stood on the Wall looking out over the downward sloping sandy plain below. The sun was just starting to rise with a thin angry red skyline. It was beautiful. The view and fresh new morning smell provided pleasure for Tee against the constant anxiety of the past few days. Thousands of tents with many thousands of GEMs were massed just outside the range of Pacifica's weapons. The only good news was they didn't appear to be forming up for an attack yet.

"I supplied water on the Wall when I was a boy," Jay said. "But I don't remember the number of GEMs ever being this massive."

"I heard Griff telling the CGG the same thing yesterday," Tee replied. "Griff was right to push hard for full mobilization. We wouldn't be in shape to defend the Wall right now if he hadn't."

"My dad told me the retired Guard has already been mobilized. He was asked to form an additional reserve squad for work below the Wall made up of retired Guard and second year Newbies," Jay said. "They're formed up and working on squad coordination exercises."

Tee and Jay continued to look out into the distance, lost in their own thoughts. Tee considered the Wall and its placement, deciding it was well thought out. The canyon below the dam had high cliffs on each side that were easily defended. That ended abruptly four hundred yards out. The belief was that the original colonists had intentionally sculpted them to create a killing field. Across this choke point was a twenty-yard-wide dry moat. It was deep and stretched across the entire width of the canyon. The moat was useful in slowing attacks and making it difficult for siege towers and other large war machines to be brought to the Wall.

The Guard Newbies in Tee's recruiting class had been formed up for Wall duty. They were another full training cycle, from being added to specialty veteran squads and platoons who might fight below the Wall.

Tee was still smarting from being ordered to arm himself with his bow for this battle.

"I want you with your bow on the Wall, Tee. You're much more effective with that than with a spear. When you go below the Wall, it's a different matter," Griff said.

"Do I join one of the Wall Archer groups?" Tee said with frustration evident in his voice.

"No. You're going to stay with me as an aide. I'll be on the Wall much of the time directing squads and platoons or we'll be plugging gaps if the Wall is breached," Griff explained. "I want you to watch the battle develop. Let me know if you have any ideas that might gain us an advantage. If you think I'm making a mistake, I want to hear that too."

"If you go below the Wall, will I go with you?" Tee said with a hint of challenge in his voice.

Griff turned and locked eyes with Tee. "You'll do what I tell you to do," Griff said in a commanding voice, continuing to stare.

Tee just nodded and automatically said, "Yes, sir," acknowledging Griff's unquestioned authority.

Griff gave him a crooked, knowing look before turning away.

The "sir" had come out without thinking. It was like he was back in recruit training again. He knew better than to call a non-com, sir. Embarrassing. At least he hadn't saluted. Griff was scary, Tee thought. He was a collaborative leader much of the time. But when he gave an order in that voice, you simply obeyed without thinking about it.

Tee was pulled out of his thoughts by Griff, motioning him that they were moving to another section of the Wall. He stayed a couple paces behind as Griff stopped to give orders to various squads and 'suggestions' to the officers. When they got near the center gate, they ran into the Apple Valley archer unit. They arrived as his mother was instructing Tia on keeping the Wall Archers supplied with arrows.

"You stay seated next to the arrow stand, handing the archer arrows when requested. She will say 'arrow' and you will hand her one with the fletching toward her, but with the arrowhead pointing off to the side. We don't want any accidents where you get stuck with an arrowhead," Arti said.

"How will I know when to go get more arrows?" Tia asked.

"Count down how many arrows are left in increments of five. For the final group, count down each arrow as you hand it to the archer. Do you understand this part?"

"Yes. I count down. Twenty-five, twenty, fifteen, ten, five, four, three, two, and one," Tia said.

"Good. The archer will decide when you should go down to the arrow bin for a new supply. Don't go down until she tells you to," Arti continued. "When you walk to the staircase, do not linger in front of the arrow slits. Keep yourself out of the direct line of an arrow or spear that might find its way through," Arti told Tia with Diana nodding in agreement just behind her.

Looking up as she finished her instruction, Arti noticed them standing there. She turned and smiled, saying, "It's a beautiful morning."

Griff grunted and lifted his hand to point out beyond the Wall and said, "I'm not sure how you see anything beautiful in that."

"My mother always insists on recognizing the good in a bad situation," she replied, hesitated, and with her smile brightening a bit said, "I admit it can be irritating at times."

"Well, wisdom can be irritating," Griff said with a grin. "I stopped by to request Diana be ready to lead the Apple Valley group. I would like to be able to have you move around to support other parts of the Wall if needed. I wouldn't ordinarily ask this, but I've seen her in action and know she can manage it."

Diana's face blushed, and she looked to the ground, embarrassed. Tee swelled with pride for Diana, knowing the truth in what Griff said.

"I agree she can handle it. How will I know if I'm needed elsewhere?" Arti asked.

"I'll send a runner with instructions. It may not happen. But I would like to be prepared for a situation needing your special skills," Griff said. As Arti nodded, an increase in noise from the GEM encampment reached them.

"Looks like they're forming up. Good luck today," Griff said, looking at them both. After they had walked a few paces away, Griff turned, grabbed Tee by both his shoulders and turned him so they were face to face. Pulling him close with an intense look in his eyes, he said in a low voice only Tee could hear, "Ad Victoriam."

Tee hesitated, surprised by what Griff said. Then, remembering, he responded saying, "Cum scuto aut in scuto."

It was an age-old private ritual of the Guard spoken in old earth Latin. It was said from a veteran to a Newbie as their first battle was about to begin. The veteran would say 'To Victory' and the Newbie would respond by saying 'With shield or on shield.' It signified the veteran believed the Newbie was required for victory. It meant the Newbie was willing to give his life to protect Pacifica. Tee had forgotten all about this ritual in the excitement. His breast swelled with pride at the honor of being addressed in this way by the Master Sergeant of the Guard. He was truly prepared to go forth and die for Pacifica and victory.

They walked down the wide staircase near the main gate and reviewed preparations for the Guard units staging for work below the Wall. Barin Phillips, Jay's father, was there with his reserve unit. He greeted them both warmly. Griff quizzed him on what he had done to prepare his hastily assembled reserve squad. He nodded approval at what had been achieved in so little time.

As they were walking away, Barin Phillips grabbed Tee's arm, pulled him off to the side and said quietly, "My son has a bunkmate to be proud of. Look out for him, Tee." Tee glowed with pride at that request. He knew everyone thought Jay protected him, not the other way around. He would indeed look out for Jay.

As they were completing the inspection, a roar erupted from beyond the Wall. Tee followed Griff as he briskly hurried back up the main staircase. They were just in time to see a full-scale assault begin to take shape. They noticed the peace offering kiosk burning brightly in the distance.

Tee watched as GEM teams carrying bridges ran up to the moat and placed their platforms across the opening. Catapults opened fire from behind the Wall and atop the cliffs to either side, dropping large stones on and just behind these structures. Many rows of women and older men fired coordinated flights of arrows to fall on the mass of GEMs queuing up to cross the bridges. While some bridges were destroyed, enough bridges survived to move a few thousand GEMs across the moat and into position to directly attack the Wall. Tee was appalled by the number of GEMs they were willing to lose just to stage an attack.

Then they came running full speed and screaming at the top of their lungs. Mixed in with the mass of GEMs attacking the Wall were scaling ladders. The Wall Archers concentrated on identifying experienced fighters associated with the ladder crews and taking them out. The early waves of attacks were oftentimes heavily populated with young warriors with a few gray beards to guide them.

"This isn't the serious assault, Tee," Griff said. "Notice the older warriors trying to organize the younger ones. This is simply an attack to give them experience and hopefully soften us up. The big push will start this afternoon or, if we're lucky, tomorrow morning. Their goal is to get us into a state of fatigue, eat up our supply of stones and arrows, and then attack with their best troops."

With this pronouncement, Tee had a sudden sinking feeling in his gut. He was intimidated. If this wasn't a serious assault, he wasn't sure he was prepared. After a few panicked moments, Tee shook off the fear and notched an arrow. He started picking off some of the older looking GEMs and battle fever took over. He replaced fear with grim determination. Tee would do whatever it took to defeat these devils or die trying.

Tee was surprised when Griff suddenly said, "Battle always starts with fear, Tee. Even for veterans. I can see you've overcome it. Not everyone does."

The rest of the day was pure exhaustion. Griff had boundless energy and Tee ran after him from section to section. Wherever the battle intensified or whenever the Wall was breached, they went into the middle of it. Twice scaling ladders had gotten set with enough time and support to get GEMs to the top. Both times Guard squads arrived to support the volunteers and throw them off. On one occasion, Tee glimpse a tired but whole Jay wiping off his sword only to have to turn around and head off in the other direction after Griff once more. He was thankful for that aspect of being Griff's aide. He had seen almost everyone he was worried about at some point in the day and knew, at least in that moment, they were safe.

As the sun was setting and the GEMs were retreating once more back across the moat, Griff turned to Tee and said, "That should be the last assault today. Did you notice when the quality of the warriors improved?"

"The third assault seemed more organized. It appeared to have less age gap between the warriors and their leaders," Tee observed.

Griff nodded in agreement and said, "They came early with their best warriors. This is either a good thing or a bad thing. It's good if they're running out of inexperienced warriors. It's bad if they have so many experienced warriors that they can send wave after wave with no letup," Griff said. "They haven't attacked at night for several decades. Nobody knows why. That makes me suspicious. If there is one thing I know about the GEMs, it's that they're patient, smart, and persistent."

Griff and Tee walked at a leisurely pace down to the Apple Valley archers' station. Griff got his mother's attention and asked, "Arti, do you have a watch supervisor schedule for the Wall Archers tonight?"

"Yes, Diana will take the first watch. Landfall and Eureka will provide supervisors for the second and third watches. We have an AC meeting after nightfall to discuss results from today and plans for tomorrow," Arti explained.

"Good, I'm going to have the volunteers keep torches lit all night every ten feet along the Wall. Please have the AC delegated night supervisors double check that the volunteers are keeping them lit during their rounds. I would like flare arrows every fifteen minutes or so. Make it random. Send out more if anything odd happens or someone hears something suspicious. Have them pay attention to the dead bodies. As you know, it's not unusual for GEMs to fake a death and try and sneak up the Wall."

"Will do," Arti said.

Griff motioned Tee over and said, "Go get something to eat, rest, and meet me here before sunrise tomorrow."

Tee was exhausted as he walked to the barracks. The sun had just set, and Jay was already there when he arrived. He looked drawn. "You okay, Jay?" Tee asked with concern in his voice.

"A couple of scratches, but mostly just tired. Spent the day warding off scaling ladders. Got in some close quarter work once when a ladder got set and GEMs reached the top. We eventually got it thrown back," Jay said. "How about you?"

"Exhausted. My arm, wrist, and fingers are sore from firing arrows. I don't think I've ever shot that many in one day before. The GEMs don't seem to care how many warriors they lose. However, when the leaders are taken out, they lose focus and eventually call a retreat," Tee said.

"What was Griff's impression?" Jay asked.

"You're not going to like it. He said he's never seen so many GEMs in reserve beyond the moat. He claims the fighting tomorrow will start to ramp up and become serious," Tee explained.

"That wasn't serious today? Really?" Jay asked. He hesitated and in a serious tone said, "Is he worried?"

"It's hard to tell, but I think he is. I don't think he's lost confidence in our ability to withstand whatever they throw at us. But I know he's disturbed by the number of casualties we're taking. I can tell my mom is worried. She hides it really well, but she can't hide it from me," Tee said.

"We'll break them tomorrow, Tee," Jay said, and Tee believed him.

Tee and Jay walked to the mess tent and had a quick dinner with Pete, Ansen, and Tia. Kale and Zeb joined them as well. With one exception, they were all visibly tired. The exception was Tia. Her bubbly, dramatic personality was in full swing. It was a needed tonic for them all. Tee sat back and listened to all the stories of the day. The excitement in their stories was mixed with fear, and it made him all the more determined. Family and good friends, what else could a man ask for in life?

As they headed back to the barracks Tee said, "I'm too wound up, Jay. I'm going to go walk a bit."

Diana found herself enjoying the quiet walk along the Wall in the early evening. It was warm, with a slight cool breeze blowing down from the dam above. She was glad the breeze was not coming from the opposite direction. The stench would be horrible. There were a lot of dead GEMs out there. Her duties were simple, which gave her time to think. Something that wasn't possible during the chaos of the past few weeks. She had decided before she left Apple Valley she was going to break it off with Ansen. But she would wait until after the battle. Ansen needed to concentrate on protecting himself on the Wall. Diana knew he'd be distracted if she had her talk with him now.

Once that was done, she was going to tell Tee how she felt about him. Tee had been rather cool to her since he was asked to join the Guard. If he didn't share her feelings, she would be devastated. What she did know was that she would only marry if she were truly in love with someone. Marrying Ansen would be logical. It could be a good life. But it would not fulfill her dreams and desires. She suspected it would not fulfill

Ansen's either. Perhaps they both would have been disappointed.

Suddenly, Tee's voice came out of the gloom. "Diana." She flinched. "Sorry, did I surprise you?"

Diana's face heated, and she hoped it was dark enough that Tee didn't notice the blush. She felt like he had caught her thinking about him. "Yes, sorry, I was thinking about Ansen."

Oh God, why did I say that?

"He's okay. Saw him with Pete and Tia at the mess tent just a few minutes ago. He asked about you and I told him you were good at the end of the day. He was relieved. He told me to look out for you and Tia," Tee said in his earnest, caring manner.

Diana was still a little agitated with herself by the Ansen remark Tee had surprised out of her. "Are you okay?" she asked. Another stupid thing to say. They had talked briefly at the end of the day, and he already told her he was fine.

Tee looked a little confused but said, "Yeah, a couple scratches. Nothing to worry about. Are you sure you're okay?" he asked with clear concern showing in his voice.

"Yes, just distracted, I guess."

Oh God, do I ever stop saying stupid things? Now he'll think I'm referring back to Ansen again.

Then the conversation smoothly evolved into the calm, casual, and easy nature they had always had with each other. They walked along the Wall talking about home, people, Friday night bonfires, and hunting trips. The last topic transitioning into what they both would like to do when the battle was over.

"When this is over, I just want to go into the woods. Do a little hunting," Tee said with a wistful smile.

"That sounds absolutely wonderful. Let's go. I tried hunting with Ansen. It was a disaster," Diana said, laughing.

"Let me guess. He did a poor job of pretending to enjoy the woods. He never stopped talking. And he scared away the game," Tee said, smiling.

"Exactly," Diana said. She opened her mouth to say more, but then bit her tongue. She had come really close to telling him how she felt about him.

There was awkward silence for a moment and then Tee quickly changed to a safer topic. "How is our arrow monkey?"

"Really good. Better than I expected. She followed her orders exactly. We were worried she would linger on the Wall when it wasn't necessary. Or worse yet, poke her head up to look out of one of the arrow slits. Neither turned out to be a problem," Diana said with pride. "Have caught her early in the morning and late in the evening at the Guards' practice range. She's already a couple of years ahead of the other girls. You better watch out or she'll knock you off your perch."

Tee smiled and said, "I have little time to practice anymore. The Guard is keeping me busy doing other stuff. It relaxes me so I get out as often as I can."

"Oh, making your excuses ahead of time? You afraid you won't be able to keep up with me?" Diana said, falling into that easy banter she and Tee had always had.

"Yeah, you caught me," Tee said, smiling.

"By the way, I caught up with Hestie at Jay's mother's house. God, it was good to see her. I have missed her horribly since she left for university." Diana hesitated, then said, "I hope Jay is as over the moon about her as she is about him," Diana said with a hint of a question in her voice.

"I can't imagine her being any more smitten with him than he is with her. I'm really happy for both of them. And to save you from having to ask, yes, Jay really is a good guy. They're a good match, Diana," Tee said with his voice and face matching his words.

Diana had been watching Tee closely as he answered. She was vastly relieved by his answer. It surprised her how much that news relaxed her. She thought she knew how her best friend felt about him. A brother, not a lover. But with Ansen constantly trying to push the two together, she had begun doubting whether she really did understand their relationship. Well, perhaps paranoia was setting in now she had woken up and gotten honest with herself. What a relief to know she wouldn't have to deal with best friend jealousy.

They stayed on safe topics for the rest of her watch. Both losing track of time. Tee had a way of making her feel comfortable, warm, safe, and peaceful. He also excited her in a way no other man did. Diana wanted to drown in all of it. But that would have to wait.

peaceful. He also excited her in a way no other man did. Diana wanted to drown in all of it. But that would have to wait.

THE WALL
DAY 2

Tee was up extra early and decided to leave Jay alone to get a bit more rest. Last night Griff had told him to meet him on the Wall "Before sunrise." Tee hadn't asked what that meant. If there was one thing that irritated Griff, it was people being late. It gave Tee time to think.

He vividly remembered stumbling upon Diana the night before. He had stopped and watched her from the shadows before he announced himself. She was simply breathtaking. Tall and strong, with a heart of gold. Nobody was more beautiful in his eyes. His heart ached thinking about her.

Their discussion started off strangely. She was obviously worried about Ansen and distracted by it. He suspected she was sending him a message by bringing him up when Tee asked her how she was. Then the sudden enthusiasm to go hunting when all this was over. He was excited and troubled by it. She obviously didn't want Ansen along. Which made sense.

Tee smiled as he thought about how he had tried that once. It was easy to guess how it had gone for Diana. However, he wasn't sure how comfortable he would be alone with Diana. He might have to come up with an excuse to get out of it. Claiming Guard duties were wearing a little thin. Especially if he was given leave after the battle was over. It just hurt too much.

"Good morning, Tee," he heard Griff say from behind him.

Tee turned around and said, "Good morning."

"Thanks for getting here early. I wanted to discuss yesterday's battle before things heat up today. What did you learn?" Griff asked.

Tee straightened and gave his report, "The GEMs seem happy to trade lives for small gains. I don't think they place the same value on life that we do. The troops I saw yesterday morning were not very well trained. You mentioned they were the GEM version of Newbies. They didn't seem to have much weapons training or knowledge and experience on how to place and support their scaling ladders."

"Why would they waste inexperienced warriors this way?" Griff asked.

"I noticed our squads getting more and more aggressive as the day went on. Archers were exposing themselves more than they should as well. Maybe they are lulling us into a false sense of security they can take advantage of. They could also believe that sacrificing tens of GEMs for a few Pacifica warriors is worth it," Tee suggested.

"So, what do you suggest we do?" Griff asked.

"Tell everyone to be cautious, pay attention to changing capabilities, and stay defensive," Tee said.

"Good. That is exactly what everyone has been told to go over with their units," Griff said with a satisfied look on his face. "Pay attention to GEM squad cohesion when a leader goes down. They have trouble with coordination. Even at the squad levels, they are overly dependent on the squad leader."

"I did notice the squad coordination issue yesterday. I'll pay closer attention to larger scale moves today," Tee said, then hesitating he added, "How much trouble are we in?"

"Nothing we can't handle," Griff replied nonchalantly, turned, and strode off.

Tee took a deep breath and followed close behind. He was troubled. He made a habit of observing those around him. He was good at recognizing cues suggesting there might be more to the story. Griff didn't lock eyes with him when he responded. That likely meant he was anything but confident. He also noticed the volunteer reserves drilling in a phalanx formation yesterday afternoon. This was an integral part of the retreat plan to get as many people as possible back behind the dam if the Wall fell.

A multi-row phalanx with large square shields and long spears would set up and retreat step by step until it slowly dissolved back near the dam for the final run up the steep and winding dam road. In essence, it was a moveable Wall, slowing down the GEMs and providing an organized, purposeful retreat. Thinking about the phalanx sparked a thought he put away for later reflection as he noticed GEMs starting to cross the moat bridges and form up. The day had begun.

After the sun had gone down, and Griff finished his squad leader reviews, Tee walked back to the barracks. He saw Jay sprawled out on his bunk, looking spent. There were a number of bandaged wounds, but nothing that looked serious.

"Looks like you're not dead yet," Tee said, trying to joke.

"It's not from lack of trying, Tee," Jay said, not cracking a smile. "It was insane today."

"Seriously, are you okay?" Tee asked in a concerned tone.

"I'll have a few new scars to impress the girls, but nothing that will keep me out of the fight tomorrow," Jay said.

"Saw you fighting alongside Ansen during a Wall intrusion late afternoon," Tee said.

"Yeah, our squad came up in support when the GEMs made the Wall. Ansen and some of the other Apple Valley volunteers were doing a good job of keeping them confined, but it was a standoff. Ended up teaming with Ansen on an attack to break through. It was pure chaos. Waded in with sword and round shield, killing everything I saw," Jay said with a weary voice. "Your cousin is a good fighter, Tee."

"And a good guy as well," Tee responded.

"How about you? You look like hell," Jay asked with a forced grin.

"Similar story, a few minor wounds, but nothing serious. I spent the day chasing Griff around again. When he wasn't moving, I was taking out GEMs with my bow. Shooting fish in a barrel. I showed up with Griff toward the end of the same Wall infiltration you stopped and helped with. Griff was amazing. I know where all the crazy stories about him come from. They're all true," Tee said with admiration.

Jay nodded, adding, "He came charging in from the other side mowing them down and just like that the fight for control of the Wall was over. Then he calmly wiped his blade on a GEM tunic and told us all to get back to our stations. Next thing I knew, he was off down the Wall with you running after him."

"He never stops," Tee said.

"We lost a lot of Guard today. I've been asked to backfill a reserve squad tomorrow for duty below the Wall," Jay said with fire in his eyes. "And no, it won't be my father's squad. They don't put family members in the same squads for obvious reasons."

"They are backfilling Wall positions with some of the older youth reserve. My cousin Pete has been called up. He's thrilled and I'm worried. He's a good fighter, but he's immature," Tee said with visible anxiety.

"They'll put him with a seasoned veteran, Tee. Major Richards knows how to blend in the young and inexperienced."

They chatted for a while about inconsequential things, which calmed them both down. Then Tee said, "Go ahead and meet the others for dinner without me. I have to go find Griff. He told me if I have any ideas to let him know."

"Another suicide mission?" Jay asked, smiling.

"I hope not," Tee said grimly, smiling back.

Tee went to Griff's private bunk room and when he didn't find him there wandered around the encampment. He found Griff deep in conversation with the CGG and some of the other officers at a side table in the officer's mess hut. He couldn't interrupt that group, so he waited until they all filtered out. Griff saw him hanging around just outside the door and beckoned him in.

"Do you have something for me, Tee," Griff said.

"You asked me to tell you if I had any ideas. Is this a good time?" Tee asked tentatively glancing over at the CGG.

"Go ahead, let's hear it," Griff said, nodding in encouragement.

"I noticed the GEMs throw everything into the kill zone quickly to try and overwhelm the Wall with numbers. When that starts to slacken, we counterattack, and they retreat just as quickly back over the bridges they installed. They seem to be very good at knowing when to retreat to avoid mass casualties. They are using the moat for defense in the same way we use the Wall," Tee said and looked at them both.

"Agreed, go on," Griff said while the CGG nodded his agreement.

"If we can trap them between the Wall and the moat just as they call for a retreat, we can hurt them," Tee explained.

"Yes, but how do we cut off their exit back over the bridges?" Griff said. His face was drawn gray from the long day.

"Jay Phillips has a friend whose father owns a warehouse storing this winter's heating oil for Landfall and Eureka Valleys," Tee said. "The cliffs on both sides of the canyon that butt up against the moat are sheer. If we build ramps on both sides, we can quickly roll barrels of heating oil down into the moat. They will break when they hit the bottom. There are trails from Landfall City to the top of both cliffs. They are just wide enough for carts, so getting the barrels there shouldn't be a problem.

"The GEMs don't pay much attention to the cliffs on either side, other than to stay far enough away to avoid getting rocks thrown down on them. If we quickly drop them at the right time, we might be able to get enough heating oil in the moat that, when lit, will trap them between the Wall and the moat. While they are confused by the moat being on fire, the Guard goes out and clears enough room in front of the Wall to have the Volunteers form up their phalanx. Then we drive them into the moat."

The CGG and Griff looked at each other, dumbfounded. Nobody had ever thought of setting the moat on fire. It seemed so obvious now. Turning the phalanx from a defensive weapon to its original purpose as an offensive one was inspired. The CGG looked at Tee and said, "What if we can't get enough heating oil in the moat to create a barrier?"

"Then we just do what we normally do when they retreat. We don't show the phalanx. If it doesn't work, we haven't lost anything other than having a colder than usual winter," Tee said.

Griff smiled, thinking that it really wouldn't matter to Apple Valley, since they burn wood for heat in the winter. "Give us a few minutes to discuss this, Tee." He flicked his hand toward the door and Tee exited the mess tent.

When they were alone, Griff said, "It's brilliant, Nate. And we don't have a prayer otherwise. Assembling and organizing the Phalanx is needed, anyway. If it doesn't work, we start the retreat to the dam."

Nate quickly shook his head in agreement and said, "Let's do it. We're out of options. It's clear we're going to be forced to retreat beyond the dam. It's a question of when not if." Nate hesitated and then said, "I have to admit Tee is impressive. The creativity he showed in training seems to translate to the battlefield. You were right, the Guard needs more people like him, regardless of stature."

"I'm afraid Tee might be unique. I'm starting to think he's the most dangerous man in Pacifica," Griff said, smiling. He then turned to walk out, stopped, turned back, and said, "Tomorrow I'm going to tell Tee he's your personal aide in case of a full retreat. He'll be very unhappy about not being in the fight. But if this plan doesn't work, we'll need some other crazy scheme to save us."

Tee was thinking about Diana and how to handle his next hunting trip when Griff walked out of the tent. He locked eyes with Tee, grinned and said, "Let's go get Jay and find his friend."

CHAPTER 27

THE WALL
DAY 3

It was another angry red skyline that greeted Tee and Jay early the next morning. They had been up all night on the special project. Unlike the confidence they felt the morning before, this was a somber morning. Pacifica's defense had been badly mauled. The veterans were voicing confidence to the Newbies, but you could tell it wasn't heartfelt. Pacifica could not continue to sustain the level of casualties they had been experiencing. The GEMs didn't seem to care how many casualties they suffered.

The day started much as it had the previous two days. The early assaults were mostly young males with limited fighting skills. These were mass assaults intended to soften up and tire the defense. As these waves of GEMs were cut down, experienced warriors started appearing, and the fighting got more intense.

Midafternoon Tee saw Jay below the Wall in a squad led by Dee, of all people. Tee still harbored some resentment of Dee. But he was glad to see that Jay was in a squad whose leader was known to be excellent. There was a reason he was in charge of recruit training.

Just then, disaster struck. Barin Phillips's squad of retired Guard and second year Newbies had successfully disabled a siege tower before it could get to the Wall. It was burning brightly. However, they were getting cut off from their retreat route.

Griff immediately sent a runner for Arti. He turned to Tee and said, "Stay here, organize the archers to focus on carving a path for Phillips's squad back to the Wall. Griff then disappeared down the stairway.

Arti, Diana, and a few of the Apple Valley archers showed up running with Tia and another arrow monkey trailing them. The two girls' arms were piled high with arrows.

Tee pointed to the Phillips squad situation and said, "We need to carve a path back to the Wall."

Arti yelled out in a firm voice, "Beth, Silvia, focus on taking out as many as you can between the squad and the Wall." Turning to Tee and Diana, she said, "Tee take the left and Diana take the right. Take the pressure off those flanks so they can focus on a retreat. I'll focus on the front. Tia with me."

And with that, a hail of arrows greeted the GEMs attempting to surround and consume the Phillips squad. It felt like the practice range and another of his mother's crazy scenarios again. In a way, it was comforting. His confidence in his mother was complete. Some in the Guard would have been outraged to be given orders by an Archer, especially their own mother. But Tee knew the best person to be in charge was giving the orders.

It was a gut punch when Tee saw Barin Phillips take a spear. He had been gaining confidence they would pull this off when Jay's dad was suddenly struck down. The squad was now leaderless, and it showed. As their formation crumbled, Dee came roaring in like an angry bear, Jay right on his heels. GEMs went down like bowling pins; Dee got them formed up properly again and hope reemerged. Jay went to check on his dad, but Dee shook his head sadly and motioned him to get back to fighting.

The GEMs recognizing Dee's leadership focused everything on overwhelming him. Recognizing the dire situation, Dee motioned Jay to lead them back to the Wall. Then he plunged headlong into the heart of the attack. When Dee went down, Jay countermanded the retreat order and led the squad back, clearing space around the badly wounded Dee. As Jay's squad floundered, Griff rushed out of the gate with Kale, Zeb, Moose, and Rilla. The GEMs were introduced to hell.

"You." Griff pointed at one of the less effective Newbies. "Grab Dee's collar and drag him along inside our formation until we get to the Wall. Jay, you're with me on the front line. Squad, retreat together one step at a time on my cadence."

Tee was amazed to see the GEMs leery of attacking Griff. Not that they didn't have good reason for caution. After the initial carnage, they stayed clear of him and focused their attack on the sides and back of the formation. Now that the squad was organized and tightly bunched, the effectiveness of the archers improved.

Under Griff's direction, the squad was soon in close enough

proximity of the Wall for additional spearman to be sent out to help. The retreat path was cleared. Looking up now that his archery skills were no longer required, Tee saw that the area between the Wall and the moat was black with GEMs. These were the experienced ones, their best. The influx of GEMs crossing the bridges was starting to wane, so Tee rushed down to find Griff. It was time to prime the moat.

When he got down the stairs, he saw Dee on a surgical table with Dr. Espers looking at Griff and shaking her head slightly side to side. The nonverbal message was clear: Dee wasn't going to make it. Griff went to Dee, bent down, and said something in a low voice. Dee, noticing Tee approaching, motioned him over and grabbed his tunic. He pulled him down close and, wincing in pain, he whispered, "Ad Victorium."

Shocked, it was all Tee could do to mumble back, "Cum scuto aut in scuto."

Dee nodded, smiled with a grimace, turned toward Griff, and grabbed his tunic to pull him close. "Take care of my boys for me Griff," he said, pleading in a barely discernible and whispery voice.

Griff locked eyes with him and softly said, "That's a promise old friend." With Griff's promise, and acknowledgment of friendship in hand, Dee died with a peaceful expression on his face.

Tee was shocked at this version of Dee. He had just given Tee the ultimate acceptance. No time to think about that now, Tee thought. He hated to interrupt but with tears threatening his own eyes he said in a clear voice, "Griff, it's time." Griff turned toward him with eyes shining. Tee saw Griff had a serious gash on his shield arm. It had been hastily wrapped with a blood-soaked bandage, but clearly needed some attention.

"Sit down. Take something for the pain. And let me sew that up," Dr. Espers interrupted.

"Work on those who really need it," Griff said.

"I make the medical decisions, Sergeant, not you," Dr. Espers said in a firm voice.

"Follow me to the top of the Wall. You can sew it up there. Save the pain medicine for the others," Griff said.

Tee had never seen Quinn and Hestie's mom back down from anyone. But she just nodded, grabbed some antiseptic and bandages, and, with sewing gear in hand, followed him up the stairs.

When they got to the top, Tee pointed at the bridges and said, "It looks like they are gambling everything on this assault. The bulk of their experienced units appear to be on this side of the moat."

Griff turned to a runner and said, "Inform the CGG that it's time to signal the drop and form up for the attack."

As Dr. Espers was stitching up his arm, he stepped forward to look up and down the length of the Wall. "Stay still a minute," she ordered in a brisk voice.

Amazingly, Griff complied and, turning his head toward Tee, said, "They aren't going to call a retreat. They have the advantage, and they know it. Here are your orders. Light the moat when the barrels have all been dropped, or if it doesn't light, retreat. The CGG will come up here after we're formed up below. You are going to be his aide in case of a full retreat from the Wall. He will listen to your suggestions. Is that understood?"

"Yes," Tee said.

"I know you want to join us in the assault. You are capable. But you can make a bigger contribution by following orders," Griff said, then he turned and hurried down the staircase.

Tee could see the barrels dropping in quick succession on both ends of the moat. Either the GEMs hadn't noticed, or they were unable to get orders to their troops to retreat. It was amazing, but the bridges still had GEM units trickling over the bridges toward the Wall. He would have thought they could smell the fumes by now.

The CGG was standing next to him when the first fire arrow disappeared into the moat. A satisfying whoosh was heard, and the moat quickly became a flaming inferno. Flames were shooting fifty feet above the top. The gates opened and defenders poured out of all the gates. Only a skeleton crew was left behind. The CGG had asked for volunteers to join the Guard in an all-out final assault below the Wall. In true Pacifica fashion, almost all men of fighting age signed up.

As predicted, when the moat erupted in flames and the gates opened with an all-out mass assault, the GEMs panicked. They shrank back away from the Wall, bunching together so tightly they couldn't fight effectively. A few of the more senior GEM squads recognized the situation and tried to disrupt the formation of the Phalanx. However, with the entire Guard below the Wall, it wasn't coordinated well enough to make a difference. The Phalanx formed quickly and started a determined march, spears forward, driving toward the moat. The GEMs hadn't seen long spears or large shields before. The Phalanx was completely foreign to them. They had no idea how to combat it. The key was keeping a tight formation. All the training done to retreat in this formation turned out to be good practice in moving forward as well. Some GEMs tried climbing the cliffs and a few even tried running back over the burning bridges. Tee had seen Griff with Jay at his side spearheading the initial assault to clear space for the Phalanx to form up. Then he spotted Pete in one of the back row slots in the Phalanx. This really was an all-out gamble when young boys were fighting below the Wall.

It soon became clear that their gamble was paying off. The GEMs were getting impaled on spears or being pushed by those trying to avoid the spears into the burning inferno of the moat. The Phalanx continued its methodical drive into the massed GEMs and what had been a fight turned into a massacre.

Tee guessed it would be a while before the GEMs would try another assault. He took a deep breath, and his muscles started to relax. A thin smile formed on his lips. Suddenly a spear flew past, threading its way between himself, the CGG, and Diana. Tee heard it hit something with a wet splat. Before he could register what had happened, he heard Diana scream in anguish. Turning, he saw an image he would never be able to extinguish from his mind.

Lying on the stone parapet, in a pool of blood impaled by the spear, was Tia. Looking quickly back in the direction the spear had come from, he saw Angus sprinting away toward the staircase.

CHAPTER 28

THE WAGER

Grant was infuriated. He had been giddy with excitement at his certainty of a big score. He had bragged about it for three days to the other members of the survey crew. He even boasted to everyone and anyone who would listen on the feeds. He was a laughingstock now. Worse, this had been his opportunity to pay off the horrendous gambling debts he had accumulated. The odds makers had predicted true humans were more likely than not to survive this latest battle. It was clear now they had set the odds correctly. The odds being given for the true humans getting overwhelmed on the next attack by the mutants weren't attractive. The true human's days would soon be over. Grant needed to win back some of his losses. He knew thinking like this wasn't logical. But he just couldn't help himself. His luck would change.

Pacifica

CHAPTER 29

HALL OF HEROES

The Hall of Heroes was a large stately granite building in the center of an expansive and meticulously manicured park. It was located on a flat knoll above Lake Landfall, across from the capital. It was situated with its large bronze front doors looking out over the Landfall Lake dam. There was a sweeping view of the Wall and beyond. It was the final resting place for anyone who died in battle protecting Pacifica. Above its entrance read 'Semper Vilgilantes.' Always Vigilant.

Inside the building was an auditorium reserved for funerals and events to honor those who gave the ultimate sacrifice. The rest of the building consisted of hundreds of rooms big and small. They were each dedicated to the year those interned had given their lives. All Pacifica citizens were cremated upon death. The rooms had enclosed shelves with clay pots holding the ashes of the deceased. Some of the jars were empty. If they were of the Guard, their final insignia was attached to the pot. Everyone had a small plaque with their name and a short message. These messages were sometimes composed by the person whose ashes were being displayed and sometimes by close relatives.

Tee and Jay were standing in front of Tee's father's jar. The message said simply 'For us all.' Arti explained to Tee when he was young that they knew what a wonderful husband and father he had been. The message was to remind ourselves and others that this sacrifice was made for everyone, not just his family.

"How much do you remember about your dad, Tee?" Jay asked quietly.

"A little. I just remember being happy when he was around. My uncle really helped after he died by including me in all their family activities. He treated me like a son and still does. My father was his partner in their blacksmith business. He introduced my mom to my dad, so lots of history there," Tee said.

Jay just nodded and stayed by Tee's side until he was ready to go. They were there for Dee's funeral. It had been a full week of funerals. They had attended more of them than they could count. The Guard had been decimated. They heard recruiting was going to be increased with many more graduates than usual, given the situation. In fact, some of the recruits who had failed the cut based on points in the past two recruiting classes were being retroactively added. They were now in the Guard for life.

Tee and Jay had been close friends before the battle. But this joint experience added a bond that would never break. Tee was there for Jay, mourning his father. Jay was providing the same support as Tee mourned Tia. As they walked toward the auditorium, the hallway was quickly filling up. They were just able to find a seat before the ushers placed a rope across the door behind them and let everyone know they could listen from outside in the hall.

This funeral started the same as all the rest. The Guard chaplain got up and read verses, extolling the virtue of sacrifice. They were reminded that time on Pacifica was short and a better future with reunion was in store. After a blessing, he asked if there was a spokesperson from the family who would like to say a few words.

To everyone's surprise, Griff got up and walked to the front. All the Guard members looked at each other with an unspoken 'I didn't know Griff and Dee were related.' Tee had gotten to know Griff pretty well over the past two weeks. While outwardly he was his usual confident self, he looked a little shaken to Tee.

Griff stood up next to the displayed urn and said, "I am not related by blood to Dee. But I am nonetheless a brother. Both of Dee's grandfathers, his father, and three younger brothers are all interned here. They were all of the Guard and died protecting Pacifica. His mother died of a heart broken by war. Few families have given so much. His only remaining family was the Guard. Many of you are here today because he forced you to be better than you could have ever imagined. His passion was to develop raw recruits to reach their full potential. He did this because he cared deeply for each and every one of you.

"For this, he is widely reviled and disliked. He accepted this as a fair tradeoff. If he could help ensure a Guard member would go home to his family, he was happy to be cursed at the dinner table for it. He thought of every recruit as one of his boys. I know it doesn't fit with the image he presented. But he loved all his boys. He died saving them. I have nothing but admiration for Dee's commitment to the best traditions of the Guard. Sleep well, my friend. I'd pray for your admittance to heaven, but I know you're already there."

With that, Griff picked up the urn and, per tradition, carried it to the new room and placed it in its cubicle. Tee and Jay waited until the crowd thinned down to go in and pay their respects. It took quite some time. Written on his plaque was the message 'For the boys.'

"I guess you never really know a person, huh?" Jay said to Tee as he wiped his eyes. "If someone told me I'd be shedding tears over Dee, I would have told them they were crazy."

Tee nodded slowly in agreement and said, "I remember him crashing into that crowd of GEMs. He saved half the squad by doing that. Most of them Newbies. He easily could have followed standard doctrine. I hope I can be that brave if I'm ever in that situation."

"Do you mind if I take a few minutes by my dad's urn again?" Jay asked.

"Of course, I'll come with you. Take all the time you need," Tee said.

Jay's father's memorial had been tough. In addition to feeling horrible for Jay, it brought back memories of his own father's death. Jay ended up giving the memorial because his mother just couldn't. She had broken down during the ceremony and leaned over into Arti's arms and sobbed quietly. It was heartbreaking. His mother was staying at the Phillips home. When she was invited, Arti told Pam, "I don't want to intrude on your family during your grief."

Pam dried her eyes and said, "You understand, Arti. You've been through this. I need your strength right now if you can give it."

"Of course," said Arti.

Later that day, when Pam learned of Tia's death, she admonished her, saying, "Arti, you've been sharing my grief. It isn't right for you to keep me from doing the same for you." And after that, they sat and talked quietly for hours.

Tia's funeral was by far the worst. It was one thing to accept that a fully grown man or woman fighting to protect Pacifica had given their life. But to accept that a child had died just seemed unnatural. Tee was in a fog during the ceremony. His Uncle Hugh had gotten up and talked about how happy and joyful Tia was. How she livened up everyone she came into contact with. How she was loved by everyone who knew her. Drying tears, he changed tone and said he had something to get off his chest. This part Tee would remember.

"There are those who say my sister should not have had a child on the Wall. They are wrong. Tia's passion was to be a Wall Archer, like her aunt. She died as a Wall Archer. She was killed by a deranged coward who should have been out fighting in the final battle with the GEMs. Arti loved Tia as much as I do, as much as her mother does. Do not dishonor Tia's name with these ridiculous accusations. Tia died as a Wall Archer, protecting us all."

After his uncle and aunt walked the urn to its final resting place, they all gathered in the hallway.

"Dinner tonight at my house?" Jay asked.

"It's really nice of your mother to include all of us. Are you sure this is okay?" Tee said.

"My mom is better when she has people she likes around her. She has really taken a liking to your mom. Feels she understands her and the pain of losing a husband. It's also important to her that she is there for your mother. She told me that losing a niece is just as bad or worse. She enjoyed meeting Diana, Ansen, Quinn, and especially Hestie. Believe me, this will be good for her," Jay said.

"Your mother actually asked my mom about Hestie. She was trying to ask whether she was a good person without insulting anyone," Tee said with a smirk.

"She didn't!" Jay said in mock horror, and they both laughed. A pleasant change from the past few hours.

"My mom told her you couldn't find a sweeter, more loving person," Tee said.

Arti walked over to them, and Tee asked, "Where's Ansen?"

"He showed up at the Phillips house late last night. He's having an especially tough time accepting Tia's death. He won't talk to anyone about it and is angry all the time. I'm getting worried," said Arti.

Tee saw Ansen, Diana, and Hestie off to the side. Ansen did indeed look angry. He left Jay and walked over. "I'm so sorry about Tia Ansen," Tee said.

"You should be!" Ansen shouted. Everyone in the hall stopped what they were doing and looked to see what was going on. "I warned you about him. You knew what he was capable of. He blames you for not getting into the Guard and for his dad being in jail. I asked you to look out for her while she was on the Wall. You said you would take care of her. Well, you didn't, and now she's dead."

Diana grabbed Ansen's arm and pulled him away, speaking softly to him. She then turned and frowned at Tee. She blames me too, thought Tee. With tears running down his face, he turned and walked briskly out into the gardens and disappeared.

Jay was the one who found him. He had to stop and think about what would make Tee comfortable and then headed to the grove of trees on the far edge of the gardens. As predicted, Tee was sitting in the middle of a mini forest. "Hey buddy, you okay?" Jay asked with concern.

Tee looked up at him for a few moments, looked back down and said, "I should have been keeping better track of Angus. I knew he was looking to get even. Ansen is right, Tia's death is as much my fault as it is Angus's. I wish I had been the one to take the spear."

"That's crazy talk, Tee," Jay said. "It's not your fault a coward threw a spear at your back and missed."

"I appreciate you saying that, Jay, but it isn't true. Tia's death is on me." Tee hesitated for a few moments and then said, "Would you do me a favor?"

"Anything, Tee," Jay responded softly.

"Tell my mom and the others I'm going hunting. Ask them to leave me alone for a few days."

"I'll come with you if it would help," Jay said.

That drew a short-lived smile from Tee. It extended briefly to his eyes, then he said, "That's quite the sacrifice. I know how much you despise 'wandering around aimlessly in the woods.' Thanks, but it's best if I'm alone for a few days."

With that, Tee stood up and walked out of the Hall of Heroes' gardens alone with his anguish.

CHAPTER 30

SOLITUDE

It had taken a few days, but Tee finally felt somewhat like himself again. He had done very little hunting. Just enough to fill his belly. His father taught him to kill only when you planned to eat it. So, he mostly hiked through areas he had never explored before. He was there for that sense of peace he got from being outdoors. It was a bit cold for camping in the open. So, he built a lean-to out of branches stacked up against a rock wall. He buried the frame under a thick blanket of fallen leaves.

At night, he brought heated rocks into his temporary home. It was cozy. He loved camping in the woods. In his opinion, this was not the hardship many others thought it was. Jay, in particular, would hate it. Diana would love it. This was where he could always find peace. Solve any problem. He had finally accepted the terrible events of the past two weeks and was ready to go back to real life.

His relationship with Ansen and Diana was never going to be the same. He had taken on the responsibility for looking after Tia and failed miserably. The look Diana had given him confirmed she agreed with Ansen. They were both good people and would forgive him in time. But it would never be the same.

Tee packed everything up, made sure the fire pit was stone cold, and set off down the trail toward Apple Valley. He tried to clear his mind. But he kept coming back to the mistakes he had made and the things he should have done differently. Grammy had warned him that everything he valued in life could vanish in an instant.

"That is why you enjoy every moment, good or bad," she always said. It had been difficult to enjoy anything the past few days. Today, however, was a bit brighter than yesterday. He knew he would survive this. He had responsibilities. Pacifica still needed protection. Perhaps he would be like Griff and Dee. Never marrying. Making the Guard his family and his life. He had a future, even if it wasn't the one he had hoped for.

Tee's hunting senses suddenly kicked in and he stopped. The forest was too quiet. He notched an arrow and turned slowly around, trying to sense if anything was there. He wasn't overly concerned. Animals rarely attacked humans. But he was always cautious when out by himself. Suddenly, he felt a sting in his neck. He reached up, pulled something out, and looked at it. It was a small dart. His vision blurred. He heard something behind him and, turning, saw two small men cautiously coming out of the woods, fear clearly on their faces. As he collapsed on the ground, his last conscious thought was saying, "What odd clothing."

Tee woke up without opening his eyes. 'What to do if you're captured' was required training for all Newbies. Tee and Jay had wondered why they spent any time on this as GEMs were known to immediately torture and kill anyone they got their hands on. Lying quietly on some sort of soft surface, he controlled his breathing and listened intently.

The air smelled faintly like antiseptic, and the light coming through his eyelids was harsh. He decided he hadn't been captured by GEMs. The two small men didn't look anything like GEMs. They looked like tiny Pacifica men. There really wasn't a reasonable explanation. There was someone else in the room, perhaps eight feet or so past his feet. Tee could hear him breathing and every once in a while he talked to himself in a low voice. The discussion he was having with himself was laced with obscenities.

A door opened somewhere to his right. It had a metallic sound, somewhat like the bronze doors at the Hall of Heroes. It was a sharper sound, however, and unfamiliar to Tee.

"Has the gorilla woken up yet?" asked a voice in a commanding tone. This voice belonged to whoever had just walked in the door. A foul odor came along with him.

"No boss, he just lays there quietly," said the voice just past his feet. Boss was said sneeringly and clearly intended as an insult.

"Don't sass me, Theo, or I'll make sure you end up in the mines instead of the Arena," said the commanding voice.

"You can stop with the empty threats. I know I have value, or I wouldn't be in one of these special cells," he said, but with the sneer gone. "You have to admit you wouldn't be too happy if our places were reversed."

"True enough. Don't give me any trouble and I won't go out of my way to make your life even more miserable. Help me out when I ask for it and I'll see you get some privileges," said the voice of the person Tee now thought of as Smelly.

"Deal. I'll pound on the Wall when he wakes up," said Theo.

The door opened and closed again. The foul smell started fading.

"Bastard! If I get my hands on you, I'll make you wish you'd never been born," Theo muttered and went back to being quiet.

The Arena? The mines? It didn't make any sense. After a few minutes, Tee decided he wasn't going to learn anything more by pretending to be asleep. He also didn't want to alert them he'd been faking it. Smelly must know how soon the drug in the dart would wear off and had come expecting him to be awake. Delaying any longer would cause suspicion. His training emphasized hiding all skills and capabilities unless a high probability of escape or death presented itself. He had to be submissive.

"Do not look your captors in the eyes. Hunch over, look at the floor, show fear," his instructor had said.

Tee opened his eyes and sat up. He looked up at Theo, forcing a fearful expression, scooched back against the Wall behind him, and cowered.

"Big as a barn, but acting like a little girl," Theo said with disgust in his voice. "What's your name, pussy?"

"Th-Theron, ah, sir," he said, affecting the voice and mannerisms of someone mentally challenged. Tee was proud of his last second addition of "sir."

Theo laughed maliciously and pounded on the Wall next to him.

Tee took a moment to glance around the area while mostly keeping his eyes locked on the floor. He was in a jail cell with bars for two of the four walls. Four cells were arranged in the corners of the room with just over two arm spans of distance between them. Only two of them were occupied. They each had a narrow bed, a toilet, and a sink. A guard came through the door on the opposite side of the two occupied cells.

"He's awake," said Theo.

"No shit, moron," said Smelly.

"I hope he's not earmarked for the Arena. If so, you guys screwed up," Theo said and laughed.

"What do you mean? He's from Pacifica. They'll love him in the

Arena," Smelly said.

"Just talk to him. Says his name is Theron," Theo encouraged.

"Tell me about yourself, Theron," Smelly said with suspicion in his voice.

"I want to go home," Tee said, enunciating each word carefully. "Mom said to hike up to the lake and back before nightfall. She said she would have sweets for me when I get back," Tee said with his mouth partially open and a vacant scared look in his eyes.

Smelly broke out laughing. "Someone is dead over this. The bribes to get even one of these monsters from Pacifica must be astronomical." Smelly hesitated, scratched his head, thinking, and then said, "Oh well, he's still worth something. Maybe they can have one of the emperor's family members fight him in the Arena to show how tough they are."

"I'd enjoy slowly carving pieces off him. There would be lots of crying and screaming. I could make it really entertaining," Theo said with a sadistic grin.

Smelly ignored him, turned around, and exited out the door. Tee clearly heard it lock.

Theo then entertained himself by explaining to Tee all the painful and humiliating things he would do to him if there weren't bars between them. Tee curled up in a ball and whimpered. He had trouble staying in character because he couldn't believe the callousness and pure evil of the man. To abuse someone who had been born with mental challenges was about as low as a human being could get. Eventually, Theo tired of the harassment, which gave Tee time to review what he had learned.

He was no longer on Pacifica. Tee had trouble just grasping that concept. It meant their planet had been discovered. Whoever discovered it was practicing slavery but having to bribe someone to capture slaves on Pacifica. He was destined for the Arena, whatever that was. Given the comments, it sounded like some sort of blood sport. Just when he thought life couldn't get any worse, it had.

CHAPTER 31

IMPROVING THE ODDS

Grant's confidence was back. It wasn't often you could improve the odds. Even by a little. What he had done was surely illegal. But there was no way he would get caught. Grant had figured out that Guard member Theron Stone was the one who came up with the idea resulting in the defeat of the mutants. He discovered this by accident as part of his job as an anthropologist. He kept it to himself. He didn't log the files, so there was no evidence of his discovery.

When the slave ship arrived and requested Survey assistance, he was happy to help. They wanted to identify a member of the Guard located remote enough to be captured without witnesses. He had gleefully supplied Theron Stone's location. Unbeknownst to the odds makers, he had just eliminated a wild card. One more battle was all it would take. Now he just had to get ahold of more money. Knowing he had altered the odds gave him the confidence to gamble everything he could beg, borrow, or steal. His luck was definitely improving.

Judgement

CHAPTER 1

SEARCH PARTY

Grammy was worried. Tee didn't show up on the fifth day, as promised. That wasn't like him. When the poor boy had shown up on her doorstep last week, he had been more distraught than she had ever seen him. He was so overwhelmed by trauma and guilt that she tried to get him to delay his hunting trip. She thought a few days talking it out would be good for him.

Tee told her he had to get by himself to sort it all out. This was how Tee solved personal problems his whole life. So, she was hopeful he would find the healing he needed in the woods. He promised her he would be back by the fifth day. He said he would spend a couple of days with her before having to report back to the Guard. She remembered their last conversation. "Where are you going to be?"

"Not telling, Grammy. If you don't know, they can't get it out of you," Tee said.

"What's wrong with you? Somebody ought to know in case you do something stupid or clumsy out there. God knows it wouldn't be the first time," she said. That actually made him chuckle, a sound that warmed her heart after an entire day of sorrow and tears.

"Sorry, but I need the time alone. Ansen and Diana will come find me if they know where to look," Tee said.

Grammy knew something had happened that Tee hadn't told her about. While they were both distraught about Tia, he seemed downright guilty about it. He also said very little about either Ansen or Diana. That was unusual. Tee tended to be on the private side. He tended not to say bad things about people. There was more to this story.

Late in the afternoon on the sixth day, Arti, Hugh, Ansen, Pete, and Diana all arrived. Instead of going home, they had all shown up on Grammy's front porch.

Arti started the conversation with, "Where is Tee, Mom?"

"He left here six days ago and was supposed to be back yesterday afternoon, latest," Grammy said with concern in her voice.

"Where was he going?" Diana asked.

"He wouldn't tell me. Said he didn't want you or Ansen to find him until he was ready to be found. That was cryptic, so I tried to find out what happened between the three of you that had him so insistent," Grammy said with a hint of accusation in her voice.

There was dead silence for an uncomfortable amount of time until Ansen spoke up. "It's my fault, Grammy. I told Tee at Tia's funeral that I blamed him for her death. I had asked him to look after her on the Wall. I told him she was dead because he failed to do that," Ansen said with tears forming in his eyes. "I know Tee loves Tia as much as I do. It was cruel and selfish to take out my anguish on Tee. I just hope he'll forgive me."

Grammy just glared at him for a few moments. Then her face softened and with compassion in her voice said, "He will Ansen, he will. The one time he did talk about you was to compliment your bravery on the Wall. Evidently you fought beside his friend Jay, who had good things to say about you. He also said you were as good a brother to him as you've always been to Pete." Ansen turned bright red, looking completely embarrassed, and Pete just looked down at the ground. Perhaps I shouldn't have said that, thought Grammy. But Ansen knows better than to say something like that. He needs to be called out on it. The two of them are like brothers.

Turning toward Diana, she asked bluntly, "Why was he worried about you Diana?"

"I don't know, Grammy," Diana said earnestly, but with something held back.

There was way more to that story. But now wasn't the time to get it out of her. Diana was like a granddaughter to Grammy. She hated pushing her in front of everyone, but her anxiety over Tee overrode any concerns of making Diana uncomfortable. Diana was definitely holding something back. It wasn't like her to lie, even by omission.

Arti spoke up. "It's time to organize a search. I'll go down to the Sheriff and see if he can help us drum up some volunteers. Most people are still making their way back from the Wall. Some decided to help the

Eureka farmers with the planting. God knows they are stretched. We aren't going to get the number of people we would usually get for something like this."

"Maybe we could get the Guard to help. I'm sure they would be interested in helping us find him," Diana offered.

"That's a good idea. Hugh, could Pete go back down the falls and find the Guard scout team we saw there yesterday?" Arti asked.

"Of course. We need to find our boy," Hugh said. "Pete, turn around and head down the falls this afternoon. Stay with your aunt and uncle tonight in Apple Falls. As soon as it's light tomorrow, go look for that scout team. Tell them Tee is missing. Diana, you go hunting with Tee. Where should we start?"

"Let's go into town and ask around. Maybe someone saw which direction he was headed in. If we know that, I can make a better guess," Diana answered.

Later that day Diana suggested they wait for the scout team because she thought she knew where Tee went. She explained her theory to Arti, "Steve at the general store said Tee bought bread and fruit to take with him. Enough for four or five days, he thought. He noticed him heading in the direction of the west side trail, which means he's probably over on that side somewhere. Tee won't kill anything he's not planning on eating, so it's a minimum of small game. That means he'll have lots of time on his hands with nothing to do. He's not a person who's going to sit around," Diana said.

"He hasn't stayed in one place since he could crawl," Arti confirmed with a sad smile.

"He likes to explore, so I think he went somewhere he hasn't fully explored. That eliminates anything that can be done on a day trip and most of the east side. We talked once about taking a few days and exploring the north end of the west side. There are a couple of small valleys up there. They are really remote, and he wouldn't run into anyone up there. Just the sort of place he would go," Diana said.

Pete showed up late in the afternoon with Scout Team 5. "We came as soon as Pete found us," Staff Sergeant Willis said to Arti. "Tee was supposed to join our team on his next cycle. We've already done some training with him. I guess I'm telling you this because we consider him one of our own. If he can be found, we'll find him."

"Thank you, Sergeant. If you need anything, just let me know. This is Diana," Arti said, motioning over to her. "She has spent many hours hunting with Tee and will go along with you. She knows his habits and his preferences, which might be helpful."

"A pleasure to meet you, Diana." Sergeant Willis studied her for a few moments and then said, "Weren't you one of the hunters who discovered the GEMs and then helped drive them off the cliffs?"

Diana blushed and simply said, "Yes."

"Sergeant Glenn is quite the fan," Sergeant Willis said with a grin to the amused chuckles of the rest of his team.

Diana's blush turned scarlet.

Noticing her embarrassment, he respectfully said, "I'm sorry. I didn't mean to embarrass you, Diana." Sergeant Willis's smile faded, and he continued. "We're all deeply appreciative of what you've done here in Apple Valley and at the Wall. Everyone in the Guard loves it when they have Apple Valley archer support."

He glanced over to include Arti in his appreciation. Willis then sighed and said, "It's already close to sunset so let's meet in the town square before first light. We need to be able to look for signs and can't do that in the dark. This is Corporal Walker. He's the best tracker in the Guard. In fact, he's the one who trains new recruits. Tell him everything you know about Tee's habits and tendencies when he's hiking. Does he go off-trail often? If so, what draws him off? Favorite places to stop and rest, things like that."

"Thank you," Arti said, sweeping her hand to encompass the entire scout team. "I can't tell you how much I appreciate your help with this," Arti added, catching all of them with her intense eyes.

"He's one of our own, ma'am. We'll look until we find him," Sergeant Willis said.

After most of a day hiking up the west side of Apple Valley, they reached the first of the smaller northwest valley trails. Sergeant Willis called for a halt and motioned Walker toward the trail. Walker was tall and rangy. He seemed to blend into the environment, moving smoothly and easily. He nodded and started up the trail, carefully staying off the main path and looking intently from side to side. He soon disappeared around a bend.

Thirty minutes later, he came back and said, "There isn't any recent activity on this trail. They told me in town that it rained two weeks ago, just before Tee left. The trail only has animal tracks on it. Let's go look at the next spot."

Four hours later, Walker strode up the next trail and came back quickly, excitement clear on his face. "There is one set of tracks going up, and none coming back," he said. "It's a Guard issue boot and on the small side. Give me ten minutes, then follow me up the trail at a slow pace." And with that, he disappeared with his long strides up the steep forest trail leading alongside a rushing stream to the valley above.

Just after sunset, Walker appeared, coming quickly back down the trail toward them with a bow, arrows, and backpack. Diana blurted out, "Those are Tee's! Is he okay?"

"Don't know, Diana. I searched the general area around where I found these and didn't find Tee," Walker said. "Staff Sergeant, would you come with me? I need to show you something. Sorry, but everyone else needs to stay put. I don't want anything disturbed until I can look the area over in full light tomorrow."

When they returned, Sergeant Willis looked grave. He turned to one of the scouts and said, "Hollings, go find Master Sergeant Ricks and tell him Tee is missing. Tell him Walker found something unusual connected to Tee's disappearance and I'm requesting his presence. Tell him we're going to search this valley until he shows up. And Hollings, go as fast as you can."

Willis looked over at Diana and could see the barely contained anxiety. He took a deep breath, let it out, and then said, "Griff will probably kill me for telling you what we found. Can you keep what I tell you a secret? That means from everyone."

"Yes," Diana said with her heart in her throat.

"Tell her Walker," Willis said.

"I think he was ambushed and taken somewhere. There isn't any blood or even signs of a fight. He appears to have just collapsed in the middle of the trail. The other signs are hard to believe. Surrounding where the person fell are a number of adolescent sized footprints with unusual soles. Strides are consistent with someone not fully grown. It looks like they picked Tee up, tried to carry him, gave up, and then dragged him to a nearby clearing. All the signs disappear in the middle of that clearing. It's like he just vanished," Walker said, clearly troubled to be telling her this.

Diana was stunned. She didn't know what to say. Then she blurted out in disbelief, "He's been kidnapped?"

"It looks that way. It certainly wasn't GEMs if that's any consolation," Sergeant Willis said. "I have no idea what to make of it. I'm hoping Ricks can help us sort this out. We will do an exhaustive search of the valley and make sure he isn't here somewhere. Would you stay and help?"

"You don't have to ask; I'm staying and looking for him regardless of whether you want me to or not," Diana said as she fought to control her emotions.

"We're glad to have your help, Diana," Willis said with a gentle voice and troubled look.

Diana might be calm on the outside, but inside she was screaming. In a way, it might be good news. She was worried he had run into GEMs or fallen off a cliff. She had even harbored thoughts of him taking his own life. Tee was the last person she thought might do that. But, he had undergone a tremendous amount of trauma in a short period of time and that can do strange things to a person.

Diana was very angry with herself. She should have gone to Tee when Ansen lost his temper. Ansen wasn't the one who needed her in that situation. Tee was. They all thought of Tee as tougher than anyone. Tee was always okay. It would be her life's tragedy if she were never able to apologize and tell Tee how she really felt about him.

CHAPTER 2

CONFRONTATION

Griff walked into the Blue Heron Tavern and sat down heavily in a chair across from Del. He had an angry, stern expression on his face.

"What? No hello, no insults," Del said, trying to lighten the mood.

"Hello," Griff said stiffly. Then he just continued to look sternly at him.

Del hesitated and then, with concern in his voice, said, "I heard Tee is missing."

Griff continued to glare at him for a few moments longer and then asked in a stern and threatening voice, "What are you hiding?"

Del replied with both hands raised and surprise written all over his face, "What do you mean?"

Griff's frown deepened. "I've known for a while you're hiding something. Your engineering department is especially fishy," Griff said accusingly.

"Why do you say that?" Del replied, looking down into his whiskey.

"You send out a new 'military history' student every few years to learn about Guard tactics and strategies. They're always young, smart, and attempting to hide their involvement in your engineering department. When I ask what they want to learn from the Guard, they give me the same answer. The same EXACT answer. It's clear they've been coached on what to say. If I try and dig deeper into their objectives, they get hesitant, cagy, and feign confusion." Griff hesitated a moment and continued. "If I wasn't in charge of Guard training and naturally paranoid, I never would have gotten suspicious. Once my suspicions were raised, I noticed other peculiarities. For instance, engineering technologies seem to flow out of the university cleanly and systematically. It's not as messy as I would expect new discoveries to be. I can also tell when you're not being completely forthright with your answers to my questions."

Del continued to examine his whiskey and did not answer.

Griff sighed, let out a deep breath and said, "Our scout teams are very good at tracking. Most people don't know that GEMs get past the cliff forts and into the wilderness occasionally. This is mostly a problem in the mountains on the western side above Landfall and Eureka Valleys. As you know, a full-scale invasion was recently attempted in Apple Valley. Our scout teams are the ones who hunt them down. We keep quiet about it because we don't want people to panic.

"When Tee went missing, we were able to identify his last location and were surprised by what we found. Based on evidence at the site, which I have seen with my own eyes, children snatched him. They tried to carry him and failed, so they dragged him to a nearby clearing. From there, he magically disappeared."

Griff hesitated and, staring aggressively at Del, said, "I'm convinced you know something about his disappearance."

Del was rarely stunned into silence. He started to reply, stopped, hesitated some more, then finally looked up from his whiskey and said, "Give me a day or two and I'll tell you what I can."

Griff's eyes bored right through him as he said, "A missing member of the Guard is involved. I can't let this go. I know you, so I'm sure you have your reasons for hiding whatever it is you're hiding. But one way or another, I'm going to get to the bottom of this." Having said what he needed to say, Griff abruptly stood up and walked out of the tavern.

Del took an especially deep breath and let it out slowly. As he sat there, he transitioned from panicked to resigned. Once again, he was left with lots to think about after meeting with Griff. *Damn him, why can't we just meet for dinner and have a pleasant conversation?*

CHAPTER 3

THE COMMITTEE

While Del was waiting for the other committee members, he reflected on how Pacifica had gotten into such a precarious position. Barlow was extremely irritating, but his accusation of a manipulated history was true. The official history of Pacifica was a lie. Barlow was clever in uncovering it. But he was entirely wrong about the purpose of the lie. There was a good reason. It was a life-or-death reason.

The irony was that a group of committed pacifists, with the best of intentions, created two of the most warlike cultures ever known. While the people of the peninsula could argue they were defending themselves, they were killing and being killed by other intelligent beings on a monumental scale.

The original emigration plan was to permanently separate from the rest of humankind. The goal was to live an isolated and peaceful life. After a long search, sabotage marooned them in a stable orbit around a planet presenting significant terraforming challenges. It was a massive planet. Gravity was higher than humans were accustomed to. It also had a slightly more extreme axis tilt than Earth's. This meant it had larger extremes of seasonal heat and cold than the environment humans are best suited for.

There was a single long narrow peninsula on the north end of the smaller of the two continents. It was situated near the equator, with deep temperate oceans surrounding it. This kept the temperature extremes of summer and winter reasonably regulated. It was the only location on the planet that could possibly support unmodified humans. One of the main motivations for permanent separation from the rest of humanity was moral abhorrence with genocide. That it was being carried out on those possessing engineered genetic alterations was not a justification for this horror.

The so-called Mutant Wars in Earth's solar system had just been lost by the genetically impure. The victors were sure of their moral superiority. They were diligent in a brutal quest to ensure genetically engineered modified humans, or GEMs, would disappear forever.

Earth had developed a standard colonization process after decades of trial and error. Triple redundant starships had been shown to have many advantages. By keeping the three starships coordinated but isolated from one another, the ravages of disease and societal dysfunction could be confined. You might lose one of the ships, but experience had shown you were unlikely to lose more than that. Spare parts and expertise could be shared as long as physical contact was kept sterile and communication was limited to specific objectives. The other requirement was locking down language and culture.

Humans were combative enough without the challenge of navigating multiple dynamic cultures. For this reason, there was a right way and a wrong way to speak and act. When the three starships recombined, people had to be able to communicate and blend back into a single culture.

Not all the Pacifica colonists were genetically pure humans. This was the genesis of the false history. Ship 2 had smuggled onboard a population of GEMs who had escaped capture toward the end of the Mutant Wars. These GEMs were a team of scientists with a pacifist bent. This GEM population had minimal modifications and was visibly indistinguishable from unmodified humans. Only extensive genetic testing could uncover the truth.

Unfortunately, extensive genetic testing was a requirement for all citizens after the war. The moral alignment, indistinguishable modifications, and addition of unique and valuable skills were too appealing for the inhabitants of Ship 2 to ignore. They felt they could not allow these scientists to be handed over for genocide.

The three-ship alliance first broke apart over the strategy of colonizing Pacifica. A planet named in honor of the colonists' intentions. After decades in space, Ship 2 was primarily populated by GEMs. The populations of Ships 1 and 3 were unmodified. Both groups agreed that some modification was likely needed to ensure survival. An analysis suggested a 70% probability of success if they confined themselves to the peninsula and avoided modification. This was considered dangerously low.

Ship 2 proposed massive genetic modifications to enable colonization of the whole planet. Ships 1 and 3 wanted to limit changes to just those calculated to be probable by natural micro-evolution. This would still limit them to the relatively mild environment of the peninsula. If done properly, it would allow the modifications to potentially remain hidden if the rest of humanity discovered them.

They finally agreed to disagree. A compatible middle ground was found. They were the descendants of pacifists, after all. There was an agreement to separate into two colonies. Ships 1 and 3 would own the peninsula and Ship 2 the rest of the habitable parts of the world.

Harmony and cooperation only lasted for a single generation. The second generation of genetically altered offspring of Ship 2 suddenly murdered what was left of the original Ship 2 colonists and attacked those living on the peninsula. War was sudden, brutal, and devastating for both races. In the end, all three spaceships were destroyed, and both races plunged into an agrarian state fighting to survive.

What the peninsula kept secret was that it retained much of its technological knowledge. Information hidden away in caves was waiting for society to recover enough to be able to invest the time and energy needed to make use of it. The crisis struck just as that had begun to be possible. Their sector had been discovered by the Commonwealth and other solar systems were being colonized.

By sheer luck, the radio operator on duty that day decided to stay silent when local microwave radio traffic was first received. Their freedom and likely their lives had been saved by that decision. It didn't take long to realize the danger they were in. Listening to their new neighbors, they learned that the violently anti-GEM society they escaped had turned into a sprawling authoritarian government spread across the universe. This Commonwealth was fanatically committed to maintaining true human purity.

This was when the Committee was first formed.

They took steps to create a false history and over many generations aggressively erased all traces of evidence contradicting that history. Oral histories were the most problematic. Traces of those written in private journals and stored with records in small town parishes were what Barlow had uncovered.

It was common knowledge that a system of caves existed beneath the university. This cave system was owned by the university and used for natural refrigeration, storing records, and archiving artifacts from the original colonists. What was known to a select few was the existence of a carefully hidden and extensive tunnel system branching off from it. This tunnel system had been carved out of the rock by the original colonists for use as a bunker. It was to a conference room in that tunnel system that the Committee convened.

There were four members of the Committee. Professor Delvin Dacy, Dr. Dorothy Espers, Kevin Wise, and President Jennifer Malrey.

"Thank you for coming so quickly. I apologize for the last-minute request and appreciate the difficulties it presented," Del said, looking around the table. "This emergency meeting is to discuss the rapidly deteriorating situation at the Wall."

"Has something changed since the last meeting?" asked Jennifer with a worried expression.

"We've intercepted more communications from the survey ship orbiting the planet," Del said. "They continue to report that the GEMs have retreated, as relayed in our last meeting. But they are not dispersing. This is new behavior. The survey ship crew is communicating to A27 that it's just a matter of time before the GEMs regroup. They expect the next attack to break into the peninsula and wipe us out."

"Remind me how the Commonwealth is structured and why their laws allow for the genocide of true humans by GEMs?" the president asked. "I'm sorry to drag you all through this, but as you know, I was just elected and am new to all of this."

"Not a problem, Ms. President," Del said.

"Please call me Jennifer for these committee meetings. We are all tied together closely in our struggle and formality will just get in the way," she declared.

"Okay, done, Jennifer. Everything I tell you is based on listening and not being able to ask questions. It means everything I say on this subject is unverified speculation. It is speculation based on lots of intercepted communications over the years, but speculation none the less," Del said. "Our understanding is that the Commonwealth is motivated by tax revenue growth and a monopoly on technology-based manufacturing. They accomplish growth by colonizing new planets and incorporating previous expeditions, like ours. They set up one planet per sector to take in raw materials produced by the colonies in that sector and turn them into trade goods. We are in Sector 27. The name for the Commonwealth owned planet in this sector is A27. The A stands for Administrative.

"We believe they base their economic model on the British Empire of the eighteenth century. Recognizing that the British system fell apart because of colonial rebellion, they have devised a system to eliminate that threat. They control trade and technology-based manufacturing by keeping the colonies at a pre-industrial level. The colonies supply raw materials, agricultural products, and cheap labor-based manufacturing. Commonwealth corporations and citizens get obscenely wealthy.

"By completely controlling transportation, they control interplanetary and intersectional trade. This is their sole source of tax revenue. Since they transport everything, it's extremely easy to administer and impossible to avoid. They don't appear to bother controlling politics on individual colony planets. As long as tax revenues and raw materials are flowing, they don't get involved. It does appear they sometimes intentionally create conflict between planets if they believe they can increase tax revenues or their own manufacturing output.

"To effectively manage such a large number of diversely located planets, they have divided it into sectors defined by permanent wormhole boundaries. Each sector has a governor whose authority is absolute as long as the Commonwealth's Edicts are being observed. We have reason to suspect our sector's bureaucracy is corrupt. We don't know if corruption is limited to our sector or a widespread attribute of the Commonwealth.

"One of the Commonwealth's Edicts is that civilizations of true humans in a pre-industrial state with only first-generation warfare capabilities are to be left alone. Evidently, they are very interested in societal evolution and want to study it. All colony planets are restricted to first generation warfare, and the Commonwealth is brutal in enforcing this Edict. They keep subject planets at a technological level that eliminates their ability to revolt. We know that whole planets have been destroyed or their populations enslaved for hiding even mildly sophisticated weapons or violating any of the technology Edicts.

"As you know, another of their Edicts is to eliminate all GEM races as they are discovered. However, it appears that the Edict to leave true humans alone extends to the current protection of GEMs on our planet. We've intercepted a communication from the survey ship stating that if the GEMs wipe us out, it validates their belief in the prohibition of genetic alterations. It's a self-serving justification for their system of genocide. Our belief is that once we use second generation warfare or cross the boundary into an industrial state, the Commonwealth will invade.

"We don't know if they will install their own government or hand us over to one of the other colonies in our sector. Slavery is common on Arista and our guess is that we would be placed under their control. On the other hand, if the GEMs wipe us out, the Commonwealth will come in. They would cleanse the planet of GEMs and strip Pacifica of its natural resources."

"Why are we only worried about Arista?" Jennifer asked.

"I would say we are more worried about Arista than the others. Arista was originally formed with a benevolent dictator advised by a Senate comprised of citizens. Citizens are the descendants of the original wealthy families that funded the colonization. Everyone else came with indentured servant status and that class system hasn't changed much in almost a millennium.

"Over several generations, the benevolence disappeared and an obsession with ancient Rome and its emperors emerged. They endorse the idea that the citizen class is superior to all other classes. That slavery is the rightful position of the lowest class. They conspire to take over the sector and the Commonwealth doesn't seem to be interested in stopping them. They may even have some level of support. There are indications that Commonwealth tax revenues can somehow be increased in that circumstance.

"The other significant planet is Liberty. They have a constitutional monarchy with strong protections for their people. It's similar to our belief in the natural rights of humans. This extends to abhorrence for the condition of slavery. The advisory body for their monarch can only make suggestions for new laws, taxes, and declarations of war. Amendments to the constitution must be proposed by their House of Lords but can only be approved by their king or queen. All decision making outside of constitutional declarations and protections are completely within the authority of the king.

"Currently, Liberty is embroiled in a civil war over succession. A younger brother is attempting to overthrow the succession and take the crown. This came soon after a long war of unification, where the current kingdom defeated the two other kingdoms on the planet. They definitely have some similarities to the class system on Arista. But each member of society is free and has rights. The Commonwealth's modeling of eighteenth-century British Empire might explain the societal class structure similarities between the two colonies.

Outside of the obligatory Commonwealth planet which manages the bureaucracy of the sector, there are seven additional colonies. They are all relatively poor agricultural societies and pose no threat."

Jennifer took a deep breath and said, "Well hearing it again doesn't make it any better. It certainly explains the extensive efforts we take to slow down innovation and hide what technology we do have."

"And we need to hide that technology regardless of how this plays out," Del said. "If they discover we have been hiding industrial technology, they will accuse us of avoiding Commonwealth taxes. If they discover we are hiding next generation weapons, no matter how insignificant, they will consider us to be in rebellion. Either way, the best case for our population is enslavement. If they discover our genetically engineered modifications, we're all dead."

"The good news is that only committee members know we have been genetically modified. We know slavers have kidnapped numerous individuals from Pacifica over the years. Given that some of the planet's population is GEM, they would have done extensive genetic testing on the captives. We assume they have not discovered our modifications, because if they had, we wouldn't be sitting here," Dorothy added. "It was brilliant to do the original modifications in a way that probabilistically fits with natural micro-evolution induced by selective breeding. We have a simple solution to keep this hidden forever."

Only Dorothy would refer to all past and present committee members committing suicide as a 'simple solution,' Del thought, smiling. "Back to the purpose of our meeting," Del said, looking around the table. "I believe it's just a matter of time before the GEMs get past the Wall and threaten the Landfall Dam. We still have a few tricks up our sleeves that don't involve second generation warfare, but we are running out of time. With that in mind, I have a proposal for the committee."

"Is this proposal within the scope of our current powers?" Jennifer asked.

"Yes, it resides within the secret addendum to the constitution that formed this committee," Del replied. "My proposal is that we add the military to the committee. In my opinion, Master Sergeant Ricks, Griff, is the best choice. The reason for this addition is to get ready for the day we have to use second generation warfare to hold off the GEMs. That will be the day we effectively announce ourselves to the

Commonwealth."

"That will mean the GEM race will be eliminated by the Commonwealth," Dorothy said with her bland expression.

If you looked closely, you could see her eyes were slightly dilated, which Del now understood meant she was troubled. Thank you, Phyllis Del thought. "I think we are all in agreement that we will avoid this until our survival is threatened. A last option," Del said.

"Okay, let's vote first on whether to add a military member to the Committee. If it passes, we can discuss who should be asked to take on that role," Jennifer said. "Kevin?"

"I vote yes. There aren't any financial implications, and I agree with Del's points."

Kevin was the finance minister for Pacifica. His responsibility was ensuring all government spending fit within the balanced budget requirement in the constitution. The only exception to this restriction were materials needed for war. Everyone knew the government could come in at any time and confiscate. They would get reimbursed, but that reimbursement had to fit within the balanced budget guidelines.

No government spending was possible without Kevin's approval. His role on the Committee was as secretary and financial controller. He had proven to be excellent at hiding the funds they needed to enact their decisions. It was a good thing for Pacifica he was a public servant because he would be filthy rich and useless to them otherwise.

"Dorothy?"

"It's a logical move, yes. This should have been proposed sooner. We don't have margin for error," Dorothy said with her deadpan expression. Del smiled once more, recalling Phyliss's advice. While Dorothy was bluntly calling out the error in not tabling this sooner, it was just an observation, not a personal attack.

"And Del?"

"Yes."

"The proposal to add the military to the Committee passes unanimously."

"Let's move to who we should add. Why are you proposing, Master Sergeant Ricks? Isn't the CGG in charge of the Guard?" Jennifer asked.

"The CGG would be the natural choice. He's an excellent administrator and highly respected by the Guard. But he's mired in tradition and doesn't think outside his own experience and the historical record. The more important point is that Griff is the real leader of the Guard. They all follow his lead on important matters. Even the CGG. Griff is intelligent, creative, open-minded, and not reluctant to collaborate as part of a team," Del explained.

"I know both Griff and the CGG well," Dorothy said. "I agree that Griff is the best choice."

"Any other nominations?" Jennifer asked. After a few moments of silence, she said, "If there are no other nominations, then let's vote. Kevin, we already have Del and Dorothy's votes. Do you agree or want to discuss further?"

"I don't know either candidate, but I trust the combined judgement of those who do. I vote yes," Kevin said.

"It's decided. We will invite Griff to join the Committee with the responsibility of leading military matters with a full vote on all decisions. I'm sure you all realize this means we can now be dead locked on decisions. Per the Committee charter, the president facilitates the Committee and only votes to break a tie," Jennifer said. "Del, since you know him best, would you deliver the invitation and bring him up to speed?" Then, hesitating, she continued with a flat smile. "I hope he's not as scary as he appears."

Del chuckled and said, "He'll be very respectful Jennifer. I think you'll like him once you get to know him." Del had never seen Griff treat any woman with anything other than respect. Most times looking uncomfortable, he thought, smiling to himself. "I will contact him immediately and get him on board."

Del relaxed a little. His opinion of both Jennifer and Kevin went up with every meeting. They both stayed within their roles and made solid contributions. Kevin was a bear defending cubs with the finances. But he didn't use that stick to try and increase his influence on the Committee.

In some ways, it was dangerous to change something that was working so efficiently. However, the need for military involvement was real, and it neatly solved the problem of having to deal with Griff's suspicions. Wasn't the first time a member of the Guard had gone missing. It will be quite a shock for Griff to learn the answer is space-based slavers. He's not going to like that answer. But once he gets the whole picture, he'll understand why our hands are tied.

As Del left the chamber, he mused over how much to tell Griff. On the one hand, the BIG secret was instrumental in Pacifica's range of possible actions. On the other hand, protecting its secrecy was life or death for all of Pacifica. He would have to figure out a way to prepare Griff for all the possible alternatives while still keeping much from him. Griff was smart and much more intuitive than most gave him credit for. It was easy to think of him as a knuckle dragger. But that couldn't be further from the truth.

Del had been verbally sparing with Griff for two decades and enjoyed every minute of it. Thinking about their many tavern discussions, Del smiled, then grew reflective. The old world of Pacifica was nearing its end. Huge changes were in store for everyone.

Those changes would happen within his lifetime. As Del reflected on what had been a wonderful life, he prayed for his people's survival.

CHAPTER 4

KING KENNETH

It was much too early in the morning for an audience. But the governor's first minister had insisted. It was infuriating that he had to obey orders from a mere bureaucrat. He was the King of Liberty! It was especially aggravating given the youth of the first minister.

Kenneth had been crowned a year and a half earlier on the death of his father. He was in his early forties, with no remarkable attributes other than showing the effects of a gluttonous life. He was pudgy, with light hair and pale skin that looked as if it had rarely seen the sun. He spent his days and evenings scheming to solidify his control over Liberty and his nights engaged in his 'hobby.'

Kenneth thought his younger brother's objections to his 'hobby' exposed a character weakness. However, his bleeding-hearted brother's objections to changes proposed for the constitution was what caused the current crisis. He was the king and should be able to do anything he desired. The concept of personal rights taking precedence over royal desires infuriated him.

The governor's first minister was a tall, handsome, dark-haired man with pale skin and penetrating eyes. He seemed young for such an exalted position. He wore simple but formal clothing, tastefully adorned with understated but expensive jewelry. He casually wore an antique twentieth century Patek Phillippe watch that screamed wealth and influence. His eyes bored into Kenneth, demanding submission.

"We've backed you in your efforts to change the constitution and defeat your brothers' armies. Once you've eliminated him, we expect you to quickly deliver on your promises," the first minister said sternly.

When his brother had staged a popular revolt, Kenneth had turned to the Commonwealth for financial help. They were reminding him of his contractual promises. He needed to figure out how to slow that down or he would risk alienating support from the wealthy landowners and privately owned monopolies.

"I will deliver the imports and exports as promised, but need time to institute the changes we discussed," Kenneth said.

"It's pretty simple. You enslave the peasants living in areas that supported the revolution. Put them to work mining natural resources and producing exportable products. Drop all tariffs on imports. This combination will increase taxes on Liberty's trade to the levels agreed upon," the emissary patiently but firmly explained.

Kenneth knew this was true. It also increased the wealthy landowner's income, but not as much as they expected. It was going to be tricky keeping their support once they figured out that the bulk of the change in wealth distribution was going to go to Commonwealth taxes and his personal coffers. The effect of dropping import tariffs on local monopolies would be a disaster inviting dissent. However, with the landowner's support and control of the military, he could weather that storm.

He had panicked when his brother organized a popular revolt. That he had done so because of the proposed changes to the constitution surprised him. Why worry about a bunch of peasants? He initially assumed General Eastbrook would back his brother. They were friends, after all. That meant he would need an influx of Commonwealth credits to secure mercenaries if he hoped to survive.

To his utter shock and surprise, he had retained General Eastbrook's support. Eastbrook's support meant the bulk of the military stayed loyal. The General had remained to protect his "rightful king." What a joke that was. In Kenneth's opinion, whoever held power was king. It was as simple as that.

The general's misplaced loyalty to the oaths sworn to his father was irrational. It was definitely something to be used to Kenneth's advantage. When he was a teenager, his father had become concerned about Kenneth's fitness to be king. He had discovered Kenneth's 'hobby' and gotten a behavioral scientist from the university to do an analysis.

The university woman who spent a great deal of time talking with him eventually told his father he lacked empathy. She even went as far as to tell the king his eldest son was best described as a psychopath. His father, being the sap that he was, decided Kenneth just needed love and understanding. It was just a phase. It was pretty easy to manipulate his father once he learned what a psychopath was and how to emulate and use empathy to his advantage. Unfortunately, his younger brother never bought the act.

"Well, my brother hasn't been defeated yet. Let's discuss details once that's done," Kenneth said, attempting a delaying tactic to end the audience.

"The governor has done her part in securing the loan. Now it's time for you to do your part. She is starting to believe you're intentionally delaying. If delays continue, it won't be hard to convince a Commonwealth judge that you've violated your contract and issue an avoidance of taxes decision," the first minister said with a knowing smile. "As you know, the governor has a reputation for being quite aggressive in these cases. My personal belief is that she enjoys meriting out justice."

Kenneth's stomach clenched and a cold sweat greased his palms. The facade dropped for a moment, and he said nervously, "This will be over quickly. Taxes will be generated. You have my word."

"I don't want your word. I want you to do what you promised and do it quickly," the first minister said coldly. Then he insultingly turned and left without saying another word.

Kenneth sat for a few minutes, trying to figure out a way to escape the trap he was in. Realizing he was out of options, he decided he needed to take a walk and plan what to do. The delays were at an end and an aggressive plan needed to be executed quickly.

General William (Perry) Eastbrook was irritated, but you wouldn't know it by looking at him. He appeared to be relaxed and sitting patiently, waiting for his audience with the king. The king was late, and punctuality was somewhat of an obsession for Perry. His subordinates learned this quickly and joked quietly about it behind his back.

Perry was of average height, slender yet muscular. He had olive skin, black hair, and a hawkish face. He took great care with his physical conditioning and personal appearance. As the second son of a poor tenant farmer, his only opportunity in life was to join the military and hope for the best. A combination of intelligence, luck, hard work, and battlefield success had culminated in his appointment as general of the Royal Armed Forces. More than anyone else, he was responsible for Liberty being under one government. After decades of perpetual war, he succeeded in conquering the despotic kingdoms that had opposed his king. He had united the planet. He could have declared himself king at that point. He was wildly popular not only with his compatriots, but also with the populations that had been suffering under oppressive governments.

A student of history, he emulated Alexander the Great's habit of recruiting his defeated enemies instead of punishing or imprisoning them. He had been successful in wooing them into his fold by treating them more honorably than their former kingdoms had. His answer to calls for him to take the crown was, "I am a simple soldier and have sworn an oath to my rightful king."

Everyone called him Perry. It was short for 'The Peregrine.' Prince Justin, the king's younger brother, had named him this after Perry saved the young, confused, and scared prince's first command from disaster. Prince Justin was an avid falconer and said the soldier reminded him of the lightning quick vicious strikes of a peregrine falcon. Perry had taken charge of the unit in the midst of chaos. He did this without having been given the authority to do so.

He opened up a retreat path with a series of precise attacks against weak points in the encircling armies' lines. Many of royal blood would have been insulted. Many would have denied they needed a common born soldier to extricate them from their mistakes. Prince Justin was an honorable man and gave Perry his well-deserved accolades. He then became his sponsor and vocal supporter, helping to move him up the ranks. The name stuck, much to his embarrassment.

The royal receptionist came over politely and said, "The king will see you now, General Eastbrook."

Perry handed his weapons over to the two guards standing to either side of an impressive set of double doors. He walked in and nodded briefly to the four guards inside the reception room. Two were just inside of the doors and two were situated to either side of the king. They were six of his best. He hated seeing them used as guards. But given his personal opinion of the king he needed to have eyes and ears close by. They must be dying from boredom he thought. Perry saluted and then stood with his hands clasped behind his back and said, "you requested my presence Your Majesty."

"It's time, Perry. Storm the castle and end this thing," the king said forcefully.

What's changed thought Perry. He could have ended this months ago. It was getting harder and harder to explain to his troops why they were just sitting around. Not that he minded giving Prince Justin more time. It bothered him deeply to be pressed into this duty, but duty it was. The prince was a longtime sponsor, friend, and a good man. But oaths took precedence over friendship. Oaths also took precedence over his conviction that the prince would make a much better king than this one.

"If we can promise safe exile for the families of the rebels, I believe I can end this without bloodshed," Perry responded.

"Why should I care about the families of those who have forsaken their rightful king?" Kenneth answered with a sneer.

"Because a castle siege, even a quick one, is a bloody affair and we need those troops to defend against Arista should they decide we are ripe for invasion," Perry responded. He had thought about his answer to this ever since they surrounded the castle. He knew the king would not be swayed by non-combatant arguments, even children. It had to be something that benefited him.

Kenneth hesitated to think it over, then said, "Give my brother assurances the rebel families will be spared if they surrender without delay. The families will be exiled to safe locations."

"I will execute that immediately, Your Majesty," Perry said. He saluted and backed out of the room.

Instead of leaving the royal apartments, he turned into the corridor leading to the crown princess's suite. He nodded at the salutes of the guards stationed outside her door and the second set of guards located just inside before he heard. "Dad, I didn't know you were coming." A beautiful young woman ran up and leapt into his arms, embracing him tightly. A single tear ran down her face, which she quickly wiped away, smiling broadly.

"It was a last-minute summons by the king. Sorry, Bria, but a note wouldn't have beaten me here," Perry said, smiling as another young woman looking remarkably like Bria walked up.

"Your Highness," Perry said as he bowed and then straightening up, he grinned.

"Oh stop, Uncle Perry," she said with an affected grimace that couldn't keep from turning into a smile. "I know you have to do that in public, but not here," she admonished him. Olivia had known Bria and her father as long as she could remember. When she was a toddler, she had heard the Guards refer to him as Perry and believed he was one of her uncles. As a toddler, she had called him Uncle Perry in front of the entire royal court to uproarious laughter. It became an endearment.

"You both look wonderful, a sight for sore eyes." Perry shook his head and remarked, "The two of you look like twins. Are you ever going to stop copying each other?"

"No," they both said simultaneously and then looked at each other and broke into giggles.

They were of a similar height, slender with pale skin, blue eyes, and black hair pulled on top of their heads. Even the combs holding their hair up matched. If you looked closely, Olivia had a softer, slightly less athletic look about her. But they definitely looked like siblings. Those who didn't know them often confused them, to their delight.

Although their physical appearance was uncannily similar, their personalities were not. Princess Olivia was a queen in the making. Intelligent, decisive, outspoken, and tough-minded when needed. Bria was also intelligent, but quiet, introspective, and soft-spoken. They both agreed Bria was actually the more stubborn of the two.

"Are you planning the wedding?" Perry asked.

This elicited frowns from both of them, with Olivia saying, "Yes, but I'm not happy about it. Lord Druango is twice my age, fat, grumpy, with no sense of humor. He's a cruel man. I know I have to marry to solidify the crown, but couldn't he have found someone a bit more suitable?"

"I'm sure he did the best he could, Olivia," Perry said.

"Uncle Perry, please don't mouth politically appropriate nonsense to me. He could not care less for my well-being, and you know it," Olivia said bluntly.

Lord Druango was extremely rich and the power behind the previous Kingdom of Druango. The actual King of Druango had been a pawn. He had been assassinated by 'unknown assailants' in the final days before Perry had marched into their capital city. It was well known who ordered his assassination, but without evidence, there was little that could be done.

The engagement was a good move politically and financially, but at what cost? Perry knew part of the reason Olivia and Bria copied each other was their fantasy of being sisters. The fantasy included having him as their father. It was humbling, to say the least. It added an extra layer of loyalty and commitment even beyond his unbreakable oath. She was the eventual Queen of Liberty. "He's your father, and you need to respect him. I'm sorry you have to do this for the crown. You know Bria and I will always be here for you."

This last promise was politically important. Lord Druango would try and take control when the current king died. Perry was the one man who could stop that and maintain Olivia's authority over the realm.

Olivia's mother had died under suspicious circumstances. Getting no love or support from her father, she begged him to go live with Uncle Perry and Bria. His reaction was to order the pre-teenage Bria to move into Hastings Castle as a companion for Olivia. The one concession Perry had gotten in return was to have them both at his ranch during the summers. This eliminated time the king was expected to spend with his daughter and provided a hostage against the good behavior of General Eastbrook when the House of Lords was in session. A win-win in his mind.

"Let's be honest with each other no matter what," Olivia said with warmth in her eyes. She then turned serious and asked, "Will the siege be over soon?"

"That's why I'm here. I'm going to go and attempt to negotiate a surrender with your uncle. If that's not possible, I'll have to take his castle," Perry said.

"Is there any way to save Uncle Justin?" Olivia said in a pleading voice.

"I'm sorry, but there isn't. He rebelled against the rightful ruler of Liberty and his fate is sealed. Your aunt and cousins will be saved if he agrees to surrender. You know your uncle; he will sacrifice himself to protect them and prevent unnecessary bloodshed. He's a good man, but there isn't anything that can be done."

They spent the next few hours discussing family, friends, and the wedding plans. Bria would be Olivia's maid of honor and had agreed to be her official companion until Bria married. While more than a little jealous, Olivia was pleased that Bria could marry whomever she wanted. She knew her Uncle Perry could gain monetary benefits from an arranged marriage, but insisted his daughter's happiness came first. Olivia was dwelling on this when Perry said, "I'm sorry, but I'd be derelict if I didn't leave now. The king insisted I get a surrender negotiated as soon as possible. Have loved seeing you both and will see you again as soon as this is over."

"Please tell Uncle Justin that I love him," Olivia said in a sad voice. Perry frowned but nodded his agreement.

Both young women hugged him fiercely and, with their eyes shining, Perry said his goodbyes, turned, and left.

As he left Hastings Castle, Perry mused on the possible reasons for the abrupt change. He was missing something. He wondered if it had anything to do with the Commonwealth dandy he saw in the hallway that morning. It would not be surprising if the Commonwealth were playing politics with the king. Their only objective was higher taxes and Perry worried about what agreements might have been made. If there was one thing Perry was good at, it was compartmentalizing problems until something could be done about them. He decided to quit worrying about this sudden change and rode off toward Prince Justin's castle.

CHAPTER 5

OATH GIVER

Griff strolled into Del's office and plopped down in one of the chairs facing his desk. The man swaggers everywhere he goes, thought Del. If anything, the stern expression he wore the last time he saw him had intensified. Griff glared at Del and said, "Since you asked me to come see you, I assume you have something to tell me."

Del swallowed the smart-ass response normal for their interactions and said, "It's conditional. I have some things to discuss but only if you agree to join a group simply known as the Committee. Once you join, you can't leave. It's a lifetime commitment."

"What kind of nonsense is this? I want to know what's going on with Tee and I expect you to tell me," Griff said forcefully, leaning forward in a threatening way.

"You're not going to learn anything unless you agree. This is for the good of Pacifica. No amount of bullying is going to get me to open up. I promise you'll agree with the necessity for secrecy once you understand what we're doing. To do that, you must join and agree to follow all rules and restrictions," Del said equally forcefully.

"What are the rules and restrictions?" Griff asked.

"I won't tell you anything until you agree to join and pledge an oath to comply. The rules and restrictions pertain to information that can't be divulged to anyone not a member of the Committee," Del said.

Griff just looked at him for a while, clearly mulling it over. Then his frown deepened, and he said, "So I have to give you my oath to keep something secret for the rest of my life without knowing anything about it beforehand."

"Yes," Del answered.

"If I join the committee and swear an oath, will you tell me what happened to Tee?" Griff said with eyes boring into Del's.

"Yes," Del answered quickly. Then a moment later he said, "And I should not have told you that."

Griff took a deep breath, grimaced, and said, "If I didn't know you as well as I do, I would never agree to these ridiculous conditions. This had better be good, or you and I are going to have a problem."

Del smiled for the first time and said, "I think you'll be satisfied with the reasons behind the need for secrecy. Do I have your agreement to join and your oath to abide by the rules and restrictions?"

Griff's frown disappeared. He visibly relaxed, clearly accepting the situation. He took a deep breath, held up his hand mockingly and said, "I swear to join the Committee and abide by its rules and restrictions. Now what the hell is going on."

Del stood up and walked to his office door. He locked it. Turning back around, he walked to a large wooden filing cabinet built into the wall. Unlocking and opening one of the bottom drawers, he reached in and fiddled with something until Griff heard a loud click. Del then rotated the entire cabinet away from the wall, revealing a hidden stairway. He lit a lamp and beckoned Griff with a wave of his hand before disappearing down the stairs into the dark.

"Pull that closed on your way down," Del called out.

Griff stepped through the doorway, peered into the darkness suspiciously, then shrugged his shoulders and closed the hidden door. A loud click let him know it was latched. He caught up with Del in a narrow hallway at the base of the stairs. "Where are we going?" he asked.

"Afraid of the dark?" Del responded, attempting to revive their usual banter.

"No," Griff replied. "If I'm going to murder someone for irritating me, I prefer to do it in the dark."

Del smiled, glad to hear his old friend sound like himself again. "We're headed to a secret complex of tunnels below the caves that everyone knows about. I'll explain more once we enter. While we are unlikely to be overheard down here, we take extreme precautions outside of that space."

They followed a downward sloping tunnel, which had a half dozen side tunnels randomly feeding into it. After a five-minute walk, the tunnel ended at a metal door that looked like the opening to a bank vault. Del took out a large key and opened the door, which swung out and away from the opening. Ten feet away was an identical door. After they stepped through, Del closed and locked the door behind him. Then he said, "When I open the next door you're going to see things you'll have a hard time believing. Once we lock that one behind us, I'll start answering your questions."

Del opened the second door, and the small metal room was filled with light. Griff could hear a low humming noise and feel warm air filtering in through the doorway. Stepping out into the room, Griff looked around in speechless wonder. The illumination was from some source other than open flame and was quite bright, daylight bright. Devices that looked like the computers in ancient children's books were glowing and had pictures and images on them. Del caught the attention of a young man who was seated at one of these stations. Griff recognized him as the kid who got punched on the Apple Valley school playground.

"Quinn, this is Griff. He's a new member of the Committee. If he has questions for you in the future, you are free to answer them just like you would any other Committee member," Del said.

Turning back to Griff he added, "Quinn is one of five engineering specialists privy to much of what I'm going to tell you. You'll want to spend some time with him after we're done."

"You're the Guard member who invited Tee to recruit training," Quinn said, smiling broadly.

"Do you know what happened to him?" Griff asked sternly.

Del held up his hands and said, "Patience Griff, there is a lot of background information you need before you can understand the situation. The short summary is that Tee is alive, unharmed, and relatively safe. He is a prisoner, and unfortunately we don't have a way to rescue him. Come into the conference room and let me sketch out what's going on."

When they sat down, Griff said accusingly, "We clearly didn't lose our technology."

"Not all of it, no. But before you ask why we aren't using it against the GEMs, you need to hear the whole story. The short answer is that if we reveal our technology, we all die." Del went on to explain how they had accidentally learned of the Commonwealth and the dangers of revealing themselves. Griff was shocked, and a bit shaken to learn Pacifica natives were actually GEMs themselves. That he was a GEM. When Del got to the part where the Committee might decide that everyone had to commit suicide, he just nodded his agreement. That's when Del knew Griff really understood the dire situation they were in. Once again, he was impressed with Griff. The man had absorbed the shocking news much faster than Del had those many years ago. Del went on to explain how Pacifica's ability to delay interacting with the Commonwealth was coming to a close.

"So, we need a plan to roll out second generation warfare. That's the purpose of my being added to the Committee," Griff said.

Del gave a sigh and said, "It goes way beyond that, Griff. We need more diversity on the Committee. We obviously have to keep the number of members to a minimum, but in doing so we have the risk of limited perspective. We are likely to miss something important when making decisions. You will be expected to weigh in on every issue that comes up. You were selected because of your intelligence, leadership, creativity, and ability to work in a team. It's not just because you are a professional soldier."

Griff considered this and then, changing the subject, asked, "So what happened to Tee?"

"Arista kidnapped him for their gladiatorial games. He's a slave. Based on intercepted communications, we believe a sizable bribe was used to get approval from the Commonwealth to do this. Our civilization is designated as a primitive culture. We're supposed to be left alone. We don't understand if this was even legal by Commonwealth law. The best case is that Pacifica gets accepted as a colony and we successfully challenge the legality of Tee's slave status. Unfortunately, because of the dangers involved, neither of us will be around to celebrate," Del said.

"So, we'll never see him again," Griff said.

"Unlikely either of us will. It's possible his family could get him back at some point," Del said. "The reason Pacifica is out of options is that the GEMs have run out of room. Their high reproduction rate has outstripped their food production. They are highly motivated to expand into the peninsula. The crisis is causing them to cooperate, which is why so many more GEMs were involved in the latest attack. The opinion of the Commonwealth survey ship orbiting Pacifica is that they will overwhelm our defenses sometime in the next two years. You know better than I how close we came to losing the Wall this last time.

"Once the Wall is breached, it won't take long until the Landfall Dam is threatened. The Committee has always thought that is when we pull out second-generation weapons to defend ourselves. Now that you are on the Committee we'll look to you for advice on timing and execution. Once we use that technology, the Commonwealth will take over. The good news is they will eliminate the GEMs. The bad news is that if we aren't incredibly lucky, everyone on Pacifica will be enslaved or killed."

"Pacifica has an abundance of natural resources. The Commonwealth wants to legally convert us from being designated as a primitive culture to a Commonwealth colony. Since we are adapted to heavy planet activities, there is motivation to enslave rather than kill. There is also speculation of turning the Guard into slave mercenaries. Turns out they believe we have the most effective warriors in the Commonwealth."

Griff considered this for a while, then he asked, "What technologies do we have access to?"

Del nodded, grinned, and then said, "We have the entire set of logs and libraries from the colony ships. It is a tremendous resource of technical information and know-how. We believe some of what we have is now banned technology. Even Commonwealth citizens don't have access to it. What we don't have is most of the technology itself. This set of rooms is contained in a structure called a faraday cage. It keeps all electrical signals from detection by the Commonwealth. The electronic equipment we have consists of a variety of radios and computer systems. This was put together just before the Colony War.

"Obviously, we were suspicious of the GEMs intentions before they attacked. We stockpiled backup systems, spare parts, and even printed service manuals for critical systems. Below us is an underground river we use to drive an electric generator that runs what you saw in the other room. We also have a fully provisioned computer operated machine shop to service and repair critical elements. We can make damn near anything with that equipment. All of these areas are shielded."

"Okay, what weapons do I have access to?" Griff asked.

"There is a planetary defense system in mothballs. But there is no way we could install and activate it. Even if we could, these systems were designed to be used in concert with space-based warships. The Commonwealth knows how to defeat these types of defensive systems, so trying to employ one would just be a form of delayed suicide. There are two space shuttles in storage as well. As far as we can tell, they both work. At least they pass their diagnostics. But until we try and use them, who knows? We can't use any high-level technology because the

Commonwealth will see that as tax evasion. Our designation as a primitive culture is basically a tax exemption for the sector. It is illegal to hide technological sophistication in an attempt to stay in a primitive state under their Edicts.

"It's even worse if we are discovered to have second-generation or later weapons of any kind. In that case, the Commonwealth would consider us to be in rebellion. Either of these situations would authorize sector government to assume control of the planet and enslave or kill the population. So, we have to 'invent' second-generation weapons in a way that is believable. And we have to destroy everything else," Del said.

"You've obviously thought about all of this, so where do I start?" Griff asked.

"Black powder. We have all the raw materials and the formula for making it. Producing guns would make it obvious have been hiding technological advances. Some sort of weapon that drops bombs in front of the Wall is an idea. Burying bombs in the sand and detonating them from the Wall is another," Del said.

"How are we going to explain black powder suddenly showing up?" Griff asked.

"A little luck has helped us there. A farmer discovered black powder by accident a decade ago. He developed it to the point where he was entertaining his family and neighbors with crude explosions. The Committee decided to buy his silence and move the discovery to the university. We intercepted communications indicating the Commonwealth detected the gunpowder. They decided that since we haven't used it for anything other than entertainment we're still below the threshold for conversion to a colony. Our story is that we hid it because we were worried about public safety. When the GEMs looked like they would overwhelm us we realized it could be used as a weapon," Del said.

Griff nodded his head thoughtfully and said, "how do we test our ideas without the Commonwealth sensing the explosions?"

"It doesn't have to work all that well. The intent is enough. Our goal is to demonstrate second-generation weapons capabilities. Once we do that, the Commonwealth will take over. We have an extensive library that includes detailed instructions for weapons manufacture from simple chemical weapons to fission, fusion, and anti-matter devices. Of course, we don't have the refined materials for the latter three, so that information is rather useless. We are confident of building something that will work." Del paused, and then said, "You can ask Quinn questions, but I'll assign one of the other students to work with you on this. Keep in mind we're looking for ideas. We must save the people of Pacifica, and perhaps there is another way."

Del got up and motioned Griff to follow him. "Let's take a break and go have a little fun."

"There isn't anything remotely fun about any of this," Griff said seriously.

Del just kept walking and turned down a corridor, which ended with another locked door. He produced yet another key from his pocket, unlocked and opened the door. "This is our advanced weapons arsenal and lab," Del said as he swept his hand around the room.

Griff was dumbstruck trying to take it all in. Along the back wall of the room was a rack of approximately one hundred devices. They had stocks and triggers like a crossbow with two round tubes aligned with where an arrow would be placed on that device. The other end of the room was clearly a firing range with silhouette targets and of all things a pumpkin on a stand. Motioning over at the racks of devices, Griff said, "What comes out of the tubes?"

"The bottom tube is a battery. That's an energy storage device. The top is the discharge tube. By the way, part of our historical cleansing was to confiscate all the adult level books describing technology. We left the children's books so that it would be less shocking if and when we trotted all this out. It was a nice story that paper books were only printed for children." Del then picked up one of the devices and continued, "This was originally a bunker built in anticipation of the Colony War. It's the only thing that survived. These weapons were for defending the bunker. It's an energy weapon. Three settings. Safe, kill, and stun," he said as he pointed to a switch clearly marked with these designations.

"When kill is activated, it will burn a hole completely through clothing and flesh, but not metal. Evidently these models were for use aboard spacecraft. You can imagine the problems with weapons aboard a spacecraft. We have plans for altering these to basically burn through anything. Not currently a high priority for us."

Del flipped the switch to kill, turned, aimed, and burned a hole right through the chest area on one of the cloth silhouette targets. Motioning Griff forward, they inspected the cherry sized hole in the cloth and the slightly blemished metal plate behind it.

"Why don't you take a few shots?" Del said, grinning like a teenage boy.

Griff smiled and accepted the offer, then blasted away for a while. At Del's suggestion, he shot the pumpkin, which not only drilled a hole but caused the pumpkin to emit smoke from the burning skin and pulp inside. Smiling broadly, he said, "That's incredible. And you're right, it's fun." He thought about this for a few moments and started asking questions. "How many shots can it fire?"

Del nodded and said, "Ninety to one hundred and then it needs to be recharged. The recharge currently takes almost a day. We have schematics for a fast charger. But it involves changes to our power grid that would be quite a bit of work. Another thing low on the priority list."

"How do you know how well it works on flesh?" Griff asked with concern.

"We didn't use it on people, if that's what you're asking," Del said with his face scrunched up in mock disgust. Smiling, he then said, "We've taken haunches of beef and drilled holes through them. Doesn't seem to matter how thick the haunch is. The hole goes all the way through."

"Tell me about the stun setting," Griff said.

"The stun setting was initially a little more challenging to test from an ethical standpoint. One of our university students long ago decided to volunteer. He reported that it was just like falling asleep. No pain, no apparent aftereffects at all. The literature on it says it immediately forces the brain into a delta wave pattern, or deep sleep. It maintains this pattern for one to three hours. The person doesn't feel pain and cannot be woken up. Dr. Espers is very enthusiastic about using it for general anesthesia. The brain eventually transitions through the normal brain wave functions you would expect from someone going from deep sleep to wakefulness. The test subject said it just feels like a good nap," Del concluded.

"How accurately does it need to be aimed? How selective is it?" Griff asked.

"That turns out to be a complicated question and one we did extensive testing to figure out. Once we were certain there weren't negative side effects, we gathered more volunteers. It seems to be a function of the field strength of the wave when it encounters the subject. Quinn can give you the details. To give you an idea, if the end of this room were filled with people, one shot would put them all asleep. In the stun setting, you only get twenty to twenty-five shots."

Griff grew serious at this point, obviously thinking it all through. He then looked to have reached a decision and said forcefully, "I will honor my oath and comply with decisions made by the Committee. We share the same primary goal of protecting our people, but my objective is victory. I don't plan on losing to the Commonwealth."

Del just nodded, showing his understanding, and decided he had made the right choice. A few moments later, he added, "You should have a high-level understanding of our technology knowledge base and sector history as we understand it. This is going to take some time to digest. I'll leave you with Quinn to start that process and see you at the next committee meeting."

As he walked away he thought, we have the same end goal, old friend. I don't know how we pull off the herculean task of beating the Commonwealth. But it doesn't mean we shouldn't try. We will likely go down, but like you, I want to go down swinging.

CHAPTER 6

THE GOVERNOR

The first minister was always nervous meeting with the governor. It wasn't the power of her office that caused his anxiety. He was used to interacting with the great and powerful in the Commonwealth. He was one of them, after all. It was the way she looked at him. She was cat-like. Her pitiless stare didn't give any indication of whether she was preparing to pounce or would just swish her tail and walk away. Her unusual appearance made her behavior even more disturbing. She had stark white hair cut short with mismatched eyes. One blue and one green. She had a trim figure with perfectly smooth bronze colored skin. Most people thought she was extremely attractive. These were people who didn't know her.

"Good afternoon, Jack. I hope you have good news for me," Governor Jacobs said, locking him with her cat eyes and sly smile.

"Good afternoon, Governor. We have a commitment from King Kenneth to finish his brother off. However, he's still arguing to delay the changes needed to increase tax revenues. He's on notice that further delays will result in a request for a tax avoidance judgement," Jack said with his hands clenched tightly together behind his back.

The governor just stared at him, not indicating pleasure or anger at his report. Finally, after an uncomfortable amount of time, she said, "Our goal is getting the legal authority in Liberty to change the constitution. Punishment of the rebels will allow him to get 'emergency changes' through a diminished House of Lords. Once fully implemented, we can move forward with the proposal from Magistrate Pluta. Anything that stops constitutional change destroys the plan. I hope you have everything in place to insure nothing unfortunate happens."

Jack had to collect himself before answering. He was very good at keeping emotions off his face. But he felt she could see right through that and was enjoying his discomfort. "The key lords have signed taxation contracts in exchange for their votes. As promised, they have used their advances to fund mercenaries who are ready for the final military phase."

"Will the mercenaries be able to force a quick marriage so that Lord Druango can eventually take control of the planet?" she asked.

"That's the plan. King Kenneth has no ethics, morals, or loyalties. He is a psychopath and megalomaniac who lacks good judgement. His ego is so out of control that he doesn't see the threat in Lord Druango. If nothing else, this is proof we can't depend on him. We can't even depend on him to make the right decisions in his own self-interest. Druango promises King Kenneth will have an accident soon after the wedding," Jack said.

"Any indications that Druango is going to change his mind with respect to the slave trade?" she asked.

"He has remained consistent with what he wants. I think we can count on him as long as he gets his cut of the revenues as proposed by Magistrate Pluta."

The governor nodded, accepting his explanation and then said, "Does our friend in Arista have control of the emperor?"

"He says he does, but I have reason to doubt that. While Pluta is the current magistrate for the Senate, there is a younger, aggressive senator who appears to be chipping away at his influence. They are both entirely motivated by money. We can probably come to an agreement with either one," Jack said.

"Have you spoken with this young senator?" the governor asked, her eyes narrowing.

"I met Senator Cereo at a party he held in his Roma Domus just last month," Jack said. "He's very charismatic. He's clearly the leader of the 'new money' senators and is slowly expanding his influence with 'old money' votes."

"That's unusual, isn't it? I thought Arista was quite stogy in their belief of old order superiority," she said with an expression on her face that indicated she didn't believe him.

"I learned at the party that he's descended from one of the original senatorial families. He's actually distantly related to the emperor. His parents squandered the family fortune and went bankrupt. He started with nothing and is now the richest man in Arista. Or soon will be. He does get insulted in private for 'dirtying his hands' by the old order senators, but it's more a respectful jibe. He is highly respected for turning around his families' fortunes. The old order sees him as proving their theory of superiority while the 'new money' senators believe he is one of their own, having come up the hard way," Jack said.

"Young and aggressive sounds better than old and stogy. Why don't we prefer to work with him?" the governor asked.

"The difficulty is we can't predict who the emperor will listen to. As you know, all real power in Arista rests in the emperor's hands. The Senate's authority stops at managing the planet. They can propose actions and decrees, but the emperor must approve them. They can't negotiate treaties or declare war. The current emperor is gluttonous, lazy, and prone to making arbitrary decisions. He's too entitled for us to work directly with him. All he really cares about are blood sports and pleasure slaves. Both senators keep their own stable of gladiators because it gives them audience time with the emperor," Jack explained.

"While we're on that subject, were our friends successful in capturing one of those Pacifica brutes for the magistrate?" the governor asked.

"Yes, they did. As you know, Pacifica is extremely remote. It will take time to execute the large number of jumps to get back to Arista," Jack replied. He thought for a moment and then said, "You might get a complaint from Sector Judicial. The first justice was not comfortable approving this, even after the outrageous bribe. Their hands have been well greased, so no one should have anything to complain about. Their excuse of indigenous research is inspired but weak. Given similar cases I'm familiar with, they will merely get their hands slapped if they get caught."

"Sector Judicial are a bunch of whiny assholes. It's no surprise they take the credits and then complain," the governor said with disdain. "So, Magistrate Pluta's excuse for requesting the kidnapping was access to the emperor?"

"Yes, but I'm pretty sure it wasn't the only reason. The senator also enjoys his blood sports a little too much," Jack said.

"You don't approve?" she said, narrowing her eyes and examining him.

"I don't approve of anyone we are depending on having distractions," Jack said.

The governor considered his answer, then slowly nodded and asked,

"Any other weaknesses to exploit?"

"He enjoys driving aristocrats who don't work hard or fall on bad luck into bankruptcy. Appears to be a hobby of sorts. If having a significant number of impoverished formerly wealthy individuals hating your guts is a weakness, then we can put it on the list," Jack explained.

"At least he's shown himself to be a clever negotiator. Let's make sure he doesn't get too clever," the governor said with an amused smile. "Keep me updated on Liberty and Arista."

"Yes, ma'am," Jack said, then turned and walked out of her office, relieved for the audience to be over. He had been unsettled with the plan from the beginning. Jack liked plans to be simple. In his opinion, a good plan relied on as few people as possible. All with a history of being predictable. Jack would be losing sleep until large shipments of slaves were actually leaving Liberty.

CHAPTER 7

SURRENDER

Why did he have to smile, thought Perry. The prince greeted him warmly, treating him as an honored guest and friend. Perry already felt terrible about doing this. An angry, accusatory posture would be much more appropriate and easier to handle.

"You look well, Perry," the prince said. "Although that frown you're wearing doesn't go well with your face."

"This isn't pleasant and you're making it harder than it already is," Perry responded with a hint of anger.

"Let's enjoy each other's company one more time, my friend. We both know this will be over soon," the prince said with a sad smile. "Tell me how Bria is doing." He said this with his trademark devilish smile, brightening a bit.

Perry remembered once again why he liked and admired this man. No matter the circumstances, no matter the station of the person, he was almost always gracious and thoughtful. So different from his brother. The prince did have a temper. He could be a devil when he thought someone was being unfair or treating others badly. They had argued when the prince had proposed deposing the king. He vividly remembered the conversation.

"My brother has a serious mental illness, Perry. He's unfit to rule. My father was deceived as to his true nature, or he would have passed over him," the prince had said.

"I swore an oath to support the succession and be loyal to the king in all regards," Perry said. "I cannot support you becoming king."

"I'm not asking you to make me king. My niece is not her father. Bria is Olivia's best friend, for heaven's sake. You know her better than I do. You know she would be an excellent ruler."

"I've sworn an oath," was all Perry would say further on the matter.

Back in the present, Perry hesitated a bit and then said in a business-like tone, "Both Bria and Olivia are fine. Olivia told me to tell you she loves you. They are both worried about you, but mature enough to understand the situation. I'm here with an offer. You surrender and the families will be spared. They will be separated and exiled to locations that will be determined later. They will be safe, and they won't be impoverished."

"Did my brother promise this?" the prince responded.

"Yes," said Perry.

"This is obviously your idea. You know his word is meaningless."

"I will die to protect the families. You have my word," Perry said.

"Now that is something I can count on," the prince said in a serious tone. "Give us this evening to spend with our families and I'll surrender at noon tomorrow. I do this based on your personal honor and nothing else, Perry."

Perry always woke two hours before dawn. This was his time to attack thorny problems, work on battle strategies, time to think without interruption. It was the best time of his day. This morning was not pleasant. Going through the motions of surrender would be easy enough. But putting the prince and old friends in chains was going to test his resolve. Many of the rebellious officers were previously trusted advisors to whom he owed a large debt of gratitude.

But what was on his mind this morning was Lord Barrows. The lord had shown up the day before with a sealed order authorizing him to accept the surrender on the king's behalf. That didn't set off alarms, but the special guard squad sent to escort him did. It wasn't a concern that the king's representative had a guard detail to protect him. It was that Perry didn't recognize any of the soldiers. Perry had a remarkable ability to remember names and faces. He had never seen any of these men before.

He called out, "Corporal, go get Captain Peters for me."

"He's likely still asleep, General," the corporal responded.

"Wake him up. I need him here as soon as he's presentable."

A few minutes later, a young, groggy, and rumpled officer showed up, saluted, and said, "Peters, here as ordered, sir."

Perry looked him over, nodding in approval at Peters's decision to forgo appearance for speed, and said, "Peters, I have a special assignment for you this morning."

Perry walked out of his tent ten minutes before the surrender was scheduled to begin. He would be five minutes early per his long-maintained habit of punctuality. As he walked out, Captain Peters and four burly veteran soldiers formed up in a protective diamond formation around him. Anyone in the Royal Armed Forces seeing this would be surprised since Perry never used bodyguards. His sword and knives were not decorative.

As they walked toward the castle gates, Perry asked Captain Peters in a low voice, "Is everything in place?"

"Yes, sir," he replied.

Perry grunted an acknowledgement, but said no more.

A large tent had been erected just in front of the castle gates to hold the formal surrender proceedings. The formal declaration of surrender had been sent the previous evening for the prince's review. This wasn't a negotiation; it was a courteous gesture by Perry so Prince Justin would know beforehand what was required of him.

Lord Barrows was incensed the previous evening when he found out. He had barged into Perry's command tent, interrupting a staff discussion, and declared, "You have no authority to write or deliver the surrender contract. That duty was given to me by the king."

Perry calmly continued the discussion he was having with one of his staff members, ignoring him. When the conversation ended, he slowly turned and stared at Lord Barrows until Lord Barrows looked away.

Then Perry said, "This is a military operation. Until the surrender is formally accepted, I am in charge. I have always written and delivered surrender agreements. In the past, I also accepted surrenders on behalf of the king. The king's orders stated you were to accept surrender on his behalf. Nothing else."

"I don't agree with the terms of surrender you offered that traitor," Lord Barrows said, looking down his nose at Perry.

"The king gave me the terms of surrender personally and asked me to negotiate on his behalf. You have no authority to change my previous orders. I was directed to complete this surrender as soon as possible, and that is what I'm going to do," Perry said firmly.

"You will answer to the king for this," Lord Barrows shouted as he turned around and walked out.

"As will you, Lord Barrows," Perry said quietly as the tent flaps swung back in place.

One of strengths of Perry's army was its surveillance capabilities. He had agents embedded everywhere. Perry had recognized the value of surveillance early in the Unification Wars. The competing kingdoms were both corrupt. That made it easy to bribe or pay retainers for information. He learned that you never knew where key strategic information would come from. The more informants, the better. Of course, this meant he had more opportunities for double agents. But as long as you treated all of them as double agents, useful information could be deciphered and corroborated.

Lord Barrows had one of Perry's agents on his personal staff. He had copied the lord's surrender document and passed it over. The terms of surrender were quite different from what had been sent to Prince Justin. It was cleverly worded. Without time to work through the language at the surrender table, Prince Justin could easily have misunderstood the agreement to be promising safety for the families of the rebels. In reality, it was an unconditional surrender with no concrete promises. This was contrary to what Perry had negotiated, and he would not allow it.

Perry and Lord Barrows stood next to the open-air tent as the castle gate opened and Prince Justin, with two retainers, walked out. Perry was the first to greet them. "Good morning, Your Highness."

To which Lord Barrows said forcefully, "He's not a prince anymore, the king removed his title."

Prince Justin ignored this and said, "Good morning General Eastbrook, Lord Barrows."

He's a better man than I am, thought Perry. Even in these circumstances, he maintains perfect decorum. Perry then said, "Let's review the terms and process steps of surrender and I'll answer any questions you have."

"Thank you, General Eastbrook, for sending the surrender document last night. It matches our discussion, and I have no questions." With that, Prince Justin motioned one of his retainers to hand over the document sent the previous evening. He took a deep breath and signed it with a flourish. His whole body visibly relaxed at that point, seemingly accepting his fate. Prince Justin then motioned to his other retainer, who made a hand signal back to the castle.

The main gate opened, and the rebels streamed out of the castle in a single file. The officers came last. Most were familiar to Perry, as he had fought alongside them in many battles. A few brought a grim, painful smile to his face. They handed in their weapons at a table set up for this purpose and then walked to another table for processing. Political leaders and officers were separated, as they would be put on trial. They expected to be hung, but accepted this fate as payment for their family's safety. Everyone else was to be let go after swearing allegiance to the king.

When the stream of rebels stopped coming from the castle, Perry sent in a squad to search for anyone hidden away. After a few hours, it was declared to be populated entirely by non-combatants. This was a testament to the trust the rebels had in Prince Justin.

Perry turned to Lord Barrows and said, "I'm satisfied that all terms of surrender have been met. You can sign for the king now."

Lord Barrows smiled and turning to Prince Justin he said, "The surrender contract you signed is null and void. I require your signature on the official one authorized by the king."

Perry said, "This is not my understanding based on discussions with the king. I will not support this."

Lord Barrows smiled even wider, turning to his Captain of the Guard and said, "Arrest General Eastbrook. He is charged with treason and will be delivered to the king for judgement along with the others."

Upon that pronouncement, one of the servants attending them drove a large knife into Lord Barrows's Captain of the Guard. The rest of Lord Barrows's men within the surrender tent were quickly overwhelmed by more of Peters's men who were also donning servant's garb. The mercenaries outside the tent were quickly cut down in a barrage of arrows.

Lord Barrows was in shock. "You can't do this. I have the authority of the king."

Perry looked at him confidently and said, "At this point, you have no authority. You're going to tell me exactly what the king told you to do."

Although full of bluster, Lord Barrows wasn't dedicated to anything other than himself. It didn't take much persuasion for self-preservation to take over. He spilled his guts while begging for mercy. The most immediate problem was an army of mercenaries on its way to take over operations. They had orders to slaughter the rebels and their families. Even the children. They were primarily off-world mercenaries, with a few from Druango. That region had a longstanding reputation for brutality. The lord of that region was Princess Olivia's fiancée. Now that Perry knew the plan, it was a simple thing to occupy the castle and eliminate the threat.

Perry walked back to join Prince Justin, sat down, and signed the surrender document.

"What are you going to do?" Prince Justin asked, a smile now on his face.

"I'm going to go have a discussion with the king," Perry responded. Turning, he beckoned his second in command over. "Colonel Fedral, you are in command. Prince Justin is under your protection and will comply with orders spelled out under the surrender agreement. You will occupy the castle and deny access to the mercenaries, who will arrive shortly. This includes the authority to arm any rebels who swear to follow your orders, and you feel are necessary to execute those orders. If opportunity presents itself, you can use your judgement and go on the offensive against the mercenaries. You are not to follow anyone's orders other than those I give you personally."

Colonel Fedral turned to Prince Justin and said, "Your Highness, will you assist me in moving everyone back into the castle?"

Prince Justin grinned broadly and said, "It would be a pleasure, Colonel. I will publicly swear fealty to your authority and encourage everyone to do the same."

"Thank you, Your Highness," Colonel Fedral said respectfully.

Perry turned to Captain Peters and said, "Pull together one hundred of your best rangers. We leave for Hastings Castle in fifteen minutes."

CHAPTER 8

SUCCESSOR

Perry surprised the king's receptionist; walking in with no advance notice, covered in dust, with a severe look in his eyes.

"General Eastbrook, we didn't know you had returned from the siege," the receptionist said with panic showing on his face. It was obvious he never expected to see Perry again. "I don't have any openings for an audience today."

Perry ignored him and walked up to the surprised throne room guards and handed them his sword. They saluted and when he motioned them to open the doors, they did.

The king was speechless as Perry walked purposefully toward him. Perry was supposed to be dead, along with the king's brother and all the rebels, including their families. Clearly Barrows had failed.

The king finally found his voice as Perry approached him. "Arrest General Eastbrook. He has committed treason against the crown."

"Stand down," Perry ordered forcefully without turning to face the guards. They dutifully resumed their positions. These guards had been hand-picked by Perry. They were from families owing allegiance to him. Families he knew to be completely loyal and trustworthy.

"What are you doing?" the king asked, fear clearly on his face.

"Something I should have done long ago," Perry said as he quickly drew a dagger from his sleeve and drove it forcefully into King Kenneth's chest, piercing his heart. He pulled the dagger out, grabbed the king by the hair, pulled his head back, and slit his throat. His training as a ranger taught him to double up on killing blows when it was critical for the enemy to stay down. It was always good to be thorough.

As the king lay with blood gurgling out onto the stone floor, Perry said casually to the guards, "You can arrest me for treason now."

"Sir?" was the nervous response from the young man in charge. He was the youngest son of a close family friend. Perry had known him since he was a toddler. He hated putting the young man in this situation. The young soldier looked terrified at the prospect of arresting the godlike personage of General Eastbrook.

"Richard," he said kindly. "Go out in the hallway and find Captain Peters. Bring him here."

"Yes, sir," Richard said, saluting. He then hurried off out the door.

Perry shook his head slowly, his face relaxing into an amused grin. He guessed he ought to accept that as a compliment. It did bother him that he could walk into the throne room, assassinate the king, and then have his orders obeyed by guards sworn to protect the king with their lives. He guessed it had as much to do with the guard's distaste for the king as loyalty to him. They must have been privy to all kinds of disturbing knowledge, including questions about the rumors surrounding the king's 'hobby.'"

"Sir," said Captain Peters a few moments later.

"The king is dead. I murdered him. Go secure the queen. Inform her of what has happened. Tell her my recommendation is to place you in charge of castle security until other arrangements can be made. Lock down the castle until you are assured of the queen's safety. You can trust the king's and queen's guards. They were hand-picked by me and will be loyal to the queen. Once she places them under your authority, do what you think is best. Arrest me and have these guards place me in the dungeon for now," Perry said, motioning to the king's guards still obviously in shock. "You have much to do, Captain. Better get going."

"Yes, sir. Thank you, sir," Captain Peters said with gratitude in his eyes. Perry continued to be impressed with Peters. He had obviously figured out what Perry was going to do and had resolved to support it anyway. Peters was bright enough to realize that Perry had not filled him in on the plan to protect him from accusations of involvement in a treasonous conspiracy. All Peters had to do was tell the truth. He had simply been following reasonable orders.

Perry spent about two hours in the dungeon before the queen showed up with Captain Peters, the chief justice, and the Queen's Guard. "I want General Eastbrook moved to a more secure location until the trial," she said, looking sternly at Perry.

She was a pretty good actress but couldn't hide the warmth in her eyes, Perry thought. Unfortunately, she would need to get much better at hiding her thoughts and emotions. His heart went out to her. She was much too young to be forced into this situation.

Turning around, the queen said, "Captain Peters. There is an unused apartment at the top of the residence tower. The only access is through a narrow stairway located in an alcove at the west end of the third-floor hallway. Bar the doors at the top and bottom of the stairway. Place whatever guards you deem necessary on both doors. There is to be no access to General Eastbrook except to provide food and housekeeping by my personal servants until further notice."

"It will be done Your Majesty," Peters said stiffly still standing in the official army version of 'at ease'".

Perry smiled. Both of them were playing their roles to near perfection. Peters was ready for the next level of command. He hoped whoever took over as general would recognize this and promote him.

The apartment at the top of the tower was opulent, but a bit dusty. For a man who usually found comfort at night on a cot in a drafty tent, it was a bit much. He did have a ranch, which was very comfortable. But those were the practical comforts of a well-to-do farmer, not an aristocrat. Perry was a frugal, practical man.

The apartment had a definite feminine quality to it. Perry had heard rumors of Olivia's grandfather keeping a mistress close by. He decided this was what the apartment had been last used for. It was a short walk down the hallway from the king's chambers.

Perry had settled in for the night when a bookcase in the bedroom suddenly clicked, swung out, and then off to one side. To his surprise, he locked eyes with Bria, who hesitated, then ran over and jumped up into his arms, hugging him fiercely. Olivia followed with a troubled smile on her face and hugged him just as fiercely when Bria was done.

Tearfully, Olivia said, "I will pardon you as soon as I can."

"You have more important things to do, my queen," Perry said with affection clearly evident. "I am deeply sorry to have put you in this situation. I am even sorrier that I felt compelled to violate my oaths and murder your father."

"I'm not going to tolerate apologies or regrets on your behalf," Olivia said in her queenly voice. "You have done the people of this kingdom a great service. Your oath was to the realm, not to a man who was violating his oath to protect its people. The realm owes you more than it could ever repay."

Olivia hesitated to gather her thoughts and then said softly, "I am sorry my father is dead; he was my father. My mother was a saint, but my father was thoroughly evil. Opening up his 'hobby room' ended any doubts I might have had about that. My parents' arranged marriage was a terrible match. I believe he killed my mother for daring to oppose him. Justice has been delivered." At that point, Olivia lost her composure and burst into tears. Bria wrapped her in a hug until the tears subsided.

They walked out into the richly appointed parlor with both Olivia and Bria wiping away tears and sat down. Perry waited until Olivia had composed herself and then said, "You need to get Prince Justin here as soon as possible. He's an expert in political intrigue and you're going to need his advice. I know you don't know him well. Your father was always worried the two of you would conspire against him. He forced the separation, which is why you don't have a close relationship with him. I know him well; he's a good man. You can trust him."

"I'll pardon you both and then we can figure out what to do together," Olivia said.

"You should not give out any pardons until you fully understand the political situation. In fact, you're likely going to have to sacrifice one of us. Prince Justin is worth far more than I am. You own the most powerful army on the planet and there are several officers who can keep the peace on Liberty. Colonel Fedral would be an excellent choice. Politics are another matter. Things could spin completely out of control if the Commonwealth is involved. And I think they are. The first threat is civil war breaking out. The bigger threat is invasion by Arista. The best defense against that is a political solution with the Commonwealth" He stopped for a moment and then asked, "I assume the hidden stairway comes up from the king's quarters, correct?"

"Yes, Mom showed it to me when I was eight. She wanted me to know about all the hidden passageways in the castle so I could hide or escape if needed. She even showed me the hidden door to the 'hobby room' but told me to never go in there. It connects to a tunnel that leads outside the castle. I showed Bria and thought you ought to know of its existence," Olivia said. "We can use it to escape if necessary."

Perry nodded and said, "My advice is to limit your trips here. Reserve them for emergencies. I know it sounds paranoid, but you don't want any evidence supporting an accusation that you were involved in a conspiracy to kill the king. This is a deadly game, Olivia. You should also have Justice Reynolds officially question Bria. Once he declares her innocent of knowledge or involvement, you can resume spending time with her. Until then, keep her confined to her rooms under guard."

"Dad, no!" Bria said. "Olivia needs my support."

"It's only for a day or two and it's necessary to protect you both," Perry said.

Olivia had lots of questions which Perry did his best to answer. When the question-and-answer session fizzled away, she said, "I'll have your military library brought up here. Can't imagine how you find that stuff interesting, but it's probably better than sending up my romance novels," she said, smiling. Then she handed him a dagger and said, "I don't want you weaponless, Uncle Perry." It was the same dagger he had used to kill the king.

Perry was struck once again by Olivia's intelligence and empathy. Giving him that dagger was a clear signal that she fully supported him and what he had done. She knew he would be second guessing his actions. Perry replied, "Probably not necessary, but thanks."

Olivia and Bria said their goodbyes and then, shedding a few tears, left the same way they came. Perry found the cleverly hidden bookcase door lock and engaged it. They would have to knock next time.

Two weeks went by with no news. Servants had been instructed not to talk to him, so he couldn't even question them on the common news of the day. He knew this was for their protection as well as the queens. For a man of action, this was a hellish life.

Deep into an ancient text describing the care and maintenance of catapults, there was a loud knock on the door. One of the guards called out, "you have visitors General Eastbrook."

"Enter," Perry said. He put his book down wondering what this was all about.

The queen, Justice Reynolds, Colonel Fedral, and Captain Peters walked in. The queen had an amused look on her face and said, "General Eastbrook. Will you please instruct Colonel Fedral to relinquish Prince Justin and his castle to my control?"

Perry was flabbergasted. He had assumed Fedral would recognize the situation and open the gates to the queen's authority. He should have known better. Colonel Fedral was an excellent administrator. He was an inspired battlefield commander, matched only by Perry himself. He was also uncompromisingly loyal and incredibly stubborn. His orders had been to control the castle and protect Prince Justin until Perry ordered him otherwise.

"If I ever had any small doubts about you following orders, they have been eliminated," Perry said to Fedral with a slow shake of his head and amusement in his eyes.

Colonel Fedral looked a little hurt and said, "Yes, sir."

"You are to follow all commands and orders given to you by Queen Olivia. Even if they countermand orders I have given you in the past."

"I understand, sir," Colonel Fedral said simply. Then he turned to the queen and said, "I'm ready for your instructions, Your Majesty. My deepest apologies for not following your earlier commands."

Queen Olivia looked him in the eyes and with a sincere voice said, "I value loyalty, Colonel. Those who follow orders regardless of their difficulty are highly valued. It's a rare man who would stand firm given the situation you were put in. You handled it admirably. Thank you for all your contributions to the realm."

Fedral visibly relaxed and with pink cheeks said, "Thank you, ma'am."

Olivia is going to be a wonderful leader, thought Perry, smiling inside.

"Colonel Fedral, you are promoted to general and are in charge of the Royal Armed Forces as of this moment onward. I would like Prince Justin to be brought under heavy guard to Hastings Castle as soon as practical. You should delegate that task as I have immediate need of your advice. We have quite a bit of planning to do."

General Fedral, nodding, turned to Peters and said, "Captain, please use your rangers for the prisoner transfer. Prince Justin is to be treated with all the respect and honors due a member of the royal family. Name a temporary replacement for yourself to head up castle security. I would also like you to carry orders for Colonel Pike and the army currently occupying the prince's castle. We'll bring the siege team back and have them take up a defensive position near the main Druango mountain pass. I will have orders ready for you within the hour. When you return, we'll discuss next steps."

"Yes, sir," said Captain Peters.

Turning back to the queen, General Fedral said, "Might I request regular access to General Eastbrook for advice on next steps for the Royal Armed Forces?"

"That is granted with the provision that Justice Reynolds is present at these meetings. No discussion of events associated with the rebel surrender or murder of the king are allowed," the queen said calmly. She then turned to Perry and said, "We'll leave you to your contemplations General Eastbrook." She hesitated a mere moment and let some warmth in her eyes show. She then exited confidently through the doorway, radiating royalty.

After the door closed, Perry allowed himself a smile of pride. She was already better at schooling her features. Even that last glance was done in a way that only he could see. Perry gave a deep sigh and was once again left to his books and his thoughts.

CHAPTER 9

GOVERNOR'S UPDATE

Jack walked into the governor's office wondering if this was his last hour of life. It had been a mistake to apply for first minister in this sector. His career had been on a steep upward trajectory. His father had certainly played a role in his decision. "Jack, you don't reach the heights of Commonwealth administration by playing it safe."

"I've heard she's brutal and unforgiving. The last first minister simply disappeared," Jack had said.

"Her next assignment is likely going to be on the High Council, Jack. She's ticked all the boxes and been incredibly effective while doing so. Revenues from that sector have doubled, and they will double again before she is done. You might not like her, but it's a chance to gain a mentor destined to go far," his father had concluded.

And so, Jack had taken the risk. It had been a poor choice. As he was called into the governor's office, he decided he would face this with courage. He might as well go out in style. So, in keeping with that theme, he would stay calm, state the facts, and hope he survived.

"Good morning Jack, I hope you have good news," the governor said in greeting. It was maddening that she always greeted him with that statement. It made giving her bad news even worse. He suspected that was her intent.

"King Kenneth is dead, and his daughter is now queen. He was murdered by General Eastbrook. The mercenary army has been eliminated. My plan is in complete ruin," Jack said simply.

The governor's face showed a cold smile. Jack decided she wasn't going to swish her tail and walk away this time. Then she said, "What did you learn Jack?"

Jack hesitated, opened his mouth to speak, and then decided to think this through before answering. Turning this into a mentoring session was not what he expected. A small hope blossomed. Then he took a deep breath and said, "There were too many unpredictable players involved. I should have reduced the plan's reliance down to fewer people and ensured they had no option but to follow the plan exactly as laid out. King Kenneth deviated from the plan by ordering one of his lords to take over the surrender from General Eastbrook.

"My guess is that he wanted to accelerate the plan by eliminating Prince Justin and General Eastbrook in one stroke. General Eastbrook obviously figured this out. I should have remained in Liberty and ensured the king stayed on plan. I underestimated the General, and this is unforgiveable. He is known to have wide-ranging surveillance capability. He is also known to have exceptional judgement on military strategy and implementation." Then he stopped and waited for judgement.

He felt good about his delivery. The governor liked her summaries simple and to the point. No excuses and clear accountability. King Kenneth had actually changed the plan twice. First, he agreed to a surrender negotiation, which in Jack's mind was an improvement. One of Jack's hidden flaws was that he did not approve of killing women and children. Sometimes it was necessary, but something he would avoid if possible. Then, unforgivably, the king actually tried to ambush General Eastbrook while he was with his army. This is a man who had successfully countered those types of attempts innumerable times. Sheer stupidity.

The governor's icy voice brought him back to the present. "What about Lord Druango?"

"While he has the right motivations for us to work with, he failed completely in carrying out the king's altered plan. He should have either ensured success or refused to do it. I would not advise having him in a role where we're relying on his judgement," Jack said.

"So, he's one of the plans dependances that should have been worked around?" she asked.

"Yes, Governor," Jack said simply.

"Who's fault is this disaster?" she asked.

"Mine entirely, Governor," Jack responded.

Then she just stared at him with those mismatched cat eyes. Were the claws coming out, he wondered. Maintaining eye contact was difficult, but he knew that showing weakness was deadly. So, he looked back respectfully and waited for her to speak.

After what seemed like a lifetime, she said, "You're right about the unforgiveable nature of underestimating Eastbrook."

"Yes, ma'am," was all Jack said, stomach roiling.

Then she stared some more and finally said, "You know I'm not a forgiving person, Jack."

"No, ma'am," Jack said, staying expressionless. She likes playing with her food, he thought grimly.

After another long and uncomfortable silence, she asked, "So how do you propose to fix this situation?"

A thin ray of hope emerged once more with that question. But Jack knew he was still in a very dangerous position. "I do have a suggestion. It pushes Lord Druango into a support role and reduces the number of people we rely on," Jack said.

"What about timing?" she said. "You know my patience is wearing thin."

This was dangerous. His plan would take time to properly coordinate all the pieces. If he promised results on too aggressive of a schedule, it might be his final act. Taking a deep breath, he said, "It adds nine to twelve months to the timeline. The risk of failure is lower and will be easier to administer in the long run."

She hesitated, smiled in all her cat glory, and purred, "Come to my apartment tonight for dinner, Jack. We'll discuss your new plan. We can also talk about how you are going to persuade me to allow your unforgiveable mistake." She then looked at him up and down openly and provocatively.

Jack's insides melted. He almost lost his composure and had to quickly lock down his facial expressions and body language. There were rumors about the governor taking liberties with her staff. While she was commonly known as 'The Cat', she was also known in whispers as 'The Black Widow.' She was almost twice his age, although she didn't look it. Life extension therapies were readily available to the upper crust of Commonwealth citizens. Visibly a very attractive woman, her other attributes gave him the shivers. Her mismatched eyes would have been easy to fix with contacts or cosmetic surgery. Jack had come to believe she liked unsettling people. He wasn't sure he could do this, but he knew he didn't have a choice.

"What time should I arrive, Governor?" he asked.

"Seven o'clock," she said with a sly smile. Then she slowly looked him up and down provocatively once more. "You can call me Julie in private, Jack."

"I'll see you at seven, Julie," Jack said as he forced what he hoped looked like an authentic smile and returned her provocative look.

As he walked out of her office, Jack was torn on whether this was a good outcome or not. His best-case scenario going in was leaving with his life. A life whose career was destroyed, destined to die of boredom in a low-level job. But alive. Of the three options, that might have been the best result. Leaving with his life was a pleasant surprise, but becoming the governor's latest toy was at best highly perilous.

CHAPTER 10

WEDDING NEGOTIATIONS

Olivia wished she could work closely with Perry and her uncle on the negotiations. Lord Druango had the backing of a minority group of Earls, Barons, and other wealthy landowners who mostly represented the two kingdoms subjugated in the Unification Wars. While she had the loyalty of the largest army on the planet, another civil war could weaken Liberty to the point of being an attractive target for Arista.

Lord Druango stood as Olivia entered the dreary meeting room set aside for her negotiations with him. "Good morning, Your Majesty, you look very pretty today," the old, fat, and indolent man said as he looked her up and down provocatively.

It made her skin crawl. How was she going to be strong enough to do this? She decided leering at her was all part of an attempt to intimidate her. "Good morning, Lord Druango," she said crisply.

He waited for her to sit and then sat himself and said with a sly smile, "Your father made a wise decision arranging our betrothal. It is the best move to solidify unification of the realm and provide long-term stability for the royal family. Everyone needs to put down their swords and forget the divisions of the past."

Olivia smiled grimly back, letting him know she wasn't intimidated, and said, "Now that I am queen, I have no obligation to continue with this betrothal. If you really believe in unification, then you will support pardons for Prince Justin and General Eastbrook. The evidence of the king's betrayal of the people of Liberty is compelling. People would rise up if either of them were punished," Olivia said forcefully.

"Opening the king's hobby room left little doubt as to his horrendous crimes. But, as you know, there is still division within the kingdom. While I believe both of them would support the royal family without question, I'm not convinced safety for the people of my province would be protected. There are rumors that Arista is contacting influential people in an attempt to convince them life under their rule would be better. As the queen's consort, I could be persuaded those fears are misplaced. If I am persuaded, I can persuade others who hold doubts. It's to everyone's benefit if we keep Arista out of Liberty," he said with a triumphant smile.

She did not believe his arguments had anything to do with a concern for people in his province. The tone of Druango's voice made it clear that being Lord Druango worked equally well under Arista as under her as queen. This lord was very good at making threats without saying anything that could be called treasonous. It was purely a power play. Unfortunately, House of Lords's support for the pardons was a trump card.

Without their support, civil war was highly likely. It was an excruciating decision. It meant sacrificing any hope of personal happiness for the good of the kingdom. She was confident the combination of Perry and her uncle would protect her from Druango's control. But Druango would have to be watched very closely. It wouldn't be a happy life. Having grown up knowing she would marry for the good of the kingdom, she had already accepted sacrifice as her fate. "I am willing to continue our betrothal once both Prince Justin and General Eastbrook's pardons are publicly supported by the entire House of Lords."

Lord Druango locked eyes with her in a flinty glare and said, "I have no problem with pardoning both, given we consummate a marriage as previously arranged. However, General Eastbrook has been quite vocal in stating he wants to retire from the army to go live on his ranch. I would expect you to ensure he does exactly that and doesn't interfere politically."

His suggestive emphasis on the word consummate made her skin crawl once more. Regardless, she couldn't let it affect her decision. The demand to exile Perry to his ranch had Olivia in turmoil. The one person of power she knew and trusted was Perry. Her experiences with General Fedral were good, but she didn't have a high level of trust built up yet. Perry had been vocal and public with his declarations of retiring to his ranch once the wars were over. He cast himself as a modern-day Cincinnatus who simply wanted to return to being a farmer. She knew the real reason for these declarations was to shore up the succession.

General Eastbrook was wildly popular broadly across the realm. If he even breathed a desire to rule, the kingdom would be his. She knew Druango was trying to divide and conquer, but she could always rescind

Perry's exile if needed. Steeling herself to her fate, she said, "I accept your conditions. I will pardon both and expect you to provide public support from the House of Lords before we are married."

"Done. I look forward to an expeditious wedding," he said, smiling.

She nodded, got up, and walked toward the door. As she did so, she was very conscious of him staring at her body once more. God, give me the strength to actually do this, she thought as she left the room.

On her walk down the hall to her uncle's accommodations, she steeled herself for the anger Prince Justin would have for her decisions. She walked into Prince Justin's suite and said, "It's good to see you out of the dungeon, Uncle."

Prince Justin was clearly anxious when she walked in. His look was clearly asking for her to explain how her negotiations had gone. Exhaling some of the stress away, she said, "It's done. I agreed to all of the concessions we discussed."

Prince Justin was visibly angry, as predicted. He looked at her and shouted, "Are you out of your mind Olivia! Lord Druango is as evil and dangerous as a snake. He was going to murder me, Perry, and the families of everyone who opposed his plan with the king. He directed those mercenaries to kill children, CHILDREN!" Justin paused to control his anger, then continued. "Lord Barlow's confession was coerced so not admissible in a trial. But that doesn't matter, since he conveniently died in an accident."

"Well, I didn't say I expected him to be a good husband," she said sarcastically as she smiled back.

"This is not a time for jokes, Olivia. Both Perry and I would be honored to be sacrificed for the good of the realm. I am not necessary, but Perry can ensure the regions stay loyal. The common people love him. The rest won't dare defy his army." He stopped a moment to collect himself and then said in a pleading voice, "I understand you need to marry for the good of the realm, but not that man!"

Olivia's expression changed from amused to warmly stern and said, "You are my only insurance. Lord Druango won't kill me before I produce an heir. He won't do this because he knows you are next in line to assume the throne if I die childless. He also knows you will be regent if he kills me after I have produced an heir. With you out of the picture, he has an easy pathway to the throne. Fedral is an excellent general, but he can't insure loyalty like Perry can."

"I hate this decision," Prince Justin said. Then he sat down and moved his glance from her to the floor, pouting like a child.

Olivia smiled, patted his arm and said, "You are the queen's advisor. I expect you to tell me when you think I'm making poor decisions. I will always listen and consider what you say. But, when I decide, I expect you to honor my decisions and do your best to implement them. I have made this decision."

"Don't worry about my loyalty. Never worry about that. I will support your decisions." Justin took a deep breath and said, "On another topic, I am also not happy with the plan to exile Perry. Fedral does not have the same level of respect and loyalty from the common soldiers that Perry does. Everyone knew your father was a horrible king, but once Perry declared his intent to honor his oath, most unquestioningly backed him. They think of him as one of their own. We need his leadership," Prince Justin pleaded.

"That was a very difficult decision. I agree we need his council and leadership. But having him in the castle is detrimental in the short term. The minority in the House of Lords will be more defiant with him around. He defeated most of them in battle. They remember being his prisoner. If a crisis breaks out, I can rescind the exile order and bring him back," Olivia said.

"His ranch is remote. We need to make sure he has a lot of security around him," Prince Justin counseled.

"I agree about the need for security. Druango and his minions would love nothing more than an accident at the ranch. I was thinking of asking him to step down and become commander of the rangers instead of retirement. He came up through those ranks and there isn't anyone better to train and organize them. His ranch is conveniently located near strategic roads connecting the three regions. Easy to argue it's a good place for an army camp. He will be living on his ranch as agreed, but this would essentially give him a good-sized elite army at his disposal. I discussed it with General Fedral, and he agrees. To be honest, Fedral believes all of this is subterfuge. In his opinion, he's still Perry's second in command. We've discussed promoting Captain Peters by jumping major directly to Lieutenant Colonel and making him Perry's second in command," Olivia explained.

"He seems awfully young," Prince Justin said.

"Believe it or not, he has fifteen years' experience in the Royal Army.

Peters was an orphan and lied about his age at thirteen to join the army. His motivation was literally to avoid starvation. He rose up the non-commissioned ranks quickly because of his fighting skills, judgement, and intelligence. Perry saw something special in him and eventually gave him a battlefield promotion to commissioned officer. Fedral told me this is extremely rare. I think Perry identifies with him. They both came from poverty and they both came up through the ranks. Peters certainly worships the ground Perry walks on. They have a high level of personal trust. I can't think of a better bodyguard. Especially since Perry won't accept a bodyguard," Olivia said, smiling.

"You are definitely sneaky enough to be queen, Your Majesty," Prince Justin said with a touch of light sarcasm and the first smile of the day.

"I wish sneaky wasn't something I needed to be good at. Would prefer to just be honest with everyone. The days of simplicity are unfortunately gone forever," she said with a sad expression on her face.

Next stop was Bria. She kept very few secrets from her best friend. Bria had encouraged her to keep her father's fate a secret until it was decided. It wasn't a selfish request; her motivation was a belief that it would make it easier on Olivia. Bria was truly a gift from heaven. In her world of royal politics, Bria was the one person her age who loved her. Bria only desired love and friendship in return. They had solemnly sworn as small girls to always stay close.

She walked into Bria's quarters and said, smiling, "I have good news. Your father has been pardoned."

Bria hesitated in answering, studying her closely. "And?" Bria asked, locking eyes with her.

"You know me too well," Olivia said with a touch of sadness in her voice. "The 'and' is that I have to exile him to the ranch for now. You can go live with your father on the ranch just like you always wanted."

Surprisingly, Bria smiled and said, "Unless you exile me too, I'm staying here."

"But you've always said you want to live near your father. That the wars have robbed you both of time together," Olivia argued with a furrowed brow.

"Dad and I already discussed it. You are going to need someone to talk to who cares about you. That would be me," Bria said with a smirk.

Olivia couldn't help but smile, then she said in surprise, "How did he find out he was going to be exiled?"

"He told me when he first got here that you would negotiate pardons with Lord Druango. He told me the right move would be to sacrifice him and break your engagement with Lord Druango. In his opinion, you are predictably guilty of letting your heart win out over your head," Bria said with a knowing smile. "If his prediction came true we agreed I would stay close to help you. Dad is really worried about you, Olivia. We both are."

"I'm glad your dad is a friend and not an enemy, Bria. He's endearing, but it's scary how well he predicts what people are going to do," Olivia said as she started to relax. One of her big fears was that Bria would be offended by Olivia's treatment of her father. That she would move to the ranch with Uncle Perry and cut off communication.

"Dad told me to give you a suggestion in case 'you insist on making bad decisions.' He suggests you build a summer house on the ranch. He said you could visit your Uncle Perry during the hot muggy season when the House of Lords is not in session," Bria said with a hopeful expression.

"God, that's a wonderful idea! I loved the ranch when we were girls," Olivia said with brightness glowing in her eyes.

"It's a bit rough, Olivia. I'm not sure you're remembering it accurately," Bria said, smiling.

"Those were the happiest days of my life, Bria. After my mother died, the castle was gloomy and filled with people who either saw me as an opportunity or an annoyance. The ranch was beautiful. My best friend was there. No courtiers. Just real people who cared about me. Aunt Beatrice was fussing over me and making me laugh instead of being surrounded by servants with cold smiles. I had work to do. Taking care of the animals and working in the fields was very satisfying. A home on the ranch where I can stay part of the year sounds like heaven," Olivia said wistfully. Then, with her face transforming into a grin, she said, "Where else can I practice my knife throwing?"

They both laughed, stood up, and hugged each other fiercely. Like Olivia, Bria was an only child whose mother had died when she was young. While growing up, she was either on the ranch, at the castle, or on a campaign. When he had a choice, arguments to leave Bria behind simply didn't work with her father. Wherever he went, she went.

Exposed to the dangers of war, and the castle, Perry decided she needed to be able to protect herself. The problem was that Bria was incredibly soft hearted. She refused to hit anyone or spar with weapons. "What if I hurt someone?" she had exclaimed in horror to her father.

"That's the whole point, Bria," he responded with obvious exasperation.

"Well then, I won't do it," she declared and then locked her face into her well-known look of absolute determination. In addition to being soft-hearted, Bria was the most stubborn person on the planet, according to her father. Frustrated, Perry finally got her to throw knives by turning it into a friendly game. They would compete with a set of throwing knives and a wooden target they took everywhere. Olivia had gotten into the act on an early visit to the ranch and turned out to have natural skill. She always beat Bria, which wasn't hard because Bria didn't care. But she also won regularly against Uncle Perry. This delighted both girls. Mostly because it frustrated the extremely competitive Uncle Perry. Making it even better, Perry's staff had gotten into the act by ribbing him about it when the girls were around.

Olivia took a deep breath, let it out, and then said, "Would you have an early breakfast with me tomorrow? The wedding is at noon, and I would love to have lots of time to get ready together."

"Of course. How about we both wear our special hair pins," Bria proposed with a grin. "Only Father will know what they are, and he'll smile when he sees them."

Their hair pins were cleverly disguised throwing knives. They were small but made of an extremely dense wood that maintained an edge. They were also heavy enough to penetrate deeply when thrown. Their decorative carved and painted sheaths successfully hid their purpose. Perry had gifted them both with the matching hair pin knives years ago. They had worn them to many royal events in the past. Given their close friendship, it wouldn't look inappropriate at the wedding.

"I love that idea. Gloria will hate it, but she'll go along if I insist," Olivia said, smiling. Gloria was the royal interior designer and dresser for Olivia. Arguably the most beautiful woman in the realm. She had a warm personality and was blessed with an eye for color and excellent taste. "I wish your dad could give me away," Olivia continued. "But politically, it has to be Prince Justin. Nothing against him, but I really don't know him all that well."

"If there was ever someone who deserves a fairy tale ending, it's you. Unfortunately, it looks like you're only going to get the best friend and her father part of the story," Bria said with a sad smile, which Olivia returned. The two best friends spent the evening sipping wine and reminiscing about their lives, knowing it was all about to change forever. As Olivia left Bria's apartment, she thought once again that she would gladly walk away from wealth and luxury for freedom. Freedom to live her life the way she chose. For her, there was little liberty on Liberty. She had pardoned her uncle that morning and would pardon Perry this evening.

The morning of the wedding, Bria was modeling Olivia's wedding dress when a loud commotion broke out in the hallway. The door burst open, and a rough-looking man ran in with blood dripping off the sharp edges of his sword. He smiled cruelly when he saw Bria and as he hurried toward her, he said, "You're coming with me, queeny."

Bria froze, not knowing what to do. There was a loud clash of swords in the hallway. It sounded like the fight was getting closer. She feared that meant the queen's guards were being overwhelmed. "I said you're coming with me," he said in an angry voice as he advanced toward Bria.

As he got close, a knife suddenly appeared in his neck. He fell and was spilling his life out on the marble floor when Bria turned and saw Olivia standing angry and defiant with her hair now loose and flowing over her shoulders.

Pushing down the bile in her throat, she forced herself into action. Bria found her voice and said firmly, "Olivia, the apartment!"

Olivia hesitated, then, nodding, ran over to a bookcase. She released a hidden catch and swung the hidden door open. She motioned Bria over, and when Bria didn't move, she refused to enter alone. Bria ran quickly over and surprised Olivia by pushing her hard into the stairway landing beyond. Bria pushed the hidden door closed. She quickly found the lock and heard it click just before more of the invaders entered the queen's dressing room.

"Grab her and let's get out of here before we have to fight off the entire Royal Army." The oldest of the men said. One of the larger men jogged over, grabbed her roughly, and threw a hood over her head. He picked her up and slung her over his shoulder. For the second time, she fought down the urge to throw up. The vision of blood pulsing out of the first man's neck kept running through her mind.

"Hey, grab the pretty one, too. She'll be worth something," the one in charge ordered.

Bria heard Gloria wail out an agonized protest about her children. Her heart sank even further thinking about the two beautiful little twin girls who visited sometimes. It was horrific to contemplate their grief. These men were slavers. They hadn't been active in Liberty for decades, given the planet's large army and rich kingdoms. The retribution Liberty could extract wasn't worth it. Bria was terrified but proud she had saved Olivia from this fate. They had obviously targeted the queen as part of a plan likely cooked up by Lord Druango. If they didn't find a queen, then they would keep looking, and Bria couldn't risk that.

Why now and not later?

Bria couldn't figure out the logic. The castle was overflowing with armed men, given the number of lords and ladies attending the wedding. She composed herself, wondering what she should do. Then she remembered her father's voice repeating one of his oft quoted axioms 'never correct your enemy's mistakes.' They thought they had captured Queen Olivia. She would not correct their mistake.

CHAPTER 11

VOYAGE

Tee was in the middle of his twice a day exercise routine. You would have to look very closely to notice muscles flexing and relaxing. He was careful to do it when the guards weren't present, and Theo was either sleeping or not paying attention to him. It was a lengthy and elaborate routine intended for use when Guard members were confined for multiple days in a small space. It was part of their scout training. The Guard wanted everyone to be prepared for just about anything. While it did not take the place of real exercise, at least it raised his heart rate a little and slowed down muscle atrophy.

Suddenly the door unlocked, opened, and two women were escorted in. They were each given orders to go into one of the two empty cells. When they didn't move quickly enough, they were roughly shoved in. The one directly across from him was stunningly beautiful. She was terrified and Tee's heart went out to her. Fortunately, Theo was asleep, or she would already be suffering his verbal abuse. The second woman across from Tee was also pretty, but more athletic looking, which appealed to Tee. She also exhibited a stoic nature against the rough treatment that radiated confidence. Another attractive quality. She examined both him and Theo carefully, but without being obvious about it.

The woman across from him said, "Hi, my name's Gloria. Do you know where we are?"

"Theron doesn't know. Theron wants to go home," Tee said, staying in character.

"Oh dear," Gloria said with compassion in her voice. "Are you scared, Theron?"

"Yes," Tee whispered. "Theron scared of Theo," Tee said, pointing toward the other prisoner and cringing away from him at the same time.

"He's simple Gloria. I can't believe they would put someone like him in a cage," Bria said softly, but with a clear tinge of anger in her voice.

The tone in Bria's voice woke up Theo. He rubbed his eyes, looked around, and smiled widely. "Well, look at what we have here, Theron, women for Theo." He stood up and moved to the bars to get as close a look as possible. Then he pointedly looked both over carefully. He turned toward Gloria and said, "You know the guards owe me a favor. I'll get them to let us spend some time together in my cell. You know there is only one thing women are good for. Can you guess?" When she turned bright red, he laughed harshly and started fondling himself. Then he proceeded to describe in disgusting detail what he thought women were good for.

"Leave her alone," Bria demanded.

Theo turned to her and smiled his evil smile and said, "You must be jealous of the attention I'm giving the pretty one. You're not bad yourself. You know the Guards owe me more than one favor. After I'm done with her, we can spend a little time together, too."

"You touch either one of us and I'll kill you," Bria said coldly. She knew it was an empty promise. Hurting people was not something she could bring herself to do. Silly to threaten anyway.

"I'm not someone you want to threaten. After I'm done with you, you'll plead for death. That's a promise," Theo said coldly, with his smile still in place.

Bria turned toward Gloria. "Ignore him Gloria. He's locked up just like we are. You're safe from him," Bria said soothingly. Then she shot a quick, cold smile at Theo and turned away. Gloria took her cue from Bria, turned away and seemingly ignored Theo's continued descriptions of their future activities together.

In the middle of what Tee had decided was the night the door unlocked and then was slammed open. Three guards stumbled in. Tee could smell the alcohol. Staying in character, he cringed on his narrow bed with his knees held in a fetal position.

"I told you they were beautiful," Smelly said, slurring his words.

"Meant for some senator's entertainment, no doubt. I like this one," the older of the two new guards said pointing at Bria.

"No! She's special. Queen of Liberty no less, and a certified virgin to boot," Smelly said firmly. We're worse than dead if we touch that one.

"Will we be in trouble with this one," the new guard with buck teeth said pointing at Gloria.

"We've been told to be careful with all of them." Smelly looked at Gloria lustfully and swaying a bit said, "she's had kids so nothing special other than being beautiful. She's only in here because they were worried the men in the holding cell would all want a go at her and damage the goods. As long as we're careful nobody will care."

"Don't touch her," Bria shouted at them.

"Shut up bitch. You're lucky you're special or I would give you to Theo for entertainment," Smelly said. Then he opened Glorias cell and as they entered Tee shut his eyes tightly. It was in character for him to turn away and shut his eyes. Tee simply could not watch what was obviously going to happen next.

The next hour was a nightmare. Gloria was crying and pleading for them to stop. Bria was shouting obscenities. And Theo was offering suggestions of what the guards should do next. Tee was sick to his stomach and enraged that anyone could abuse another human being like this. When Gloria's crying weakened into whimpering, Tee started to hope they were finally finished with her.

"Well, that was fun. Can we do this again," Buck Tooth said as the door to Gloria's cell clanked shut.

"It will take a couple of weeks to complete all the jumps to Arista," Smelly said, chuckling. "We have to be careful not to get caught. But we'll have lots of time with her."

"Hey, how about you let me have some time with her? There are suggestions I was keeping to myself you might enjoy watching," Theo said with hope in his voice.

"No. You're not leaving that cell until we get to Arista," Smelly said, sounding like he was sobering up. He turned to the other two guards and said, "This disgusting excuse for a human being loves to torture and kill people. He likes to do it slowly. They are going to use his skills at the Arena. The emperor likes that sort of thing to start the games. He's only in here because he would damage the goods if he were in the holding cells."

"If you won't let me have a go at her, how about letting Theron provide a bit more entertainment?" Theo said, chuckling.

"That's not a bad idea," Buck Tooth said. "A video might make a little extra money on the black market. There are people into all kinds of weird shit."

"No way we let that monster out of his cell," Old Guy said.

"He's a moron, you idiot. The extraction team fucked up big time and heads are going to roll. He's still in this section because he's from Pacifica and has value in the Arena. I can only imagine what they will do to him. We might as well have a little fun while we have the chance. I think it could be worth a few credits," Smelly said, smiling.

Bria started in with insults and obscenities again as Tee heard his cell door unlock. He opened his eyes and said, "Theron wants to stay here," in a pleading voice. He could see the guards visibly relax and then smile in anticipation.

"Help me get him into her cell," Smelly said, motioning to Buck Tooth, and then he said. "We're probably going to have to help him figure it out." They all chuckled.

Bria was more disgusted than she had ever been in her life. She had heard stories of rape. She had been warned to be aware of her surroundings from a young age. She even knew women it had been rumored to have happened to. But she never thought there were people so sick as to do the things she had just witnessed. And now this! She watched the guards guide the huge simpleton out of his cell. Smiling and cracking jokes, they roughly pushed him along. Hunched over and whimpering, he timidly allowed them to guide him toward Gloria's cell door.

When all three of the Guards were within arm's length, the simpleton transformed. To her horror, in the blink of an eye, all three guards were on the floor and appeared to be dead. Blood was pooling beneath them. The simpleton had turned into a killing machine. It happened so quickly Bria couldn't quite understand what had just happened. Once she did, she vomited violently and quickly backed up away from her cell door, terrified by what she had just witnessed.

"Don't be afraid. I'm not going to hurt you," Tee said to Gloria as she stood glued to the back wall of her cell. He stood erect, confident, and calm, with a soothing voice. His eyes had transformed from vacant to warmly penetrating. He took one step toward Gloria, then stopped when she squealed in terror, cowering. Turning to Bria, he said softly, "Why don't I unlock your cell, and you can help her?"

"Don't come near me," Bria said firmly but in a quavering voice.

"Hey tough guy, how about letting me out to comfort her if Her Majesty doesn't want to," Theo said.

Tee bent down and relieved Smelly of his keys. Then he calmly walked over and unlocked Theo's cell door. As Tee entered, Theo suddenly lost his macho attitude and feinted to one side, then attacked. Just as blazingly fast as before, Theo was dead on the floor after having his head bashed against the wall. Bria vomited again from the sight of Theo's brains stuck on the wall but starting to dribble down to collect on the floor.

Tee then calmly dragged the three guards into Theo's cell and covered them with Theo's sheets. He locked Theo's cell door, then turned to Bria. "Don't throw whatever that is in your hair at me." Hesitating, he locked eyes with her and said, "If I harm you or Gloria in any way, you have my permission to kill me." Then he walked into his cell, locked the door, and threw all the keys to Bria. "There, I hope that helps you feel a little safer. You should get Gloria over to your cell. She is in shock and needs someone to help her." He stopped for a moment and then said with a grim smile. "I prefer to be called Tee, by the way."

Bria was in shock, and it took a few moments to compose herself. She had to gather her courage before venturing over to guide Gloria back to her cell.

"Can we have a little privacy, please?" Bria said in a sharp tone.

"Anytime. All you have to do is ask, but please let me know when you're done," Tee answered.

As far as Bria could tell, Gloria didn't have any permanent physical damage. Emotional damage was a whole other matter, especially given Gloria's history. She couldn't imagine Gloria escaping from what she had experienced in her life without permanent scars. Bria wasn't sure she herself would ever escape the horror of the last hour.

As she gently cleaned up Gloria, she stole glances at Tee. No longer bent over or cringing. He appeared to be honestly concerned for them. He was handsome and this new version of him had kind, intelligent eyes. Seemingly blessed with an easy manner, Bria could imagine him being very attractive to most woman.

However, Bria couldn't get past the Jekyll and Hyde transformation. The sudden change from a harmless simpleton to the deadliest thing she had ever seen terrified her to her core. She had been completely fooled by Theron the simpleton. Was this new version just another masterful acting performance? She decided to be wary of Tee. To watch him carefully. The fact he had known she had a weapon and was considering using it was almost magical. Yes, she would watch him carefully.

A few hours later, another guard unlocked the door, walked in, and froze. Eyes wide, he quickly turned and ran out, locking the door behind him. Tee could hear yelling in the hallway beyond. Tee allowed a grin to surface as he imagined the discussions. He glanced back over at Bria again, worried he had gone too far. He had broken training. He wasn't sorry he'd done it.

There was no way he was going to continue to play a role waiting for an opportunity to escape. He had been enraged and thoroughly disgusted by the three guards. But that wasn't why he killed them. The women needed protection. What he had done was the only way he knew to protect them against these particular guards and Theo. She surely understood justice had been served. Anyone who would do what was done to Gloria didn't deserve to live. She hadn't yet heard Theo's stories of what he had done to countless men, women, and, yes, children. Somehow, he knew Theo's stories were true. Tee felt he had an obligation to end Theo's horrendous abuse. More importantly, he felt an obligation to protect the two women from this collection of monsters.

The security officer for the ship was terrified. Three guards and a slave with highly valuable skills were dead. Worse, that particular slave had been personally requested by the emperor. The guards were his men, his responsibility. He had locked up the acquisition team on the captains' orders when their Pacifica captive turned out to be a simpleton. Laughing at them, he had explained that the captain wanted to make sure they lived long enough for their benefactor to decide what to do. He was remembering their evil grins as he took their place. He wished at least one of those three idiots had lived. Someone would have to pay the price for the lost revenue and the emperor's ire.

He was the only one left.

CHAPTER 12

PLUTA

A polite and efficient butler dutifully took the first minister's hat and coat, then escorted him to an austere but spacious office. "Thank you for seeing me on such short notice, Magistrate," Jack said in greeting.

"Always happy to serve the Commonwealth," replied Pluta, smiling. Pluta was a vigorous man in his sixties who took pride in his appearance. He had steely colored hair covering an intimidating face highlighted by dark, penetrating eyes. He made most people uncomfortable. This was intentional.

Pluta didn't like the first minister. He thought there was something undefinably soft about him. Weakness was a good thing in enemies or junior partners. But not in the person controlling the Commonwealth's involvement in a delicate and lucrative endeavor. He had only met the governor once. That was someone you could rely on to do what was necessary. Someone after his own heart, or lack thereof, he thought, smiling grimly.

"The governor's plan has changed. We would like you to take on a larger role," Jack said.

"I don't like it when plans change," Magistrate Pluta said forcefully while staring at Jack. His philosophy was to negotiate all changes to a plan. His pretended outrage at proposed changes was heightened if he thought the other sides negotiator was weak. And he thought Jack was weak.

Jack locked eyes with him and calmly said, "I misspoke. Your continued involvement in this venture requires you to take on a larger role."

Magistrate Pluta had to collect himself before he said something he would regret. The gall of this insolent puppy to threaten his involvement in a scheme that was his idea. The first minister was crucial to his future and had to be appeased. A subservient approach, however detestable, was required here. "My apologies, First Minister. I did not mean to indicate I was unwilling to do whatever the Commonwealth requires. I just get concerned when plans change midstream."

"Understandable. This change is to your advantage, Magistrate. The governor has authorized an increase in your share of the tax revenue from this venture to twenty percent," Jack said.

Pluta was sure the first minister had seen his shock at that news. He had allowed greed to show on his face. Pluta's share had just doubled! His original forecast from this venture was already astronomical. The first minister had been clever in delivering the news. He might sense weakness in the man, but he needed to make sure he didn't underestimate him.

Jack let a knowing smile cross his face, communicating that he had indeed noticed the reaction. He hesitated a moment to let that sink in and then said, "The governor is proposing raising the stakes. We would like you to continue owning the Arista side of this and take over Lord Druango's role."

Pluta was confused and he let it show on his face. He shook his head slightly side to side and said, "You want me to marry the Queen of Liberty?"

Jack laughed and said, "We want you to control the queen. You don't have to marry her yourself."

"How do you expect me to control the Queen of Liberty?" Pluta asked, his confusion deepening.

"By contracting with the slave ship to pick her up on their way back from Pacifica," Jack said, continuing to smile.

"That would be extremely expensive. The emperor would have to approve. That is an act of war," Pluta said.

"The slave ship is an independent contractor as far as the Justice Ministry is concerned. They are authorized to capture slaves from any planet. As long as they sell them at a Commonwealth authorized public auction, it's perfectly legal," Jack explained. "Liberty might declare war, but they are hardly in a position to do so. The whole planet is reeling from decades of war followed by a coup. In addition, General Eastbrook and Prince Justin have recently been pardoned for their roles in a coup dividing the planet further."

"I'll have to think about this," Pluta said. The shock of this news overwhelmed him.

"Think about the best way to control the queen. The slavers have already picked up the queen on your behalf. The acquisition cost will be deducted from the sale price at auction," Jack said, obviously enjoying putting Pluta on his back foot.

Pluta looked away from Jack so he could concentrate. He had invested heavily in slave acquisition ventures to the minor planets in the sector. The Justice Ministry had been bribed from his own coffers to allow the Pacifica acquisition. An accusation that the bribe included a stop on Liberty would stick. He was trapped. He had paid the bribe for the Pacifica captive to impress the emperor. Pluta enjoyed the blood and gore of the games. But he didn't enjoy it as much as the emperor. He would have to explain this was a major contribution to the emperor's plan to conquer Liberty. Something the emperor loved to talk about. Yes, it could be made to work. If it didn't, he might end up as entertainment at the Arena.

"I will talk to the emperor and get him on board with the new plan. When does the slave ship dock?" Pluta asked.

"Next week. As agreed, communications on the slave ship schedule are locked down. The public auction can be as private as you would like it to be," Jack said, smiling.

Pluta took pride in not underestimating people. He had underestimated the first minister. He could see now why the young man had risen so fast in the Commonwealth. He wouldn't make that mistake again.

It was insane to make enemies of any citizen of the Commonwealth. Much less one who had power. It would be difficult, but he resolved to put this child in his place at some point. That enjoyment would have to wait. There was a lot to do. He would instruct the auction house to open very early in the morning and reverse the order of bidding. High value slaves first and then wait until normal business hours to sell the more common ones. Most bidders at the slave auctions were a late-night bunch. If news of the auction didn't leak, he should be able to secure both the Pacifica fighter and the queen. As in chess, the queen was the key piece. What he would do with his queen was a mystery. But it was an exciting mystery to work out.

Judgement

CHAPTER 13

THE AUCTION

Someone was going to pay, thought Pluta, seething in anger. A few minutes before the slave auction was to start, Senator Cereo walked in. As usual, he was attended to by his valet and security team. Pluta was jealous of Cereo's security team. They were six ex-gladiators who had all gained their freedom by winning the required thirty bouts.

Pluta had tried bribing several of them over the years, but to no avail. Obviously, his own personal servants weren't averse to bribes. Either that or the emperor was pitting them against each other. Cereo's presence at the auction was proof of foul play.

"Good morning, Magistrate." Caius Cereo greeted Pluta with a smile that didn't quite reach his eyes. "Looks like we both stumbled on this auction. They usually advertise them in advance."

Caius was extremely charismatic. It required work to dislike him. It was a mistake to think he was just an unusually good salesman. What set him apart was that he rarely, if ever, made a bad business decision. This good judgement had followed him into the political arena, where he had slowly become a serious threat to Pluta and his cronies.

"It is odd, isn't it? Unusual to see you this early in the morning, Senator," Pluta said, suggesting his presence might not have been accidental.

"Was just on my way home when I noticed the auction house doors open. I decided to peek in," Caius said. "Do you know what they are auctioning this morning?"

"It's about to start, so I guess we'll find out together," he lied. "Hopefully, something interesting. We have a Senate hearing tomorrow. I look forward to seeing you then," Pluta said as he turned and walked to his bidding station.

The first slave they brought out was stunningly beautiful. One of the most beautiful women Pluta had ever seen. Pleasure slaves were usually brought out nude. This one was dressed in a sheer chemise that was cut low, barely covering her breasts and high enough to show most of her legs. It left little doubt about what was underneath without actually showing it. The woman was attempting to cover herself, the cold room accentuating two of her attributes. One of the handlers barked a stern command for her to put her arms down. She flinched, clearly terrified of him. Eyes cast toward the floor, she had tears streaming down her face. She was distraught, humiliated, and completely submissive to the instructions from her handlers.

"You won't find a prettier or more willing pleasure slave than this one. Already broken in, she will do anything you ask. Previously, she was the Dresser for the Queen of Liberty. She is experienced in interacting with nobility and can provide entertainment for those of the highest station. Bidding starts at five thousand credits," the auctioneer said.

Bidding was enthusiastic until it got to 15,000 credits. To Pluta's surprise, Caius raised his hand and bid 20,000 credits. That silenced the other bidders, and the gavel was struck. As the woman was taken away, he caught Caius's eye and gave him a knowing smile and nod. Caius just nodded back with the corners of his mouth slightly upturned.

Pluta was surprised. Caius had lots of slaves. All those of high station did. He kept the bulk of them on his massive villa properties, where he had located the bulk of his agricultural and manufacturing businesses. Caius had few house slaves in Roma and didn't offer any of them for entertainment. This was unusual for someone of his wealth and station.

One rumor was that he was prudish. His wife was from a common farm family. She went everywhere with him, so perhaps he was under her control. Another possibility was that he was extremely paranoid about his security. None of his slaves were in residence at his Roma Domus for long. He rotated them between Roma and his villa. Pluta had been unable to bribe any of Caius's house slaves. Threats hadn't worked either. As soon as he had one of them threatened, they disappeared. Presumably back to Caius's villa.

His purchase of this woman gave him an idea. Perhaps Caius did have a weakness. Maybe he enjoyed pliant, submissive pleasure slaves. Could he use this weakness to sneak a spy or even another assassin into Caius's villa? Something to consider.

Next up was the Pacifica Guard captive. He was brought out in heavy chains surrounded by a large team of rough looking handlers. Although the handlers looked tough, they also looked a little frightened of their charge. The small crowd naturally shrunk back a little. The man was massive, although Pluta thought he was smaller than expected. There was no fear in this man. Just a quiet confidence that radiated danger. When he looked at you, your instinct was to back up and look away. The primal threat was palpable.

"Next up, we have the ultimate killing machine. This man was born and bred on Pacifica and his capture was authorized by the Justice Ministry for indigenous peoples' research. As anyone who loves the Arena knows, members of the Pacifica Guard are unequaled in combat. On the voyage here, guards made a minor mistake in handling him with four dead as the result. The most challenging task you will have managing the star of your stable is finding credible opponents. Bidding starts at a hundred thousand credits."

A gasp came up from the small crowd with that announcement. A top tier gladiator usually topped out at 50,000 credits. However, it had been years since the Commonwealth had authorized capturing one of the Pacifica Guards and they were unique. Pluta knew the acquisition cost from the slavers was partially responsible for this exorbitant starting bid. He had expected this. Pluta started the bidding out at 100,000 credits and gritted his teeth, hoping Caius wasn't interested. He was. They went back and forth until Pluta bid 150,000 credits. At that point, the auctioneer stopped the bidding.

"Apologies from the Auction house, but we need to pause for a few minutes to discuss the latest bid. Magistrate Pluta, would you meet with me and the import minister at the auctioneer's table?"

Pluta stormed over to the auctioneer's table, intending on tearing this low-level slave dealer a new orifice. "What is your problem?" he said, making it personal with the malice in his voice.

"I apologize for stopping the bidding, but you are five hundred credits short of that bid in your account," the auctioneer said respectfully.

Pluta was stunned. The Commonwealth required all import and export transactions to be in cash. This was done so tax revenues could be immediately credited to the Commonwealth. His bidding account was tied to his main cash account at his bank. There were millions of credits in that account. He turned to the import minister and said, "Can we delay bidding until I can get this straightened out with my bank?"

The import minister was unaffected by Pluta's demeanor. A representative of the Commonwealth had nothing to fear from a colonist, no matter how rich and powerful. He calmly said, "No, Magistrate. You know the Commonwealth's rules. I've already allowed a minor violation by stopping the process to discuss this with you. It was a courtesy, nothing more. All planned sales have to be executed in a timely fashion once the bidding starts."

Pluta just nodded, turned, and rushed away to the communication portal supplied by the Commonwealth. He called his bank president's private line. "Why are automatic account transfers down this morning?" Pluta asked angrily without any attempt at a greeting.

The bank president had obviously been asleep when the call came in. He was clearly frightened, as evidenced by the sweat starting to form on his brow. Pluta was his largest customer. "I'm sorry, but the Commonwealth's communications services company told us late yesterday they needed to shut down transfers for a few hours this morning. They said it was standard maintenance. We were told we'd be back online well in advance of normal business hours. I had no idea you would need a large transfer of cash so early in the morning."

"We'll discuss this later," Pluta said curtly and broke the Commonwealth provided connection. He was beside himself with frustration and anger.

As he walked back into the auction room, he remembered that Caius had an interest in a company that provided local communications support services for the Commonwealth. Few Commonwealth citizens wanted to suffer the inconvenience of living in the colonies. So, a limited number of carefully scrutinized locals were trained and contracted for services. Communications were completely controlled by the Commonwealth and could only be used for financial transactions and communications regarding them.

This was allowed because it sped tax revenues to the Commonwealth. The bank had no control over the movement of money or the choice of when maintenance would be performed. The stranglehold the Commonwealth had on its colonists was oppressive.

Word had gotten out once the bidding had started, and the auction room was now starting to fill. As he got to his bidding station, Queen Olivia was brought out. She was young, beautiful, and radiated health. The auction house had her decked out like the queen she was. Instead of provocative clothing, she had on a formal dress that would have been appropriate for a state function. They presented her with liveried handlers, adding to her regal posture and attitude. She looked every bit the queen of a substantial kingdom as she looked disdainfully down at the crowd. The auctioneer announced the start of bidding.

"In front of you is the Queen of Liberty. As is well known, that kingdom is in disarray and a claim to the kingdom could be made by anyone who legally marries the queen. Of course, you have to do more than conquer her to do it." The sexual innuendo brought out a round of chuckles. It also pinked the queen's cheeks slightly, adding to her allure. "If you can legally marry and conquer the planet, Commonwealth recognition of legal ownership is assured. Bidding starts at one hundred twenty-five thousand credits."

Caius raised his hand and called out in a clear voice, "One hundred fifty thousand." There was stunned silence as the other bidders considered his bid. On the one hand, ownership of the queen could be extremely lucrative. At the very least, you could sell her back to Liberty for a fortune. On the other hand, it was extremely dangerous to play planetary politics. Anyone who had any sense at all was terrified of the Commonwealth. Driving up the price on something Senator Cereo clearly wanted was also a risk. If the emperor was somehow orchestrating this, it was suicide. The other bidders considered their futures and decided to stay quiet.

"No other bids?" asked the auctioneer. "Sold to Senator Cereo for one hundred fifty thousand credits."

Pluta left the auction house at once. It was a short walk to his office, and he set a fast pace. Surrounded by his security team, he noticed they were keeping their gazes off of him. They were close enough to hear his conversations with both the auctioneer and the bank president. While his face and demeanor were controlled, they understood what had happened. Anyone who worked for Pluta was terrified of getting on the wrong side of him.

When he reached his office, he looked at his security team and said, "You are not to talk to anyone about this morning. Understood?" He looked at each of them in turn as they nodded their understanding.

There in his office, he let his emotions run free. "Humiliating!" he yelled. "I should have crushed him when I had the chance!" When upset, he tended to talk to himself. Part of the reason his office was soundproof.

Pluta wasn't one to obsess over the mistakes of the past. However, there was one mistake he regularly whipped himself over. Once more, he punished himself by reviewing that horrible decision of thirty years ago.

He remembered being tired from long hours of work. His eyes had burned. He had been going over the accounts in his various businesses. As he completed that task, he was re-energized, knowing the next order of business was the final phase of a project he delighted in. Nothing was more satisfying than breaking those who had inherited great wealth and weren't smart, competent, or hardworking enough to hold on to it. He was especially disgusted by those who partied their lives and fortunes away. If they couldn't hold on to their wealth and position, they deserved to have it taken away.

There was a knock on his office door. "Come in."

"Good news," Phillip, his lawyer, said as he came through the door. "The bank called in all loans this morning and foreclosed."

"Excellent," Pluta said with a satisfied smirk on his face.

"It gets better," Phillip said as he sat in the chair opposite Pluta's desk. "This afternoon he and his wife drank themselves nearly into a stupor. They left the bar, stumbled their way to the canyon bridge, and jumped off. There are two wet smears at the bottom of the ravine."

"Oh, how I would have loved to have seen that," said Pluta, delighted. "So, the heir to the Cereo fortune will be out on the street soon."

Phillip hesitated, and looking a bit guilty said, "No, I imagine he'll stay at the villa until they run out of food, or taxes are due. The villa wasn't used as collateral in the last round of loans."

Pluta glared at Phillip said, "Why didn't you get the villa?"

"I decided you would enjoy watching them try and be farmers on that worthless piece of property. Jenny was always bragging about how it was completely sustainable. This has been so much fun I was reluctant to see it end. How could I know they'd jump off a bridge? Jenny was the one who bought the property out in the middle of nowhere because she wanted to be closer to nature," he scoffed. "It just ended up being a place to park their kid while they gambled and partied."

"Well, she is close to nature now," Pluta joked. They both laughed. "So, what about the villa now?"

"The son just turned sixteen, which is the age of maturity in that backward region. His slaves will likely kill him, steal everything, and run away. They certainly know there isn't anyone to inherit. Nobody will have an interest in chasing down a few slaves," Phillip explained. "We could argue his contract with us is vague enough to cover the villa and claim a debt equal to or greater than the value of the land, slaves, and livestock. As you know, his idiot father signed a contract no one in their right mind would sign."

"Starving amidst pastoral beauty. Murdered by slaves. Almost poetic," Pluta said. "He'll fail on his own. Might provide some entertainment." Pluta considered his options, then he said smiling, "Sign off on the debt and let probate go through. When he tries to borrow money or is late on taxes, let me know." Pluta hesitated and said, "Tell Henry to pull a case of the ten-year-old Gold Coast pinot noir out of the cellar and deliver it to your Domus.

"That's quite a gift, sir," Phillip said with suspicion in his voice.

"Continue to deliver value and I'll continue to be generous," Pluta said, smiling but with a tinge of threat the way he said, 'continue to deliver value.'

"You know my weakness." Phillip laughed nervously.

Pluta just gave him a tight smile and dismissed him, saying, "See you at the board meeting next week. Henry will see you out."

Pluta smiled at the memory of Phillip joking about Pluta's knowledge of his 'weakness.' His weakness wasn't wine. Not in the traditional way that alcohol was a weakness. But it was what triggered his downfall. His weakness was having a mother who was a common pleasure slave. His father had fallen in love with her and concocted an orphaned nephew story that had been accepted by the aristocracy. Pluta privately released this information. Phillip was blacklisted, debarred, and eventually bankrupt. The last bit was delicious. Phillip's sin? He had built a private wine cellar to hide his stock of Cereo's wines. Caius had initially built his fortune on wine and every wine snob on the planet had a collection of it. Pluta did not accept any hint of disloyalty from his employees or associates.

Coming back to the present, Pluta knew he had to find Caius Cereo's weakness. He must have at least one. As far as his sources could tell, Caius didn't bilk, bribe, or steal in his business dealings. He hadn't been caught cheating on his wife. He had never been accused of breaking any laws. Pluta had a lot of pride in his ability to hide his indiscretions. Caius was obviously a master at it as well. Pluta would not directly attack Caius's business interests. That was far too dangerous. Others had tried and failed. Some quite dramatically. He would have to wait, be patient. Everyone makes mistakes, and Caius would too. When he did, Pluta would relish finishing him and his entire family.

TRAJAN

Trajan, Fifth of his Name, was lounging in the central courtyard of the Palatium Trajan. The large garden was located in the center of the sprawling complex. The garden was a maze of walkways and seating areas surrounded by meticulously maintained ornamental vegetation. Numerous fountains added a pleasing background noise amidst the bright colors and fresh scents of flowering plants.

Trajan was stocky and had been ruggedly handsome in his youth. Now past middle age, he was showing the effects of a life of excess. He was recovering from the previous night's activities, and unhappy with the progress of his grand project. The year was Trajan 5-27, or the twenty-seventh year of his reign. Other than the grand construction of Palatium Trajan, he felt he hadn't accomplished much as Emperor of Arista. He fancied himself an equal of the roman emperors of antiquity. The grand accomplishment of the roman empire was conquest. His namesake had expanded the roman empire to its greatest extent. Trajan felt his destiny was to equal or exceed that accomplishment. It was taking too long.

Tajan looked up from his musings and saw Caius Cereo approaching with his ever-present valet, walking a few steps behind him.

"Good morning cousin," Trajan said jovially. There were multiple messages in his now standard greeting. The first was a bit of a jab at the ever-present sycophants nearby. Caius was an actual distant relative. They had a common paternity that split off generations ago. He had started calling Caius his cousin when he first achieved visible power in the Senate. He had noticed Magistrate Pluta visibly wincing the first time he jokingly did this in public. That cemented his use of the appellation.

On the other hand, Trajan had publicly executed a number of his cousins after they had formulated a coup on his first anniversary as emperor. He had been young when his father died. His relatives had thought him weak. They had underestimated him. He knew it was a whispered joke that being related to Trajan was more dangerous than being his enemy.

While not the most intelligent of emperors, he was a cunning and vicious man. He knew it was important to keep the Senate divided. Anything other than constant bickering and positioning for power between the senators was a threat. He privately preferred Caius over Pluta. He believed much of Caius's success was due to the superior blood line they shared. However, his primary goal was to keep the two of them at each other's throats.

"Good morning to you, Trajan," Caius said, smiling.

Caius had cleverly responded the first time he was addressed as "Cousin" by simply calling him Trajan. He was unique in the Senate by referring to Trajan as a family member would. Rather than being offended, Trajan had been amused. He appreciated a quick wit and bold moves. He felt the empire was suffering from a lack of risk taking and he valued the clever quick-thinking Caius. "The senatorial magistrate was here earlier and in a foul mood," Trajan said with a penetrating look.

"I can imagine he was upset with this morning's slave auction," Caius said with a conspiratorial smile.

Trajan then took on a more serious look and said accusingly, "You have upset plans. Magistrate Pluta proposed to accelerate our conquest of Liberty."

Caius took on a determined look and said, "Yes, I did that intentionally. Magistrate Pluta's plans were inspired, but not aggressive enough. Liberty should be a submissive region of the empire, not a subject kingdom. The plan's flaws were a limitation on your control and a cap on eventual revenues. You should accept nothing less than complete domination."

Trajan unknowingly reacted to Caius's use of the words submissive and domination. He had an unquenchable thirst for control. Watching others die at his whim was his ultimate satisfaction. The Arena satisfied some of this obsession. His punishment of criminals was akin to a sexual experience for Trajan. Nothing satisfied him more than having someone screaming in pain, begging him to take their life. Trajan shook himself out of the fog he had been induced into and asked, "What are you going to do with the Pacifica gladiator?"

"I was planning on making him a New Year's present," Caius said.

"Why not now? That was Pluta's offer," Trajan asked, frowning.

"Turns out he's smaller than previous captives. While still impressive, it's not clear he's up to the standards set by previous Pacifica captives. If he performs well in the Arena on New Year's, then I'll give him to you. I didn't want to gift him now just to find out later he's mediocre. That would be an insult to you and an embarrassment for me," Caius said.

"You are always thinking, cousin," Trajan said with a grin breaking out on his face. "There is no need to risk the reputation of my stable. We'll see how he stacks up." Trajan paused and affected a leer as he said, "I heard the queen's servant was uncommonly beautiful. That might have made an appropriate gift to compensate me for the change in plans."

"The queen and her servant are both part of the plan to conquer Liberty. If you are not supportive of my proposal, I will hand them both over to you. It will take some time to explain the intricacies of the new plan. Would it be possible to pull in your war planners and review?" Caius asked.

"Intriguing. As you saw on the way in, there is a long line of people to see today. This short audience was to get an explanation of why you interfered this morning. I'll get an extended session scheduled." Trajan then affected a threatening tone, saying, "I hope it's a good plan. Cousin or not, I won't be happy if you've slowed down Arista's conquest of Liberty."

"Understood Your Eminence," Caius said as he smiled, bowed low, and exited the courtyard.

CHAPTER 15

THE GLADIATORS

As Tee was being led out of the auction house, his concern was for Olivia and Gloria's safety. He had gotten to know both of them well during the weeks of travel. They were good-hearted moral people. He would be happy to call them friends in better circumstances. His blood still boiled over the obscenely revealing dress they made Gloria wear. His anger had been further heightened by the comments he heard coming from that crowd of decadent bastards during her auction. He didn't know what would happen to the two women, but he swore an oath to find them if he ever escaped.

Queen Olivia had surprised him. The Pacifica history books had led him to believe royalty thought themselves better than others. Olivia didn't treat Gloria or himself that way at all. He was treated just like someone from home would treat him. He had to admit he was attracted to her. She was smart and witty. Although tiny by Pacifica standards, she had an athletic look he found appealing.

What was really surprising was her knowledge of agriculture and animal husbandry. He didn't expect royalty to have that sort of working knowledge. In many ways it was like talking to someone from Apple Valley. Thoughts of home brought back thoughts of Diana. He had to move on from that fantasy, as difficult or impossible as that might be. He cautioned himself that life now simply revolved around staying alive. "Tee, you have a habit of being attracted to unobtainable women," he said out loud, shaking his head slowly in self-depreciating amusement.

They arrived at the Arena soon after leaving the auction house. It was an impressively large building with a number of smaller buildings enclosed within a high wall off to one side. It was to one of these buildings he was taken. He was placed in a cell much larger than the one he had on the slave ship. On board the ship, he only had a short narrow bed with a toilet and sink. This one had a large bed, a table with two chairs, a bookcase, toilet, sink, and what appeared to be a large shower.

Obscene luxury compared to his Guard accommodations.

While all areas of his cell were open to viewing by the guards, the solid walls were arranged so that the other prisoners couldn't see into each other's cells. A barred window looked out into what appeared to be an exercise yard. It had shutters on the inside of the window. Privacy of a sort. On the slaver, they had arranged a system where Olivia or Gloria would simply say, "Privacy please," and he would turn around until they said, "Done." It was embarrassing for everyone. He was glad he had some limited privacy.

Once he was locked in a cell, and his chains were removed, all but one of the contingent of guards left. The remaining guard was the oldest of the group and seemed to be in charge. He was a small thin man with grey hair and the look of someone who had lived a hard life. However, his eyes were bright with intelligence and Tee had noticed him carefully studying his new prisoner.

The old man looked him over once more and said blandly, "This is where you'll live until you die in the Arena or survive thirty matches. I've never seen a Pacifica gladiator win his freedom. The emperor tends to spread out matches for you folks and reserve them for special occasions. The good news is that you'll likely grow old here. You keep yourself and your cell clean, or we'll be forced to hose everything down. That gets everything wet, which is uncomfortable. We'll bring you three meals a day. When you're done, just slide the tray back out under the door. You'll get time in the training yard every day. This is for exercising and working on your fighting skills.

"Your owner will assign a handler. They are responsible for ensuring you're healthy and ready for the Arena. Your handler will likely want to see you demonstrate your skills this week, so he knows what you can do. You are free to spar with the others if they agree to it. There will be blunt weapons and the like for that. If you seriously injure a guard or another gladiator, your exercise privileges will be revoked. The Arena is the only place you are allowed to seriously injure anyone."

He stopped talking for a moment, looked Tee in the eyes and said in a more friendly and slightly pleading voice, "You are from Pacifica. I'm sure if you decided to kill me, it wouldn't take much effort on your part. The guards aren't your enemy. We are slaves just like you. Our lives depend on doing what we're told. If you kill one of us you won't be killing an enemy."

Tee was touched by this revelation. He had been looking for ways to get at the guards. Knowing they were slaves changed his opinion of them. They weren't his captors; they were fellow captives. He looked the guard in the eye and said, "In Pacifica, slavery is outlawed. We believe it's a crime against God. Only God has dominion over humankind. Don't worry about me. I understand your situation and don't resent you for the actions of others. I have no reason to harm you." While Tee couldn't trust the guards to go against their own self-interest, they were potential allies. He would treat them with kindness and respect.

The guard looked visibly relieved and said, "my name is Dobler. If you cooperate I'll do what I can to make your life as pleasant as is possible in this place."

"Thank you, Dobler. You can call me Tee." And with that Dobler turned and walked off down the hall.

The next morning after breakfast Dobler showed up. "You have the morning shift in the exercise yard today. There will be a number of other gladiators there and they might challenge you to spar. Like I said yesterday, please don't kill or seriously injure anyone. It would be really boring sitting in your cell all day, every day." Then he opened Tee's cell and motioned him out.

"Aren't you going to chain me?" Tee asked.

"No, I have a feeling you're a decent human being. If you kill me, I'll go to my maker knowing I've had a better life than most," Dobler said seriously. Then he hesitated and, smiling, said, "And the knowledge that I'm not as good a judge of character as I think I am."

Tee smiled. He liked Dobler. Deciding to be honest, he said, "I'm not planning to live the rest of my life here. But I won't kill innocent people in exchange for my freedom."

"Fair enough. Can't hold it against you if you try to escape. Just so you know, we've never had anyone succeed," Dobler said conversationally. Then with a grin he said, "I would appreciate you not escaping on my shift."

Tee grinned and replied, "I won't promise, but I'll keep it in mind."

Walking down the hallway, they passed cell after cell of small but rough-looking men. They were quiet and studying him intently. They were clearly measuring their chances against him. One of them finally asked Dobler, "Is he from Pacifica?"

"Newly arrived," Dobler replied.

They soon stood in front of a short corridor leading to the exercise yard. The corridor had locked gates on each end. Dobler opened the first gate and motioned him into the corridor. As he locked the gate behind Tee he said, "At noon we switch to another group. You have six hours if you want them. Call out to the guards in the observation booth if you want to go back early." Then he motioned Tee to walk to the gate on the far end, where a new guard stood waiting for him. This guard was young and looked nervous. He hesitated, then said in a questioning voice that quavered a bit, "My name is Eric. Dobler says you won't kill me if I open this gate."

"I have no reason to harm you," Tee said in a soft, reassuring voice.

Eric unlocked the gate, backed away, and quickly disappeared through a doorway to his right. Tee entered the courtyard and looked around. Above and behind him was a large balcony with heavy bars protecting the observing occupants. As he scanned the men and women watching him, Eric emerged and gave him a nervous wave.

There was an oval running track alongside the walls of the large rectangular courtyard. In the middle was a round ring that looked like a place to spar. Spread across the rest of the open area were weights and various devices. Some he was familiar with; some he was not. There was an archery and spear range with a high and wide wooden barrier up against the inside of the track at one end to protect the runners. It had been over a month since he had gone for a run, so he started with that.

The lower gravity made it easier, but a month without a hard run eventually earned him a burning sensation in his side. While he was running around the track, he noticed a large older man with a long-braided ponytail watching him. He was certainly large enough to be from Pacifica. But no one from home would disgrace themselves by wearing their hair in that fashion.

After an hour, he stopped running. His breathing was even, but he was having to breathe deeper than he normally would. It would take a few days, but he would get back into shape. Next, he worked hard with the weights and went through his entire regiment of Guard exercises. Six days on, one day off, was the mantra and he would stick to it. It felt good to be out of confinement. Then he realized his cage was simply a bit larger.

Just before the change in shifts, a voice called out from the observation deck, "Challenge him."

One of the larger gladiators approached and asked, "Would you like to spar? No weapons, just hand to hand."

Tee considered this and then agreed. "Okay, what are the rules?"

"Bruises are okay but nothing serious. If either of us says Halt, that ends the match."

Tee nodded, and then the man said, "Are you really from Pacifica? You're not as big as the other one."

"Yes, I'm from Pacifica," Tee said forcefully, tension in his voice. He was angry. The older man was obviously 'the other one' and was parading around with braided hair. Nobody from the Guard would do that. It was even more insulting for a common citizen to affect it.

His opponent backed away a step until Tee waved him forward and they began. Tee's opponent said, "Halt," after being knocked to the ground for the fifth time without landing a blow. Two others challenged and just as quickly ended their engagements with him. Tee was actually drawing the matches out, not showing his true skills. The Guard had taught him to do that. He would only show enough to win and no more.

After the third sparring match, Dobler was there to let him back into the gladiator residence hall. Tee looked up before re-entering the corridor and studied the man who had directed the other gladiators to challenge him. They locked eyes, and the man nodded.

"Who was the man with Eric in the observation room?" Tee asked.

"That's your handler," Dobler said. "Would you like to meet him?"

"Do I have a choice?" Tee asked.

"You do. But it's to your advantage to get to know him. Like me, he's a slave and the only friend you'll have in this place. You'll never get close to your owner, or any citizen, for that matter."

"Okay, how and when?" Tee inquired.

"Now and in your cell. The reason there are two chairs with your table is that you can have visitors. We lock you in, but you can have guests. Most of the gladiators avoid each other except to train. You never know who you're going to have to kill later," Dobler said with a sad tone in his voice.

"How about you? Can you visit me in my cell?" Tee asked.

"I'm your keeper. I'm not someone you should trust. I have to report on everything you say and do. But yes, we can share a few stories in the evening if you like." Dobler hesitated a moment and then said with a friendly grin, "I'll add honesty to your list of attributes."

"Why do you say that?" Tee asked.

"Last night you told me you wouldn't kill innocents for your freedom. Today, you told Eric you had no reason to harm him. You never promised either one of us safety. Most will lie when we ask them and give an empty promise." Dobler paused, then said, "Honesty is measured here by only lying when you have to."

Tee smiled at that description. He had to admit he wasn't the most honest person he knew. That was Quinn's domain. His personal rule for honesty was not to lie about something that would benefit himself unfairly or harm another person. He wasn't perfect. But he was very disappointed in himself when he failed. The rule had to be different in this situation. He liked Dobler's definition and decided to adopt it until he escaped this nightmare.

The man he had seen in the observation room walked up with Dobler and introduced himself. "My name is Leo. My master decided I'm to be your handler. It's less controlling than it sounds. I'm to ensure you are getting what you need to be your best in the Arena. From what I saw today, you don't need any help from me on training. I can also take requests back to our master for you."

Tee studied the man for a few moments before responding. Leo was heavy set but shorter than Dobler, who Tee had decided was of normal height based on his observations so far. He had dark hair and a coppery complexion with green eyes. Tee then turned to Dobler and said, "Let him in. He'll be safe."

Leo sat down at Tee's table and said, "Let me start by explaining who I am and a little about our master. I'm our master's personal valet. That means I'm constantly at his side providing services. As a consequence, you won't see me often. I was born on our master's estate as a slave. I will be a slave for the rest of my life. Our master never frees slaves. He says it's for our own good." This last bit was said with a hint of a smirk.

"Thank you for being honest with me and not giving me false hope. I will return that honesty by telling you that no man is my master," Tee said firmly.

Leo smiled at that and said, "I respect your beliefs, Tee. But you need to accept your reality. I will help you as much as I can. But there is nothing you can do to gain your freedom."

Tee nodded grimly. They had an understanding; he didn't like it, but at least Leo seemed to be a decent person. Broken, but decent.

Leo nodded back at him and said, "I'm not sure when I'll be back, so let me tell you what I know about your immediate future. Your first visit to the Arena will be in four months at the Harvest Celebration. That is a yearly national holiday to give thanks for the blessings Arista has bestowed on us. I don't know who or what you'll face. It might be some of the other gladiators here or it might be criminals or captives of some sort. Likely it will be more than one at the same time. Assuming you survive that, you'll definitely be included in the New Year's celebration. This is the biggest and most elaborate event of the year at the Arena."

Tee accepted this news and then leaned forward. "What can you tell me of Olivia and Gloria? I know your master purchased them as well."

Leo sat back and considered this. "I have met them both and they are well. It would have been far worse for both of them had the other bidder won. Before you ask, I won't take any messages to them." He said this last bit firmly.

"Thank you. If you change your mind, tell them I'll be coming for them," Tee said with ice in his eyes.

This visibly surprised Leo. After a pause, he seemed to be delighted by it as well. "I might actually do that," he said and chuckled. "Let Dobler know if you need anything from me. He can always get in touch." Still smiling slightly with his gaze remaining on Tee, he called out, "Dobler, I'm ready to go." Dobler came quickly. He must have been just around the corner.

"See, I told you he wouldn't tear you into a hundred pieces," Dobler said in an amused tone, unlocking his cell. They both disappeared down the hallway.

The next two days were much like the first in the recreation yard. The only exception was that Tee could tell his wind was returning. As before, gladiators would challenge near the end of their allotted time, and he would quickly defeat them. On the third day, the other Pacifica gladiator was in the yard, continuing to watch him.

When he was done with his run, he limped over to Tee and said, "You want to spar?"

Tee looked daggers at him, barely able to keep his anger in check. He bit off a quick, "Yes." Then he settled in to punish this pretender for his insult. Tee feigned to his right, intending to unbalance the big man by putting his weight on what was obviously a bad leg. He was aiming to grab his braid and yank him to the ground. The next thing he knew, he was on his back seeing stars.

"That was pathetic," the old man said with disgust on his face. "Get up and try again."

Tee got up and decided to be a bit more cautious this time. A different result this time. Now he was face down in the dirt. He tried a more defensive approach for the next round. Other than bruises in new places it wasn't any different. After a few more rounds, Tee was covered in dirt, which his sweat was turning into mud. His opponent was untouched, unsoiled, and seemingly accomplishing this with little to no effort.

"Who are you?" Tee finally asked.

"My name is Victor. Are you actually in the Guard?" he said with anger in his voice.

"Yes, first year Newbie. Are you really Vic?" Tee asked.

"Only my friends call me that. You call me Victor," he said sternly. Then turning his head toward the sky he said, "God, what has happened to my Guard!"

Turning back to glare at Tee, he seemed to consider what to say for a few moments and then said, "Tell Dobler yes when he asks if you'll accept me as a guest tonight. We have things to discuss." He then turned around and walked off. Instead of the uncoordinated limping and stooped posture that had been affected since Tee arrived, Victor walked like a panther, smooth, graceful, and radiating danger.

Tee couldn't have been more embarrassed. Even walking away, Victor was insulting him for being so stupid as to underestimate an opponent, buying into false deficiencies. The man wasn't insulting the memory of Vic; he was Vic! In the lore of the Guard, there wasn't a more godlike figure. In recruit training they make you shave your head the first time you lose a bout. The instructors made sure this happened during their initial physical fitness assessment. Your hair stayed shaved for the rest of your life in the Guard. The idea being that you shouldn't have hair long enough for an opponent to grab. Victor never shaved his. As a recruit, he never lost a bout. Even the instructors couldn't best him. Victor was a nickname from his recruitment days when every bout declared him

'The Victor.'

How could this be? Tee asked himself. Victor disappeared before he was born. The story was that he went out on a scouting mission and never returned. But it must be him, Tee thought. While he wasn't the best hand-to-hand fighter, he always managed to get in a strike here and there. Even when sparring with Jay. He never got close to that with Victor. "Well, it ought to be interesting to hear what he has to say," Tee said aloud.

Later that evening, Victor didn't waste any time on pleasantries. "If you are what's in the Guard now, something horrible has happened. Tell me what's happened since I was captured."

That set Tee back a bit, but he could understand Victor's conclusion, given Tee's unconventional path to the Guard. Tee proceeded to update Victor on news and battles with the GEMs since his disappearance. When he got to the one he had participated in, he slowed down and gave a detailed description of every day of the battle. He kept it general and didn't mention his role or activities.

"Setting the moat on fire and marching out with a phalanx was clever. I would have liked to have seen that. We never had a chance to try the phalanx out. It was always intended to be a last-ditch surprise to cover a retreat to the dam."

"Who is master sergeant now?" Victor asked.

"Griffith Risk," Tee answered.

"No shit. Griff's still alive? That warms an old man's heart. Is he still grumpy?" Victor asked, again with the corners of his mouth slightly upturned.

"Yes, very," Tee said, trying a smile back.

The conversation progressed through old Guard members still around who Victor knew. Victor's interest peaked when he mentioned his mother was a Wall Archer. "What's her name?" asked Victor.

"Arti Stone," Tee answered.

"Maiden name Green?" Victor asked with interest.

"Yes," Tee answered.

"Your mother is little Arti Green?" Victor asked incredulously and then said nostalgically. "She was an arrow monkey the last time I saw her.

I remember her because she was wicked with a bow. Already better than most of the experienced Wall Archers. They all talked about her. God, that makes me feel old." He hesitated, looked Tee over anew and then said, "That explains why you pay attention to the archers." Victor stopped thoughtfully and looked Tee in the eye and asked in a low voice. "How good are you? No false modesty."

Tee hesitated; he had been avoiding the archery range, hiding that skill. This was Victor, however, and if he wanted to know, Tee would give him an honest answer. "My mother is the only one who can best me."

"And how good is she?" Victor asked.

"She's won the archery competition in every game held since she reached maturity," Tee said in a low voice brimming with pride.

"I should have guessed," Victor said, berating himself. "It's obvious. The callus patterns on your hands and the uneven musculature. Have seen the same thing on some of the better Wall Archers. Can't believe I didn't put it together." He stopped for a few moments to consider what he had just learned. "Continue to keep it a secret. You should practice. Don't do it very often or they will get suspicious. Just enough to stay sharp. Aim at something different every time and convince everyone you're worthless at it. Show frustration. We can't afford to ignore something that might give us an advantage."

Victor stopped then and asked, "Who invited you to recruit training?"

"Griff," Tee answered.

This clearly surprised Victor. He paused for a while, looking at Tee with more interest. "Are you related to him?" he asked suspiciously.

"No, the Guard doesn't allow that sort of thing," Tee answered, looking back defiantly, more than a little insulted.

"Thank God that hasn't changed. Okay, I'm missing something." Victor paused to think it through. After a while, he said, "Griff used to say the Guard needed to be more than a bunch of brutes bashing about. What else can you do besides archery?"

Tee sighed deeply, turned red, embarrassed by the question. Then he said, "Griff told me he wanted me in the Guard because I'm good at coming up with unconventional battle plans."

Victor just looked at him in confusion for a few moments and then asked, "Can you give me an example?"

"Lighting the moat and driving the GEMs into it with a phalanx was my suggestion," Tee said, with his face turning even redder.

"I'll be damned," Victor said, clearly delighted. "Griff has you earmarked to be an officer, doesn't he? If that idea is an example of your contributions, maybe he was right all along. We all used to make fun of him for saying that." Victor stopped and stared at Tee for a few moments, making him uncomfortable.

"There is no excuse for your incompetence in the ring," he said as his eyes bored into him. "They trained you for defensive fighting. It's better than your laughable offensive skills, but it's far short of acceptable. I've lived here longer than I lived on Pacifica. Someone is going to pay for that, and I want you to help me. To do that, you have to be turned into a competent fighter. You want to help me make them pay?"

"Nothing would make me happier," Tee said honestly.

"Good, then reserve three hours every day in the yard for practice. We are also going to have dinner together whenever I have something to discuss with you. You'll do exactly what I tell you to do. We'll have to start your training from scratch, so plan on being frustrated and angry most of the time. No sparring with the other gladiators. It will just give you bad habits and you have enough of those already," Victor said sternly. Then softening his tone, he added, "Some advice. Don't talk to the other gladiators. They are used to my aloofness and will figure it's a Pacifica thing. You are likely going to have to kill many of them in the Arena. It makes it easier if you don't know anything about their personal lives."

And with that he yelled, "Dobler, we're done."

The next day Tee asked Eric. "Can I get a bow and some practice arrows?"

"I thought archery was a women's thing on Pacifica?" Eric asked, confused.

"It is, but I'm bored. It will give me something new to do," Tee replied. Then he thought, it will also give me something to be secretly good at while Victor humiliates me in front of everyone.

Judgement

CHAPTER 16

ARCHERS AUXILIARY

It had taken several long frustrating sessions, but the CGG finally agreed. Ultimately, it was two of Griff's staff sergeants who convinced him. The CGG decided to bring them in to ask questions, given how often Griff kept referring to them in his arguments. Their enthusiasm surprised him. It wasn't that the CGG didn't believe Griff. It was that he didn't think the rank and file would accept this kind of change. The Guard's self-identity was very strong. Sergeants Willis and Glenn had strong opinions about the excellence of Apple Valley Wall Archers. They were convinced the group was much better than the other two regions. When asked if they would support a few Wall Archers becoming a permanent part of the Guard, they enthusiastically supported it.

As Sergeant Willis put it, "Arti Stone is the reason the Apple Valley Wall Archers are so effective. Just having her spend full time training across all the regions would enhance effectiveness. If we coordinated training with the Guard, I think the improvement would be tremendous."

Sergeant Glenn chimed in as well. "Our scout teams would be greatly enhanced by some of their better archers. Diana Wells and her small team decimated the GEMs guarding the rope ladders during the upper east valley invasion. It saved lives and was the reason for our quick victory. Just one or two archers per scout team would make a difference."

After the two scout team leaders left, the CGG said, "Okay Griff, I'm sold. Let's pull together a proposal for President Malrey. I would like to start small and see how it goes before commissioning a full-blown organization. Perhaps two archers from each of the regions. I believe the proposal hinges on Arti Stone agreeing to lead this. We need a name for the group. The Guard and its traditions are something specific. I don't want that to change. The Wall Archers aren't going to go through recruit training and other Guard type processes, so we don't need to muddy the water by trying to completely combine them. Perhaps we should ask Arti to figure all this out."

One week later, President Malrey brought the council back to order. "I believe we're ready for the last item on our agenda. This is a proposal I'm asking the council to vote on even though it is within my authority to decide. I'll hand over the floor to the CGG to explain."

"Good afternoon. In our most recent struggles with the GEMs, it's become clear to the Guard how vital Wall Archers are to overall success. It's also become clear that the training Apple Valley has been doing has greatly increased their effectiveness in battle."

The CGG paused, looked at Councilwoman Ricks, and gave a slight smile and nod of appreciation, knowing her history.

"It's common knowledge that Arti Stone is responsible. Our proposal is that we fund a permanent unit of Wall Archers that is separate from but under the command structure of the Guard. By having full-time focus and the ability to jointly train, we believe we can significantly improve our defensive capabilities. We would like funding approval for six full-time Wall Archers, two from each region. Arti Stone would be asked to lead this unit. Questions?"

Councilwoman Ricks spoke up, "What if Arti says no?"

"Then we drop the idea. We believe Arti could eventually train a replacement for herself, but to start this up, it will take her unique knowledge, skills, and reputation among the Wall Archer community."

"Great answer. I fully agree," Ricks said with a smile.

Barlow jumped in and said, "I don't think we ought to approve anything for the military until we agree to make a serious attempt at peace negotiations. After seeing thousands of dead from the latest battle, they might be more inclined to stop this madness."

"You are well within your rights to call for an agenda item to discuss peace negotiations, Councilman Barlow. But I recommend we not tie agenda items together. It will likely impede progress," President Malrey cautioned.

"I have a vote and will cast it anyway I like Ms. President," he said with a sneer.

Jennifer just stared at him for a moment, collecting herself. Barlow had progressively gotten more and more combative in the past few months. He seemed to think she was the problem when she was simply a facilitator for the Pacifica Council. She had hoped bringing a decision to the council that was wholly hers to make would be an olive branch. It appeared that collaborative gestures weren't going to make things better.

"If there are no more questions or comments I move, we vote," Jennifer said stiffly and waited. After a few moments of silence, she started.

"Councilwoman Ricks?"

"I vote yea. Arti is a national treasure, and this will make us safer."

Councilman Rickets?

"I vote nay. Barlow is right. We are too militaristic. Death and destruction seem to be our answer for everything. I, for one, am sick of it."

Jennifer was shocked. Looking quickly over at Councilwoman Ricks, she could read the surprise on her face as well. She knew Rickets had lost a son at the Wall. Perhaps he was angry about that. She could certainly emphasize having just lost a younger brother during the last day of battle. Losing the full support of Apple Valley was extremely disturbing from a number of perspectives.

The rest of the voting was quick and predictable. Landing Valley voting yea and Eureka Valley voting nay.

Jennifer looked around the room and, after catching everyone's eye, said, "I brought this issue to the council to test the appetite for military spending. I can see we need to restart discussions on how to approach the GEMs with peace proposals. We lost a good portion of our Guard and Volunteer forces at the Wall in the most recent battle. Given the situation, I don't believe we can wait on proposals that potentially increase our effectiveness. For that reason, I will break the tie with a yea vote."

"Councilman Rickets. Given your strong stance on it, will you come back with a proposal for peace negotiations? Feel free to work with any of your fellow councilpersons."

"I appreciate the offer, Ms. President. Can I have two weeks to prepare?"

"Yes. I'll add it to the agenda two weeks from today. This Pacifica

Council session is now completed."

Griff's visit to Apple Valley wasn't going as expected. It was confusing, to say the least. He had expected Arti to be warm and friendly. She was not. Her treatment of him had been coldly professional. This wasn't the Arti he had come to know. After explaining the Wall Archer leadership role that was being offered, she had a few questions.

"How often will I be working directly with the Guard?" Arti asked.

Griff hesitated a moment, still confused by her seemingly angry disposition. Then he said, "That is something you will propose. You know how the Guard operates at the Wall. I think you're in the best position to decide what is most efficient. I would like to discuss how archers can be deployed alongside our scout teams. Diana's success at the upper east valley incursion has sparked a lot of ideas to improve those teams' effectiveness as well."

"How often will I have to work with you?" she asked pointedly with ice in her eyes.

"As much or as little as you think necessary," he said. His heart was in his throat as he wondered what he had done to make her this angry.

Just then, the door to Arti's house opened and Grammy strolled in. She didn't seem any happier than Arti. Without so much as a hello Grammy said with iron in her voice, "I heard you were here. You know something about Tee's disappearance. I want to know what you know."

"What makes you think I know something?" Griff replied.

Grammy huffed out a big breath, composed herself and said, "Diana is like a granddaughter to me. At times I know her better than she knows herself. She has been cagy about what was found over on the east side. That isn't like her. She's also acting like Tee isn't dead. She hasn't said anything to anyone. But I know that girl. I also know that if she knows something, you know something."

"If you think Diana knows something, ask her," Griff replied with his voice becoming stern.

"I have, and she lies to me," Grammy said. "You must have scared her into keeping what happened to Tee a secret."

"I have not threatened Diana. I'm also not going to lie, so don't ask me anything else about this," Griff said in a loud voice.

"I think you should leave now. I will accept the position offered, but I would appreciate keeping our interactions to a minimum," Arti said in a raised but quavering voice.

Griff just stared at her for a moment, his heart going out to her. Then he said, "I'll assign Jay Phillips as your primary Guard contact. He is working for me as an aide, and most of what needs to happen can happen through him. And before you ask, Jay doesn't know anything about Tee's disappearance." He hesitated for a few moments and said, "One more thing. They found Angus Willard hanging from a tree in a remote area of the Armstrong Reservoir. The Landfall Valley Sheriff isn't investigating, and neither is the Guard." After delivering that news, Griff opened the door and left. He was heartsick. Tears threatening to form in his eyes. But he would honor his oath to keep everything about the committee secret. His personal desires were insignificant compared to the safety and security of Pacifica.

Judgement

CHAPTER 17

CAIUS

Senator Cereo was in the entry hall to personally greet him when the first minister arrived. They walked a short distance down the hall and into a small but warm office. "Thank you for making the time to meet with me, Senator," Jack said with a polite smile.

"Good to see you again, Jack. I enjoyed our conversation at my little party. Thank you again for taking the time to attend." He hesitated a moment and then continued. "I'm not much on formalities so please just call me Caius."

Jack was struck once again by the senator's easy-going nature. He didn't have the upper-class snobbery common among the colonist elite. Perhaps it was his rural upbringing. However, Jack had seen glimpses of steel in his nature at the senator's party, so he would proceed cautiously. "I have some delicate topics to discuss. Is it possible to have some privacy?" he asked, glancing over at a slave sitting in a corner of the room.

"You can discuss anything you want in front of Leo. He's my valet and you can trust him to keep his mouth shut. He's not stupid enough to cross me. Nor is he smart enough to take advantage of anything you say," Caius said disdainfully.

Jack had heard the senator was unusually paranoid about his safety. Evidently, several assassination attempts have been made over the years. One recent attempt was reported to have been made by a highly regarded and expensive professional. That man had gotten into Caius's private suite at his remote villa. But he only killed one elderly servant before being killed himself. Jack studied the senator's valet. He was heavyset, and with his buzz cut, he looked more like an army sergeant than a house servant. Jack was sure this was part of his personal security, so unlikely to be a threat.

"I wanted to discuss one of your recent acquisitions at the slave market," Jack said.

Caius looked at him, smiled and said, "You can be blunt with me, Jack. Outside of the games that must be played at parties, I prefer to speak plainly. You strike me as an intelligent person. I'm sure you have specific things you'd like out of our conversation. Feel free to dive in."

He couldn't let it affect his decision making; but he couldn't help but like the senator. Jack gave Caius a conspiratorial grin and said, "That will certainly save us time and eliminate confusion." When Caius nodded, he continued, "You have possession of Queen Olivia. Magistrate Pluta had plans for her that he claimed would increase tax revenues for the Commonwealth. We would like to know what you have planned for her."

"Is the Commonwealth going to ask if she can be released to Magistrate Pluta?" Caius asked.

"No, certainly not. As you know, we can't legally compel you to do that," Jack said, emphasizing the word legally in a way that insinuated this really wasn't a barrier. "The Commonwealth is always interested in supporting colonists within the boundaries of the Edicts."

Caius gave a warm smile and said, "My initial objective was to be a pain in the ass. As you know, Jack, Pluta and I are business and political competitors. I didn't know at the time what he had planned for her but wanted to ensure it didn't create a problem for me."

"That makes sense. But, again, what do you have planned?" Jack asked.

"I was originally thinking I would ransom her. It would fill my coffers and keep her away from Pluta. However, after studying the situation in Liberty I've concluded a bigger play might be possible," Caius said. "I'm not being evasive, Jack. I still haven't come up with a plan that doesn't have significant issues. But I'm working on it."

"Is it something the Commonwealth could help with?" offered Jack.

"Perhaps," Caius said thoughtfully. "Can I share some thoughts and have them stay private?"

"I have to report all conversations with colonists to the governor. But I am authorized to commit on her behalf that she will keep anything you say in confidence. The Administration function is not obligated to share information we obtain from planetary governments or colonists with Judicial. Unless, of course, something violating Commonwealth Edicts is proposed or exposed," Jack said in a tone that insinuated once again that legality was a negotiable topic.

Caius tapped his finger lightly on the table as he considered Jack's conditions. Looking Jack in the eye, he said, "I'm intrigued by the possibility of conquering Liberty and putting the population to work. The emperor has long had a desire to conquer that planet. But he doesn't have a plan to accomplish it without taking on an unacceptable level of risk. Worse yet, he doesn't have a plan of what to do if he's successful. Their army is smaller than ours. But long supply lines and decades of war producing excellent military leadership steers me away from the direct approach. So, it has to start with a political solution, and we have their queen."

"How about forcing a state marriage between the queen and a member of the emperor's family? Over time, you could take control," Jack said, voicing the plan he had with Pluta. "Once you have control, you change their constitution to allow slavery and start with the regions that have recently rebelled."

Caius appeared to be considering this carefully before saying. "In my opinion that isn't good enough. There are too many things that can go wrong. We have to eliminate Prince Justin and neutralize General Eastbrook for starters. Once that's done, we have to eliminate the queen's power without it looking like a coup. Assuming we accomplish all that, the House of Lords would have a say in the succession. They would likely deem a prince consort from Arista as an unqualified foreign national." Caius hesitated a moment and then said, "We need to conquer them. Their constitution needs to be torn up. Trying to work within their system is unlikely to work and even if it did, it would limit profits. We have to divide their kingdom and then conquer it. But it has to be done very carefully."

Jack had to think about that for a minute. Trying to buy time, he asked, "What is your interest in this?"

"I would like to be the emperor's Governor of Liberty once it's conquered. I would sign a tax revenue agreement with the Commonwealth in exchange for its assistance. My compensation would be based on a percentage of the increased taxes that are collected."

Jack nodded, acknowledging his understanding. He wondered if Caius had grander goals in mind, perhaps as ruler of an independent Liberty? Needing more time to consider this change in plans, he said, "I'm sure the governor would be interested in your thoughts on a tax revenue contract. Let me discuss it with her and get back to you."

"While you're doing that, I'm going to fix the mess Pluta created. Liberty will naturally blame Arista for the queen's kidnapping. This weakens any plans the emperor might have by unifying Liberty rather than dividing it. I have a message to Prince Justin and the House of Lords, ready for the emperor's seal. It exposes a plot by unknown parties in Liberty who bribed the slavers to capture the queen and transport her for sale to Arista," Caius explained.

Jack's brow wrinkled, and he said, "Doesn't that mean you'll have to hand her over to Liberty and lose our leverage?"

"No. In his message, the emperor will express paternal concern for the queen's well-being. He'll state that he doesn't know who paid to have her kidnapped. Given that, he has no idea who he can safely release her to," Caius said, smiling. "He'll go on to say that he is very interested in working with the Kingdom of Liberty to expose whoever is trying to create problems between their two worlds."

Jack was clearly still not convinced and said, "Given that message, won't Queen Olivia just decide to return to Liberty?"

"It will be pointed out that Queen Olivia has not reached the age of maturity, according to Arista law. The emperor will state that he is so concerned for her safety that he personally designated one of Arista's leading citizens as guardian. He states in the message that his only goal is to ensure long-lasting peace with Liberty," Caius said with his winning smile. "It turns out I'm a hero of the empire by recognizing Queen Olivia and quickly taking control of her safety. As a show of good faith, the servant who was taken along with her will be immediately released. She has been well treated since leaving the auction house and her account of time spent on Arista will align with the emperor's message."

Caius hesitated then, with a smug expression, said, "This did present a personal challenge. Her servant was unusually attractive. I was very tempted to keep her. However, the needs of Arista and the Commonwealth come first."

Jack was very impressed. He wasn't sure what the next steps were, but Caius's plan kept them in control of the queen while causing strife and confusion in Liberty. Jack considered everything and then asked, "Is there anything you need from the Commonwealth in the short term?"

"It would be helpful if the Commonwealth didn't refute the claim that someone on Liberty paid for the queen's transportation to Arista. By declining to confirm or deny Liberty based involvement, the natural assumption will be that the Commonwealth confirms the accusation." Caius hesitated, then he said with a knowing look, "I believe Magistrate Pluta has been ignoring messages from Lord Druango."

At this point Jack wasn't surprised Caius knew their plans. His ability to take control meant his sources of inside information were excellent. "Yes, he doesn't know what to tell Druango, so he's been buying time."

"You might let Lord Druango know privately that the rumor on Arista is that Prince Justin is the culprit. That he's trying to supplant the queen now that her father is gone. Expressing concern for Druango's health at the same time might be a nice touch," Caius suggested. He let that sink in for a few moments and then continued, "In addition, it would be ideal if General Eastbrook's surveillance network intercepted a message indicating Lord Druango provided the slavers bribe. His plan was to convict Prince Justin on a second count of treason, execute him, and then negotiate with Arista to get the queen returned.

"The nice touch here is to have plans to eliminate Justin's and General Eastbrook's extended families as part of the intercepted message. The conspiracy clearly intends to isolate the queen and leave her as the only living member of the royal line."

Jack's head was spinning. This was much more aggressive and devious than their original plan. The financial windfall would be enormous if they pulled it off. But it would mean another delay. He wasn't looking forward to delivering a schedule change to the governor. On the other hand, she might be intrigued by Senator Cereo's plan. The confusion he was going to sow didn't present a problem for the Commonwealth. Another civil war was obviously Caius's goal here and there was only upside to that outcome. He would have to come up with an alternative plan for the governor to consider. Just going in with Caius's plan would make him look weak.

"Thanks again for seeing me. I'll be in touch once I've discussed this with the governor. I'm looking forward to seeing what we can accomplish together," Jack said.

Caius walked him all the way out to his carriage, asking about his family and how he was enjoying his new role as first minister. It was a nice touch. Most powerful people hand that duty off to a servant and wouldn't bother to ask personal questions. As his carriage drove off, he realized with alarm that he liked the senator. The extent of the man's deviousness made him extremely wary, but he was oddly likeable. He counseled himself that having personal regard for anyone was dangerous.

You never knew when they would need to be sacrificed.

SALT THE EARTH

The messenger arrived late in the afternoon through driving rain. The lieutenant was wet, grimy, exhausted, and escorted by a small contingent of rangers. The roads had gotten dangerous since the queen's kidnapping. Criminal elements were taking advantage of the military prioritizing preparations for renewed civil war, rather than chasing down criminals. They hadn't gotten so bold as to attack a military unit yet, but safety on the roads was getting worse every day.

When he was ushered into the ranch house, Perry was having a late dinner with Olivia, Colonel Peters, and a few of his staff officers. The rangy young man hesitated at the door, clearly intimated by those seated at the table. Perry, recognizing his hesitancy, rose and warmly greeted him, "Come sit and have dinner with us. Lieutenant Graves? Is that right?" he asked.

"Yes, sir," Graves answered, clearly surprised Perry knew his name.

Turning to one of the two soldiers serving them, he asked, "Would you get another place setting and some hot tea for the lieutenant? I'm sure he's chilled to the bone."

"Thank you, sir, but I don't want to impose," Graves said, clearly uncomfortable dining with the top army officers.

Perry noticed Graves self-consciously looking down at his mud splattered uniform and remembered his own days as a young lieutenant. "Please join us. You can give your report and get a decent meal at the same time. What kind of soldier turns down a meal or a chance to sleep?" Perry said, conveying his origins as an ordinary soldier.

"A stupid one, sir," Graves answered with a shy smile, quoting the axiom learned in basic training.

Perry had noticed the look Graves had given Olivia when introductions were made. If memory served him, he had seen the young man on duty at the castle before the kidnapping. He had likely seen both Olivia and Bria up close. His wide-eyed glance at Olivia had given him away. His shocked look betrayed that he knew this was not Bria. Oh well, he thought, another soldier to add to the list of those not allowed to leave the ranch.

"I can see that you recognized the queen, Lieutenant," Perry said in a serious tone.

"Yes, sir," Graves said nervously. Then, turning to Olivia, he bowed low and said, "My apologies for not addressing you correctly, Your Majesty."

Olivia smiled warmly and said, "Please sit down and have dinner with us, Lieutenant. You were right to play along with our little secret. I would appreciate it if you would refer to me as Bria for the time being. At some point, we can get back to Your Majesty, or ma'am, depending on the circumstances. For now, it's vital we continue the pretense that I'm the General's daughter."

"What do we do when an enemy makes a mistake, Lieutenant?" Perry asked with a tight grin.

"We don't correct them, sir," Graves answered, smiling. Clearly becoming more comfortable.

"Good man," Perry said. "Please eat your dinner and then we can review your message packet and verbal report." Perry was pleased to see the young man attack his dinner with gusto. His guess was that the man hadn't stopped to eat anything since he left the castle. That told him much about the importance of the information he would deliver.

When Lieutenant Graves folded up his napkin and placed it on his plate, Perry said, "Give us your report, including what's in your packet. I'm also interested in any thoughts or impressions you have on morale among the troops, given all the strife." He then looked around the table and said, "We'll wait until you're finished before we ask questions."

Graves took a deep breath and gave his report. "In the packet is a copy of a message from Emperor Trajan of Arista. The summary is that he claims shock and anger at the kidnapping of the queen and strongly states his dedication to finding those responsible. He goes on to say that his belief is that someone from Liberty is responsible. He says he will protect the queen's safety until the guilty parties are identified and neutralized. Since he doesn't know who to trust, and the queen is considered a minor under their laws, he will take on a paternal role and keep her safe on Arista." Graves paused at that point given everyone was leaning over the table clearly wanting to ask questions.

"Please continue, Lieutenant," Perry said calmly but greatly relieved to have news of his daughter's whereabouts and situation. Perhaps he could even get a good night's sleep tonight.

Graves nodded and resumed his report. "Also in the packet are three messages from Prince Justin. The first details the latest developments in the House of Lords, along with rumors the prince thinks may be legitimate. The second and third are written in code and for your eyes only," Graves said, looking at Perry, then nervously at Olivia. Continuing he said, "The summary of the first message is that the House of Lords has closed its session with the various members leaving for home.

"Arguments over the missive from Arista resulted in a brawl on the floor of the House of Lords. A faction comprised of pre-unification lords accused Prince Justin of a power grab by stopping the wedding. Those backing Prince Justin have the view that Lord Druango concocted this. His objective being to eliminate the prince so that when the marriage is consummated, he can exercise control over the queen without interference. The rumors all have to do with pre-unification lords forming militias under the guise of self-protection."

Perry caught, held the young man's eye and asked, "What do you think, Lieutenant?"

Graves was ready for this question. General Eastbrook was famous for asking people at all levels in his army their opinion. Everyone knew there were no negative consequences when honestly answering. "None of it makes sense, sir. Druango would have been better served to marry the queen and then act to take control." He glanced quickly and nervously at Olivia after delivering that opinion, but then continued. "General Fedral assigned me as Prince Justin's military aide, and my observation is that he's completely devoted to the queen. Even if he wasn't loyal, stopping the wedding in this fashion would be stupid, and the prince is anything but that."

When Lieutenant Graves finished giving his opinion, Perry decided he was impressed. Justin had made a good decision sending this young man. He was an excellent communicator and insightful. Given he couldn't leave the ranch, Perry would add him to his personal staff. Perry then opened it up for discussion and questions. As the poor young lieutenant was being peppered by questions from all sides, he excused himself and asked Olivia to accompany him. Walking to the buffet where the message packet had been placed, he pulled the coded messages out and they retired to his office. After decoding the first message, they read.

Olivia,

It's likely going to end in war. Not clear to me who kidnapped Bria or what their end game is. Druango is using this to stir up the former non-aligned regions. Given that Arista claims they will return 'the queen', he feels he has the upper hand in appealing to those who love her. The fact I openly rebelled against the king makes me look like the guilty one too many.

It's time to make some decisions. The first is whether to announce that the kidnappers missed. That Bria is the one being held by Arista. The upside is that this would remove the excuse Druango has for building up the militias. The downside is that we don't know who is behind all of this and it's possible the revelation could play into their hands. Bria's safety is a large concern of mine in this scenario.

The second decision is whether to demand the newly formed militias be immediately disbanded. This is likely to launch a civil war. You both know my opinion on Lord Druango and the inevitability of conflict, so I won't bother to restate it.

My advice? Keep the fact that the kidnappers missed their target a secret. Authorize me as regent to recall Perry as general of the Royal Armed Forces. I would further advise you to direct him to get on a war footing as soon as possible. If you agree with my advice, I recommend you stay with the army and lie low until we can recover you safely.

Your faithful servant,

Justin

Opening and decoding the second message they both read.

Perry,

I know you're going to recommend we announce the queen's presence in Liberty and avoid an immediate war. Sacrifice for the greater good is in your nature. However, I caution you that war is sometimes the greater good. I believe that to be true in this instance.

We will get Bria back, but we need your sacrifice along with hers until we are certain we understand who is pulling strings and what the endgame is.

These messages were sent with Lieutenant Graves. He is an intelligent and unusually insightful young man. Take some time and question him before you send him back. I've found him to provide excellent observations and advice.

Your faithful friend,

Justin

Perry sat with Olivia and they both thought about the new developments and what they meant. Olivia finally broke the silence by saying, "I agree with Justin's advice. My gut tells me I made a mistake trusting that Lord Druango could be controlled. My guess is that he's behind all of this but agree with Lieutenant Graves that none of it makes sense."

Perry considered that for a moment, and then responded, "The Commonwealth is involved in this somehow. There has to be a third player. They were acting behind the scenes with your father. That means Lord Druango is in league with them. Since the Commonwealth only cares about tax revenues, this means whatever plan they have is not good for our people. My advice is…"

A loud crash startled them both. It sounded like a door being broken in. This was followed by breaking glass. Likely from the windows in the next room. The next thing they heard was a series of whistles. Peters always kept a whistle around his neck and used it on the battlefield to communicate commands to his rangers. This one was an order to converge on him if Perry remembered the commands correctly. Perry immediately motioned Olivia to stay put while going to his weapons rack and pulling out an arming sword and parrying knife.

Stopping for a moment, he grabbed his cavalry saber as well. Rushing through his office door, he was met with complete chaos. A melee was taking place in the dining room, with Graves and Peters in the middle of it. Graves was the only one with a sword, having brought it in when he arrived. Peters was a brawler. He was brandishing a chair as a defensive weapon to buy time.

Perry yelled, "Sword," at Peters while throwing the arming sword handle first. Peters turned and grabbed the sword out of the air and went on the offensive, brandishing both sword and chair. Perry then caught Colonel Pike's eye and tossed him the cavalry sword. He stayed put guarding the doorway until Peters, Graves, Pike, and the rest of his staff were in danger of being overwhelmed. He yelled, "Barricade the door," over his shoulder as he dove in.

Peters, Graves, and Pike were shoulder to shoulder bearing the brunt of the attack while the rest of his staff officers, armed with table knives, did what they could. Pike went down first, followed soon after by Graves.

This left Peters trying to hold all the attackers off. Perry jumped in and grabbed Grave's sword, and they reestablished a stalemate. Suddenly, Perry was separated off and in danger of being overwhelmed. Peters, swaying on his feet from multiple stab wounds, yelled in frustration and launched himself into the middle of the swarm of those around Perry. The rest of Perry's staff followed.

All of a sudden, cutlery knives started spouting randomly in the attackers. This caused a lull in the fighting as the attackers struggled to adjust to this new threat. As Olivia started running out of table knives, Peters's rangers showed up in force. It was quickly over once they arrived.

Olivia hurried over to check on Pike, who appeared to be badly injured. She had known him since she was a little girl. She checked his wounds, turned to Perry, and shook her head. There was a new opening on Perry's staff. Graves had a serious gash on his sword arm, but it was not life threatening. A blow to the head had knocked him out. He was now awake, but a bit confused as he slowly recovered. She went to a battered and bloodied Peters.

To her surprise, she discovered he was still alive. He had clearly offered his life to the attackers in exchange for Perry's. Serious wounds, but still living. "Get a doctor in here immediately," she ordered one of Perry's staff officers, who only had a few minor injuries. Then she started compressing the more serious wounds using dinner napkins and strips of cloth from her dress.

"You shouldn't be doing this, Bria," Peters said seriously.

Although she was extremely worried about him, she smiled at his discomfort of being cared for by his queen. It was amazing to her that he was clear-headed enough to maintain the ruse. She then said in a joking voice, "I'm a farm girl, Timothy. I know how to take care of the animals."

Peters smiled with difficulty, and then with an amused expression on his face, said, "Thank you. You are truly an animal angel."

She realized they were flirting with each other. He seemed to have realized it as well, to his embarrassment. It was even a bigger surprise when she realized how much she liked it. He was a very attractive man who she greatly enjoyed being around. His quick thinking and unwavering support immediately after the king had been killed had shown his intelligence and compassion. She also felt incredibly safe when he was around. Of course, any thoughts in that direction were worse than useless. She would marry for the kingdom, not for love. That was Bria's future, not hers.

The doctor showed up and gently guided her out of the way so he could get to work. She looked around the room and caught Perry's eye. He had been barking out orders, getting some semblance of a defense organized and established around the house. She realized it might not be over yet. Still in a daze, she looked further around the room and realized there were only eight attackers dead on the floor. It had seemed like so many more to her. Seeing Colonel Pike lying dead in a pool of blood was incredibly sad. Sadness slowly turned to anger. This was a man who had survived much hardship for the security of the kingdom. This was a man who had always been kind to her. He ought to have enjoyed his final years in peace. A peace he had fought hard and sacrificed much for. She resolved he would not die in vain. The kingdom would have peace.

Later, when order had been established, and a careful sweep had been done around the ranch house, Olivia and Perry continued their conversation. Olivia looked at Perry with steel in her eyes and said, "I know you believe we ought to be compassionate with our enemies. That punishing them just leads to making sure they will always oppose us."

"Hold on, Olivia," Perry said calmly, but with purpose in his voice. "It's true. I believe it's better to turn your enemy into your friend rather than punish them." Olivia started to break in, but Perry put his hand up, stopping her. "But, there are times when your enemy has proven they are evil. Sometimes all your attempts to redeem them fail." He paused as his face took on rock hard determination and he said, "It's time to salt the earth."

Olivia understood the biblical reference and shuttered inside.

Judgement

CHAPTER 19

HARVEST FESTIVAL

The past four months of training with Victor had been hell. Battered and bruised, Tee was having a hard time seeing the benefit of getting beaten senseless every day. Every time he ended up in the dirt, or was declared dead, Victor would tell him in colorful language what he had done wrong. Then they would focus on specific exercises intended to fix that specific deficiency. Every one of his weaknesses was attacked over and over and over again until Victor was satisfied.

After one such session, Tee had been visibly frustrated and angry. Instead of consoling him, Victor said, "Size and strength are useful, but it's not what separates good fighters from mediocre ones. It's what you have between your ears that matters. You don't suffer from a lack of size; you suffer from letting your stature be your excuse. You're surprisingly tough, Tee, but you have to stop giving yourself excuses."

At first, Victor's lecture just made him angrier. Heartless asshole, thought Tee. But calming down later, he reluctantly admitted that it was true. His whole life, others had told him his lack of size and strength meant he had limitations. He was guilty of accepting this. It wasn't their fault for having an opinion. It was his fault in accepting that opinion and making it his own.

Oddly enough, the next morning, Victor's accusation was starkly confirmed. Someone unfamiliar was sparring with Victor. Although smaller than Tee, he was challenging Victor and making him work. Not that the stranger was anywhere close to winning, but he did make it interesting.

When the time came for Tee's daily training regimen, he asked, "Who's the guy you were sparring with this morning? I thought you didn't spar with the other gladiators."

"His name is Forti. He's not a gladiator, He's a citizen. Won thirty bouts in the Arena and was given his freedom," Victor said.

"If he's a citizen, why is he here?" Tee asked.

"He wants to keep his fighting skills sharp. He's the head of Senator Cereo's security team, and assassination attempts are common here," Victor answered. He then added, "And he's a friend."

"You have a friend?" Tee asked, before realizing how that sounded.

Victor laughed loudly, causing the other gladiators to glance over at them. Then continuing to smile he said, "Yes, I am human, Tee." Then, settling back into his normal training voice, he said, "And being human, I am sometimes a hypocrite. I didn't learn my lesson right away. When I first got here, the other gladiators would challenge me. It was irritating. Since I had nothing to gain from sparring with them, I would accept their challenge and make the experience as painful as possible without losing my exercise yard rights. That caused them to leave me alone. It didn't work with Forti. He kept coming back. So, I asked him, 'Do you have a pain fetish?'

"Instead of being insulted, he laughed and said, 'No. Perhaps a lack of brains, but no fetishes.' Then he looked me in the eye and said, 'Winning doesn't make me better. Only losing does that.' This was a man I could respect. I became his mentor and eventually his friend. He claims he gained his freedom because of me. It would have been horrible if I had been forced to meet him in the Arena. Thank God that didn't happen."

Tee's natural stubbornness took over at that point. He was guilty of exactly what Victor had accused him of. He pledged that his excuses for himself were going to stop. Once he accepted this, he started to progress rapidly, surprising even Victor. Instead of backing off, Victor pushed harder, became more intense. When he first realized Victor had not been going full speed, it momentarily depressed him. Then he realized the change in Victor was a compliment, so he worked even harder.

Then one day it happened, Tee knocked Victor to the ground. As he moved in for the kill, Victor rolled quickly to the side and up and then put him down, match over. Instead of frowning, Victor smiled. Helping Tee up, he said, "I've been waiting for the right time to tell you this. You have progressed from being an embarrassment to being adequate." Then, holding up one hand, he said, "Before you start puffing up your feathers, you still aren't what I would call good. Not even close."

Tee was bursting with pride at that announcement. He knew he was much better than he had been when he left Pacifica. It made the last few months of pain and embarrassment worth it.

"Now we're going to focus on something you're already much better at than most. Paying attention," Victor said. "I lied when I said size and strength don't matter, they do. But I'm not a good fighter because of physical attributes. It's because I pay attention."

Victor then started spending time coaching Tee on what to look for in weaknesses. Tee always thought this was a strength of his, and it was, but he quickly discovered it wasn't nearly as refined as it could be. Victor was an expert in human anatomy. He could watch you walk and know the condition of your ankles, knees, hips, and back. All of which might have potential weaknesses to exploit. He passed on this knowledge, constantly testing Tee whenever someone new showed up. It didn't have to be a gladiator, anyone could be analyzed, taken apart, and exposed.

After the initial lecturing on this, Victor started imitating a variety of weaknesses. Bad knee, sore back, stiff hip, etc. Tee was expected to immediately identify the vulnerability and quickly devise a plan to take advantage of it. Once he had devised an acceptable plan, he had to practice it over and over and over again. No detail was too obscure. No advantage too small.

One day Victor pulled Tee off to the side and asked, "What are Sam's weaknesses?" Sam had only been there a few days but had immediately gone to the Arena and survived.

"He isn't bilateral. Attacks primarily with his right side, sword, strike, and kick. His right shoulder appears to be damaged, as he doesn't lift it all the way over his head. He ducks with his arm at an odd angle when faced with a high attack on that side," Tee explained.

"How would you attack him?" Victor said.

"Force him into a block with his right arm high. He will likely adjust rotating to his right and lowering his center of balance. Depending on how his stance changes would determine the next move," Tee said.

"Wrong," Victor said. "Part of the reason you believe this is you've seen him get caught off balance during sparring." Hesitating, Victor then asked, "What weapons did Sam have on him when he went to the Arena?"

"Sword, round shield, long knife," Tee said, looking a bit confused.

"How did he sheath his long knife?" Victor asked.

"Where it's easy to grab with his left hand," Tee answered. Frowning in concentration, his face took on a knowing look. "He's fooling the other gladiators into thinking he has a weakness he doesn't have."

Victor nodded, pleased. "There isn't anything wrong with his shoulder. The other secret he hides is that he's ambidextrous. I saw Eric toss him a knife, and he grabbed it out of the air effortlessly with his left hand without thinking about it. I saw him frown slightly as he realized he had screwed up. Don't just watch them fighting, watch everything."

"So now how would you attack Sam?" Victor asked.

"Same way, except the high strike would be a feint to try and get him to commit to dropping his shield and attacking with his knife hand. Since he would think he has me fooled, he might be coaxed into overextending. But I wouldn't rely on surprise or assume I have him fooled. Now that he's shown himself to be clever, I need to consider that any scenario might have been part of his overall plan," Tee said.

Victor nodded, obviously pleased with that answer. "The smart ones are the dangerous ones, Tee. Make sure you study that aspect of your enemies even most closely than their physical traits."

Victor then took a deep breath, let it out, and then said, "Tonight is the last night of the Harvest Festival. It's traditional to get a special meal tonight. Way more than anyone needs. Wine will be offered as well. "Don't make the mistake of overeating or having anything other than water to drink tonight. You'll go to the Arena tomorrow and the last thing you need is to be weighed down and sluggish because you overindulged," Victor said.

Of course, Victor had advice about dinner, Tee thought, he had advice about everything. "Yes, Master," Tee said sarcastically.

Their relationship had improved since he had been deemed barely adequate. Tee could even joke around with him a bit. He was nervous about going into the Arena the next day and nervousness tended to heighten his sarcasm. He was a bit touched by the fact that Victor seemed to care what happened to him in the Arena and that tended to heighten his sarcastic nature as well.

"Don't be a smart ass," Victor said bluntly and walked away.

The next day, while he was getting suited up, Victor was all business. "Get stretched out but save your energy for the Arena." Victor hesitated, locked eyes with him and said, "Remember what I told you. Take them out as quickly as you can without overreaching. It's a blessing for them if it's quick. Anyone injured who stops fighting disappoints the emperor, and they die a very painful death later."

Taking a deep breath, he said in a low voice only Tee could hear, "Forti told me they are going to release three at a time and a total of five groups. Not clear if it's on a schedule or whenever you dispatch the previous three. There are hidden doors in the walls so they can appear at any time from any direction. Listen to the crowd. If you hear anything new, a change in volume or tone, quickly check your surroundings."

Tee just nodded. Now wasn't the time for jokes. The only thing new was that he would be facing five groups of gladiators, three at a time. The fact that Victor was repeating himself told Tee how concerned he was.

As he was being led to the tunnel system leading underground to the Arena, he stopped and simply said, "Thank you, Victor."

Victor hesitated, grabbed Tee's shoulders with both of his hands, turned him around, and then, locking eyes with him, said in a whisper, "Ad Victoriam."

Tee stood a little stunned and went weak in the knees. He hadn't expected this. Taking a deep breath and squaring his shoulders, he gave the correct response. "Cum scuto aut in scuto." Victor gave him a quick nod, patted his shoulders, turned around, and walked away.

It wasn't Tee's first battle as a member of the Guard. It was his first appearance in the Arena. Performing the ritual was not strictly appropriate. But Victor was sending multiple messages by claiming the honor of a mentor. It meant Victor truly respected him. That Tee was necessary for winning the battle and Victor would be honored to fight alongside him. It was a message that they were still of the Guard and Arista was the enemy. 'To Victory' meant much more than an inspirational message. It was a reminder they were committed to ultimate victory. Or at the very least, in Victor's own words, making sure the bastards pay. It had the intended effect; Tee was committed to victory beyond simply preserving his life.

Tee couldn't see the Arena from the holding cell they had him in awaiting his bout. But he could hear. The festivities started off with a man loudly begging for mercy, then screaming in pain, followed by more begging. This progressed to deep mournful sobs and ultimately a plea for death. It seemed an eternity before that plea was answered. Tee was disgusted by the audible enjoyment of the crowd. The next hour was spent listening to a series of bouts being played out with the occasional roar from the crowd. He supposed it was an advantage to hear all this. It prepared him for what would follow.

When his time came, Tee walked purposely down the corridor to the Arena. He could feel the excitement in the waiting crowd. As he walked out onto the Arena floor, a roar went up that he not only heard but felt. His eyes struggled to adjust to the brightness and when he was able to see clearly, the sight stunned him. He had never seen so many people in one place. This was his first time seeing the inside of the Arena. The seating had multiple levels that rose steeply into a cloudless blue sky. Looking at the packed sand floor of the Arena he saw blood stains scattered here and there.

There were discarded weapons strewn around as well. Perhaps the weapons of the defeated. He would have to pay attention as he could trip over them, or his opponents could pick them up and use them. He knew this was the final bout of the harvest festival. They called it the finale. He located the emperor's box. It was one level up, but directly across from him. The emperor was easy to spot. He sat in the middle, richly adorned, and had a smug smile that suggested the truth of what Tee had heard. This man had no morals.

Tee walked forward and positioned himself in front of the emperor. Having been coached on what to do, he took his right fist and slammed it against his chest in a salute and loudly declared, "For the honor of Emperor Trajan." At the same time thinking that this man had no honor.

The emperor was seemingly bored with Tee's declaration. He maintained his smug smile as he made a shooing motion, indicating the bout should begin.

Tee moved to the middle of the Arena and slowly turned around, waiting for things to start. He cautioned himself to ignore the crowd. Except as an audible indication of what he wasn't currently seeing. A shout went up and he whipped around as a gate behind him opened up and three men came out. All had small, round shields, but two had swords and one had a spear. He didn't recognize any of them.

Victor had told him that he would likely see a combination of criminals, captured warriors, and gladiators he was very familiar with. Warriors who were captured but not purchased as professional gladiators were unlikely to be highly skilled. Criminals were often sent out who hadn't even held a weapon before. For the most part he needed to worry most about those he saw every day. However, there were exceptions, so he was cautioned to be careful.

The three rushed forward, spreading out in an obvious attempt to surround him. Their haste indicated they were more afraid of the emperor's wrath than Tee. All three looked terrified. Tee let them separate, then he rushed the one who held his weapon as if he knew how to use it. He purposely forced the man to turn so he could engage while still keeping an eye on the other two. The man was dead in seconds. The other two yelled and tried to rush him together. It was over quickly, none of them having much skill.

Tee moved toward the emperor's box, suggesting he was ready to accept his victory. The emperor shooed him back, indicating his day wasn't over yet. Victor said it was important to protect Forti, so he played out the ruse. They could not allow any indication that he had been coached on what to expect.

Tee quickly moved back into the center of the Arena and started his slow turn, waiting for whatever was coming next. He glanced up at the emperor and got a nod of approval, which just made him feel sick. It was an abomination to be a part of this disgusting entertainment. This time two came out from the same gate he had entered by. He heard the crowd grow quieter.

Alarmed, Tee whipped around and caught the third of this set, trying to sneak up behind him. He charged the lone gladiator, eliminating one threat before the other two could converge. Again, it was over quickly. None of his opponents had been capable of causing concern.

It wasn't until the fourth set that a real challenge emerged. Two of the three were men he was familiar with. They weren't the best of the gladiators, but they were skilled and thus dangerous. They also stayed together instead of spreading apart. He dispatched the loner and then had a protracted fight against the two gladiators.

They had a good, coordinated plan to wear him down. He was forced to fight them both at the same time, which drew out the fight. He eventually prevailed with one minor cut on his upper arm. When he was pinked, the crowd erupted. They had evidently become bored with the slaughter and wanted some of his blood as well.

He was breathing deeply and feeling his legs when the last three came out of the gate just below the emperor's box. They were the three best gladiators in the yard. Having knowledge of them was a double-edged sword. While he knew them, they knew him. They had been watching his bouts with Victor for months. The other advantage they had was his inexperience in fighting smaller men. Victor had insisted he spend as much time as possible sparring with Forti, the only other sparring he allowed. However, Forti's availability was sporadic, and it wasn't the same as regular bouts with various fighters of that size.

These three stayed together, mirroring the strategy of the prior group. Two of them were armed with spears and the third was armed with a sword. The spears were on the outside and the swordsman on the inside. They marched forward together. Searching for anything to give him an advantage, he noticed a large rectangular shield that had been left from a previous bout. He picked it up and charged. This caused the spearmen to extend their spears, which he was relying on. As he engaged, he swept the spears off to the side with his sword, causing them all to react by retreating a few steps in unison to reestablish their defense. Instead of stopping, he swiveled the shield sideways in mid stride and barreled into the tightly packed group of three before they got set.

There was a lot that could have gone wrong with this tactic. But it seemed luck was on his side. Instead of getting tangled up in the pile of bodies, he rolled clear. Popping up, he immediately dispatched one of the two spearmen before the unfortunate man could regain his bearings.

The crowd roared its approval, evidently enjoying his trick. The next few minutes were exhausting, and he decided to take more of a defensive posture. It was a gamble. If another three emerged before he dispatched these two, his life was likely over. He prayed Forti was a trustworthy source as he waited for his opponents to make a mistake. The spearman stumbled slightly on a piece of equipment left behind from one of the earlier groups and lost his right hand as a consequence. This left him face to face with Sam. Everything Victor had suspected about Sam had been confirmed during the fight so far. Strikes and lunges intended to subtly test his supposed weaknesses convinced Tee those weaknesses were a ruse. Trusting his instincts, he attacked as if Sam had a bad shoulder and was rewarded with a knife attack from Sam's left hand. Sam's head flew off his body to the raucous approval of the crowd.

Instead of immediately going forward for the emperor's approval, he turned and walked purposely back to the spearman, who had lost a hand. The man was still alive and in shock. Tee was not going to leave the poor man to suffer whatever sick torture was in store for him. What he had heard earlier had hardened his resolve that he would only go so far with this travesty. He drove his sword into the man's chest, ending his suffering. The crowd roared its approval.

He went back to the center of the Arena and, holding his sword and shield up, screamed out a challenge for the next test. When he had turned around enough to see the emperor, the man motioned him to come toward him. Tee positioned himself in front of the emperor's box and saluted with his fist to his chest, waiting for a decision. The emperor frowned and hesitated. Any wounded who stopped fighting were supposed to be left for the emperor's judgement. Or perhaps more accurately, the emperor's enjoyment. Perhaps thinking Tee didn't know the correct protocol yet, he smiled and said in a loud voice. "One."

Twenty-nine more wins and I gain my freedom, thought Tee with disgust. He knew his freedom would never be allowed, but he would play along with their tradition.

"Twenty-nine," he shouted, bringing the crowd back to its feet and cheering him on as he walked off.

Victor greeted him as he entered the gladiator's compound. "Am happy to see you survived. Pray for those you were forced to kill today. They are not our enemies." When Tee nodded his understanding, Victor added, "Forti watched your matches today. He'll stop by tomorrow so we can review your performance. Rest." And with that, Victor walked off with a sad look on his face.

Tee was deeply troubled. He sat, reflecting on the men he had faced. He had no idea how many GEMs he had killed. But today's fifteen deaths laid heavily on his conscience. Protecting himself and others didn't hold any regrets for him. But what had happened today bothered him to his core. He knew their faces would show up in his nightmares and guilt over their deaths would not go away. Victor had told him a quick killing was a blessing for those men since the alternative was a long and protracted death full of pain and suffering. But it just felt wrong. And it always would.

A beautiful young woman was brought to his cell that evening. She had a light, sheer cloak on and nothing else. There were catcalls from the other gladiators as she had made her way down the hall. Tee noticed that Dobler was clearly unhappy with his role in bringing her, but was trying not to let it show. Tee had become even better at reading people due to Victor's training. His already good opinion of Dobler was further enhanced.

Dobler stopped in front of his cell and spit out, "The emperor was appreciative of your efforts today. This is your reward." Then he unlocked Tee's cell door and gently encouraged the girl to enter. Saying nothing further, he locked the door behind her and walked back down the hallway.

The poor girl was trembling. He towered over her. Tee knew how intimidating that must be. His blood was boiling. He tried to keep the rage off his face. She was frightened enough already. Tee was grateful that Victor had warned him of this. Her knuckles were white, and her hands shook as she gripped the cloak high on her chest. When she tentatively started to open her cloak, he stepped forward, closed it firmly, and said softly, "I'm not going to abuse you." Then he turned, grabbed one of his robes and draped it over her, motioning her to pull it closed as well.

"It's too cold in here for just that. My name is Tee. What's yours?" Tee said.

"Ca-Ca-Cara sir," she finally got out. Then with tears pooling in her eyes she said, "They will beat me or worse if I don't satisfy you." The poor girl was terrified.

He considered what to say and then responded with, "Cara, I'll tell them you satisfied me. I'll ask if you can stay longer and if you can come back from time to time." He hesitated and then gently lifted her head with his fingers on her chin. Locking eyes with her, he said, "Where I come from, we don't believe in slavery. We do not abuse women. You're safe here."

That seemed to give her hope, but she was still trembling. He hesitated and then said, "My grandmother always says to find something to enjoy even in the worst of times. She believes being happy is a choice, not a result of circumstances. I've found her advice to be very wise."

The girl looked at him like he was crazy. That was clearly not the right thing to say. Great, Tee, he thought. Way to make her relax. He sighed and thought that perhaps she would consider Grammy's advice at another time. Grammy or Hestie would have known what to say. God, he missed them both at times like these. Feeling incompetent, he considered how to make the poor girl more comfortable. He ended up giving her the bed and sleeping on the floor. Turned out ignoring her was the best thing he could do.

Dobler knew something was going on. Victor and Tee were up to something. He didn't know what, but he knew he should report the various inconsistencies and oddities he was seeing. His life depended on it. But some things were more important to him than his empty life. His wife and youngest daughter had been captured along with himself by slavers years ago. The girl the emperor had supplied as a reward for Tee's Arena performance looked just like his daughter had at that age. Could have been her twin. It broke his heart when she showed up.

Dobler was not surprised to discover the next morning that Tee had treated the girl with respect. He realized he would have been surprised if he hadn't. Victor had always done the same with the girls supplied. Not that Tee admitted it. No, Tee had told him enthusiastically that the girl had 'greatly satisfied' him. He turned a little red at that point and then requested she stay with him for longer. It was a bit too enthusiastic, and the slight blush didn't help. The look on the girl's face ratted him out as well. It was heartwarming. Tee had gone to too much trouble to try and provide the poor girl with a few hours of decency.

Tee was scary as hell. Almost as scary as Victor. He was a horrible liar. But clearly an honorable man. Dobler thought he had gotten the measure of Tee from their late-night talks. This confirmed his suspicions. He didn't know where his wife or daughter were. The last he saw of either of them was at the slave auction. His image of them being led off the auction block by different owners was burned into his brain. He prayed nightly they had found some semblance of happiness.

Later that day Leo, Senator Cereo's valet, showed up to collect the girl and ask about Tee. "Did you see Tee fight in the Arena?" Leo asked with enthusiasm.

Dobler looked down at the tabletop in front of him and said, "No, I never watch the Arena fights. I'm around the gladiators so much I get too attached." The truth was that he was disgusted by the Arena and everything it represented.

"Too bad. It was a once in a lifetime experience. Everyone will be talking about it for months. The emperor decided to test our new Pacifica gladiator. He told people beforehand he wanted to find out how tough he really was. Tee did not disappoint. Fifteen dead in a little over fifteen minutes. They were released three at a time and told they would be part of the after games entertainment if they didn't engage quickly," Leo said.

So, a choice between a quick death and an excruciatingly painful one, thought Dobler. He nodded his understanding and waited to see if Leo had anything else to say.

"How did Tee like the emperor's gift?" Leo asked with a knowing smile.

The emperor was known for awarding the owners of the winning gladiators for special events with beautiful and untouched, newly captured slaves. The understanding was that the gladiator got to go first. It was too much for Dobler. She reminded him too much of his daughter and he was outraged. He had lived long enough. Years of frustration caused him to drop his façade and say, "Your gladiator is a better person than that. He was respectful of the girl. He refused to take advantage of her. He might be a slave, but he has morals. More than you can say about most citizens of Arista." He was dead. Perhaps it was for the best, he thought. His life had been better than most. But it was getting increasingly harder to accept the tradeoffs.

Leo's expression surprisingly changed from haughty to concerned. He hesitated, clearly thinking about his response. Then he said, "I'm not going to report your outburst. But I will tell you something in return that I trust you'll keep between us." Leo stopped, waiting for an acknowledgment from Dobler. When Dobler nodded, he continued. "Senator Cereo will not be informed of Tee's behavior or your comments. Given your concerns about the girl, I'll tell you that he doesn't allow his slaves to interact with anyone at his Roma Domus. Do their job yes, interact with others no. We'll move her into his Domus as a serving girl and maid. She will be safe, at least until she's moved to his villa."

Dobler was stunned, and he took a few moments to collect himself and consider what had been said. He took a deep breath and dived in, saying, "Tee requested she stay with him longer and be sent to him on a regular basis. He's trying to provide a place for her to occasionally relax and feel safe. He thinks he's fooling me, but he's not."

"That won't be possible. As I said, Senator Cereo doesn't allow his slaves to interact with others, even other slaves. Security is a serious issue for him. For the same reason, he never sells his slaves. I trust you will keep this between us, Dobler," Leo said, staring him down.

Well, that sounded better than the typical fate of a pretty young slave girl, thought Dobler. He nodded his understanding and agreement, then walked Leo out to the exit gate.

"Anything said between us stays between us," Dobler said.

"Thank you. I don't see a need to come around often. It seems like Tee is getting what he needs. But let me know if there is anything you think he needs."

Dobler considered the conversation with Leo and wondered about it. His sudden change in demeanor was a surprise. Perhaps the man had his own secrets. He thought he would check in on Tee and wandered up to the recreation yard observation room. Eric was watching Tee practice his archery. There were arrows in the barrier wall behind the target and a few on the outer edges of the target. One had surprisingly hit dead center. "He is hopeless with a bow," Eric said, smirking. "The others won't even run on the track when he's out there," he continued, chuckling. "The one in the bullseye was Victor challenging him to hit the same section on the barrier wall an earlier arrow had hit. He's a demon with every other weapon, but a duel with bows and arrows at a hundred feet would favor me."

Dobler nodded. Then he narrowed his eyes in thought.

As he was walking Tee back to his cell, Dobler casually said, "Your archery isn't improving. Try relaxing your arms as much as you can and release the arrows smoothly. Use the same motion and rhythm every time. I'm not sure you'll ever be any good. Archers are born, but you should be able to improve."

Tee froze inside, hiding his reaction as he thought about this. Dobler had been a frequent visitor to his cell at night. Tee knew Dobler had been a warrior as a young man. He also knew Dobler had little to no experience with archery. Dobler had never given him advice before, either. It was obvious he knew Tee was faking his incompetence. No matter how bad someone was, practice would improve their skills. Tee mentally flogged himself and then calmly said, "Thanks, Dobler. I'll try that the next time I practice." Dobler nodded as he locked Tee into his cell. He hid a smile as he turned away and started walking back down the corridor.

CHAPTER 20

NEWS FEED

Jennifer looked around the table and gave all the committee members 'the look.' This was combined with a warm smile that made you want to pay attention. She had a way of getting people to stop their private conversations without being blunt about it, without saying a word. One of her many subtle skills. Once she had everyone's attention, she said, "I want to start by thanking everyone for getting up extra early this morning. The council is still in an uproar over issues surrounding the delayed planting, and I have a full day with them right after this meeting." Jennifer paused and her face brightened a bit. "The good news is that the current crisis is pulling everyone together. A significant number of Landfall and Apple folks volunteered their labor to help make up for Eureka's late start to planting. I also want to thank Griff and Del one more time for assigning Guard and university students to help out as well."

"It's good for them," Griff said with a mischievous grin. "They need a reminder of where their food comes from."

"And it dispels the idea that farmers have it easy," Del added with his own grin.

Jennifer smiled inside. She knew they both grew up on farms and were a bit disdainful of those who hadn't. Although she grew up in the city, she agreed that city folk generally have it easier. Jennifer was no stranger to hard work. But spending summer 'vacations' on her relatives' farms meant she knew what life was really like on the farm.

Jennifer continued. "Not only will those efforts pay off in improving our food supply, but the tension between the regions has gone down dramatically. I've been told by several people that the mistrust of the university and Guard that began with the call for full mobilization has gone away as well. I'm hopeful it will last. The bad news is we are going to have to ration. It's not nearly as bad as we originally thought, thanks to everyone pulling together. But we will have to be frugal with our food supply until the fall harvest next year. The other issue you all know about is heating oil. Everyone will have to wear extra layers this winter."

Jennifer looked at Griff when she said this. She had false accusation in her tone and amusement in her eyes and everyone chuckled. Del had been right. Now that she knew Griff better, she had grown to trust, like, and admire him.

Jennifer turned back to the group and said, "We only have one item on the agenda today. Del will review the latest intercepted communications and offer opinions on what it might mean. This is informational only. As I understand it, there aren't any actions being proposed."

Del had a worried look on his face as he started his report. "Jennifer's correct. While there isn't anything of immediate concern, there was a report transmitted on the GEMs that is alarming. The anthropologist who studies Pacifica cultures is claiming the GEMs are evolving their social interactions. The latest report says they are becoming more collaborative. Even more disturbing is the claim they are markedly more compliant to orders given by their leaders. The report stated that their common warriors 'don't need to be beaten into submission anymore.'"

Griff grunted and said, "When you read accounts of battles with the GEMs over the past two hundred years, you see a steady change that aligns with that view. Even a hundred years ago, it wasn't unusual for an attack on the Wall to stop because the GEMs started killing each other instead of trying to kill us. Most recently, it was clear that the attempted Apple Valley invasion was a joint exercise between two warlords. Their struggles to coordinate have always been one of our main advantages."

Del nodded in agreement and continued, "The report did confirm that we hurt the GEMs badly. While their main army isn't dispersing as usual, they are currently in no shape to organize another attack. It was clear the author of this report was angry with our success. It's odd and I don't have an explanation for it."

"Maybe he just wants to go home," offered Kevin.

"Perhaps. But it is concerning that at least this one individual sees some sort of advantage to our demise. I'll continue to look for clues to help us sort out their motivations. But given the sporadic nature of our intercepts, I don't have a lot of confidence in getting a firm answer."

"Why are the intercepts sporadic?" asked Griff.

"Good question," Del said with a smirk, which Griff returned. Jennifer found it mildly annoying when the two of them bantered back and forth without explaining what was obviously a private joke. Del then replaced the smirk with his professor's personality and explained, "The communications network consists of a system of satellites orbiting Pacifica. You can actually see them as tiny dots zipping across the sky on a moonless night. They communicate with each other and any spaceship in the vicinity with lasers. We don't have the ability to intercept those signals.

"However, these satellites also have microwave radios that transmit everything going over the network to the ground. We think it's there to support occasional visits to the surface for survey purposes. That signal we can collect. The reason our information is sporadic is twofold. First, all official Commonwealth traffic is encrypted with something we're not familiar with. We've tried to crack it over the years but have been unsuccessful.

"However, the Commonwealth requires personal communications to be transmitted with an encryption scheme we can decrypt. It's a simple one and easy to crack. I believe the Commonwealth doesn't trust its citizens. I believe they listen in on all personal communications.

"The second reason is that survey ships aren't always in orbit around Pacifica. They only come when they believe something interesting is happening or is about to happen. When they aren't here, there are no communications to listen in on."

"So that means we're only getting their private letters to each other?" Jennifer asked.

Del's head nodded as he answered, "Basically, yes. That and what they call news feeds. Their version of a newspaper." Del hesitated a second and added, "Speaking of news feeds. There was some good news about Tee Stone. Well, relatively good. He was reported to have survived his first visit to the Arena as a gladiator. I have a copy of the news article that goes into some detail. Evidently, he fought a total of fifteen individuals and defeated them all. The article seemed to indicate that Commonwealth citizens can somehow watch these events."

Griff huffed out his disapproval and said, "Thanks for showing me that earlier, Del. It makes me angry to know those bastards find human suffering and death entertaining. But it's good to know Tee's still alive. Even better to know the competition is obviously not very good. Tee was never the best at hand-to-hand combat."

"Why would an anthropologists report be sent in a personal communication?" Jennifer asked. "Are all of their survey reports sent that way?"

"No, we don't believe they are. It's also interesting that these reports are only being sent to one recipient. We don't know why," Del answered.

There was a pause in the conversation and then Dorothy stated bluntly, "Phillis Osman is asking questions."

"What kind of questions?" Jennifer asked.

"She named the five of us and asked me what we're doing in secret," Dorothy answered.

"Damn it!" Del said loudly before he could catch himself. "Sorry, that slipped out. I swear that woman is a mind reader. I do everything I can to avoid her, but obviously she's picking up on something."

"It's not just you, Del," Kevin piped in. "I've found myself telling her all kinds of things I didn't intend to say. Nothing about the committee or the Commonwealth, but plenty about other concerns."

"What did you tell her?" asked Jennifer.

"The truth," Dorothy answered blandly. The room expelled a collective gasp. Then she calmly added, "I told her we are of like minds and discuss the challenges of Pacifica. I told her we meet to brainstorm."

"What did she say to that?"

"She asked if she could join. I told her it was invitation only, and we already had university representation. I asked her to keep our group's existence a secret, and she agreed," Dorothy responded, seemingly nonplussed by the whole thing.

Del let out a deep breath, then said, "I've actually thought quite a bit about situations where she might be useful. I concluded she would be perfect as an advisor on a negotiation team. Perhaps negotiating with the Commonwealth if that ever came to pass. Her ability to manipulate people without them knowing they are being manipulated is unbelievable."

"Can we trust her to keep what she knows secret?" Jennifer asked.

Del and Dorothy both said simultaneously, "Yes."

Jennifer gave that some thought and then said, "Okay, Del, I would like you to engage her on this and set up regular meeting to hear her thoughts on the big challenges we face as a people. We either need to keep engaged with her or ask her to join. I'm reluctant to add anyone simply to keep them quiet. Let's add an agenda item to discuss how we ensure she is seen as the leader of Pacifica if the Commonwealth comes in and we're all, um, unavailable." Jennifer paused and then said, "I think that's it for today. We'll still meet at the regular time because I think I'll have news from the council to discuss."

Del was distressed about having to meet regularly with Phillis. That woman is going to break down my barriers one of these days, he thought. "Griff, stay here for a few minutes. I have something to discuss. I'll be right back." Griff just nodded and sat back down.

The door opened a few minutes later, and Del had Quinn in tow. He sat down and said, "I've been keeping one last secret from you. Quinn knows, and it's time you know, too."

Judgement

CHAPTER 21

WINE TASTING

The governor and first minister were riding in an opulent carriage in the early evening on their way to Domus Cereo. They passed through the squalor of the inner city and entered an exclusive neighborhood with elaborate gas streetlamps. The lamps cast a pleasing warm light bright enough to hint at the elegance of large mansions on both sides of the road. Governor Jacobs was not used to primitive transportation, having spent most of her career on Commonwealth planets. The colonies did not have cars, trains, and shuttle craft commonly used by Commonwealth citizens.

"What's that horrible smell?" Governor Jacobs asked, wrinkling her nose.

"It's a mixture of dung and horse sweat," Jack answered. He hesitated a moment and then added, "If you're around it long enough, you get used to it."

"Gross," said Jacobs, wrinkling her nose. Looking over at him, she asked, "Tell me a little about tonight's event."

"It's a special wine tasting hosted by Dry Brook Vineyards. That's Senator Cereo's foundational business. It's what took him from poverty to a serious businessman," Jack explained. "There will be a mix of politicians, business magnets, plus ladies and gentlemen of leisure in attendance. It's invitation only so it won't be a large crowd. Senator Cereo is really good at using these events to endear himself to the elite and the poor. Every year they pull out a small number of older vintages of a wine called Jenny's Acre and auction them off for a homeless charity. This year's highlight is a single bottle from his first vintage. Bidding will be fierce."

"How did you get an invitation? The governor asked.

"I think it's his way of signaling that he wants alignment with the Commonwealth. His friends and enemies will notice the

Commonwealth's presence. It's a political statement, if nothing else. After his initial surprise, he'll see your arrival as a boon to his prestige. Everyone will assume he has a working relationship with you and the rumors will fly. It should give us an advantage in negotiations. Perception is everything with these people," Jack said with a smile.

"We've established he's smart. Let's see if he has balls," Jacobs replied with a predatory smile.

The carriage pulled up to an elegant Domus with its own gas-powered lamps, providing added illumination to its entrance. A large number of security personnel protected the narrow entry to the drive. They were allowed to proceed up the drive after showing their fancy printed invitation.

Dry Brook Vineyards is pleased to invite

Jack Spenser and Guest

to its annual auction for the hungry

Featuring the first vintage of Jenny's Acre

After pulling up in front of the entry, they were met by liveried footmen opening their carriage door. One of them offered to help Governor Jacobs out. Receiving an icy glare, and a sharp wave of her hand, he backed off, letting her navigate her own way out of the conveyance. Governor Jacobs did not like anyone helping her, especially men.

Domus Cereo wasn't the largest or grandest in Roma. But it was impressive. Jack had been told it was the original Cereo hereditary home lost by Senator Cereo's parents in bankruptcy. Evidently, the senator had reacquired the property once he had the financial resources to do so. Handing over the printed invitation, they were allowed to enter the large double doors at the entrance. The massive entry hall was an odd combination of grandeur, coupled with a feeling you were actually visiting someone's home.

In Jack's experience, most of these grand mansions had a cold clinical feel to them. This one was somehow warm and inviting. Remembering his last visit, he told the butler they could find the library on their own. The library was a good-sized hall set up for entertainment and could comfortably hold up to fifty people. It was much smaller than the ballroom he had been escorted to for the last party. It had a cozier, more intimate feel to it.

Senator Cereo greeted them with a smile at the doorway to the library. "Welcome back to my home, Jack. Always good to see you," he said. Turning to Governor Jacobs, he introduced himself. "My name is Caius Cereo, Governor. I am delighted you were able to join us for our Dry Brook wine tasting. Please call me Caius."

"Delighted to meet you, Caius. I do enjoy a good glass of wine, so I'm looking forward to the evening," the governor said as she smiled and surveyed her prey. She had a way of making people uncomfortable, even when saying all the right things.

"I hope you don't mind but I have a private room set up for discussions with Jack after the auction. Obviously, you are welcome to join us," Caius said, seemingly nonplussed with the governor's body language.

Most people visibly wilted when she openly broadcast her predatory nature. Jack's respect for Caius grew.

Caius turned and swept his arm across the room, saying, "Please visit the various tables. Each one is dedicated to a particular wine. Each table has an expert to answer your questions. They also have small plates that pair well with that particular wine. If you start just to your left and follow the tables around the room, you'll get the best experience. But feel free to wander. Olympia is our winemaker. She's the woman over by the fireplace holding court. Enjoy."

They spent the next half hour wandering around the room with Jack, introducing people to the governor. As always, she was gracious, but intense. She had a way of impressing and intimidating people all at the same time. Jack knew she liked wine but was surprised how much she was enjoying the experience. He decided he needed to learn more about wine, as it was the first non-work topic she seemed to enjoy. Jack started to relax as she was almost purring with her enjoyment of the event.

They were introduced to Senator File, who was Caius Cereo's longtime wine distributor. The governor immediately started an aggressive interrogation of the older gentleman with questions about Cereo's businesses. Jack was amused by the man's ability to divert her questions. As she was breaking down his walls, Caius approached with a man in tow. Jack froze, paralyzed as Caius announced his guest. "Governor Jacobs, I found Chief Justice Evans wandering around."

Evans was Jacobs's rival in the sector. They hated each other. This was the first time Jack had ever seen Jacobs caught off guard. However, she recovered quickly and said, "Justice Evans, what a pleasure to see you. I had no idea you were here on Arista."

"I've been a fan of Dry Brook Vineyards since discovering it last year. Senator Cereo was kind enough to invite me and I decided to accept," Evans said with a lightly flushed face broadcasting an overindulgence in the evening's entertainment.

"I told Justice Evans we were going to discuss the current situation with Liberty tonight and he asked to attend. I hope I didn't overstep," Senator Caius said with an air of innocence and subservience that was completely believable.

"It's wonderful the good justice is here tonight. By all means, he should attend if he isn't otherwise engaged. We want to ensure that all Commonwealth Edicts are strictly followed. I wouldn't want anyone on Arista to have an accidental violation that would cause work for his organization," Jacobs said with an expression that almost made you believe she meant it.

"Sorry to run away, but I have to get the auction started. If you want to bid on anything, just raise your hand. If you win, don't worry about payment tonight, just enjoy." And with that, Caius walked off toward the Podium at the far end of the library.

Jack had noticed Caius's wine distributor quietly slipping away during the exchange. Caius's associates are loyal, thought Jack. Few would risk offending Governor Jacobs by avoiding her questions. Jack was relieved the auction started as soon as Cereo reached the podium. Standing between Evans and Jacobs as they avoided even looking at each other was unnerving.

The auction was fun. Watching the wealthy bid against each other in sums that were meaningless to them was a lesson in local politics. The political, social, and business power structures were obvious after a few rounds. Jack watched carefully and took notice of who deferred to whom. The cold knot in his stomach returned after Jacobs and Evans started bidding against each other for the evening's last bottle. The colonist bidders withdrew immediately, knowing their place.

Jack had recently learned enough about Arista wine to know the original vintage of Jenny's Acre was extremely rare. But as the bid price grew to an outrageous level, he realized Jacobs was just playing with her food again. It ended as he thought it would. Jacobs deferred to Evans as it appeared he was becoming uncomfortable with the price. She gave him a respectful bow of her head, acknowledging his victory and then turned her face away, unable to hide a thin feral smile.

Senator Cereo walked over to congratulate Justice Evans. "Congratulations, Justice. Your bid will feed a lot of hungry people. Your generosity is much appreciated. If you are a collector, I would be happy to provide a signed certificate of authenticity. Believe it or not, there have been fakes produced of this wine."

"I would appreciate that, Senator. While I would love to have a taste of it, I do have a collection of rare wines from across the Commonwealth. This will be given a special place in my cellar," Evans responded with a smile.

Later that evening, they retired to what appeared to be the senator's expansive office. As they sat down to start their discussion, Caius's valet entered with a bottle of Jenny's Acre and four glasses.

"I thought we might enjoy the same vintage you both bid on tonight. Justice Evans will know what he has in his wine cellar, and Governor Jacobs will discover whether she should have bid higher. Seems like a way for everyone to win," Caius said with a smile.

Jack was floored. Given what the auctioned bottle had sold for, this was beyond extravagant. Caius's observation that everybody wins wasn't lost on anyone. A perfect way to start the discussion. Evans was beside himself with glee. The senator was perfectly using one of the justices weaknesses to manipulate him into a sense of obligation. An expensive but highly effective move.

Jack took a tentative sip of his wine and was surprised. He wasn't sure what he had expected. It was very smooth and dry, with a subtle, tart taste that flowed over his palette. While he wasn't a wine drinker, this was pleasing. Evans was using the situation to rub in his winning bid by effusively complimenting the wine. Jacobs just watched him with that hidden smile of hers, privately pleased that she had manipulated him almost as well as Cereo had.

After Evans's compliments tailed off, Governor Jacobs kicked off the conversation. "You've invited us here so that the Commonwealth is aware of Arista's plans with regards to Liberty."

Caius smiled and then said, "We understand the Commonwealth wants to be informed of any plans that may affect tax revenues. You've been very clear that the Commonwealth has strict Edicts on non-interference in colony politics. In other words, the Commonwealth would like to be aware of plans and developments but will not take sides."

"I'm really pleased to have my faith in Governor Jacobs confirmed. There have been sector governors who have violated the non-interference Edicts. It's gratifying to work with a governor who sets a high ethical standard," Evans said while indicating the opposite with his tone of voice and body language.

At this point Caius jumped in and said, "Let me outline the emperor's plans. First, let me assure you that Emperor Trajan is very supportive of the Commonwealth being aware of his efforts. His goal is to increase the wealth of the Commonwealth. He believes the Commonwealth would be enriched if Liberty were as well managed as Arista. You are all aware of how segmented and divisive Liberty is today. The result of the current chaos is a lower standard of living for everyone. We even feel it here on Arista. To contribute to the welfare of the Commonwealth, he intends on invading and subjugating Liberty. The plan is to separate the population into those who can lead and those who are most effective being told what to do. Any questions so far?"

"Assuming you are successful, is Trajan intending on changing the constitutional protections for the people of Liberty?" Evans asked.

"Trajan believes the bulk of the population's lives would be improved if they were slaves. It would be a transition from constant warfare and suffering to one of efficient societal contribution. Clearly a better result for the people of Liberty as well as the Commonwealth," Caius responded.

"You make it sound like Trajan is sacrificing for the Commonwealth. Clearly, Arista has other goals in mind for such a large and risky investment," Jacobs said with a smirk.

Caius smiled knowingly back at Jacobs and said, "The emperor's plan is to expand Arista governance to include both planets. In addition to increased trade, the wealth of the two planets combined will be enhanced. Adding to the emperor's motivation is a personal desire to emulate his namesake. While personal goals are secondary to the wealth of Arista and the Commonwealth, they do play a part."

"You currently have the Queen of Liberty in your custody. What are your intentions? She is head of state for one of the Commonwealths colonies after all," Evans asked.

"What we have told Liberty is that we don't know who we can safely release her to. So, for her safety, we await their resolution of who was to blame for her kidnapping. We believe this is what is best for the people of Liberty," Caius said. Then changing tone, he lowered his voice as if sharing a secret and said, "To be completely transparent, Trajan's real intent is to magnify their dysfunction. The goal is to force her to perform a subservient role after our invasion has been successful."

"Who was responsible for her kidnapping?" Evans asked sincerely.

"We really don't know," Caius said, looking at Evans innocently. "It's a happy coincidence that it probably isn't safe to turn her over to anyone on Liberty until that is known."

"My understanding is that her servant is going to be turned over. How do you know that is safe?" Jacobs asked.

"She is a servant. On Arista, a slave would perform her functions. We are not overly concerned with her safety. However, you are making an excellent observation. It was my recommendation that she be released as a goodwill gesture. The emperor decided we should ask Liberty to send a delegation to retrieve her. Best case, it drives further division on Liberty. Worst case, we end up negotiating with both sides before our invasion."

Evans was nodding and said, "Please keep me updated on developments. As you know, the Commonwealth does not have jurisdiction over interplanetary politics. In fact, it is a violation of our founding Edicts to get involved." Evans swung his head to look directly at Jacobs and smiled coldly. It was an obvious accusation.

Caius nodded and said, "Let me assure you that Arista is not asking for anything from the Commonwealth. We believe that keeping the Commonwealth abreast of plans and developments that could impact tax revenues is a responsibility of a well-managed colony."

As Caius walked them out to their carriages, Jack reviewed the evening. He wasn't sure whether to be pleased or panicked. Julie was going to rip him to shreds by being surprised by Evans's attendance. 'Never let your superior be surprised' was an axiom to live by. On the other hand, Caius had played Evans perfectly. He had hidden their involvement in the scheme while justifying continued communication on the topic. Any follow-on meetings discovered by Evans could be explained as 'just getting an update.' Jack was so distracted with worry that he didn't even hear what Julie and Caius had discussed on the way out. That was dangerous, and he scolded himself to be more careful.

Once in the carriage and on their way, Julie said, "Senator Cereo is much more impressive than I imagined. His manipulation of the situation was masterful. In one fell swoop, he put us in our place while making sure Evans wasn't going to be a problem."

"My apologies for not anticipating this move. I should not have let you be surprised tonight," Jack said with his head slightly turned down in a submissive gesture.

"I wasn't surprised. I know everything Evans does. That's the reason I asked to join tonight. The senator is good, very good. He's proven to be everything you said and more. He would make an excellent first minister," she said, smiling in a way that indicated his performance in that role was marginal. "But don't worry, you have your value as well," Julie said in a soft and intimate but predatory tone while patting his arm. Clearly indicating his extracurricular activities partly made up for a lack of professional attributes.

He shivered inside for what seemed like the millionth time and said, "So we're going forward with Senator Cereo's plan."

"No, Jack. He's too smart. Evans was surprised by my arrival. Senator Cereo wasn't. I will have to root out how he acquired my travel schedule. Cereo would be impossible to predict and control. Unless we find a weakness to exploit, he's too dangerous. I admire him. But I've learned those you admire are the ones who can destroy you. Something is going to have to be done about his relationship with Evans. I'll handle that part. It's time for you to put pressure on Pluta and Trajan to get moving on a Liberty invasion. There isn't anything Senator Cereo can do if the emperor is supporting Pluta. Let's enjoy the evening and discuss tomorrow how you'll arrange an understanding with Trajan and Magistrate Pluta."

She was probably right. While Cereo could be a powerful partner, he was very dangerous. Pluta, also dangerous, was more predictable and thus easier to control. In thinking ahead to the rest of the evening, Jack shivered once again. He would have to perform again tonight. He realized that the one thing he could honestly claim to have gotten out of working for the governor was a deep gut level empathy for those forced into prostitution.

CHAPTER 22

THE DARK SECRET

Hestie was in the small library alcove where she enjoyed doing her genetics research. After Gloria caught her looking at raw DNA code in the commons area, she decided she needed to be more careful. Soon after arriving at the university, she had gotten lost looking for biological reference materials.

She had wandered into a side tunnel of the natural cave system beneath the university library. She found herself amongst rows and rows of ancient history books that had decades, if not centuries, of dust on them. She was intrigued. Perusing this section of old title storage turned into a hobby for her when she needed a break.

One day, after a couple of months of random reading, she discovered gold. In a back corner, buried in dust, and clearly mis-shelved, were three hardbound books. They were each very thick and contained nothing but human genome data. Hestie was in heaven.

She had immediately known it wasn't a complete genome. There were simply not enough pages for that. But with no title page, table of contents, or appendix, she was lost trying to figure out what she had. She did finally crack the unusual notation code that identified where in the genome each of the documented sequences were located. It took weeks of study to realize that each book contained sequences from a different individual. Comparing the books, she determined they were focused on specific differences between the three individuals.

Then the fun began as she started to tease out what those differences were. After much study, it slowly began to take shape. Two had brown eyes and one had blue eyes. Two were female and one was male. One was dark-skinned, one was light-skinned, and the third was somewhere in between. One was tall and two were short. Two were slender and one was robust. All three had brown hair.

Today she was hit by a thunderbolt. She suddenly realized something that shocked her to her core. She sat for a long time before deciding what it meant. Then she had to determine what to do with the information. Should she just keep it a secret? Would people be angry with her? Had she broken the laws around genetics research? In the end, she decided she needed to test her hypothesis with the one person on the planet who might be able to find a flaw in her logic. Her mother.

Her head was spinning as she walked from the library to the medical research building. She was lucky her mother was on one of her frequent trips to the university. Hestie found her in the office the university provided for her. She knocked on the door, entered, and closed the door behind her. Her mother just looked at her with owlish eyes and waited for Hestie to tell her why she had come. It would have been mildly rude if anyone else had done this. It didn't bother Hestie at all. This was her mother, and she loved her.

"Mom, I've been researching DNA for the past few months. I've stumbled on something confusing. Unless I'm missing something, it's also disturbing," Hestie said plainly.

"What did you discover?" her mother asked.

Hestie always watched her mother closely. Growing up, she had learned to discern emotions that were invisible to everyone else. Her mother was worried. This was a woman who was unnaturally calm, even in the worst situations. Hestie swallowed, took a deep breath, and explained.

"A few months ago, I found three hardbound books in the library archives that contain DNA information. After studying them, I decided each of the three were different individuals and the books detailed their differences. Eventually, I figured out that two of them were parents of the third. What was initially surprising was that the child had genes indicating it was much larger than the parents. I thought that odd and dug deeper. I discovered the child had higher bone and muscle density, larger lung capacity, and a larger heart.

"What I suspect is that this child mirrors current Pacifica humans while the parents appear to be from the original colonist stock. What is disturbing is that this change doesn't mirror micro-evolution over forty or fifty generations. It's a single generation set of changes." Hestie stopped for a moment before concluding, "It suggests we're GEMs, Mom."

Her mother had gone from worry to shock. Hestie couldn't remember her mother ever being so distraught. Perhaps she was misreading her mother because she herself was so upset. Hestie watched her mother gather herself and finally ask, "How long have you been able to read the genome without guidance, a map, or notes?"

Hestie turned a light shade of red. This was embarrassing, she thought. Then she confessed. "Since you brought home the first genetics book from the library."

"Why didn't you tell me you could do this?" her mother asked.

"I was embarrassed," she admitted in a soft voice.

Then, to Hestie's horror, her mother started to do something Hestie had never seen her do before. Her mother started to cry.

TRAJAN'S CHOICE

There was a light tap on the door, dragging Pluta out of the financial details of his sprawling slave trading business. "What is it?" he said in an angry voice. Pluta did not like being disturbed when he was buried in a business review.

Henry opened the door and said in a hushed voice, "Apologies, sir. The first minister is in the entry hall asking for an audience. Shall I tell him to come back another time?"

What does that weasel want now, thought Pluta. It's clear the Commonwealth is backing Cereo, and I really don't have time for meetings with no purpose. He wanted to instruct Henry to tell Jack he would have to schedule an appointment sometime later next week. But, he took a deep breath and said, "Take him to the library and tell him I'll join him in five minutes." Hesitating as a thought occurred, he flashed a spiteful grin and continued. "Henry, pull out a recent vintage of Jenny's Acre and offer him a glass. Pour me a glass as well and position the bottle so the label is visible to the first minister."

"Yes, sir," said Henry.

When his information network informed him that the governor had attended a Dry Brook Vineyards wine tasting, he was incensed. Caius had purchased the old Domus Cereo successfully through anonymous agents. It was galling that the governor had met with Cereo at a property that should still be his. He had been talked into letting it go because an offer had come in at twenty percent above market. His previous real estate manager told him he would never get a better price for the old broken-down mansion. That man learned what happens when you disappoint Pluta. The wine will let Jack know that I am aware of the governor's meeting with Cereo, he thought.

"Welcome Jack, what a nice surprise," Pluta said with his false smile as he entered the library.

"Thanks for seeing me on such short notice, Magistrate. I know you're a busy man," Jack said, matching Pluta's phony smile with one of his own.

"Not a problem Jack, you are always welcome here."

"Your choice of wine for this occasion is appropriate. I wanted to discuss Senator Cereo and the results of a meeting the governor had with Emperor Trajan," Jack said as his smile faded and was replaced with a businesslike one.

So that's it. Jack has come to gloat. How immature. Just one more reason to try and break this puppy at some point, thought Pluta. "I am always ready to do whatever the emperor desires. If that aligns with the needs of the Commonwealth all the better," Pluta said, straining to keep his voice pleasant. He knew his façade was starting to crack and silently barked at himself to get under control.

"Trajan decided he wants to hear your ideas on the Liberty situation once more. As you know, the Commonwealth really doesn't get involved in colony politics. However, the governor is supportive of your proposed plan to increase tax revenues," Jack said.

Pluta just stared at Jack in shock. He was sure he had been outmaneuvered by Cereo. Speechless, as he thought through the implications, he finally said, "I'm glad the emperor has decided to hear more about my plan for Liberty. Did the emperor have any additions or alterations to what has already been discussed?"

"He did discuss some ideas, but he wanted to deliver those thoughts to you personally. Since the emperor knew I was planning to visit this afternoon, he asked me to relay his desire for an immediate audience," Jack said with a knowing smile. Jack took a final sip of his wine and said, "Excellent vintage. I'll have to procure some of this while I'm here." Then he stood and said, "I'll show myself out. The governor and I look forward to seeing progress."

The comment about procuring Jenny's Acre caused a jolt of anger to hit him. That bastard really knows how to pull my strings. I need to stop underestimating him, Pluta concluded.

Pluta waited until he heard the door close and then called out to Henry, "Pull out my best suit and have the carriage brought around. I've got an appointment to see the emperor. Move quickly." As he was getting ready to depart, Pluta thought, I really do need to do something about Jack.

Pluta was led under guard through the reception areas of the palace and eventually into the expansive central garden. He was guided down a series of stone walkways to one of Trajan's private alcoves. The central garden was a mix of large open areas and carefully hidden alcoves. The emperor was fond of picking these intimate alcoves for meetings with individuals. It was considered an honor to be invited to one. While Pluta had been to the large meeting area in the center of the garden many times. Being invited to an alcove was a rare experience. This will put the bastard in the right frame of mind, thought Trajan.

Pluta entered the small intimate garden and said, "Good afternoon Your Eminence."

"Pluta, thank you for coming so quickly. It's a pleasure to see you," Trajan said, smiling. The smile was a sham, which he didn't even try to hide. Trajan was wary of Pluta and his influence. While he had more confidence in Cereo, the governor had made it clear the Commonwealth preferred Pluta. It irritated him that they would interfere in his internal affairs. However, Trajan was a realist. He might be the undisputed ruler of this planet, but the Commonwealth could squash him like a bug if they decided they wanted him gone.

"I am at your command," Pluta responded.

"Review your plan for Liberty. I've heard it before, but want to ensure I'm up to date," Trajan said.

Pluta brightened and reviewed the plan he had previously presented. "As I'm sure you'll remember, Lord Druango is eager to form a coalition with Arista to take control of the planet. He proposes maintaining the current monarchy. After victory is achieved, he will ensure that Prince Justin is convicted and executed, along with his extended family. That leaves Queen Olivia as the sole member of the royal family. He plans to marry the queen, then force her to comply with his rule.

"Per Liberty's succession rules, he would have to do that as the queen's consort. This has historical precedence in Liberty whenever the king or queen is unable to perform their royal duties. In return for assisting him, he'll pledge a tribute equal to sixty percent of Liberty's share of the Commonwealth's increased tax revenues. He also pledges to remove natural rights clauses in their constitution. That will permit slavery to be legally practiced. He will also sign a treaty in which Arista will be given a license to manage all of Liberty's slave trade."

"Senator Cereo made some good arguments for making Liberty a region of Arista rather than a subject kingdom. Why isn't that a better plan?" Trajan asked in a tight voice.

Pluta quailed and was obviously trying to come up with an answer. After a long minute, he said, "Legate Ricci believes our legions will be three times the strength of the Liberty Rebel Army when the war ceases. We can decide then which system to enable. Perhaps we can convince Lord Druango to rid himself of the royal family and become governor of the planet rather than ruler," Pluta said, smiling.

"Why wait. We have the upper hand here. General Eastbrook will put down the rebellion if they don't get help from us. Just tell Druango what his role is going to be. You're a businessman. You should know how to negotiate. I want Liberty to be a region of Arista and NOT a subject kingdom. Do you understand?"

"Yes, Your Eminence," Pluta said, clearly shaken.

"Good, good," Trajan said in a satisfied voice. "I have decided you will head up Arista's post war consolidation efforts. The military strategy and invasion will, of course, be handled by a Legion Legate. You will act as a consultant in those matters. I have grown impatient with Senator Cereo and expect you to do better. However, I like his plan better and expect you to deliver a new region to our rule and nothing less," Trajan said.

"I am humbled and pleased to perform whatever service you desire," Pluta responded with a true smile on his face. "Does Legate Ricci know of his role yet?"

Trajan gave a twisted and obviously satisfied smirk and said, "I have decided that Legate Vincentius Cereo will command the invasion. The Second Legion has been informed they are to proceed to Roma to await orders. They will spearhead the attack. The Commonwealth has agreed to supply transport immediately and can move one legion at a time. I am expecting you to move quickly." Trajan was delighted to see how uncomfortable Pluta was with this proclamation. Having Caius Cereo's eldest son head up the invasion would further divide the Senate to his benefit.

Pluta took his time digesting this information and finally said, "I understand and will do whatever is necessary for success." He waited for Trajan to acknowledge his submission. With a head nod from Trajan, he continued. "Given the need for quick action, I recommend Liberty's queen and her servant be moved to Roma under my protection. This will assist in accelerating negotiations with Druango and planning for post war consolidation."

"I'm leaving her where she is for now. She's isolated from Roma intrigues. I want to ensure that continues. We'll hold on to her until Liberty is mine. If all goes well, she can offer me a little personal entertainment. After than perhaps she ends her days at the Arena. Everyone should witness her ultimate submission to my rule," Trajan said firmly.

"I will contact Lord Druango and get started immediately," Pluta said and started to rise up off his chair.

"Lord Druango is on his way to Arista as we speak. You and Legate Cereo will finish negotiations with him and submit a plan as quickly as possible." Trajan hesitated and then said, "The war will be over soon after we land our legions. You better ensure consolidation is done just as quickly." The implied threat was abundantly clear.

"Yes, Your Eminence," Pluta said and then hurried off, clearly shaken by the encounter.

It made Trajan smile to see Pluta terrified of him. Just another attribute of a weak blood line. Cereo would never show fear like that. Trajan sat for a while, dreaming about his legacy. He would be a true namesake to the original Trajan. Liberty first and then Pacifica. Once those dominos dropped, the other planets in the sector would be easy to add as well. There were two other sectors in the Commonwealth under the control of a single planet and Sector 27 was going to be the next. He smiled, imagining Pluta's reaction when he referred to the young Vincentius as cousin. He just hoped Cereo's son was as quick-witted as his father and name him Trajan in return.

Frowning, he thought through the challenges. He didn't trust Pluta, Druango, Cereo, or the Commonwealth. All of them want power and will rob whatever they can from my legacy. Best to keep them all guessing. Even assuming each does their part, it doesn't guarantee success. He reflected once more that blood lines were important. He worried Pluta would not be up to the task. Oh well, he thought, if Pluta fails, I can always fall back on Cereo. One way or another, Liberty will be mine and then work can start on acquiring the rest of the planets in the sector.

NAVIGATION

Hestie turned to Quinn, smiled, and said, "Match." "Match," he agreed. Then, with his cheesy grin, he added, "I never get tired of doing these calculations. Especially when we're pushing the distance."

"Explain to me why we're even doing this," Hestie said with concern. Her passion was diving into the original colony ships' medical and biological databases. The technologies were incredible. She was awestruck by the lives they could improve, extend, and save. The upside for Hestie in discovering they were GEMs was being allowed to dive deep into the vast information resources of the original colonists.

Quinn's smile faded just a bit, and he said, "Professor Dacy says we have to be prepared to take advantage of a Commonwealth spaceship. He says we can't just give up, no matter how bad it looks."

"But what is the probability of gaining control of a spaceship," Hestie said, Then she quickly raised both hands and added, "No don't tell me. If you do, you'll have to explain how you arrived at your answer, and I'm not interested." Hestie smiled brightly at her brother. Quinn always made her smile inside and out. He was so uncomplicated. Of course, that actually made life complicated for him. Since he seemed unaware of the complications, it was, in reality, a blessing. It was just good to see him so happy. People thought she was the one always helping him. The truth was that he helped her just as much, perhaps more.

They had been working on a navigation simulator for local wormhole jumps. These were temporary wormholes that could be artificially created. It involved extremely sensitive sensors that created an accurate 3D map of the far end of the envisioned wormhole. The sensors were the distance limitation. Since quantum computing was a required step, a probabilistic result was the output. It was never perfect. Large amounts of computing time were required.

As an additional safety factor, each spaceship had two independent navigational mapping systems to calculate the wormhole construction. When their answers matched, the likelihood of a mistake was near zero. It bothered Hestie that it was near zero and not zero. A mistake would place the other end of the wormhole somewhere in the universe better matching the model. You could end up anywhere with no path home. Of course, Quinn had no such reservations.

All of this took advantage of an epiphany in physics that had uncovered the mystery of gravity. With it, a new standard model devoid of proxies like dark energy and dark matter. The old standard model was a grand accomplishment given the information available. But since adjustments to the theory had to be made every time a more sensitive telescope was deployed, it was clear something was missing. It turned out that the early theories of quantum gravity were not quite right. The answer was quantum in nature, but not in any of the ways physicists had imagined for hundreds of years.

Allen's Law was actually named after a janitor. Allen was a savant with puzzles. His home was filled with intricate 2D and 3D cardboard, wooden, and metal puzzles he had collected and built over the years. It was rumored he could simply look at all the pieces laid out on a table and instantly know where each piece fit. To fund his obsessive-compulsive hobby, he took a job cleaning offices at CERN.

One day, while emptying a trash receptacle, he asked CERN's director why everyone in the building was working on the same thing. Amused, the director asked him why he thought it was all the same. The answer shook him to his core. Five years later, a large research team, which included Allen as a consultant, had worked out the math, performed measurements, and validated the theory. CERN's director refused to be named primary discoverer. He maintained until his death that Allen's insight was wholly responsible. His summary was "I just did the math." From this discovery, interstellar and intergalactic travel was made a reality.

Hestie and Quinn were part of a six-person team required to operate the spaceship described in their simulator. Artificial Intelligence, AI, had almost destroyed humanity in the twenty-first century, and limitations on computation were strictly adhered to. Those living through that horror had discovered that nuclear weapons weren't the biggest threat to humanity.

The biggest threat to humanity was an AI enabled world wide web.

Limitations could be broken down into three areas. The first prohibited AI algorithms from making decisions. Any decisions. The second was strict limitations on how computer systems communicated. Most systems were constrained to either send information and commands or receive them. Those allowed to have two-way communication were prohibited from having AI software of any kind. The third was limiting access to data for computing systems that utilized AI.

Systems were designed for limited capabilities, and only the data required for them to perform their function was allowed. Navigation was composed of three separate systems. First was plotting a desired path through local space. These systems had maps of the sector they were operating in. The second was a wormhole description, which Hestie and Quinn had just simulated. This system knew the vector math of the path but had no understanding of anything but the two points in space it was navigating between.

The final piece of navigation was the wormhole generator. As far as the last two components of this system knew, they could be anywhere in the universe. Each of these three steps required human interaction and agreement. Redundancy of human judgement and manual data entry was the key to maintaining control. An autonomous, self-aware, computer-controlled spaceship was technically possible. History had shown the grievous mistake of allowing these types of systems to be created.

"My other question is why we are simulating a small warship?" Hestie asked.

"Professor Dacy says the only ship worth working on is one that allows us to fight. Everything else would be a waste of time," Quinn said while he looked away from her.

There it was again. A lie! Well, maybe not a lie, but certainly he was withholding information. Quinn knew something he wasn't allowed to tell her. Oh well, she thought, once again resigned to being in the dark. And it wasn't like she didn't have a secret she kept from Quinn. It was bad enough learning Pacifica natives were GEMs. What could possibly be worse than a death sentence? She was pretty sure she didn't want to know.

That train of thought led her back to thinking about Jay. Her eyes still misted up when he entered her thoughts. It had been weeks since she last saw him and her despondency over their breakup wasn't getting any better. Perhaps worse. She had met him at the Blue Heron Tavern.

She had been procrastinating having the discussion and had talked herself out of doing it that evening. They were having so much fun and there was nothing she loved more than just hanging out with Jay. Then Jay said, "I think Tee is still alive."

"Really? Why do you think that?" Hestie asked, forcing a look of confusion on her face. She hated lying to Jay, even if it was only a facial expression.

He looked at her with concern for a few moments and said, "Partially because you're keeping something about him from me. I know you. While you're good at hiding your thoughts, you can't completely fool me. I wouldn't press you on this if it was anyone other than Tee." Jay turned to the side to show her his first insignia and pointed to the thin red stripe on it. "This means he's always with me. It means I have an obligation to help him in any way I can. He's like a brother to me, Hestie. More even."

Hestie's eyes teared up, and she blurted out, "I've been meaning to tell you this for a while. I've decided we are not a good match, and it's better if we stop seeing each other."

He just sat there staring at her for an uncomfortable couple of minutes before responding. "I don't believe you," Jay said with no malice on his face, only concern. That was one of the things she loved about him. He was trying to understand her pain and grief instead of focusing on his own. Swallowing hard, she said, "I've decided it just isn't going to work." And then, because she couldn't keep her emotions under control any longer, she got up and hurried out. The last thing she heard as she was walking away was, "Something is going on. Just tell me and we'll figure it out." She didn't respond.

Diana sent her a letter a couple of weeks later asking, 'what the hell is going on with you and Jay.' Hestie didn't respond to that either. She couldn't think of anything to say. Diana was her best friend and knew her better than anyone. She simply couldn't come up with a story Diana would believe. She knew Jay was going to ask her to marry him. She would have said yes enthusiastically before the GEM discovery happened. It would have been a dream come true.

But she couldn't say yes, she couldn't do that to him. She couldn't marry him and then kill herself without him knowing why she'd done it. He would decide she had serious mental health issues that were hidden and breaking up with him was a symptom of that. She knew he would be sad at her death. It was much better this way for him, and for her.

CHAPTER 25

TREATY

In the end, Trajan couldn't resist toying with Lord Druango. Once the Commonwealth ship had landed, Pluta had been summoned to the Palatium. Trajan sent a message informing him that Lord Druango was on his way to a meeting with the emperor. *Trajan wants to intimidate the poor bastard before discussions even start,* Pluta thought. *He loves to scare the crap out of people and can't resist.*

Everyone except Cereo, Pluta remembered. That thought peaked his hatred of the man. *Trajan treats him like a long-lost relative.* Those thoughts were bouncing around in his head as he entered the central garden. Before he could greet Trajan, Vincentius Cereo entered the garden on his heels.

"Hello cousin," Trajan said with a twisted smile, moving his head to the side to look past Pluta as he greeted Vincentius Cereo first.

Vincentius hesitated, realizing the slight just given Pluta, and then said deferentially, "A pleasure to see you again Trajan."

Pluta's brain almost exploded. *Bad enough the father was referred to as a family member, but now the upstart Legate?* The obviously pleased Trajan smiled back at Vincentius and then turned to Pluta, frowning a bit. "Glad you found your way here, Magistrate."

"At your command, Your Eminence," he said respectfully, trying very hard to hide his outrage.

At that moment, an overweight, pasty looking man well past his prime was led into the central garden by the first minister.

Jack motioned the man to stand in front of Trajan and said, "It is my pleasure to introduce Lord Druango, Your Eminence."

"Very pleased to meet you, sir," Druango said.

"The proper way to greet me is by referring to me as Your Eminence, Your Majesty, or Your Primacy. Although that last one has fallen out of favor lately," Trajan said, frowning.

"My apologies, Your Eminence," Druango said haltingly. His demeanor going from confident to uncomfortable. Well, get ready to be even more uncomfortable, thought Pluta, smiling.

"If it pleases Your Eminence, I will retire and let the four of you discuss colony business," Jack said in a submissive fashion. What a suck up thought Pluta. But I have to admit, he does a good job of managing Trajan. Most Commonwealth citizens would treat him as someone of little regard. Jack seemed to understand the man had true power here on Arista, which meant indirect power in the sector. Hard to use that power against a Commonwealth citizen, but it was power, nonetheless.

"Thank you for accompanying Lord Druango to my home. I understand you've found temporary quarters for him while he's here," Trajan said. Plura wondered if Lord Druango realized Trajan was insulting him. Anyone of significance visiting Roma was housed in the guest wing of the Palatium. It was a collection of elegant apartments meant to impress. It appeared that Trajan didn't care to impress the lord.

Jack nodded in acknowledgement and said, "Yes. I'll wait out in the reception hall for your meeting to conclude. Then I will accompany Lord Druango to his quarters. I'm sure he's exhausted from the trip."

Yeah, he sure looks like shit, thought Pluta. This was exactly the sort of man Pluta despised. Overweight, doesn't take care of himself physically, likely unable to defend himself. Obviously, a lazy man. Disgusting.

"Thank you, First Minister. We appreciate all the support the Commonwealth gives to its colonies," Trajan said in an appreciative tone.

Jack gave a half bow and backed his way out of the garden. Acting like one of Trajan's subjects, thought Pluta, further irritating him. Jack really was a man who shouldn't be underestimated.

"Tell me why you've come, Lord Druango," Trajan said, as if he didn't already know.

Druango hesitated, clearly confused. He gathered his thoughts and said, "I have a proposition for your consideration. Our offer will greatly increase the wealth of your kingdom, Your Eminence."

"And what proposition is that?" Trajan asked.

"The queen's uncle has rebelled against her succession to the throne by having her kidnapped and sent to Arista. I think he hoped I would be blamed for this. Instead, the House of Lords has declared him to be the culprit. Our army has cornered him, and we are asking for your assistance so that he can be quickly brought to justice," Druango said.

"Why should I care what happens on Liberty?" Trajan pressed.

Druango grew angry then and said, "You don't need to care. I've been negotiating with Overlord Bennett of Sector 3. General Harris, his top mercenary commander, is available. I just thought it would be better to keep this within Sector 27," he said defiantly.

"Come now Lord Druango. Do you think I'm an idiot? General Eastbrook is the one who has cornered you, not the other way around. If you don't get immediate assistance, your life is over. I know what kind of fees Bennett charges. You had better offer us something better than that."

"If you send two legions back with me, I will transfer forty percent of the increased tax the Commonwealth has agreed to apportion to Liberty to Arista. A conservative estimate is at least five billion credits per year," Druango said, smiling.

"Why don't I send three legions and just take over the planet? Why do I need you?" Trajan said in a thick voice, leaning forward with his chin jutting out.

Sweat broke out on Druango's forehead, and he stuttered. "I was assured by the first minister that you were in favor of an arrangement."

"The Commonwealth doesn't get involved in colony politics. It violates their non-interference Edicts. If I want to have you provide entertainment at our next Arena event, they don't care. If I want to conquer Liberty and turn it into a slave planet, the Commonwealth would just turn its head. I merely need to increase tax revenues. Which isn't hard if I control the planet," Trajan said in a tone that was just short of shouting. Lord Druango melted at that point. He was clearly terrified of Trajan and his eyes were darting wildly about, looking for an escape.

At that point, Trajan barked out, "Lord Druango." And when Druango's eyes jerked back to him, he said, "You are fortunate. I like having local governance for the regions of my empire. The first minister and Magistrate Pluta seem to think you can effectively provide that. While I'm not yet convinced, I am willing to let you try and convince me.

"Before you ask about your fiancée, she is being well taken care of. I doubt we need royalty on Liberty, but just in case, I'll keep her safe for now. Work with Legate Cereo and Magistrate Pluta on a plan to conquer and govern Liberty as a region of Arista. When you're ready to plead your competence, request an audience."

Then, instead of dismissing him, he smiled and said in a conciliatory voice, "Tomorrow you are invited to attend the Arena in my private suite. It's the first day of our New Year's celebration. You might as well enjoy a little entertainment while you're here." After that announcement, Trajan shooed them away.

As they exited the central garden, Pluta was thinking it was a little surprising the man hadn't had a heart attack. Or at the very least, wet his pants. Trajan excelled at being rational one minute and unhinged the next. It kept a person guessing what was really going on. He hoped Druango was made of stronger stuff than was evident. In any case the man now knew his dreams of being the King of Liberty were over.

The following day, Jack declined the emperor's invitation to attend the Arena. His excuse was that he had an important Commonwealth issue to deal with. Pluta didn't believe his excuse, and it solidified his suspicion that Jack was soft. A weakness to be exploited, perhaps. Lord Druango didn't realize that the Arena was more than gladiator bouts. The entertainment the emperor had mentioned the day before was much more gruesome than anything Druango had likely witnessed or even imagined. Pluta was really looking forward to watching Druango's reaction.

At the last minute, Trajan had sent word that he would not be attending that day, but wanted everyone to enjoy the festivities. Pluta knew this was twofold. First, it insinuated that perhaps Trajan was working privately with Jack. If not, it was clearly another insult. It was classic Trajan. Put people in their place and keep them guessing.

The day's activities started with an announcement of the first event. A man with a large megaphone walked out onto the sandy surface of the Arena floor to the cheers of the crowd and announced, "First up today is administering justice for dereliction of duty."

A door opened up across from the emperor's suite and a nude man in chains was led out. He stumbled badly. Instead of letting him get up, he was roughly dragged to a post, picked up, and slammed against it.

Then he was chained so that he had no choice but to stay upright. He sported a number of open sores and untended wounds all over his body. He had clearly been tortured.

"This man was in charge of security on one of the Commonwealth's transport ships. They were transporting slaves for Arista. He neglected to ensure that newly captured slaves were being properly secured. As a result, he was responsible for three guards and one highly valued slave being killed. These are the four the Pacifica gladiator Tee murdered onboard ship."

A roar of approval went up from the crowd when Tee's name was mentioned. The announcer waited for the cheers and applause to die down before continuing.

"The slave Tee murdered was intended to be the one providing justice in the Arena. So, it's fitting that the murdered slave's replacement is the one to administer this judgement. In the meantime, since the murdered slave was originally requested by the emperor, this scum has been getting special attention from the emperor Trajan himself." More applause. Then the announcer said, "Let justice be served."

As the announcer walked off, a gaunt, cruel looking man with various implements on his belt walked forward to the terrified, cringing man chained to the post. The man started screaming before it even began.

Pluta couldn't remember the last time he had enjoyed himself this much. He had watched Lord Druango go from horrified to sitting frozen with a vacant look on his face. The best part was when he couldn't hold on to the contents of his stomach. It was clear Druango understood Trajan's threat to have him provide entertainment at the Arena was the same fate he was witnessing. He had gone into shock when the tortures grew more inventive, and eventually extremely personal. This was when the screams grew sharper and louder.

When the screaming, sobbing, and begging weakened, the man was told to beg for his death. A megaphone was held up to his ruined mouth so that the entire crowd could hear his plea. After the man made an impassioned plea, the torturer decided to keep at it, to the delight of the crowd. The torturer finally ended it when he sensed the crowd was growing bored. The rest of the day at the Arena was uneventful.

Druango eventually decided to take advantage of the suite's refreshments and drank himself senseless. He just sat and stared, neither enjoying the gladiator bouts nor turning his head away at the more gruesome parts. Pluta was pleased. Lord Druango was now in the right frame of mind for negotiations.

CHAPTER 26

NEW YEAR'S FESTIVAL

Tee was holding his own against Victor. Then suddenly he wasn't. Lying on his back in the dirt, Victor laughed and held his hand out to help Tee up.

"Don't feel bad, Tee," Victor said with his smile still in place. "Even Griff doesn't know that trick. One of my failures is not completing Griff's training before I was kidnapped. One of the traditions of master sergeants was to withhold certain techniques until the person you're training as a replacement is considered worthy. With years to think about it, I've decided this is a bad tradition. All Guard members ought to know all the tricks. For the Guard, important knowledge needed has likely been lost forever. If you get back to Pacifica, I want you to promise you'll teach all the special techniques I teach you to Griff. Then make him promise to teach it widely."

"When we both get back to Pacifica, we can share that duty," Tee said, grinning.

Victor just looked at him oddly. Talk of getting back to Pacifica had started a few weeks ago when Tee told Victor, "I have an idea of how we might kill the emperor." As he said it, he thought of Jay. Jay would smile and say it was just another suicide plan. Shaking himself out of his nostalgia, he said in a low voice, "Speaking of getting back to Pacifica, did Forti measure the wall yet?" Tee asked in a hushed whisper.

"Yes, and you were right. It's almost the same height as the arrow and spear range barrier. Perhaps a bit less. Test out your idea tomorrow during practice. Don't be obvious, Tee," Victor said in his mentor's voice while glaring for good measure.

Tee shot him his 'you don't need to state the obvious' look. Then he grew pensive, keeping his eyes on the ground for a while. Looking up, he said, "Do you really think this will work?"

"It all depends on whether you get in a kill shot quickly enough. I'm certain of giving you enough time for one but uncertain if you will have time to get off two," Victor said, staring intently at Tee.

Tee stared back at Victor for a few moments and then said patiently, "I used to practice doing exactly this. Taking an unknown bow and executing a kill shot with the first arrow. I can get off a second arrow very quickly. I am confident of placing the second arrow where it's needed. Forti told me the bows used in the Arena match what I practice with. They are standard legion issue. But they are not high-quality bows. There will be minor differences between them. I just don't know what those differences will be."

Victor huffed and said, "If nothing else, it's a good plan. My idea of the two of us rushing the emperor's suite was doomed to failure. There are way too many security personnel around him and the archers placed on top of the walls would make pincushions out of us. Distracting everyone while you attack from across the Arena feels like something that might work.

"The people behind you will obviously see what you're doing, but surprise will give you some time. They will most likely panic seeing one of us on top of the wall. Forti will be in that general area, along with a few others. That could buy us some time. As long as that bastard emperor dies, I'll go to my maker a happy man."

"Why is Forti helping us?" Tee asked suspiciously. He had never quite gotten to the point of trusting the man. Much of that suspicion had to do with Forti working for Senator Cereo. How could he trust a man who thought he owned him, or anyone, for that matter? He was also chummy with Leo, who Tee definitely didn't trust. There was something false about him.

"It's a sad story. He was a legionnaire who helped a slave girl escape. She had been assigned to him. It's one of the benefits given when a warrior reaches that status. She cooked, cleaned, mended his wounds, and provided company. After a few months, he realized he was in love with her. It was impossible for him to buy her from the legion. They don't allow the soldiers to have a future with the camp girls. They believe that would cause too many problems in the ranks.

"So, when she was scheduled to be rotated, Forti helped her escape. The emperor himself got involved. One of the Legates mentioned the situation, and the emperor decided to administer what he calls justice. They made Forti watch as the slave girl was tortured in the Arena. Then, as they were dragging her dead body out of the Arena his first match started.

"After Forti won, Trajan announced that he was being given a chance to redeem himself because of his years of service to the legion. Thirty hard fought bouts later, he was a free man once more," Victor finished, shaking his head. "The emperor is a monster. He needs to be put down. Don't worry about Forti. He's all in."

"I'm all in too, Victor. Training to kill innocent people is not a life I care to continue. If we can provide some real justice, it's enough for me," Tee said.

"Forti says there is a chance we can trigger a revolution. Everyone is terrified of the emperor, but once he's dead, they may be confident enough to throw down his government. The aristocracy is hated by most of the people of Arista. Citizens are a minority. I've told you what to say. Make sure you say it before you let go your first arrow. Make sure everyone around you hears it," Victor said sternly. "We have to spur them to action."

Tee smiled grimly. He didn't mind dying if he could protect others. If they could really kill the emperor, then maybe the kidnappings and Arena atrocities would slow or even stop. If so, it would be enough.

The next day, during archery practice, Tee placed an arrow in the very top of the barrier. Eric had a ladder he used to retrieve these types of errant shots, but he wasn't around. Tee glanced around and up to the observation room. Seeing no one, he casually walked over to the barrier and jumped. He caught the top of the barrier with one hand and then swung up to grab it with his other hand. He quickly pulled himself up and stood on top.

He reached down and pulled out the errant arrow, then jumped down. The other gladiators were staring at him. Damn, that wasn't inconspicuous at all, he thought. Victor was glaring at him. Oh well, another lecture at dinner tonight. The good news was that jumping to that height was easy. He could get on top of the Arena wall anywhere he chose.

Standing back in the shadows of the observation room was Dobler. His jaw almost hit the ground when Tee did a standing jump and ended up on top of the barrier. The athleticism of the Pacifica gladiators was simply astounding. He never would have guessed anyone could do that. His eyes narrowed. But why? Why would Tee allow himself to be seen doing that? Was he testing an idea?

Just then, he realized the height of the barrier was similar to the height of the protective wall around the Arena. Everyone thought it was plenty high enough to protect the spectators. This sudden realization made him smile. He knew he should report it. He knew that if something happened, they would interrogate him and discover he had been holding back. If so, he might end his days as Arena entertainment.

But every time he thought about giving a report, the memory of the girl who looked so much like his daughter reappeared. Victor and Tee are good people, he thought. Victims like himself. He would wait and see what happened. The next time they would appear in the Arena was New Year's. They pulled out all the stops for New Year's and both would definitely play a part. It would be just like Trajan to have them fight some ridiculous number of gladiators together. Perhaps he would buy a ticket this year.

As the New Year's Ascension holiday drew nearer, Victor's training grew even more intense. Lately, Victor was a maniac. There was a new technique almost every day, and he was expected to do them perfectly. Tee took his lumps and learned. He wondered how he might fare against Jay these days. Those bouts had always been decidedly one-sided. His confidence had grown from the months of training with Victor. He believed his new skills might even test Jay. That would be fun.

"Okay, that's enough for today," Victor finally said as daylight began to dim. "Tomorrow we do a light workout to loosen up and then rest. Let's have dinner and discuss the plan again. I want to make sure we both know what to do in various situations," Victor announced with a light sweat showing. It used to be that Tee was the only one sweating. The fact Victor worked up a sweat sparring with him was all the validation Tee would ever need. While he lost all the bouts, he was making Victor work, and that was something to be proud of.

Dinner that night turned into a quiz session. Tee knew all the answers, but Victor wanted to hear them from him one more time. Tee had seen this behavior before when Victor was anxious. Tee guessed his obsessive nature was one of the things that made Victor special. His preparation was incredibly detailed, with multiple backup plans. If they failed, it would not be because of a lack of planning.

As they were finishing dinner Victor said, "Make sure you shout out the call for revolution before you let the first arrow loose."

Tee rolled his eyes and in an exasperated voice said, "For heaven's sake, Victor. You've told me that five times today. I think it's more important to see him dead than worry about starting a revolution. Yes, I'll make sure I say exactly what you taught me."

Victor stared daggers at him and said, "Just make sure."

New Year's Day came, and Tee had been too nervous to sleep. Was he nervous or already feeling guilty about the men he would be forced to kill today? Perhaps a combination of both. His expectation was that sleep wasn't going to matter after today, anyway. Looking out his window as the sun was rising, he was thinking about Grammy. She would tell him to fully enjoy his last sunrise. So that was what he was attempting to do. The beauty of the sunrise got him to think about Diana and the many shared sunsets and moon rises they had seen at the beach. He missed his family and friends terribly, but her most of all.

As the gloom started to fade into light, he noticed Victor sitting across from Forti at one of the training ground tables. They were both leaning forward and having an intense conversation. How did Victor get permission to be in the yard that early? Tee was distrustful of Leo and Forti. He hoped Victor hadn't been taken in by a story of freedom invented by a slaver.

Perhaps their plan was known to the emperor and was part of today's entertainment. He trusted Victor completely. He would just have to hope Victor wasn't trusting someone he shouldn't. His only worry should be doing his part exactly as planned. It would feel good to have a bow in his hand with something other than practice arrows. It would be especially satisfying to have the chance to dispense justice.

Victor had told Tee what their strategy would be if they fought together. It was similar to what Jay and Tee had used early in recruit training. Victor would go on the offensive and Tee would watch his back. However, what they had practiced was vastly more intricate than what he and Jay had done. His training in these techniques had been done in the evenings in Tee's cell. Victor didn't want the other gladiators to know how they would coordinate. Before Tee had explained his plan to Victor, he had been intense with his training. Tee realized later than it was anxiety more than anything else. Victor remained an uncompromising taskmaster, but he seemed confident in their new plan. At least someone thought it might work.

Victor explained what he had learned just that morning as they were led into the tunnel for the Arena. "Forti told me the plan is to swarm us with a mix of gladiators, newly acquired slaves, and criminals. He wasn't sure how many would be released or when. The newly acquired slaves might be captured warriors from another world. What this means is that we have to focus on identifying and taking out the best fighters early. They will try and hide in the crowd to get close. They may even have a coordinated plan."

"How sure are you of Forti's information?" Tee asked.

"I'm confident of Forti. He's confident of his information. That's all you need to know," Victor said sternly, obviously irritated with Tee's continued suspicion of Forti.

"I will do my part, Victor," Tee said with steel in his voice.

"I'm confident of that," Victor said softly. There was something approaching affection in his voice. He recovered his usual gruff manner and added, "Just like we practiced. It's a dance and I'm leading. Watch my back, but keep me in your peripheral vision. I may suddenly move at any time in any direction. You must stay positioned to protect me from what I can't see."

Tee swallowed a deep sigh and thought, he's told me this almost as many times as he's mentioned making the call for revolution before my first arrow. Well, I have to admit it's burned into my brain at this point.

As they arrived at one of the gladiators' doors to the Arena, they heard the announcer say, "A special treat for your New Year's enjoyment. We are recreating the Battle of Thermopylae. Playing the part of the Spartans will be the Pacifica gladiators. Perhaps Sparta will be victorious this time. Perhaps history will be repeated."

With that introduction, the door opened, and Victor and Tee walked out. He noticed Victor's swagger and affected one for himself. The crowd did have an effect, and he smiled to think his ego might be getting a bit inflated. They had brought in large boulders and sprinkled them around on both sides of a wall they had built bisecting the Arena. It did give the appearance of a narrow mountain pass. It had an opening just wide enough that Victor and Tee standing side by side could easily defend it. Thermopylae indeed. Victor and Tee walked over in front of the emperor's suite and did their customary roman salute. Then they both declared in unison, "For the honor of Emperor Trajan."

Trajan shooed them away with a limp wrist and a bored expression. They jogged over and positioned themselves to protect the opening in the wall. Victor was actually smiling as he said, "This helps our plan as long as the main attack comes from the emperor's side. And that egomaniac will want the best view, so that's guaranteed. We stay here until the bodies pile up and the flow of new warriors diminishes.

"When the doors open behind us, we start our dance. At my signal, you retreat to the far side. Be defensive, be boring. We need everyone to focus on me. I'll do everything I can to draw the crowd's attention. When I think the time is right, I'm make my declaration and then you do your part."

"Tee grinned back at him and said in a singsong voice, "And I'll make my declaration before I loose the first arrow." They both chuckled.

"As all the doors on the emperor's side of the Arena opened, Victor said, "It's truly been an honor, Tee." And before Tee could respond, insanity arrived.

After months of training, Tee thought he had a good grasp of Victor's abilities. What he was witnessing was something else entirely. His speed, agility, and ability to kill with a single sword thrust were amazing. It also became obvious that he could pick out who was dangerous, regardless of how they tried to blend in. Several times Tee had to lecture himself to stop being a spectator. He had a job to do. It was hard not to just watch the legend at work.

As predicted, bodies started to pile up. Victor had been grabbing the dead and dragging or throwing them into positions that helped slow the main attack. He was building a wall of bodies. The fighting slowed and then stopped. Quiet filled the Arena until the doors underneath the emperor's suite opened once more and a new mob of fighters emerged.

Victor grunted and said, "I'm guessing this is day two. If so, we won't have anyone attacking from behind until the next set."

"I'll keep watch," Tee managed to say before the next wall of fighters hit them.

After the fighting started to diminish once more, Tee heard the crowd gasp. He turned his head to see a handful of gladiators pour out behind them. "Looks like they shortened it to two days," Tee said. Victor signaled a progression to their original tactic. Victor was the aggressor, with Tee protecting his back. With both tiring and dripping with sweat, the number of gladiators started to diminish. There were just two behind the wall now and a dozen or so trying to get over the dead body barrier. Victor had manipulated the action to get this result. He then signaled Tee to separate.

Tee turned his attention to the two remaining on their side of the wall. Out of the corner of his eye, he saw Victor run and leap over the bodies piled in the doorway and then lost sight of him. From the swell of crowd noise, he guessed there was quite a bit of carnage going on. Neither of the two he was fighting had much skill. One was young, younger than anyone should be in the Arena. The boy was clearly panicked and was not thinking clearly. He had no skills but was pushing forward, regardless. The threat of ending up as special entertainment at the Arena was a powerful motivator. The other was a middle-aged man who had some skill with the sword, but not much. It was easy to manipulate a quick retreat to the back side of the Arena just under the far side archers' station.

The stadium had archers stationed every fifty feet along the periphery of the wall. They were not expected to get involved in the Arena battles. They were window dressing to make the spectators feel safe. Tee glanced up and the archer was intently watching the battle on the other side of the wall. Victor must be just underneath the emperor's suite by now. All of a sudden the crowd was cheering wildly. Then the mood completely changed with the crowd quieting, and then they let out a collective gasp. All the archers started notching arrows with their eyes locked on the other side of the separator wall. Victor must have made his declaration.

Tee didn't hesitate. He killed the older, more skilled attacker and slammed his shield into the adolescent, knocking him to the ground. At least that death won't be on my conscious he thought. Dropping his shield and sword, he jumped, grabbed the top of the wall, and in seconds was standing on top, right next to the archer.

The man who had been ready to fire an arrow was stunned to look up and see Tee towering over him. He just stared dumbly, as if he couldn't believe what he was seeing. Tee grabbed the man's tunic with one hand, pulled the bow away from him with the other. Then he tossed him off the wall. He felt good that perhaps this man would live as well. Broken bones perhaps, but a chance to live. All hell was breaking loose around Tee as the crowd scrambled in a panic to get away from him. Tee stepped to the arrow stand and quickly selected two arrows. He notched the first and as he pulled back, he turned, looked up, and located the emperor. Trajan was still sitting down and looking wide eyed down below. He imagined Victor was causing enough havoc to captivate him.

Out of his peripheral vision, he saw the other archers letting loose their arrows. He caught himself and hesitated long enough to loudly shout his declaration before letting the arrow loose. He mentally thanked Victor. He had almost forgotten to do that with all the chaos. With the first arrow on its way, he quickly notched the second. He had known almost immediately that his first arrow was at least three or four inches too high.

Wincing internally, his thoughts went to his mother. She would be disappointed with that shot. Although he heard movement behind him, he took an extra moment to make sure of his aim and let it loose. He had a moment of satisfaction knowing this arrow was flying true. Then his world went black.

SOVEREIGN

CHAPTER 1

PALATIUM

Tee woke without opening his eyes or moving. His Guard training kicked in just like it had on the slave ship. His first thought was that he was dead. Whatever he was lying on was warm and unbelievably comfortable. He thought it smelled lightly of lavender. Then he noticed a headache intruded on his comfort. He decided the afterlife should not be a mix of comfort and headache. It should either be wonderful or horrible, but not something in between. Given the things he had done lately, horrible was likely the proper judgement. He could hear someone softly breathing a few feet to his left. After a few minutes, the person sighed as if impatient and moved slightly. Perhaps getting more comfortable in a chair? Curiosity overcame his paranoia. He opened his eyes, turned his head, and found Forti sitting in a chair by the side of his bed, reading a book. Tee was in the biggest bed he had ever seen.

He swept his eyes quickly around the room and was stunned by what he saw. He had never seen anything so extravagant. At first he thought it might be a one room home given its size. However, he didn't see a kitchen, so perhaps it was in a separate room on the other side of the door. If so, this would be a very large home. The ceiling had three-dimensional features with a large mural painted on it. The walls were a soothing color with artwork adorning them. There was a full set of plush parlor furniture arranged around an elaborately decorated fireplace. Opposite the fireplace was a large desk made of almost black wood. It was placed in front of floor-to-ceiling glass windows. Bright daylight was streaming in. It made no sense to him.

Forti was patient while Tee looked around, trying to get his bearings. When his eyes wandered back Forti said, "Am glad to see you awake. The doctors always worry with a head injury."

Tee, remembering his last moments from the Arena, reached up and felt the back of his head. There was some sort of bandage there. Touching it lightly, he immediately identified this as the source of his headache.

"Sorry about your head. I was a step too late," Forti said, grimacing a bit in empathy.

"Where is Victor?" Tee asked.

"I'm sorry, Tee," Forti said with compassion in his voice. "He didn't make it. It's the stuff of legends, but he's dead." After giving Tee a few moments to absorb the bad news, he continued. "I have a lot to tell you, and it's going to be hard to accept."

"How do I know I can trust you?" Tee said bluntly. He couldn't imagine why he was in such an opulent place. Even more confusing was Forti saying he was going to explain it to him.

"Excuse me for just a second, Tee," Forti said as he got up. He walked over and cracked the door open, and spoke quietly to an unseen person on the other side. He came back, sat down, took a moment, and then said, "Victor thought we should have a conversation with just you and me. He wanted us to establish trust. He told me to apologize for not telling you everything about the assassination plan. His apology will make sense later. The important thing to know is that you were successful. The emperor is dead. You are safe."

Tee forced himself to bury his grief over Victor's death. He needed to worry about self-preservation for now. He pushed himself up into a sitting position and was immediately woozy. His headache increased, adding nausea to his list of 'not in heaven' ailments. He gritted his teeth and propped himself up by leaning back against an elaborately carved headboard.

He waited for his head to clear, then looked at Forti and said, "Why should I trust you?"

Forti smiled and said, "Victor told me it would be difficult to explain this if he didn't survive. The short answer is that 'I am of the Guard, and we are brothers.'"

This was a formal greeting ritual used to start briefings. It communicated the close relationship between all Guard members and the need to trust and believe in the presenter. "What?" Tee asked, clearly stunned by the reference, especially given it was said within its intended purpose. In disbelief, he said, "You can't be a member of the Guard."

"Victor told me he is Master Sergeant of the Guard. He said that since he hasn't been notified of a change in status, he has the authority to invite, test, and approve new recruits. He said he was convinced I could provide capable service below the Wall. Whatever that means. Perhaps you can explain it to me later. All of this came out early in the morning before the two of you entered the Arena. When he gave me that phrase to say to you, he said he also has the authority to graduate you into full Guard membership. You're not a Newbie anymore," Forti said.

It sounded like something Victor would say. But why? I'm supposed to be dead along with Victor, Tee thought. The plan was to make them pay. There was always a hope that their actions would spawn an uprising, but Tee never put any faith in that.

"Why am I still alive?" Tee asked in an angry voice.

"Now that's where this gets really interesting. Do you remember the call for uprising that Victor made you memorize?" Forti asked.

"Yeah, 'overthrow the tyrant' or something like that," Tee said, confusion deepening. "It was supposed to encourage the crowd to overthrow the emperor and his family."

"Well, he lied. It was a clever lie, because in a sense, it's true. You shouted out 'Provoco ius Imperandi,' correct?"

"Yes," said Tee with a questioning look on his face.

"The correct translation is 'I challenge the right to rule,'" Forti said. "By ancient custom, anyone can challenge the emperor's right to rule on his ascension anniversary. In Arista, this is also called New Year's Day. That's why he was so heavily guarded. It originally meant personal combat in the Arena. Centuries ago, one of the early emperors successfully argued that an emperor's weapons included his army, guards, family, servants, and slaves. So, if challenged, all could be utilized for the emperor in 'personal combat.' The other key change was that a weapon of the emperor cannot be used against him. This guaranteed safety from those closest to him."

Tee held up his hand at that point and in frustration said, "Please just tell me what this means."

"It means you are Emperor Theron, First of his Name," Forti said with an amused grin.

Tee just stared at him. He couldn't believe what he had just heard. Although he had lots of questions, one thing needed to be resolved before anything was going to make sense. He furrowed his brow and asked one more time, "Why should I trust you?"

Forti's face showed a mild frustration, then it took on an amused expression, and he said "Victor said you would be a tough nut. He admired your 'pig headed ways,' as he put it. He told me two things that might help. First, he told me to remind you to balance your stance."

It was the very first thing Victor had harped on in their training sessions. He had pointed out that Tee took on a defensive posture, even when positioning for an attack. Victor had likened him to a little girl confronting a mouse. In typical Victor fashion, he insulted him brutally in creatively colorful language before telling him why it was important. In this case, Tee was limiting his options while telegraphing weakness. Tee considered this and then said suspiciously, "Anyone who watched our early training sessions might come up with that."

"The other thing he told me was what happens between a mentor and a Newbie before the Newbies' first battle." Forti walked over and whispered the call to victory, along with the correct response in his ear. "Victor told me he said that to you just before you entered the Arena for the Harvest Festival."

Tee just stared at him. It was all too much to process. Victor would never have given Forti that particular piece of Guard lore if he hadn't met Victor's stringent requirements. That meant Victor trusted Forti without reservation. It meant Tee had to trust Forti with his life. He was trying to make sense of it all when Forti said, "If Victor didn't make it, I was to tell you he would like you to call him Vic the next time you see him."

To Tee's horror, his eyes formed tears and as one started running down his face, Forti thankfully turned away. Tee had to get his control back. There had been way too much death this past year to say nothing of having his freedom taken away from him. After gaining control, Tee said, "What else do I need to know?"

Forti raised his eyes and said, "Senator Cereo is someone to trust and he's waiting just outside the door."

Once again, Tee was caught speechless for a few moments. Then he said "You have to be kidding me. The man who thinks he owns me is someone Victor wants me to trust?"

"Senator Cereo doesn't believe in slavery any more than you do. And yes, he's trustworthy. It's a long story. Let's have him come in. It's important that we pull a plan together for the next few days. You are the emperor, but it's a very dicey situation and much needs to happen before it all falls apart," Forti said.

Tee thought about that for a few moments and then nodded.

Forti rose and went to the door. Then he paused and turned back around. "Victor knew you had succeeded. Your first arrow severed the carotid artery, the second pierced his heart. Both were kill shots. I was told Victor clearly recognized this and smiled just before he died."

Caius could hear them talking as he waited with Leo just outside the door. The doctors had been worried about the head injury. All three of them had waited nervously all night, hoping he would awaken. Not only had Theron awoken, Forti said his mental faculties were intact. He still couldn't believe the two Pacifica gladiators had pulled this off. Forti had come to him the week before with his confession of helping Victor plan the emperor's assassination. He explained that he had kept it from Caius, so there was deniability if they got caught. He pressed Caius to take control if they were successful.

By sheer luck, his son's Second Legion was in the barracks right next to the Arena. They were days away from transport to Liberty. His efforts to delay that invasion had ended in failure, and he had accepted it. After a tense thirty-minute discussion with Leo, they decided to throw the dice. Leo was aware of the ancient law of challenge by combat. They would risk everything if Victor and Theron were successful. Leo was the one who really pushed for this decision. He still remembered his plea.

"Caius, we have a chance to make a difference for millions. We can free everyone in our family. This opportunity will never happen again. We can't turn away from this." It really wasn't all that hard to convince him. Caius had always been known as the risk taker in the family. But Leo now wore that crown. They purchased all the remaining New Year's Day tickets still available that were across the Arena from the emperor's suite. Those seats had been filled by Forti's security team and selected members of his son Vincent's legion.

Waiting patiently, Caius reflected on when this crazy path in life started. It was almost thirty-five years ago. He had just turned sixteen. He was terrified. His parents were dead, and he had no idea what to do. He was deeply ashamed when he realized he wasn't overly upset about them being dead. It was the uncertainty of how their deaths would affect everyone he loved that haunted him. The overseer, a brutal alcoholic who did nothing unless his parents were in residence, left as soon as the news arrived. He pulled Caius off to the side before leaving and said, "Make a few examples of the slaves if you want to live. They'll slit your throat by the time I get to the front gate if you're not tough on them."

His parents had left him when he was just a baby at their remote villa with June, her daughter Olympia, his half-brother Leo, and June's father, Sage. His half-brother was only a month older than him, and June had been recruited to be Caius's wet nurse. His parents rarely visited, and when they did, it was a horrifying experience. His father was always drunk and, at some point, would say horrible things to June and drag her into his bedroom. His mother would act as if nothing were happening. He despised them both for it.

When he was twelve, he told his father to stop doing bad things to June. His father just laughed, grabbed June's arm, and drug her toward his bedroom telling Caius he could come watch if he wanted. Caius picked up a walking stick and hit him with it. His father responded by beating him mercilessly.

After exhausting himself, his father calmed down and said with a smile, "Okay, she's getting a bit old anyway. You can keep her for yourself if you want." Then he laughed as Caius lay humiliated on the floor.

Later, with his face flushed red, he haltingly told June he only wanted her to be safe. June, with a warm but sad smile, said, "Caius, you are not your father. You're the good-hearted young man I've always known you would be."

The first night after receiving the news, they sat around the dinner table and June informed him, "All of the slaves not part of my family left the villa this afternoon. We gave them food but didn't let them steal anything."

Caius just shrugged and announced his plan. "I'm going to free everyone, sell the ranch, and split the proceeds."

June smiled, hesitated a moment, and then gently asked, "And then what are you going to do?"

"I don't know. I guess I'll go to Roma and find a job."

"What kind of job Caius? What skills do you have?" June asked softly.

"I haven't really thought it through yet, but that's what I'm going to do," he said and glared defiantly back at her.

"You know, if you sold us and the villa, you could probably afford to go to college. You would have to be frugal, but you could do it," June offered.

"NO!" Caius shouted. "That's disgusting! It's insulting you think I would sell you, my brother, my sister, and grandfather!"

"Well, Oly isn't really your sister, is she?" June countered.

"She's my brother's sister which makes her mine," Caius said with his lower lip protruding outward and his body language conveying an immoveable conviction.

June's concerned look turned into an amused grin. "You've always been a headstrong and stubborn child. You would be easy to dislike if you weren't so sweet." Her smile flattened and mist formed in her eyes. Caius blushed and looked down. Then with tears welling in her eyes she said, "Since you were a baby, I have loved you as my own. You are a loving brother and treat all of us as family." This stunned Caius, June NEVER cried. "Your stupid, doomed to fail plan just confirms we really are a family. If so, we're going to keep our family together. We have land and we're going to work it."

A calmness and determination fell over Caius. He would free them all. If they wanted to continue to live at the villa with him as a family, it would be a dream come true.

The only hope they had of paying their real estate taxes was the one-acre hobby vineyard his mother had ordered planted. She knew the owner of Gold Coast vineyard, the most renowned winery on Arista. She had been sold cuttings from their Pinot Noir stock at an outrageous price. Gold Coast never shared cuttings or any other secrets about their wine business. But the owner liked Jenny and was confident that nothing would come of it. His mother insisted she was going to be a vintner. She purchased a library full of books on grape growing and winemaking, but never got around to reading more than a few of them.

Years ago, this initiated a 'family meeting' where it was decided they had to produce drinkable wine. If they didn't, they would be blamed for sabotaging his mother's vineyard. It was decided that Sage, Caius, and Leo would grow the grapes and Oly would learn how to make wine. Oly was the natural choice because she possessed an uncanny sense of taste and smell, critical in winemaking according to one of the books. Caius's participation in this was, of course, voluntary, but he put in as much effort as anyone. It was incredibly hard work, as there wasn't an irrigation system. The vineyard had to be watered by hand.

This was in addition to the daunting task of growing enough crops and livestock to feed everyone. His mother, again, had the opinion that her refuge from the world had to be disconnected from it. It had to be self-sustaining. Much like the vineyard, his mother's only contribution to this was supplying an extensive library of books on sustainable agriculture. Mixed in were books on agri-business. With wet winters and bone-dry summers, it was challenging, but possible. His mother's 'live off the land' fantasy was the reason they would survive.

The hobby vineyard was currently in its sixth year and its first harvest had been the previous year. They had produced 250 cases. His parents had been delighted with that first year's wine. His parents had expensive tastes, so if they liked, it might actually be good. Leo said that if they could sell two hundred cases for ten credits a bottle, they could pay their property taxes and have enough left over to cover their other expenses. Even then, Leo was the brains behind the business. He had devoured the business-related books in the library. He was passionate about building a successful winery business. Leo immediately pushed for expanding their vineyard. He told them that with only one acre, a bad year could break them. For this, they needed a more reliable source of water than a single well. With no power available, Sage came up with the idea of building a gravity flow irrigation system. This was eventually done by forming a reservoir in a large ravine uphill of the farmable area of the property. Of course, this just added more work. But because it was their collective future, the familial bonds grew stronger.

If they were going to successfully sell their wine, Caius thought they had to have a gimmick. Caius's mother had been extremely popular, even if she was considered a bit of a crackpot. She had a natural charisma combined with a way of making people around her feel comfortable. He suggested they name the wine Jenny's Acre and combine it with Sage's suggestion of Dry Brook Vineyards. The latter being an inside joke about their plan to build a reservoir based on a brook that was dry most of the year.

At first Caius had been hesitant about using his mother's name. He had not forgiven her for his father's abuses. She should have stopped him, he thought. After mentioning this to June, she sat him down and said, "You will never be free if you don't find a way to forgive. It will control you, Caius. Honoring your mother by naming the wine after her is the right thing to do. For whatever reason, she was not strong enough to stop your father. But she was always pleasant, kind, and considerate to everyone in the villa. She is the reason we will survive. What is most important, however, is that she is your mother. You have an obligation as her son to honor her."

Caius had spent little time in Roma. But he had spent a whole summer there when he was fourteen and knew many of his parents' friends. So, they gambled. Money was extremely tight. They strapped two cases of wine to one of their plow horses and sent Caius off with blankets, a handful of credits, and a lot of prayers.

When he finally arrived in the capital, he hesitated. An entire week of sleeping by the side of the road meant he looked and smelled a bit rough. He knew his parents' best friends, but was hesitant to knock on the door of an elegant domus while holding the reins of a plow horse.

His father and mother's best friends were avid wine collectors. Not an unusual hobby for the elite. The Files had a reputation for offering the best Arista had to offer at their parties. Deciding this was the best place to start, he gathered his courage, tied up the horse, then walked up and knocked on the massive front door.

The butler took one look at him, wrinkled his nose, and said politely, "The service entrance is around back young man."

As the butler moved to close the door, Caius put a hand up and said, "Jeffery, it's me, Caius Cereo."

Jeffery looked shocked. He wasn't used to seeing a member of the elite looking like a lost farm boy. Recovering, he took a few moments to respond. He knew the Cereo family had been broken with Adrian and Jenny committing suicide. While no one cared much for Adrian, Jenny was loved by everyone, including himself.

"I'm sorry. I didn't recognize you, Caius. What can I help you with?" Jeffery assumed Caius was looking for a handout and if his master didn't give him one, Jeffrey would do what he could. Unlike most wealthy citizens, Jenny had always been very kind to him. She didn't treat him like a servant. He wasn't alone in this regard, as other members of the staff had shed a few tears when the news about Jenny had been delivered.

"My parents built a vineyard at the villa, and I have wine to sell. I was hoping Mr. File could help me find a buyer?" Caius asked with desperation clearly in his voice and manner.

Jeffery considered this for a minute, then said, "Go around to the service entrance and I'll meet you there."

When the servants' entrance door opened, Jeffery was there with a man Caius didn't recognize. Jeffery smiled and said, "This is Oliver, our sommelier. Can he sample what you have?"

"Sure," said Caius, holding out a bottle he had pulled from one of the cases. He watched them both closely as Jeffery supplied a wine glass and Oliver carefully removed the cork. Oliver smelled the cork and then poured a small amount.

Oliver tentatively took a sip. After a moment's hesitation he looked surprised. He then swirled the wine in the glass, sniffed it, and sipped again. He let it stay in his mouth longer this time. He smiled, handed the glass back to Jeffery, and then raised a brow. He turned to Caius and asked, "How much are you asking for your wine?"

"Fifteen credits a bottle," Caius said. The question had surprised a higher price out of him. The plan was to sell individual bottles and perhaps a case. With enough sales, they could then bring the rest of the wine to Roma and hopefully sell it all.

Another look of surprise crossed Oliver's face, and he asked, "Do you mind if Jeffery and I take this to Mr. File for his opinion?"

"Of course not. Do you want me to stay here?" Caius asked.

"Why don't you do that? I'm sure he would be pleased to see you, but he might be in the middle of something," Jeffery said. He then hesitated a second, and then turned to one of the servants and said, "Would you ask Gloria to make Master Cereo something for breakfast?" He then turned back to Caius and said, "We'll be back in a little while."

Jeffery politely knocked on Jovan File's office door and waited for a response.

"Come in," Jovan called out.

Jeffery and Oliver entered with Jeffery quickly saying, "Begging your pardon, sir. Adrian and Jenny's son is in the kitchen asking to meet with you. Jenny's hobby vineyard has produced some wine, and he would like you to help him sell it. I didn't want to put you in a delicate situation, so I got Oliver to give an opinion."

Oliver leaned forward and said with excitement, "It's not just good sir, it's exceptional. For new wine it's unusually smooth, like velvet on the tongue. The fruit is a complex mix that is, in my experience, unique. It's quite delicious. I need to spend some time with it to fully understand its complexity. But with age, it will only get better."

"It's from Jenny's vineyard, really? I thought that was just a fantasy," Jovan said. "Do you have some of it with you?"

"Yes, sir," Jeffery said and produced a wine glass with a small amount in it. Jovan swirled the glass, sniffed it, and then took a sip. His gaze quickly rose to look at Oliver with a pleasantly surprised expression on his face.

Jovan came down and greeted Caius warmly just as he was about to start in on an amazing breakfast. "Caius, it's so good to see you." He hesitated and his face took on a sad expression and he said, "I am so sorry about your parents; Jules and I loved them."

"The card you sent was very much appreciated, thank you," Caius replied. One of the reasons he had come to the Files was the thoughtful card they sent. Few of his parents' friends had bothered. They had even invited him to visit them the next time he came to Roma. It was that offer that emboldened him to knock on their door.

"So, you want to get into the wine business? Oliver tells me you are offering to sell it for fifteen credits a bottle. How many cases do you have?" Jovan asked.

"Two hundred cases, most of this year's vintage," Caius answered.

"Is it here in the city? Your villa is quite distant," Jovan said with a slight frown on his face.

"No, I just have two cases with me," said Caius.

Jovan thought for a minute. "How about I buy all of it from you for ten credits a bottle? I'll pay to ship them. As soon as I find a buyer, I'll send you the credits. Of course, I'll give you two hundred forty credits right now for the two cases you have with you. Jules will be delighted to have your mother's wine in our cellar."

Caius was ecstatic but tried not to show it. Two hundred forty credits in hard cash was double what they found squirreled away in the villa. One of Caius's gifts was the ability to read people. He knew Oliver had been very impressed with the wine; he also knew Jovan was going to make a good profit on the deal offered. His dad always said Jovan was an excellent negotiator. But the offer on the table was their minimum asking price, and they didn't have to pay for shipping.

Deciding not to look like a rube, he said, "If you buy all two hundred cases, and pay for shipping, I'll settle for twelve credits a bottle." Caius was proud of himself for not taking the first offer.

"Done," said Jovan immediately, a bit more enthusiastically than Caius expected. He pulled Jeffery off to the side and whispered something to him. Then he turned to Caius and said, "I hope you can join us for dinner tonight. Jules would love to see you and I would enjoy catching up and hearing all about your vineyard." Smiling, he waved and exited the kitchen.

Jeffery smiled at Caius and said, "Mr. File would like you to stay here tonight so you can rest up for the trip back. I'll show you to one of our guest rooms and let you rest and freshen up. Dinner will be at eight o'clock. Don't worry about your horse. We'll brush him down, feed him, and find a spot in the stable tonight.

It was the start of a wonderful day. He had a hot shower and was given clean clothes to wear. He ended up spending much of the day in the library marveling over the selection of books the Files had. Leo would be in heaven here, he thought. He ended up writing down titles of books on business he thought Leo would like. Perhaps someday he could surprise Leo with one of them as a present.

Dinner at the Files' was fancy, lengthy, and reminded him of the summer he had spent in Roma as a young boy. His parent's home, Domus Cereo, was large, elegant, and that summer was one long endless party. While he enjoyed people, and they liked him, everyone young and old seemed pretentious and uncaring.

The Files were no different, although he did like them both. Seeing them now with a more mature eye, he decided they just didn't understand what life was like for ordinary people. After some reminiscing about his parents, Mr. File asked, "You said the two hundred cases were most of the vintage. How much more do you have?"

This increased his suspicion that the wine was worth much more than twelve credits a bottle. He considered his answer and said, "We have another fifty cases in storage, but I'm going to hold on to that for a rainy day." Leo had insisted they hold on to the additional cases because he said if their wine was really good, it would grow in value. It was Leo's opinion that they should never borrow money to fund their business. He said they were used to living modestly and they should salt away as much as possible for unforeseen expenses and future investment.

"Well, let me know if you would like to sell them. Be happy to give you the same price," Mr. File said with a smile.

That offer convinced him he had not gotten as good a deal as he could have. Oh well, compared to expectations, he was very happy with the way the day had worked out.

The next morning after another amazing breakfast Caius said goodbye to the Files and left feeling like the world was indeed a wonderful place. He was wearing clean secondhand clothes, courtesy of Jeffery. He had a bag filled with fancy sandwiches from Gloria, their chef. But best of all were the 288 credits he was on his way to deposit in the family's bank account. He couldn't wait to get home and tell everyone.

The conversation Caius had with Leo when he got home set the stage for their future business dealings. Everyone was thrilled he was able to sell all the cases. But Caius could tell Leo was not completely happy with how the negotiations had played out. Leo took a deep breath, and seemed a bit hesitant, but ended up saying gently, "Caius, you should have asked them what they thought it was worth instead of offering up a price."

"Sorry, you're right. I guess I got excited that they wanted to talk price so quickly. I knew it was a mistake at the time. I won't make that mistake again," Caius said sheepishly.

"You also should have told them we would take care of the shipping and payment was due on delivery," Leo said.

"Why do it that way?" Caius asked, confused, but with a facial expression and tone indicating he was honestly interested in the answer.

"Basically, they got three credits per bottle for shipping, which comes to seventy-two hundred credits. We could have shipped all one hundred ninety-eight cases for around two thousand to twenty-five hundred credits total. In the future, we should think about buying a cart and some oxen so we can do our own shipping," Leo said calmly.

"I'm sorry! I didn't realize that cost us so much money," Caius said, feeling horrible.

"We're learning, Caius. We'll make mistakes. It's okay as long as we learn from them," Leo said in a soft voice. "I just realized I made a mistake in saying we ought to charge ten credits per bottle. I did that based on how much money we needed instead of what the wine was worth. We should have investigated that. I'm really impressed you were able to sell the whole lot, and for more than our minimum. We thought you would sell the first two cases bottle by bottle and then come back for more. Your trip turned out much better than we dreamed it would," Leo said, complimenting him.

He hesitated and then continued to explain. "There are two reasons for getting cash on delivery. The first one is the scenario where one of the cases falls off a shelf and bottles break. Who pays for that if the agreement is that we get paid when they are sold? The second is that with this agreement, we are basically loaning them money at zero interest to stock their inventory."

Caius pondered this for a while. Then he said, "You should be making our business decisions. But you're legally a slave, so we can't present you as the head of the business. I know many of the elite families in Roma, and that is our customer base. So, I can act as our salesman." Caius stopped catching his brother's eyes and said, "I have an idea. How about you go everywhere with me? I will present you as my valet. You will sit in on all the meetings and tell me privately what decisions need to be made. It's a bit odd, but if anyone asks, I'll say you're providing security. You are quite a bit larger than I am." Then he stopped and, looking embarrassed, said, "You're not my servant, Leo. I hate asking you to act like one."

Leo brightened and smiled. "That's a brilliant idea. We both know we complement each other. I'm no good at selling. Not really good with people. And you're not really interested in the business details." He hesitated and then said, "I've never felt like anything other than your brother, Caius. I can play any role the family needs me to play. You would do the same."

It was just like Leo, pretending Caius didn't care about the business details. The truth was that he didn't have the business sense and good judgement Leo had. "Truth be told, the family needs you more than they need me," Caius said.

"Truth be told, you're full of shit, Caius," Leo said, and they both laughed. Leo's expression turned serious, and then he said gravely, "I'm really worried about whether we can pull this off. I just have to look stupid. But you're going to have to convince people you're smart." Leo's frown turned into a sly smile, and they both laughed again.

They found out later their wine sold for upward of one hundred credits per bottle. Jenny had been well known and loved by the partying elite. Her orphaned son selling Jenny's Acre wine had a certain cache driving up the price. However, the real reason for its success was that it was a truly exceptional wine. The owner of Gold Coast Winery was outraged with their success. Dry Brook was a new competitor at the highest end of the wine business.

He decided to try to take some of the credit by letting everyone know that Jenny's Acre was based on his root stock. Instead of diminishing Dry Brook Vineyards reputation, it had the opposite effect. Most wine connoisseurs agreed that Jenny's Acre was a superior wine to Gold Coast's pinot noir. Knowing they used the same root stock resulted in the conclusion that Dry Brook's soil conditions and wine making skills were superior.

What still caused an emotional reaction for Caius was Mr. File's treatment of the increased price. He decided to split the increased price instead of pocketing it. While it was motivated by charity for the son of his good friends, it was the best investment he ever made. Jovon File was, and always would be, the sole distributor of Dry Brook Vineyards wines.

Caius was yanked out of his nostalgia when the door opened. Forti stepped through the door, looked at the two brothers, and said in an amused and mildly sarcastic tone, "Theron, First of his Name, will see you now. As predicted, he's more than a little suspicious and very confused." They all shared a grim smile and walked in together.

Sovereign

CHAPTER 2

GENERAL HARRIS

Jack had informed Lord Druango a few days before that Trajan had been assassinated. The man seemed to be having trouble accepting Trajan was really dead. They had gone over the details several times already, and Jack was getting frustrated

That it had happened in the Arena by one of the gladiators made it all the more unbelievable to him. Jack could tell the man was traumatized by his experience on Arista. Druango did not understand how anyone could get into the emperor's suite, much less carry out an assassination. Druango was visibly relieved once he finally realized that Trajan was truly dead. But he was terrified by the fact that General Eastbrook was days away from overwhelming his rebel coalition.

"Lord Druango, we need to stop discussing the past and move to time critical matters. You are most fortunate that General Harris just completed a contract in Sector 26 and is relatively close to the wormhole. He can have troops on the ground in less than a week. To expedite matters, I took it upon myself to invite him for discussions. He will arrive late this evening. I expect you will want to hold a meeting with him first thing in the morning."

"Yes, of course. We are fortunate that General Harris is available. I understand he is considered the best of the mercenary generals," Lord Druango said.

"He has a reputation for quickly and efficiently defeating his enemies. He has never failed to collect full price on a contract. That makes him unique. It also makes him expensive," Jack said, emphasizing the last comment.

"What does he want?" Druango asked.

"I don't know," Jack lied. "As you know, the Commonwealth doesn't get involved in colony negotiations beyond providing mediation. Our role is to maximize trade across the Commonwealth. We do not interfere in colonial affairs."

Jack knew the price for Harris was astronomical. It would impoverish the planet for decades. It would spike tax revenues due to contract payments. But it was a bad deal for Sector 27 in the long run. Julie being so supportive meant she must be getting some sort of kickback. It also meant the deal was being supported all the way to the High Council. Jack was amazed at how quickly Julie could recover in a crisis. He cringed a bit internally, realizing his failed plans had caused more than a few crises for her recently. Arista having control of Liberty was clearly better for Sector 27 financials. But she didn't hesitate to change course when it became clear the Arista plan had failed.

"I guess it doesn't matter at this point. We really have no other alternatives," Lord Druango admitted, revealing he had no bluster left to expend. "We can start at 10:00 AM if he is available that early. I really don't want to waste time getting this done."

Jack had never been impressed with Druango, but this further degraded his opinion. He thinks ten o'clock is early! The man is weeks, perhaps days away from the gallows and he wants to sleep in. Unbelievable! "I will have him in your command tent at 10:00 AM," Jack said. With nothing further to discuss, he nodded, indicating an end to their discussions, turned around, and headed back to his shuttle. No need to rough it tonight when he could have the conveniences of his space yacht. It would also be good to go over the plan with Harris one more time. The man was a narcissist and Jack needed to insure he didn't go off script.

The next morning, General Harris and his staff had taken over the command tent by the time Lord Druango arrived. They had been poring over battle maps and grilling his army staff. Jack had agreed to touch down at 5:00 AM so that Harris and his senior staff could get a better idea of what they were up against before the meeting started.

"Lord Druango, let me introduce you to General Harris," Jack said with a tight smile.

"A pleasure to meet you, sir. I've heard much of your abilities and am anxious to see them in person," Lord Druango gushed.

"A pleasure to meet you as well, my lord," Harris said respectfully. "I am not in favor of non-combatants actually witnessing the fighting, as you might well guess. I like to keep the person promising to pay me safe," he continued with a smile.

"We have common goals, General," Druango replied with his own smile. Hesitating, he ventured a question. "I understand your men have already spent a good many hours poring over the battle map."

"Not only that. We have a battle plan that should turn the situation around rather quickly. But before we get into that, I would like to agree on payment terms," Harris said with a penetrating look.

"I'm glad to hear this should be an easy campaign for you. I hope that lowers the cost for this venture," Druango said before he even knew what was going to be asked.

Harris seemed irritated by the clumsy attempt to negotiate. "It doesn't," Harris said bluntly and sternly. "Our price is non-negotiable. My men just finished one contract and are due their normal rest and relaxation between campaigns. I have to pay a large bonus for each and every one of them to compensate for having no rest between campaigns. Even if that weren't the case, you are not in a position to negotiate."

Druango was used to being in charge. He was clearly angry at the tongue lashing he just got. But given the circumstances, he could not afford to insult General Harris. With his face bright red, he gained control of himself and asked, "What do you propose?"

"Ten million credits up front. After we suppress the revolution, you will award us eighty percent of Liberty's portion of increased tax revenues for twenty years. There will be a twenty million credit completion bonus. It is customary that my army gets thirty days of free rein in the areas under rebellion. In addition, we will receive one thousand slaves from the rebel areas with first choice in their selection. We will pay a fair price for property damage, or any slaves killed or permanently disabled during that time."

Druango was stunned. He had not envisioned this costing that amount of money, and for twenty years! He finally spit out, "That is an outrageous sum, sir. How do you justify this highway robbery?"

Turning to Jack, Harris said, "First Minister, can you take us back up to your ship so we can coordinate our travel home? I'm wasting my time here."

"No, wait!" Druango said in desperation. "I'm sorry. I don't mean we won't pay. I was just surprised at the cost. If you've looked at the battle map, you know we don't have other options. We are forced to pay and pay we shall."

Harris stared at him for an uncomfortable amount of time. He was clearly driving home the reality that he didn't need this contract and could simply leave at any time. "I accept your apology. Papers for you to sign have been prepared. I expect to have signed copies before I leave this tent."

"I can facilitate getting the documents signed and apply the Commonwealth's notary stamp. You can have the legal part of this wrapped up this morning," Jack said. Harris was a little full of himself, he thought. I hope he's not overconfident with Eastbrook. Too many have made that mistake already.

"Agreed," Druango said, still collecting himself. He took a deep breath and said, "My men are prepared to review the current situation and offer advice on how to proceed."

"That won't be necessary my lord," Harris said with clear disdain. "Eastbrook's army is unsophisticated and has never gone up against a credible opponent. This isn't unusual in the backwaters of the Commonwealth. In addition to greater experience and expertise, we outnumber your rebels significantly. As I said earlier, this won't take long."

"Eastbrook is very devious. He does things you don't expect. His armies have a history of overcoming larger forces. He has extensive knowledge of geography and how to take advantage of it. I implore you not to underestimate him," Druango said with great concern showing on his face.

Harris's senior staff broke into raucous laughter. After they quieted down, Harris said, "We don't mean to be insulting, but your concerns are unnecessary. The best thing you can do at this point is relax and wait for us to remove your problem. My men will make landfall in three days. Just make sure you hold on that long and all will be well."

Later, as Jack walked General Harris back to his shuttle, he said, "I know your reputation. It is very impressive and unblemished by failure. I've watched General Eastbrook's tactics closely these past few years. I have no doubt you will prevail. But I would caution you to be wary. The General has done some rather remarkable things."

Harris looked at him with amusement and said, "I know you're not a military man, First Minister. Let me assure you there is nothing to worry about. I know what I'm doing. You can tell the governor this contract should be closed out in a few weeks."

Jack would relay Harris's message to the governor. He would also caution her that the man was overconfident, so she shouldn't be surprised if it takes longer than predicted. Jack hoped the man was right. If he wasn't, Jack knew she would ultimately blame him for the failure.

CHAPTER 3

THE SENATE

Tee had been in meetings all morning. He retained his sanity only because he had worked out with Forti early and then went for a swim. He was still amazed that he had his own private pool. It was unbelievably large and the one thing he truly liked about living in the Palatium. The extravagance of the emperor's home boggled his mind. When he first woke up in the Palatium, he thought his bedroom was an entire home. It disgusted him, knowing how many of Arista's citizens struggled simply to eat every day while he lived in outrageous luxury.

Listening to wealthy people complain about money was not something he enjoyed. His butt was sore. It was not the first time he had longed for the black and blue of Victor's training sessions. And it likely would not be the last. In his opinion, getting the crap beaten out of him was much better than the life of an emperor.

His frustration of having to participate in these ridiculous meetings was offset by his appreciation of Leo's and Caius's ability to manipulate these people. They were masters at preparing Tee for these small private meetings. He knew what decisions needed to be made before the meetings began. Caius guided these sessions without seeming to be the one in charge. While not everyone was happy with Tee's decisions today, no one seemed unduly offended. He guessed that meant a successful morning. Caius had explained how the power structure worked. His guiding advice was that the powerful had to be fed. And fed they were. It was disgusting to approve decisions resulting in riches being given to people who didn't seem to need or deserve them. God, he just wanted to be back on Pacifica with family and friends. His obligations as a member of the Guard hadn't changed. He had committed his life to protecting Pacifica. This was the only way for him to do that for now.

Next up on the agenda was his first meeting with the Senate. He had already met Pluta, the Magistrate of the Senate. It had been one of his first private meetings. At that meeting, Tee informed the magistrate that

401

he required the Senate to loan him Senator Cereo as an advisor. He explained that he needed the senators' help in acclimating to his role. It was a very tense meeting given Pluta claimed that honor should be his as Magistrate. Tee had to get forceful and demanding before Pluta relented. Tee could tell this man was going to be trouble.

With Forti's team surrounding him, Tee was suddenly outside the Palatium for the first time since becoming emperor. It was strange to be outside again. No jailors, no shackles, but still not free. He walked down cobblestone streets past multi-story granite buildings. There was even a fleeting look at a large ornate marble fountain down one of the side streets. He would have enjoyed being a tourist for the day. But the harsh realities for this planet's citizens soured his enthusiasm. It was clear this was a paradise only for the privileged few. Several times during his walk to the Senate, he saw those who appeared to be beggars. Barefoot slaves in thin, worn-out clothing were also evident. This might be a wealthy planet, but it was clear that the necessities of life were hoarded and withheld from those who desperately needed them. So different from Pacifica.

The Curia Julia was a reproduction of the Senate meeting hall commissioned by Julius Caesar and completed by the Imperator Augustus. The choice was symbolic, as its construction represented the transition from a republic to a monarchy. Tee had learned from Leo that democracy had disappeared since the collapse of democratic forms of government on Earth. He was told that Pacifica's republican government with elected officials was out of favor across the Commonwealth. Why this had happened was a mystery for Tee. From what he could see, Arista's form of government wasn't working very well for its people.

As Tee walked into the Senate building, he felt uncomfortable once again. He towered over everyone. It was strange to be unusually tall and muscular. To have others think of him as physically imposing. He was much more comfortable just being part of the crowd. A low murmur had arisen as he entered the building. A hum of whispered conversations as they all stared openly at him. He stepped up on the dais, sat down, and per Caius's instructions turned to Magistrate Pluta, nodded in greeting and said, "You may proceed, Magistrate."

Magistrate Pluta gave him an oily smile, held his hands out to the assembled Senate and said, "Thank you all for responding to the compulsory order to meet today. As magistrate, I declare this meeting to be in session. First on the agenda is a proposal for a special vote from Senator Ricci. Senator, you have the floor."

Senator Ricci walked to the open area between the rows of senators. He was a robust man for those of Arista's stature. He was a warrior by training and a senator by birth. He stuck his chin out and said, "Thank you, Magistrate. Fellow senators. I propose a vote negating the succession."

He stopped for a few moments to let the gasps die off. After the room became dead quiet, he continued. "As you know, the man currently calling himself emperor is doing so under the pretense of archaic legal interpretations. Legal succession requirements have changed over the centuries. This is a fact. Succession by combat is not legal. The changes to the laws of succession over the years have been a natural evolution.

"Our society has matured. The colorful and brutal history of Arista leadership is valued by all of us. It is part of our inheritance. But it is far in the past. A sense of pride motivated previous Senates to alter the law of combat rather than remove it entirely. They did so because they wanted to honor our glorious past. The alterations they made were clearly meant to eliminate personal combat as a legitimate avenue for succession. And rightly so.

"Limiting it to Ascension Day and declaring that the emperor's own weapons cannot be used against him was clearly meant to disable this as a method of succession. I also think it worth noting that the man calling himself emperor is not even from this planet. He is a slave, nothing more. We do not have to accept this. I do not accept this."

Tee marveled once again at Caius's prescience. Or perhaps he simply had a good spy network. In any case, he had accurately predicted what would be said, and who would say it? Tee had been waiting for the personal declaration. Caius had said it would come, and he rose to play his part. "I accept your challenge," Tee declared loudly as he stood up and pulled his large ceremonial knife out of its sheath. As he stepped off the dais, striding in the direction of Ricci. Caius stood up and moved to intercept him with one hand raised and said, "Your Eminence, I'm certain Senator Ricci did not intend to challenge your right to rule."

Although a military man, Ricci turned white. He gripped his own ceremonial knife but left it in its sheath at his belt. He had terror in his eyes and appeared to be getting ready to flee. He slowly composed himself once he saw Tee had halted. Then in a shaky voice he said, "What is this Cereo? I did not challenge Theron."

"Your confusion is understandable, Senator. A careful review of the law was performed after the events of the Accession Day celebrations. As head of the justice committee, I had intended to deliver this information today and apologize for not requesting that the magistrate let me go first. Just this morning, the Justice Council came to a unanimous decision that Theron was within his rights to challenge Emperor Trajan. In addition, it was determined he did so within the legal guidelines. One of the conclusions from that analysis is that anyone who questions the emperor's authority is considered to have challenged him to personal combat," Caius explained patiently. He hesitated a few moments and then said, "I would also recommend you refer to him by his title instead of his name to avoid the appearance of a challenge. You are not family, after all." Cereo then looked to Pluta and smiled, his subtle reminder of how Trajan used to refer to him obvious to all.

Pluta flushed at the last statement, then turned to the bench where the justices sat and asked, "Justice Wright, is that description accurate?"

"Yes, Magistrate. The law is old and the legal language archaic, but its meaning is clear. The emperor can be challenged at any time. Acceptance of a challenge is only automatic on Ascension Day. Senator Caius is correct that questioning the emperor's authority in public is legally considered a challenge to combat. The Senate floor is considered a public place."

"Your Eminence, can you please forgive Senator Ricci this once? He clearly did not understand that his motion constituted a personal challenge. His confusion is understandable. I can vouch for his personal integrity."

Tee delayed long enough to peak the tension in the room, as Caius had instructed him to do, and then said, "I've been educated on my authority and responsibilities as emperor. I understand that my authority can be challenged and am happy to defend it." Tee glared at Senator Ricci. "During my education, I have also come to appreciate the complexity of Arista law. It is reasonable to assume Senator Ricci was confused. Given your assurance of his personal integrity, Senator Cereo, I will forgive it this once."

You could feel the Senate breathing a sigh of relief. They were accustomed to sitting safely in the stands while gladiators cut each other to ribbons. They were not used to being physically threatened in their hall of power. They had all watched Tee in the games and had no illusions about what would happen if he perceived a challenge. Magistrate Pluta paused a few minutes to confer with one of his lieutenants and then said, "Senator Ricci, do you withdraw your motion to vote based on the legal guidance from our Justice Council?"

Ricci couldn't get his response out fast enough. "Yes, Magistrate, I withdraw my motion."

"Good then, that matter is closed," Pluta declared and then he turned to Caius. "Senator, would you please lodge your requests for floor time before the meeting? Following our standard process would have avoided unnecessary confusion today."

"I agree with you, Magistrate, and beg forgiveness. I will endeavor to be more diligent in the future," Caius said as they looked knowingly at each other. They both knew Caius had created this confrontation to shut down questioning of the validity of Theron's rule.

"That would be much appreciated, Senator Cereo. Let's move onto the next proposal for a vote. Senator Potts, you have the floor," Pluta said.

"Thank you, Magistrate. With the approval of the emperor, I'll read the motion."

Potts looked over to the emperor's dais and received the traditional head nod to continue. That this courtesy had been missing from the first motion proposal was obvious to all. Caius had counseled Tee to ignore the initial minor insults because it would make his sudden challenge all the more dramatic.

"The sudden nature of the succession has caused unease in Roma. Malicious rumors are flying around with regard to the intent of the Second Legion's proximity to our capital city. There is a growing fear that property and lives are at risk. While the Senate believes these to be false, we must face the reality of the current mood in the city. I propose we direct the Second Legion to remove itself to a minimum of thirty miles from Roma. The proposal being that this requirement is in place until the Senate votes to revoke it. As always, our vote is dependent on the emperor's approval," Potts said, looking to Tee, who nodded approval.

Magistrate Pluta asked, "Are their comments before we proceed to vote?"

"Magistrate, might I have the floor?" Caius asked.

"You have the floor, Senator Cereo."

"I want to voice my strong support for Senator Potts's proposal. We must do what we can in these times to calm everyone down. There are no immediate threats that require any of our legions to be within thirty miles of Roma. Given that, let's put this requirement on all our legions. A minor change to what Senator Potts has proposed," Caius said, to the surprise of the entire Senate. Everyone knew that Pluta's supporters wanted to separate Caius from the legion under the command of his son. Caius had lost some of his support with the succession. Many were suspicious that he instigated the entire thing as a means of grabbing complete control. It was rather obvious that he had something to do with it, given Tee's insistence that his former owner become his key advisor. A role traditionally held by the magistrate.

Pluta looked pleased with this turn of events and quickly proposed, "If there are no further comments from the Senate I move that we vote on Senator Potts's proposal." It passed unanimously.

Caius raised his hand and said, "Magistrate, I have one more motion for consideration by the Senate."

"Proceed Senator Cereo."

"I move that we vote to confirm Theron, First of his Name, as Emperor of Arista. Having the Justice Council announce their accension decision helps, but nothing would solidify public confidence and reduce fear like a clear public statement from the Senate."

You could see the wheels spinning as Cereo's foes looked for a way out. If they argued against confirming, Theron could rightfully view that as a challenge to his authority. Nobody wanted to die today. On the other hand, voting to confirm would publicly commit the entire Senate to serve under Theron's rule. Pluta recovered first and said, "We all recognize His Eminence's legal right to rule. I think we can dispense with having to vote on it."

Tee was again impressed with Caius's premonitions. Pluta pushed back but used an honorific instead of his name. He glared at Pluta and recited his lines. "Given the earlier confusion, I think a vote would inspire public confidence. The only argument against a vote would be one that questions my right to rule."

The motion passed unanimously.

The rest of the afternoon was boring, as seven other votes on mundane topics were made. As Tee walked back to the Palatium, Caius whispered that he had done an excellent job. While Tee was gratified by the praise, he was disgusted by his role. He disliked bullies, and that was the role he played today. The political intrigue and positioning disgusted him. But he knew he had to fulfill the role laid out for him. He just kept reminding himself that this was truly the only path he currently had to protect Pacifica.

When he returned to the Palatium, Tee walked to one of the smaller courtyards in the large central garden. This courtyard was surrounded by a grove of dwarf trees. It was his favorite place in the Palatium. It was the closest to nature he could get these days.

Next on the schedule was something he had been looking forward to. A reward for the long and frustrating weeks of playacting. He waited patiently until Dobler was led in. Expecting a smile, he was surprised to see Dobler looking frightened, maybe even terrified. Tee mentally kicked himself. He was the God cursed emperor. Dobler was a slave. Not only was he a slave, but he was also Tee's previous jailor.

Tee stood up, smiled, and held his hands out wide in greeting. "Dobler, you're safe here." When the tension eased slightly, Tee added with a grin, "You've given me no reason to harm you."

That got a nervous laugh out of Dobler remembering their first conversation. "I thought you would be merciful. But I did have the keys to your cell for quite a while," he said. Tee noticed Dobler had visibly started to relax. Then Dobler smiled and said, "I remembered on the way over here that I once threatened to hose down your cell with you in it," to which they both shared a laugh.

"Let's take a walk," Tee said as he beckoned Dobler toward a winding path heading deeper into the garden.

Tee could see Dobler's head on a swivel as he took in the gross grandeur of it all. Perfectly manicured stone walkways with beautiful flowering plants all around. Hummingbirds flitting from flower to flower made it seem like something out of a dream. They eventually came to an impressive set of double doors, with guards stationed at each side.

With a nod, they quickly unlocked the doors and ushered them into a mantrap corridor, much like the one used in the gladiator residence. The purpose of this one was obscured by marble designs on the floor, flower stands, and gilded artwork on the walls. The painted mural on the ceiling was inappropriate, in Tee's opinion. The nude woman that was its centerpiece was shocking the first time he had seen it. Tee was sure most would not guess the corridors' true function. He was sure Dobler would.

When the iron gates at the other end of the corridor were locked behind them by a second set of guards, Tee stopped and said, "This is my personal residence. A good portion of my hometown of Apple Valley could live here in luxury." He smiled and shook his head, still amazed by it all. "The tables are turned, Dobler. I'm now your jailor. But before I explain why I asked you to come here, I'd like you to meet your fellow prisoners."

They turned down a hallway and Tee continued. "There are three guest apartments. Trajan used them for visiting family members. They are quite large, and you'll have to share yours." They walked down a long hallway and out into a small courtyard garden with a pair of small fruit trees and a fountain gurgling in the middle. Tee turned and walked over to one of three ornate doors positioned along the outer walls.

Tee knocked, and the door opened immediately, revealing an attractive woman with blonde hair that was starting to turn white. Her eyes were vividly blue and lit up with excitement. There was a younger woman standing behind her. Those blue eyes locked onto Dobler, searching. After a few moments, she whispered, "Dobby? Is it really you?"

Dobler froze with his mouth slightly open in stunned silence. When he recovered, he said with recognition and deep emotion in his voice, "Jessie." He stepped briskly toward her and wrapped her in his arms. They just held each other for a long time. Then he stepped back, took both of her hands in his and just looked at her. "I can't believe it. It's really you." Then, with tears streaming down his face, he turned toward the other woman and with sudden recognition said, "Sally?"

"Yes, Dad. We got here late yesterday and have been waiting all day to see you." Sally pointed to Tee and said, "We couldn't believe it when he told us what was going to happen. I didn't even know if you or Mom were still alive." And then she broke down crying as Dobler scooped her up into a bear hug.

After it all settled down a bit, Tee said, "I can't free you and your family, Dobler. At least not yet. You know my thoughts on slavery, so I won't say more about it now. Politically, I can't do anything in the short term. You'll have this apartment within my private residence for your extended family's use. I would like you to be my personal valet and your family to help provide services in this private area of the Palatium. It won't be difficult; you know I have modest needs. I'll pay for any work your family does. I need those closest to me to be people I trust. Is that acceptable?"

With eyes still glistening, and voice choked with emotion, Dobler said, "There isn't anything I wouldn't do for you, Tee. We can never repay you for this. Whatever you want, we'll be happy to provide." And looking for approval from his wife and daughter, he was rewarded with enthusiastic heads nodding up and down.

"We'll talk more when you're ready, Dobler. Until then, take all the time you need with your family," Tee said. Then he turned and walked away.

As they walked into the apartment together, he heard Jessie say, "You have three grandchildren and a son-in-law to meet." And with that, they disappeared into their apartment and closed the door.

Tee was delighted. This couldn't have worked out better. Tee remembered explaining to Forti, Caius, and Leo that he wanted his private quarters to be a sanctuary. That it only be accessible to those he trusted. After some debate, they agreed to pull Dobler from the Arena and search for his family. Caius was supportive but warned him, "It may be more painful for Dobler than not knowing Tee. But I agree, he has a right to know. Years ago, we searched for Leo's mother's husband and found he had been murdered by his overseer. We also searched for Leo's uncle. In some ways, that news was worse, as there was no way to free him. He still toils in slavery today. This was all very distressing for Leo's mother. That was the bad news. The good news is that we discovered Leo had a half-sister. His mother views her as a daughter. Eventually I fell in love with her, and we married. My family is a tangled web, Tee. But I could not have asked for a better one."

Walking back to his quarters, it was the first time since just before the last GEM war Tee felt a measure of happiness. He was going to spend the rest of the evening enjoying that feeling.

CHAPTER 4

PARTIAL MOBILIZATION

As soon as Jennifer started the committee meeting, Del held up his hand. "You'll all find this hard to believe. I certainly did. Tee Stone is now the Emperor of Arista."

They all sat and stared at him for a few moments until Griff said sternly, "That isn't funny, Del."

"It wasn't intended to be. It's simply the truth," Del said with a slightly bemused expression.

Jennifer knew Del was a bit of a practical joker, especially when Griff was around. In fact, when they were together, it was sometimes hard to distinguish them from twelve-year-olds. However, she could tell Del was serious.

"He's finally lost his mind," Griff said, looking around at the other committee members.

"Perhaps. Always possible," Del said. "But we have intercepted communications that lead me to believe what I just told you. I have copies for everyone so you can judge for yourselves."

The room was quiet while they all read through Del's materials. Jennifer started reading and her disbelief slowly lessened and was replaced with amazement. The further she read, the more she agreed with Del's conclusion. It was unbelievable. But it was hard to refute. No doubt something drastic had happened on Arista. One of the communications simply claimed Trajan had been assassinated. Another claimed that Trajan had been killed during the Arista New Year's games. A third reported that a gladiator had killed Trajan. That same communication claimed the event had triggered an ancient rule by combat clause resulting in the gladiator being named emperor. Multiple communications referred to the new emperor by his title. Theron, First of his Name, Emperor of Arista. Theron was a name unique to the Stone family, according to Del's write up. It had been passed down for generations. This had to be Tee!

Griff put his report down and said, "If there was ever anyone who could have pulled something this crazy off, it's Tee. But if true, what does it mean?"

"It means there is a ray of hope. It means we might have someone on Arista with our best interests at heart. It doesn't mean he can do anything about it," Del said.

"If he's the emperor, why can't he do whatever he wants?" Griff asked.

Jennifer spoke up and said, "We don't know what their actual form of government is. A monarchy can range from complete and total control to merely being a figurehead with no power. We believe Arista is more the former, but we don't know for sure."

"And, to top it off, the Commonwealth has ultimate control of Pacifica. It may not matter what Arista wants," Del added. "The good news is that it appears Tee is still alive and might be safe. Although it's just as likely he's in greater danger now than when he was a gladiator. We just don't know."

They all sat for a while, musing over the implications, until Jennifer spoke up and said, "Let's move to our agenda, as we don't have a lot of time. Del, would you keep us updated on this situation?" Jennifer asked and with a head nod of agreement from him she continued. "Our agenda item is to discuss the massing of GEMs just over the horizon. You've all seen the report, so I won't go into specifics. Griff has a recommendation, Griff?"

"At the end of the last conflict, we were preparing to retreat back to the Landfall Dam. The force coming up against us is much larger. We need to recognize that we cannot stop the GEMs at the Wall. My recommendation is that we do two things. The first is to call for partial mobilization. If we strip the coastal forts and backfill with volunteers, we can execute a retreat with only Guard and Wall Archers. It's critical the retreat be well planned and executed. Confusion or panic at the wrong time would result in a massacre." Griff stopped and looked around the room. "Any questions so far?"

Kevin spoke up, "What happens to all the materials stored below the dam?"

Griff nodded and replied, "That's the second recommendation. We should move everything not needed for the retreat to storage facilities in Landfall City."

Jennifer let out a soft breath, steadied herself, and said, "Once we start moving war materials, people will quickly figure out we're giving up on the Wall. We're going to have to go to the Pacifica Council with both of these recommendations. We need their support to keep everyone calm. Any attempt to do this quietly will result in chaos."

"Del and I can talk the CGG into proposing both of these," Griff said with a slight frown. His face then took on a mischievous grin, and he said, "Del can create another bullshit report. That and his ability to lie with a straight face will convince everyone it's real."

Del looked down at the table then and when he looked back up, he appeared to have been hurt by Griff's remark. He took a breath and said, "My grandfather told me he would always be proud of me for telling the truth, no matter what it was. I'm not sure what he would think of me these days."

Griff went stone faced. He hesitated for a few moments and then said with conviction, "I think he would be very proud, Del."

Wasn't it just like men to apologize without an apology, Jennifer thought. All this craziness must be getting to Del. He's never shown weakness before. It was so out of character. That made it especially disturbing. The last thing they needed right now was for Del to fall apart. Breaking the uncomfortable silence, she said, "Let's vote. All those in favor of proposing a partial mobilization and relocation of war materials to Landfall City raise their hands." She looked around the room and said, "The motion passes unanimously."

Not wanting to end the meeting on a sour note, Jennifer asked Del, "How is Hestie working out?" Jennifer stole a glance at Dorothy. She could see an emotional reaction from the woman and that worried her a little. Another person on the committee to worry about.

Del shot a quick look over at Dorothy as well and then answered, "Perfectly. Quinn needed someone who could keep up with him on a few of his special projects. While I knew her biological knowledge was excellent, I was surprised by her knowledge of math and physics. It's obvious she's been hiding her abilities."

"Good. We'll meet day after tomorrow to discuss whatever comes out of the Council meeting. Adjourned."

Early the next morning, President Malrey was sitting in her office reviewing military logistics. She had been preparing for the two council agenda items she would facilitate today. She had a good view of Landfall Lake and the city as sunlight winked on the horizon to start the day. She took a few minutes to watch the city awaken before taking a deep breath and getting back to work. Jennifer was exhausted. It wasn't lack of sleep or her workload. Although both of those contributed. It was the constant bickering at council meetings.

Today would be emotional. A partial mobilization wouldn't be a big deal by itself. But coupled with a motion to move most of their war materials to Landfall City was going to make for a difficult day. Those two votes coming together would make it obvious they were giving up on the Wall. Barlow would, of course, propose negotiating with the GEMs again. She would be able to stop that nonsense without too much trouble. His diminished support from the vote of no confidence fiasco continued. She continued to worry that his isolation would eventually cause even greater problems.

She was thankful Pacifica still had one trick up their sleeve. Unfortunately, it could only be used sparingly. After that, it was a choice of retreating all the way to the protection of Apple Valley or spurring the Commonwealth into action. It really wasn't much of a choice. Their estimate was that half the population, maybe more, would perish in a retreat of that magnitude. Even if half the population reached Apple Valley, many would likely starve. The only responsible action was to hurl a few black powder bombs toward the GEMs and wait for the Commonwealth to arrive. She shuddered, remembering what she would be required to do next.

A few hours later, President Malrey opened the council meeting. "Del and the CGG have come today to provide background for the first two motions. Del will give an update on GEM activity and the CGG will offer solutions to counter the implied threat."

Barlow jumped in and said, "Whatever is going on, we should counter it with an offer for peace. If we're going to abandon the Wall anyway, perhaps we offer them Landfall Valley."

Well, that came sooner than she thought it would. Obviously, details on the two motions had leaked. Looking around the room, she saw nothing but disgust on everyone's faces. Well, almost everyone.

Councilman Rickets looked like he was sympathetic to Barlow's request. Those two were going to cause trouble at some point.

Jennifer didn't hesitate. She immediately said, "All those in favor of adding an agenda item to discuss negotiations with the GEMs raise your hands."

Only Barlow raised his hand.

"All those opposed?" Five hands shot up. "I'm sorry Councilman Barlow, but it doesn't look like there is appetite for that discussion today," Jennifer said crisply and then immediately followed it with, "Del, you have the floor."

The next three hours were completely dysfunctional. Councilwoman Ricks even joined the craziness by calling the CGG a coward. In her opinion, they needed to stop the GEMs at the Wall no matter the cost. To his credit, the CGG stayed calm. He pointed out once again that they had narrowly escaped a full retreat the last time the GEMs attacked. That retreat would have been a disaster. Children and non-combatants would have been trapped in a mass of people trying to escape.

To make matters worse, they would have lost all their war materials, further strengthening the GEMs. He told them the Guard would stay disciplined and that a retreat did not require as many warriors as holding the Wall. Especially since the GEMs would be surprised. In the end, both motions were approved.

Unfortunately, they both won by four-to-two votes. Barlow and Rickets had both voted no to both measures. Jennifer could have understood a vote to block mobilization. That cost money. But leaving their vast military stores in a location that was likely to be overrun made no sense. Rickets had her worried. Since his son died, he was voting irrationally. She hoped the disease would stay confined to the two of them.

Jay was tired. They had been spending mornings practicing a retreat from the Wall and afternoons moving materials. The Tram did most of the work lifting sacks of grain and armory inventory to the top of the dam road. But it all still had to be loaded and unloaded. He was tired. But not so tired that he wanted to go back to the barracks. So, Jay wandered the streets until he ended up in front of the Blue Heron Tavern. Suddenly remembering it was Friday night, nostalgia drove him to enter and look around. To his surprise, he spied Hestie and Diana sitting across from someone in a Guard uniform. Before he could exit quietly, Diana recognized him and, with a big smile, waved him over.

"Jay, it's great to see you. Pull up a chair and join us," she said with enthusiasm as she glanced sideways at Hestie.

Diana seemed to do most things with enthusiasm, Jay thought. It made it difficult to say no, even if sitting across from Hestie was going to be awkward.

"Do you know Glenn?" she said, motioning to the man he was now sitting next to.

They just looked at each other for a moment and then Glenn smiled and, glancing back at Diana, said, "Yes we've met. Jay knows some of the members of my squad."

Jay smiled, remembering when they met. It was in jail the morning after the brawl with Glenn's squad. He noticed Hestie's mouth had turned up slightly, obviously remembering the story. "Good to see you again, Sergeant. I've heard we have special assignments from Griff in common."

Glenn laughed and said, "Yes we do. At least it keeps us both in good shape."

Jay smiled and turned to Diana, asking, "Are you staying at Mom's?"

"Yes, she's incredibly gracious. Arti and I just arrived today, and she insisted we stay with her. Turns out I'm staying in your room," she said.

"You're welcome to it," Jay said. Then, with concern in his voice, he asked, "How's Arti?"

"She's an incredibly strong person. But it's difficult," Diana said, losing the electricity in her smile.

Jay suddenly remembered what he had been keeping in his pocket. He pulled Tee's insignia out and offered it to Diana. "I took this off of Tee's spare uniform. I've been meaning to give it to Arti. Would you give it to her for me?"

Diana just looked at him for a few moments and, with eyes misting up, said, "Don't you want to keep it?"

Jay took a breath and then, pointing at the red stripe on his own insignia, said, "This means Tee is always with me, Diana. This one belongs with his mother."

Jay had been watching Hestie out of the side of his eyes the whole time he had been sitting there. She had been looking down and avoiding eye contact. As soon as he finished talking, she looked over at Diana and said, "I have to go." Then, looking at Jay for the first time, she said in a soft but shaky voice, "It was nice to see you, Jay." Then she simply stood up and left.

Diana looked confused, stood up, and as she went to follow Hestie said, "I'll be right back."

There were a few moments of awkward silence until Glenn said, "I'm sorry about Tee. Everyone I've talked to seems to think he was something special. I'm not sure Diana is ever going to get over it."

"Are you and Diana friends?" Jay asked.

"Not in the way you're asking. But we have become really good friends. We spend time together, but her heart belongs to Tee," Glenn answered, insinuating he would like it to be more.

"Really? Wow! She's all he talked about in recruit training. Claimed she was his cousin's girlfriend. But he did a horrible job of hiding how he felt. It was sad," Jay said.

At that point, Diana walked back in and sat down. "Everything okay?" Glenn asked.

"Yeah, she's upset. She's leaving tomorrow to go back up to Apple Valley." Diana looked over to Jay and said, "Grammy isn't doing well. With Arti and I down here, more help is needed."

"Isn't she in school? Won't that be a problem?" Glenn asked.

"She'll just work out some self-study program and get her professors to approve it," Diana said. Then, with the corners of her mouth turned up slightly, she said, "She's likely the smartest person you'll ever meet."

Jay suddenly stood and said, "I have to go, too. One of Griff's special assignments starts early tomorrow morning."

He started to walk away, and Diana rose, saying, "I'll walk out with you, Jay." Once they got outside, she put a hand on his arm to stop him. When he turned toward her, she said with her blazing blue eyes locked on his, "I don't know what's going on either."

"What?" he said, although he knew full well what she meant.

Diana stepped a little closer and said, "Hestie. She's either lost her mind or there is some secret she's hiding. Knowing her, it probably involves sacrificing herself for some reason. She and Quinn are both hiding something. She is the least selfish person I know. One thing I am sure of is that she's wildly in love with you. She left because she just couldn't keep up the façade with you sitting there." Diana stopped for a moment and then said, "Don't give up on her, Jay. The two of you are perfect together."

The only thing he could think to say was, "I haven't yet." Then he turned and walked off. He was embarrassed a few minutes later when he realized he hadn't thanked Diana for her encouragement. He hadn't even said goodbye. His voice had been cold and angry. It was rude. He needed to think, so he took the long way back to the barracks.

Diana said one thing he strongly agreed with. Whatever was going on probably involved Hestie sacrificing herself. Jay could not imagine what that might be. He decided it was a good thing Hestie was heading up to Apple Valley. The GEMs were coming, and she would be far safer up there than down near the Wall.

CHAPTER 5

CAVERNS

Colonel Peters came out of his field staff tent to a red sun dying on the western horizon. The cold mountain air was thin, and he was breathing a bit more deeply than normal as he walked uphill toward the command tent. After a few days at high altitude, his body was starting to adjust. Putting that minor annoyance aside, he focused on what was troubling him.

The war had been going badly ever since the mercenaries landed. The Royal Army was exhausted and in danger of becoming despondent. It took great effort for Peters to remain enthusiastic and pretend optimism in front of the men. He didn't think they bought the act. It seemed like they had been running and running with no apparent purpose.

Occasionally, they would stop, backtrack, and perform a surgical strike, resulting in a surge of confidence. But then they would start running again. That they had lost few men after all these weeks was a testament to Perry's brilliance. That they were in a strategically perilous position was a testament to Perry's fallibility.

Peters had read in one of Perry's military history books that the most brilliant of generals were also the ones most likely to make disastrous mistakes based on overconfidence. Perry had perhaps proven that observation these past months.

The worst of the blunders was allowing General Fedral and about a third of their army to get split off from the main body. The last reports of Fedral and his troops were from a scout who had watched them run away from battle in a panic. He described it as a complete rout. And for God's sake, where were the auxiliaries? Fully half the Royal Army were militias that could be called up and quickly incorporated into the professional army. The mercenaries had arrived so quickly that the process of calling them to duty had been late. The recently promoted Captain Graves had been sent out to assemble as many of the widely distributed militias as possible. He was tardy in returning with them. Was

Graves too young and inexperienced for the mission? Did the militias refuse to honor their commitments? Had they joined up with General Fedral's command? Had some of them joined the rebels? Was the army currently under Perry's direction all they had? There were far too many questions without answers.

Thank God they had set up camp three days ago in a defensible valley near the peak of the main mountain pass between Druango and the vast flatlands leading to the Royal Castle. The troops desperately needed the rest. But they would run out of food within the week. Now the difficult decision. Do they try and fight their way back into Druango or fight a running battle down the mountain retreating all the way to the Royal Castle? Waiting while their enemy strengthened the two ends of the mountain pass would be a grievous mistake. It was a trap that would close soon. They needed to choose a direction and attack. The only other option was surrender. Reports from the areas under occupation were bleak. Rape and pillage were commonplace. Citizens were being treated as slaves. Surrender was not an option as far as Peters was concerned.

The odd thing was that Perry didn't seem to be overly concerned by any of this. Perhaps he was exhausted, perhaps he had given up. Peters didn't know what they should do, but they would have to act soon. Generals had been taken out of command by their staffs before in these sorts of situations. If Perry didn't start making rational decisions soon, something would have to be done. The thought was deeply troubling. Perry was like a father to him. He could never repay the man for what he had done for himself and his sister. The difficulty, perhaps impossibility, in removing him was that his staff and the common soldiers worshipped him. They would follow Perry to hell. Unfortunately, that seemed to be the direction they were headed.

As he entered the command tent, he looked around and saw discouraged faces all around. Perry walked in and looked around, seemingly checking for something. He seemed to have found what he was looking for and started the meeting with a stern face. He turned to his head of security and said, "Sergeant Greaves, place Lieutenant Yelling under arrest."

There was a sudden surge of movement from behind the staff officer as Yelling was roughly placed in restraints by a couple of Greaves's men.

"Search his tent. You should find a quantity of spice there and perhaps more evidence of treason. Bring anything you find back here by 2100 so we can hold a field trial." With that, the man was pulled roughly from the room, his face a picture of terror and panic.

"Gentleman we've had a traitor in our midst," Perry said with his face an angry mask. He looked around the room at all of them. "What do you do when you don't know who to trust?"

"Don't trust anybody," came the chorus. And for the first time that evening, the corners of Perry's mouth turned up just slightly.

"I am sorry for the confusion and anxiety caused by my decision to withhold information from you. It's been difficult trying to explain our movements the past few weeks without being able to explain the end game. I trust everyone in this room with my life. Unfortunately, letting our actual plans get into the hands of our enemy would cause more than the loss of my life. It would cause the loss of our freedom, of our future, of our humanity. We are literally fighting for our way of life. Our enemy intends to enslave us. They would force our families and descendants into a brutal life of endless work and poverty. All in the name of greed. They would do this without remorse." Perry hesitated then and looked around the table, engaging each one of them with his eyes. Then he said, "Before I outline our current situation, are there any questions?"

Colonel Pike spoke up. "What did Yelling do, sir?"

"He exchanged information for spice. He's an addict. He's likely been one for quite some time. As you'll remember, we spent months in Druango at the end of the unification war. I'm guessing he was recruited then. As you know, spice is an extremely addictive drug that can only be produced by Commonwealth technology. It's not only prohibited by Liberty but also by the Commonwealth. That makes it extremely expensive. He was hooked and decided to betray us instead of getting help."

Perry's chief logistics officer, Captain Lowell, then asked, "How long have you known?"

"I noticed early on that our enemy seemed to know details of our general plan. It was small things, nothing blatant. They did a pretty good job of hiding their knowledge. So, I tested my concern and discovered it was valid. At the time, I didn't know who the traitor or traitors were. But I knew we had a leak. It took about six weeks to identify and verify that Yelling was selling information. I did this with the assistance of Bria and Sergeant Greaves. Bria's sudden interest in cooking was her way of gaining access to our stores to help with the investigation. Just so you know, she does not enjoy cooking, so expect that to stop immediately."

The command staff groaned at this news. She may not have enjoyed cooking, but she did produce excellent meals. The corners of Perry's mouth lifted once more. The thin smile disappeared, and he continued.

"Captain, we'll talk later on how the spice was hidden in our ration deliveries. It was cleverly done. I don't hold you responsible, but I think it's a good learning experience. The only good thing I can say about Yelling is that it appears he didn't reveal our royal secret," Perry said. This was as close as anyone ever came to acknowledging that the woman they all called Bria was actually the queen.

Colonel Peters spoke up once more and asked, "So, what we've been doing the past few months has been part of a plan?"

Perry smiled broadly for the first time and said, "Colonel Peters, I can always count on you to ask the question everyone wants to ask. The answer is yes, I have not lost my mind quite yet."

This comment caused an outbreak of nervous laughter. They were all thinking it, thought Perry.

He paused a moment and then said, "If there are no more questions, I'll dive into our situation and what we're going to do about it." Perry paused again, looking around the table for any more comments or questions and then said, "Gather around the map table and I'll explain. Our movements have led us to this mountain pass on purpose. As some of you know, I like hiking in the mountains. As a young man, I enjoyed exploring caves. There happens to be two large caves that connect, creating a tunnel from one of the minor canyons off of this valley to a hidden shelf just above the valley below."

Perry's staff leaned in toward the map table as Perry pointed out the locations of the cave entrances. "From that shelf is a narrow but navigable trail to this minor canyon extending off the valley below. The entrance to that canyon is narrow and well hidden by brush. That entrance is just behind the enemy's defensive position at the bottleneck. Years ago, before the first unification war, another ranger and I concealed both cave entrances."

Perry smiled and looked around the table. "You could say this plan has been coming together for twenty years. As you know, our scouts are reporting that the lower valley has been filling up with enemy troops in anticipation of an assault. They would be better served to starve us out, but since they see us run at every opportunity, they think they can end the war quickly. General Fedral was made aware of the traitor before he split off. Yes, that was a planned ruse. His orders were to retreat and locate Captain Graves.

"His units, along with Graves's militias, should now be well hidden near the base of the mountain pass. General Fedral will be positioned to either ambush their retreat or attack their rear based on his judgement of the situation. We will leave just enough troops at the mountain pass above to hold off an assault from that direction. Our main attack will be just before dawn.

"Colonel Peters will take his rangers and slip in behind them by utilizing the caves. His orders are to attack after the main attack has begun or when he judges it most expedient." Perry stopped and looked around the table once more and said, "Even with General Fedral and the militias, we will be outnumbered tomorrow. Surprise is essential. We must quickly overwhelm them. We get one shot at this." Perry paused and asked, "Any comments or questions?"

Then Captain Brush, a brash young man of great potential and a quick wit, said, "Welcome back, General, we've missed you." The staff laughed, relieving the tension. Young Brush was well liked and probably the only one who could have pulled off saying something like that to the General. They all appreciated seeing Perry smile broadly once again.

The staff meeting broke up an hour later after the details of the next day's assault were discussed and finalized. Peters always marveled at how Perry could get each officer to internalize and own their own plan. Perry always let his staff determine the execution details for their units as long as it fit within the overall strategy of the battle plan. A young Lieutenant Peters once asked him, "Why don't you just tell us what to do?"

"Because you will execute your own plan better than one I give you. I might come up with a better plan, but it's only going to be better for me. As a leader, your primary job is to delegate, not direct. Giving and obeying orders is critical, but your role is really one of support and mentorship. You just need to make sure that each one of your delegates understands the general plan and can do their job."

As Perry's staff filtered out of the command tent on their way to organize the assault, Perry said, "Walk with me, Colonel. I'm going to show you where the upper end of the cave system is." They walked in silence until out of earshot of the others. Perry then said, "You're wondering why I didn't include you in the people who knew we had a spy."

"I admit it's a question I have. It's hard to accept that you didn't trust me," Peters said with sadness in his voice.

Perry stopped walking, forcing Peters to do the same. He turned toward him moving close and said, "It has nothing to do with trusting your loyalty. I trust you with my life. I trust you with the queen's life. I don't trust your acting skills."

"Acting skills, sir?" Peters said, confused.

"One of the reasons your men admire and trust you is because you're an open book. There are no secrets. If you're angry, they know. If you're proud of them, they know. They aren't wondering if you have hidden opinions or agendas. Everything is there for everyone to see," Perry said. "If the entire command staff were concerned about my decisions and you weren't, Yelling would have known something was up. If you knew Yelling was the spy, he would have seen the accusation in your eyes. I couldn't risk that."

Peters gave it some thought and decided the General was right. He was a terrible liar and hopeless at acting a part. He huffed a breath and said, "My sister always says I couldn't tell a decent lie to save my life."

Perry smiled, and as he slapped him on the back said, "It's a strength. I admire and value you because of it. However, it does have its drawbacks given this situation. You're a successful leader because of who you are. Don't think you need to change anything."

Early the next morning, General Harris was a happy man as he walked briskly to his command tent. The Liberty contract was almost complete. By tomorrow, the day after at the latest, he could go enjoy the fruits of this planet for a month and then head back home. He was still trying to decide how to spend the money. If successful, this was an outrageously rich contract. And success was assured.

The famous General Eastbrook turned out to be a dolt. No coherent strategy. Running away at every opportunity. A complete buffoon. He was ineffective at coordinating even simple battle plans. Something any of Harris's lower-level officers could have done successfully. Allowing his army to be split apart was gross incompetence. On the other hand, his focused surprise attacks were impressive. But perhaps that was Colonel Peters and not Eastbrook.

It took more than good special forces to win a war against credible military men. He might look into purchasing Peters and perhaps a few of his officers. Decent special forces officers were hard to find. Offered a choice between the life of a mercenary and death by hanging was typically an easy one for his defeated opponents to make.

Harris's command tent was a bustle of activity. He frowned when he noticed Lord Druango and his cronies assembled around the coffee stand. Nothing worse than customers thinking they have something to contribute. They lost their war against this same army. Any advice they might offer was worse than useless.

He grumbled with a tight smile, "Good morning Lord Druango. Are you here to witness our victory?"

"Good morning General. We are excited to see you so close to achieving the end of this," Druango said with a smile that didn't reach his eyes. "I would be remiss however if we didn't warn you once more than Eastbrook is not always what he seems. History would recommend caution."

General Harris just stared back at Druango, attempting to get his anger under control. This was the worst part about being a mercenary. The customers. If you irritated them, they could decide to delay payment. While the Commonwealth would mediate mercenary contracts, they couldn't care less about enforcement. That was between the colonies. His home planet wasn't even in the same sector. The only other option was to completely conquer the planet and hold it for ransom. A costly and lengthy process at best. No, he would have to feed this clown's oversized ego.

"Your advice is appreciated, but Eastbrook is badly outnumbered and bottled up. He is trapped in an indefensible position. The portion of his army we routed has disappeared like the morning fog and their militias never materialized. One good push and he's done."

"As you say, he's bottled up. Can't we just back off and starve him out? Seems the more prudent strategy," Lord Druango said, clearly concerned.

"No need. His army is done. This effort has taken longer than I planned. Eastbrook's habit of running away from every battle has delayed the inevitable long enough. I'm happy for your group to witness this final assault but please stay back from the fighting. Getting too close to the action is an unnecessary risk."

Just stay the hell out of my way, he thought, although it would be amusing to see one of them get skewered.

"Now, if you don't mind, we have a lot of work to do this morning."

To General Harris's annoyance, they did not take the hint and leave. They did, however, stop offering advice. As his staff was discussing the order of battle, a commotion was heard.

"Probably a localized raid," his chief of staff offered. "They do that sort of thing a lot."

General Harris nodded his agreement, and they focused back on their planning. Suddenly the command tent flap was swept aside, and a wild-eyed young lieutenant ran in and said, "We are under attack!"

General Harris turned to the overwrought young man and said, "Of course we are. That's what happens when you decide to become a fighting man." His comment elicited a derisive laugh from his command staff.

The lieutenant was nonplussed by the insult, however, and continued. "Colonel Beaty said the upper defensive line has been overrun with enemy units attacking it from above and below. Somehow, they flanked the main line of defense. He's ordered a general retreat and recommends moving to the other end of the valley to set up a new line of defense."

Harris felt a cold sweat break out. Colonel Beaty was a solid, experienced officer. If he took it upon himself to call for a general retreat without discussing it with Harris, the situation was really bad. This was obviously a last-ditch effort by Eastbrook. No reason to panic, but every reason to move quickly.

"Gentleman, you heard the report. Execute a general retreat to the far end of the valley and set up a line of defense. You have your orders." And with that, the staff members ran out of the command tent, shouting orders to their officers.

"General, we warned you about Eastbrook. He's lured you into a trap," Druango said with fury in his voice.

"Shut up and stay out the way, Druango. If you hurry, you'll avoid Eastbrook's troops who likely don't have a good opinion of you," Harris said as he hurried out of the tent to organize the retreat.

At the base of the mountain pass, a scout traveled quickly but silently to the hidden encampment. Giving the correct passwords to the pickets, he made his way to General Fedral's command tent. The assembled staff had been waiting all night for his report. "Excuse me, sir," the scout said as he entered the command tent. "The attack you predicted has started. It appears to be successful so far. Fighting is heavy and enemy troops are retreating down the valley. They are making efforts to set up a line of defense at the lower end of the valley."

"Any signs of them planning to retreat beyond the end of the valley, Sergeant?" File asked.

"No, sir," the scout responded.

Well, Perry's done it again, Fedral thought. If he hadn't known Perry as long as he did, he would have thought the original plan crazy. But Fedral had seen too many crazy Perry plans exposed as brilliance. Perry had somehow manipulated General Harris's movement and timing precisely. Right down to the day, location, and situation Perry told him to be prepared for. The news of the leak had been one of the more shocking experiences in Fedral's life. A punch in the gut. That someone from the inner circle would betray them was hard to believe. Almost impossible to believe. The loyalty of Perry's troops was legendary. His direct staff was more a family than anything else. Regardless of who the traitor was, it would be a sad day when he was exposed.

Fedral shook himself out of his thoughts and said, "We're going with Plan B. Captain Graves, hold the second and third militias in reserve a half mile back as we've discussed. Be ready to move up in support on my orders, or at your discretion if conditions warrant. Gentlemen, let's move."

Late in the afternoon, after a long day of fighting, Perry barked, "Colonel Peters!"

"Yes, sir."

"We need to break this line before they further stabilize their position. Take your rangers and attack the right flank centered on where that small stream flows through. They don't have earthworks setup properly yet to defend that streambed. It will be hard fighting, but we need to break through."

"Yes, sir. Do you want to signal the attack, or should we go when ready?" Colonel Peters said.

"Go when ready, but Signal as you do," Perry said. He took a deep breath and reviewed their situation. Their initial attack had been a complete surprise. Harris's army had been forming up for an attack and was not prepared to defend. Peter's flanking maneuver had been executed flawlessly, creating a rout.

While they had already captured roughly one third of Harris's men who had been positioned to attack that morning, the rest had escaped the trap. They moved quickly down the valley until facing resistance about three quarters of the way down. By midafternoon they had taken the valley but had gotten stopped by Harris's second line of defense.

As always, mistakes were made. Perry had given orders for Fedral to attack, if their retreat resulted in them abandoning the valley, or wait until Perry's troops reached the end of the valley. He realized now that he should have ordered both ends attacked simultaneously. Given what his scouts on the cliff tops were reporting, he believed Fedral had been discovered when he moved into position early that morning.

Waiting for Perry had given them time to position themselves to protect against attacks from both sides. Harris had turned the bottleneck at the end of the valley into a fortress. Perry had to admit that Harris was a credible opponent. His army kept their composure and quickly established a defense against both ends of the pincher. It was a shaky but defensible position. These were well-led disciplined troops.

Perry and his staff were standing together on a low hill with a partial view of the fighting. Their growing assessment of Peter's heroic charge was that the enemy had pulled troops from elsewhere and plugged the gap. The gambit had failed. Many rangers had been lost.

"Ideas, gentlemen?" Perry asked. And as his staff shuffled their feet trying to come up with an alternative plan, a messenger ran up the low hill out of breath.

"General! They're surrendering. The mercenaries are surrendering."

Turning to examine the battlefield once more, Perry saw that the defense of the stream bed had suddenly collapsed. What was left of Peters's rangers were now pouring into the gap. How and why this had happened was a mystery.

What turned the tide was Captain Graves and his militias. The enemy had stripped defenders from the back side of the stream bed to stop Peters's assault on the front side. One of Graves's scouts noticed the paucity of defenders in the area where the small stream flowed through. Graves could hear a major assault that seemed to be somewhere further up the stream bed. He recognized the situation, abandoned caution, and quickly drove right through it. Once the line was breached, small mercenary units started surrendering. Graves soon connected up with Peters's rangers. Harris's defense was cut in half. They now had gaps that couldn't be closed on both upper and lower defensive lines. Isolated groups began surrendering in mass. It all fell apart quickly.

One of Perry's genuine pleasures was awarding battlefield promotions. It was especially gratifying when the promotion was for an unusually noteworthy accomplishment. Captain Graves had thrown the dice at exactly the right time. If he had faltered, if he had exercised caution, they would likely be back to running for their lives. Perry had little confidence he could fool Harris twice.

Captain Graves was standing at attention in front of Perry's command staff. He looked awfully young, Perry thought. He also looked awfully nervous. Perry could remember his own days as a young officer hugging the walls at senior officer meetings. Being called to attention before all of them was intimidating.

"Captain Graves. For your courageous and meritorious service given during this campaign, the command staff have approved promoting you to the rank of major. You are being assigned to Colonel Peters as a ranger unit commander. Let me thank you personally for your bravery and quick thinking. A lot of good men died creating the breach you so quickly took advantage of. Due to your actions, they did not die in vain."

"Thank you, sir," Graves said, keeping his features locked.

"My queen," Perry said, turning it over to Olivia.

"Major Graves. At General Eastbrook's recommendation, and my concurrence, army officers of special distinction are awarded the Royal Cross. This is in recognition of the enormous contribution you have made to the kingdom. Those holding this distinction are rare. You'll find you're in good company," she said as she glanced towards Perry's Royal Cross, pinned to his uniform. "My thanks, and the thanks of the kingdom for your service." The queen then stepped forward and pinned the Royal Cross to his uniform.

"Thank you, Your Majesty," Graves finally got out.

Olivia looked him in the eye and, with a smirk, said in a conversational tone, "You can go back to calling me Bria now." This caused a general low chuckle among Perry's staff officers. Perry smiled, thinking his adopted daughter was really stepping into her role. A queen to love and admire.

"Yes, ma'am," Graves said with a smile breaking through.

Now that the pleasant portion of the day was complete, it was time for Perry to do his duty. It was a duty he took no pleasure in. A duty that would haunt him. But a duty that must be done.

Lord Druango was led in chains into the command tent, along with twenty-two other members of the nobility. This group represented the core leadership of the revolt.

"Lord Druango. You and your followers are being charged with treason and rebellion against your rightful ruler and the kingdom. After the unification wars, you all swore pledges of loyalty, which you have broken. I am convening this court to dispense justice," Perry said with iron in his voice.

"You can't do that Eastbrook. Only the queen can declare war. She is also the only one who can authorize a Royal Army and name its leader. She is off world. The reconstituted House of Lords found her uncle guilty of treason. He was found wholly responsible for her abduction and transportation to Arista. This judgement voided his authority to act on her behalf. As you know, he is still a fugitive. As Queen Olivia's fiancé, I was given the legal authority by the House of Lords to act as regent until she returns. You have no authority. I command you to set us free immediately. If you don't stop this nonsense now, you'll hang for it," Druango confidently said.

As he finished talking, Queen Olivia stepped out in her royal finery from behind a screened entrance. Druango's eyes grew huge, and his mouth dropped open. Those with him audibly gasped.

"Lord Druango. You are mistaken on a number of topics. Top of the list is the obvious fact that I am not off world. I have directed General Eastbrook to command the Royal Army and put down a rebellion against the crown. He is authorized under my declaration of war to hold military court hearings and dispense justice." Olivia paused and grimly smiled at

Druango, who was speechless with horror clearly showing in his eyes. "I'll also take this opportunity to break our engagement," she said, tossing her engagement ring to his feet. "Now that the legality of these hearings is settled, I'll step out of the way and let General Eastbrook do his job." She left as quickly as she had arrived.

It took all morning to review the evidence, hear pleas for mercy, and pronounce sentence. It was a bit of a farce, given everyone knew what the outcome would be. But Perry insisted they follow proper procedure. Executing the sentences, however, was over quickly.

Twenty-three corpses were swinging gently with the breeze as General Harris was led past them and into the command tent. He was clearly angry at being shackled and didn't hesitate to complain about it. "Will you take these ridiculous restraints off? I am willing to negotiate a surrender, but I expect to be treated with dignity during those negotiations," Harris said in a condescending tone. "Trying to scare me with those idiots hanging from the gallows isn't going to work. I have friends in the Commonwealth. They won't be pleased if I'm treated badly."

Perry looked at Harris calmly and said, "This isn't a negotiation. The only option open to you is unconditional surrender. If you refuse, we'll simply mop up the few units you left back in Druango's capital. It won't be difficult."

"I know Sector 27 is far away from the center of the Commonwealth, so perhaps you don't understand how these things are done. My benefactor will offer a reasonable ransom for myself and my army. He'll agree to some restitution, again provided it's reasonable," Harris said, softening his aggressive tone a bit.

"I am not the one who's uninformed," Perry said. "Once you landed on this planet, you placed yourself under the laws and authorities of the crown. You are not a prisoner of war, General Harris. You are under arrest for violating the laws of this nation. A full set of charges awaits an investigation by our legal system." Perry paused and then added, "You are under a misperception if you think credits will take the place of justice for those who died and those who were abused."

Harris had a cold, sinking feeling in his gut. He sensed that General Eastbrook was being completely forthright. He really wasn't negotiating. The general was intent on extracting some form of revenge. He had to admit the man had lived up to his outsized reputation. Underestimating the man was a grievous mistake. But he was clearly a rube. Harris's benefactor was an obscenely wealthy dictator of a collection of the oldest and richest colonies in the Commonwealth. His tentacles reached all the way to the High Council.

His reputation depended on fulfilling his obligations. Harris had a contract with his benefactor and could expect it to be honored. The powerful Commonwealth authorities taking his benefactors' bribes couldn't interfere directly given the strict non-interference Edicts. But it didn't mean they wouldn't act aggressively to assist his benefactor if properly paid. The bribes would be large, but Harris knew his benefactor's reputation was important enough to him to force payment. This was simply how things were done. He would have to bide his time and suffer this humiliation for now. Justice would prevail. Revenge would be sweet.

CHAPTER 6

COMMAND PERFORMANCE

Caius was intimidated and overwhelmed. Since boarding the governor's space yacht, he had been inundated by technologies denied to the colonies. It was the simple things that were the most appealing. He had spent a ridiculous amount of time turning lights on and off in his suite with voice commands. He kept changing the temperature and humidity just to see what it felt like. His bathroom was a marvel. Being wealthy, he was used to indoor plumbing.

But his toilet had an amazing range of capabilities, from a heated seat to multiple options involving water cleansing. The shower was so complicated he gave up trying to figure it out. He was able to set the water temperature to his liking, which was good enough.

Having water come from above and all sides was an experience. His skin was drying out from all the showers he was taking. He quickly became addicted to the information retrieval capabilities and entertainment. This was all accessed through a large screen above the desk in his assigned suite.

After an entire day of playing with technology, he realized it was distracting him from planning through his various alternatives. The challenge with lies is that you have to remember all the details, he thought. So far, he had been able to tell a simple story. That simple story was going to require revisions that made it complicated. He had been a bystander. Now he was a major player. In the beginning, he had simply been trying to delay an invasion of Liberty. Now he had to consider the complicated politics of three planets, plus the Commonwealth.

What gave him indigestion was that he had no idea why the governor asked for a private meeting. The expense, time, and effort it must have cost to set up a meeting on A27 meant it was very important to her. He knew colonists were rarely invited to Commonwealth planets. What was her game?

The invitation had come in the form of two Commonwealth representatives showing up unannounced in the early hours at Domus Cereo. They explained they were there to escort Caius to A27 for a compulsory meeting with the governor. Caius was told he had an hour to prepare and that he would be gone for an entire week. He was also told the governor wanted this meeting to be kept strictly private.

Luckily, Leo had not gone to the Palatium yet. Leo had been in the habit of getting up early and working with Dobler on basic self-defense skills. As his brother had jokingly noted, "With all the crazy things you've been getting us into, I thought I better learn how to defend myself." Caius also thought he was using it as an excuse to watch Forti and Tee train. Leo was fascinated by the raw athleticism of the two and enjoyed learning more about the martial arts.

Caius spent five minutes throwing clothes and toiletries in a bag and the rest of the hour planning out the week with Leo. They decided to hide the fact Caius wasn't in Roma. It was fortunate the governor insisted on privacy. Pluta had observers everywhere and they would need help from the Commonwealth escorts to avoid detection. They would all go to the Palatium together and then the two Commonwealth escorts would appear to leave by themselves. Leo would leak out that the emperor had received a private message from the governor.

That same morning, the emperor was going to come down with a contagious illness. There would be enough concern that a quarantine would be placed on the private residence portion of the Palatium. Caius and Leo would unfortunately be caught up in it. Leo could navigate all the correspondence that would naturally flow back and forth. There was a planet plus a business empire to run, after all. If something especially tricky came up, it would be communicated that Caius was very ill and would be unable to respond for a few days. It would work.

Caius decided the governor's insistence on him visiting A27 was based on intimidating him. The travel was already doing a good job of that. A simple threat to force him to take some sort of action could have easily been communicated through Jack. No, there was more to it. He was still working through his alternative stories when the shuttle from the space yacht landed. From there, he was whisked off into an air taxi.

Once again, he was overwhelmed with technology. Transportation on Arista was simple. You walked, rode on something involving a horse, or traveled by boat. He had flown through space, been transported on some sort of moving walkway, and was now flying through the air in a pod that had whirling blades above it.

When he first arrived in his suite on the space yacht, the large display above the desk was showing a technology tutorial. It had clearly been created for colonists to enable them to use the common forms of communication, transportation, and personal comfort available on a Commonwealth world. How these things were accomplished was noticeably missing. While he had become aware of these conveniences from the tutorial, it scrambled his brain to experience them.

Taking a deep breath to ease the anxiety of flying through the air, Caius looked out over the countryside. It appeared to be an undeveloped paradise. Colonists believed the Commonwealth always took the best planet in each sector for themselves. What he had seen so far supported that belief. He passed over forests, grass-covered plains, a major river, and numerous lakes. Snow-covered mountains could be seen on the far horizon.

Suddenly, the air taxi cleared a series of low hills, and he saw a building sitting in a small, picturesque valley on the shoreline of an idyllic lake. It was the only sign of human habitation he had seen in the past hour. He wondered if the air taxi was the only way to get to this location. He hadn't seen a road since just after leaving the vicinity of the spaceport. The planet seemed to be almost entirely uninhabited.

Humankind had learned from the environmental disasters of the twenty-first century. Colonists kept their terraformed planets lightly populated. It wasn't enough to limit greenhouse gases. A healthy planet was one that didn't feel the footsteps of its human inhabitants. A27, however, was an extreme case of being kept in a natural state.

When they landed, he was led along a stone walkway to what he now recognized as a residence. The formal garden that was off to one side looked almost as extravagant as some of the many courtyards in the Palatium. It was in the garden area he first noticed that servants had thin silver bands tightly wrapped around their necks. Then he noticed they all had blank expressions on their faces. It was creepy, to say the least.

"Senator Cereo, thank you for making the trip," the governor said as she stood up from a small table positioned on a covered deck overlooking the lake. "Please join me for lunch."

"You have a beautiful home, Governor," Caius said.

"This is my getaway. My main house is in the city, but I wanted to insure privacy, and I thought you might enjoy seeing some of the planet," the governor said, smiling with her mouth while her eyes stabbed into his.

"The entire trip has been amazing. Thank you for hosting me," Caius said, keeping his warm smile in place.

One of the blank-faced servants shuffled over to the table with a bottle of wine and two glasses. Caius looked up at him and froze. He was unable to hide his shock. Caius glanced over at the governor, and she had that unblinking stare of hers in place. The corners of her mouth were slightly upturned in a smirk.

She turned her head to look at the waiter and said, "I think you recognize Evans Senator Cereo. His new responsibilities are now more in line with his abilities."

She turned back toward Caius and gave him a predatory smile. After an uncomfortable pause, she continued. "Evans made the mistake of taking bribes from slavers. The Pacifica gladiator you know so well was the result of one of those bribes. That was a minor violation. He would have easily recovered if it were only that.

However, being part of a conspiracy to kidnap the reining ruler of a Commonwealth colony violates the non-interference Edicts. Violation carries an automatic life sentence of service. I was fortunate enough to be assigned his caretaker," she said as Evans poured wine for them both and then stepped back from the table. He was the perfect waiter.

Caius noticed the bottle he poured from was the original vintage of Jenny's Acre. June was a very good artist and had hand drawn all the first year's labels. They were unique and very distinctive. It was likely the same bottle of wine Evans had purchased at his charity event. The effect was a deeply chilling one.

They both knew Evans didn't have anything to do with the kidnapping of Queen Olivia. Caius knew Pluta had been involved but was likely innocent as well. Pluta was too cunning to take that kind of risk. He must have been trapped into it. That meant Jack and the governor planned and executed it.

Caius made a show of thinking about this and then asked, "Are all your servants criminals?"

"You're very perceptive, and yes. The beauty of our system is that we create low-cost labor for our society's needs instead of spending credits on prisons. The practice originated from the strict rules governing the separation of Commonwealth and Colony. Colony citizens, even slaves, are prohibited from populating Commonwealth planets," the governor said, continuing her icy stare.

"Creative and efficient. I'm not one who likes to waste people or credits either," Caius said, pretending to be impressed instead of horrified. "What have you done to make them so docile? It appears Evans doesn't even know who I am."

"He doesn't. It really isn't him anymore. He only knows you are a guest, and he must do whatever you ask him to do. The process involves permanent changes to specific parts of the brain," the governor explained.

"What's the purpose of the collar?" Caius asked.

"It's for training purposes. Pain and pleasure are useful tools for optimizing their contributions."

"Interesting. Is the process exportable to the colonies?" Caius asked.

"No, it involves prohibited technology. It's only used for the needs of Commonwealth planets."

"A shame. I could get more output from workers who aren't burdened by emotions and thoughts of things that will never be," Caius said with a conspiratorial smile. The governor relaxed a little and Caius could tell he had passed some kind of test. While he couldn't be sure, he thought she was unaware of how disgusted he was by this practice. This was evil beyond even slavery.

The governor looked at him for a few moments with her intense stare, seemed to come to a decision and said, "I asked you to come to A27 because I have an offer. I want you to be Sector 27's first minister." The governor gave him a warmer smile, although her smiles never reached her eyes. Even her smiles were chilling.

Caius just looked back at her for a few moments, thinking through his carefully constructed set of alternatives. While this specific situation wasn't on his list of possibilities, one of his alternatives fit it reasonably well. "I'm stunned and flattered, Governor. I didn't know colony citizens could take on administrative roles in the Commonwealth."

"They can't. Part of the process is making you and your immediate family Commonwealth citizens. This is extremely rare and involves patronage from the Commonwealth's High Counsel. Fortunately, I have connections, and this offer has already been approved."

Which meant corruption went to the very top of the Commonwealth, thought Caius as he asked, "Why me, Governor?"

"When you drop the façade, you get right to the point. I like that," she said, keeping her smile in place. "You started off being an annoyance and graduated rather quickly to a significant disruption. I decided to support Senator Pluta because I was concerned you would keep out maneuvering my first minister. Then suddenly your gladiator slave becomes emperor through an archaic succession law and you now control the planet. To say I was outraged is an understatement.

"Next, the Liberty Royal Army was successful against the best mercenary army in the Commonwealth. More plans up in flames. That this was something you warned me about made it all the more aggravating. After giving it quite a bit of thought, I decided I needed a fresh start. I decided your creativity and ability to manipulate people to benefit yourself needed to be harnessed by the Commonwealth. So here we are."

Caius wondered what was going to happen to Jack, but he knew better than to ask. It would either be seen as worrying about trivial issues or, worse, having concern for the young man. Caius didn't trust Jack, but there was something likable about the man. Dangerous as a scorpion, but likable. "What's in it for me? I already control a planet."

"Control of Arista is child's play compared to what you can do in the Commonwealth. I have meetings in the city this afternoon. I'll leave a compensation package for you to examine. I think you'll be delighted. Evans will give you a tour of the house while I'm gone, as well. I'll answer any questions you have when I get back. I will want an answer tomorrow morning when you leave to go back to Arista," she said.

"Greater wealth is attractive, but it isn't my primary motivation. I'm interested in how aggressive you want to be in the sector. I wonder whether we can agree in principle on priorities and strategy. I'm not impressed with what Jack has been attempting to do. I assume that has been at your direction," Caius said with a frown. He knew it was a risk confronting her, but thought she would respect rather than resent that kind of approach.

"You do have a rather large set of balls; I'll give you that," she said with her smile turning feral. "I am interested in your thoughts, but I will set priorities and strategies. What do you think Jack should have been doing? If we agree on that, we are likely going to be in alignment longer term," the governor said with her most intimidating stare.

Caius made a show of coming to a decision. He huffed out a breath and said, "Okay. First of all, the strategy for Liberty has always assumed a military solution. This is unwise. The planet has been in a state of war for twenty-five years. The army is battle hardened. General Eastbrook was going to have a prominent place in military history books before this latest fiasco. He is a brilliant military strategist, and his men will follow him anywhere. His victory against General Harris just reinforces his reverence with the population. You want to harness that not go up against it. There will be a way in, but it must take the form of a trojan horse, not the launch of a thousand ships."

When the governor nodded in agreement, he continued. "But that isn't what's interesting in the sector. Pacifica is the prize. While its natural resources are attractive all on their own, its human resources are special. The people there can be utilized for heavy planet labor. Also, the wars they have been fighting against the GEMs for more than a thousand years have created a military that makes Liberty's Royal Army look like children playing. Can you imagine what a mercenary army of Pacifica warriors would bring in fees? My guess is that you benefit when services from your sector are paid for by another." Caius stopped and got a head nod from the governor. He continued. "Jack's attention would have been better utilized on efforts to turn Pacifica into a colony."

"It's easy to make that observation, but do you have a plan that could achieve it?"

Caius sighed, then took a deep breath and said, "I guess I might as well go full disclosure." He looked at the governor once more and, taking another deep breath, he said, "My plan all along has been to control Arista as a steppingstone to convert Pacifica into a vassal state. Theron is a member of their Guard. That has great prestige on Pacifica. I did some research on the original colonist manifest and their Ship 3 captain was a man with the last name of Stone. Theron's last name is Stone.

"All of their technology and most of their history was lost in the original GEM war. That means we can create a history and claim he is the rightful hereditary ruler. Now that he is officially the ruler of a Commonwealth colony, he can make requests of the Commonwealth. What if he requests admission to the Commonwealth for his home world? The key here is that he is now aware of Commonwealth technology and has a legitimate claim as ruler of Pacifica. Under those conditions, I imagine approval could be obtained. My attempts at developing a relationship with Evans were for that purpose, not just to be annoying." He gave her a mischievous smile.

The governor was clearly surprised by this idea. She gathered herself and considered it for a while. Finally, she said, "That might be possible. I'll need to investigate and perhaps have a conversation with my mentor on the High Council. Conquest of one colony by another is allowable, but having one colony pull another out of its protected status isn't straightforward. There has to be evidence of industrial technology or second-generation warfare. But an argument could be made that knowledge of either of those is sufficient. It would take a while to prepare, and longer for the bureaucracy to approve, but perhaps possible." She stopped and thought some more and then said, "What would be your plan to increase revenues from Liberty?"

Caius gave her his best sneaky smile and said, "Our trojan horse is a marriage between Theron Stone and Queen Olivia. He saved her from abuse onboard the slave ship and then they spent weeks living side by side. They think they're in love," he exclaimed with a smirk.

"The first step is to orchestrate a marriage between the two of them. However, this does not unite the planets. Theron would only be the queen's consort. All power would reside with the queen. If attempts to change Liberties constitution through her fail, then we will need to assassinate the queen, her uncle, and General Eastbrook. It would then be revealed that rebellious members of the House of Lords paid for an assassination.

"Outraged, Theron lands with the Pacifica Guard and lays waste to the government. A new constitution encompassing all three planets is then approved. That new constitution would be based on Arista's. Timing of events is critical, but I believe it can be done. However, this cannot be done quickly. A complex scheme like this takes time to develop. I strongly recommend a focus on Pacifica and to deal with Liberty later."

She nodded in approval and asked with a puzzled expression, "If you are first minister, then who would have ultimate colony control?"

"Magistrate Pluta."

"Pluta? I thought the two of you were sworn enemies," she said again, clearly surprised.

"We are. But as I mentioned before, I don't like to waste credits or people. He would be an efficient if unimaginative dictator. If you study his business practices, he is very good at maximizing profits. He enjoys the detailed process of squeezing them out of every nook and cranny. He would initially hate being under my control. But once he realizes the vast power he can wield, he would get past it," Caius said, smiling.

"Document your plan and we'll review this evening. I have to admit I'm impressed, and I'm not easily impressed. It should be obvious by now that I don't handle disappointment well. If you can deliver, we'll work well together."

"I'll put something together for you to review when you get back. By the way, what happens to Jack?" Caius said.

"Jack is a useful emissary but lacks the creativity and ruthlessness to operate at a first minister level. His family is wealthy. He will be sent back to enjoy a simple life of luxury. His father will attempt to disown him. He is a vicious little climber and will attempt to maintain his own career amidst this embarrassment. His motivation for his son's success is a selfish one. His mother will win the argument and make sure Jack lives a comfortable life," the governor said with a smirk.

"He's young and stupid. No question about that. But I think he did a passable job executing his plans. I agree he is acceptable in the role of emissary. Given those two attributes I might have something he could add value with," Caius said.

"Okay, we can discuss that sort of detail later. Will let you know when I've returned." And with that, the governor got up from the table and left.

Caius spent the rest of the afternoon sitting at the small table, trying to enjoy the spectacular view. He alternated between writing up his bogus plan and being paralyzed by sheer terror. The compensation offered was staggering. It included high paying careers for his son and daughter. It all amounted to an obscene amount of generational wealth for his family. The governor's get away was part of the package. She really knew how to sell. On the other hand, she really knew how to threaten. All the lake house servants came with the property. Evans was obviously intended to be a constant reminder of what might happen if he failed.

Looking out over the placid lake, he thought this was much worse than the worst-case scenarios he had imagined on his way here. He had been forced to go with the alternative Leo had named 'pure insanity.' Then Caius smiled, remembering the governor's reaction when he proposed Pluta as dictator for Sector 27. That threw her off track. Keeping her a little off balance was useful. He knew the job offer was absolute. He either took it or would have an unfortunate accident in the near future. He would likely never get back to Arista if he didn't accept. He might even be added as a servant to her household. There wasn't anything he thought her incapable of. He kicked himself for throwing out the lifeline for Jack. Nothing but trouble could come from that.

How is my family going to survive this? Is it better to adopt Commonwealth citizenship and do the horrible things required with the hope he could make a difference in other ways? Is it better to sacrifice himself and hope his family survived? He knew what June would tell him. It was her mantra for tough decisions.

"Just do the right thing, Caius. You know deep down what that is."

With that in mind, he thought furiously on various options, scheming away the sun-drenched afternoon.

CHAPTER 7

GRAMMY

Grammy was relaxed and satisfied at the end of the day. Her chores were complete, and she sat on the porch enjoying a spectacular sunset. The sky was a light blue smeared with clouds that were a riot of white, yellow, and red.

Her conversation with Hestie earlier had gone much as expected. She could count on that girl to ensure her wishes were honored. Hestie had been reluctant to leave that afternoon, and Grammy had been reluctant to say goodbye. But other responsibilities beckoned and Hestie finally gave her a tight hug and hurried off.

Continuing to sit out on the porch as it slowly grew dark, Grammy was delighted to be entertained by the first dance of the fireflies that summer. It was her favorite time of the year. Eventually, she realized she was nodding off and in danger of falling asleep out there. So, she stood up and went into the house. She changed into her nightclothes and laid down on the old bed, thinking of her Pop.

As she drifted off, she transformed into Gertrude, the young, vibrant woman she once was and always would be. Suddenly her younger self was standing at the kitchen sink satisfied that the dishes were done. As she was hanging the dish towel up to dry, a handsome young man opened the screen door and peaked in. "Looks like your work is done Gerty, time to come sit on the porch with Tia and I."

"But Tee hasn't come home yet, Pop," Gerty said with concern.

Pop gave her a warm, compassionate smile and said, "He will, Gerty, he will. His work isn't done yet. But yours is finished. Time to come rest."

Happiness and joy filled her as she walked out the door and onto the porch to be with her true love once again.

Grammy passed peacefully in her sleep with a smile on her lips.

CHAPTER 8

RETREAT

Diana was on watch, which was troubling. It gave her too much time to think. As always, she wondered about Tee. How was he? Would he ever return? If he did, would he share her feelings? Which led to Glenn's question at the Blue Heron a few days ago.

"I really enjoy your company, Diana. Is it possible we could be more than friends some day?" Glenn had asked with an expression she wasn't sure was concern or desire.

Diana hesitated before answering. Glenn had become a really good friend. She liked his ethics, his humor, and his easy-going manner. His quick acceptance of her plan for the archers during the Apple Valley east incursion said a lot about his acceptance of women leaders. This was important to her.

Looking him straight on, she said, "I'm not interested in any sort of relationship, Glenn."

"If that changed, would I have a chance?" he asked, probing.

She paused again, giving it some thought. "If it changes, then yes." And then she gave him a grin and teased him, saying, "Along with all the other handsome men running around here these days."

"That's all I wanted to hear," he said, smiling. Then, turning serious, he asked, "Until then, can we continue to be good friends?"

"I would like that," she said and smiled. Then she felt guilty. She was in love with Tee. She was sure he was still alive. Arti and Griff were both hiding something about Tee, and she guessed it was more good than bad. Perhaps he was gone forever.

But her heart still belonged to Tee.

She wouldn't consider anyone else until she knew for sure he was gone. As she berated herself again for not telling Tee how she felt, alarms sounded from sentries on the wall, followed by a deafening roar. Torches on the wall were quickly lit, and Diana gave the command to the two archers nearby to light the bonfires. Griff had insisted they not be complacent at night. He believed GEMs were intelligent and crafty.

While they hadn't attacked at night in many decades, he thought it was a ruse. At his insistence, they had placed numerous piles of oil-soaked wood far enough out to be barely visible from the wall. They all went up with a whoosh and what it revealed was terrifying. There was a horde of GEMs running full speed toward the wall with ladders and other siege equipment. This was a full-scale attack. She hoped it would be a long night. The alternative was too horrible to contemplate.

Jay was sleeping soundly when the alarms went off. This was followed rather quickly by a horn signaling a full call to arms. This must be a significant raid, he thought, as he donned his breastplate and helmet. GEMs don't do full scale attacks at night, he thought. He left off the rest of his armor, as he didn't think they would go below the wall at night. That was best done when visibility was good. Strapping his round shield to his back, he jogged out the door of the barracks and toward his station on the wall.

"Jay, what's going on?" said a deep voice in the misty night air. Moose appeared out of the mist and ran alongside him toward the Wall.

Jay recognized him and said, "I don't know, Moose. We've never had a full call out in the middle of the night. Wouldn't surprise me if Griff decided we had gotten lazy and wanted to shake things up a bit. They took the stairs two at a time and when they got to the top, they stopped and stared.

"Jay recovered first and said, "Better get to your station Moose. This is a full-blown attack."

"I wish Tee were here," Moose said before he took off running. Tee, Moose, and Rilla had been constant targets of Dee during recruit training. It had forged a bond between the three of them. He knew what Moose was thinking. Tee would figure out something to stop the GEMs. As Jay watched Moose running to his post, he thought he was never going to accuse Griff of going overboard again. Everyone knew the GEMs didn't attack in the dark. He had been grumbling about the nighttime drills Griff had forced them to do. He even forced them to practice a full Phalanx retreat in the dark. Lots of people were grumbling after that one. Never again, he swore.

Arti had given orders for the Wall Archers to slow their rate of fire. This was so they could randomly limit their exposure in the arrow slits. With the height advantage of the Wall, the archers had always prioritized GEM archers. The goal was to never let them get close enough to be effective. The GEMs had put out the bonfires almost immediately and had successfully moved their archers into effective range. They hid their archers in the gloom while their targets were well lit up by torches on the Wall. It was suicide to stand in front of the arrow slits and shoot continuously as they normally did.

"Arti, Griff says the Guard is slowly leaving the Wall to form up in the courtyard for the retreat. He apologizes but says we need to keep the GEMs off the wall," Diana said, clearly concerned.

"Okay, signal the girls to double their rate of fire. Have the arrow monkeys bring us three sheaves of arrows and then head for the Dam Road. Tell them to run and that we'll be right behind them," Arti said. She was deeply worried. They had held the Wall so far, but the GEMs had not yet retreated. These were experienced warriors, not the untested ones that usually came with the first wave. The plan had been to retreat as the GEMs were retreating and hope they didn't notice and turn back. Although they had practiced a retreat while still engaged, they always thought of it as the unlikely worst-case scenario.

Her arrow monkey looked terrified as she dropped off the extra arrows. Arti gave her a confident smile and said, "Everything will be okay, Louise. Run for the Dam Road and don't stop until you get behind the fortifications. You've done a wonderful job. I'm proud of you." That seemed to bolster Louise's spirits as she gave a faint smile and then took off running.

Arti took a deep breath and disobeyed her own orders. She stood tall and proud in her arrow slit and took down as many GEMs along the Wall as fast as she could. Almost through her second sheaf, she was knocked off her feet with intense pain in her shoulder. When the shock from the blow lessened, she looked and saw an arrow sticking out of her and blood spurting out from the wound. As her eyesight failed, she thought, I hope Louise makes it. Then she passed out.

"There're on the Wall," came a chorus of voices up and down the length of their fortifications. Jay and Kale had ended up fighting side by side. While their section of the Wall was still under the control of the Guard, it was clear the time to leave was now. "Let's go," Jay said, and they headed to the stairway with GEMs starting to come over the Wall behind them.

They bounded down the stairs and sprinted toward one of the openings that had been set up in the Phalanx. They were assigned to be part of one of the roving squads who would protect the ends and plug gaps as they emerged. Kale tapped Jay on the shoulder and said, "Look, Moose is in trouble."

Jay's immediate thought was that Moose was on his own. In a full retreat, they were ordered to go immediately to their new stations. Anything else just created chaos. Looking back, he saw that Moose was carrying someone. Another violation of the rules during a full retreat.

"Who is he carrying?" Jay asked just as he recognized the long, braided red hair. It was Arti. Jay stopped and out of the corner of his eye he saw Rilla charge into the mass of GEMs that were starting to swarm around Moose. Jay couldn't help himself and charged into the fray as well.

"I couldn't leave her," Moose said in a weak voice. That's when Jay noticed he was bleeding profusely from several wounds. He had obviously fought hard to get Arti this far. Then Moose collapsed and Jay thought, this is the end. Kale had followed him and so far they had held the GEMs at bay but were starting to get surrounded.

That's when Griff showed up with the rest of Jay and Kale's roving squad. They quickly opened up a corridor for retreat. Rilla had forgotten all his training and turned into an out of control killing machine. He wasn't responding to the retreat order. Griff yelled. "Rilla, drag Moose back behind the lines." Hearing his bunkmate's name and a promise of safety for his friend, he stopped moving even deeper into the GEMs and did as Griff ordered. "Jay, Kale, right and left. On my cadence."

Jay got safely back behind the Phalanx just in time to see Moose breathe his last. Rilla was sitting on the ground next to him, holding his hand. He turned to Jay and Kale and said, "He was the best bunkmate ever. Thanks for helping. At least those bastards won't abuse his body. I know Griff is going to be pissed, but I'm forever grateful."

Jay looked for Arti and saw she was being tended to by a medic. Griff was standing over her with a look of desperation on his face. That was new. Griff exchanged some words with the medic and seemed satisfied with her answers. The anxiety melted away and determination took its place. Griff turned and hurried off, shouting orders.

As Jay glanced back at Rilla. An image of Tee flying up and over the training Wall suddenly entered his mind. Moose and Rilla, what a pair. He was going to miss Moose. But this was not the time for nostalgia. The Phalanx was backing its way toward the dam quickly, and thankfully, it seemed to be working reasonably well. Time to get back to work. "Rilla, get your ass over here. We have work to do," Jay shouted, bringing Rilla out of his grief. He and Rilla then chased after Griff, who was plugging yet another hole in the line.

It was mid-morning, and Del was standing on top of the dam with President Malrey and Griff. They were looking out over the mass of GEMs in the valley below the dam. They were clearly trying to bring equipment in to undermine the dam. If successful, it would leave Landfall Valley indefensible. Eureka Valley would fall quickly as well. Tourists, he decided. It made no sense for them to have any more of their warriors in the valley below than it took to destroy the dam. Such was the unorganized, chaotic nature of GEMs. They were celebrating. Well, that was about to change, he hoped.

When the Landfall Dam had been constructed, it was done with all the technology available to the original colonists. Advanced metallurgy had enabled gates to be placed near the bottom of the reservoir for the purpose of cleaning out sediment. They did this every few years at night on the ocean spillover side, which hid it from view.

There was another route that followed one of the original bypass tunnels when the dam was first built. This one emptied out in the valley below. They had never opened this one. Much was riding on it working after all these years. If opened, the valley below would quickly and dramatically flood.

They heard it before they saw it. Suddenly, the rock camouflage covering the old tunnel entrance below exploded outward with an impressive torrent of water. Panic ensued as the GEMs realized they were all about to drown. As predicted, the Wall created a barrier and a dam of sorts at the far end. Thousands and thousands of GEMs flailed in the rising water and died. This was even more catastrophic than lighting the moat had been.

"Signal them to close the gate," Griff said as he looked over his shoulder at the alarmingly low level of Landfall Lake. "We might be able to do this one more time, even if they quickly regroup. Hopefully, this slows them down enough to refill, but we shouldn't count on it." Griff hesitated a few moments and then said, "They're even worse at swimming than we are." It was a good attempt at humor, but it only elicited a few strained smiles.

"We need to be realistic," Jennifer said quietly. "We owe it to the people of Pacifica to consider executing our alternative. Even if none of us wants that."

"If we're going to be realistic, we need to consider what happens to them if we do execute that alternative. I'm not convinced we should do that until all our options are exhausted. They are likely to be enslaved rather than saved," Del said in a whisper. "In any case I agree it needs to be discussed."

Griff huffed and said, "We are a long way from being defeated. Once the waters recede, we'll reclaim the Wall. My hope is they will decide the retreat was merely a ruse to drown them. Given enough time, we'll be back to a full lake. They will tread carefully approaching the dam after this."

"Tomorrow morning, we'll regroup and discuss the way forward. Griff, I want to thank you for the tremendous job the Guard did fighting off the nighttime attack. You're mostly intact, even though losing the CGG is a big blow. For now, you are the acting CGG," Jennifer said.

Griff respected Jennifer too much to make a scene here. He would not join the officer corps even if he were temporarily in charge. She would have to make it a political position of some kind. He was proud of Nate. On the other hand, he was disappointed in himself. Perhaps his training had been insufficient. The man had never learned to retreat properly. But he had gone down fighting, taking quite a few GEMs with him. That was what every member of the Guard aspired to do.

It had been a busy couple of weeks for Griff. The Guard had been working long days and nights to clean up the mess. The dead GEMs had been a horrible clean-up job. The stench of the burning bodies had choked Landfall City for days. He was glad that part was over. Getting the Wall back in shape was much easier than he thought it would be. There was sand everywhere, but that was much easier to deal with than mud. Not that there wasn't a lot of backbreaking work to do. The bad news was that the moat was now partly filled with sand. At this point, they weren't going to risk anyone trying to dig it back out. It was still deep enough to be serviceable.

Arti was out of the hospital and convalescing at the Phillips residence. She had almost died from blood loss and was lucky the arrow didn't cause permanent damage. She would be back on the Wall, eventually. That was a big relief to Arti. Griff had visited her in the hospital as soon as they would allow visitors. It was so good to see her out of danger. He had been beside himself with anxiety when he first saw Moose carrying her across the battlefield. Then he had rushed in to help, breaking his own rules.

Later, he lectured Jay and Kale about not following their retreat orders. They had just stared back at him incredulously until all three of them broke out laughing.

He intended to just check in on her, given that she had made it clear she didn't want to see him anymore. He should have stayed away but couldn't help himself. He remembered their conversation with a smile. "Just wanted to make sure you're okay and see if you need anything," Griff said stiffly. He was alarmed at her appearance. She was shockingly pale and looked completely exhausted. Her shoulder was heavily bandaged up. It was obviously painful from the way she was holding it.

"Come sit on the bed beside me," Arti said softly. Griff dutifully sat down. "I want to apologize for getting angry with you over whatever is going on with Tee. He's my only child, and his disappearance has torn me apart. I took that out on you and I'm sorry. I realized after giving it some thought that you must have a good reason for keeping whatever is going on secret. I know you. I should have realized you would tell me if you could." She smiled weakly and then said, "I would like to be friends again if you'll have me."

"You don't need to apologize," Griff said firmly.

"Yes, I do!" Arti said even more firmly, with color rising in her face. "Accept the apology with some grace instead of telling me I don't owe you one."

This was the Arti he knew and loved. "Yes, ma'am. I accept your apology. You are forgiven," Griff said softly with a half-smile breaking out on his face.

"That's better," she teased, her voice soft again. And then they spent the next two hours talking about everything and nothing at all until the nurse showed up and kicked him out.

Griff arrived early in the evening at the Phillips home. It had become a daily ritual. Pam greeted him at the door. "Good evening, Griff. Am guessing you're here to see Arti again," she said, smiling with just a hint of a smirk.

"Yes. Sorry to be interrupting your household, Pam," Griff said.

"You are never a problem, Griff. Arti loves your company and I'm rather fond of you myself," Pam said warmly.

They talked for hours until Griff finally blurted out. "There is something I've been wanting to ask you." He could feel his face reddening. "Well, I um, I mean we've been seeing a lot of each other and um." And then he was at a loss for words.

Arti looked at him with a mixture of pity and amusement. Then she said simply, "Yes, I will marry you." Griff was dumbstruck. This wasn't how this was supposed to happen. He sputtered and tried to formulate a response when she added, "That is what you were working yourself up to ask?"

Griff just stared at her for a moment and then stuttered, "Yes, but I mean, um."

"Griff, we're too old to be wasting time. Once I saw the real you, I fell in love. It's hard to tell, but I'm guessing you feel the same," Arti said with a smile.

At a loss for words, Griff lunged forward and kissed her, pulling her into a bear hug. "Ouch, I'm still healing, Griff," she said sharply but with good humor. "Goodness, you are going to have to work on the 'sweep me off my feet' part of this."

Griff grabbed her again, but more gently this time, and they both laughed with joy.

CHAPTER 9

RUINED

Grant Parsons was ruined. He alternated between bouts of deep depression and outrage. How could the survey's engineering team have missed the hidden bypass tunnel? How could they not see such an obvious way to protect the dam? His job as an anthropologist did not include making those kinds of assessments. This was entirely the fault of the engineers.

His bookie didn't care. Grant had gambled everything. More than everything. The worst part was that he had been so confident he borrowed from loan sharks. All his legal means for borrowing money had been exhausted. So, he utilized not so legal means. These people would not accept a bankruptcy filing. His debt would never be easily wiped away by the justice system. Those who lived in the shadows would take nothing less than his life if he didn't agree to do what they demanded.

Grant would be working hard the rest of his life with all of his money going toward paying interest on a debt he would never be able to pay off. The major financial institutions of the Commonwealth were all powerful. They had made borrowing money from unauthorized sources just as illegal as providing the funds. They completely controlled the business of credit.

While those who had loaned him the money could disappear, he didn't have the knowledge or means to do the same. The bastards would gladly provide evidence of his avoidance of borrowing from legal sources if he tried to turn them in.

What was even worse was that he was blacklisted. These people were well connected with the bookies. None of them would take his bets, even small ones. Perhaps it was a good thing he was stuck out here in the middle of nowhere. His luck would change. This run of bad luck would turn. He just had to be patient.

CHAPTER 10

ACQUIESENSE

Pluta was aggravated as he walked up the stone walkway toward a deck overlooking the lake behind him. It had taken three days aboard the governor's wasteful space yacht to get here. Three days his business managers were free to make idiotic decisions. He told Henry to inform his callers he was on a weeklong vacation. The man had just stared at him for a few moments. He finally accepted the explanation and simply said, "Yes, sir."

Surprising the unflappable Henry had provided Pluta with some entertainment to offset his foul mood that morning. After Henry recovered, he hurried about packing Pluta's personal effects. At least his butler could do simple jobs reasonably well. He had written out detailed instructions for Henry to deliver to his managers. He didn't trust any of them to execute those instructions correctly, but what other options did he have?

A bunch of idiots, he thought.

The worst part of all was not having access to his business records. Those were all contained in handwritten journals too voluminous to bring. He was told in no uncertain words that he could only bring one bag. He did discover once aboard ship that he had access to his bank accounts. So, he contented himself with watching the financial transactions for his businesses as they were taking place. He took detailed notes on these transactions so he could grill his idiot business managers when he returned.

He was pulled out of his ruminations by a cold voice, "Magistrate Pluta, welcome." Looking up, he saw two differently colored cold eyes staring at him. He kicked himself for not paying better attention on the walk up.

"Thank you for inviting me, Governor. It's been a very pleasant experience," Pluta replied while trying to smile convincingly. Her stark white hair and disturbing eyes made him uncomfortable. The trip so far had not been pleasant. But it had been illuminating. Pluta guessed most would be impressed with the conveniences provided by technology. He was disgusted. They indicated an indulgence in wasteful activities. The Commonwealth was obviously soft.

"Please join me for lunch," she said, sweeping her hand toward a small table on the deck.

After sitting down, she dispensed with small talk. "I know you dislike wasting time as much as I do. So let me get straight to the point. All of your plans to increase Commonwealth taxes and trade revenues have failed. I've watched Senator Cereo systematically outmaneuver you at every step along the way. What excuses do you have to offer?"

Pluta was not used to being treated this way. He hesitated, turned beat red, took a shallow breath to try to calm himself, and in a fit of panic decided to blame Jack. "It's not my fault your first minister can't do his part." He was trying to hide his fear with false bravado. It was clear from her expression that it wasn't working.

She nodded, as if verifying what she already knew. Then, after a few uncomfortable moments, she said, "My first minister did fail to perform. That doesn't excuse your incompetence. The plans relied on you having the situation on Arista in hand. You obviously had no clue what Cereo was doing and were completely unable to stop it once you did."

"I can hardly be blamed for a gladiator killing the emperor. I'm not responsible for Arena security. Who could have guessed that an archaic succession law would make the slave emperor? I will admit Cereo moved quickly to take advantage of the situation. For that, I am guilty," Pluta said after deciding she wanted a confession.

"Well, I'm glad you take some accountability. Perhaps there is hope for you after all," she said sarcastically. Then she just stared at him.

Finally, Pluta gathered his courage and said, "What can I do for you, Governor?"

"I hesitate to ask you to do anything." Then, pointing a finger at the waiter, she said, "I might as well ask Evans." For the first time, Pluta looked at their waiter and noticed the blank expression. He also noticed the thin silver collar around his throat. He recognized the former first justice with alarm. A sharp stab of fear hit him in the stomach as he realized the implied threat. He either performed or he would end up performing similar tasks to Evans.

Fear turned into anger, and he blurted out, "I have nothing to fear from you. I am a colonial citizen. The Commonwealth protects colonial citizens if they haven't broken any laws." Pluta immediately regretted losing his temper and saying something stupid. The woman made him crazy

She just stared at him some more. The long silence was extremely uncomfortable. Then she said, "I'm afraid you have broken Commonwealth laws. You paid a large bribe to the first justice to kidnap the ruler of one of our colonies. That violates the non-interference Edicts. Being a colonial citizen does not protect you from complicity in that crime."

He was trapped. There was nowhere to go except to accept his fate and do whatever the governor wanted. She would not have paid to have him travel here just to murder him. Would she? So, if she wasn't going to murder him, what did she want?

"I am at your disposal, Governor. What do you want me to do?" Pluta asked contritely.

She looked at him with an unblinking stare for another uncomfortable minute and then said, "I want to you to be dictator over all the colonies in Sector 27."

Pluta just stared back at her longer than was polite before recovering from the shocking statement. He swallowed hard and said, "I would be honored, Governor." He hesitated a few moments and said, "How am I going to accomplish this?"

"That's the first intelligent thing you've said. Recognizing your incompetence to figure this out on your own is a good start. Given your business success I assume you can implement better than you can plan," she said, then waited for his submissive head nod to continue, "We are going to set up your good friend Senator Cereo to fail and then you'll pick up the pieces."

"Nothing would give me greater pleasure, Governor," Pluta said with a real smile on his face.

"Now you're worrying me again, Magistrate. I don't care about your childish competition with Cereo. The only goal should be an increase in tax and trade revenues. Are you capable of maturity?" she said sarcastically.

"Yes, Governor. My apologies," Pluta said. She made him feel small. Something he hadn't felt since he was a child. It made him angry and desperate for revenge. He stopped himself from that train of thought when he realized she just offered him dictatorship of the sector. This was beyond his wildest dreams. Perhaps he could kowtow to this bitch long enough to gain control of the colonies. That damn bribe to get a Pacifica gladiator was the worst of disasters. She had banking records and the ship manifest to burn him anytime she chose.

Another long silence with her eyes locked on his. Then she said, "This is strictly private. Jack will have his role, but he has been told to support what Cereo is doing. He does not know you and I are having this conversation. You will remain in the background for now until I give you instructions. Instructions I expect to be followed to the letter."

"Yes, ma'am," was all he said.

Her face took on a thoughtful expression, and she said, "What assets do you have within Cereo's businesses or residences?"

"None. The man is incredibly private with his slaves. His business associates are heavily compensated. I have been unable to turn any of them," Pluta said with a straight face. He hoped she didn't see his lie. He did have one deeply entrenched operative. He was very proud of how he had accomplished it. The assets value was too great to reveal.

"Well, I guess that aligns with your general level of incompetence on anything not strictly business related. Keep trying. Even a fool gets lucky sometimes," she said dismissively.

"Yes, ma'am," he said, thinking it was the only thing he had said to her so far that hadn't resulted in demeaning criticism.

"Finish your lunch and then get back to Arista. Wait there until I tell you what to do. Do not take any actions against Cereo in the meantime." She stared at him until he nodded once more. Then she slid her chair back, and without saying goodbye, stood up and walked into the house.

He just sat there for a while, somewhat in shock. He felt he had come out of this better than expected. Being handed the dictatorship of the sector was better than any of his guesses at what this meeting had been about. The downside was that he didn't trust a word she said. He had to admit that Jack delivered everything he said he would deliver. So perhaps this would all work out in his favor. If the only thing that happened was the destruction of Cereo, he would be satisfied. So, given the situation, he needed to consider how he could increase the rate of receiving intelligence from his agent. It had to be done without jeopardizing the situation. Reports once a month were not sufficient, given what he had just been told. Something to ponder on his way back.

459

CHAPTER 11

VILLA CEREO

Against her better judgement, Bria felt at home. She and Gloria ended up on a country estate that reminded her of her father's ranch. June, the head housekeeper, had greeted them warmly that first day. She moved them into an older, medium-sized, no-frills home that was on the other side of a very large vegetable garden from the big house. Bria was told they would live with June and her father. They were each given two small but clean rooms next to each other.

June was an older woman with hazel eyes, short gray hair, and a slim figure. She obviously spent a good part of her day in the sun, as her skin was tanned to a caramel color. What struck Bria the most, however, was June's warmth. Although she was Bria's captor, she instantly sensed that June was a good person.

The next day, June sat the two of them down and said, "All slaves are well treated here. Senator Cereo expects everyone to do their job, but he doesn't allow mistreatment." She turned to Gloria and in a soft voice said, "I heard you had a horrible experience during your travel from Liberty. That won't happen here. If anyone makes you uncomfortable, tell me, and I'll take care of it."

"What is expected of us?" Bria asked defiantly.

"Nothing from you. We know you're not used to physical labor or housework. Gloria can continue her duties as your servant, and if she agrees, I could use some help redecorating the senator's villa. I heard she was responsible for redecorating Hastings Castle in Liberty. Senator Cereo told me reports from our ambassadors say it's spectacular. We aren't fancy here, but adding a little flair for the main house wouldn't hurt," June said, smiling.

"I'm going to need something to do. We aren't idle in Liberty," Bria said.

June frowned, considered what Bria said, and then offered, "This is a working villa. We grow our own food. There is a large vegetable garden, fruit trees, and a small vineyard the household staff manage. The villa also raises animals, but that's done at another location. Senator Cereo doesn't think our guests from Roma would appreciate the smell, so it's well away and downwind from the house," June said with a grin. "If you want to help me in the garden and vineyard, that would be greatly appreciated."

This is not what Bria had expected when she left the auction house. Senator Cereo had a calculating smile that didn't reach his eyes. The other man bidding for her seemed cold and angry, so she guessed she should be grateful he didn't win. Gloria had been quite upset when they were separated from Tee. He was going to the oft-mentioned Arena, which sounded horrible. Bria had to admit she felt safer with Tee around. Even when he was chained up. A few days after his murder spree, the new guards started making lewd comments. Tee firmly told them to stop being disrespectful. Even with him locked behind bars, the threat emanating from him was enough to change their behavior. She wished she knew what happened to him.

Life at Villa Cereo was predictable and peaceful. She rose early and joined Gloria, June, and June's father, Sage, for breakfast. Sage was an ancient but agile man. He was consistently polite and considerate. It was an easy household to blend into.

After breakfast, Gloria would go off with Sage on her main house redecoration project. Gloria had confidentially told Bria that the main house was plain and drab. That it desperately needed a makeover. Gloria was given a modest but adequate budget and, between herself and Sage, she was transforming the place. Gloria had slowly relaxed and was happy to be doing something she enjoyed. This helped lower Bria's anxiety over their situation.

Bria and June would spend mornings in the garden and afternoons doing house chores. Months of working in the garden had tightened her muscles and slightly darkened her pale skin. She actually had a tan, which delighted her. Not that it was all that noticeable to anyone but herself.

At first, June tried to give her tasks that were easy to perform. She soon learned that Bria could match her work output. They fell into an easy companionship that was comforting. Perhaps too comforting.

While June had informed them that she and her father were slaves, everyone treated them as if they owned the place. It was actually hard to believe any of the people she came into contact with were slaves. June mentioned one morning that she had known Senator Cereo since he was a baby. Another time she had casually mentioned that her son was Senator Cereo's valet. What was somewhat odd is that when talking about the senator, her voice was always warm. It was understandable that she might avoid speaking badly of her owner. Nothing good could come from that. But it seemed like she admired and cared for him. Perhaps her family held a special place within his slave hierarchy. It was a little suspicious, but then Bria knew she tended to be a bit paranoid.

She wasn't the only one with suspicions. One morning, a couple of weeks after Bria arrived, June said in an offhand manner, "Your Majesty, If I didn't know better, I would think you grew up on a farm."

They had visited the villa's livestock fields and yards the previous afternoon. Bria had asked a few questions. Thinking back on the conversation, she realized they were questions someone with livestock knowledge would ask.

Bria hesitated and then said, "Please call me Olivia. There is no need for formality in the garden." Bria paused and held up her dirt covered hands, smiling. "I told you we keep busy in Liberty."

June just nodded an acknowledgement. But her face clearly showed she had doubts. She liked that about June. Questions were common, but Bria's answers were never questioned. Her adoption of Grace perhaps had something to do with June's suspicions as well. While visiting the fields, one of the field hands told June, "The runt of the litter isn't going to work out." He pointed to a young Australian Sheppard. "She has a good temperament, but she's too stubborn to be useful."

"What's she stubborn about?" June asked.

"She's really smart and great at herding. But she herds the sheep where she thinks they ought to go. Not where anyone else wants them to go," he said with a smile. "Would be a good family dog if you want another one up at the villa?"

"I'll take her," Bria said quickly. She couldn't help herself. It was tricolor and beautiful. It appeared happy and friendly. She was used to having working dogs around her on the ranch. "I mean, I'll look after her if that's okay."

June had searched Bria's face until it was almost uncomfortable and then said, "Okay, she's yours." And that was that.

Late in the afternoon, June slipped away and went to the main house. She walked in the back door and wrapped her arms around Leo and then Caius. "I'm so glad you're both here. Sorry, but the two of you will have to stay here at the main house. I put Queen Olivia and Gloria in your bedrooms. I wanted to keep a close eye on them. Cara has blended in nicely with the household staff as well. She's staying in the women's bunkhouse."

"Is Cara still terrified of everyone?" Leo asked.

"She's better. But she still looks at your shoes when she's talking to you. Probably just the trauma of it all. Imagine being kidnapped and sold into slavery on another planet. Then she gets thrown into that Pacifica gladiator's cell as a prize. That he treated her kindly doesn't change the horror of being told what was expected of her. This was followed by a slow walk to his cell. She was a simple farm girl before all of this," June said with concern.

Caius nodded and asked, "How is Queen Olivia going to take our story?"

June thought for a few moments before answering. "She's smart, courageous, stubborn, and levelheaded. The big issue is going to be trust. Living with Grandpa and I these past few months will help. I think she does trust the two of us for the most part. When it's clear we're slaves in name only, she may feel she's been lied to. That won't help. She's a good person. We should eventually get her to a good place. My concern is that we don't seem to have much time."

"You're right, things are quickly spinning out of control," Leo said. Then turning to Caius he asked, "If we get agreement on a plan, can we delay the Commonwealth?"

Caius shook his head slightly in the negative and said, frowning, "If we get agreement on the plan proposed to the governor we can only slow its implementation a little. Anything else is going to cause her to change course. I can't predict what that new course would be."

"Let's meet with Queen Olivia in the garden tomorrow morning. Since you're going to expose everything, we need to be careful we don't get overheard by the house staff," June said.

Bria had gotten into the habit of taking Grace on a long walk every morning before breakfast. Instead of her usual path, she decided to go take a peek at the main house. Last night, the main house had been glowing brightly, which was new. She wondered if that meant Senator Cereo was in residence. As she rounded a corner, she almost ran into Leo. "Excuse me, Your Majesty. I didn't see you."

Bria was startled, but recognized Leo from the auction house. He had been polite but distant, which she had appreciated. "My apologies as well. It's Leo, right?" When he nodded yes, she said, "I'm not used to seeing people out early in the morning."

"Well, it appears we both enjoy an early walk. I find it clears my head for the day," Leo said conversationally.

There was an awkward silence until Grace padded over to Leo and gave him a good sniff. He held his hand out to her, and she licked it. Bria couldn't have been more surprised. She wasn't sure why, but she had expected Grace to dislike Leo. Grace had strong opinions about people. She mostly liked everyone, but those she didn't, Bria had learned to be cautious of.

Leo bent over and petted Grace for a few moments and then said, "Senator Cereo came in last night and would like to talk to you this morning.

My mother, June, thought right after breakfast would make sense."

"I look forward to it," Bria said, cutting off further conversation. She had to stop and motion for Grace to follow her, as she was obviously enjoying Leo's attention. I'll never figure that dog out, Bria thought.

Breakfast started out uncomfortably as Bria waited for June to bring up the morning meeting with Senator Cereo. After everyone had served themselves, June said, "Senator Cereo came in last night and asked to meet with you this morning. I hope you're okay with that."

"If he's here to set me free, then I'll meet with him. If it's anything else, he might as well go back to Roma," Bria said briskly. She had given the meeting quite a bit of thought since she had run into Leo. She decided she needed to make a strong statement about her displeasure at being held against her will.

June looked at her with sympathy for a few moments and said, "That's a reasonable stance, Olivia. Can't say I would feel any different if I were in your shoes." She then took a deep breath and let it out. "Would you do me a personal favor and just listen to what he has to say?"

Bria looked at her for a long while, thinking it over. June had been nothing short of wonderful to her, given the situation. While it galled her to give in, this was a small request given the relationship they had built. "Okay, I'll listen. But I won't promise to be polite or compromising," Bria said sternly.

June grinned and said, "I would expect nothing less."

Senator Cereo was sitting with Leo on a bench up against one of the covered garden boxes. It was a popular place for private conversations. Bria and June sat down across from them. "Good morning, Your Majesty."

"Good morning, Senator," Bria said coldly. Grace was acting odd. After sitting down, she pressed her body against Bria's leg and growled once low in her throat. Grace was looking at the senator while she did this, which confirmed Bria's opinion of the senator.

Senator Cereo smiled grimly, then took a deep breath and let it out. "I know you want your freedom and to be allowed to return to Liberty. That is our desire as well," he said, motioning around to Leo and June. "However, simply letting you go at this time has serious adverse consequences for three planets. To explain all of this, I have to reveal secrets about my family that have been kept for thirty-five years. Secrets that could destroy us. I'm going to trust that you'll keep them in confidence regardless of how this plays out."

"I can't promise that. I will do what is right for my people. If that involves revealing information detrimental to you and your family, I won't hesitate to do it," Bria answered with her head held high and a defiant look in her eyes.

Caius hesitated a moment, and with the corners of his mouth upturned slightly, he said, "Well, I suppose that's fair. June claims you are a good person, and I trust her instincts. We'll just have to trust you." Taking a deep breath he said, "The story starts fifty-one years ago when Leo and I were born..."

Two hours later, Bria was in shock. That was the only word for it. Everything she thought she knew about the senator, Leo, and June had been upended. If any of it could be believed. She did admit it went a long way toward explaining the oddities she had seen. Sage and June's authority. The way servants were treated. The affection for Senator Cereo June had been unable to hide.

The story made all of these make sense. That Tee had somehow become Emperor of Arista was simply impossible to believe. Could this all be some kind of elaborate ruse? The wonderful news, again if it could be believed, was that her father had defeated Lord Druango, who had been backed by Commonwealth funded mercenaries.

Eliminating the threat from Lord Druango and his cronies was almost too good to be true. That her father supposedly hung the whole lot of them saddened her. Not because of who had been executed, but how she knew those deaths would haunt her father. She knew he would feel he had failed somehow. The hope that her father and Olivia were safe lifted her spirits. If the war was won, why hadn't they admitted the wrong person was kidnapped?

This meant there must still be a threat to the kingdom. It was possible they were simply concerned for her welfare and waiting to play that card. If Tee truly was the emperor, she couldn't imagine him doing anything other than letting her go. If everything is true, then the threat from the Commonwealth was real and the answer to all her questions. Only time would solve this mystery.

Until then, she would follow her father's advice. "If your enemy makes a mistake, don't correct them."

"You must have some plan in mind?" Bria asked.

"Any plan for dealing with this must ultimately come from you and Tee. You are the legal decision makers for Liberty and Arista. I am happy to share ideas once we can include Tee in our discussions. For now, I would like your agreement to travel to Roma. Gloria will also be asked to join us. She can go home as soon as we can secure transportation,"

"I need to give all of this some thought," she finally said. "Can we meet again tomorrow?"

"That's fair," Senator Cereo said. "Your head has to be spinning from our crazy story. If you have questions, just walk over to the main house. We will answer any questions you have. Just remember that the house servants think we're reasonably nice slave owners. They don't know we are anti-slavery revolutionaries." He smiled at Bria, stood, and started to walk past her toward the main house.

Grace stood up and approached him. He held out his hand, and she gave it a sniff. Then she licked it and sidled up to him. After a few pets, she turned back toward the bench where Senator Cereo had been sitting and growled low again. Crazy dog, she thought. Crazy or not, she seems to like Senator Cereo after all. In Bria's mind, this was no small thing.

"Maybe there's something in the planter. Grace doesn't normally act like that," June said. "I'll have someone clean it out later."

As they walked away, a small figure hidden under the tarp shifted slightly. Hours of lying motionless had left Cara stiff and sore. That was all forgotten in her excitement. She knew this might be a place they would meet to talk and had decided to gamble. This was better than her wildest dreams.

Now what to do with the information?

Should she go directly to the Commonwealth with it?

If so, how can I do that safely?

Should she sell the information to Pluta and let him go to the Commonwealth?

Given what she had just learned about Pluta, should she blackmail him?

Maybe a combination of both?

She would think carefully through her alternatives before acting. This was the opportunity of a lifetime. One thing was certain. She needed to escape and be well hidden before revealing anything. She had dealt with men like Pluta many times. They had a habit of killing those they thought knew more than they should. She would need to disappear for good.

Turning to more immediate concerns, she gritted her teeth. That damned dog almost ruined everything. Cara hated dogs. They were simpering parasites. She should have poisoned the mutt weeks ago, when it was obvious it didn't like her. Her motto had always been to eliminate anything that could cause a problem.

However, at this point, she needed to lie low and escape as soon as possible. Her escape would have to wait until the courier showed up. They had an extraction agreement. Pluta knew nothing about that alternative plan. Cara always had a backup plan. Then she smiled again, thinking about what she would do with the enormous sum of money that was surely coming her way.

CHAPTER 12

MEMORIAL

Griff and Del were sitting in a quiet corner of the Blue Heron having a whiskey. Del took a sip and asked, "You hungry?"

"You buying?" Griff responded in his typically blunt manner.

"You get the drinks, and I'll get dinner," Del replied.

"Then I'm hungry," Griff said.

Del smiled seeing his old friend's brusk manner return. Griff had gotten almost solicitous after his emotional outburst in the committee meeting. He was embarrassed that he had lapsed like that in front of everyone. Perhaps he needed more sleep. That had certainly been lacking the past few weeks. It had touched him when Griff seemed to care that he had hurt his feelings.

Del had been brought up in a strict household where lying was simply unacceptable. He had prided himself on honesty as a young man and resented the circumstances that led him to develop the ability to lie convincingly. He put that talent to use frequently these days. He knew the lies were necessary, but it bothered him anyway.

"Have you given our earlier conversation any more thought?" Del asked.

"I've been thinking about it all day." Griff shifted in his chair and leaned forward. "In battle, sometimes you just have to say screw it and charge. You might not have enough knowledge of your enemy. They might be uphill of you and well protected. Command might be clueless. They usually are. Sometimes the only answer is an immediate all-out charge," Griff said.

"Well, I haven't thought of it in those terms, but it's an appropriate analogy. What about asking command for direction first?" Del said, taking the analogy further, knowing what Griff's opinion was of asking for direction.

Griff actually smiled. "You know my opinion of whether it's better to ask for permission or forgiveness." Griff hesitated, then said, "In this case, it's a reasonable question. Like Hestie's secret, this one has dire consequences if the wrong people find out." Being in public, they really couldn't discuss this openly. But Griff had cleverly delivered his decision on the difficult question posed earlier.

"So, you agree we keep this to ourselves and perhaps even execute without telling the rest of our group," Del said, thinking that even referring to the committee was something best left unsaid in public.

"Yes," Griff said, and then asked, "I know Quinn is fully briefed but how many more need to know?"

"Hestie and four more. They will all need extensive training. I already know who they are. As you can guess, they're already doing work in the Dungeon." Griff had dubbed the secret shielded tunnel system under the university the 'Dungeon.' The name had caught on. Del continued. "If we decide to execute, then a total of twelve more will be required. The skills needed for those responsibilities can be trained quickly. You and I can fill in if we run short," Del said.

Griff grunted and said, "I don't like keeping this from them. But I'm convinced it's the right thing to do." They both examined their whiskeys for a few moments until Griff asked, "I heard Hestie is back from Apple Valley."

"Yes, and thank God for that. She's as smart, perhaps smarter than her brother. She just isn't as obvious about it." Del said.

"Perhaps she just has a healthier ego," Griff said with a grin.

"Contrary to what some people think, Quinn does not have an oversized ego. He just loves to discuss what he knows and thinks everyone else is equally excited and knowledgeable," Del said. He had been getting progressively more paternalistic with Quinn. His earlier frustrations had turned into admiration for the boy's simple outlook on life. He identified with how being the smartest kid in class can create jealousy and resentment. He had been that kid once.

"Knock it off," Griff said loudly, glaring at him. "Stop being so touchy." The glare softened a little, and he continued in lower voice, almost a whisper, which was good because people had turned around and were staring with worried looks at them, "This isn't like you. Besides, I like the kid. He's honest, hardworking, and never complains. Unlike some people I know," Griff said, referring to the fact that Del had been giving in to a little grousing lately.

Griff was right. He needed to get ahold of himself. Anxiety over what was going to happen to the people of Pacifica was going to disable him if he didn't toughen up. Del just nodded in agreement.

Dinner was served, and they moved onto more mundane topics. Griff was a good friend, Del thought. He was uncomplicated. He wasn't full of himself like so many of his colleagues in academia. Best of all, he told simple truths. Sometimes they were truths you didn't want to hear, but they were truths.

Hestie was walking with Quinn to the Phillips house. She was going there to fulfill her obligations to Grammy. There had already been a small gathering in Apple Valley with the list of people Grammy said were family. Grammy did not limit her interpretation of family to blood relatives. She and Quinn were examples of that.

She was really nervous about seeing Jay. Scared she might give in. The surprise meeting at the Blue Heron before she left for Apple Valley had shaken her badly. She had barely made it out the door before she broke down in tears. She had held onto Diana and sobbed just outside the tavern until she grew concerned that Jay might come outside. Then she just turned and walked away. And then there was Grammy's letter.

"Did you finish your simulation?" Quinn asked, pulling her out of her internal turmoil.

Hestie took a breath to clear her head and said, "I did, but we didn't match. There is something wrong with our initial conditions. I noticed that when the target has unusually low density, our simulations differ by a set value. It's a three-dimensional matrix of whole numbers, so I think it's built into one of the two programs to jettison unrealistic locations."

"Okay, I'll take a look at it after Grammy's service," Quinn said, frowning.

Hestie knew the frown was sadness over Grammy, not her simulation results. "It's not a service, Quinn. Grammy was very clear that she wanted laughter, not tears."

Quinn looked sideways at her for a moment and then smiled with all his teeth and said, "I don't think Grammy is going to get what she wants today."

Hestie was once again surprised by her brother. It was easy, even for her, to fall into the belief that he was socially clueless. You could even convince yourself that he was terminally happy because he didn't recognize what was going on around him. Then he would surprise you with an insightful comment. It was good to see his smile back in full force.

The front door opened, and Pam greeted them with a smile, shooing them inside. Then they were surrounded by everyone. Arti wrapped Hestie in a tight hug and said, "It's so good to see you again, Hestie. I can't thank you enough for looking after my mother. I got a letter from her sent a few days before she died telling me how much she enjoyed having you there."

"It was my pleasure. She really didn't need much help. You know how independent she was. I think she helped me more than I helped her," Hestie said. Off to one side, she saw Jay looking anxious. To avoid having to talk to him, and also to get the hard part over with, she said, "Would everyone sit down? I have something Grammy wrote that she asked me to read."

At first they looked surprised, and then that knowing look invaded everyone's face. Hestie's face brightened slightly, and she said, "Well you know she had to get in the last word." This caused everyone to laugh. Then satisfied this was starting out the right way, Hestie read Grammy's letter.

Dear Family,

I felt the need to write this so I can lecture all of you on the need to stop crying. Remember all the good times instead. I asked Hestie to gather everyone together so she could deliver this.

I have had an incredible life. No person could be more fortunate than to have the love of our dear departed Pop. I'm likely sitting with Tia on the front porch right now, both of us laughing at one of Pop's ridiculous stories. Who could have had better children than Arti and Hugh? Only Ansen, Tee, Pete, or Tia might have been an improvement. In addition to my blood relatives, I've had the joy of expanding my family with Hestie, Quinn, and Diana. Some of my happiest and most fulfilling memories were watching over my grandchildren, which includes the three of them. Lots of laughs, a few tears, and I thank God for all of it.

Now none of this means I feel my work is done quite yet. To finish off my worldly responsibilities, I've left each of you a short note. Yes, one more piece of advice from Grammy. Please think about what I have to say. I expect you to follow my advice. I will ask about it later.

Love you all Dearly,

Grammy

Well, if her intention was to get everyone to stop crying, she failed miserably, Hestie thought as she looked around the room with tears streaming down her own face. Only Grammy was capable of lecturing and advising at her own funeral. It made her smile. Smiles slowly infected the room and then the 'crazy Grammy' stories started. Perhaps Grammy's letter did have it right.

Handing out the letters caused another round of tears. It was no surprise that she had letters for Arti, Diana, and Quinn. The surprise was that she had letters for Jay, and of all people, Griff. Arti and Griff's engagement happened after her passing. How did she know? Nobody opened theirs in public. More than a few snuck off to see what she had to say. They all knew their letters would contain something very personal and private. Grammy knew everybody's deepest fears and secrets and offered advice on all of it.

Hestie opened hers the day Grammy died. It was a good thing she did because she would have melted if Jay were anywhere around. Hestie had found Grammy tucked into bed with a smile on her face. At least that's how it looked to her. Late in the afternoon that same day, Hestie went down to the beach and, sitting on Grammy's bench, opened her letter.

Dearest Hestie,

Have loved all of our time together. The deep conversations and the silly ones. You have always been wise beyond your years. I have a special place in my heart for you. For you, I have a simple request. Look after them for me.

You have never needed much advice from me. But you know I never pass up the chance to interfere. Look after yourself first. Don't make life decisions based on what you think is best for others.

Follow your heart and not your head.

Love Grammy

P.S. That Jay is a keeper.

How did she know?! Perhaps Tee or someone else had told her they were dating. She had wondered why a letter had been left for Jay. She had been tempted more than once to open it. But no, that would be a violation of not only Jay but Grammy as well. It had been horrible the last time she saw Jay. When he pulled Tee's insignia out and handed it to Diana, she almost lost it. It was just like Jay to be thoughtful. A tremendous gift for Tee's mother. God, she loved that man.

Grammy was spooky. At an early age, Hestie had called out Grammy for her fortune telling. She would hold court at the table on the front porch with her deck of cards and give them all their fortunes. Her fortune telling was always vague enough that they would invariably come true.

"You're just making all this up," Hestie had said accusingly.

"Well, don't go spoiling it for the others, Hestie," Grammy had scolded her. "They are having fun with it and so am I." Then Grammy had winked at her and said, "It will be our secret."

Not for the first time, Hestie wondered if she was wrong about Grammy's fortune telling. Her predictions always seemed to have a lesson embedded in them. They always did seem to come true. Grammy seemed to just know things. Jay had been on the top of her mind the whole time she had been taking care of Grammy. One benefit of taking time off of school to help with Grammy was that it gave her time to think.

Perhaps there was some truth to the old adage that distance made the heart grow fonder. She wasn't sure her heart could have gotten any fonder of Jay. How did Grammy know Jay was on top of her mind? That she was trying to come to a decision. Or more accurately, that she was trying to reverse a decision. She was privately worried she wasn't being rational. She had definitely been swept off her feet and that was scary, which complicated things.

Diana approached her, wiping her eyes, "You already opened yours, didn't you?"

Hestie hesitated a moment and then said, "I did, the day she died."

"Did you follow her advice?" Diana asked with a humorous smirk. A glimmer of the old happy Diana showing through.

"No. Not yet anyway," Hestie admitted. Then she wondered why she qualified her answer the way she did. Then, of all people, Jay walked up.

"Thank you for delivering the letter, Hestie," Jay said. Then he smiled and added, "She just had to get one more piece of good advice in."

"Did you open yours?" Diana asked.

Jay's smile faltered a little and then glancing at Hestie he said, "Yes I did. She cautioned me to be patient. She said the best things in life are worth waiting for."

Hestie's stomach lurched. More Grammy spookiness, she thought, as a tickle raced up and down her spine. She steeled herself and said, "Well sometimes you do have to move on. You shouldn't wait for something that's never going to happen."

Jay smiled grimly, then continuing to look directly at Hestie, he said, "I think Grammy's right. Some things are worth waiting for." Turning to Diana, he said, "It's been nice to see you again, Diana. Glenn said you're meeting at the Blue Heron this Friday and asked if I wanted to come along. Will probably see you there." Then, nodding at Hestie, he walked off.

They watched him walk away in silence. Then Diana turned to Hestie and pulled her into a hug. They held onto each other for a while, soaking in each other's friendship. Diana stepped back and said, "I have no idea what's gotten into you. I'm on your side, even if I think you're making horrible decisions. I know you're going to drop out of Friday night now that Jay is coming. I'm hoping you will explain it to me someday."

Hestie's eyes welled up. Jay had intentionally brought up the Blue Heron to give her an opportunity to avoid him. Thoughtful. Just like him. Her heart was truly broken. Looking at Diana, she thought she had the best friend a person could have. She settled herself and said in all honesty, "I hope I can explain it someday, too."

Sovereign

CHAPTER 13

BLACKMAIL

Pluta was excited, frightened, and angry all at once. His initial elation at getting Cara placed in Cereo's villa had slowly turned into agonizing frustration. It had been months, and the contract was not yet complete. He supposed this was his fault. He had insisted Caius and Vincentius be assassinated together. The scheduling obligations of the Senate and those of the Second Legion did not naturally line up. Hard to blame Cara for that.

Now he was being blackmailed. Or was it her way of proving she had a valuable source of information? That had been her claim. Her documentation of a large number of his questionable business practices would cause significant trouble in the right hands. Civil lawsuits at a minimum. With a prosecutor who was in the pocket of Cereo, he would stand a good chance of being convicted of fraud. Either could ruin him. She never threatened him in the letter. She didn't need to.

She claimed she had information on Cereo that was even more damaging than what she had on him. That was exciting. The frightening news was that it intersected in some way with the governor. She claimed she could sell the information to the Commonwealth for a fortune. After his visit to A27, he was committed to having as little interaction with the governor as possible. Trying to sell information to her would likely backfire in dramatic fashion. She would assume he should just give it to her. It was also possible that Cara would reveal to the governor that he had been hiding things. His blood ran cold at the thought.

Cara was a highly respected and prohibitively expensive assassin. Within the criminal world she had a reputation for efficiency and integrity. As Pluta started to calm down, he realized his anger had quite a bit to do with her competence. She had disappeared with no notice from the villa. Then she had compiled and documented evidence from public sources on his indiscretions. After receiving her letter, Pluta had searched frantically for a few days before giving up. It wasn't even clear she was still on Arista. Cara had covered her tracks well.

A bank account had been provided, and his only decision was whether to deposit the demanded amount or not. She had given him ten days to comply. It infuriated him to pay a fortune for something sight unseen. Objectively, he knew he had to pay. She had left him no options to negotiate or maneuver. Perhaps the worst part was knowing he could never extract retribution for the way he was being treated. Rational people did not try to have top level assassins assassinated. They had their own little inbred world, and the likely result was ending up dead. If you were lucky.

CHAPTER 14

DIPLOMACY

Bria and Gloria arrived at the Palatium late in the day. It had been a tiring trip, but their first view of the Palatium shocked them out of their lethargy. The building was enormous. It sat on a hill and was a mix of Roman columns and fortress-like walls. It had clearly been designed to provide security while maintaining an elegant visage. Tee came out to personally greet their coach. His security team was obviously irritated by this. Bria thought their concern a little ridiculous given the large number of armed men guarding the entrance to the Palatium. If anyone got past all of that, they would still have to deal with Tee. She couldn't imagine anyone brave or stupid enough to do that.

Gloria flew out of the carriage once it stopped and wrapped Tee in a tight hug. She told Bria that Tee reminded her of her brother. She just felt safer when he was around. It was strange that Gloria, who was generally suspicious of men, was so trusting of Tee. The poor woman had been through hell.

Orphaned at sixteen, it had not taken long for her vulnerability to be noticed. A local pimp kidnapped her and took her to a neighboring kingdom, where he sold her into prostitution. Gloria's last name was Peters. Her brother, the now Captain Peters, had searched frantically for her. But at thirteen it was well beyond his ability to do more than search their hometown. Starving, he had joined the military to get enough to eat. But he never forgot her. He searched for her everywhere he was deployed.

Bria's father had noticed Sergeant Peters taking a few days off every time they deployed somewhere new. Otherwise, he never took leave. Worried about what might be going on, he had him followed. It turned out Peters was searching for his sister. Having sisters himself, Perry took an interest and used his surveillance network to track down what had happened to Gloria. Although slavery had always been illegal in Liberty, she was basically a slave in Druango serving the high and mighty. Once found, Perry gave the then Lieutenant Peters permission to take a small group of volunteer rangers into enemy territory and rescue her. Once freed, her father talked Olivia into taking the woman on as a servant. So perhaps Gloria saw Tee as a replacement for her savior brother.

"It's good to see you both," Tee said warmly, turning to catch Bria's eye.

"Are you really the emperor?" Gloria asked.

Tee grinned and shaking his head in disbelief looked back to Gloria said, "That's what they tell me Gloria. It does seem crazy, doesn't it?" Disengaging with Gloria, he held his hand out toward Bria and said, "Let's go inside and get you both settled. We have a private apartment for the two of you. If you are up to it, we can have dinner later and catch up. I'm sure you have as many stories to tell as I do."

Leo showed up the next morning and escorted Bria to a covered roof top patio with a view of Roma's city center below them. It was magnificent.

"Tee is finishing his morning exercises and thought you might want breakfast before we begin," Leo said.

"Is he going to join us?" she asked.

"No, he's been up for hours already. If he doesn't exhaust himself first, we can't keep him engaged in conversations. Says he's always done this," Leo said, shaking his head.

"He exercised constantly in his cell on the trip here. It got on Gloria and my nerves enough that we had to get him to agree to limit it to certain hours," Bria said, smiling.

Contrary to what Leo had just told her, Tee and Senator Cereo walked in.

"Good morning Your Majesty. I hope you were comfortable last night," the senator said, smiling.

"Gloria and I were both very comfortable. The apartment is more than adequate," Bria said with a neutral expression. The apartment was more extravagant than Olivia's quarters in Hastings Castle. Given the poverty she had seen in her travels on Arista, the extravagance sickened her. Tee had expressed the same thoughts at dinner. Bria had stayed up late with Gloria and Tee, trading stories. Their stories were bland compared to the craziness Tee had been through.

"If you're okay getting started, I would like to reveal more of my conversation with the governor," Caius said.

"You haven't told me everything yet?" Bria asked.

"I haven't told you or Tee everything yet," Caius replied.

Bria looked at Tee and saw he was angry as well. "This is unacceptable. The deceptions have to stop if you hope to include Liberty in your schemes."

Caius held up his hands in a peaceful gesture and said, "Agreed. The secrecy needs to stop. Please accept my sincere apologies to you both for keeping some things hidden. If the governor got wind of what I'm trying to do, it would doom all three planets. Hear what I have to say and then decide what you both want to do."

For the next few hours, Bria listened in amazement to Cereo's story of discovering her kidnapping and thwarting the governor's plans. When he got to the part of the story where he said he had promised a marriage between Tee and Olivia, she had to stop him.

"What gives you the right to promise anything that has to do with Liberty?" she asked, glaring at him.

"Nothing gives me that right. What gives me the motivation is a deeply personal abhorrence of slavery. While abolition is years away on Arista, anything I can do to prevent it elsewhere is something I consider to be an obligation."

He said this with such intensity that Bria tended to believe him. She softened a little, realizing she had her own secret, and said, "I can't fault your motivation. Please continue."

When he was done explaining all that had happened, Bria was speechless. She was worn out by the intricate political intrigues. It wasn't in her nature to be manipulative. But it seemed every path out of this involved playing a role that went against her nature. She wished Olivia were here to handle all of this. Bria, a simple country girl, was a poor substitute for Olivia, the rightful Queen of Liberty. The saving grace was that Prince Justin and Chief Justice Roberts would be here tomorrow.

After that, her only role would be to report on what she knew. She didn't have the authority to make decisions. Realizing this, she calmed herself and said, "Your entire strategy has been a series of delays. You don't have a plan that results in freedom for the three planets."

"Guilty. I don't have a plan. The reason I think delay tactics might work is that the governor doesn't care what happens to Sector 27 after she leaves. This is a career steppingstone for her. If we can figure out a way to make her successful without forcing our populations into slavery, we've won. She will leave and we'll hopefully get a better governor. That's the best I've come up with," Cereo said, clearly exasperated with their situation.

"Why is Pacifica in danger? My understanding is that we have been designated as a pre-industrial civilization and must be left alone," Tee asked.

"With another governor, there might not be an immediate danger from the Commonwealth. But it's just a matter of time before the GEMs break through. The Commonwealth would be satisfied with letting it all play out and cleansing the planet for its nature resources. However, Pacifica's human capital is seen as having high value. Heavy planet slave labor and mercenary armies are lucrative. Pacifica's military capabilities would be in high demand. The governor is motivated to find a way to step in before the GEMs succeed," Caius explained.

"Your plan is to help the Commonwealth turn us all into slaves?" Tee said, clearly angered.

"If we do nothing, that is exactly what the Commonwealth will do. I am hoping we can agree on a plan to keep as many people free as possible. If the Commonwealth doesn't need to force us to do what they want, they won't care how it's done. This is about power and money. A hard life for many? Yes. If we can stay in control, it's one that can evolve over time into the free societies we all want," Caius said.

Tee thought about that for a few moments and then said, "I'm not sure how I'm going to talk my government into naming me king."

"You won't have to. We'll go to Pacifica and reveal the reality of the situation to them. They already know the GEMs are going to break through. Our proposal would be that they accept a constitutional monarchy. That means you're a figurehead for the Commonwealth to justify naming Pacifica a colony. They view democracies as barbaric remnants of the past. They believe they are dangerous to the Commonwealth. If successful, your form of government stays intact. Unlike your status on Arista, you would be king in name only," Caius explained.

"Your plan is to announce a betrothal, but delay the marriage as long as possible?" Tee said.

"Tee, it's our plan. You both have more control of it than I do," Caius said, looking back and forth at them both. "But you're correct. My proposal is to do exactly that. I will do everything I can to delay or change the plan so the two of you aren't forced into marriage. If I fail, you both need to accept that the marriage will happen," Cereo said firmly. "I don't want you to think I can work miracles. The governor is capable of all sorts of horrors. The reality is that we may all regret whatever decision we make."

Later that afternoon, Bria was sitting by the side of an enormous pool with Tee. They were watching three children squealing in delight and splashing each other. They were Dobler's grandchildren. Tee had been teaching them to swim. His rule was that they weren't allowed in the pool unless he was with them. Tee had been walking Bria back to her apartment when the three children spied them.

"Tee, Tee, Tee," they clamored and came running. The eldest eventually asked in a pleading voice, "Can you watch us swim?"

Holding the smallest who had jumped into his arms, with another hanging on his leg, Tee laughed and said, "Sure, let's do that." Turning to Bria, he said, "Do you like to swim?"

"I do, but I think I'll just help you watch them," Bria said, smiling. She had met Dobler and Jessie earlier that morning and heard their tale. They couldn't say enough good things about Tee. The story of him being an imprisoned gladiator under Dobler's control, then suddenly becoming emperor, had terrified Dobler. The story of their family being reunited brought tears to Bria's eyes.

"I should have known better," Dobler said. "I saw his character every day at the Arena. When he realized the children were terrified of him, he made a point of spending time with them. They adore him. I'm ashamed that I doubted him."

Sitting next to Tee by the pool, Bria exhaled, letting go of her anxiety. She realized she was enjoying herself. Tee was easy to be around. His natural optimism helped her control her anxiety. Like Dobler, she was a little ashamed of herself. She didn't fully trust Tee. She liked him. She respected him. She even admired him. And being completely honest with herself, she was attracted to him. Handsome with the body of Hercules wasn't the main attraction, although it didn't hurt. It was his toughness mixed with empathy and compassion.

But could she ever fully trust someone who had so thoroughly fooled her?

Maybe it was the explosive and efficient way he killed the three guards. She had grown up surrounded by soldiers and had often been in military camps. She had seen death. She had seen a number of horrible things she wished she hadn't. But she had never seen anything like that. It was over in the blink of an eye.

While Bria was still in shock trying to understand what she had just witnessed, Tee calmly unlocked the door to Theo's cell and murdered him as well. Not that humanity would miss any of them. They were animals. It was better described as justice than murder. But, at that instant, she truly believed she and Gloria were next. The experience still made her wary of Tee, and she felt guilty about it.

The three of them had shared quite a bit of time talking during the weeks of space travel. There was really nothing else to do. Tee explained what life was like on Pacifica. His family, joining the Guard, what they did for fun, and the latest GEM war. He explained that everyone was a warrior. This included women and children. He talked about the role of Wall Archers. He seemed very proud of his mother.

Pacifica had a republic form of government, which was odd and interesting. She had been taught these forms of government always devolved into tyranny. It certainly didn't sound like tyranny. What did sound horrible was the never-ending war with the GEMs. While Bria had been subjected to war most of her life, the enemy was human. Their enemies were interested in control and owning property, not committing genocide. She could understand how that environment might produce the sort of violent outburst she had seen from him.

"Do you trust them?"

The question from Tee jerked her out of her inner thoughts. Bria smiled and then said in mock seriousness, "I'm not sure I trust you." They both laughed, and she felt another twinge of guilt at the partial truth in her reply.

"Timmy stop! No running on the side of the pool," Tee said in a deep voice. The boy slowed to a quick jerky walk. "That boy pushes all the rules," Tee said with obvious affection. Then, with a serious look, he turned back to Bria and said, "Honestly, you've been at their villa for almost a year. Do you trust them?"

Bria thought about that for a few moments and then said, "I trust Sage and June. I'm convinced they're good people. Whether Leo and Caius are trustworthy, I don't know. June loves the two of them dearly, but you know how a mother's love works."

Tee nodded. "I'm in a similar situation with Forti. I'm obligated to trust him. I know that sounds weird, but he is a member of the Guard and trust in each other is absolute. Forti trusts the two of them. I believe his trust is real. I've also come to believe Forti is a good judge of character."

"But you don't trust them yourself?" Bria asked.

Tee hesitated, clearly thinking about how to answer that. "I have no reason not to trust them. The situation with the GEMs on Pacifica leaves me with no other option. If I don't support their plan, I believe my people are lost," Tee said. "You and Liberty are not in an immediately dire situation. I will completely understand if you decide to take a less risky approach for Liberty."

Tee's head snapped back toward the three children as sounds of distress came from that direction, "Timmy! What did I tell you about sisters?" Tee said firmly. Timmy had been splashing water in the older sister's face with a little bit too much exuberance.

"I have to protect them," Timmy said, looking down.

"Who do you have to protect them against?" Tee asked.

"Everyone. Including me," Timmy said, clearly reciting something Tee had obviously made him say more than a few times before.

Bria smiled. That was an interesting way to correct Timmy. Tee was going to be a good father someday. She went back to the difficult question she needed to resolve. They sat in silence for several minutes until Bria came to a decision. Tee's concern for the inhabitants of her planet in light of what that would mean for Pacifica is what swayed her. She appreciated that Tee didn't claim trust when it was clearly in his best interests to do so.

Instead, he gave an honest answer.

When Prince Justin and Chief Justice Roberts showed up tomorrow, she would support Cereo's plan. Not that she really had a vote, of course. She was Bria, not Queen Olivia.

Bria broke the silence and said, "Even if Leo and Caius are trustworthy, I'm certain the first minister is not."

"Amen to that," Tee replied.

The next morning, the first minister opened the meeting by saying, "I hope we can resolve the current conflict between Arista and Liberty. Given Arista has a new emperor, perhaps there is an opportunity for a resolution that benefits you both. I want to remind everyone that my role is one of mediation. The Commonwealth has no wish to interfere in the internal affairs of its colonies."

And if you believe that… thought Bria. She took on her best impersonation of royal disdain and said, "I will go no further with this meeting until I've had the chance to consult privately with Prince Justin and Chief Justice Roberts."

Prince Justin came quick on her heels with, "It's outrageous that my queen has to ask permission to speak with her uncle. While we don't want war, we are highly skilled at it. We will stop at nothing to gain her freedom."

"We are not going to release Queen Olivia until His Eminence is convinced she is safe. Lord Druango was very clear in his belief that you Prince Justin do not have her best interests at heart," Caius said, glaring at the prince while pointing his finger. Tee nodded in agreement.

"I ask both of you to please step back and remember why we are here. Recriminations are not going to achieve the result you want. I think it's completely within my authority as mediator to recommend that Queen Olivia be allowed a private conference with Liberty's regent," Jack said calmly.

"Queen Olivia does not have nor need a regent. She simply needs to be set free," Prince Justin said, snarling.

"My mistake," Jack said, showing mild frustration. Then he continued in a lightly sarcastic, singsong tone. "I support Queen Olivia having a private conference with her uncle. Any objections?"

When no one spoke up, Tee gently said, "Please take the morning to get caught up. Feel free to meet anywhere you choose. There are no restrictions." He then looked nervously at Caius until he got a nod of approval.

Bria's regal manner dropped. She showed softness for Tee as she said, "Thank you, Tee. I'll take Prince Justin and Chief Justice Roberts to my apartment where we can be comfortable." Turning to Jack, her manner switched back to stern and added, "Given how long I've been gone from Liberty, I will need the whole day."

Jack hesitated and then said, "We'll meet again tomorrow morning then."

Well, that had gone exactly to script, Bria thought. Even Prince Justin had played his part without realizing he had a part to play. When they had planned this out the day before, she had guessed he would show outrage early, and he had. While Justin was ordinarily gracious and calm by nature, he had a hot temper when he perceived injustice. When they had gotten out of sight, Prince Justin grabbed Bria and gave her a hug. Being a close personal friend of her father's while she was growing up, they had a family-like relationship. Taking a deep breath he said, "It's so good to see you safe, Olivia. We've been out of our minds with worry."

She held onto him for a while, then disengaging she said, "When we get to my apartment, we can talk. It's private and I believe it's safe there," clearly indicating it wasn't safe to talk in the main garden.

When they walked into the apartment, Gloria was waiting for them.

Prince Justin dispensed with a greeting and immediately said, "The girls are healthy, safe, and as happy as can be expected."

"Thank God," Gloria blurted out before burying her head in her hands and bursting into tears. She recovered after a minute and said, "Thank you, Your Highness. That news means the world to me."

"They are at General Eastbrook's ranch and being taken care of by his sister Beatrice. They miss you horribly. I assured them you were okay, and that I was going to personally bring you home." He smiled then added, "The last time I saw them they were learning to ride ponies. You'll remember that Aunt B is quite the character. There is a lot of laughter. She loves those two girls and is going to have a hard time letting them go."

Gloria dried her tears and said, "I can't tell you how much it means to me to hear they are healthy and safe. Thank you. I know you have much to discuss, so I'll leave you alone for now. If you need anything, just let me know. I'll bring some lunch around noon."

Prince Justin stopped her with a look and said, "Gloria, I can't express how much the royal family appreciates your service this past year. If there is ever anything you need, you have only to ask." Gloria nodded, curtsied, and quietly left.

Once, when Tee was asleep, Gloria silently moved to stand at the bars of her cell and said in a soft whisper. "I won't tell them how close you are to General Eastbrook, given your friendship with Bria. You know General Eastbrook would do anything for you. If they knew, they might try to tempt him into a betrayal. It was Gloria's way of saying she wouldn't betray her. At the same time, it would tempt them to contact her father, which might present an opportunity. It was cleverly done. Bria had developed an enormous level of respect for Gloria through the extremely troubled times they had shared.

Once Gloria left, Justin said, "Bria and her father asked me to tell you they miss you horribly and can't wait for you to get home. We are all concerned for your safety."

Bria gave a slight smile and said, "You can call me Bria here. Things are not what they seem. I'm reasonably safe here on Arista. That wasn't entirely true until Tee became emperor. The Commonwealth is the real enemy."

Justice Roberts frowned and said, "How can the colonies be in danger? The Commonwealth's non-interference Edicts are strictly enforced. Just recently, the first justice for this sector was convicted of violating them and was quickly replaced. He was caught taking a bribe involving your abduction. No one knows what happened to him. But we do know the Commonwealth is brutal with these cases."

Bria sighed, remembering her first conversation with Caius. "It's a long story. Be patient and I'll tell you what I know. I'll also tell you what Senator Cereo is proposing as a way forward."

Hesitating a moment, she added, "The governor is responsible for my abduction and Lord Druango's rebellion. If they hadn't gotten involved, Olivia would be married to Lord Druango and we would have that to worry about. Perhaps it has worked out better for Liberty that this happened. But I'm convinced we are in real danger from the Commonwealth. Executing those who committed murder and rape on Liberty outraged General Harris and irritated the governor. Harris is evidently very influential in the Commonwealth. While the governor can't do anything openly, Senator Cereo says she can cause a lot of trouble."

By early afternoon, they had finally gotten to the point of discussing their decision. Or more accurately, Prince Justin's decision. There were two options. Go along with Cereo's plan or simply go back to Liberty. Bria had gotten a commitment from Caius and Tee that they would simply let her go. However, they requested Liberty stage a big fight over it. Tee would step in, declaring he was letting her go. The story to the first minister being that Tee was in love with her. The danger of Arista giving in too soon was that the first minister might tell the governor Caius hadn't done everything he could to force a three-planet pact.

"Are you really prepared to marry that monster?" Prince Justin asked, frowning.

Bria frowned back at him. "Tee is anything but a monster. Yes, he's huge. That makes him incredibly intimidating. But warm and compassionate is a better description. Lord Druango was a monster, and Olivia was going to marry him for the good of our people. Can I do anything less? The plan doesn't work without the promise of a marriage."

Prince Justin considered that. "I apologize, Bria. He's been nothing but polite and considerate so far. I also know he did what he could to protect you and Gloria on that damned slave ship. And it appears he continues to treat you well," he said as he waved a hand around indicated the luxurious apartment. "I just hate the idea of you being forced into a marriage."

"Well, it wouldn't be the worst thing that ever happened to me," Bria said with a smirk. "He is quite handsome and if you got to know him, you would like him. I guarantee you Olivia would have traded Lord Druango for him."

Prince Justin chuckled. Turning back to being serious again, he said, "We do need to have the option of revealing Olivia. It gives us the ability to declare any agreements null and void. But I am worried about what will happen when Tee learns the truth. He thinks he's marrying a queen."

"To be honest, I think he would be delighted. Tee doesn't want to be an emperor. He doesn't want to rule a planet. He wants his simple life back. Reminds me a lot of my father. He's driven by an obligation to protect others and is willing to sacrifice everything to do it. His selfish desires are simple and meager," Bria said.

"It almost sounds like you're in love with him," Justin said accusingly.

"I almost am," she said, surprised at herself to have admitted it.

That evening Bria left her apartment and wandered through the expansive and opulent emperor's residence in search of Tee. She eventually found him in the pool, swimming back and forth. He never sits still, she thought. Bria sat down and waited for him to stop. When he finally finished, she said, "Where are the kids?"

"I decided to be selfish. Told them I would watch them tomorrow evening for as long as they wanted. That seemed to satisfy them. Needed some exercise after sitting all day," Tee said, smiling as he got out of the pool with water dripping in rivulets down his face and body.

She was glad when he dried off and donned a robe. Tee had been almost naked in his skimpy swimsuit. His body glistening from the water had caused a somewhat pleasant physical reaction. That was the last thing she needed right now. "I came to tell you we agree with the plan. Prince Justin has his script and won't deviate from it. It was difficult for them to agree to this. However, we believe the Commonwealth was the root of the problems in Liberty. Defeating their plans for us means we need friends. For that reason, we have decided to join in the pact."

Instead of being delighted, Tee's face took on a somber look. Quiet for a while, he finally said, "I'm sorry you're being forced into this. I know you have agreed to do it based on what's best for your people. I admire that." He looked at her for a few moments and then said, "On Pacifica marriage is a choice, but it's also a lifetime commitment. We believe this is best for the children. And what's best for the children is what's best for the whole community. When I marry, I will work hard to be the best husband and father I can be. I won't give up on that." Tee hesitated, then lowering to one knee he said, "Olivia Hastings, will you marry me?"

Bria was stunned. She had not expected him to formally ask for her hand in marriage. Tears started to form in her eyes as the seriousness of the situation hit her all at once. However, she was committed to this and would see it through. "Yes, I will marry you, Theron Stone."

He stood, hugged her, and then said, "Let's take this slow. Perhaps things will work out, so we don't have to do it." He hesitated, and then with a roguish smile said, "I will admit it's not entirely distasteful." She laughed, suddenly releasing the anxiety of the moment. As strange and unnatural as his proposal was, she wasn't sure she could have gotten a more romantic one.

They announced their engagement the next day to howls of protest from Prince Justin and Justice Roberts. Caius was actually the first to talk over the din to voice his disapproval. "Your Majesty, marriage is a very serious move. It must only be done after understanding the political consequences. I can't object strongly enough."

"As much as I hate to say it. I wholeheartedly agree with Senator Cereo, Your Majesty. You simply cannot agree to a betrothal with this man," Prince Justin said, waving his hand toward Tee. "You will be subjugating your people to a brutal non-representative government. They don't even have personal rights protections in their constitution. Citizens are not protected. You simply cannot do this."

"I can and I will. You forget yourself, Uncle. We have agreed that while on Liberty, Theron will be the queen's consort and on Arista, I will be the emperor's consort. We will alternate living arrangements between the two planets. You have proven you can act on my behalf while I'm away. Tee trusts Senator Cereo to do the same. What we do with our children remains to be decided. We both agree with Senator Cereo that changes to government need to be made on both planets."

Bria was especially proud of her acting here. They gave the first minister everything he wanted. She hoped it would buy enough time to put themselves in position to control the situation. As Caius had observed, "They only care about money. If we can deliver significantly increased tax revenues, they will leave us alone." Bria hoped he was right. This tradeoff would come at a high cost for their citizens. But being poor was better than being enslaved. When the current governor was replaced, perhaps they could turn it back around.

"Would a marriage resolve all the issues between your two planets?" Jack asked, clearly questioning whether it did.

Prince Justin and Caius both started to talk at the same time when Bria held up her hand. "First Minister, I appreciate your efforts to mediate our differences. You can report back to the governor that you have been successful. Theron and I will resolve this between ourselves. We are of like mind on the issues and don't believe we need further assistance." As she said this, she looked pointedly at both Senator Cereo and Prince Justin.

As Caius was walking Jack out he said, "I'm sorry you've come all this way just to be told you're not needed."

Jack smiled conspiratorially and said in a low voice, "The governor told me what your plan is. It looks like everything is falling into place."

Caius lowered his voice as well and said, "We still have a long way to go. The Commonwealth has to approve the plan for Pacifica. Once that's done, Pacifica's government will have to be convinced to accept Theron as their figurehead king. Their culture will rebel against having royalty. However, if it's announced as a requirement to be accepted as a colony, we should be able to push it through. They should be so delighted that the GEM threat is being eliminated that anything is acceptable."

"But what about Liberty? Why not push for a quick marriage and then move to make constitutional changes? That's the question the governor is going to ask."

Caius showed some frustration at that point and said, "The two of you need to recognize that Pacifica is the prize here. Anything that slows down progress risks losing their human capital. You've seen the reports on GEM collaboration and the massing of their troops. Pacifica is running out of options."

"Yes, we've both heard your thoughts on that. It doesn't change what questions the governor is going to have," Jack said with an empathetic grin.

"As soon as I have approval, I will get Theron and Olivia to Pacifica. After we gain colony status, and everything calms down, we will have a wedding on Liberty," Caius said.

"Why Liberty and not Arista?" Jack asked.

"Because Theron is an absolute ruler here and can do as he pleases. The queen has to have a good relationship with the House of Lords to run that government. To make changes to the constitution we can't start off by insulting everyone," Caius said. Then he stopped to consider something and added, "If I can get approval for Prince Justin and Chief Justice Roberts to travel with us to Pacifica, we can finalize wedding plans. They will want to see Pacifica and meet members of their government to feel comfortable with this, anyway. That will speed up the timeline for the wedding."

Jack was clearly not convinced. Caius knew Jack was concerned he didn't have a strong enough message for the governor. "What can you do to move the Pacifica timeline along faster?" Jack asked.

Caius pretended to give this some thought. He was thrilled that Jack had pushed on the topic. After enough time to convince Jack that what he had to say wasn't pre-planned, he said, "I've been suggesting to Theron and Olivia that an investment in a mercenary army could be lucrative. An army led by General Eastbrook that includes the Pacifica Guard could charge an enormous premium. His defeat of General Harris had to have been noticed across the Commonwealth. If I can get approval to bring the General to Pacifica, he can evaluate what it would take to form such an army. That would push our plans forward faster."

Jack mused over this for a while and finally said, "Okay, you have my support. I'll let you know what the governor says."

"Safe travels Jack," Caius said with a convincing smile.

"And to you as well," Jack said, shaking his hand and then climbing up into his carriage. As he drove away, he thought Caius Cereo was up to something. It's certainly an aggressive plan with enormous potential. But what is he really trying to do?

CHAPTER 15

THE COMPLIMENT

Jack had mixed feelings as he left Julie's apartment. It wasn't how the evening had gone. It was another humiliating experience followed by the now familiar self-loathing. She had a way of forcing you to do disgusting things, then feeling like you were a bad person for doing them. It was slowly destroying his sense of self-worth.

What was unusual was how their business meeting had gone earlier in the day. As he walked out of her building and down the street toward home, he reviewed everything they had discussed.

"Good morning, Jack. You look really good in that suit," Governor Jacobs said.

Jack froze for a moment. She never complimented him like this. "Well, thank you, Governor. You are looking quite nice yourself," he said, deciding to flirt a bit. Perhaps that's what she was going for.

The governor actually smiled and said, "Give me an update on Liberty and the negotiations on Pacifica." She did not ask if he had 'good news'.

Jack put on his dutiful underling voice and body language and began, "I was able to get Prince Justin to release Harris and what was left of his mercenaries. A number of them had already been executed for crimes against civilians. Liberty wasn't happy letting criminals go free. But I got them to understand that relations with other colonies are important, even if they are located in another sector."

"Did they demand compensation?" she asked.

"No. Prince Justin said that no amount of credits could compensate people for the abuse suffered. He was quite forceful in saying that Liberty would not accept blood money," Jack replied.

"How sanctimonious," Julie said. "It's childish to take that sort of position. However, it's good, since Overlord Bennett is already incensed. Executing perfectly good mercenaries has him demanding justice. As you know, Bennett is well connected on the High Council. It would do Liberty good for them to make amends."

"I will mention this again when I meet with Queen Olivia on Pacifica," Jack said. "Our meetings went surprisingly well after an initial shouting match. What forced agreement was Theron and Olivia announcing their engagement. They told their advisors they would resolve issues between Liberty and Arista. They both support adding Pacifica if the Commonwealth approves them as a colony. There really wasn't much for me to do."

"So Cereo's plan is evolving as he predicted. Good. I want you to support him completely. Our interests are in excellent alignment with his," she said.

"Cereo says he can move things forward faster if General Eastbrook is allowed to join the discussions on Pacifica. He asked me to make that request. Do you approve?" Jack asked.

"No, I think the original proposal is good enough. No need to make those discussions more complicated than they already are," she said calmly. "I have to congratulate you on how well you've handled Cereo. While he has done some surprising things, you responded to them in a way that maintains our control of the situation." The conversation went on to inconsequential details. Her parting comments had been warm instead of cold. Weird!

Jack realized he had been standing in front of his apartment door for a while, just staring at it. Why does she want General Eastbrook to remain on Liberty? She had never denied a request that claimed to accelerate a plan. He was at a loss for words when she complimented him. And he was at a loss to explain it now. In the entire meeting, she had not insulted or demeaned him once. And then an actual compliment. Something was wrong. Something was very wrong.

CHAPTER 16

MORNING RUN

Jack was insistent that discussions with the Pacifica government happen privately. "The Commonwealth's Edicts on non-interference of pre-industrial civilizations are rigorous. Until they agree they have a monarch, and that monarch agrees to accept our offer to join the Commonwealth, this must remain private."

"What if they agree to join but claim they are a republic?" Caius asked.

"Then they will either sit to the side and watch the GEMs take over or declare the government dysfunctional and invade. The key is whether they can justify knowledge of second-generation warfare or industrial technology. My guess is that they will invade. Their justification will be that the human capital on Pacifica is too valuable to waste." Jack looked at Tee when he said this with an apologetic smile.

"The Master Sergeant of the Guard knows all the politicians. If I can talk to him, he can help," Tee said. Then he added, "He trains teams all the time, so we have a good chance of catching him away from the city."

It took nearly a week to make the jumps necessary to enter Pacific's orbit. Unfortunately, after locating and tracking Griff for three days, the man seemed to be spending the majority of his time at the university. Way too many people around him to organize a private conversation. Even out of uniform, Tee was too well known to show up in public. Then Tee recognized Jay while he was with Griff and told the Commonwealth crew to track him as well. The next morning, they were rewarded with a view of Jay on an early morning run up a trail alongside the Armstrong River.

"Tee?" Jay said with disbelief.

"Yes, it's me," Tee said.

Jay walked over briskly and picked him up in a bear hug. Tee hugged him back just as vigorously. After a few moments, Jay put Tee back down. With his hands now on Tee's shoulders, he asked with a face masked in confusion, "Where the hell have you been?"

Tee smiled back sheepishly. "You're going to find the answer hard to believe. Pacifica is in grave danger, and we don't have time for a long discussion. I'll explain more later, but you are going to have to just trust me for now."

Jay hesitated, then said soberly but with conviction, "I trust you, Tee."

Tee then quickly described what had happened to him, why they were in a crisis, and what needed to be done quickly.

Jay listened without interrupting. Tee could tell it was difficult for him. When Tee was done, Jay looked down at his feet for a while, considering what he had heard. Then he looked up and said with a straight face, "Let's see if I have this straight. Space pirates kidnapped you. They took you to a planet ruled by a sadistic emperor and sold you into slavery as a gladiator. The legendary Vic turns out to still be alive, having suffered the same fate. You talk Vic into a scheme to kill the emperor with one of your crazy suicide plans. The plan works and somehow that makes you the new emperor of the planet. Then, to protect Pacifica, you enter into an engagement with the ruling queen of yet another planet."

Jay hesitated a moment and then continued. "Oh, and I almost forgot. The queen happens to be smart, courageous, sweet, and drop dead gorgeous. So far, so good?"

"That's about it," Tee said with a slightly embarrassed grin.

Jay just looked at him for a while. "The really weird part is that I believe every word of it. Only you could get sold into slavery and figure out a way to conquer the planet responsible," Jay said and then grinned.

Tee grinned back for a moment and then his face turned serious. "I would love to explain more and catch up, but we have to get Griff to set up the meeting. The GEMs are massing and unless we agree to the Commonwealth's terms, their next attack will likely succeed.

"Okay, you stay here. I'll go get him." Jay started to run down the trail, stopped, and then turned around and said, "I can't tell you how good it is to see you, Tee."

"You too Jay," Tee said and looked away so that Jay wouldn't see his eyes misting up. Jay then turned and took off running, but not before Tee saw the mist in his eyes as well.

Almost two hours later, Jay and Griff came running back up the trail. Griff hesitated a minute, standing directly in front of Tee. Then he stepped forward and embraced him. Well, that was a more emotional greeting than I expected, Tee thought.

"God, it's good to see you again, Tee. Jay told me what I need to know for now and we don't have time to waste, so let me explain what we're going to do. Professor Dacy has access to President Malrey. He lives in a house on the university grounds that back up to this river downstream. We're going to sneak you in his back door and then I'll go get him. He will know how to contact the president."

Griff hesitated for a few moments and looked over at Jay. They both looked uncomfortable. He appeared to come to a decision and then said, "Your mother ought to be the one to tell you this, but since everyone you'll be talking to knows, I better tell you now. Your mother and I were married about a month ago."

Then, in typical Griff fashion, he turned and started running back down the trail, obviously expecting Tee and Jay to follow. Tee looked at Jay who simply shrugged and, nodding in the direction of the quickly disappearing Griff, ran after him.

When Griff said he had something to tell him, Tee's mind had gone blank with terror. In a flash, his mind had gone through all the terrible things the news could have been. Stuck in that reflection, he wasn't sure if he had heard Griff right. His mother and Griff were married? Then he remembered when he had seen her talking to Griff at his graduation ceremony. His first thought had been that they were flirting with each other. But that seemed so ridiculous he dismissed it. Looks like I had that right after all, he thought.

Then, to his horror, he realized that Griff was now his stepfather. After they had been running for several minutes, he finally calmed himself down. Under control now, he took a deep breath and said in all sincerity, "Congratulations, Griff."

Griff turned his head around to look at Tee and with a tight grin simply said, "Thank you, Tee."

Glancing over at Jay, he could see him relax a little. So, you've been worried about how I was going to react, Tee thought.

The next morning, President Malrey, with an unreadable expression, opened up a special closed-door session of the Pacifica Council. "Thank you all for being here today. I apologize for the cryptic description given to get you here, but you will soon understand my reasoning." She took a moment to look around the room and then said, "Please bear with me. You'll all have questions, but it will go much smoother if I can explain what I know without interruption." She looked around the room and got head nods of acknowledgement then continued, "The civilization our ancestors left two millennia ago have colonized this section of our galaxy."

A collective gasp went up from those assembled. Jennifer held up her hand and resumed, "Many of the local planets originally surveyed have been colonized by what is now known as the Commonwealth. We have been left alone for the past few hundred years because we are what they consider to be a pre-industrial civilization. Those types of civilizations are protected from interference under their laws. The first minister of this segment of the Commonwealth is here and would like to present the conditions under which we can be admitted as a colony. If admitted, the Commonwealth will protect us from the GEMs. They will grant us all the rights and privileges of their other colonies."

There was dead silence in the room as they all internalized this shocking development. Councilwoman Ricks was the first to recover. "Have you had discussions with the first minister?"

"Yes, but only to organize this meeting. He requested that everyone hear what he has to say together," Jennifer answered.

Barlow, in particular seemed pleased by that. He then said, "Will he help us negotiate with them?"

"I don't know. He just said that we won't need to fear them after colony status is conferred. He said he has the authority to take immediate action to stop the violence once we agree to their conditions," Jennifer said.

"What do you think of him?" Ricks asked. Ricks was a big advocate of listening to your gut.

"I'm not sure," Jennifer said, her face mirroring her confusion. "He's polite and considerate but seems overly anxious for us to agree with whatever their conditions are. But you can make your own assessment. I've spent little time with him and have as many questions as I'm guessing you all have." She looked around once more and said, "If there are no more questions for me, I'll go get the first minister."

"Good morning. My name is Jack Spenser. I am First Minister for Sector 27 of the Commonwealth. The Commonwealth was born out of the horrible wars your ancestors successfully escaped. Our mission has been to provide intergalactic peace for all humans. Our analysis indicates your lives are in immediate mortal danger from Pacifica's GEM population. I'm here to offer you an alternative. That alternative is an invitation to join the Commonwealth as a colony." Jack paused for a few moments and, looking around the room, asked, "Any questions so far?"

Barlow recovered first and asked, "Our failure has been our inability to negotiate in good faith. Will you help us negotiate with the GEMs?"

Jack seemed confused by the question. He mused over it for a while and then said, "There is no need for you to negotiate with the GEMs. We have technology that can be used to deny incursions into or out of the peninsula. Think of it as a fence neither of you can get over. Since your populations are separated by clear and distinct territorial boundaries, this will immediately put a stop to the bloodshed."

"You will give us this technology?" Barlow asked.

"No. This is something the Commonwealth can put in place and manage. Your question highlights one of the requirements for acceptance as a colony. Pacifica must restrict its technology to pre-industrial levels. This is basically where your civilization is today. This requirement is absolute. I'm sure you can appreciate that all advanced technologies can be used for war. By restricting technology use, we have provided peace and prosperity for nearly two millennia," Jack said.

"What other requirements do you have for acceptance of a colony?" Councilwoman Ricks asked, giving him a suspicious look.

"There is one that will likely cause consternation. We require that each planet have a form of government that has demonstrated the ability to survive the test of time. Democracies have consistently devolved into tyranny. They have all done this in a relatively short period of time. History has shown these types of governments to be warlike in nature. This is a threat to peace. Your republic has survived as long as it has because of a common enemy. We don't restrict colonies from having elected representatives or guaranteed rights for their citizens. However, we insist it be led by a monarch. All long-living governments have been managed in this fashion. The Kush, Roman, Egyptian, Zhou, and

Ottoman empires are just a few examples. The latest example is the Commonwealth."

The room was silent as each of the council members absorbed this news. Jennifer finally said, "We don't have royalty on Pacifica."

"Not currently. But there are representatives from two of our colonies in the sector who have a proposal. The proposal team is led by Theron Stone of Apple Valley." With that shocking news, everybody started talking at once.

Jennifer finally got the council under control. She did this by shouting at them. It was so out of character it successfully silenced the room. With her face flushed and eyes blazing, she turned to Jack and said, "Perhaps it would be good for you to back up and give us some background on this proposal. A description of the colonies and the individuals on the proposal team would be a good start. And we are all dumbfounded by the news that Theron Stone is involved? Please explain that in detail. He disappeared over a year ago. We have been assuming he was dead. When Professor Dacy showed up with you this morning, the fact that Theron Stone is alive wasn't mentioned."

Jack looked a bit chagrined and said in a conciliatory voice, "My apologies. I am so concerned with your safety that I neglected to give you the background you need to make sense of all this." He spent the next hour giving a quick history of the Commonwealth and a more thorough one for Sector 27. He then moved onto Tee's kidnapping and the subsequent trial of the first justice for Sector 27. Jack then explained Arista's challenge by combat secession law and how that made Theron Emperor of Arista. This was followed by a description of the representatives from Liberty and Arista.

Jack stopped at that point and said, "You're probably wondering why Liberty has chosen to be involved. The simple answer is that Theron Stone is engaged to be married to Olivia Hastings. Olivia Hastings is the Queen of Liberty." Jack hesitated for a moment and then said, "You probably need time to absorb this. I have to admit it boggles my mind as well. We've never had so much political interconnection between colonies. Since the Commonwealth is dedicated to non-interference, we simply want to mediate the discussions. My role is to provide support for your decision process. I hope you will agree to our conditions for acceptance as a colony."

Stunned silence. It was simply too much information at once. Jennifer recovered and said, "Thank you, First Minister. We will need time to discuss this privately. Can you return at noon?"

Jack smiled and said, "Yes, I'll walk over and see if I can wait in Professor Dacy's office for the rest of the morning."

As Jack was meeting with the Pacifica Council, Griff was sitting in Del's courtyard having a light breakfast. As he finished, Tee and Jay walked out. The previous evening, Tee had filled them in on everything that had happened to him since he was kidnapped. Griff would not have believed it except that all the evidence said it was true. He also knew Tee. He knew the boy wouldn't be part of a plan to deceive.

"When do you think Professor Dacy will be back with news from the council?" Tee asked.

"Not until afternoon, at least. Might take the entire day. It's an awful lot to absorb and near impossible to make sense of," Griff said as he finished his meal.

"Will you spar with me, Griff?" Tee asked out of the blue.

Jay's head shot up and looked surprised that Tee would challenge Griff like that. Griff grinned and said, "You sure you don't want to try Jay first?"

"I'm sure. How about we use wooden practice swords," Tee said and smiled.

"Okay, it's your funeral," Griff answered.

It was conventional for Newbies to challenge each other to spar. This was expected. It was usually painful to challenge one of the experienced Guard members. They considered it an insult. They usually made sure the Newbie would think twice before doing it again. It was unheard of for a Newbie to challenge the Master Sergeant of the Guard. Griff smiled, wondering why this had come about. Did it have to do with his marrying Tee's mother? Then he decided it didn't matter. Perhaps Tee has a big head from his successes in the Arena. He would put this pup back in his place.

They faced each other, and Griff gave Tee the hand signal to start. He immediately thrust in toward Tee's left side, pressing the weakness of Tee's standard defensive position. Well, he has improved on that slightly, but not enough, Griff thought. Remembering another of Tee's weaknesses, he came down with his sword over Tee's left shoulder, causing Tee to stumble backward. Having confirmed what he remembered as Tee's major weaknesses, he thrust weakly down low, allowing his sword to be blocked, and then went in for the kill. The next thing he knew, he was on his back with Tee's sword at his throat.

Tee smiled down at him, reached into his tunic, and pulled out an envelope. "This is from Victor."

As Griff got up, he glanced at Jay and saw the smirk on his face. "You got something to say, Jay?"

The smirk disappeared, and he said, "No, Master Sergeant." It reappeared once Griff's eyes left him.

Satisfied that he had regained a little of his dignity, he brushed himself off and sat down on the bench. He opened the envelope and pulled out a letter. Recognizing Vic's handwriting, he took a deep breath and started reading.

Griff,

If you're reading this, I am dead, and Tee has figured out a way to make it back to Pacifica. I hope you've received this laying on your back in the dirt. If so, this is my final lesson. If not, then I'm impressed.

Let's assume I'm not impressed. You had two major faults the last time we spoke. I have recently become aware of a third deficiency.

Aggressiveness is your greatest strength and your greatest weakness. Don't hesitate to act. Continue to move quickly, but always have a backup plan. Consider this and improve.

When you perceive a weak opponent, you have a habit of probing twice and then going in for the kill. Your enemies are watching. Being predictable is not acceptable. Consider this and improve.

You underestimated Tee. He arrived as an embarrassment. I give you back an adequate fighter. Consider this and improve.

The student has become the teacher. I would not have seen Tee's immense value. You were right that the Guard needs to be more than brutes bashing about. Having spent much time with him, I believe he is the leader we need for the future. I have considered my lack of vision at length. Thank you for helping me improve.

You started out as a Newbie project and became an excellent warrior. From my discussions with Tee, it's obvious you have become an exceptional leader as well. You are much more than adequate.

Most important to me is that you are my friend. I wish you love, happiness, and a long life. No one deserves it more.

Your brother,

Vic

Griff paused for a few moments, smiled, and then turned to Tee and said, "So Vic put you up to this?"

"Yes. He made it part of our daily practice sessions for weeks," Tee said. "It's still hard for me to believe how accurately he emulated your movements and predicted your actions."

"There will never be another Vic," Griff said wistfully. Then he hardened his features and said, "Now that you and Vic have had your fun, how about another bout?"

Tee was startled. He hesitated, then he grinned and said, "Yes."

After their session was finished, Griff held out his hand and helped Tee to his feet. He was battered and bruised, but elated. It was just like sparring with Vic. He was badly outclassed but got instruction from it instead of frustration. *I wish I could do this every day instead of sitting on my butt pretending to rule a planet,* he thought.

"Vic was right. You are adequate," Griff said with a knowing smile.

Tee heard echoes of Victor's voice. It was the way Griff said the word *adequate*. He realized Victor must have used it to acknowledge Griff's progress long ago. With that realization, he smiled back at Griff and said, "Well, it doesn't get any better than that."

Griff's smile warmed in agreement. Then he nodded gravely in acknowledgment of their shared experience.

CHAPTER 17

BENEFACTOR

Julie's yacht was waiting in a line for its turn to transit through the final wormhole from Sector 3 to Sector 1 and Earth. One benefit of being a sector governor was that the wait was measured in hours instead of days. Traffic between the home world and the rest of the Commonwealth was heavy. She looked forward to the day when she would jump past all these idiots to the front of the line. She had been making this trip twice per year since she was posted as governor of Sector 27.

This would be her final meeting with her benefactor as governor of that sector. She had exceeded her original commitments to the High Council and was near to delivering those she had boasted of. Rising to the top involved taking calculated risks. It was not a game for the weak. She was looking forward to her triumphant return to Earth in a few months to join the elite of the Commonwealth.

Chairman Amala had been her mentor since she was awarded her first promotion. He had noticed her unusual success in increasing tax revenues. He was especially interested in her ability to exceed goals through aggressive negotiations. She had initially been intimidated by the attention of one of the elites. The spotlight grew with his ascension to chairman. Anxiety had lessened over the years but had not disappeared. Having the favor of the Chairman of the High Council was exhilarating and terrifying. It meant she was close to the ultimate in power. I also meant she was only a misstep away from being just another bureaucrat for the rest of her life.

"Governor Jacobs, it's nice to see you," Amala said. Julie had been assigned one of the apartments usually reserved for the highest level of visitors to Earth. An opulent penthouse with a rooftop garden overlooking Central Park had greeted her. A bevy of silver-collared servants had provided for her every whim since she had arrived. It was an indication of Amala's approval and of his expectations. Nothing was ever given without a cost.

"It's good to be back on Earth, Chairman. The apartment you arranged for me was amazing. Thank you," Julie said, smiling. As she beamed back at him, she wondered what her amazing accommodations would cost her.

"If your plans are achieved, I think you'll be back soon," Amala teased. He then transitioned into mentorship mode and said, "Give me an update. I hope you have some good news."

She had learned the technique of putting her underlings on the defensive from Amala. There was always an expectation of exceeding goals or at least achieving them faster than planned.

"I can commit to having the enhanced plan for Sector 27 wrapped up within two months," Julie said.

"You're late," Amala said bluntly. Frowning as his eyes bored into hers.

"I am," Julie said. After pausing for effect, she continued. "Pacifica coming under our control will be added to my commitments. The opportunity presented itself and I decided it was worth the slip." She had learned long ago that Amala appreciated initiative and respectful defiance. Be accountable, but never act submissively.

"How will you get that past Justice? Pacifica remains pre-industrial in the judgement of those academic idiots who own those kinds of decisions," Amala said.

"It was partly luck. Arista has an archaic law allowing for their emperor to be replaced via succession by combat. A Pacifica gladiator assassinated him in the one place, on the one day of the year, when that law would apply. Senator Cereo recognized that this gladiator was now a monarch who could submit legal requests to the Commonwealth. Since he is also a citizen of Pacifica, he can request his home world be granted colony status."

"Has Justice approved this?" Amala asked.

Julie nodded and said, "They have given provisional approval with the understanding that the requestor be the legal ruler of Pacifica. This way, the ruler of Pacifica is making the request. That satisfies the non-interference Edicts and bypasses the pre-industrial civilization protections. Senator Cereo is on Pacifica getting this accomplished."

Amala just stared back at her for an uncomfortable amount of time. She waited patiently, understanding his intimidating management techniques, having adopted them as her own. "That is good news. What financial return are you committing to?"

"The initial first year target is an improvement of fifteen percent. An additional ten percent will be delivered with the creation of a mercenary army incorporating Pacifica units. However, the value to the Commonwealth will be enhanced beyond Sector 27 revenues. The additional ten percent will be flowing in from other sectors, further enhancing Commonwealth tax revenues," Julie said, her face and manner all business.

Amala nodded and favored her with the corners of his mouth slightly upturned. Then his face darkened in concern. "Since we're on the topic of mercenaries. I've been told Overlord Bennett is incensed with Liberty. Evidently, they executed a number of General Harris's men instead of ransoming them back.

"He's asking for Commonwealth support to exact revenge. He will fund an invasion from his own coffers if the Commonwealth agrees to provide transportation and stay out of the way. His only financial request is that he be allowed to recover his cost for the invasion from Liberty."

Julie gave that some thought, smiled, and then said with enthusiasm, "That works perfectly. I'll get back to you once I've discussed it with Bennett. When Pacifica becomes a colony, there will be a wedding on Liberty, with the leadership from Pacifica and Arista in attendance. This marriage will unite the three planets. Once united under one government, a coup that originates from one of those three planets will satisfy Justice. I just need to connect the players."

Amala was visibly pleased. "Clever. That should simplify Sector 27 administration nicely. Bennett has two other requests. The first is that he be given the judges who passed sentence on Harris's men. The second is that the queen be given to General Harris as compensation. He originally asked for General Eastbrook, but I said no. I'm assuming you want Eastbrook to lead your new mercenary forces?"

"Yes, his defeat of Harris will ensure a premium for his services. It doesn't speak well of Harris that he is motivated by something as unproductive as revenge. But he can have the queen as long as she never reappears in the sector. The last thing the next governor needs is a legitimate legal challenge to the rule of Liberty," Julie said.

"Harris has always had an outsized ego. Up to now it's been deserved. Let's throw him that bone, but make it clear that General Eastbrook and his entire staff must be preserved," Amala counseled. He hesitated a few moments and asked, "Do you already have someone to lead the coup?"

"Magistrate Pluta of Arista. He is awaiting instructions."

"How will you control him?" Amala asked.

"I have evidence that his bank account was the true origin of the bribe to Evans," Julie said with a glimmer in her eyes.

"Well done, Ms. Jacobs. Impressive," Amala said, giving rare praise. "How is progress going with our other Justice issue?" he asked with a penetrating look.

"I have enough failures documented to send Spenser's son home in disgrace," Julie said. "He is currently mediating the three-planet pact on Pacifica. Once the coup succeeds, I'll dismiss him."

Amala nodded in approval. "As we discussed don't let the son know you have documented evidence tying him to the Evans bribery. I want it to come as a complete surprise to Justice Spenser. He will be given the opportunity to drop his High Council corruption investigation. His alternative will be seeing his son in a silver collar serving the High Council. It should be an easy choice."

"Isn't it dangerous to leave Justice Spenser in place?" Julie asked.

"I've been unable to trap him into anything personally compromising. There are advantages to leaving him in place. He can hardly say no to reasonable requests," Amala said. "Going back to your plan. Do you intend on making Senator Cereo first minister after you remove Jack?"

"I haven't decided yet. I lean toward having him die in the coup. He's much too clever and I don't trust him," Julie said.

"I am intrigued by your Senator Cereo. His rise from poverty to control of Arista speaks for itself." Amala paused and, staring intently at Julie, said, "As you rise in the Commonwealth, you need to take advantage of clever people. Those who pose a threat to you professionally are the same as those who are the most useful. There are many uses for untrustworthy people, Ms. Jacobs."

Julie understood. He wanted her to utilize Cereo. Amala was making a not-so-subtle point. He didn't trust her. But he didn't need trust to take advantage of her capabilities.

"Understood, Chairman Amala," she said.

Amala examined her again. And again, it was for an uncomfortable amount of time. Then he said, "Katanna will resign from the High Council in three months and Norden will be elevated. This opens up a High Council Advisor's position." He paused and then said, "Finish your work in Sector 27 quickly, Ms. Jacobs."

His tone made it clear the interview was over. Julie rose to leave and simply said, "Yes, sir." There was never any chit chat with the Chairman. He made it clear early on that his time was valuable and not to be wasted. As she left his office suite, she wondered how she was going to get Harris's army housed in Sector 27 while keeping it a secret. A27 was off limits legally and Cereo's network would immediately discover something of this magnitude on Arista.

Any of the other planets in the sector would require Pluta to negotiate multiple contracts. That would take too much time to execute. She would need to take some additional risk. A more aggressive plan was needed. As her air taxi left for the spaceport, she allowed her anger and outrage to surface in her mind. Amala had humiliated and abused her as a wide-eyed young woman trying to make a name for herself.

Once he was done satisfying his desires, he never called her by her first name again. Amala will beg me for mercy someday, she thought. And when he does, I'll put a silver collar on him but leave his mind intact. She spent the rest of the short flight entertaining herself with all the degrading things she would make him do.

CHAPTER 18

REUNION

Tee started arguing heatedly with Del as soon as the professor got home from the council meeting. Griff glared at Del and said, "Tee has gone through hell. It's reasonable for him to see his family. They can be sworn to silence. Even if they spill, so what? It will be public soon enough."

Del glared right back, saying, "All of this has to flow out in a way that doesn't cause panic. People are already terrified. They know another GEM attack is coming. We can't have uncontrolled rumors about the Commonwealth and other planets popping up everywhere."

"I'm going to go see my mother and other members of my family. I'm doing this whether anyone agrees to it or not," Tee said calmly but firmly.

"I'll go with him," Griff said defiantly.

Del huffed out a breath. He glared at both of them for a while and finally said, "Okay, how about this for a compromise? Griff goes and gets your mother; you can see her here."

"No, not good enough. Jay told me Hestie, Quinn, and Diana are in town. They are all part of my family," Tee countered.

Del took a deep breath and wilted a bit. Looking defeated, he lowered his gaze and, shaking his head slightly from side to side, said, "Okay, but they all need to swear to keep this quiet until the president makes an official announcement." He hesitated and then said, "She's going to skin me alive for this."

"So, you come out ahead," Griff said. "I was going to do something far worse if you tried to get in the way."

The door opened and his mother hesitated an instant, taking her first look at him in over a year. Then she flew into his arms and started sobbing quietly. Tee was worried for a second because this was so unlike his mother. She had always been a rock. But then his tears started to flow as well. Then he finally relaxed into the joy of really being home again.

"Let me look at you," she said, wiping away her tears and examined him head to toe. "You're a little taller. You've put on quite a bit of muscle. It doesn't look like your little vacation was all that bad," she said with a tearful smile.

This was more like his mother, making light of difficulties. It warmed his heart. "It wasn't all horrible," he admitted, paused, and then added, "Just most of it," which made everyone laugh.

"Well, there are others here that want to get reacquainted," she said and stepped to the side. Suddenly Hestie grabbed him in a tight hug and said, "It's so good to see you, Tee. Don't have to tell you we've been worried sick." Quinn stepped up next and gave him a quick hug as well. This was unusual. Quinn didn't tend to hug people. Tee could tell Quinn had been worried and was thrilled to see him. Then he was face to face with Diana. They both hesitated, locked eyes, and simultaneously stepped forward into yet another hug. This one lingered a little longer than the others. He noticed she hugged him straight on, a full body hug not to the side, which made him wonder.

After they separated, his mother looked suddenly grave and said, "Before we start sharing stories, we have some bad news. Grammy passed away a few weeks ago." This hit Tee like a thunderbolt. His elation at being reconnected with those he loved disappeared and was replaced by sudden bone numbing grief. His mother continued, "She didn't suffer and seemed to know it was coming. She wrote her own funeral service and individual letters to everyone before she died. Hestie has a copy of the funeral service and your letter."

Tee didn't know what to say. He just wanted to run away. As he wondered what to do, his mother stepped in again. "Here, take the funeral service and letter from Hestie and go out in the garden," she said, pointing over his shoulder at Professor Dacy's small enclosed garden. "When you are ready, come back in. We'll be waiting for you. Take your time."

He was so grateful he didn't know what to say. His mother knew him. She knew he needed to be alone to process this horrible news. She knew being outside would help with that, even if it was just a small garden."

Tee walked out into the garden numb. He sat down, turned away so nobody could see his face, and cried for a while. Then he pulled out the funeral service and cried some more, but not for long. Suddenly an image of Grammy shaking her finger at him and lecturing him on all manner of things came to mind. He laughed. With a smile still on his face, remembering other endearing qualities of hers, he pulled out her letter.

Dearest Tee,

I would have loved to see you one more time. Knew you would return. But it was not to be. I can't tell you how much joy you have given me in this life. Truly blessed to have had you as my grandson.

Not that you're perfect! And for that reason, I have one final piece of advice. TELL HER! You know what I'm talking about.

Love,

Grammy

How did she know I was still alive? How did she know I would return? Of all the things the Commonwealth had stolen from Tee, this might be the worst. He never got a chance to say goodbye. His last memory of Grammy was waving to him standing on the porch, a concerned look on her face. He promised he would see her in a few days. He sat there thinking about Grammy until he realized everyone was waiting for him. So, he stood up and walked in to tell them his story.

It was an emotional story to tell. While he had told much of it before, it hadn't been to those he had known his whole life. They were outraged with his captivity and being forced to kill innocent people. They were amazed that Victor had not died those years and years ago. They were proud Victor had looked out for him and had become his mentor.

They cried when Victor sacrificed his life so that justice could be served. They laughed when he described waking up thinking he was dead only to find out he was somehow Emperor of Arista. But the strongest reaction was when he explained that he was engaged to the Queen of Liberty and was going to have to marry her.

"No!" his mother said. "You've given too much all ready. There has to be another way."

She had startled him because he had actually been watching Diana without looking directly at her. Diana reacted very strongly to this news. Was there something more than pity in her reaction? His mother's outburst had startled him back to paying attention to her.

He took a breath and said, "Mom, Victor gave his life. Senator Cereo is gambling his entire family's lives. Liberty has been under constant attacks from mercenaries trying to enslave them. Our freedom and perhaps all our lives are at stake. It's a sacrifice I will gladly give. You and Grammy always told me that an opportunity to defend our people is an obligation, not a choice. I have an obligation."

There was silence in the room. Diana looked like she was going to burst into tears when the door opened, and Professor Dacy entered with Queen Olivia. "I hope I gave you enough time to get caught up. We stayed at the restaurant as long as we could without drawing too much attention." Diana just stared at her, seemingly in shock. Since she was standing closest to the door, Del introduced Olivia to Diana first.

"Your Majesty, may I introduce Diana Wells," Del said.

"Please call me Olivia," she said, looking around the room. "I don't want to be formal with people who are sacrificing so much," Bria said graciously.

Diana recovered quickly, a trait that had benefited her greatly as a Wall Archer. "In that case, I really like your dress, Olivia," Diana said brightly in an attempt to lighten the mood. Tee smiled seeing the old Diana again. Diana succeeded by making Bria smile.

"Thank you," Bria said and then added, "I feel like I already know you, Diana. Tee spoke of you so often." She hesitated a moment, looking Diana up and down and then smiled and said, "It's hard to believe, but you're as beautiful as Tee described."

Diana blushed and said, "Thanks. Tee does tend to exaggerate, and it's nice of you to cover for him." Tee felt himself turning red. He guessed he had gushed about Diana more than once.

Bria smiled at Diana's deft deflection, realizing she had made things a bit awkward. She had blurted out what she was thinking. The real Olivia would do a much better job, she thought. However, in her own defense, Diana really was a beauty. Recovering, she asked, "So you're an archer? Do you really fight on the Wall?"

"As you probably know, we are all warriors. We have no other choice. But let me get out of the way so you can meet everyone else," Diana said gracefully.

His mother was tongue tied when she met Diana. This was not the way to meet a future daughter-in-law. He would get an earful later. He decided she really couldn't say much, given how he learned about having a stepfather. After the introductions were completed, Del said, "Sorry to interrupt, Tee. But I thought everyone would want to meet Queen Olivia. I'll talk to you later about what to expect tomorrow." And with that, they left the front room and retired to the back of the house.

Later in the evening, Tee noticed Diana was out on the bench in the garden. He turned to Hestie and said, "I'm going to go out and talk to Diana for a while."

Hestie gave him a nod and said, "We'll leave you two alone." She then gave him a look that he interpreted as 'there are things the two of you need to discuss.'

Fantasizing about the impossible again, Tee thought.

"Hey," Tee said.

"Hey," Diana replied. Then she gave him a weak smile and slid over to give him room to sit down next to her.

"I'm surprised Ansen isn't here," Tee said, testing the waters. He was a little ashamed he didn't just say what he needed to say. Grammy shaking her finger at him popped into his mind once more.

Diana turned to look at him and finally said sadly, "A lot has changed since you've been gone. Ansen is up in Apple Valley with his girlfriend."

"Oh, I'm so sorry, Diana," Tee said. But he was secretly thrilled with the news. Not that it mattered anymore.

"Nothing for you to be sorry about. I broke it off. I did it because I'm in love with someone else," Diana said and seemed heartbroken saying it.

"You seem really sad. Didn't it work out?" Tee asked.

"No, it's not going to work out," she said. "There is somebody I'm seeing, though, and perhaps that will work out."

Tee was suddenly deeply saddened for Diana. Whatever she thought of him, he loved her deeply and always would. Olivia was a wonderful girl, and they would have a happy life together if it came to that. Well, he would be much more than just happy. But there was only one Diana.

They sat in an uncomfortable silence for a while until Tee decided he needed to follow Grammy's advice, no matter what. He would always wonder otherwise. "Diana," Tee said and waited for her to turn her head to look at him. "I'm going to say this before I lose my nerve. I hope it doesn't ruin our friendship." Tee hesitated, took a deep breath, and said, "I'm deeply in love with you. I think I've loved you since you sat down next to me under that oak tree."

Diana just looked at him, searching. Then suddenly she wrapped her arms tightly around him and started crying. He didn't know what to do. What did this mean? He guessed it meant they could still be friends.

After a long time of just holding onto each other, Diana gently pushed him away and wiped her eyes. She looked down, seemed to gather herself, and looking him in the eyes said, "I am deeply in love with you too, Tee. Realized it way before you were kidnapped. Almost told you that last night on the Wall. I'm sorry I didn't come to you when Ansen accused you of being responsible for Tia's death. That was wrong. You always seem so solid. So able to take on anything and recover from it. I meant to come back once Ansen settled down. Then you were gone."

Tee just stared at her, not believing what he had just heard. Then he leaned forward and kissed her deeply and passionately. She responded by pressing her body close to his. It was incredibly exciting and frustrating all at the same time. Heaven, if only for a moment. When they disengaged, he said, "I've been wanting to do that for a long time."

"Me too," Diana said, and their grins turned into laughs.

They talked long into the night. Smiling at shared memories. Crying more than once over their lost future. They agreed that Tee had to go forward with the marriage. Pacifica's future depended on it. It was a sacrifice they both had to make. When the eastern sky started to lighten Tee wondered where the night had gone. They could talk for hours, or they could just be comfortable with silence. His heart ached. They said their goodbyes in the garden. Both knowing this was the end.

As they left the garden, a curtain ruffled on Bria's bedroom window. Sleep had evaded her. She had guiltily stolen a few looks at the two of them on and off during the night. She had convinced herself she had a right to know what her future husband's true feelings were. But it still didn't feel right.

She had liked Diana instantly when she met her. From Tee's stories, it was hard not to admire her as well. Imagine going to war alongside the men. It was all so confusing. Her feelings were ridden with guilt. She wondered what Tee would do when he found out the truth about who she really was.

Diana was walking close to Hestie on their way to her dorm room. Griff had wisely decided to walk well behind to give them privacy. Arti and Quinn had decided to go get some sleep earlier in the evening, with Griff agreeing to walk Hestie and Diana home.

"He loves me," Diana said in amazement mixed with grief. "I love him too. I've kept it hidden for so long."

"You only hid it from each other. It's been obvious to everyone else for a long time," Hestie said softly.

"Really? Why didn't you say anything?" Diana asked.

"If you didn't admit it to yourself, it would do no good for me to point it out. You do remember me constantly reminding you to look deep into your heart whenever you used to talk about your future with Ansen. And why do you think Ansen was always trying to push Tee and I together," Hestie said.

"God, I'm such an idiot," Diana said, a little louder than she intended.

Hestie stopped and made Diana turn to her. Then she said, "No, you were confused, and you ran away from something that scared you."

Diana thought about that for a while as they walked through the empty streets. "Hestie, you're the best friend a person could ever have." Then she hesitated and with a grin said, "We are both a mess, aren't we?"

Hestie turned, grabbed her and they both hugged and cried while Griff stood off to the side looking uncomfortable.

Shrugging and rolling his eyes, Griff muttered quietly, "Men are so much easier to deal with."

CHAPTER 19

THE PACT

Jack gave an honest smile and said, "I am pleased Pacifica has agreed to the Commonwealth's conditions. I will get the exclusion fence in place as soon as possible. Please warn your people not to cross those boundaries. Have them stay on this side of the moat and off the beaches. We don't want any unfortunate accidents." He looked around the table and concluded, "If there are no more questions then I'll leave you to your discussions."

Jennifer was still vibrating from the earlier session with the council. In the end, they voted unanimously to accept the Commonwealth's offer. They really didn't have a choice.

To Jennifer's surprise, the incorporation of a monarchy into their constitution was quick and easy. They would model the later part of twenty-first century Briton and create a figurehead. Jack made it clear this was acceptable with the provision that their monarch would be solely responsible for interactions with the Commonwealth. That included making commitments for the planet. This meant that they truly would have an all-powerful monarch as far as the Commonwealth was concerned.

This had everyone worried. They decided they would figure out how to deal with it later. The lone dissenting voice was Barlow's. He was adamant that, "We can't have a king who comes from the Guard. This will just perpetuate military solutions to everything." When it was pointed out that Pacifica didn't have a choice in the matter, they were able to move on. Jennifer did worry once again that with every defeat of Barlow's strongly held opinions, he would get more and more unstable.

Then the really difficult discussion. Arista and Liberty would have two attendees to the initial discussions. The planet's decision maker and an advisor. They had requested Pacifica offer the same. This flew in the face of Pacifica's republic form of government. There really was no one decision maker. That Tee, as King of Pacifica, could make responsible decisions, was too silly to even consider. Councilwoman Ricks finally resolved the uproar by proposing that Pacifica counter with a negotiator and advisor. The idea being that negotiations could take place but would have to be ratified by the council.

In the end, the Pacifica Council agreed that Jennifer would be the negotiator and Griff, her advisor. Since a military alliance was one of the key proposals, it made sense for the Guard to be in attendance. Again, this passed with Barlow dissenting.

The meeting to negotiate the pact started early the next morning. Jennifer looked around the table, trying to judge the other participants. She was quite adept at reading people. She smiled grimly, realizing that the range of attitudes around that table were similar to a typical council meeting. Tee and Olivia were clearly fond of each other. But she didn't think they were the actual decision makers. She suspected this from the way they interacted with their advisors.

Senator Cereo was the consummate politician. Polished, smooth, and engaging. She instantly liked him, so she would have to watch him carefully. He could just be an accomplished con man. Prince Justin, Queen Olivia's uncle, was angry. Jennifer suspected this was disguised fear and who could blame him? She would tread lightly with him.

Prince Justin opened the discussion. "What keeps Pacifica from landing a few thousand warriors on Liberty and simply taking over?"

Griff looked like he hadn't slept in a while. He huffed. Then he said in an irritated voice, "Nothing." Griff stared at Prince Justin for a few moments and then added, "We have to trust each other because we have no other choice." His voice and body language made it clear he didn't trust Liberty any more than Prince Justin trusted Pacifica.

Well, so much for treading lightly, thought Jennifer, having trouble keeping a smile off her face.

"We talked about this on Arista, Justin. We have no other choice than to trust each other. The Commonwealth is the real enemy," Caius said.

"That's rich coming from you. You've admitted you've been lying to everyone. You were advising the previous emperor on how and when to invade Liberty," Justin said, raising his voice. "You've made recommendations to the governor of how to turn Pacifica into a slave planet. Why should anyone trust you?"

"Enough!" Bria said firmly, surprising everyone. With her voice firm and unyielding she said, "I've spent a lot of time with Senator Cereo's family and with Tee. I'm not the most trusting person. But I trust them both." Turning to Prince Justin, she said meaningfully, "You're right. It's time for the lies to stop."

"No, Olivia," Justin said in a small voice beseeching her.

"It's what she would want," Bria said firmly. Then she looked around the table, catching everyone's eye, and said, "I am not Olivia Hastings. I am not the Queen of Liberty. My name is Bria Eastbrook." Justin just looked down at the table in front of him. He was obviously embarrassed. Everyone else just stared at Bria. Jennifer noticed that Tee was as shocked as everyone else, perhaps even more so.

Eventually Jennifer found her voice and asked, "So, what does this mean?"

Tee looked at Bria for a few moments. His confused and suspicious expression gradually softened, and he visibly came to a decision. He looked around the table and in a calm voice said, "It means we need to trust each other. I've seen what the Commonwealth does to people. The Commonwealth is our enemy. Fighting amongst ourselves serves their purpose, not ours." Then, motioning toward Bria, he said, "If Bria is an example of the people of Liberty, then I trust the people of Liberty." Turning his head to look at her, he hesitated and as a mischievous smile started to form he said, "I'm guessing this means the engagement is off."

There was a hesitation. Then the room rang with laughter. Prince Justin was laughing along with everyone else. Jennifer noted that the mood in the room had changed. The tension had broken. Griff had told her Tee was a natural leader. He predicted the boy would eventually be the CGG. Here was proof of that claim. When the laughter died down, Prince Justin said, "Okay, you're right. I don't like any of this, but we do have a common enemy." He stopped for a moment and looked at Caius. "I apologize. We've been at war so long it's hard not to see threats everywhere. But that is no excuse to accuse you of something I'm just as guilty of." Caius nodded graciously. Prince Justin continued. "As you can guess, I can't legally agree to anything on behalf of Liberty. We need Queen Olivia for that."

While the negotiation of a pact was taking place, Jack wandered around until he found Barlow sitting on a bench in front of their government building. "Good morning Mr. Barlow. Is there somewhere we can talk privately?"

"Sure, we can talk in my office," Barlow said pleasantly. They walked in silence into the medium-sized marble-faced building and up two flights of stairs. Barlow finally noticed that Jack was huffing and puffing as they reached the third floor. "I'm sorry, First Minister. I know you aren't used to Pacifica's gravity. That was inconsiderate of me. We should have taken a break on the second floor."

Jack caught his breath before answering. "Don't worry yourself. Being here takes the place of my usual workout. Better even."

"Well, no more stairs for now. My office is just down the hall," Barlow said with a guilty smile. After they entered Barlow's office and closed the door, they sat down at a small table. Jack was impressed with the workmanship of the table. Joints fitted together perfectly. Amazing what could be done with primitive tools, he thought. It was the little things the colonies did that were impressive.

Barlow smiled and said, "What can I help you with, First Minister?"

"As I mentioned in the council meeting, the Commonwealth is dedicated to peaceful coexistence. I am concerned that a majority of your council is going to struggle with this given the history with your neighbors," Jack said. He was quite proud of how he framed it. He had often gone fishing with his grandfather and knew the importance of choosing the right bait.

Barlow visibly reacted. He had to collect himself before responding. When he did, there was still an abundance of passion in his voice. "They would commit genocide if the opportunity presented itself. They have no interest in peace. The Guard is a collection of homicidal maniacs. They altered our history to hide the fact that we are the cause of our never-ending wars."

Barlow took a deep breath further, calming himself, and observed, "With a fence of sorts in place, I guess it's not really an issue anymore. I'm pleased the Commonwealth has invited us to join as a colony."

Well, that was certainly the right bait, thought Jack. I'll press and see if anything interesting comes out. "My concern, Mr. Barlow, is that when there is no longer an external enemy, an internal one will appear. Our experience with warlike cultures is that the fighting never stops."

"That's exactly my concern as well," Barlow said with a frown. He hesitated and then asked, "Are there examples of where the

Commonwealth has helped cultures mature?"

Jack smiled. He would have to tread carefully with Barlow. The man was smart. He already understood the non-interference Edicts and was looking for a way around them. "The non-interference Edicts are absolute. This governmental innovation is central to insuring peace across the universe. The Commonwealth will do nothing to interfere in your government as long as it has the correct form. As first minister, I am expected to offer advice and consultation. The more I know about your situation, the more I can help."

Jack paused, pretending to be concerned and searching for a solution. Then he said, "The Commonwealth does have an opportunity to help guide your government formation. I have to sign off on the form of government. Given Pacifica's preference for a monarchial republic, a key role is advisor to the king. This should be someone from your council who can help guide him. Theron Stone is an inexperienced and impressionable young man. He needs proper guidance. The role of his advisor is going to be critical." Jack paused again and then said, "At this point, I don't know enough to decide who would be best for that role."

Barlow nearly jumped out of his chair to start talking. Hooked! Jack thought gleefully. For the next thirty minutes, Jack was subjected to every perceived sin committed by the president and council. It took great patience to nod and look concerned at the appropriate times.

His patience finally paid off when Barlow said, "I shouldn't say this." Then he took a deep breath and, lowering his voice to just above a whisper, said, "President Malrey, our illustrious university dean, our financial controller, a medical researcher, and the Master Sergeant of the Guard are part of a secret group. They meet privately in hidden tunnels beneath the university. I don't know what they do down there. But I'm convinced it's not in the best interests of the people of Pacifica."

"How do you know this?" Jack asked, quieting his voice as well.

"Councilman Rickets discovered it by accident. He inadvertently left a report in President Malrey's office and went back to get it. Her office door was locked. She didn't answer when he knocked. It was very suspicious because her secretary claimed she hadn't left. He started checking her door when her schedule said she was going to be unavailable and had last been seen entering her office. That led to discovering others on the council having the same peculiarity. We got access to Kevin Wise's office, that's our finance minister, when he went on a vacation.

"After almost an entire day of looking, we found a hidden door in the back of his closet. A tunnel led to a locked steel door. There were other tunnels we suspect led to other offices in the Administration building and the university. When leaving, we noticed a key hanging on a hook just inside the tunnel entrance. We think it fits the steel door. We made a copy, but have been too cautious to go any further."

"Why are you afraid to go further with your investigation? You're both council members and nothing should be off limits," Jack said.

"These people are homicidal maniacs. They have a secret. It's reasonable to worry that they would kill to protect it," Barlow said in a whispery voice.

Jack pondered this for a minute and then said, "Can you show me the hidden door and give me the key? It's my responsibility to make sure the Commonwealth understands what is actually going on before it approves membership for a new colony. I will not reveal you or Councilman Rickets involvement in any of this."

Barlow considered this and then said, "They tend to have early morning meetings the day after something of consequence has happened. My guess is that we'll find Kevin Wise's office locked early tomorrow morning. If you meet me here at 5:00 AM, Rickets and I will get you into the tunnel system."

As Jack walked to Professor Dacy's office to wait, he wondered what the extreme secrecy was all about. He could certainly understand wanting to have meetings without Barlow. The man was paranoid, conspiratorial, and perhaps even a bit delusional. Hidden doorways and secret tunnels suggested a need to hide something significant. There was more to this than mere political disagreement. Hopefully, something he could play to his advantage.

CHAPTER 20

DISCLOSURE

The money had shown up. All of it. She was rich. Filthy rich. She carefully used a variety of agents to convert most of it into land, small private business ventures, untraceable precious metals, and Commonwealth certified bearer bonds. Nothing worse than keeping all your money in one place. By the time the money stopped moving, it would not be traceable to her or her holdings. It wouldn't even be possible to figure out which planet it was on. It was important to stay out of the view of colonial governments and the Commonwealth. She had decided years ago to retire on Athena. It was a pretty place that was sparsely populated. It was an agricultural planet with excellent soil and predictable weather.

But it was a relatively poor planet, given it had few other natural resources. That meant nobody cared about it. The other nice attribute was the lack of corruption. A corrupt government is a good thing if you need to bribe someone. It is generally bad if you are hiding from powerful people. They had money for bribes, too.

She wondered if Pluta would be satisfied. Not that she feared him. He would be stupid to try to do anything to her. She had been careful to build up favors, overpay for information, and make sure those who crossed her were never seen again. It tended to make decisions easy for those who were inclined to sell information. They could safely sell the inquiry to her at a premium instead. But you never knew what men like Pluta would try. She would keep her eyes open and her spies well paid.

Pluta could not believe his good luck. Cara had asked for a fortune; it was worth five fortunes. This information would destroy Cereo's political power. It would make his family social outcasts and ultimately drag his business into ruins. There was one earth-shattering revelation after another. The one he had to read twice was the news that his wife was a slave. She had always seemed provincial and unrefined, but he never suspected she was anything other than a well-to-do rural farmer's daughter.

The story of her father's land being next to the Cereo estate was believable. That one of the elites of society would marry such a girl made sense given how poor Caius was after his parents lost their fortune. The common people loved the story. Pluta now had documentation detailing how a birth certificate of a local girl who had died as a baby was used to create a false identity. His valet turned out to be his half-brother. Not that this by itself was all that unusual. Slave women had their uses.

But it turned out Leo was the one making all the business decisions. Caius was little more than Leo's mouthpiece. Slaves could easily be denied access to business meetings. That should make life difficult, perhaps even crippling. This was enough for him. The information confirming Cereo was behind Trajan's assassination was too risky.

Pluta thought he could control Theron once Cereo was out of the way. He had suspected the boy was an unenthusiastic ruler, and that was now confirmed. The last thing he wanted to do was initiate a succession debate. They might end up with an emperor who actually wanted to rule. As he was gleefully considering what to do with the information, there was a knock on his office door.

"What is it?" he snarled, irritated that his good mood was being interrupted.

"There is a woman who insists on seeing you immediately sir," Candice, his receptionist said. Her voice quavering.

"Tell her to request an appointment and I'll review it later. You should know better than to interrupt me," Pluta said angrily.

"I'm sorry, sir, but she said to tell you her name is Julie Jacobs. She was sure you would want to see her. She is quite forceful, sir," Candice said, clearly distraught.

Pluta's mind went white with terror. Cara's report started shaking slightly in his hands as he attempted to collect himself. After he somewhat gained control of his panic, he said, "I'll be right out, Candice."

He immediately took Cara's report and put it in his desk drawer. Wondering how to handle her arrival, he decided to let the governor lead the meeting. If she asked about the report, he would admit he had just received it and was about to report back. He stood and went to greet her.

"Ms. Jacobs, what a pleasant surprise," Pluta said with his best false smile. He had immediately noticed she was disguised and played along. She obviously had contacts in to hide her mismatched eyes. This couldn't be good, he thought.

"I hope you'll forgive me for the surprise visit. But I was in the city and decided to come by and see how you're doing. It's been much too long since we've seen each other," the governor said with her own false smile.

"Please come into my office Julie, I would love to catch up," he said, noticing Candice's alarm turning to confusion. Pluta was never this nice to anyone. He could see the wheels spinning as she tried to make sense of it. He would have to invent some story about a distant relative or long-lost friend.

After the office door closed, the governor said coldly, "Well at least you had the intelligence to not call me 'Governor' in front of your doxy." Pluta just nodded in agreement. He didn't dare tell her that Candice was just an office worker and nothing more. She stared at him with her inhuman eyes for what seemed to be an eternity. He was surprised to discover that contacts making them the same color didn't change their chilling effect in the slightest. Finally, she said, "When were you going to inform me you had a resource at Cereo's villa?"

"She was an assassin I placed there almost a year ago. Given our latest conversation, I changed her assignment to gathering information and hadn't gotten around to telling you yet," Pluta lied.

"If you lie to me one more time, it will be the last time," she said. The threat was clear and Pluta had no doubt she would carry it out. His hands started shaking again. If he hadn't just used the toilet, he thought he might pee his pants.

"Yes, ma'am," was all he could manage.

"You're fortunate I don't have time to replace you. But let me be clear. This is the last time you do anything independent of me. Is that clear?" she said.

"Yes, ma'am," Pluta said, thinking once again that this was the one thing he could say that seemed to mollify her.

She stared at him for another uncomfortable period of time before saying, "Tell me everything you've been keeping from me." The dam burst and Pluta confessed everything. He even told her why he had been keeping Cara a secret and that he was surprised when she claimed to have information damaging to Senator Cereo.

"And what are you going to do now that I know?" she asked with a threatening half smile.

"Whatever you direct me to do?" Pluta answered.

"An intelligent decision. One you claimed to make before but didn't carry through with," she said and just sat there watching him as he grew more and more uncomfortable, wondering what she would make him do. Then she said menacingly, "It's too bad you're not as competent as your assassin. Now there is someone with potential. She kept her fee reasonable so you would have no reason to be resentful. She did an admirable job of anonymously getting off planet and diversifying her money in a way that was near impossible to track.

"But what was really impressive is how she took the information she gathered to discover documented evidence that could be used against both you and Cereo. I especially like the seating charts based on tickets to the New Year's festival purchased by a servant of Vicentius Cereo. It shows twenty experienced soldiers under his command directly adjacent to where Theron shot his arrows. She has put information in your hands to destroy Cereo politically, socially, and bring him up on charges of high treason. My only question is whether you have the intelligence and balls to take advantage of this?"

"Yes, ma'am," Pluta said, relying on his mantra when it came to the governor.

"Okay, I'm doubtful, but this is exactly what you're going to do," she said with a threatening smile. Then she described precisely what was expected of him.

REVOLUTION

The committee started especially early that morning. They were all yawning. Jennifer bit back yet another yawn and decided to get things started. There was a lot to do outside of the committee today.

"Thanks again for coming so early. The Commonwealth showing up is a blessing for our people and a crisis for all of us. Before we get into a discussion of how we dissolve this group, let Griff and I review the decisions that were made yesterday." Jennifer was proud of herself for calmly referring to the dissolution of the committee. Everyone knew she mean 'when we all commit suicide.' It just sounded better and more abstract.

"The three planets have decided to form an alliance. We've agreed on a framework of the major issues. At some point, we'll have to formalize a treaty. But for now, we'll keep it at a high level. The council will meet today to hear all of this as well. I don't expect much disagreement, as we really aren't agreeing to anything controversial." At least for everyone except Barlow, she thought. "The one odd wrinkle is that the woman we thought was the Queen of Liberty is actually her best friend. The kidnappers mistakenly took her instead of the actual queen and she didn't inform them otherwise."

Del raised his hand and was acknowledged with a nod. "Does that mean that Tee isn't marrying the Queen of Liberty?"

Jennifer smiled, remembering the banter around that topic the previous day, and said, "No, the plan for all of us to retain some semblance of freedom is to have the wedding. Tee has agreed to marry the real queen."

"That sucks," Griff said angrily. "The boy should be able to choose his own wife, for God's sake."

"I agree. It's an incredible sacrifice. Tee said that being a member of the Guard meant he would do whatever was necessary to protect

Pacifica. You would have been proud of him. You've told me he's a natural leader, and I saw that yesterday," Jennifer said, mollifying Griff.

"Other than that, our agreements are fairly mild. We agreed, in principle, to negotiate a peace agreement that states we will not war on each other. The other two planets are very intimidated by us. I can see their point given how much more robust we are. But they should realize we have been yearning for peace for almost two thousand years. The last thing we want is war. They also proposed eliminating import and export tariffs. Since we have no trading experience, I have no idea if this is a good thing or a bad thing. Del, can you have someone in the history department investigate it before we sign any agreements?"

"Sure, not a problem. To be honest, Barlow might be a good resource for this. He used to teach a course on the history of economics. I know he's a pain in the rear, but he is knowledgeable and insightful as long as the topic doesn't get ensnared in one of his conspiracy theories."

"I'm fine with you using Barlow, as long as it doesn't create more confrontation in the council." There, she thought, proud of herself, batted that ball right back to him.

Griff raised his hand and said, "My understanding is that mercenaries actually invaded Liberty. Is this something the Guard is going to have to learn how to deal with?"

Jennifer sat back in her chair and in frustration said, "The first minister talks eloquently about how the Commonwealth has provided peace. But in talking to Senator Cereo and Prince Justin, it seems they do everything but that. I…"

Just then, the conference room door opened. The first minister entered holding what appeared to be a weapon in his hand. He quickly cautioned them, saying, "Stay where you are. This is a stun gun. It will put you all down the instant I pull the trigger" With a tense expression, he slowly backed himself into the furthest corner of the room. He motioned toward Griff and said, "I've seen you spar and know how fast you can move. Please no sudden movements."

Jennifer's gut turned into ice. They had been caught. Worse, there wasn't time to eliminate knowledge of their origin. They had doomed their people to extermination. As her mind screamed for an opportunity to turn the tables on the first minister he continued, "The four young people in the computer room were not harmed. They are sleeping and will stay that way for a few hours. I have some questions."

Jennifer thought, perhaps I can talk him into solving our problem for us. "The general population knows nothing of what's down here. No harm should come to them. You've made the consequences of violating technology restrictions clear. Why not execute our sentences here and now?"

The first minister looked surprised, and a little confused. After a moment he said, "What are your real plans with Liberty and Arista?"

Jennifer took a deep breath and let it out. Then she said, "Exactly what you've been told. Theron Stone and Olivia Hastings marry. We cooperatively work on increasing tax revenues from all three planets."

"Why hide all of this?" he said, clearly indicating their hiding of technology.

Never the most patient of people, Griff said, "So we can destroy the Commonwealth."

Jennifer actually smiled. Griff consistently said that Pacifica should go down swinging. She suddenly found herself caught up in his defiance and said sternly, "Why don't you grow yourself a pair and get on with it." Jennifer was oddly delighted to notice the rest of the committee was shocked at her words. She never said things like that. Her mother would be horrified, she thought, and smiled again.

Jack just stared at her for a few moments. Then, with an amused expression beginning to show, he said, "That might just be the advice I needed." Another pause, then he explained. "Uncovering hidden technology and a plot against the Commonwealth would make my career. At the very least, I can be sure of being assigned first minister of a much more lucrative sector." He hesitated again, and with a determined look said, "The truth is that I want to help you."

There was a long period of stunned silence. Finally, Del asked, "Why would you want to do that?"

Jack huffed out a nervous breath and said, "It's complicated." Pausing a few moments to collect his thoughts, he said, "No that's not true. It's actually very simple. I can't continue to do what the Commonwealth asks me to do. I've done horrible things in the name of the Commonwealth. I can't justify what I've done with that excuse any longer."

The committee members all looked at each other with surprised hope in their eyes. Jennifer then said, "So how can you help us?"

"I've been working with Senator Cereo for quite some time now. It's clear his strategy was to slow things down while generally giving the governor what she wants. It's a good strategy. Most of the Commonwealth's governors just want to maintain the status quo. Most of them got their jobs because of political influence, not merit. Her replacement should be vastly easier to work with. I can assist you through the transition."

"What do you get out of this?" Del asked bluntly.

Jack just stared back at him for a few moments and finally said, "Self-respect." Then, in a sad voice, he added, "As soon as the current governor has transitioned, I will resign my position and leave government. I'm not sure what I'll do. But it will be something I can be proud of."

Jennifer noticed that Griff and Del were giving each other looks. Griff then nodded and Del spoke up. "How far are you willing to go? Would you act against the Commonwealth? Are you willing to strike a blow?" Del asked.

Jack considered this for a long time. Then with firm conviction he said, "The Commonwealth is corrupt from top to bottom. Its original founders had good intentions. But it has evolved away from those good intentions. It's an amoral system completely controlling humankind for the benefit of a few power-hungry people. My father is a high-level bureaucrat in the Justice Ministry trying to fight corruption. He is an idealist. I believe the Justice Ministry is supporting him as a way to gain more power on the High Council. They don't want to eliminate corruption. They are as corrupt as everyone else. If there was a way to revolt against the Commonwealth, I would join the revolution."

Del smiled at Jack and said, "There is a way." He stopped, frowned at Jack's weapon, and added in the haughty professor voice he used with undergraduates, "If you're joining the revolution, please put your weapon away and sit down." Looking over at Jennifer with a sly smile, he said, "Griff and I have a secret we need to share."

CHAPTER 22

FORT PACIFICA

Jack's shuttlecraft landed at the designated location on the largest of Pacifica's two moons. He had informed the survey ship that he enjoyed visiting moons as a hobby. It was a ridiculous excuse for the shuttlecraft to be there. But being first minister meant that nobody would question his right to have a crazy hobby.

Large enough to be a small planet, it was perfect for hiding what they believed was there. They had landed next to what appeared to be a naturally formed cave. In fact, the opening seemed too small for what was described to be inside. Donning spacesuits, the team walked into the cave, which enlarged past the opening.

At the end of a corridor sized cavern was a large metal door. Quinn located a touch pad alongside the door and entered a code. To everyone's amazement, the door swung open to reveal an airlock. This was the tricky part. If the airlock didn't work, the warships said to be within the base would likely be damaged. If that were the case, their gamble would fail.

When the next keypad code was entered, the first door closed, lights came on, and a whooshing noise was heard. Quinn checked a readout on his space suit arm and after a few minutes announced with glee, "One atmosphere, seventy-eight percent nitrogen, twenty-one percent oxygen with traces of argon and CO_2. It's still very cold, so don't take your suits off."

Del added, "The entry door to the base will unlock when temperatures match. Let's keep these suits on until we are on the other side, with the airlock completely closed."

After shedding their spacesuits, they ventured down a hallway and entered what appeared to be a small reception area. A large screen on the back wall suddenly came to life. A GEM was looking at them. The group gave a collective gasp. Everyone except Griff and Tee stepped back. The two of them reached for nonexistent weapons at their belts. Just when they all wondered if they should run, the GEM smiled and began to speak in a warm and rich voice.

"Welcome. I hope this greeting is being received by the descendants of Ships 1 and 3. If not, I beseech our own descendants to search for their humanity and honor your ancestors' greatest desire. Peace for all.

My name is Donald Pearce. I am a direct line descendant of the original genetically enhanced research team given asylum by Ship 2. Our team was given asylum because we refused to participate in a plan to eradicate unmodified humans. We strongly believe there is no justification for genocide. We believe all life must be honored and protected.

I am first generation, which means I was genetically altered physically for life on Pacifica. Those likely still alive on Pacifica are second generation. Those alterations were intended to make them stronger emotionally and mentally. As you surely know, those alterations went horribly wrong. Most of the first generation volunteered to remain in orbit once it became clear what we had created. We told our offspring we were doing it to support them. In reality, we were debating what to do. Our shared goal had been to enable our descendants to enjoy all the fruits of Pacifica. And to do so in peace. We intended to live alongside the inhabitants of the peninsula in harmony, honoring our common roots. It became clear this wasn't going to happen.

Our paranoia was justified. Autonomous shuttle craft pretending to be carrying supplies were used to destroy Ships 1 and 3. Their plan had been to simultaneously board Ship 2 while launching an invasion of the peninsula. We uncovered their subterfuge, and with great reluctance, destroyed the shuttlecraft approaching our ship. We did not realize the danger to Ships 1 and 3 until it was too late. For that failure, we are deeply sorry.

We now faced another difficult choice. We could have used our technological capabilities to wipe out our progeny. But then we would have been as immoral as the civilization we escaped. They are human, perhaps with the worse attributes of our race, but human, nonetheless. We knew about the secret bunker beneath Landfall Valley. After witnessing the devastation of the civil war, we knew it would be many generations before that technology would be useful. We were extremely concerned that remnants of the civilization we escaped would discover our technology. Some advocated destroying it, but others, including myself, advocated storing it away in the hope that Pacifica could someday use it for peaceful purposes.

The research project the original modified colonists were working on was QW, or Quantum Warfare. Allen's Law laid out the groundwork for making incredibly sensitive measurements of gravitation. So sensitive, in fact, that locating and identifying objects in the vastness of space was possible by simply looking for emanations from concentrations of mass. Not only could minute concentrations of mass be located, but their nature could be determined. For instance, a spaceship is easily identified, given its three-dimensional distribution of mass compared to its volume. Our original goal was to confuse these measurements. Our research turned out to be much more successful.

Not only could we confuse measurements, but we also found we could create false readings. We have the means to present whatever we want our adversaries to see. Including nothing at all. This means a QW enabled warship can travel undetected and deliver a QW enabled warhead that is similarly undetectable. The warhead seemingly detonates out of nothing. If our technology had been intended to defeat those who wanted to eradicate us, we would have enthusiastically supported that effort.

However, it became clear that hatred had infected our leadership and QW technology was going to be used for genocide. We simply could not contribute to that cause. Our hope is that this technology will be used to protect all forms of human life, not destroy them.

To enter, we ask that everyone individually pledge to use the technologies within for the betterment of all of humanity. Please say your name and make your pledge. When all pledges have been accepted, you may enter. Every time you reenter, you will have to make your pledge again. Whomever you have chosen to lead should go first. After entering, merely state your name and what you would like to accomplish. Automated systems will do the rest.

May peace be with you.

They all looked around at each other in wonderment. After a few moments, Del stepped forward and said, "My name is Delvin Dacy. I pledge to dedicate my life to the betterment of humanity. This pledge includes all humans, whether genetically altered or not."

The voice from the video simply said, "You speak the truth. Your pledge is accepted."

The rest of the group stepped forward individually and repeated the same pledge Del had made. Quinn was the last one to make his pledge. After his pledge was accepted, the voice said, "Welcome to Pacifica's archive of technology." A hidden door in one of the side walls popped open.

Even after three days of discovery, the group was still in awe but wary. This seemed too good to be true. Everyone had a sense that disaster must surely be just around the corner. Well, almost everyone. Quinn seemed to be on his dream vacation. It would be nice to exist in such a state of bliss all the time, thought Del. While he had seen Quinn nervous or uncomfortable at times, these were rare and never lasted for long. It was a good thing the boy wasn't moody. He was key to unlocking this technology.

While Hestie was also capable of understanding it, she wasn't as passionate about the engineering side of things. Her passions were focused in other areas. Quinn's contributions were critical in protecting them from the Commonwealth. Del was very happy he did not have to deal with someone as irrational as he had been at that age.

The three warships were much larger than they had guessed. They were designed to be operated by six crew members. But they were outfitted to comfortably hold twelve for long periods of time. There was a shuttle craft on board each ship for planetary excursions. These were small but could transport a crew of up to six for short distances. They were not equipped with jump capability. The warships had clearly been intended to do everything from destroying planets to boarding spaceships and performing limited scouting missions on planet. "Where are we in getting the warships operational?" Del asked.

"Donny says all calibrations and tests have been completed on Gerty. It's ready to go. The Aguila has an issue with its propulsion system. It's repairable but we need to create replacement parts and perform a full service. I recommend we leave that for later. Peregrine is currently being calibrated," Quinn said.

One of the political agreements was that each planet would crew one of the three warships. They committed to making sure these vessels were only used for sector defense and not planetary war. Pacifica did this with the restriction that they alone controlled the technology. The Liberty and Arista ships' maintenance and support would be solely provided by Pacifica. Jennifer asked Tee to name Pacifica's ship. He named it after his grandmother. Prince Justin and Senator Cereo named the other two. Donny was what they had all taken to calling the voice that seemed to control everything. It was the same warm and friendly voice that had originally welcomed them. It had a calming nature and, by now, seemed to be part of the crew.

"I've finished testing our inventory of fusion and anti-matter munitions. They are all QW enabled," Quinn said, smiling.

Del wasn't sure how anyone could talk about that kind of destructive power and not seem concerned, but again, this was Quinn. "What are they designed for?" Del asked.

"There are two types of fusion devices. The first is small and would destroy a building, bridge, or spaceship. The larger would incinerate an entire valley on Pacifica. The anti-matter devices could destroy an entire planet. We only have five of those," Quinn said with a smile still intact.

Del shuddered to think they had the means to destroy five entire planets. "How many of each type of fusion device do we have?"

"One hundred and twenty of the small and thirty of the large. We also have full production capability to build more. The limiting material is anti-matter. If we keep in reserve what has been set aside for munitions, we can build approximately one thousand more devices. The triggers for the fusion devices use a tiny amount of anti-matter. We can also produce more anti-matter, but would need to invest quite a bit of time and resources to build that capability out," Quinn concluded.

In other words, we have way more than we should ever need, Del thought. "How about crew related activities? When will we be able to launch Gerty?"

"Communications, propulsion, environmental, and ordinance have reported they are ready to go. Hestie has the navigation system up and running. I need to finish here and go through the navigation checklist with her on Peregrine," Quinn said.

After deciding Quinn had everything under control, he went looking for Griff. He finally found him on board Gerty, checking ordinance. He said, "For a man terrified of the Tram, you seem to have overcome your fear of technology."

Griff grinned and replied, "Knowing you had nothing to do with designing any of this gives me great comfort."

Del smiled back and then changed to a serious tone. "Griff, is Tee really ready to take this on?"

Griff stopped what he was doing and looked calmly at Del. After a few moments he said, "Yes. The boy has many lifetimes of experience in highly stressful situations where judgement and timing are critical. He is Pacifica's best military strategist. There isn't anyone I trust more to lead this, including myself." Then, Griff smiled and said, "Plus, he'll have the benefit of my vast knowledge and experience to fall back on."

Del retained his serious expression and simply nodded. "That's all I needed to hear, Griff."

Griff seemed surprised at the lack of a comeback. "Were you thinking of using your authority to make a change?"

"I was. He just seems so young. It's also clear he doesn't desire leadership," Del said.

"He is young. But after Arista, he's far older than either of us. While he doesn't pursue command, he never hesitates to take it on and excel. Having power over others isn't important to him. People sense that and are drawn to him. He's the kind of leader the Guard and Pacifica needs," Griff said with conviction.

Just then, Donny's voice permeated the inside of Gerty, saying, "We have detected movements of two Commonwealth warships that appear to be offensive in nature. Of immediate concern is a Commonwealth warship on a vector to Pacifica, utilizing fast jumping. This warship will arrive in the vicinity of Pacifica in approximately twenty-seven hours at their current jump rate. A second Commonwealth warship, together with three large transport vessels, is vectoring for Liberty. This configuration is typical for transporting an invasion force. Given its current standard jump rate, an invasion force could be on the ground in three days."

Fast jumping was dangerous. By shortening the processing time to generate a wormhole, you increase your risk of miscalculating. While rare, ships have simply disappeared forever when operating in this mode. This meant the Commonwealth was suspicious of a threat from Pacifica and decided to take aggressive action. "We need to get everybody together and decide what to do," Griff said with worry in his voice.

"The governor has obviously decided to accelerate the plan," Jack said. "If she understood what we're doing, she would send more than one warship to Pacifica."

"But why send a warship here at all?" Jennifer asked.

"She doesn't like loose ends. Having legal authority for three planets in one location would be seen as a risk. It might look like an overreaction, but this is typical of her," Jack said.

"So, we still have the opportunity for a surprise attack," Griff said.

"In my opinion, yes," Jack said.

"What about providing immediate support for Liberty? You've agreed to provide for the defense of Liberty," Justin said suspiciously.

"We've all agreed to support each other," Griff shot back. "We will get to Liberty as soon as possible, but it has to be in the context of an overall battle strategy."

"Gentleman, we are all friends here. We have a common enemy. Can we please discuss alternatives in an atmosphere of trust?" Cereo said. "Griff, you've told me that Tee is our best strategist. Perhaps we should listen to his council on what we should do with our warships."

They all looked at Tee, and he momentarily leaned back in his chair. He looked down and said, "I've been giving this some thought. "We need to maintain the element of surprise as long as possible. This should drive our decisions until we decide to reveal ourselves. The first priority is to keep our base of operations hidden. That means this moon."

"But what about Liberty!" Justin blurted out.

"Give me a few minutes to describe what I think our strategic priorities should be, and then I'll make a recommendation on how to achieve them," Tee said, looking calm and confident. Jennifer smiled. He really is quite mature for his age, she thought.

Justin took a deep breath, obviously settling himself. "I'm sorry, Tee. My anxiety over the queen is making me crazy. I need to trust everyone here, which is obviously still a challenge for me." Jennifer was starting to like Prince Justin. He might be overly emotional at times, but he owned up to it and made the necessary changes in his behavior.

Tee continued, "We are badly outnumbered, and that suggests we cut their military supply line as soon as possible."

"What does that mean?" Del asked.

"It means we control movement through the Sector 27 wormhole. Cut them off from the Commonwealth," Tee explained.

Del scrunched his eyebrows together, obviously giving this some thought. Then he said, "We can also shut down their ability to communicate. Quinn told me we could capture key nodes in their network and control communications. If we do this properly, we can communicate with ourselves and the Commonwealth, but they can't communicate with each other."

Del noticed that everyone was giving him confused looks. He hesitated a few moments and then added, "I know all this technology is confusing. Let me explain a bit more. The way real-time communications happen across the sector is through permanent stationary artificial wormholes that are enlarged just enough to transmit optical information. A very thin beam of light. As we've discussed with the warships, the energy required to grow and keep artificial wormholes open is tremendous. By keeping the distances between nodes reasonable, and the size of the wormholes very small, a real-time network can be built and reasonably operated. To control information flow, we simply select key nodes in the system and replace them with our own. Quinn built two of these long ago as a hobby project. He can build more if we need them."

Tee nodded at that information and continued, "The lowest risk short-term move is to leave one warship here and take the other straight to the wormhole. However, that is likely just going to end up in a war of attrition. That is a war we will lose." Tee stopped and looked around the table. Then he said, "Are you willing to gamble?"

CHAPTER 23

SIEGE

Olivia knew they had been extremely lucky. Without warning, troop transports had landed just outside the capital. The luck was having Hastings Castle currently overcrowded with Colonel Peters's rangers. If they had landed a few days later, most of those men would have been on their way back to their barracks near Perry's ranch.

They were cut off from the main Royal Army units. But they had an adequate number of defenders to withstand a lengthy siege. The castle had its own well, so water wasn't an issue. But they only had about three weeks of food stored away. Perry had immediately issued orders for reduced rations, but that would only add another three weeks, best case.

Perry was shocked to see General Harris riding up to the main gate with four armed Guards under a white flag. A messenger relayed that he was asking to speak with whomever was in charge.

After a short conversation with Olivia, Perry walked out of the gate to meet with him. He had Colonel Peters and another robust ranger as his only security. Olivia smiled. She remembered Perry had been outnumbered two to one in his previous confrontation with General Harris. Well, that's a creative way to insult him without saying a word, she thought.

"General Eastbrook and Colonel Peters. So good to see you both," Harris said jovially.

"What are you doing here, Harris?" Perry asked sternly.

"I've come to take control of Liberty for its rightful ruler," Harris said with his smile still in place.

"Queen Olivia would never engage mercenaries," Perry said dismissively.

"Queen Olivia is no longer Liberty's rightful ruler," Harris countered, paused, and then with an evil grin said, "Why don't I explain what's happened? That will speed up discussions of your surrender." Harris paused again, then continued. "Arista's Senate has determined that Theron Stone and Olivia Hastings are legally married. They met the three qualifications of a common law marriage on Arista. They both had the legal capacity to enter into a marriage. They expressed an intent to be married. And they were engaged in cohabitation at Theron's private residence in Arista's Palatium.

"Once married under Arista law, Olivia Hastings falls under the authority of her husband. That means he became the legal ruler of both Arista and Liberty. Theron's chief advisor, Senator Cereo, was discovered to be secretly fomenting a slave rebellion. This was known to Theron and is in violation of the articles of property in the Arista constitution.

"This caused the Senate of Arista to issue an arrest warrant for Senator Cereo and declare Theron unsuitable to rule Arista. Magistrate Pluta, in the name of the Arista Senate, now claims authority over both planets. The Commonwealth's Justice Ministry supports the legality of Arista's claim."

Perry just stared at him for a while. Just as it got uncomfortable, he said, "I don't believe you. Pack up and leave, or this time the courts will decide your fate." He turned around and walked back into the castle.

Harris shouted at him as he strode away, "It's just a matter of time, General. Something I have in abundance. My men will simply enjoy all your planet has to offer until you accept reality. Your only decision is to decide how much suffering you want the citizens of Liberty to endure."

Perry walked directly from his confrontation with Harris to Olivia's quarters. She was currently hiding away in the old apartment he had occupied for a number of months. As soon as he walked in, Olivia could see his anxiety. She said softly, "I heard everything. What do you think we should do?"

Perry took in a deep breath and said, "It's time to reveal that they kidnapped the wrong person. The welfare of Liberty must come first. It may put Bria in danger, but it's what she would want us to do."

"Agreed. How do you propose we announce this?" Olivia asked.

Perry steeped his hands together and said, "I recommend we tell Harris we're willing to discuss surrender if the first minister mediates the discussions. Harris insisted on this the last time, so he can hardly object now. We'll need to prove you are the queen. Pretty much everyone knows what you look like, so it shouldn't be difficult. It's why it's been so hard to hide you. If we don't get the Commonwealth involved, Harris will just claim you're a fake."

Olivia looked troubled. She gave it some thought and finally said, "I don't like leaving our people defenseless against that army. Perhaps it's better to declare it now. It might cause enough worry that he controls his men until the first minister shows up."

"It will likely cause him to storm the castle instead. If he suspects that he has no legal authority, he will take steps to change that situation. I have no doubts he will kill everyone in the castle to cover this up. Given the Commonwealth is involved, anyone who knows the truth will be hunted down," Perry said firmly.

Olivia's expression grew firm and, raising her voice, she said, "I am not willing to hide behind these walls while our people are murdered and abused."

As Perry opened his mouth to respond, they heard a loud whooshing noise outside the window. Both walked over to look outside and froze, dumbfounded. Perry recovered first and shouted, "Peters! Full complement on the main gate walls. Assemble a raiding party for an assault in case hostiles emerge from that shuttlecraft." And with that, he briskly followed Peters, who was running to comply.

Olivia joined him a few minutes later in the watchtower above the main gate. Everyone she had walked past to get there recognized her. Shouts of "Queen Olivia has returned," were ringing in the courtyard below.

"I guess you've made your decision," Perry said with mild sarcasm.

"You always told Bria and I that sometimes you just have to make a decision," Olivia said.

Perry frowned at her and, looking back to the shuttlecraft, said, "What do we have here?"

Just then, the door to the shuttlecraft opened and a man walked out.

"It's Uncle Justin," Olivia said in surprise. A woman exited next. "And Bria!" And with that, she ran down the stairs and out the gate to greet them. Colonel Peters quickly detailed his rangers waiting by the gate to surround the queen. She ran and jumped into Bria's arms, both of them laughing and crying all at once. Perry joined them and pulled Bria into his own tight hug, rocking her back and forth.

"I can't believe you're back. I've been worried sick about you," Perry said.

Justin smiled broadly watching the reunion, and then looked toward the shuttle door and said, "Come on out."

The three largest people Olivia had ever seen stepped out of the shuttle. "Surround," Colonel Peters barked as his ranger pulled their weapons and, keeping their distance, quickly encircled the newly embarked passengers.

"Stop!" Justin yelled. "They're friends. Put your weapons away."

Olivia noticed the rangers didn't comply with Prince Justin's order. Only when Colonel Peters ordered them to 'stand down' and 'escort' did they put their weapons away. Even then, they kept their hands near their weapons. They closed in around their queen but maintained their encirclement of the group.

"Your Majesty, would you allow me to make introductions?" Prince Justin said. After she gave him a nod of approval, he continued. "First let me present Theron, First of his Name, Emperor of Arista."

"It's a pleasure to meet you, Your Majesty," Olivia said smoothly, which surprised even her, given the shocking news that she was talking to the emperor of a planet she thought utterly immoral. She paused and then said, "Do you realize the mercenary army camped out on the plain believes they are acting under orders from Arista?"

Tee smiled grimly at her and said, "We suspected that was the case when we arrived. We saw the Commonwealth troop transport vessels and decided to come straight to your castle. There is much to discuss, but know we are here to support you," Tee said quickly. Then he stopped and, grimacing in embarrassment, said, "It's nice to meet you as well."

Prince Justin continued with introductions, "With Theron is Griffith Ricks, acting Commander General of the Pacifica Guard, and Diana Wells, Captain of the Apple Valley Wall Archers. I'm sorry to rush introductions, but can we retire for a private conversation?" Looking over at Perry, he said, "I will vouch for Theron and his companions. They are our friends and, as Theron said, they are here to help."

"What about the rifles?" Diana asked Griff.

"Keep them in the shuttle for now. We'll offload them after we've explained everything to Her Majesty and General Eastbrook. In the meantime, if the army camped out there, attacks take off and dissuade them with the shuttle's armaments," Griff said with a grin.

"Yes, sir," Diana said, smiling.

As they were walking to Olivia's reception room, Perry turned to Justin and said in a hushed voice, "What's this all about?"

Justin turned and looked at Perry warmly. He grinned and said, "I've joined another revolution. I'm hoping to do a better job of recruiting you this time."

The next morning, Olivia, Justin, Chief Justice Roberts, Bria, and Perry met to discuss what they had learned the day before. Justin started the conversation. "I've asked Bria to join us because she has spent considerable time in Senator Cereo's household and knows Tee well." He hesitated and continued, "Our path forward has much to do with our level of trust in these people."

"And where do you stand on the trust issue?" Olivia asked.

"Senator Cereo has a golden tongue, which makes me nervous. He's been a master manipulator in Arista politics and with the Commonwealth. But I've become convinced he has helped Liberty in the process. I'm convinced he has good intentions." Justin stopped for a moment and looked around the table. "The real threat is Pacifica. A more warlike culture is hard to imagine. They control military technology that appears to exceed even the Commonwealth's capabilities. That combination terrifies me."

Olivia pondered his answer for a few moments and then turned to Bria. "Would you tell everyone what you told me about Tee last night?"

"Terrifying is a good description of Tee. I saw him kill three of the Guards on the slave ship without seeming to exert any effort at all. It happened so fast I can't tell you how he did it. As I'm sure you've noticed, he is smaller than others of his race." Bria then took a breath, smiled slightly, and said, "On the other hand, I'm convinced Tee is a man of honesty, integrity, and compassion. I trust Tee." She twitched a little mentally at the conflict that remained within her. She had come to realize she was scared of what Tee could do, but she did trust him to do the right thing.

Perry spoke up at this point. "Early this morning, I watched Tee and the one they call Jay spar. We teach smaller soldiers to take advantage of their quickness when fighting larger opponents. The unusually large can sometimes be a bit ponderous. That is clearly not the case with these two. They are lightning quick and extraordinarily skilled."

Perry smiled grimly and said, "And then there are the women. If Diana is typical, they are equally impressive. The men heard Prince Justin introduce Diana as a Wall Archer. While we were meeting yesterday, they challenged her to a contest. They gave her one of our siege bows, thinking of having a little fun. These bows are intended to launch heavy bolts over high walls from a distance. The bolts generally have large glass vials for arrowheads filled with a flammable liquid and are used to start fires. Very few are strong enough to use them. They confused pretty with weak. She used it effortlessly. She humiliated our best archers. According to those who were there, it wasn't even close to competitive."

Olivia sighed and then said in a quiet voice, "Can we trust them?"

Justin nodded and summarized, "I think the best evidence of trust is what they have offered us. Instead of demanding concessions, they will share their technology. The only restriction will be military technology. Medicines, transportation, power generation, and computer knowledge will all be available. They are asking Liberty to join Pacifica and Arista as equal partners in managing and disseminating it. The only price is that we join the revolution."

Justin hesitated, clearly going through a checklist in his head, and then said, "One more thing. Senator Cereo proposed that Pacifica announce they are the ones behind this. That Pacifica is merely evicting squatters. They will claim they achieved ownership of the sector by discovery when they arrived almost two millennia ago. It's a good idea because if this doesn't go our way, Liberty can claim we were forced to comply. Gives us an opportunity to avoid having our planet cleansed."

"It sounds too good to be true," Olivia said. "But then again, I don't see how we have another choice. If we sit on the sidelines and the Commonwealth wins, our people will still suffer. Their actions over the past few years prove that." She looked around the table and asked, "Does anyone disagree that our best option is to accept the offer?" Olivia looked at each person and received head nods from each. "Okay, it's decided. Justice Roberts, would you see what they have written down?"

Justin spoke up quickly, "Olivia, we don't have time to argue over wording. Events are unfolding quickly. We have to act immediately. If we agree, then Perry will join one of the warships as its commander. And…"

"Wait a minute. I don't know anything about space travel or modern weaponry," Perry said with exasperation.

"You don't have to. The ships operate on voice command. There is a crew of five that will propose actions, and the commander simply gives the command to execute or belay. I observed this on the trip here. You will have no trouble with it. This is all part of the sharing. We have two warships currently operating. One will be commanded by Tee, and the other by you. The third, once it's up and running, will be commanded by Senator Cereo until he can retrieve his son Vincent. All are staffed by Pacifica for now. In the future, we will have our own operators. Our warship is named the Peregrine, by the way."

"Peregrine?" Perry said, "You didn't!"

"Yes, I did. If you didn't want to be constantly reminded that you saved the life of a young and stupid prince you never should have done it," Justin said, obviously pleased with himself. "One more thing. You heard Diana mention rifles yesterday. With something called an optical scope, they can accurately hit a target from over a mile away. Fifty of these are being loaned along with Diana for training. This should keep General Harris at bay until we can spare one of the warships to come back and mop up. It should only be a few weeks at most. The other item we'll leave behind is a communications console. For now, it's been set up so you can call any of the three warships or President Malrey. Diana will train a couple of operators for you."

Justin hesitated and then said, "I know this is difficult. I had a hard time accepting it as well. But time is critical. We need to let them know we agree. Once that's done, Perry must get with Tee and Griff to agree on a battle strategy."

Tee greeted Perry warmly, "I'm happy Liberty decided to join General Eastbrook."

"Call me Perry. We aren't much on formality, Theron."

"Then call me Tee," he said, smiling. "Let me give you a summary. You'll get a chance for a more in-depth understanding once onboard and on your way. The advantage we have is invisibility. The Commonwealth warships can't see us or our munitions until they explode. They can't hide from us. But we can hide from them. When we arrived at Liberty, we destroyed the Commonwealth warship that accompanied the troop transports. The transport ships were then boarded and disabled.

"The Commonwealth is so worried about their own citizens revolting they do not allow anyone but the military to have weapons of any kind. The transport vessels are in stable orbits but unable to do anything until we return. The Commonwealth will think their sector communications network has gone down. They will eventually figure out its sabotage. General Harris has certainly realized something is horribly wrong at this point." Tee waited to see if Perry had questions, then continued.

"Did you offer to let the Commonwealth warship surrender before you destroyed them?" Perry asked with a frown.

Griff looked surprised. He considered the question, then nodded and answered, "It's a good question. Prince Justin recommended this when we arrived. However, we didn't know what action the warship might take. It might have used the demand as an excuse to attack the planet. He eventually agreed it was a risk we couldn't afford to take. Griff hesitated and then sheepishly said, "Don't think badly of us. We've been fighting a never-ending war against an enemy where surrender wasn't an option. We've never been in a position to consider humanitarian alternatives."

Perry gave that some thought and then nodded in understanding. Then he looked at Tee and asked, "What do you propose we do next?"

Tee looked a bit guilty as he said, "My thoughts are that we need to cut their supply lines and blockade A27."

"That makes sense," Perry said, nodding in approval. "Are you suggesting we try to stop all traffic into and out of the sector? Is that even possible?"

"Yes, we think so. We announce we are embargoing Sector 27 and then destroy anything that enters or tries to exit through the wormhole. We do the same for A27. We need to be careful with communications anytime there is a nearby threat. This is because our location is revealed when we transmit. In those situations, the recommendation is to only communicate when it's an emergency. In that case, the process is to send short messages and then move immediately. They can't tell where we are if we just receive messages from the network."

Perry considered this and said, "So one of us goes to the wormhole and the other to Planet 27?"

"Yes," Griff said, "Our suggestion is that you proceed to A27, and we'll take care of the wormhole. You have much more experience with offensive warfare than we do. A27 is where we believe we might need to go on the offensive. The wormhole is a defensive action that we feel we are best suited for. Tee and I propose you take the lead on military decisions. Our experience is one dimensional while yours is not. All three planets have agreed to this."

Perry was pleased. These are reasonable people, he thought. Their proposal makes sense based on experience and relative strengths and weaknesses. Giving up the lead on military decisions says they will do the right thing even if it's to their disadvantage. "Well, let's get going then. We can discuss this in more detail once we're on our way. The warships can communicate with each other, right?"

"Yes, sir, except when we're traversing a wormhole." Tee frowned slightly and continued. "I wish I could explain this better. Quinn started explaining radio communications to me, but I didn't have enough time to spend with him to truly understand it. I don't understand everything Quinn tells me, but I believe everything he says."

"Okay then, I'll believe him too," Perry said and gave Tee an approving nod of the head.

CHAPTER 24

TRESPASS

Gerty's main console came to life with an image of President Malrey sitting at her desk. Griff noted wryly that they had done a good job of cleaning off the top of that desk. It was normally piled high with paperwork. Quinn was explaining in excruciating detail how video cameras work when Jennifer started talking.

"My name is Jennifer Malrey. I am the duly elected President of Pacifica. This message is a declaration that we will no longer accept the Commonwealth's trespass in our sovereign domain. Our ancestors discovered this sector one thousand eight hundred and fifty-three years ago. At that time, our ownership of all planets within the sector was established. We desire to live in peace with other like-minded people. It's clear from our observations of the Commonwealth that this is not possible.

"We believe all people are created equal. That the form of government people live under is one they have collectively agreed to. We believe that tyranny is an abusive form of government. Our belief is that slavery is an expression of the worse attributes of the human race. It's become obvious from our observations that the Commonwealth does not share these values. We've decided that peace and freedom can only be obtained through separation."

Jennifer paused, glanced down at her notes, and then continued, "We feel it is important to give examples of why we have come to this decision. The Governor of Sector 27 has violated the Commonwealth's non-interference Edict. This is just one instance of the corruption that appears to be commonplace. She coerced the Arista government to declare war on Liberty. The people of Arista hold no blame in this. Their government was clearly operating under the duress of a tyrant. A puppet government controlled by the governor was established for the purpose of enslaving the populations of Arista, Liberty, and Pacifica. This is an act of war."

Jennifer paused and changed her tone to one of triumph, saying, "Pacifica has come to the defense of Liberty. The Commonwealth warship threatening that planet has been destroyed and the troop transports orbiting the planet have been boarded and placed under our control. Pacifica has no desire to oppress the citizens of Liberty or any other Commonwealth colony. They will be offered the opportunity to join a Confederation of Planets and live in peace, freedom, and security."

Jennifer's face took on a firm look and continued. "Due to the tyranny and lawlessness of the Commonwealth we require all Commonwealth citizens to leave the sector. As of this time forward, no vessels will be allowed to enter our sovereign domain without permission. This includes any traffic through what is commonly referred to as the Sector 27 wormhole. Any attempt to do so will result in those vessels' immediate destruction.

"A27 is similarly embargoed with the same result to any vessel attempting to land or leave the planet. We also control communications within the sector and through the wormhole. You may request permission to communicate so that plans can be generated to expedite your travel back to the Commonwealth. These communications will be individually reviewed. They will only be approved if we deem them appropriate."

Jennifer then paused and softened her expression. "Our hope is to live in peace with the Commonwealth. We ask your government to reply with its compliance so we may assist you with safe transportation back to your homes. May peace be with you."

Griff had a slight grin on his face as he turned to Tee and said, "Well that does it. It's official. The next ship that comes through that hole in space gets blown to hell." As soon as he said it, a large Commonwealth warship appeared.

"Detonate S1," Tee ordered and after a slight pause the ship's sensors were overwhelmed with energy blinding them momentarily. After the sensors recovered, there was nothing left to see but debris.

Jay immediately announced, "Device S2 ready for launch." Jay had only gotten one day of training to be Gerty's munitions officer. It was a simple job, but given the requirement of human interaction for every step, it was vital. The AI debacle in ancient times altered for eternity what computers would be allowed to do on their own.

"Destination match," Quinn said, indicating that the jump for Device

S2 was ready for launch.

"Destination approved. Launch Device S2," Tee ordered, and the device immediately arrived at the mouth of the wormhole, awaiting a detonation command.

Two more ships appeared and were added to the cloud of debris when Quinn said, "That last one didn't have any occupants. It was an empty vessel."

Tee considered this for a few moments and then asked, "Can we determine if there are any occupants before they have time to jump?"

Quinn considered this and then, with a frown, said, "Probably not. The minimum processing time for a fast jump is roughly the same as the time to analyze the contents of a ship."

Tee frowned and gave this some thought, "Is the Aquila fixed yet?" Tee asked. The Aquila was the third warship and Caius named it after the Roman symbol of authority. Caius told him that he thought Arista's Senate would feel pride with that choice and wanted to do everything possible to mollify them. When this was over, Caius had an insurrection to deal with. The more he could bow to the Senate's vanity, the better.

"No. They sent me test data and their conclusions. I'm not allowed to respond to them this close to the wormhole. I don't agree with their conclusions, so I doubt Aquila will leave Fort Pacifica anytime soon," Quinn concluded.

Tee sighed, frowned, and then said, "Colonel Peters, you are in command until I return. Continue to destroy anything that comes through."

"Yes, sir," came the response.

"Griff, can you join me in the dining room?" Tee asked.

With a quick nod, Griff turned and walked from the bridge with Tee close behind him.

As soon as the door closed Tee said, "We're screwed. They can continue sending junk vessels until Gerty runs out of munitions. We can't rely on Aquila for resupply. The danger has always been that we get overwhelmed. If they don't care how many vessels they lose, it's just like fighting the GEMs. Eventually, they will wear us down. If they can flood the sector with warships, they will eventually find Fort Pacifica. If that happens, we lose."

Griff just smiled at him and said, "You have some crazy plan you're reluctant to share."

"You've been listening to Jay," Tee accused with a weak smile.

Griff narrowed his eyes at Tee and said, "I've been watching you closely since you were stupid enough to challenge someone twice your size on the playground. You don't give up and you always have a plan. Sometimes the plan is insane. Your insane plans tend to work more often than not."

Tee shrugged in a self-depreciating way and said, "We have to change the rules. It might get messy."

CHAPTER 25

THE BUNKER

Governor Jacobs's mismatched eyes were bugged out more than Jack had ever seen them. Even parsecs away, it frightened him. He wasn't sure he would ever get over the trauma of working for her. "How dare you broadcast your ridiculous message directly to the Commonwealth and our A27 citizens," she said loudly, glaring out from the monitor.

Jennifer stared back at her confidently and said in a calm, matter-of-fact voice, "I don't have time to waste on inconsequential banter. We simply need to discuss your surrender and exit from this sector." Jack had become tremendously impressed with Jennifer Malrey. He had watched her orchestrate the Pacifica Council with graceful collaboration. He thought Julie Jacobs would chew her up and spit her out. But instead, she was showing a spine made of steel.

"Let me tell you what's going to happen. The Commonwealth will spare no expense to wipe out your pathetic little revolution. You might blow up a few transports trying to take off or land. But it doesn't change the outcome. The Commonwealth has hundreds of warships with nothing else to do. They will love having a conflict to resolve. It will temporarily relieve them of their boring lives. I've always thought the military was grossly bloated. A waste of credits. But I have to admit they are capable. I don't care what technology you have hidden away on Pacifica. You will be completely destroyed," Jacobs said with an evil smirk as Jack imagined a cat tail twitching behind her.

"If you are unwilling to recognize reality, then we will have to introduce it to you in a more dramatic fashion," Jennifer said confidently.

"Spare me your empty threats. If you surrender, I will see what I can do to ensure your people are enslaved instead of exterminated. Otherwise, you can go to your grave knowing you've caused their extinction. You'll be on your knees begging for mercy before this is over," Jacobs said with the intense stare of a cat ready to pounce. She hesitated, seemingly gathering her thoughts, and said, "By the way, what have you done with Queen Olivia, Senator Cereo, and my first minister?"

"Queen Olivia and Senator Cereo have been offered sanctuary. Your first minister is in a holding cell awaiting your surrender. We can negotiate his release once you've agreed to our terms," Jennifer said.

"Do whatever you want with Jack. It would be kinder if you simply eliminated him. Failure of this magnitude is dealt with harshly by the Commonwealth," Jacobs said and then her face took on a smile that caused chills. "Tell the queen and senator to start practicing their begging. It's going to have to be good." Then she severed the link.

Jennifer slumped a bit in her chair, took a deep breath and let it out. "What do you think?" she asked Olivia, Caius, and Jack, who were all shown on separate monitor windows.

"She believes what she's saying," Jack said. "Even if we invade A27, there is a bunker she can retreat to. Only the governor and the local commander know where it's at. She's probably already there. She won't care if we kill everyone on A27 if she wins in the end. Her stance that she has time is credible."

They were all silent for a while, then Olivia said, "I have to commend you, Jennifer. I'm not sure I could have stayed as cool and collected as you did with her."

"I agree," Cereo quickly said. Then he observed, "She was right about one thing. The threat is empty. We need A27 to surrender, but are likely to run out of time if something dramatic doesn't happen."

Colonel Askook was irritated with Governor Jacobs, but decided to try not to show it. She didn't seem to understand that the Pacifica rebels had technology the Commonwealth did not have. "We can't detect them, Governor. They're invisible. The only encouraging aspect is that it appears they only have two vessels."

Julie Jacobs starred daggers at the colonel and in a sarcastic tone said, "If you can't detect their warships, how can you possibly know how many there are?"

Askook kept his face normal and his response professional, although he couldn't keep the fire completely out of his eyes. "This comes from a well-reasoned military assessment. It's the best analysis we have. I agree with its conclusions. The assessment is based on the timelines of when various parts of the communications network went down. We first lost contact with Pacifica.

"Then, seventy-two hours later, we lost connection to Liberty. This is the proper amount of travel time between Pacifica and Liberty. The local A27 and wormhole communication paths were shut down as if two ships left Liberty at the same time, arrived on normal transit schedules, and shut down each of those communication links when they arrived. Could there be more than two? Yes, of course. But our current information suggests two ships."

"Why weren't we notified prior to Pacifica's broadcast that our communications network had been compromised?" Julie asked as she continued to glare at Askook.

"We failed to consider the possibility of sabotage. The network support team believed this was a cascading systematic failure likely caused by the latest software update. In their defense, we haven't had anyone take physical control of a space borne portion of our communications network since the military took control of the networks after the Mutant Wars. However, this is clearly a failure of military leadership. We should have had a contingency plan, assuming this would occur. It will need to be addressed once this crisis is over."

Chief Justice Reginald, the highest legal authority in the Commonwealth, said, "I appreciate your candor, Colonel. However, the hijacking of our networks is not the main issue here." He then turned his attention to Julie and said, "Administration is responsible for Survey operations. How was it possible for Pacifica to hide technology for seven hundred years?"

The room was silent as Julie fumed. She was visualizing the things she would do to Reginald if she ever got the chance when Askook spoke up. "The rebels clearly have technology we don't have. Our advantage is time. Pacifica can't possibly defeat the overwhelming number of warships the Commonwealth can deploy. Finding the bunker will be difficult and time-consuming. We just need to wait."

"What if they do find us, Colonel?" Reginald asked.

"If they find us, our only option is surrender. We have to assume they have disruptors. As you know these devices disable anything electronic. Gunpowder was obsolete as soon as a way was invented to remotely identify it and then cause it to explode. That means that unless we can isolate ourselves in a metal tube, like a warship, we are limited to hand-to-hand combat. The few shielded assault vehicles we have on A27 would get instantly vaporized from the warship currently in orbit. Having seen videos of Pacifica warriors in action, I can assure you we have no chance to defeat them."

"Colonel Askook, do you have any idea of where their stealth technology came from?" Justice Reginald asked.

Askook nodded slightly and said, "We've had little time to investigate, but there is a theory we're running with. There was a rumor of a Mutant military research and development team that was never accounted for. They were supposedly engaged in a research project around the time the Pacifica emigration fleet left Earth. It's possible one of the three ships in that fleet had the Mutant research team on board. If so, they may have brought along a few military prototypes. What confirms this as a possibility are results from sequencing the Pacifica Mutants. What Pacifica calls GEMs seems to be based on a Mutant strain known to be associated with that timeframe.

Reginald lost his temper at that point. He turned and pointed his finger at Governor Jacobs and said, "Another Survey failure! How could you possibly miss that?" Reginald paused for a few moments, clearly trying to calm himself and think through the situation. "Are the other Pacifica natives really true humans or are they GEMs as well?"

"They're true human. This has been analyzed by multiple experts time and time again. Whenever there is a subject to sample, Survey fully examines their genome for any hint of genetic engineering. The latest sample analyzed was the Arista gladiator, Theron Stone. He is true human," Askook said with confidence.

With her unblinking eyes ablaze, Julie said, "It doesn't matter if they are true human or not. Once we get control of the sector, I'll lay waste to every single planet and start over with new colonists."

"You are no longer in charge here, Ms. Jacobs," Reginald shouted at Julie. He visibly calmed himself and then said with disdain, "As a representative of the High Council, I have the authority to dismiss governors who exhibit gross incompetence. No governor in history has lost control of their sector. Congratulations, you've made the history books." He turned to Colonel Askook and said, "As the representative of the Commonwealth Military, you are witness to Governor Jacobs being relieved of her duties. I will take over responsibility for all decisions in this sector including negotiations with the rebels.

"I verify I have witnessed this transition. The military will comply with your orders, Chief Justice."

Sovereign

INCURSION

This was the dangerous part in Tee's mind. They had to avoid the growing cloud of debris and enter the wormhole at an oblique angle with low relative velocity, hoping they don't ram a ship coming through the other way.

"Destination match," Quinn called out.

"Destination approved. Launch Gerty," Tee ordered. He had gotten used to seeing the background star field abruptly change. But having six Commonwealth ships suddenly appear was discomforting. He hadn't gotten used to being invisible, so the sight caused a sudden internal panic. Calming himself, Tee said, "Analysis Quinn?"

"Processing." A long minute later Quinn said, "They don't know we're here. There are two warships and four empty vessels that appear to be transports. The way they are configured, it's likely they are queuing up to send the four empty hulls through."

"Okay, good! Let's execute the two jumps to M26. We'll clean this up later. I don't want to alert them we've entered their space," Tee said as he relaxed. Ramming something by accident had been a real concern. If they had been sending one of the hulks through at high speed, the Gerty might have joined the cloud of debris littering Sector 27's side of the wormhole.

Back on Pacifica, Tee had questioned Jack on what lay beyond the wormhole. He learned that each sector had an additional planet on the Commonwealth side of every wormhole. This additional planet was dedicated to the military. Their wormhole led to Sector 26 and thus, there was a military planet designated M26. Jack said that anything involving the military for Sector 27 would be managed from there.

When they came out of the final jump, the sight was staggering. The planet had a huge space station in a high orbit, teaming with Commonwealth warships. There appeared to be no room left to dock any more. There were several more warships scattered about that appeared to be waiting for an open dock. In addition, there were three large installations on the planet, for God knew what. The scale of it was intimidating. Tee wondered how they could possibly win against something of this magnitude. After a few minutes of shocked silence, Tee finally said, "Options?"

"One of our large fusion devices should take out the space station and connected ships. All of that is pretty fragile. We can clean up anything we miss with the smaller devices. The planet buster will take out everything on the planet. Probably make it uninhabitable," Quinn said clinically, without his usual happy enthusiasm. They were discussing killing hundreds of thousands of people, and it obviously bothered him.

While he didn't like the idea either, these people had joined a military organization they knew oppressed the Commonwealth's colonies. They had made a choice, and it was an evil one. The faces of those he was forced to kill in the Arena came to mind as he said, "We'll take out the space station first. We don't want any of those warships to escape. Jay, load up one of the large fusion devices. Quinn plot a destination."

The crew quickly went through their process and after the large fusion device had been placed, Tee gave the command. "Detonate L1."

Even though they were prepared for it, the result was almost incomprehensible. Large segments of the space station were slowly pinwheeling in random directions, with fires clearly visible. Quinn had placed the device close to the center of the docking station side and whatever was left of the warships was hard to pick out in the flotsam. Complete and utter destruction.

"The local communications network is getting overwhelmed," Quinn reported.

Not that this affected them given they were in receive only mode. Tee thought everyone on the planet must be trying to communicate at once. Tee hesitated as he imagined what would be going on down there. The space station was so large that it would be visible from the planet's surface. The explosion must have been quite traumatic for those below. Families would be huddled together. Mothers would be rushing to their children's schools. Friends would be calling each other, hoping they weren't on the space station. His heart went out to those who were probably just caught up in a system they had no part in building. He turned to Griff and said, "What do you think we should do now?"

Griff looked at Tee with surprise and said, "I think the entire planet is a military installation and we should destroy it."

Tee just looked at Griff for a while, considering his options. Perry's lecture on not killing indiscriminately had resonated with him. He had asked Bria once why she didn't throw her knife at him on the slave ship. Her answer had floored him.

"I won't kill," Bria had said. "I would rather lose my life than live with the guilt of taking someone else's life." She had stopped after saying this, realizing he might be offended and observed, "I might feel differently if I grew up on Pacifica. It seems the consequences of refusing to fight there are much greater than on Liberty."

That led to remembering Victor's comments about the Arista gladiators. They were victims, not enemies. It made him pause. What were his moral responsibilities? Griff was right when he told General Eastbrook that the Guard had never been in a position to consider anything other than killing their enemy on sight. This was a different situation. There were other options.

"Quinn, what do we need to do to destroy the three large installations but leave the surrounding residential areas relatively intact?" Tee asked.

"One of them is a space port and one small device on the launch area should be enough. The other two are spread out and will require larger devices. Since those two are remote from the major city, we can minimize casualties," Quinn said.

Tee was once again surprised by Quinn's insight. He had correctly guessed what Tee's concern was. "Quinn, Jay, execute to that plan." He looked over at Griff and saw he was confused and a bit miffed. Griff wanted to see the whole planet destroyed. Tee thought that was the best purely military solution, but he just couldn't do it.

They destroyed all the military spacecraft they could locate in the vicinity of M26. They had seen a few wink out, hopefully heading away from Sector 27. Then they jumped back to the wormhole and took out the lone warship there. Once back in Sector 27, they contacted Pacifica.

"Gerty, you were under orders not to transmit close to the wormhole," Jennifer said with a questioning look.

"There isn't anyone left to listen," Tee responded. "I violated one other order as well. A video file with commentary is being sent. It explains everything. The summary is that we've destroyed the

Commonwealth's military capabilities on M26. Jack can explain what that means." Tee hesitated a moment and then said, "General Eastbrook did say to use my initiative if I saw an opportunity."

On the Peregrine, they watched the video, and the crew broke into applause. Perry turned to Colonel Peters and dryly said, "I'm going to like our Mr. Stone. I think we'll go easy on him at the court martial." They both laughed.

Jennifer looked shocked and turned to Jack with a questioning look. He smiled and said, "I think we just bought some time. Commonwealth citizens think the Commonwealth is invincible. Showing this will prove they are not. I have an idea."

President Malrey's image suddenly appeared on the Gerty's main screen. Sitting once again at her desk, she looked confident but stern. "Good morning, this is President Malrey with an update for the Commonwealth and inhabitants of A27. The response to our offer for peace has been rejected. Instead, an attack on our border security was made by the Commonwealth. Our response was the utter destruction of all military facilities orbiting and occupying M26." A video showing the orbital platform and multiple military bases on M26 as they were being destroyed took the place of Jennifer's image. "We had the capability to destroy the entire M26 planet but refrained from taking this action to show that we can be merciful. It is a mistake to underestimate us. We can strike anywhere in the Commonwealth with impunity."

An old picture of Earth taken in antiquity from its moon briefly made its appearance. The image slowly faded back to Jennifer.

She hesitated a few moments and then said, "Let me repeat what I've said before. We desire peace with all our neighbors. Our only demand is that you vacate our sector." Jennifer stopped and, with a look of regret, said, "I don't like to threaten. But it seems your government doesn't understand peaceful negotiations. The Pacifica Guard will arrive at A27 within a week. If your government doesn't surrender before that time, we'll take the planet by force. The Pacifica Guard does not take prisoners."

The image switched to a still photo of Rilla in battle gear covered in gore and affecting a crazed expression. Then the monitor went black.

They had all been disgusted when Jack explained that the Commonwealth secretly recorded Arista gladiatorial events and the

Pacifica wars. They consider it entertainment. They even had something called fan clubs who would gather to watch and root for whomever caught their fancy. Griff was a favorite. Tee had become quite popular after killing Trajan. Those who enjoyed these sorts of things would replay his bow work on the Wall. Even Arti had her followers.

Rilla had recently become popular because of how berserk he had gone trying to save Moose's life. His killing spree had been replayed over and over on the feeds. Jack thought his image would have a gut level impact on the ordinary citizens of not only A27 but the whole of the Commonwealth.

Later that evening, Jennifer's monitor signaled that a connection was requested. She sent out permissions for the rest of the group to view and then allowed it. A harassed looking middle-aged man greeted her. "My name is Jackson Depond. I am the mayor of A27. We only have a single city on this planet. There is a small military facility, but that is different. I, um, well, this is quite unusual."

Jennifer interrupted him since it seemed he might just keep blabbering, "What do you want Mr. Dupond?" she asked.

The question caused him to blanch. He visibly settled himself and said, "We would like to discuss your terms for surrender."

"Where is Governor Jacobs? Isn't that who I should be discussing this with?" Jennifer said.

"She is, um, she is indisposed at the moment," he said, clearly uncomfortable discussing the governor.

"Well, have her call back when she isn't indisposed," Jennifer said and acted as if she was going to break the connection.

"No, wait," Jackson said desperately. Then he took a deep breath. "A member of the High Council is on A27 visiting his daughter and decided it was best for him to take over decision making. He's asked me to negotiate on his behalf."

"I'm not going to negotiate with intermediators. Have him call me when he's ready to discuss terms," Jennifer said and cut off the connection.

An hour later, another connection request was made. When Jennifer accepted, an older gentleman appeared and said with annoyance, "Hello, I am Chief Justice Reginald, a member of the High Council for King Archibald. We will vacate A27 and leave the sector. We require all transport ships to be released immediately. It will take six months to pack up our property, which will be taken with us. I have no authority to surrender the Commonwealth's claim on this sector. I wouldn't do that even if I could. This is the best offer you'll get."

"Thank you, Chief Justice Reginald, for your offer. I will consider it. If I don't get back to you within the next five days, you'll know I've rejected your offer. In that case, you can expect the Guard to land. Those negotiations won't be pleasant," Jennifer said curtly and cut off the connection.

Jack immediately spoke up. "This is really good news. I was hoping for a grass roots coup. Reginald is the leading Justice Minister on the High Council. He is not going to risk himself or his daughter for a minor backwater sector."

The next call was from Governor Jacobs, "I would like to speak with my first minister."

"Okay, hold on a second," Jennifer said and passed the connection to Jack.

"Hello, Governor," Jack said with a stone face. She just stared at him for a long time.

"If you can't think of anything to say, please call back when you do," Jack said coldly.

"This isn't making anything easier for you when we get back," Jacobs said threateningly.

"I've been offered sanctuary and have accepted it," Jack said bluntly.

She showed some surprise at his news. Unusual for her to reveal anything. After a few moments, she smiled evilly and said, "I'll be sure to say hello to your mother and father for you, Jack."

"If you do that, it will be on A27. Commonwealth citizens who are granted sanctuary will have the opportunity to offer the same to their close relatives. None of the high-ranking members of the Commonwealth will be allowed to leave until this happens," Jack said and forced a triumphant smile on his face. He would be damned if she saw any fear in him.

"This isn't the end, Jack. Remember that," Jacobs said and cut the connection.

In the end, Reginald agreed to all of Jennifer's demands. They would leave everything behind and evacuate as soon as possible. A surprisingly small number of Commonwealth citizens requested sanctuary. Those who did had few relatives. Getting them to A27 was done quickly. Jack's parents reluctantly agreed to sanctuary, recognizing their life in the Commonwealth was over. When the last Commonwealth transport disappeared through the wormhole, Jack breathed a sigh of relief. Now all he had to do was ask for forgiveness. That and spend the rest of his life trying to repent for all the horrors he had helped inflict on his new friends.

CHAPTER 27

BLUE HERON TAVERN

Jay and Hestie both arrived at the Blue Heron early. Their greetings were cordial but strained. After sitting for a while in silence, Hestie finally said, "I think it's time to tell you why I pushed you away."

"That would be nice," Jay said with a mildly biting voice.

"I found out about our military technology when they needed help with navigation. I volunteered with the understanding that I would have to commit suicide if the Commonwealth gained control of Pacifica. They would have killed everyone if they knew. They call it cleansing," Hestie said with a look asking for understanding.

"Go on," was all Jay said.

Hestie continued. "I couldn't take our relationship further knowing you were going to discover I had committed suicide with no explanation. I just couldn't do that to you."

Jay looked down at the table in front of him and pondered that for a while. Then he looked up and said, "So you didn't trust me."

"I do trust you, Jay. More than anyone else in my life," Hestie said, with tears starting to form in her eyes.

"You didn't trust me to survive. Instead, you took what should have been months of happiness away from us both. When the world was coming apart, you took away my refuge," Jay said. Then leaning forward, he added, "My purpose in life is to risk it saving others. I could have died at any time. But I trusted you to carry on, to survive."

"I'm sorry, Jay. I hope you can forgive me," Hestie said with her voice trailing off and her eyes looking off to the side.

"How can I trust you when you don't trust me? How can I know I can depend on you when life gets difficult?" Jay said. When she looked back at him, he added, "I also think something else is going on. You have some other secret you're not telling me about. You might be able to hide from others, Hestie, but you can't hide from me."

Hestie just stared at him for a while, wondering what to say. Then she decided to stop pretending. "I do have another secret. A terrible one. Something I cannot and will not tell you or anyone else. I'm sorry, Jay, but there are things more important than our happiness."

"A secret that protects us all?" Jay said, adjusting the Guard credo.

"Yes," Hestie said.

"That's all you ever needed to say, Hestie. I wish you had said it months ago," Jay said with sadness in his voice.

As Hestie started to answer him, Jay looked up in recognition. With his frown slowly turning into a grin, he said loud enough for the whole tavern to hear, "Theron, First of his Name, Emperor of Arista, Liberator of Worlds. Your Eminence, have you come to mingle with the common people?"

Hestie face transformed into a smile, and she laughed. Tee turned bright red as the entire tavern turned to look at him. A few people chuckled, recognizing Jay and the sarcasm. More than a few people simply smiled to see him. Tee had become a celebrity.

Tee now had to wade through well-wishers to get to their table. Standing over Jay he said quietly, "Did you really have to do that?"

"Yes, I did. If I don't make fun of you, you're likely going to get a big head," Jay said, continuing to smile.

Hestie got up and gave Tee a big hug. "It's good to see you. You've been gone too long."

Tee sat down in front of the beer Jay had already ordered for him and said, "I've been on Arista this whole time. I am no longer the emperor. The new emperor is Caius, Third of his Name." This was said with a hint of sarcasm.

"How did you pull that off?" Jay asked.

"By their constitution, an emperor can abdicate to any blood relative of any of the previous emperors. I could have abdicated to my cousin Pete. He would have loved that. Well, at least for a few days," Tee said, smiling. "Senator Cereo is a distant relative of Emperor Trajan, the previous emperor."

"The one you murdered," Jay said. Hestie punched him lightly in the arm for that comment. He grinned and rubbed it as if it were painful.

"Yes, the one I murdered," Tee said, smiling at them both. "I had to go to their Senate one more time to officially abdicate. But the real reason Cereo wanted me there was to threaten people."

"Why did you need to threaten anyone?" Hestie asked.

"Cereo's main rival is the magistrate of their Senate. He's the one who headed up the coup, resulting in mercenaries invading Liberty. His argument that the Commonwealth forced him to do it had enough truth in it to absolve him. The elite are all former slave owners, and the majority support him. While the emperor's authority is absolute, it is tenuous. Civil war is a very real possibility. I met individually with many of Cereo's opponents before abdicating and told them I would be back if they caused trouble. They naturally assumed that meant with the Guard. They've seen Victor and I in the Arena, and black-market videos of our GEM wars have been circulating," Tee said.

Jay looked at Tee with concern and asked, "Do you trust Cereo?"

"No, I don't trust him. He's too manipulative. But I like him, which is weird," Tee said with a confused grin on his face.

"How can you like him if you don't trust him?" Hestie asked with concern. Then she glanced over at Jay with an odd look. That's strange, Tee thought.

"I don't know, I just do. It's probably because every time I've seen him manipulate people, it's for good reasons. While that isn't a good enough justification for me, he's been in a pretty extreme situation his whole life," Tee said, and after hesitating he added, "His situation has improved enormously, but it's still dangerous. The magistrate's supporters now know he counts slaves as his family. They know he was secretly working to free them. They suspect he talked Pacifica into supporting him."

"It makes sense to me," Jay said. "Sometimes people you don't trust can be appealing." He gave his own odd look back at Hestie. Definitely something there, thought Tee with some concern.

After a few moments of uncomfortable silence, Tee decided to change the subject, "Where is Diana? I thought she would be here tonight."

Well, that didn't calm things down, he thought as he saw Hestie react strongly. She just stared at him for a moment and then said, "She said she was meeting Glenn tonight."

Tee's brain boiled over with that news. He had been extremely busy with commitments since the warships were revealed. There had been no time to have a private discussion with Diana since their night in the garden. She knew the engagement was off, and he assumed she would just wait for him to return. Not wanting to talk about it, he quickly changed the subject. "I've been court martialed," he said.

"What!" Jay said, loud enough for people at adjoining tables to look over at them.

Tee just smiled and said, "General Eastbrook turns out to be a practical joker. He pulled President Malrey, Queen Olivia, Emperor Cereo, Griff, and a few of his top officers together and put me on trial for disobeying orders. I was found guilty and sentenced to thirty days restricted duty. If I complete the thirty days successfully, then the guilty verdict will be expunged. In other words, it's like it never happened. I've basically been sentenced to take a vacation. After that, Queen Olivia awarded me their Royal Cross, Emperor Cereo pined some olive leaf thing on my uniform, and President Malrey gave me a hearty handshake."

Tee took a deep breath and said, "I was hoping to talk to Diana tonight." He hesitated and then said, "General Eastbrook offered to take me hunting with him in the mountains close to his ranch. I wasn't going to go, but I think I'll accept. Will be nice to see Bria again." And with that, he got up, hugged Hestie once more, slapped Jay on the shoulder, and said, "Will see you both in a couple of weeks."

Tee walked out of the Blue Heron with Jay and Diana staring at his back with an open mouth, surprised. Jay recovered first. "What the hell is going on between him and Diana?"

"I don't know. She seems confused and this will just make it worse," Hestie said.

"I know that look from Tee. He's decided something," Jay replied. Then they just sat in silence for a while.

Finally, Hestie said, "Do I have a chance to fix things?"

Jay huffed, but the anger on his face had disappeared. His mouth went from relaxed to firm and he said, "Can I trust you to trust me?"

"I trust you, Jay. Maybe the problem is that I didn't trust me," Hestie said. "Anyway, if you'll give me the time to prove it, I'm willing to wait. As Grammy said, some things are worth waiting for."

CHAPTER 28

FINAGLED

It was early in the morning with mist heavy in the air. The day would end up being hot and dry. Perfect for growing grapes, Caius thought wryly. The sky was just starting to lighten, and the birds were waking and giving their opinion of the morning. The air was full of the earthy smell of vegetation. Caius was deep in thought on his favorite bench in the family vegetable garden. It was here he had spent a good deal of time as a young man desperately dreaming up schemes to protect his family.

In some ways, nothing had changed. There were still great dangers that would need to be navigated. There was no margin for error. The elite of Arista hated him. They would find a way to channel that hate.

He knew their hatred was well earned. The elite had retained their wealth. But they did not wield the power they once had. A power they believed was their right by birth. In their minds, outrageous changes had been forced upon them. Slaves had been freed. Private armies eliminated. But what caused the most angst was the elimination of corruption. Government funded projects were not for sale anymore. Legal matters could no longer be settled with a bribe. A whole new way of life was being shoved down their throats. It was too much change too fast.

He was proud of what he had negotiated. He had been the one convincing the Confederation of Planets that Pacifica should appear to be acting alone. An outraged property owner dealing with squatters. The idea emerged when it became clear Pacifica would retain control of their military technology. Pacifica, standing alone, had its merits in dealing with the Commonwealth. But it wasn't the primary reason he had proposed it. No, his real purpose would come later.

Caius wanted drastic change on Arista. One way to accelerate change was to convince Pacifica to set conditions for joining the Confederation. Any planet declining would get an eviction notice. Their alternative would be to fall on the mercy of the Commonwealth. Everyone knew the Commonwealth would show no mercy. The challenge was to get everyone to agree that slavery would not be allowed anywhere in the Confederation. There was a strong bias that each planet guide its own future. He agreed with this bias, but he had to find a way for an exception. The key was gaining agreement from Pacifica.

His mother, his real mother, had given him excellent advice once. "If you want people to agree with you, get them used to saying yes. Once they get in the habit, they're likely to continue." He found this to be surprisingly true.

So, his first proposal to the Confederation was that A27 be recognized as belonging to Pacifica. The people of Pacifica were insistent that the GEMs be left alone, which meant they had no room to grow. This was wildly popular with everyone. Jennifer reported that Councilman Barlow, in particular had been effusive in his praise of the idea. He even pulled out the original surveys and declared this would have been their home had they not lost their jump capability. They even named it all those years ago. It had originally been named Eirene after the Greek goddess of peace. There was no controversy in retaining the name.

At their next meeting, he proposed that Arista provide significant funding for two new schools on Eirene. The first was an extension of the university on Pacifica and the other a technical training school. These schools would be open to applicants from all planets in the Confederation. It was an extremely popular proposal, with Liberty immediately agreeing to match Arista's contributions.

With those pledges, Pacifica committed to making Landfall University an extension of what would become the main university on Eirene. There wasn't anyone happier with this than Del. That evening, after a few too many whiskeys, Del had slurred his thanks to Caius over and over again. "All I ever wanted to do was research and teach. Being told about our hidden technology was the worst day of my life. This is the best day."

Now with two yes votes under his belt, he proposed the Confederation of Planets adopt as constitutional law a prohibition on slavery. Since no law is valid without enforcement, he proposed that the Confederation Defense Force be tasked with compliance. That required Pacifica support.

Liberty quickly agreed. They had a prohibition of their own in the Liberty constitution. Having the same for the Confederation aligned with their beliefs. Although Pacifica had the same prohibition in their human rights clauses, they were not in favor of interfering in other planets' politics. They saw the hands-off intention of the Commonwealth's non-interference Edicts as one of the few good things about that system. After much debate, Caius asked Jennifer to be allowed to directly address the Pacifica Council. She agreed.

The Pacifica Council was just as reluctant as Jennifer had been. "I don't like telling people what to do in their own homes," Councilwoman Ricks had said.

"Your own constitution prohibits slavery by declaring that everyone has the right to freedom," Caius countered. "How is this different?"

"It's different because we have control of military technology and it's a slippery slope toward becoming just another tyrannical Commonwealth," Ricks shot back.

"I agree," Barlow said forcefully. "We need to keep the military tightly reined in."

After a couple of hours of this, Caius was exhausted. He had complimented, disparaged, pleaded, and appealed to their humanity. All to no avail. He was out of ways to manipulate the situation. When his efforts to get his way ran out of steam, June used to smile at him and say, "When you don't know what to say, just tell the truth."

So, he told his story. An hour later, there were tears on a few of the council members' cheeks. He had told them everything about his family. Confessed that he had used every manipulative trick in the book to change things. That he was out of tricks.

The vote was three-to-three. Surprisingly, Barlow was the one who switched sides. "Yea. I am voting for this because I believe he's telling the truth. And it's a compelling truth. My only request is that the constitution clearly state that this is a singular exception to the Confederation Defense Force non-interference rule."

Barlow's addition was unanimously added to the vote and, again, the result was three-to-three.

Jennifer took a deep breath and said, "The vote is deadlocked and there is no proposal for an alternative." She looked around the table and as her eyes met with Barlow's she said, "I vote yea."

He had been stunned. Given Jennifer's strong disagreement with this at the Confederation of Planets meetings, Caius thought he had failed.

The garden workers arriving to start the day brought him back to the present. He realized he was very satisfied with his life. Who would have guessed that the ragged farm boy who knocked on Mr. File's door would end up realizing his dream? Being distrusted by most in the Confederation and hated on Arista was a small price to pay.

CHAPTER 29

JACKPOT

Grant had been terrified when the small shuttlecraft docked with their survey ship and demanded they open the hatch. The communications network had gone dark a few hours before. It had done this just as a Commonwealth warship entered orbit.

As soon as it arrived, the ultimate symbol of Commonwealth power simply disintegrated into billions of tiny pieces. Data from their sensors identified the cause of its demise as a small anti-matter triggered fusion device. War was thought to be a thing of the past. Commonwealth citizens knew their government was all powerful and citizens had nothing to fear. Well, nothing except the government itself.

The shuttlecraft claimed to be under the command of the Pacifica Guard. It was all too surreal to be believed. Their captain was told his options were to open the hatch or suffer the same fate as the warship. It was an easy decision. Enormous human beings with frowns on their faces and swords in their hands entered. They looked so much bigger and deadlier in person than they had when viewed on a video screen. Grant was certain they were all about to be slaughtered. He knew the Pacifica Guard didn't take prisoners. He just hoped they would make it quick.

Grant chuckled, thinking of how he had gone from utterly terrified to wildly ecstatic. He had initially dismissed sanctuary when it was offered. He was a Commonwealth citizen and didn't want to live in some backwater sector. Then he remembered what was waiting for him back home. Grant made the decision to request sanctuary fairly quickly after that.

When the dean of the newly formed Eirene University found out he had a doctorate in anthropology, he was offered a teaching position. It even paid more than his old job of survey anthropologist. When you looked at the whole thing, it was like hitting an enormous jackpot. His luck had turned just like he knew it would. Now he just had to find a good local bookie.

CHAPTER 30

CLOSURE

Jennifer, Del, Caius, and Olivia were viewing the cockpit of Gerty.

"Destination match," Quinn said.

"How certain are we this will work?" Olivia asked.

"I am confident it will close. I'm less certain if it will close permanently," Quinn answered brightly.

Del added, "Nobody has ever explained why permanent wormholes exist. Where they get the energy to stay open or how they are formed in the first place. We've learned how to create temporary ones of our own from analyzing them. But our artificial ones are simply not the same. Since permanent wormholes are viewed as immensely valuable, nobody has been motivated to find a way to close them. Until now."

"Does that mean it could come back at any time?" Olivia asked.

"We don't know. It could disappear forever, or it could come back instantly. It's possible that Quinn's hypothesis is wrong, and nothing happens. Although I doubt it," Del replied.

Jennifer looked at everyone and said, "I would feel a lot better if it disappears and never comes back. If everyone is in agreement, then I'll give the command." She looked around the table and got approving head nods. Then, with a slight nod of her own head, she said, "Tee, give the command to launch."

They all heard Tee say, "Destination approved. Launch Closure Device."

A few seconds later, they saw the magnified wormhole on their screen simply wink out. After a full minute of anxiously watching the screen, the room slowly broke into applause and then congratulations. They were finally safe from the Commonwealth.

CHAPTER 31

EPILOGUE

Griff entered the Hall of Heroes and was struck by the silence. It seemed he was the only one here this morning and was glad for it. The display case wasn't large, but it certainly caught your attention entering the hall. Urns had never been displayed out here before. They made an exception for Vic. Eventually, Tee would be housed right next to him. There was an impressive gold-plated plaque detailing how peace and freedom had been won for Pacifica. They were doing the same for all the war rooms, detailing the story for each battle. The Hall of Heroes was turning into a museum.

"Well, old friend. You never got to enjoy the fruits of your labor," Griff said quietly. Then he just stood there, as if searching for more to say. "I came to thank you. Have regretted not doing that before you disappeared. It feels good that you knew I was promoted to Master Sergeant. That would not have happened if it wasn't for you. Your obsession on excellence is what kept me alive."

Griff paused and then said, "You were right about Tee. He was capable of being a much better fighter than I imagined. That was quite the dramatic final lesson."

Griff paused, smiled, then continued, "It reminded me of all the times I ended up laying in the dirt during your training sessions. You'll be pleased to hear Tee's been promoted to CGG. Our president had to negotiate hard to get him to accept. He truly does not seek power or influence. One of the reasons he should have both. She had to supply a shuttlecraft so he could travel back and forth to Apple Valley. He says it's his home, and he's never living anywhere else. The wonders of technology.

She felt compelled to do this because Pacifica may need his influence. There are challenges with the Confederation of Planets. Tee has become somewhat of a legend across the confederation. Arista calls him Theron the Great. The former slave population there seems to think he personally freed them and then abdicated in order to ensure slavery is stamped out everywhere. Liberty calls him Theron the Liberator." Griff smiled a little broader and said, "Pacifica is not so grandiose. We just call him Tee. But he is rightfully viewed alongside you as Pacifica's liberators.

Speaking of Tee, I'm married to Tee's mother. Yeah, I know, she could have done better. Should have done better." He hesitated again and said in a hushed voice, "I'll fill you in on a secret. Arti is pregnant. Dr. Espers says the medical knowledge in the archives will eliminate most of the risk to a woman her age giving birth. She did some sort of scan and said the baby was healthy. She was even able to tell us it's going to be a girl."

His smile faded, and he said, "It's not all good news. The Guard is changing. There isn't as much motivation to excel. The fear and anxiety of the GEMs is missing. That would piss you off. I know it pisses me off. But in my opinion being able to bring up my daughter in a time of peace is worth any price. I just have to accept things for what they are. That doesn't mean I'll let the Guard get too complacent."

Griff took a deep breath and let it out. Then he said, "I'll stop in from time-to-time Vic. I hope you'll look in on me as well. Again, thank you for everything my friend."

Griff wandered off to visit the other ghosts of his past.

Olivia and Bria were sitting on the porch of the Eastbrook ranch house enjoying their afternoon tea. It was sunny, hot, and muggy. But they were enjoying the House of Lords summer break. Getting the kingdom back in order meant the two of them had had no time to get caught up until now. But being best friends since childhood meant being together was instantly comfortable.

Olivia frowned and said, "I'm worried about Gloria. Her relationship with Jack seems to be getting serious. She told me he's the only man she's met who understands what she's been through. She says he doesn't look down on her because of it. She says he's patient, kind, and gentle with the girls. Treats them both like princesses."

"I can testify that princesses don't always get treated well," Bria quipped, trying to lighten the mood. She had been struggling to get Olivia to relax. She was stuck in problem-solving mode and needed to come up for air.

"He's done some horrible things, Bria," Olivia said, ignoring her efforts to avoid the subject.

Bria saw that Olivia's eyebrows were scrunched together when she turned to look at her. "Well, Grace likes him," Bria replied, refusing to get into a discussion of Jack's prior life as she worked to get Olivia to settle down.

Olivia's frown softened a bit at that. "You seriously think everyone that dog likes is a good person?"

"Yes, I do. She's got some sort of sixth sense about people. But then again, she likes you," Bria said with a smirk, locking eyes with Olivia.

That caused Olivia to roll her eyes and crack a smile. Then she asked, "Does she ever leave your side?"

Bria turned her head toward Olivia and said seriously, "No. She saved me on Arista. I saved her. We're both grateful."

After a few minutes of the comfortable silence best friends enjoy, Bria suddenly smiled and said, "Seems to me the ruggedly handsome Colonel Timothy Peters is never far away."

Olivia's eyebrows scrunched together again, and she looked troubled. She took a breath and sighed. Finally, she said, "Yeah, that's a problem I'll have to deal with." She hesitated a few moments longer and then said, "I asked him to marry me."

Bria's tea went down the wrong pipe and came back out through her nose and mouth in a spray. After sputtering for a few seconds, she said dumbfounded, "You did what! Why?"

"I asked him to marry me because I love him. He never would have asked me," Olivia said in all seriousness. Bria just stared at her, obviously at a loss for words. So Olivia continued her story. "It wasn't very romantic. Instead of saying yes, his answer was, 'I can't do that to you.' Then he just stared at me. Kind of like what you're doing now." Olivia smiled and continued. "After a long and arduous discussion of what was in my best interests, he reluctantly agreed to marry me. Something I'll remind him of from time to time."

"But what about the House of Lords? What about your uncle? I thought he was looking for the best political match?" Bria asked.

"Well, sometimes you just have to make a royal decision. We don't really have any serious political problems right now. So, I've decided to be selfish," Olivia said smugly. She then looked thoughtfully at Bria and said, "Were you really going to marry Theron Stone to protect me?"

Bria smiled reflectively for a few moments and finally said, "You and everyone else."

"You know, I spent time with him when you were off catching up with your father. I don't think that would have been much of a sacrifice," Olivia said, and they both laughed. Bria was happy to see the old Olivia again.

Bria's smile turned wistful as she said softly, "It wouldn't have been entirely distasteful." Catching herself, she forced a grin and said, "My dad is still rooting for it. Tee is everything he ever wanted in a son-in-law." They both chuckled.

"Well, now you get to choose," Olivia said, looking a little concerned. She had finally picked up on Bria's mood.

"Yes I do," Bria said softly. Then under her breath she added privately to herself, "If only it were that simple."

June was working in the garden when she heard someone approach. A man's soft voice said, "June?" She turned to greet him, started to reply, then stopped. She studied his face for a long moment as she tried to figure out what to say. Then, with tears welling in her eyes, she simply said, "Henry." They both stepped forward and wrapped each other up in a long embrace.

They eventually separated but held onto each other's hands. "You've left your position," she said.

"I can't believe it, but here I am," Henry said with a relaxed smile. "Although I could have continued to provide useful information, Leo and Caius insisted."

"Your sacrifice has already helped free millions," June said firmly.

"Leo told me the same thing. I told him it was a small part compared to what others have done. He's an impressive man, June; you must be very proud," Henry said.

"Just as proud of my little brother," she said with warm light dancing in her eyes. She hesitated a few moments, trying to decide whether to open up. Then, remembering how Henry was the one person she would share secrets with as a child, she finally said in a quiet voice, "I'm very proud of both my sons. I will never disrespect Caius's mother by claiming that honor in his hearing. But between us, he is as much my son as Leo is.

Let's go in and have some tea. We have fifty years to catch up on."

Tee and Diana were married under the large oak tree where they had met as children. Representatives from all confederation planets were in attendance. The Guard showed up in force along with what seemed to be the whole of Apple Valley. The public reception took place on the school playground and spilled out into the streets. It would be talked about in Apple Valley for decades.

The private family reception started at sunset, with a bonfire on the beach. Late that evening, Tee was standing off to the side watching his family and friends laughing and having fun. It was as if no time had gone past. Ansen was entertaining a large group with one of his outrageously funny stories. Jay and Hestie were sitting on Grammy's bench where they had been for quite some time. They seemed to be going back and forth between a serious conversation and laughter.

He noticed they had been slowly inching closer together as the evening progressed. It was obvious by the way they were now pressed close together, and the way they looked at each other, that they were getting past whatever it was that caused their problems. Then he caught Diana looking at him. She smiled and nodded slightly in a gesture that said it was time to retire for the evening. He needed no encouragement.

In that moment, he thought he would like things to stay like this forever. Then he remembered the last time he had wished for that on this very same beach. Smiling, he reminded himself once again that Grammy was wise. Everything changes and it's best to simply enjoy whatever fate has in store for you. The good, the bad, and yes, even the regrets. He took Diana's outreached hand. As they walked around saying their goodnights, he thought, thanks for everything, Grammy.

A young and vibrant woman sat on the front porch, surrounded by those she loved. She was wearing a self-satisfied smile as she enjoyed the dance of the fireflies. They had read their letters and followed her advice. Her work was truly finished.

ABOUT THE AUTHOR

Tom Burrell resides with his wife in Northern California. When not writing, Tom is busy with their five children and five grandchildren. He has a degree in mechanical engineering from Cal Poly San Luis Obispo. Before becoming an author, Tom enjoyed a career in the electronic test and measurement industry.

Prior to becoming a responsible adult, Tom spent a decade of his youth wandering aimlessly, working a long list of jobs. These included lifeguard, swimming instructor, janitor, security guard, grill cook, painter, greenhouse worker, midnight shift convenience store clerk, residential liquor delivery driver, waiter, too many factory jobs to count, day laborer when immediate cash was required, and maker of handmade deer skin cowboy hats. These custom hats were sold by traveling around California to county fairs and other events where people tend to drink too much and make impulsive buying decisions.

If you enjoyed The Revelation Trilogy please consider giving a review. Feedback is a generous gift.

More stories from this universe are forthcoming. For more information on T.E. Burrell and his books visit www.teburrellpublishing.com